TALES OF MYSTERY &

General Editor: David Stuart D

THE DEAD OF NIGHT

THE DEAD OF NIGHT
The Ghost Stories of Oliver Onions

with an Introduction by
David Stuart Davies

WORDSWORTH EDITIONS

For my husband
ANTHONY JOHN RANSON
with love from your wife, the publisher.
Eternally grateful for your unconditional love,
not just for me but for our children,
Simon, Andrew and Nichola Trayler

Readers interested in other titles from
Wordsworth Editions are invited to visit our
website at www.wordsworth-editions.com

For our latest list and a full mail-order service contact
Bibliophile Books, Unit 5 Datapoint,
South Crescent, London E16 4TL
Tel: +44 020 74 74 24 74
Fax: +44 020 74 74 85 89
orders@bibliophilebooks.com
www.bibliophilebooks.com

This edition published 2010 by
Wordsworth Editions Limited
8B East Street, Ware,
Hertfordshire SG12 9HJ

ISBN 978 1 84022 640 9

Typeset in Great Britain by Roperford Editorial
Printed by Clays Ltd, St Ives plc

CONTENTS

INTRODUCTION

Oliver Onions's ghost stories are as unusual as his name. Indeed he is unique in the realms of writers of the supernatural in that his tales are so far-ranging in their background and substance that they are not easily categorised. Remarkably for a writer born in the mid-nineteenth century his style is very modern and his approach is as psychological as it is supernatural. One of the well-regarded commentators of the ghost story genre, Mike Ashley, observed: 'Onions's best stories are powerfully charged explorations of physical violence, their effects heightened by detailed character study and a preparedness to challenge the accepted.'

Onions's fiction is also graced with a powerful poetic elegance often missing in even the best of ghost stories. While other writers may create moods and images designed to chill, Onions is able to add a richness to the prose giving it a depth and beauty which enhances the development of the plot and cultivates living, breathing characters who are more than just pieces to be moved about the chessboard of a plot. In simple terms Oliver Onions goes for the cerebral rather than the jugular. However, make no mistake, his ghost stories achieve the desired effect. They not only unnerve the reader, but disturb him also and stay with him long after the book has been closed.

One of the pleasures of these stories is that Onions lets his ideas breathe and develop slowly. Most of these tales are quite long and, indeed, some are regarded as novellas. There is no headlong gallop to the dénouement with his work. We are led gently but inexorably to the climax. Nevertheless, it may well be that Onions's subtle technique and style is responsible for his ghost stories having been overlooked in the past. We hope that this bumper volume will help to redress that balance.

George Oliver Onions (pronounced like the vegetable) was born in Bradford, Yorkshire, in November 1873. He had the bluff, no-nonsense characteristics of the native Yorkshireman and, although proud of his unusual name, he was taunted at school because of it. In 1918 he changed it to George Oliver, partly to please his wife, who found it distasteful, and probably also to prevent his two young sons suffering the same humiliation that he had experienced. However, by this time he had established himself as a successful author and so he continued to publish his work under the name of Oliver Onions.

From an early age, Onions demonstrated an artistic and imaginative talent. As a young man he studied at the National Arts Training School in London. He continued his studies in Paris where he indulged himself in the artistic, bohemian life of the Left Bank. It was here that he got his first taste for writing by editing a student journal, *Le Quartier Latin*. One of the contributors to this publication was a certain Berta Ruck, who had been born in India in 1878. He was to marry her in 1908. Ruck later became a popular romantic novelist, penning over eighty books. She outlived her husband to reach the age of one hundred.

On Onions's return to England, he made his living as a book and poster designer and magazine illustrator. It was the American humourist and illustrator Gelett Burgess who encouraged Onions to try his hand at writing fiction. He was hesitant to begin with but after the success of his first novel, a light-hearted comedy of manners, *The Compleat Bachelor* (which was dedicated to Burgess) the die was cast. There then followed a whole series of novels and short stories which, because of the range of tone and theme, prevented the author from being categorised. The scope of his fiction not only included ghost stories and human interest dramas, but also a murder mystery, *In Accordance with the Evidence* (1912); a science fiction novel, *The New Moon* (1918), set in a utopian Britain of the future; and an historical romance set in Yorkshire, *The Story of Ragged Robyn* (1945). In 1946 Onions won the James Tait Black Memorial Prize for the Best Novel of the Year with *Poor Man's Tapestry*. He was writing until his death in 1961 and indeed this collection contains a story, 'Tragic Casements', which was found in his papers and not published until some years after his demise by a small press.

However, it is with Onions's forays into the dark realms of supernatural fiction that we are concerned here. His best-known and probably his most effective collection was *Widdershins*, which appeared in 1911. It is this fascinating bubbling cauldron of spookiness that first gave the world 'The Beckoning Fair One', Onions's most famous and most anthologised of stories. While E. F. Bleiler, an eminent scholar and critic of ghostly fiction, regarded *Widdershins* as a 'landmark book' in the genre, such notable and respected practitioners of the art of penning strange fiction, Algernon Blackwood and H. P. Lovecraft regarded 'The Beckoning Fair One' as one of the most effective and subtle ghost stories in all literature.

Indeed this story illustrates most effectively the skill and brilliance of Onions's writing. It is in one sense a haunted house tale, but to regard it simply as that is to be blind to its depth and nuances. It is the first story in this collection and chosen to be so for a definite purpose. It is the ideal introduction to the dark, subtle and challenging psychological nature of Onions's writing. When the story's protagonist Paul Oleron goes to live in the old house in the 'little triangular "Square"', he is at a pivotal point in his life: both his writing career and his relationship with his lady friend Elsie have reached a crucial stage. As the spirit of the house and the central character in his unfinished novel begin to take hold of him, Oleron's mental outlook begins to change rapidly. As the air of strangeness grows, Onions seems to be challenging the reader to decide whether this unsettling and bizarre state of affairs is a result of supernatural forces beyond Oleron's control, or if the character is suffering the onset of madness brought about by his inability to complete his novel. This multi-layered work can also be regarded as a tale of psychic vampirism as Oleron's fictional heroine feeds on him and drains his strength and sanity.

Onions imbues the text of this fascinating story with his first-hand knowledge of the pleasures and pains of the creative writing process and the terrors of writer's block which now hold Oleron in its thrall.

As in time past he had known, in his writing, moments when his thoughts had seemed to rise of themselves in words not to be altered afterwards, so now the questions he put to himself seemed to be answered even in the moment of asking. There was exhilaration in the swift, easy processes. He had known no such joy in his own power since the days when his writing had been a daily freshness and delight to him. It was almost as if the course he must pursue was being dictated to him.

Whatever causes Oleron's world to implode upon him, we, through the persuasiveness of Onions's prose, sympathise with him and therefore experience the same shivers of uncertainty and dread. We follow and understand his moods. In other words, we see the world through his haunted eyes. The story is a master-class in involving the reader in the emotions of the author's central character.

The connection between creativity and insanity is explored in other tales in this collection. For instance there is 'Rooum', whose central character is a clever engineer who is haunted by a ghost who can penetrate matter; and 'Benlian', a story which is narrated by a painter of miniatures who now resides in a madhouse, and which concerns a sculptor who, rather like Oleron in 'The Beckoning Fair One', becomes increasingly obsessed with his creation.

Onions seemed intrigued with the power of the imagination which allows the mind to bring into reality artificial constructs, whether they are fictional characters or works of art. This idea is explored with a tinge of dark humour in 'The Real People' in which the fragile barrier between reality and fantasy is explored when characters created by a romantic novelist take on a wonderfully disruptive life of their own. Similarly in 'Hic Jacet', Onions presents us with the strange scenario of a mystery writer who writes the biography of a friend as detective story.

The stories I have mentioned so far are from *Widdershins*, Onion's first foray into what he termed 'the ghostly spectrum'. His other two collections were *Ghosts in Daylight* (1924) and *The Painted Face* (1929). It was in these volumes particularly that Onions explored his fascination with the idea that the events of the past have a great influence on the life and destiny of an individual. In 'The Rosewood Door' from *The Painted Face* we are presented with what might be termed 'a living ghost', a character who, influenced in some mystical fashion by the antique door of the title, reveals varied past lives which impinge tragically on the present. A ghost story, yes, but also a tale of a doomed romance and again one involving a possible mental breakdown. As with so much of Onions's fiction, the characters are wonderfully drawn and the plot is multi-layered. The idea of a dark reincarnation, the power of past personalities to inhabit and influence the living, is also found in one of Onions's masterpieces, the title story from *The Painted Face* collection. It is the tale of a Sicilian girl on holiday in Tunis who falls in love with a young Englishman. The passion aroused in her by this affair causes the girl to experience dramatic personality changes. It turns out that this heroine is a temptress who through the ages is reincarnated to fool and entrap men. On this occasion, however, she has really fallen in love. The resolution of the plot is both ingenious and imbued with a touching sadness. In some ways it has the feel of a Greek tragedy about it.

This theme of past influences and reincarnation can be found in other stories including 'The Ascending Dream' in which the same portentous dream is experienced by three separate individuals through history. There are a number of what one might refer to as traditional ghost stories in this collection also: for example 'The Woman in the Way', which concerns the spirit of a young woman from the seventeenth century who haunts a meadow; and 'The Cigarette Case', which involves an attractive silver cigarette case that is the souvenir of a ghostly visitation.

I have no intention of touching on all the stories in this collection in my Introduction. I just wanted to give you a flavour, an appetiser if you like, of what to expect in this rich and varied *mélange* awaiting you. As intimated earlier, Oliver Onions is unique in the world of ghost stories; neither he nor his work can be easily compared with other practitioners of the art. One can often say, with other writers, something like 'there is a touch of M. R. James to this story' or 'one can detect the influence of E. F. Benson with that particular plot', and so on, but not so with Onions. He really does stand alone.

In this volume we have tried to present the reader with all of Onions's ghost stories, but it may well be that one of two elusive tales have escaped the net. However, there are four stories included here that have not found their way into any collection of Onions's work in recent times. Two are what he referred to as trifles: 'The Ether Hog' and 'The Mortal', and they merit special comment because of the whimsical and humorous nature of their narrative, so at odds with the bulk of this volume. 'The Ether Hog' is a kind of cheery Christmas ghost story involving a cantankerous but well-meaning ghost who is sent on an errand by the 'Special Committee on Ethereal Traffic and Right of Way' and disobeys their instructions in order to save lives. It is an amusing, fanciful and heart-warming tale which clearly demonstrates the author's versatility. 'The Mortal' is even more of a trifle and is rather like a comic sketch or an amusing fairy tale with a medieval setting where the main character risks his ghostly existence to carry out a haunting.

The third 'extra' tale is 'The Master of the House', a rare foray for Onions into werewolf territory; and the fourth is the aforementioned posthumously published 'Tragic Casements' which, rather like 'The Rosewood Door', involves the ghostly past intruding upon the present by means of an antique object – in this instance ancient window glass. Written towards the end of Onions's ghost-writing career, this story does not touch on any new territory, and if the ideas are by now somewhat familiar, nevertheless the story reveals that

Onions's ability to turn a chilling phrase and inject touches of dry humour into his prose remained undiminished.

These rare examples of Onions's work are the icing on this rather majestic cake. It was over twenty years ago that Gary William Crawford, one of the great commentators on and publishers of Gothic literature, stated that Onions's ghost stories were overdue for a revival. Well, it has been a long time coming but at last you hold in your hand a treasure-trove of some of the best supernatural writing ever penned. I hope you find the contents as exciting, engrossing and indeed as pleasantly uncomfortable as I did.

DAVID STUART DAVIES

THE DEAD OF NIGHT

Credo

Ghosts, it is advanced, either do not exist at all, or else, like the stars at noonday, they are there all the time and it is we who cannot see them. The stories in the following pages were written on the second of these assumptions.

At first sight it would therefore appear that the writer of ghost-stories in this sense has unlimited material to his hand; but actually this is not so. All-the-time manifestations, pervading the whole of nature with a ghostly element, are for all practical purposes no manifestations at all. What the writer has in practice to invest-igate is the varying 'densities' of the ghostliness that is revealed when this surface of life, accepted for everyday purposes as stable, is jarred, and for the time of an experience does not recover its equilibrium.

Nevertheless his realm is no narrow one. True its Central Province is of strictly limited extent, but, as this provides only the class of story so plainly labelled "ghost" that it cannot be mistaken for anything else, the spectre is apt to be swamped by the traditional apparatus that makes the stock illustration for the Christmas Number, and there is little to be said about this region except that here the ghostly texture is found at its coarsest.

But this place of shrouds and moans and bony fingers is surrounded by territory no less haunted than itself, and with far subtler terrors. This is the ghost-belt that never asserts its spectre, but leaves you in no doubt about his presence. Above all, only rarely is he seen, and I myself have never been able to understand why the unvarying question should be, "Have you ever *seen* a ghost?" when, if a ghost cannot exist apart from visibility, his being rests solely on the testi-mony of one sense, and that in some respects the most fallible one of all. May not his proximity be felt and his nature apprehended in other ways? I have it on excellent authority that such a visitor can in fact be heard breathing in the room, most powerfully smelt, and known for a spirit in travail longing for consolation, all at one and the same time, and yet not be seen by the eye. And even short of signs so explicit as these, who at some time or other has not walked into a room, known and familiar and presently to be known and familiar again, but that for a space has become a different room, informed with other influences and charged with other meanings? Something has temporarily upset the equilibrium, which will be restored by and bye. Much less dense, I take it, is the texture of the spirits that make this secondary zone their habitat, but ah, how much more shiveringly it gets to the marrow than do the groans and clankings of the grosser spook!

But nobody who has thought much of the poise of contending forces that keeps matter in its place, or of that other mystery by which spiritual entities deviate on the whole so little from type – nobody who has given his mind to these things has not sometimes also surmised the existence of a class of beings of a composition so unstable, yet of so plausible an exterior, that they are hardly known to have been ghosts till they have passed. To some of us these are the most disturbing simulacra of all, not because they contradict nature, but because they actually join hands with it. Surely that voice was a *real* voice, that touch a *real* touch? That that passed us in the twilight just now, surely that was substance and not shadow? For all is twilight here, and before we come out into the world of men and women again we have to traverse a territory peopled, not by graveyard figures seen by their own spectral light, not by daunting presences that creep in at our pores, but by such as look like men and women, at first arouse no fear, but yet hover so on the confines of ghostliness that it is but a step and lo, from the very verge of happy unhaunted earth they lapse back into the dread company. Should not these auto-haunts, that we have rubbed shoulders with without realising their nature, have information about both realms? Alas poor susceptibles, so near immunity, but blighted with one fatal particle, one vulnerable cell, which do but touch and they are haled back and claimed, as Xena in one of these stories was haled back to the darkness of the making of the world, to be branded on the breast with the trident of her lord Poseidon! But for some other compulsion such a ghost perhaps should I be, such a ghost you. Precariously we move among perils we do not know, saved only by a sanity stronger than our own. And when, either in ourselves or in another, such an osmosis takes place before our very eyes, does not a ghost write his own story? Who are The Real People?

For these reasons I claim that the tales that follow all range themselves somewhere between the ultra-violet and the infra-red of the ghostly spectrum. The three books, *Widdershins*, *Ghosts in Daylight* and *The Painted Face* were published in the years 1911, 1924 and 1929 respectively, and, with one or two stories comparatively recent in date, are thus a record of my own timid excursions into these regions over a period of twenty-five years. They are all that at present I care to collect. *Painted Faces*, in particular, can make both waking and dreaming far too uneasy.

OLIVER ONIONS

The Beckoning Fair One

The three or four 'To Let' boards had stood within the low paling as long as the inhabitants of the little triangular 'Square' could remember, and if they had ever been vertical it was a very long time ago. They now overhung the palings each at its own angle, and resembled nothing so much as a row of wooden choppers, ever in the act of falling upon some passer-by, yet never cutting off a tenant for the old house from the stream of his fellows. Not that there was ever any great 'stream' through the square; the stream passed a furlong and more away, beyond the intricacy of tenements and alleys and byways that had sprung up since the old house had been built, hemming it in completely; and probably the house itself was only suffered to stand pending the falling-in of a lease or two, when doubtless a clearance would be made of the whole neighbourhood.

It was of bloomy old red brick, and built into its walls were the crowns and clasped hands and other insignia of insurance companies long since defunct. The children of the secluded square had swung upon the low gate at the end of the entrance-alley until little more than the solid top bar of it remained, and the alley itself ran past boarded basement windows on which tramps had chalked their cryptic marks. The path was washed and worn uneven by the spilling of water from the eaves of the encroaching next house, and cats and dogs had made the approach their own. The chances of a tenant did not seem such as to warrant the keeping of the 'To Let' boards in a state of legibility and repair, and as a matter of fact they were not so kept.

For six months Oleron had passed the old place twice a day or oftener, on his way from his lodgings to the room, ten minutes' walk away, he had taken to work in; and for six months no hatchet-like notice-board had fallen across his path. This might have been due to the fact that he usually took the other side of the square. But he chanced one morning to take the side that ran past the broken gate and the rain-worn entrance alley, and to pause before one of the inclined boards. The board bore, besides the agent's name, the announcement, written apparently about the time of Oleron's own early youth, that the key was to be had at Number Six.

Now Oleron was already paying, for his separate bedroom and workroom, more than an author who, without private means, habitually disregards his public, can afford; and he was paying in addition a small rent for the storage of the greater part of his grandmother's furniture. Moreover, it invariably happened that the book he wished to read in bed was at his working-quarters half a mile and more away, while the note or letter he had sudden need of during the day was as likely as not to be in the pocket of another coat hanging behind his bedroom door. And there were other inconveniences in having a divided domicile. Therefore Oleron, brought suddenly up by the hatchet-like notice-board, looked first down through some scanty privet-bushes at the boarded basement windows, then up at the blank and grimy windows of the first floor, and so up to the second floor and the flat stone coping of the leads. He stood for a minute thumbing his lean and shaven jaw; then, with another glance at the board, he walked slowly across the square to Number Six.

He knocked, and waited for two or three minutes, but, although the door stood open, received no answer. He was knocking again when a long-nosed man in shirt-sleeves appeared.

'I was arsking a blessing on our food,' he said in severe explanation.

Oleron asked if he might have the key of the old house; and the long-nosed man withdrew again.

Oleron waited for another five minutes on the step; then the man, appearing again and masticating some of the food of which he had spoken, announced that the key was lost.

'But you won't want it,' he said. 'The entrance door isn't closed, and a push'll open any of the others. I'm a agent for it, if you're thinking of taking it – '

Oleron recrossed the square, descended the two steps at the broken gate, passed along the alley, and turned in at the old wide doorway. To the right, immediately within the door, steps descended to the roomy cellars, and the staircase before him had a carved rail, and was broad and handsome and filthy. Oleron ascended it, avoiding contact with the rail and wall, and stopped at the first landing. A door facing him had been boarded up, but he pushed at that on his right hand, and an insecure bolt or staple yielded. He entered the empty first floor.

He spent a quarter of an hour in the place, and then came out again. Without mounting higher, he descended and recrossed the square to the house of the man who had lost the key.

'Can you tell me how much the rent is?' he asked.

The man mentioned a figure, the comparative lowness of which seemed accounted for by the character of the neighbourhood and the abominable state of unrepair of the place.

'Would it be possible to rent a single floor?'

The long-nosed man did not know; they might . . .

'Who are they?'

The man gave Oleron the name of a firm of lawyers in Lincoln's Inn.

'You might mention my name – Barrett,' he added.

Pressure of work prevented Oleron from going down to Lincoln's Inn that afternoon, but he went on the morrow, and was instantly offered the whole house as a purchase for fifty pounds down, the remainder of the purchase-money to remain on mortgage. It took him half an hour to disabuse the lawyer's mind of the idea that he wished anything more of the place than to rent a single floor of it. This made certain hums and haws of a difference, and the lawyer was by no means certain that it lay within his power to do as Oleron suggested; but it was finally extracted from him that, provided the notice-boards were allowed to remain up, and that, provided it was agreed that in the event of the whole house letting, the arrangement should terminate automatically without further notice, something might be done. That the old place should suddenly let over his head seemed to Oleron the slightest of risks to take, and he promised a decision within a week. On the morrow he visited the house again, went through it from top to bottom, and then went home to his lodgings to take a bath.

He was immensely taken with that portion of the house he had already determined should be his own. Scraped clean and repainted, and with that old furniture of Oleron's grandmother's, it ought to be entirely charming. He went to the storage warehouse to refresh his memory of his half-forgotten belongings, and to take measurements; and thence he went to a decorator's. He was very busy with his regular work, and could have wished that the notice-board had caught his attention either a few months earlier or else later in the year; but the quickest way would be to suspend work entirely until after his removal . . .

A fortnight later his first floor was painted throughout in a tender, elderflower white, the paint was dry, and Oleron was in the middle of his installation. He was animated, delighted; and he rubbed his hands as he polished and made disposals of his grandmother's effects – the tall lattice-paned china cupboard with its Derby and Mason and Spode, the large folding Sheraton table, the long, low bookshelves (he had had two of them 'copied'), the chairs, the Sheffield candle-sticks, the riveted rose-bowls. These things he set against his newly painted elder-white walls – walls of wood panelled in the happiest proportions, and moulded and coffered to the low-seated window-recesses in a mood of gaiety and rest that the builders of rooms no longer know. The ceilings were lofty, and faintly painted with an old pattern of stars; even the tapering mouldings of his iron fireplace were as delicately designed as jewellery; and Oleron walked about rubbing his hands, frequently stopping for the mere pleasure of the glimpses from white room to white room . . .

'Charming, charming!' he said to himself. 'I wonder what Elsie Bengough will think of this!'

He bought a bolt and a Yale lock for his door, and shut off his quarters from the rest of the house. If he now wanted to read in bed, his book could be had for stepping into the next room. All the time, he thought how exceedingly lucky he was to get the place. He put up a hat-rack in the little square hall, and hung up his hats and caps and coats; and passers through the small triangular square late at night, looking up over the little serried row of wooden 'To Let' hatchets, could see the light within Oleron's red blinds, or else the sudden darkening of one blind and the illumination of another, as Oleron, candlestick in hand, passed from room to room, making final settlings of his furniture, or preparing to resume the work that his removal had interrupted.

2

As far as the chief business of his life – his writing – was concerned, Paul Oleron treated the world a good deal better than he was treated by it; but he seldom took the trouble to strike a balance, or to compute how far, at forty-four years of age, he was behind his points on the handicap. To have done so wouldn't have altered matters, and it might have depressed Oleron. He had chosen his path, and was

committed to it beyond possibility of withdrawal. Perhaps he had
chosen it in the days when he had been easily swayed by something a
little disinterested, a little generous, a little noble; and had he ever
thought of questioning himself he would still have held to it that a life
without nobility and generosity and disinterestedness was no life for
him. Only quite recently, and rarely, had he even vaguely suspected
that there was more in it than this; but it was no good anticipating the
day when, he supposed, he would reach that maximum point of his
powers beyond which he must inevitably decline, and be left face to
face with the question whether it would not have profited him better
to have ruled his life by less exigent ideals.

In the meantime, his removal into the old house with the insurance
marks built into its brick merely interrupted *Romilly Bishop* at the
fifteenth chapter.

As this tall man with the lean, ascetic face moved about his new
abode, arranging, changing, altering, hardly yet into his working-
stride again, he gave the impression of almost spinster-like precision
and nicety. For twenty years past, in a score of lodgings, garrets,
flats, and rooms furnished and unfurnished, he had been accustomed
to do many things for himself, and he had discovered that it saves
time and temper to be methodical. He had arranged with the wife of
the long-nosed Barrett, a stout Welsh woman with a falsetto voice,
the Merionethshire accent of which long residence in London had
not perceptibly modified, to come across the square each morning to
prepare his breakfast, and also to 'turn the place out' on Saturday
mornings; and for the rest, he even welcomed a little housework as a
relaxation from the strain of writing.

His kitchen, together with the adjoining strip of an apartment
into which a modern bath had been fitted, overlooked the alley at
the side of the house; and at one end of it was a large closet with a
door, and a square sliding hatch in the upper part of the door. This
had been a powder-closet, and through the hatch the elaborately
dressed head had been thrust to receive the click and puff of the
powder-pistol. Oleron puzzled a little over this closet; then, as its
use occurred to him, he smiled faintly, a little moved, he knew not
by what . . . He would have to put it to a very different purpose from
its original one; it would probably have to serve as his larder . . . It
was in this closet that he made a discovery. The back of it was
shelved, and, rummaging on an upper shelf that ran deeply into
the wall, Oleron found a couple of mushroom-shaped old wooden
wig-stands. He did not know how they had come to be there.

Doubtless the painters had turned them up somewhere or other, and had put them there. But his five rooms, as a whole, were short of cupboard and closet-room; and it was only by the exercise of some ingenuity that he was able to find places for the bestowal of his household linen, his boxes, and his seldom-used but not-to-be-destroyed accumulations of papers.

It was in early spring that Oleron entered on his tenancy, and he was anxious to have *Romilly* ready for publication in the coming autumn. Nevertheless, he did not intend to force its production. Should it demand longer in the doing, so much the worse; he realised its importance, its crucial importance, in his artistic development, and it must have its own length and time. In the workroom he had recently left he had been making excellent progress; *Romilly* had begun, as the saying is, to speak and act of herself; and he did not doubt she would continue to do so the moment the distraction of his removal was over. This distraction was almost over; he told himself it was time he pulled himself together again; and on a March morning he went out, returned again with two great bunches of yellow daffodils, placed one bunch on his mantelpiece between the Sheffield sticks and the other on the table before him, and took out the half-completed manuscript of *Romilly Bishop*.

But before beginning work he went to a small rosewood cabinet and took from a drawer his cheque-book and pass-book. He totted them up, and his monk-like face grew thoughtful. His installation had cost him more than he had intended it should, and his balance was rather less than fifty pounds, with no immediate prospect of more.

'Hm! I'd forgotten rugs and chintz curtains and so forth mounted up so,' said Oleron. 'But it would have been a pity to spoil the place for the want of ten pounds or so . . . Well, *Romilly* simply *must* be out for the autumn, that's all. So here goes – '

He drew his papers towards him.

But he worked badly; or, rather, he did not work at all. The square outside had its own noises, frequent and new, and Oleron could only hope that he would speedily become accustomed to these. First came hawkers, with their carts and cries; at midday the children, returning from school, trooped into the square and swung on Oleron's gate; and when the children had departed again for afternoon school, an itinerant musician with a mandolin posted himself beneath Oleron's window and began to strum. This was a not unpleasant distraction, and Oleron, pushing up his window, threw the man a penny. Then he returned to his table again . . .

But it was no good. He came to himself, at long intervals, to find that he had been looking about his room and wondering how it had formerly been furnished – whether a settee in buttercup or petunia satin had stood under the farther window, whether from the centre moulding of the light lofty ceiling had depended a glimmering crystal chandelier, or where the tambour-frame or the picquet-table had stood . . . No, it was no good; he had far better be frankly doing nothing than getting fruitlessly tired; and he decided that he would take a walk, but, chancing to sit down for a moment, dozed in his chair instead.

'This won't do,' he yawned when he awoke at half-past four in the afternoon; 'I must do better than this tomorrow – '

And he felt so deliciously lazy that for some minutes he even contemplated the breach of an appointment he had for the evening.

The next morning he sat down to work without even permitting himself to answer one of his three letters – two of them tradesmen's accounts, the third a note from Miss Bengough, forwarded from his old address. It was a jolly day of white and blue, with a gay noisy wind and a subtle turn in the colour of growing things; and over and over again, once or twice a minute, his room became suddenly light and then subdued again, as the shining white clouds rolled north-east-wards over the square. The soft fitful illumination was reflected in the polished surface of the table and even in the footworn old floor; and the morning noises had begun again.

Oleron made a pattern of dots on the paper before him, and then broke off to move the jar of daffodils exactly opposite the centre of a creamy panel. Then he wrote a sentence that ran continuously for a couple of lines, after which it broke on into notes and jottings. For a time he succeeded in persuading himself that in making these memoranda he was really working; then he rose and began to pace his room. As he did so, he was struck by an idea. It was that the place might possibly be a little better for more positive colour. It was, perhaps, a thought *too* pale – mild and sweet as a kind old face, but a little devitalised, even wan . . . Yes, decidedly it would bear a robuster note – more and richer flowers, and possibly some warm and gay stuff for cushions for the window-seats . . .

'Of course, I really can't afford it,' he muttered, as he went for a two-foot and began to measure the width of the window recesses . . .

In stooping to measure a recess, his attitude suddenly changed to one of interest and attention. Presently he rose again, rubbing his hands with gentle glee.

'Oho, oho!' he said. 'These look to me very much like window-boxes, nailed up. We must look into this! Yes, those are boxes, or I'm . . . oho, this is an adventure!'

On that wall of his sitting-room there were two windows (the third was in another corner), and, beyond the open bedroom door, on the same wall, was another. The seats of all had been painted, repainted, and painted again; and Oleron's investigating finger had barely detected the old nailheads beneath the paint. Under the ledge over which he stooped an old keyhole also had been puttied up. Oleron took out his penknife.

He worked carefully for five minutes, and then went into the kitchen for a hammer and chisel. Driving the chisel cautiously under the seat, he started the whole lid slightly. Again using the penknife, he cut along the hinged edge and outward along the ends; and then he fetched a wedge and a wooden mallet.

'Now for our little mystery – ' he said.

The sound of the mallet on the wedge seemed, in that sweet and pale apartment, somehow a little brutal – nay, even shocking. The panelling rang and rattled and vibrated to the blows like a sounding-board. The whole house seemed to echo; from the roomy cellarage to the garrets above a flock of echoes seemed to awake; and the sound got a little on Oleron's nerves. All at once he paused, fetched a duster, and muffled the mallet . . . When the edge was sufficiently raised he put his fingers under it and lifted. The paint flaked and starred a little; the rusty old nails squeaked and grunted; and the lid came up, laying open the box beneath. Oleron looked into it. Save for a couple of inches of scurf and mould and old cobwebs it was empty.

'No treasure there,' said Oleron, a little amused that he should have fancied there might have been. '*Romilly* will still have to be out by the autumn. Let's have a look at the others.'

He turned to the second window.

The raising of the two remaining seats occupied him until well into the afternoon. That of the bedroom, like the first, was empty; but from the second seat of his sitting-room he drew out something yielding and folded and furred over an inch thick with dust. He carried the object into the kitchen, and having swept it over a bucket, took a duster to it.

It was some sort of a large bag, of an ancient frieze-like material, and when unfolded it occupied the greater part of the small kitchen floor. In shape it was an irregular, a very irregular, triangle, and it had a couple of wide flaps, with the remains of straps and buckles. The patch that had been uppermost in the folding was of a faded yellowish brown; but the rest of it was of shades of crimson that varied according to the exposure of the parts of it.

'Now whatever can that have been?' Oleron mused as he stood surveying it . . . 'I give it up. Whatever it is, it's settled my work for today, I'm afraid – '

He folded the object up carelessly and thrust it into a corner of the kitchen; then, taking pans and brushes and an old knife, he returned to the sitting-room and began to scrape and to wash and to line with paper his newly discovered receptacles. When he had finished, he put his spare boots and books and papers into them; and he closed the lids again, amused with his little adventure, but also a little anxious for the hour to come when he should settle fairly down to his work again.

3

It piqued Oleron a little that his friend, Miss Bengough, should dismiss with a glance the place he himself had found so singularly winning. Indeed she scarcely lifted her eyes to it. But then she had always been more or less like that – a little indifferent to the graces of life, careless of appearances, and perhaps a shade more herself when she ate biscuits from a paper bag than when she dined with greater observance of the convenances. She was an unattached journalist of thirty-four, large, showy, fair as butter, pink as a dog-rose, reminding one of a florist's picked specimen bloom, and given to sudden and ample movements and moist and explosive utterances. She 'pulled a better living out of the pool' (as she expressed it) than Oleron did; and by cunningly disguised puffs of drapers and haberdashers she 'pulled' also the greater part of her very varied wardrobe. She left small whirlwinds of air behind her when she moved, in which her veils and scarves fluttered and spun.

Oleron heard the flurry of her skirts on his staircase and her single loud knock at his door when he had been a month in his new abode. Her garments brought in the outer air, and she flung a bundle of ladies' journals down on a chair.

'Don't knock off for me,' she said across a mouthful of large-headed hatpins as she removed her hat and veil. 'I didn't know whether you were straight yet, so I've brought some sandwiches for lunch. You've got coffee, I suppose? – No, don't get up – I'll find the kitchen – '

'Oh, that's all right, I'll clear these things away. To tell the truth, I'm rather glad to be interrupted,' said Oleron.

He gathered his work together and put it away. She was already in the kitchen; he heard the running of water into the kettle. He joined her, and ten minutes later followed her back to the sitting-room with the coffee and sandwiches on a tray. They sat down, with the tray on a small table between them.

'Well, what do you think of the new place?' Oleron asked as she poured out coffee.

'Hm! . . . Anybody'd think you were going to get married, Paul.'

He laughed.

'Oh no. But it's an improvement on some of them, isn't it?'

'Is it? I suppose it is; I don't know. I liked the last place, in spite of the black ceiling and no watertap. How's *Romilly*?'

Oleron thumbed his chin.

'Hm! I'm rather ashamed to tell you. The fact is, I've not got on very well with it. But it will be all right on the night, as you used to say.'

'Stuck?'

'Rather stuck.'

'Got any of it you care to read to me? . . . '

Oleron had long been in the habit of reading portions of his work to Miss Bengough occasionally. Her comments were always quick and practical, sometimes directly useful, sometimes indirectly suggestive. She, in return for his confidence, always kept all mention of her own work sedulously from him. His, she said, was 'real work'; hers merely filled space, not always even grammatically.

'I'm afraid there isn't,' Oleron replied, still meditatively dry-shaving his chin. Then he added, with a little burst of candour, 'The fact is, Elsie, I've not written – not actually written – very much more of it – *any* more of it, in fact. But, of course, that doesn't mean I haven't progressed. I've progressed, in one sense, rather alarmingly. I'm now thinking of reconstructing the whole thing.'

Miss Bengough gave a gasp. 'Reconstructing!'

'Making Romilly herself a different type of woman. Somehow, I've begun to feel that I'm not getting the most out of her. As she stands, I've certainly lost interest in her to some extent.'

'But – but – ' Miss Bengough protested, 'you had her so real, so *living*, Paul!'

Oleron smiled faintly. He had been quite prepared for Miss Bengough's disapproval. He wasn't surprised that she liked Romilly as she at present existed; she would. Whether she realised it or not, there was much of herself in his fictitious creation. Naturally Romilly would seem 'real', 'living', to her . . .

'But are you really serious, Paul?' Miss Bengough asked presently, with a round-eyed stare.

'Quite serious.'

'You're really going to scrap those fifteen chapters?'

'I didn't exactly say that.'

'That fine, rich love-scene?'

'I should only do it reluctantly, and for the sake of something I thought better.'

'And that beautiful, *beau*tiful description of Romilly on the shore?'

'It wouldn't necessarily be wasted,' he said a little uneasily.

But Miss Bengough made a large and windy gesture, and then let him have it.

'Really, you are *too* trying!' she broke out. 'I do wish sometimes you'd remember you're human, and live in a world! You know I'd be the *last* to wish you to lower your standard one inch, but it wouldn't be lowering it to bring it within human comprehension. Oh, you're sometimes altogether too godlike! . . . Why, it would be a wicked, criminal waste of your powers to destroy those fifteen chapters! Look at it reasonably, now. You've been working for nearly twenty years; you've now got what you've been working for almost within your grasp; your affairs are at a most critical stage (oh, don't tell me; I know you're about at the end of your money); and here you are, deliberately proposing to withdraw a thing that will probably make your name, and to substitute for it something that ten to one nobody on earth will ever want to read – and small blame to them! Really, you try my patience!'

Oleron had shaken his head slowly as she had talked. It was an old story between them. The noisy, able, practical journalist was an admirable friend – up to a certain point; beyond that . . . well, each of us knows that point beyond which we stand alone. Elsie Bengough sometimes said that had she had one-tenth part of Oleron's genius there were few things she could not have done – thus making that genius a quantitatively divisible thing, a sort of ingredient, to be added to or subtracted from in the admixture of his work. That it was a qualitative thing, essential, indivisible, informing, passed her comprehension. Their spirits

parted company at that point. Oleron knew it. She did not appear
to know it.

'Yes, yes, yes,' he said a little wearily, by and by, 'practically you're
quite right, entirely right, and I haven't a word to say. If I could only
turn *Romilly* over to you you'd make an enormous success of her. But
that can't be, and I, for my part, am seriously doubting whether she's
worth my while. You know what that means.'

'What does it mean?' she demanded bluntly.

'Well,' he said, smiling wanly, 'what *does* it mean when you're
convinced a thing isn't worth doing? You simply don't do it.'

Miss Bengough's eyes swept the ceiling for assistance against this
impossible man.

'What utter rubbish!' she broke out at last. 'Why, when I saw you
last you were simply oozing *Romilly*; you were turning her off at the
rate of four chapters a week; if you hadn't moved you'd have had her
three-parts done by now. What on earth possessed you to move right
in the middle of your most important work?'

Oleron tried to put her off with a recital of inconveniences, but
she wouldn't have it. Perhaps in her heart she partly suspected the
reason. He was simply mortally weary of the narrow circumstances
of his life. He had had twenty years of it – twenty years of garrets and
roof-chambers and dingy flats and shabby lodgings, and he was tired
of dinginess and shabbiness. The reward was as far off as ever – or if
it was not, he no longer cared as once he would have cared to put out
his hand and take it. It is all very well to tell a man who is at the point
of exhaustion that only another effort is required of him; if he cannot
make it he is as far off as ever . . .

'Anyway,' Oleron summed up, 'I'm happier here than I've been for
a long time. That's some sort of a justification.'

'And doing no work,' said Miss Bengough pointedly.

At that a trifling petulance that had been gathering in Oleron came
to a head.

'And why should I do nothing but work?' he demanded. 'How
much happier am I for it? I don't say I don't love my work – when it's
done; but I hate doing it. Sometimes it's an intolerable burden that
I simply long to be rid of. Once in many weeks it has a moment,
one moment, of glow and thrill for me; I remember the days when it
was all glow and thrill; and now I'm forty-four, and it's becoming
drudgery. Nobody wants it; I'm ceasing to want it myself; and if any
ordinary sensible man were to ask me whether I didn't think I was a
fool to go on, I think I should agree that I was.'

Miss Bengough's comely pink face was serious.

'But you knew all that, many, many years ago, Paul – and still you chose it,' she said in a low voice.

'Well, and how should I have known?' he demanded. 'I didn't know. I was told so. My heart, if you like, told me so, and I thought I knew. Youth always thinks it knows; then one day it discovers that it is nearly fifty – '

'Forty-four, Paul – '

' – forty-four, then – and it finds that the glamour isn't in front, but behind. Yes, I knew and chose, if *that's* knowing and choosing . . . but it's a costly choice we're called on to make when we're young!'

Miss Bengough's eyes were on the floor. Without moving them she said, 'You're not regretting it, Paul?'

'Am I not?' he took her up. 'Upon my word, I've lately thought I am! What *do* I get in return for it all?'

'You know what you get,' she replied.

He might have known from her tone what else he could have had for the holding up of a finger – herself. She knew, but could not tell him, that he could have done no better thing for himself. Had he, any time these ten years, asked her to marry him, she would have replied quietly, 'Very well; when?' He had never thought of it . . .

'Yours is the real work,' she continued quietly. 'Without you we jackals couldn't exist. You and a few like you hold everything upon your shoulders.'

For a minute there was a silence. Then it occurred to Oleron that this was common vulgar grumbling. It was not his habit. Suddenly he rose and began to stack cups and plates on the tray.

'Sorry you catch me like this, Elsie,' he said, with a little laugh . . . 'No, I'll take them out; then we'll go for a walk, if you like . . . '

He carried out the tray, and then began to show Miss Bengough round his flat. She made few comments. In the kitchen she asked what an old faded square of reddish frieze was, that Mrs Barrett used as a cushion for her wooden chair.

'That? I should be glad if you could tell *me* what it is,' Oleron replied as he unfolded the bag and related the story of its finding in the window-seat.

'I think I know what it is,' said Miss Bengough. 'It's been used to wrap up a harp before putting it into its case.'

'By Jove, that's probably just what it was,' said Oleron. 'I could make neither head nor tail of it . . . '

They finished the tour of the flat, and returned to the sitting-room.

'And who lives in the rest of the house?' Miss Bengough asked.

'I dare say a tramp sleeps in the cellar occasionally. Nobody else.'

'Hm! . . . Well, I'll tell you what I think about it, if you like.'

'I should like.'

'You'll never work here.'

'Oh?' said Oleron quickly. 'Why not?'

'You'll never finish *Romilly* here. Why, I don't know, but you won't. I know it. You'll have to leave before you get on with that book.'

He mused for a moment, and then said:

'Isn't that a little – prejudiced, Elsie?'

'Perfectly ridiculous. As an argument it hasn't a leg to stand on. But there it is,' she replied, her mouth once more full of the large-headed hat pins.

Oleron was reaching down his hat and coat. He laughed.

'I can only hope you're entirely wrong,' he said, 'for I shall be in a serious mess if *Romilly* isn't out in the autumn.'

4

As Oleron sat by his fire that evening, pondering Miss Bengough's prognostication that difficulties awaited him in his work, he came to the conclusion that it would have been far better had she kept her beliefs to herself. No man does a thing better for having his confidence damped at the outset, and to speak of difficulties is in a sense to make them. Speech itself becomes a deterrent act, to which other discouragements accrete until the very event of which warning is given is as likely as not to come to pass. He heartily confounded her. An influence hostile to the completion of *Romilly* had been born.

And in some illogical, dogmatic way women seem to have, she had attached this antagonistic influence to his new abode. Was ever anything so absurd! 'You'll never finish *Romilly* here.' . . . Why not? Was this her idea of the luxury that saps the springs of action and brings a man down to indolence and dropping out of the race? The place was well enough – it was entirely charming, for that matter – but it was not so demoralising as all that! No; Elsie had missed the mark that time . . .

He moved his chair to look round the room that smiled, positively smiled, in the firelight. He too smiled, as if pity was to be entertained for a maligned apartment. Even that slight lack of robust colour he had remarked was not noticeable in the soft glow. The drawn chintz curtains – they had a flowered and trellised pattern, with baskets and oaten pipes – fell in long quiet folds to the window-seats; the rows of bindings in old bookcases took the light richly; the last trace of sallowness had gone with the daylight; and, if the truth must be told, it had been Elsie herself who had seemed a little out of the picture.

That reflection struck him a little, and presently he returned to it. Yes, the room had, quite accidentally, done Miss Bengough a disservice that afternoon. It had, in some subtle but unmistakable way, placed her, marked a contrast of qualities. Assuming for the sake of argument the slightly ridiculous proposition that the room in which Oleron sat *was* characterised by a certain sparsity and lack of vigour; so much the worse for Miss Bengough; she certainly erred on the side of redundancy and general muchness. And if one must contrast abstract qualities, Oleron inclined to the austere in taste . . .

Yes, here Oleron had made a distinct discovery; he wondered he had not made it before. He pictured Miss Bengough again as she had appeared that afternoon – large, showy, moistly pink, with that quality of the prize bloom exuding, as it were, from her; and instantly she suffered in his thought. He even recognised now that he had noticed something odd at the time, and that unconsciously his attitude, even while she had been there, had been one of criticism. The mechanism of her was a little obvious; her melting humidity was the result of analysable processes; and behind her there had seemed to lurk some dim shape emblematic of mortality. He had never, during the ten years of their intimacy, dreamed for a moment of asking her to marry him; none the less, he now felt for the first time a thankfulness that he had not done so . . .

Then, suddenly and swiftly, his face flamed that he should be thinking thus of his friend. What! Elsie Bengough, with whom he had spent weeks and weeks of afternoons – she, the good chum, on whose help he would have counted had all the rest of the world failed him – she, whose loyalty to him would not, he knew, swerve as long as there was breath in her – Elsie to be even in thought dissected thus! He was an ingrate and a cad . . .

Had she been there in that moment he would have abased himself before her.

For ten minutes and more he sat, still gazing into the fire, with that humiliating red fading slowly from his cheeks. All was still within and without, save for a tiny musical tinkling that came from his kitchen – the dripping of water from an imperfectly turned-off tap into the vessel beneath it. Mechanically he began to beat with his finger to the faintly heard falling of the drops; the tiny regular movement seemed to hasten that shameful withdrawal from his face. He grew cool once more; and when he resumed his meditation he was all unconscious that he took it up again at the same point . . .

It was not only her florid superfluity of build that he had approached in the attitude of criticism; he was conscious also of the wide differences between her mind and his own. He felt no thankfulness that up to a certain point their natures had ever run companionably side by side; he was now full of questions beyond that point. Their intellects diverged; there was no denying it; and, looking back, he was inclined to doubt whether there had been any real coincidence. True, he had read his writings to her and she had appeared to speak comprehendingly and to the point; but what can a man do who, having assumed that another sees as he does, is suddenly brought up sharp by something that falsifies and discredits all that has gone before? He doubted all now . . . It did for a moment occur to him that the man who demands of a friend more than can be given to him is in danger of losing that friend, but he put the thought aside.

Again he ceased to think, and again moved his finger to the distant dripping of the tap . . .

And now (he resumed by and by), if these things were true of Elsie Bengough, they were also true of the creation of which she was the prototype – Romilly Bishop. And since he could say of Romilly what for very shame he could not say of Elsie, he gave his thoughts rein. He did so in that smiling, fire-lighted room, to the accompaniment of the faintly heard tap.

There was no longer any doubt about it; he hated the central character of his novel. Even as he had described her physically she overpowered the senses; she was coarse-fibred, over-coloured, rank. It became true the moment he formulated his thought; Gulliver had described the Brobdingnagian maids-of-honour thus: and mentally and spiritually she corresponded – was unsensitive, limited, common. The model (he closed his eyes for a moment) – the model stuck out through fifteen vulgar and blatant chapters to such a pitch that, without seeing the reason, he had been unable to begin the sixteenth. He marvelled that it had only just dawned upon him.

And *this* was to have been his Beatrice, his vision! As Elsie she was to have gone into the furnace of his art, and she was to have come out the Woman all men desire! Her thoughts were to have been culled from his own finest, her form from his dearest dreams, and her setting wherever he could find one fit for her worth. He had brooded long before making the attempt; then one day he had felt her stir within him as a mother feels a quickening, and he had begun to write; and so he had added chapter to chapter . . .

And those fifteen sodden chapters were what he had produced!

Again he sat, softly moving his finger . . .

Then he bestirred himself.

She must go, all fifteen chapters of her. That was settled. For what was to take her place his mind was a blank; but one thing at a time; a man is not excused from taking the wrong course because the right one is not immediately revealed to him. Better would come if it was to come; in the meantime –

He rose, fetched the fifteen chapters, and read them over before he should drop them into the fire.

But instead of putting them into the fire he let them fall from his hand. He became conscious of the dripping of the tap again. It had a tinkling gamut of four or five notes, on which it rang irregular changes, and it was foolishly sweet and dulcimer-like. In his mind Oleron could see the gathering of each drop, its little tremble on the lip of the tap, and the tiny percussion of its fall, 'Plink – plunk', minimised almost to inaudibility. Following the lowest note there seemed to be a brief phrase, irregularly repeated; and presently Oleron found himself waiting for the recurrence of this phrase. It was quite pretty . . .

But it did not conduce to wakefulness, and Oleron dozed over his fire.

When he awoke again the fire had burned low and the flames of the candles were licking the rims of the Sheffield sticks. Sluggishly he rose, yawned, went his nightly round of door-locks and window-fastenings, and passed into his bedroom. Soon he slept soundly.

But a curious little sequel followed on the morrow. Mrs Barrett usually tapped, not at his door, but at the wooden wall beyond which lay Oleron's bed; and then Oleron rose, put on his dressing-gown, and admitted her. He was not conscious that as he did so that morning he hummed an air; but Mrs Barrett lingered with her hand on the door-knob and her face a little averted and smiling.

'De-ar me!' her soft falsetto rose. 'But that will be a very o-ald tune, Mr Oleron! I will not have heard it this for-ty years!'

'What tune?' Oleron asked.

'The tune, indeed, that you was humming, sir.'

Oleron had his thumb in the flap of a letter. It remained there.

'*I* was humming? . . . Sing it, Mrs Barrett.'

Mrs Barrett prut-prutted.

'I have no voice for singing, Mr Oleron; it was Ann Pugh was the singer of our family; but the tune will be very o-ald, and it is called "The Beckoning Fair One".'

'Try to sing it,' said Oleron, his thumb still in the envelope; and Mrs Barrett, with much dimpling and confusion, hummed the air.

'They do say it was sung to a harp, Mr Oleron, and it will be very o-ald,' she concluded.

'And *I* was singing that?'

'Indeed you wass. I would not be likely to tell you lies.'

With a 'Very well – let me have breakfast', Oleron opened his letter; but the trifling circumstance struck him as more odd than he would have admitted to himself. The phrase he had hummed had been that which he had associated with the falling from the tap on the evening before.

5

Even more curious than that the commonplace dripping of an ordinary water-tap should have tallied so closely with an actually existing air was another result it had, namely, that it awakened, or seemed to awaken, in Oleron an abnormal sensitiveness to other noises of the old house. It has been remarked that silence obtains its fullest and most impressive quality when it is broken by some minute sound; and, truth to tell, the place was never still. Perhaps the mildness of the spring air operated on its torpid old timbers; perhaps Oleron's fires caused it to stretch its old anatomy; and certainly a whole world of insect life bored and burrowed in its baulks and joists. At any rate, Oleron had only to sit quiet in his chair and to wait for a minute or two in order to become aware of such a change in the auditory scale as comes upon a man who, conceiving the midsummer woods to be motionless and still, all at once finds his ear sharpened to the crepitation of a myriad insects.

And he smiled to think of man's arbitrary distinction between that which has life and that which has not. Here, quite apart from such recognisable sounds as the scampering of mice, the falling of plaster behind his panelling, and the popping of purses or coffins from his fire, was a whole house talking to him had he but known its language. Beams settled with a tired sigh into their old mortices;

creatures ticked in the walls; joints cracked, boards complained; with no palpable stirring of the air window-sashes changed their positions with a soft knock in their frames. And whether the place had life in this sense or not, it had at all events a winsome personality. It needed but an hour of musing for Oleron to conceive the idea that, as his own body stood in friendly relation to his soul, so, by an extension and an attenuation, his habitation might fantastically be supposed to stand in some relation to himself. He even amused himself with the far-fetched fancy that he might so identify himself with the place that some future tenant, taking possession, might regard it as in a sense haunted. It would be rather a joke if he, a perfectly harmless author, with nothing on his mind worse than a novel he had discovered he must begin again, should turn out to be laying the foundation of a future ghost! . . .

In proportion, however, as he felt this growing attachment to the fabric of his abode, Elsie Bengough, from being merely unattracted, began to show a dislike of the place that was more and more marked. And she did not scruple to speak of her aversion.

'It doesn't belong to today at all, and for you especially it's bad,' she said with decision. 'You're only too ready to let go your hold on actual things and to slip into apathy; *you* ought to be in a place with concrete floors and a patent gas-meter and a tradesmen's lift. And it would do you all the good in the world if you had a job that made you scramble and rub elbows with your fellow-men. Now, if I could get you a job, for, say, two or three days a week, one that would allow you heaps of time for your proper work – would you take it?'

Somehow, Oleron resented a little being diagnosed like this. He thanked Miss Bengough, but without a smile.

'Thank you, but I don't think so. After all each of us has his own life to live,' he could not refrain from adding.

'His own life to live! . . . How long is it since you were out, Paul?'

'About two hours.'

'I don't mean to buy stamps or to post a letter. How long is it since you had anything like a stretch?'

'Oh, some little time perhaps. I don't know.'

'Since I was here last?'

'I haven't been out much.'

'And has *Romilly* progressed much better for your being cooped up?'

'I think she has. I'm laying the foundations of her. I shall begin the actual writing presently.'

It seemed as if Miss Bengough had forgotten their tussle about the first *Romilly*. She frowned, turned half away, and then quickly turned again.

'Ah! . . . So you've still got that ridiculous idea in your head?'

'If you mean,' said Oleron slowly, 'that I've discarded the old *Romilly*, and am at work on a new one, you're right. I have still got that idea in my head.'

Something uncordial in his tone struck her; but she was a fighter. His own absurd sensitiveness hardened her. She gave a 'Pshaw!' of impatience.

'Where is the old one?' she demanded abruptly.

'Why?' asked Oleron.

'I want to see it. I want to show some of it to you. I want, if you're not wool-gathering entirely, to bring you back to your senses.'

This time it was he who turned his back. But when he turned round again he spoke more gently.

'It's no good, Elsie. I'm responsible for the way I go, and you must allow me to go it – even if it should seem wrong to you. Believe me, I am giving thought to it . . . The manuscript? I was on the point of burning it, but I didn't. It's in that window-seat, if you must see it.'

Miss Bengough crossed quickly to the window-seat, and lifted the lid. Suddenly she gave a little exclamation, and put the back of her hand to her mouth. She spoke over her shoulder.

'You ought to knock those nails in, Paul,' she said.

He strode to her side.

'What? What is it? What's the matter?' he asked. 'I did knock them in – or, rather, pulled them out.'

'You left enough to scratch with,' she replied, showing her hand. From the upper wrist to the knuckle of the little finger a welling red wound showed.

'Good – gracious!' Oleron ejaculated . . . 'Here, come to the bathroom and bathe it quickly – '

He hurried her to the bathroom, turned on warm water, and bathed and cleansed the bad gash. Then, still holding the hand, he turned cold water on it, uttering broken phrases of astonishment and concern.

'Good Lord, how did that happen! As far as I knew I'd . . . is this water too cold? Does that hurt? I can't imagine how on earth . . . there; that'll do – '

'No – one moment longer – I can bear it,' she murmured, her eyes closed . . .

Presently he led her back to the sitting-room and bound the hand in one of his handkerchiefs; but his face did not lose its expression of perplexity. He had spent half a day in opening and making service-able the three window-boxes, and he could not conceive how he had come to leave an inch and a half of rusty nail standing in the wood. He himself had opened the lids of each of them a dozen times and had not noticed any nail; but there it was . . .

'It shall come out now, at all events,' he muttered, as he went for a pair of pincers. And he made no mistake about it that time.

Elsie Bengough had sunk into a chair, and her face was rather white; but in her hand was the manuscript of *Romilly*. She had not finished with *Romilly* yet. Presently she returned to the charge.

'Oh, Paul, it will be the greatest mistake you ever, ever made if you do not publish this!' she said.

He hung his head, genuinely distressed. He couldn't get that incident of the nail out of his head, and *Romilly* occupied a second place in his thoughts for the moment. But still she insisted; and when presently he spoke it was almost as if he asked her pardon for something.

'What can I say, Elsie? I can only hope that when you see the new version, you'll see how right I am. And if in spite of all you *don't* like her, well . . . ' he made a hopeless gesture. 'Don't you see that I *must* be guided by my own lights?'

She was silent.

'Come, Elsie,' he said gently. 'We've got along well so far; don't let us split on this.'

The last words had hardly passed his lips before he regretted them. She had been nursing her injured hand, with her eyes once more closed; but her lips and lids quivered simultaneously. Her voice shook as she spoke.

'I can't help saying it, Paul, but you are so greatly changed.'

'Hush, Elsie,' he murmured soothingly; 'you've had a shock; rest for a while. How could I change?'

'I don't know, but you are. You've not been yourself ever since you came here. I wish you'd never seen the place. It's stopped your work, it's making you into a person I hardly know, and it's made me horribly anxious about you . . . Oh, how my hand is beginning to throb!'

'Poor child!' he murmured. 'Will you let me take you to a doctor and have it properly dressed?'

'No – I shall be all right presently – I'll keep it raised – '

She put her elbow on the back of her chair, and the bandaged hand rested lightly on his shoulder.

At that touch an entirely new anxiety stirred suddenly within him. Hundreds of times previously, on their jaunts and excursions, she had slipped her hand within his arm as she might have slipped it into the arm of a brother, and he had accepted the little affectionate gesture as a brother might have accepted it. But now, for the first time, there rushed into his mind a hundred startling questions. Her eyes were still closed, and her head had fallen pathetically back; and there was a lost and ineffable smile on her parted lips. The truth broke in upon him. Good God! . . . And he had never divined it!

And stranger than all was that, now that he did see that she was lost in love of him, there came to him, not sorrow and humility and abasement, but something else that he struggled in vain against – something entirely strange and new, that, had he analysed it, he would have found to be petulance and irritation and resentment and ungentleness. The sudden selfish prompting mastered him before he was aware. He all but gave it words. What was she doing there at all? Why was she not getting on with her own work? Why was she here interfering with his? Who had given her this guardianship over him that lately she had put forward so assertively? – 'Changed?' It was she, not himself, who had changed . . .

But by the time she had opened her eyes again he had overcome his resentment sufficiently to speak gently, albeit with reserve.

'I wish you would let me take you to a doctor.'

She rose.

'No, thank you, Paul,' she said. 'I'll go now. If I need a dressing I'll get one; take the other hand, please. Goodbye – '

He did not attempt to detain her. He walked with her to the foot of the stairs. Half-way along the narrow alley she turned.

'It would be a long way to come if you happened not to be in,' she said; 'I'll send you a postcard the next time.'

At the gate she turned again.

'Leave here, Paul,' she said, with a mournful look. 'Everything's wrong with this house.'

Then she was gone.

Oleron returned to his room. He crossed straight to the window-box. He opened the lid and stood long looking at it. Then he closed it again and turned away.

'That's rather frightening,' he muttered. 'It's simply not possible that I should not have removed that nail . . . '

6

Oleron knew very well what Elsie had meant when she had said that
her next visit would be preceded by a postcard. She, too, had realised
that at last, at last he knew – knew, and didn't want her. It gave him a
miserable, pitiful pang, therefore, when she came again within a week,
knocking at the door unannounced. She spoke from the landing; she
did not intend to stay, she said; and he had to press her before she
would so much as enter.

Her excuse for calling was that she had heard of an enquiry for
short stories that he might be wise to follow up. He thanked her.
Then, her business over, she seemed anxious to get away again.
Oleron did not seek to detain her; even he saw through the pretext of
the stories; and he accompanied her down the stairs.

But Elsie Bengough had no luck whatever in that house. A second
accident befell her. Half-way down the staircase there was the sharp
sound of splintering wood, and she checked a loud cry. Oleron knew
the woodwork to be old, but he himself had ascended and descended
frequently enough without mishap . . .

Elsie had put her foot through one of the stairs.

He sprang to her side in alarm. 'Oh, I say! My poor girl!'

She laughed hysterically.

'It's my weight – I know I'm getting fat – '

'Keep still – let me clear these splinters away,' he muttered between
his teeth.

She continued to laugh and sob that it was her weight – she was
getting fat –

He thrust downwards at the broken boards. The extrication was no
easy matter, and her torn boot showed him how badly the foot and
ankle within it must be abraded.

'Good God – good God!' he muttered over and over again.

'I shall be too heavy for anything soon,' she sobbed and laughed.

But she refused to reascend and to examine her hurt.

'No, let me go quickly – let me go quickly,' she repeated.

'But it's a frightful gash!'

'No – not so bad – let me get away quickly – I'm – I'm not wanted.'

At her words, that she was not wanted, his head dropped as if she
had given him a buffet.

'Elsie!' he choked, brokenly and shocked.

But she too made a quick gesture, as if she put something violently
aside.

'Oh, Paul, not *that* – not *you* – of course I do mean that too in a sense – oh, you know what I mean! . . . But if the other can't be, spare me this now! I – I wouldn't have come, but – but – oh, I did, I *did* try to keep away!'

It was intolerable, heartbreaking; but what could he do – what could he say? He did not love her . . .

'Let me go – I'm not wanted – let me take away what's left of me – '

'Dear Elsie – you are very dear to me – '

But again she made the gesture, as of putting something violently aside.

'No, not that – not anything less – don't offer me anything less – leave me a little pride – '

'Let me get my hat and coat – let me take you to a doctor,' he muttered.

But she refused. She refused even the support of his arm. She gave another unsteady laugh.

'I'm sorry I broke your stairs, Paul . . . You will go and see about the short stories, won't you?'

He groaned.

'Then if you won't see a doctor, will you go across the square and let Mrs Barrett look at you? Look, there's Barrett passing now – '

The long-nosed Barrett was looking curiously down the alley, but as Oleron was about to call him he made off without a word. Elsie seemed anxious for nothing so much as to be clear of the place, and finally promised to go straight to a doctor, but insisted on going alone.

'Goodbye,' she said.

And Oleron watched her until she was past the hatchet-like 'To Let' boards, as if he feared that even they might fall upon her and maim her.

That night Oleron did not dine. He had far too much on his mind. He walked from room to room of his flat, as if he could have walked away from Elsie Bengough's haunting cry that still rang in his ears. 'I'm not wanted – don't offer me anything less – let me take away what's left of me – '

Oh, if he could only have persuaded himself that he loved her!

He walked until twilight fell, then, without lighting candles, he stirred up the fire and flung himself into a chair.

Poor, poor Elsie! . . .

But even while his heart ached for her, it was out of the question. If only he had known! If only he had used common observation! But those walks, those sisterly takings of the arm – what a fool he had been! . . . Well, it was too late now. It was she, not he, who must now act – act by keeping away. He would help her all he could. He himself would not sit in her presence. If she came, he would hurry her out again as fast as he could . . . Poor, poor Elsie!

His room grew dark; the fire burned dead; and he continued to sit, wincing from time to time as a fresh tortured phrase rang again in his ears.

Then suddenly, he knew not why, he found himself anxious for her in a new sense – uneasy about her personal safety. A horrible fancy that even then she might be looking over an embankment down into dark water, that she might even now be glancing up at the hook on the door, took him. Women had been known to do those things . . . Then there would be an inquest, and he himself would be called upon to identify her, and would be asked how she had come by an ill-healed wound on the hand and a bad abrasion of the ankle. Barrett would say that he had seen her leaving his house . . .

Then he recognised that his thoughts were morbid. By an effort of will he put them aside, and sat for a while listening to the faint creakings and tickings and rappings within his panelling . . . If only he could have married her! . . . But he couldn't. Her face had risen before him again as he had seen it on the stairs, drawn with pain and ugly and swollen with tears. Ugly – yes, positively blubbered; if tears were women's weapons, as they were said to be, such tears were weapons turned against themselves . . . suicide again . . .

Then all at once he found himself attentively considering her two accidents.

Extraordinary they had been, both of them. He *could not* have left that old nail standing in the wood; why, he had fetched tools specially from the kitchen; and he was convinced that that step that had broken beneath her weight had been as sound as the others. It was inexplicable. If these things could happen, anything could happen. There was not a beam nor a jamb in the place that might not fall without warning, not a plank that might not crash inwards, not a nail that might not become a dagger. The whole place was full of life even now; as he sat there in the dark he heard its crowds of noises as if the house had been one great microphone . . .

Only half conscious that he did so, he had been sitting for some time identifying these noises, attributing to each crack or creak or knock its material cause; but there was one noise which, again not fully conscious of the omission, he had not sought to account for. It

had last come some minutes ago; it came again now – a sort of soft
sweeping rustle that seemed to hold an almost inaudibly minute
crackling. For half a minute or so it had Oleron's attention; then his
heavy thoughts were of Elsie Bengough again.

He was nearer to loving her in that moment than he had ever been.
He thought how to some men their loved ones were but the dearer
for those poor mortal blemishes that tell us we are but sojourners on
earth, with a common fate not far distant that makes it hardly worth
while to do anything but love for the time remaining. Strangling
sobs, blearing tears, bodies buffeted by sickness, hearts and mind
callous and hard with the rubs of the world – how little love there
would be were these things a barrier to love! In that sense he did love
Elsie Bengough. What her happiness had never moved in him her
sorrow almost awoke . . .

Suddenly his meditation went. His ear had once more become
conscious of that soft and repeated noise – the long sweep with the
almost inaudible crackle in it. Again and again it came, with a curious
insistence and urgency. It quickened a little as he became increasingly attentive . . . it seemed to Oleron that it grew louder . . .

All at once he started bolt upright in his chair, tense and listening. The silky rustle came again; he was trying to attach it to
something . . .

The next moment he had leapt to his feet, unnerved and terrified.
His chair hung poised for a moment, and then went over, setting the
fire-irons clattering as it fell. There was only one noise in the world
like that which had caused him to spring thus to his feet . . .

The next time it came Oleron felt behind him at the empty air with
his hand, and backed slowly until he found himself against the wall.

'God in Heaven!' The ejaculation broke from Oleron's lips. The
sound had ceased.

The next moment he had given a high cry.

'What is it? What's there? *Who's* there?'

A sound of scuttling caused his knees to bend under him for a
moment; but that, he knew, was a mouse. That was not something
that his stomach turned sick and his mind reeled to entertain. That
other sound, the like of which was not in the world, had now entirely
ceased; and again he called . . .

He called and continued to call; and then another terror, a terror
of the sound of his own voice, seized him. He did not dare to call
again. His shaking hand went to his pocket for a match, but found
none. He thought there might be matches on the mantelpiece –

He worked his way to the mantelpiece round a little recess, without for a moment leaving the wall. Then his hand encountered the mantelpiece, and groped along it. A box of matches fell to the hearth. He could just see them in the firelight, but his hand could not pick them up until he had cornered them inside the fender.

Then he rose and struck a light.

The room was as usual. He struck a second match. A candle stood on the table. He lighted it, and the flame sank for a moment and then burned up clear. Again he looked round.

There was nothing.

There was nothing; but there had been something, and might still be something. Formerly, Oleron had smiled at the fantastic thought that, by a merging and interplay of identities between himself and his beautiful room, he might be preparing a ghost for the future; it had not occurred to him *that there might have been a similar merging and coalescence in the past.* Yet with this staggering impossibility he was now face to face. Something did persist in the house; it had a tenant other than himself; and that tenant, whatsoever or whosoever, had appalled Oleron's soul by producing the sound of a woman brushing her hair.

7

Without quite knowing how he came to be there Oleron found himself striding over the loose board he had temporarily placed on the step broken by Miss Bengough. He was hatless, and descending the stairs. Not until later did there return to him a hazy memory that he had left the candle burning on the table, had opened the door no wider than was necessary to allow the passage of his body, and had sidled out, closing the door softly behind him. At the foot of the stairs another shock awaited him. Something dashed with a flurry up from the disused cellars and disappeared out of the door. It was only a cat, but Oleron gave a childish sob.

He passed out of the gate, and stood for a moment under the 'To Let' boards, plucking foolishly at his lip and looking up at the glimmer of light behind one of his red blinds. Then, still looking over his shoulder, he moved stumblingly up the square. There was a small public-house round the corner; Oleron had never entered it; but he entered it now, and put down a shilling that missed the counter by inches.

'B–b–bran–brandy,' he said, and then stooped to look for the shilling.

He had the little sawdusted bar to himself; what company there was – carters and labourers and the small tradesmen of the neighbourhood – was gathered in the farther compartment, beyond the space where the white-haired landlady moved among her taps and bottles. Oleron sat down on a hardwood settee with a perforated seat, drank half his brandy, and then, thinking he might as well drink it as spill it, finished it.

Then he fell to wondering which of the men whose voices he heard across the public-house would undertake the removal of his effects on the morrow.

In the meantime he ordered more brandy.

For he did not intend to go back to that room where he had left the candle burning. Oh no! He couldn't have faced even the entry and the staircase with the broken step – certainly not that pith-white, fascinating room. He would go back for the present to his old arrangement, of workroom and separate sleeping-quarters; he would go to his old landlady at once – presently – when he had finished his brandy – and see if she could put him up for the night. His glass was empty now . . .

He rose, had it refilled, and sat down again.

And if anybody asked his reason for removing again? Oh, he had reason enough – reason enough! Nails that put themselves back into wood again and gashed people's hands, steps that broke when you trod on them, and women who came into a man's place and brushed their hair in the dark, were reasons enough! He was querulous and injured about it all. He had taken the place for himself, not for invisible women to brush their hair in; that lawyer fellow in Lincoln's Inn should be told so, too, before many hours were out; it was outrageous, letting people in for agreements like that!

A cut-glass partition divided the compartment where Oleron sat from the space where the white-haired landlady moved; but it stopped seven or eight inches above the level of the counter. There was no partition at the farther bar. Presently Oleron, raising his eyes, saw that faces were watching him through the aperture. The faces disappeared when he looked at them.

He moved to a corner where he could not be seen from the other bar; but this brought him into line with the white-haired landlady.

She knew him by sight – had doubtless seen him passing and repassing; and presently she made a remark on the weather. Oleron did not know what he replied, but it sufficed to call forth the further remark that the winter had been a bad one for influenza, but that the spring weather seemed to be coming at last . . . Even this slight contact with the commonplace steadied Oleron a little; an idle, nascent wonder whether the landlady brushed her hair every night, and, if so, whether it gave out those little electric cracklings, was shut down with a snap; and Oleron was better . . .

With his next glass of brandy he was all for going back to his flat. Not go back? Indeed, he would go back! They should very soon see whether he was to be turned out of his place like that! He began to wonder why he was doing the rather unusual thing he was doing at that moment, unusual for him – sitting hatless, drinking brandy, in a public-house. Suppose he were to tell the white-haired landlady all about it – to tell her that a caller had scratched her hand on a nail, had later had the bad luck to put her foot through a rotten stair, and that he himself, in an old house full of squeaks and creaks and whispers, had heard a minute noise and had bolted from it in fright – what would she think of him? That he was mad, of course . . . Pshaw! The real truth of the matter was that he hadn't been doing enough work to occupy him. He had been dreaming his days away, filling his head with a lot of moonshine about a new *Romilly* (as if the old one was not good enough), and now he was surprised that the devil should enter an empty head!

Yes, he would go back. He would take a walk in the air first – he hadn't walked enough lately – and then he would take himself in hand, settle the hash of that sixteenth chapter of *Romilly* (fancy, he had actually been fool enough to think of destroying fifteen chapters!) and thenceforward he would remember that he had oblig-ations to his fellow-men and work to do in the world. There was the matter in a nutshell.

He finished his brandy and went out.

He had walked for some time before any other bearing of the matter than that on himself occurred to him. At first, the fresh air had increased the heady effect of the brandy he had drunk; but afterwards his mind grew clearer than it had been since morning. And the clearer it grew, the less final did his boastful self-assurances become, and the firmer his conviction that, when all explanations had been made, there remained something that could not be explained. His hysteria of an hour before had passed; he grew steadily calmer; but the disquieting conviction remained. A deep fear took possession of him. It was a fear for Elsie.

For something in his place was inimical to her safety. Of them-selves, her two accidents might not have persuaded him of this; but she herself had said it. '*I'm not wanted here* . . . ' And she had declared

that there was something wrong with the place. She had seen it
before he had. Well and good. One thing stood out clearly: namely,
that if this was so, she must be kept away for quite another reason
than that which had so confounded and humiliated Oleron. Luckily
she had expressed her intention of staying away; she must be held to
that intention. He must see to it.

And he must see to it all the more that he now saw his first impulse,
never to set foot in the place again, was absurd. People did not do
that kind of thing. With Elsie made secure, he could not with any
respect to himself suffer himself to be turned out by a shadow, nor
even by a danger merely because it was a danger. He had to live
somewhere, and he would live there. He must return.

He mastered the faint chill of fear that came with the decision, and
turned in his walk abruptly. Should fear grow on him again he would,
perhaps, take one more glass of brandy . . .

But by the time he reached the short street that led to the square
he was too late for more brandy. The little public-house was still
lighted, but closed, and one or two men were standing talking on the
kerb. Oleron noticed that a sudden silence fell on them as he passed,
and he noticed further that the long-nosed Barrett, whom he passed
a little lower down, did not return his good-night. He turned in at
the broken gate, hesitated merely an instant in the alley, and then
mounted his stairs again.

Only an inch of candle remained in the Sheffield stick, and Oleron
did not light another one. Deliberately he forced himself to take it up
and to make the tour of his five rooms before retiring. It was as he
returned from the kitchen across his little hall that he noticed that a
letter lay on the floor. He carried it into his sitting-room, and
glanced at the envelope before opening it.

It was unstamped, and had been put into the door by hand. Its
handwriting was clumsy, and it ran from beginning to end without
comma or period. Oleron read the first line, turned to the signature,
and then finished the letter.

It was from the man Barrett, and it informed Oleron that he,
Barrett, would be obliged if Mr Oleron would make other arrangements for the preparing of his breakfasts and the cleaning-out of his
place. The sting lay in the tail, that is to say, the postscript. This
consisted of a text of Scripture. It embodied an allusion that could
only be to Elsie Bengough . . .

A seldom-seen frown had cut deeply into Oleron's brow. So! that
was it! Very well; they would see about that on the morrow . . . For

the rest, this seemed merely another reason why Elsie should keep away . . .

Then his suppressed rage broke out . . .

The foul-minded lot! The devil himself could not have given a leer at anything that had ever passed between Paul Oleron and Elsie Bengough, yet this nosing rascal must be prying and talking! . . .

Oleron crumpled the paper up, held it in the candle flame, and then ground the ashes under his heel.

One useful purpose, however, the letter had served: it had created in Oleron a wrathful blaze that effectually banished pale shadows. Nevertheless, one other puzzling circumstance was to close the day. As he undressed, he chanced to glance at his bed. The coverlets bore an impress as if somebody had lain on them. Oleron could not remember that he himself had lain down during the day – off-hand, he would have said that certainly he had not; but after all he could not be positive. His indignation for Elsie, acting possibly with the residue of the brandy in him, excluded all other considerations; and he put out his candle, lay down, and passed immediately into a deep and dreamless sleep, which, in the absence of Mrs Barrett's morning call, lasted almost once round the clock.

8

To the man who pays heed to that voice within him which warns him that twilight and danger are settling over his soul, terror is apt to appear an absolute thing, against which his heart must be safe-guarded in a twink unless there is to take place an alteration in the whole range and scale of his nature. Mercifully, he has never far to look for safeguards. Of the immediate and small and common and momentary things of life, of usages and observances and modes and conventions, he builds up fortifications against the powers of dark-ness. He is even content that, not terror only, but joy also, should for working purposes be placed in the category of the absolute things; and the last treason he will commit will be that breaking down of terms and limits that strikes, not at one man, but at the welfare of the souls of all.

In his own person, Oleron began to commit this treason. He began to commit it by admitting the inexplicable and horrible to an increasing familiarity. He did it insensibly, unconsciously, by a neglect of the things that he now regarded it as an impertinence in Elsie Bengough to have prescribed. Two months before, the words 'a haunted house', applied to his lovely bemusing dwelling, would have chilled his marrow; now, his scale of sensation becoming depressed, he could ask 'Haunted by what?' and remain unconscious that horror, when it can be proved to be relative, by so much loses its proper quality. He was setting aside the landmarks. Mists and confusion had begun to enwrap him.

And he was conscious of nothing so much as of a voracious inquisitiveness. He wanted *to know*. He was resolved to know. Nothing but the knowledge would satisfy him; and craftily he cast about for means whereby he might attain it.

He might have spared his craft. The matter was the easiest imaginable. As in time past he had known, in his writing, moments when his thoughts had seemed to rise of themselves and to embody themselves in words not to be altered afterwards, so now the questions he put himself seemed to be answered even in the moment of their asking. There was exhilaration in the swift, easy processes. He had known no such joy in his own power since the days when his writing had been a daily freshness and a delight to him. It was almost as if the course he must pursue was being dictated to him.

And the first thing he must do, of course, was to define the problem. He defined it in terms of mathematics. Granted that he had not the place to himself; granted that the old house had inexpressibly caught and engaged his spirit; granted that, by virtue of the common denominator of the place, this unknown co-tenant stood in some relation to himself: what next? Clearly, the nature of the other numerator must be ascertained.

And how? Ordinarily this would not have seemed simple, but to Oleron it was now pellucidly clear. The key, *of course*, lay in his half-written novel – or rather, in both *Romilly*s, the old and the proposed new one.

A little while before Oleron would have thought himself mad to have embraced such an opinion; now he accepted the dizzying hypothesis without a quiver.

He began to examine the first and second *Romilly*s.

From the moment of his doing so the thing advanced by leaps and bounds. Swiftly he reviewed the history of the *Romilly* of the fifteen chapters. He remembered clearly now that he had found her insufficient on the very first morning on which he had sat down to work in his new place. Other instances of his aversion leaped up to confirm his obscure investigation. There had come the night when he had hardly forborne to throw the whole thing into the fire; and

the next morning he had begun the planning of the new *Romilly*. It
had been on that morning that Mrs Barrett, overhearing him humming a brief phrase that the dripping of a tap the night before had
suggested, had informed him that he was singing some air he had
never in his life heard before, called 'The Beckoning Fair One' . . .

The Beckoning Fair One! . . .

With scarcely a pause in thought he continued.

The first *Romilly* having been definitely thrown over, the second
had instantly fastened herself upon him, clamouring for birth in his
brain. He even fancied now, looking back, that there had been something like passion, hate almost, in the supplanting, and that more
than once a stray thought given to his discarded creation had – (it
was astonishing how credible Oleron found the almost unthinkable
idea) – had offended the supplanter.

Yet that a malignancy almost homicidal should be extended to his
fiction's poor mortal prototype . . .

In spite of his inuring to a scale in which the horrible was now a
thing to be fingered and turned this way and that, a 'Good God!'
broke from Oleron.

This intrusion of the first *Romilly*'s prototype into his thought
again was a factor that for the moment brought his inquiry into
the nature of his problem to a termination; the mere thought of
Elsie was fatal to anything abstract. For another thing, he could
not yet think of that letter of Barrett's, nor of a little scene that
had followed it, without a mounting of colour and a quick con-
traction of the brow. For, wisely or not, he had had that argument
out at once. Striding across the square on the following morning,
he had bearded Barrett on his own doorstep. Coming back again a
few minutes later, he had been strongly of opinion that he had
only made matters worse. The man had been vagueness itself.
He had not been to be either challenged or browbeaten into anything more definite than a muttered farrago in which the words
'Certain things . . . Mrs Barrett . . . respectable house . . . if the
cap fits . . . proceedings that shall be nameless,' had been constantly
repeated.

'Not that I make any charge – ' he had concluded.

'Charge!' Oleron had cried.

'I 'ave my idears of things, as I don't doubt you 'ave yours – '

'Ideas – mine!' Oleron had cried wrathfully, immediately dropping
his voice as heads had appeared at windows of the square. 'Look you
here, my man; you've an unwholesome mind, which probably you

can't help, but a tongue which you can help, and shall! If there is a breath of this repeated . . . '

'I'll not be talked to on my own doorstep like this by anybody . . . ' Barrett had blustered . . .

'You shall, and I'm doing it . . . '

'Don't you forget there's a Gawd above all, Who 'as said . . . '

'You're a low scandalmonger! . . . '

And so forth, continuing badly what was already badly begun. Oleron had returned wrathfully to his own house, and thenceforward, looking out of his windows, had seen Barrett's face at odd times, lifting blinds or peering round curtains, as if he sought to put himself in possession of Heaven knew what evidence, in case it should be required of him.

The unfortunate occurrence made certain minor differences in Oleron's domestic arrangements. Barrett's tongue, he gathered, had already been busy; he was looked at askance by the dwellers of the square; and he judged it better, until he should be able to obtain other help, to make his purchases of provisions a little farther afield rather than at the small shops of the immediate neighbourhood. For the rest, housekeeping was no new thing to him, and he would resume his old bachelor habits . . .

Besides, he was deep in certain rather abstruse investigations, in which it was better that he should not be disturbed.

He was looking out of his window one midday rather tired, not very well, and glad that it was not very likely he would have to stir out of doors, when he saw Elsie Bengough crossing the square towards his house. The weather had broken; it was a raw and gusty day; and she had to force her way against the wind that set her ample skirts bellying about her opulent figure and her veil spinning and streaming behind her.

Oleron acted swiftly and instinctively. Seizing his hat, he sprang to the door and descended the stairs at a run. A sort of panic had seized him. She must be prevented from setting foot in the place. As he ran along the alley he was conscious that his eyes went up to the eaves as if something drew them. He did not know that a slate might not accidentally fall . . .

He met her at the gate, and spoke with curious volubleness.

'This is really too bad, Elsie! Just as I'm urgently called away! I'm afraid it can't be helped though, and that you'll have to think me an inhospitable beast.' He poured it out just as it came into his head.

She asked if he was going to town.

'Yes, yes – to town,' he replied. 'I've got to call on – on Chambers. You know Chambers, don't you? No, I remember you don't; a big man you once saw me with . . . I ought to have gone yesterday, and – ' this he felt to be a brilliant effort – 'and he's going out of town this afternoon. To Brighton. I had a letter from him this morning.'

He took her arm and led her up the square. She had to remind him that his way to town lay in the other direction.

'Of course – how stupid of me!' he said, with a little loud laugh. 'I'm so used to going the other way with you – of course; it's the other way to the bus. Will you come along with me? I am so awfully sorry it's happened like this . . .'

They took the street to the bus terminus.

This time Elsie bore no signs of having gone through interior struggles. If she detected anything unusual in his manner she made no comment, and he, seeing her calm, began to talk less recklessly through silences. By the time they reached the bus terminus, nobody, seeing the pallid-faced man without an overcoat and the large ample-skirted girl at his side, would have supposed that one of them was ready to sink on his knees for thankfulness that he had, as he believed, saved the other from a wildly unthinkable danger.

They mounted to the top of the bus, Oleron protesting that he should not miss his overcoat, and that he found the day, if anything, rather oppressively hot. They sat down on a front seat.

Now that this meeting was forced upon him, he had something else to say that would make demands upon his tact. It had been on his mind for some time, and was, indeed, peculiarly difficult to put. He revolved it for some minutes, and then, remembering the success of his story of a sudden call to town, cut the knot of his difficulty with another lie.

'I'm thinking of going away for a little while, Elsie,' he said.

She merely said, 'Oh?'

'Somewhere for a change. I need a change. I think I shall go tomorrow, or the day after. Yes, tomorrow, I think.'

'Yes,' she replied.

'I don't quite know how long I shall be,' he continued. 'I shall have to let you know when I am back.'

'Yes, let me know,' she replied in an even tone.

The tone was, for her, suspiciously even. He was a little uneasy.

'You don't ask me where I'm going,' he said, with a little cumbrous effort to rally her.

She was looking straight before her, past the bus-driver.

'I know,' she said.

He was startled. 'How, you know?'

'You're not going anywhere,' she replied.

He found not a word to say. It was a minute or so before she continued, in the same controlled voice she had employed from the start.

'You're not going anywhere. You weren't going out this morning. You only came out because I appeared; don't behave as if we were strangers, Paul.'

A flush of pink had mounted to his cheeks. He noticed that the wind had given her the pink of early rhubarb. Still he found nothing to say.

'Of course, you ought to go away,' she continued. 'I don't know whether you look at yourself often in the glass, but you're rather noticeable. Several people have turned to look at you this morning. So, of course, you ought to go away. But you won't, and I know why.'

He shivered, coughed a little, and then broke silence.

'Then if you know, there's no use in continuing this discussion,' he said curtly.

'Not for me, perhaps, but there is for you,' she replied. 'Shall I tell you what I know?'

'No,' he said in a voice slightly raised.

'No?' she asked, her round eyes earnestly on him.

'No.'

Again he was getting out of patience with her; again he was conscious of the strain. Her devotion and fidelity and love plagued him; she was only humiliating both herself and him. It would have been bad enough had he ever, by word or deed, given her cause for thus fastening herself on him . . . but there; that was the worst of that kind of life for a woman. Women such as she, business women, in and out of offices all the time, always, whether they realised it or not, made comradeship a cover for something else. They accepted the unconventional status, came and went freely, as men did, were honestly taken by men at their own valuation – and then it turned out to be the other thing after all, and they went and fell in love. No wonder there was gossip in shops and squares and public houses! In a sense the gossipers were in the right of it. Independent, yet not efficient; with some of womanhood's graces forgone, and yet with all the woman's hunger and need; half sophisticated, yet not wise; Oleron was tired of it all . . .

And it was time he told her so.

'I suppose,' he said tremblingly, looking down between his knees, 'I suppose the real trouble is in the life women who earn their own living are obliged to lead.'

He could not tell in what sense she took the lame generality; she merely replied, 'I suppose so.'

'It can't be helped,' he continued, 'but you do sacrifice a good deal.'

She agreed: a good deal; and then she added after a moment, 'What, for instance?'

'You may or may not be gradually attaining a new status, but you're in a false position today.'

It was very likely, she said; she hadn't thought of it much in that light –

'And,' he continued desperately, 'you're bound to suffer. Your most innocent acts are misunderstood; motives you never dreamed of are attributed to you; and in the end it comes to – ' he hesitated a moment and then took the plunge, ' – to the sidelong look and the leer.'

She took his meaning with perfect ease. She merely shivered a little as she pronounced the name.

'Barrett?'

His silence told her the rest.

Anything further that was to be said must come from her. It came as the bus stopped at a stage and fresh passengers mounted the stairs.

'You'd better get down here and go back, Paul,' she said. 'I understand perfectly – perfectly. It isn't Barrett. You'd be able to deal with Barrett. It's merely convenient for you to say it's Barrett. I know what it is . . . but you said I wasn't to tell you that. Very well. But before you go let me tell you why I came up this morning.'

In a dull tone he asked her why. Again she looked straight before her as she replied:

'I came to force your hand. Things couldn't go on as they have been going, you know; and now that's all over.'

'All over,' he repeated stupidly.

'All over. I want you now to consider yourself, as far as I'm concerned, perfectly free. I make only one reservation.'

He hardly had the spirit to ask her what that was.

'If *I* merely need *you*,' she said, 'please don't give that a thought; that's nothing; I shan't come near for that. But,' she dropped her voice, 'if *you're* in need of *me*, Paul – I shall know if you are, *and you will be* – then I shall come at no matter what cost. You understand that?'

He could only groan.

'So that's understood,' she concluded. 'And I think that's all. Now go back. I should advise you to walk back, for you're shivering – goodbye – '

She gave him a cold hand, and he descended. He turned on the edge of the kerb as the bus started again. For the first time in all the years he had known her she parted from him with no smile and no wave of her long arm.

9

He stood on the kerb plunged in misery, looking after her as long as she remained in sight; but almost instantly with her disappearance he felt the heaviness lift a little from his spirit. She had given him his liberty; true, there was a sense in which he had never parted with it, but now was no time for splitting hairs; he was free to act, and all was clear ahead. Swiftly the sense of lightness grew on him: it became a positive rejoicing in his liberty; and before he was halfway home he had decided what must be done next.

The vicar of the parish in which his dwelling was situated lived within ten minutes of the square. To his house Oleron turned his steps. It was necessary that he should have all the information he could get about this old house with the insurance marks and the sloping 'To Let' boards, and the vicar was the person most likely to be able to furnish it. This last preliminary out of the way, and – aha! Oleron chuckled – things might be expected to happen!

But he gained less information than he had hoped for. The house, the vicar said, was old – but there needed no vicar to tell Oleron that; it was reputed (Oleron pricked up his ears) to be haunted – but there were few old houses about which some such rumour did not circulate among the ignorant; and the deplorable lack of Faith of the modern world, the vicar thought, did not tend to dissipate these superstitions. For the rest, his manner was the soothing manner of one who prefers not to make statements without knowing how they will be taken by his hearer. Oleron smiled as he perceived this.

'You may leave my nerves out of the question,' he said. 'How long has the place been empty?'

'A dozen years, I should say,' the vicar replied.

'And the last tenant – did you know him – or her?' Oleron was conscious of a tingling of his nerves as he offered the vicar the alternative of sex.

'Him,' said the vicar. 'A man. If I remember rightly, his name was Madley; an artist. He was a great recluse; seldom went out of the place, and – ' the vicar hesitated and then broke into a little gush of candour ' – and since you appear to have come for this information, and since it is better that the truth should be told than that garbled versions should get about, I don't mind saying that this man Madley died there, under somewhat unusual circumstances. It was ascertained at the post-mortem that there was not a particle of food in his stomach, although he was found to be not without money. And his frame was simply worn out. Suicide was spoken of, but you'll agree with me that deliberate starvation is, to say the least, an uncommon form of suicide. An open verdict was returned.'

'Ah!' said Oleron . . . 'Does there happen to be any comprehensive history of this parish?'

'No; partial ones only. I myself am not guiltless of having made a number of notes on its purely ecclesiastical history, its registers and so forth, which I shall be happy to show you if you would care to see them; but it is a large parish, I have only one curate, and my leisure, as you will readily understand . . . '

The extent of the parish and the scantiness of the vicar's leisure occupied the remainder of the interview, and Oleron thanked the vicar, took his leave, and walked slowly home.

He walked slowly for a reason, twice turning away from the house within a stone's-throw of the gate and taking another turn of twenty minutes or so. He had a very ticklish piece of work now before him; it required the greatest mental concentration; it was nothing less than to bring his mind, if he might, into such a state of unpreoccupation and receptivity that he should see the place as he had seen it on that morning when, his removal accomplished, he had sat down to begin the sixteenth chapter of the first *Romilly*.

For, could he recapture that first impression, he now hoped for far more from it. Formerly, he had carried no end of mental lumber. Before the influence of the place had been able to find him out at all, it had had the inertia of those dreary chapters to overcome. No results had shown. The process had been one of slow saturation, charging, filling up to a brim. But now he was light, unburdened, rid at last both of that *Romilly* and of her prototype. Now for the new unknown, coy, jealous, bewitching, Beckoning Fair! . . .

At half-past two of the afternoon he put his key into the Yale lock, entered, and closed the door behind him . . .

His fantastic attempt was instantly and astonishingly successful. He could have shouted with triumph as he entered the room; it was as if he had *escaped* into it. Once more, as in the days when his writing had had a daily freshness and wonder and promise for him, he was conscious of that new ease and mastery and exhilaration and release. The air of the place seemed to hold more oxygen; as if his own specific gravity had changed, his very tread seemed less ponderable. The flowers in the bowls, the fair proportions of the meadowsweet-coloured panels and mouldings, the polished floor, and the lofty and faintly starred ceiling, fairly laughed their welcome. Oleron actually laughed back, and spoke aloud.

'Oh, you're pretty, pretty!' he flattered it.

Then he lay down on his couch.

He spent that afternoon as a convalescent who expected a dear visitor might have spent it – in a delicious vacancy, smiling now and then as if in his sleep, and ever lifting drowsy and contented eyes to his alluring surroundings. He lay thus until darkness came, and, with darkness, the nocturnal noises of the old house . . .

But if he waited for any specific happening, he waited in vain.

He waited similarly in vain on the morrow, maintaining, though with less ease, that sensitised-plate-like condition of his mind. Nothing occurred to give it an impression. Whatever it was which he so patiently wooed, it seemed to be both shy and exacting.

Then on the third day he thought he understood. A look of gentle drollery and cunning came into his eyes, and he chuckled.

'Oho, oho! . . . Well, if the wind sits in *that* quarter we must see what else there is to be done. What is there, now? . . . No, I won't send for Elsie; we don't need a wheel to break the butterfly on; we won't go to those lengths, my butterfly . . . '

He was standing musing, thumbing his lean jaw, looking aslant; suddenly he crossed to his hall, took down his hat, and went out.

'My lady is coquettish, is she? Well, we'll see what a little neglect will do,' he chuckled as he went down the stairs.

He sought a railway station, got into a train, and spent the rest of the day in the country. Oh, yes: Oleron thought *he* was the man to deal with Fair Ones who beckoned, and invited, and then took refuge in shyness and hanging back!

He did not return until after eleven that night.

'*Now*, my Fair Beckoner!' he murmured as he walked along the alley and felt in his pocket for his keys . . .

Inside his flat, he was perfectly composed, perfectly deliberate, exceedingly careful not to give himself away. As if to intimate that he intended to retire immediately, he lighted only a single candle; and as he set out with it on his nightly round he affected to yawn. He went first into his kitchen. There was a full moon, and a lozenge of moonlight, almost peacock-blue by contrast with his candle-frame, lay on the floor. The window was uncurtained, and he could see the reflection of the candle, and, faintly, that of his own face, as he moved about. The door of the powder-closet stood a little ajar, and he closed it before sitting down to remove his boots on the chair with the cushion made of the folded harp-bag. From the kitchen he passed to the bathroom. There, another slant of blue moonlight cut the windowsill and lay across the pipes on the wall. He visited his seldom-used study, and stood for a moment gazing at the silvered roofs across the square. Then, walking straight through his sitting-room, his stockinged feet making no noise, he entered his bedroom and put the candle on the chest of drawers. His face all this time wore no expression save that of tiredness. He had never been wilier nor more alert.

His small bedroom fireplace was opposite the chest of drawers on which the mirror stood, and his bed and the window occupied the remaining sides of the room. Oleron drew down his blind, took off his coat, and then stooped to get his slippers from under the bed.

He could have given no reason for the conviction, but that the manifestation that for two days had been withheld was close at hand he never for an instant doubted. Nor, though he could not form the faintest guess of the shape it might take, did he experience fear. Startling or surprising it might be; he was prepared for that; but that was all; his scale of sensation had become depressed. His hand moved this way and that under the bed in search of his slippers . . .

But for all his caution and method and preparedness, his heart all at once gave a leap and a pause that was almost horrid. His hand had found the slippers, but he was still on his knees; save for this circumstance he would have fallen. The bed was a low one; the groping for the slippers accounted for the turn of his head to one side; and he was careful to keep the attitude until he had partly recovered his self-possession. When presently he rose there was a drop of blood on his lower lip where he had caught at it with his teeth, and his watch had jerked out of the pocket of his waistcoat and was dangling at the end of its short leather guard . . .

Then, before the watch had ceased its little oscillation, he was himself again.

In the middle of his mantelpiece there stood a picture, a portrait of his grandmother; he placed himself before this picture, so that he could see in the glass of it the steady flame of the candle that burned behind him on the chest of drawers. He could see also in the picture-glass the little glancings of light from the bevels and facets of the objects about the mirror and candle. But he could see more. These twinklings and reflections and re-reflections did not change their position; but there was one gleam that had motion. It was fainter than the rest, and it moved up and down through the air. It was the reflection of the candle on Oleron's black vulcanite comb, and each of its downward movements was accompanied by a silky and crackling rustle.

Oleron, watching what went on in the glass of his grandmother's portrait, continued to play his part. He felt for his dangling watch and began slowly to wind it up. Then, for a moment ceasing to watch, he began to empty his trousers pockets and to place methodically in a little row on the mantelpiece the pennies and halfpennies he took from them. The sweeping, minutely electric noise filled the whole bedroom, and had Oleron altered his point of observation he could have brought the dim gleam of the moving comb so into position that it would almost have outlined his grandmother's head.

Any other head of which it might have been following the outline was invisible.

Oleron finished the emptying of his pockets; then, under cover of another simulated yawn, not so much summoning his resolution as overmastered by an exhorbitant curiosity, he swung suddenly round. That which was being combed was still not to be seen, but the comb did not stop. It had altered its angle a little, and had moved a little to the left. It was passing, in fairly regular sweeps, from a point rather more than five feet from the ground, in a direction roughly vertical, to another point a few inches below the level of the chest of drawers.

Oleron continued to act to admiration. He walked to his little washstand in the corner, poured out water, and began to wash his hands. He removed his waistcoat, and continued his preparations for bed. The combing did not cease, and he stood for a moment in thought. Again his eyes twinkled. The next was very cunning –

'Hm! . . . *I think I'll read for a quarter of an hour,*' he said aloud . . .

He passed out of the room.

He was away a couple of minutes; when he returned again the room was suddenly quiet. He glanced at the chest of drawers; the comb lay still, between the collar he had removed and a pair of gloves. Without hesitation Oleron put out his hand and picked it up. It was an ordinary eighteenpenny comb, taken from a card in a chemist's shop, of a substance of a definite specific gravity, and no more capable of rebellion against the Laws by which it existed than are the worlds that keep their orbits through the void. Oleron put it down again; then he glanced at the bundle of papers he held in his hand. What he had gone to fetch had been the fifteen chapters of the original *Romilly*.

'Hm!' he muttered as he threw the manuscript into a chair . . . 'As I thought . . . She's just blindly, ragingly, murderously jealous.'

*   *   *

On the night after that, and on the following night, and for many nights and days, so many that he began to be uncertain about the count of them, Oleron, courting, cajoling, neglecting, threatening, beseeching, eaten out with unappeased curiosity and regardless that his life was becoming one consuming passion and desire, continued his search for the unknown co-numerator of his abode.

10

As time went on, it came to pass that few except the postman mounted Oleron's stairs; and since men who do not write letters receive few, even the postman's tread became so infrequent that it was not heard more than once or twice a week. There came a letter from Oleron's publishers, asking when they might expect to receive the manuscript of his new book; he delayed for some days to answer it, and finally forgot it. A second letter came, which also he failed to answer. He received no third.

The weather grew bright and warm. The privet bushes among the chopper-like notice-boards flowered, and in the streets where Oleron did his shopping the baskets of flower-women lined the kerbs. Oleron purchased flowers daily; his room clamoured for flowers, fresh and continually renewed; and Oleron did not stint its demands. Nevertheless, the necessity for going out to buy them began to irk him more and more, and it was with a greater and ever greater sense of relief that he returned home again. He began to be conscious that again his scale of sensation had suffered a subtle change – a change that was not restoration to its former capacity, but an extension and enlarging that once more included terror. It admitted it in an entirely new form. *Lux Orco, tenebrae Jovi*. The name of this terror was agoraphobia. Oleron had begun to dread air and space and the horror that might pounce upon the unguarded back.

Presently he so contrived it that his food and flowers were delivered daily at his door. He rubbed his hands when he had hit upon this
expedient. That was better! Now he could please himself whether he
went out or not . . .

Quickly he was confirmed in his choice. It became his pleasure to
remain immured.

But he was not happy – or, if he was, his happiness took an
extraordinary turn. He fretted discontentedly, could sometimes have
wept for mere weakness and misery; and yet he was dimly conscious
that he would not have exchanged his sadness for all the noisy mirth
of the world outside. And speaking of noise: noise, much noise, now
caused him the acutest discomfort. It was hardly more to be endured
than that new-born fear that kept him, on the increasingly rare
occasions when he did go out, sidling close to walls and feeling
friendly railings with his hand. He moved from room to room softly
and in slippers, and sometimes stood for many seconds closing a
door so gently that not a sound broke the stillness that was in itself a
delight. Sunday now became an intolerable day to him, for, since the
coming of the fine weather, there had begun to assemble in the
square under his windows each Sunday morning certain members of
the sect to which the long-nosed Barrett adhered. These came with a
great drum and large brass-bellied instruments; men and women
uplifted anguished voices, struggling with their God; and Barrett
himself, with upraised face and closed eyes and working brows,
prayed that the sound of his voice might penetrate the ears of all
unbelievers – as it certainly did Oleron's. One day, in the middle of
one of these rhapsodies, Oleron sprang to his blind and pulled it
down, and heard as he did so his own name made the subject of a
fresh torrent of outpouring.

And sometimes, but not as expecting a reply, Oleron stood still and
called softly. Once or twice he called 'Romilly!' and then waited; but
more often his whispering did not take the shape of a name.

There was one spot in particular of his abode that he began to
haunt with increasing persistency. This was just within the opening
of his bedroom door. He had discovered one day that by opening
every door in his place (always excepting the outer one, which he
only opened unwillingly) and by placing himself on this particular
spot, he could actually see to a greater or less extent into each of his
five rooms without changing his position. He could see the whole of
his sitting-room, all of his bedroom except the part hidden by the
open door, and glimpses of his kitchen, bathroom, and of his rarely

used study. He was often in this place, breathless and with his finger on his lip. One day, as he stood there, he suddenly found himself wondering whether this Madley, of whom the vicar had spoken, had ever discovered the strategic importance of the bedroom entry.

Light, moreover, now caused him greater disquietude than did darkness. Direct sunlight, of which, as the sun passed daily round the house, each of his rooms had now its share, was like a flame in his brain; and even diffused light was a dull and numbing ache. He began, at successive hours of the day, one after another, to lower his crimson blinds. He made short and daring excursions in order to do this; but he was ever careful to leave his retreat open, in case he should have sudden need of it. Presently this lowering of the blinds had become a daily methodical exercise, and his rooms, when he had been his round, had the blood-red half-light of a photographer's darkroom.

One day, as he drew down the blind of his little study and backed in good order out of the room again, he broke into a soft laugh.

'*That* bilks Mr Barrett!' he said; and the baffling of Barrett continued to afford him mirth for an hour.

But on another day, soon after, he had a fright that left him trembling also for an hour. He had seized the cord to darken the window over the seat in which he had found the harp-bag, and was standing with his back well protected in the embrasure, when he thought he saw the tail of a black-and-white check skirt disappear round the corner of the house. He could not be sure – had he run to the window of the other wall, which was blinded, the skirt must have been already past – but he was *almost* sure that it was Elsie. He listened in an agony of suspense for her tread on the stairs . . .

But no tread came, and after three or four minutes he drew a long breath of relief.

'By Jove, but that would have compromised me horribly!' he muttered . . .

And he continued to mutter from time to time, 'Horribly compromising . . . *no* woman would stand that . . . not *any* kind of woman . . . oh, compromising in the extreme!'

Yet he was not happy. He could not have assigned the cause of the fits of quiet weeping which took him sometimes; they came and went, like the fitful illumination of the clouds that travelled over the square; and perhaps, after all, if he was not happy, he was not unhappy. Before he could be unhappy something must have been withdrawn, and nothing had yet been withdrawn from him, for nothing had been granted. He was waiting for that granting, in that flower-laden, frightfully enticing apartment of his, with the pith-white walls tinged and subdued by the crimson blinds to a blood-like gloom.

He paid no heed to it that his stock of money was running perilously low, nor that he had ceased to work. Ceased to work? He had not ceased to work. They knew very little about it who supposed that Oleron had ceased to work! He was in truth only now beginning to work. He was preparing such a work . . . such a work . . . such a Mistress was a-making in the gestation of his Art . . . let him but get this period of probation and poignant waiting over and men should see . . . How *should* men know her, this Fair One of Oleron's, until Oleron himself knew her? Lovely radiant creations are not thrown off like How-d'ye-do's. The men to whom it is committed to father them must weep wretched tears, as Oleron did, must swell with vain presumptuous hopes, as Oleron did, must pursue, as Oleron pursued, the capricious, fair, mocking, slippery, eager Spirit that, ever eluding, ever sees to it that the chase does not slacken. Let Oleron but hunt this Huntress a little longer . . . he would have her sparkling and panting in his arms yet . . . Oh no: they were very far from the truth who supposed that Oleron had ceased to work!

And if all else was falling away from Oleron, gladly he was letting it go. So do we all when our Fair Ones beckon. Quite at the beginning we wink, and promise ourselves that we will put Her Ladyship through her paces, neglect her for a day, turn her own jealous wiles against her, flout and ignore her when she comes wheedling; perhaps there lurks within us all the time a heartless sprite who is never fooled; but in the end all falls away. She beckons, beckons, and all goes . . .

And so Oleron kept his strategic post within the frame of his bedroom door, and watched, and waited, and smiled, with his finger on his lips . . . It was his duteous service, his worship, his troth-plighting, all that he had ever known of Love. And when he found himself, as he now and then did, hating the dead man Madley, and wishing that he had never lived, he felt that that, too, was an acceptable service . . .

But, as he thus prepared himself, as it were, for a Marriage, and moped and chafed more and more that the Bride made no sign, he made a discovery that he ought to have made weeks before.

It was through a thought of the dead Madley that he made it. Since that night when he had thought in his greenness that a little studied neglect would bring the lovely Beckoner to her knees, and had made use of her own jealousy to banish her, he had not set eyes on those fifteen discarded chapters of *Romilly*. He had thrown them back into the window-seat, forgotten their very existence. But his own jealousy of Madley put him in mind of hers of her jilted rival of flesh and blood, and he remembered them . . . Fool that he had been! Had he, then, expected his Desire to manifest herself while there still existed the evidence of his divided allegiance? What, and she with a passion so fierce and centred that it had not hesitated at the destruction, twice attempted, of her rival? Fool that he had been! . . .

But if *that* was all the pledge and sacrifice she required she should have it – ah, yes, and quickly!

He took the manuscript from the window-seat, and brought it to the fire.

He kept his fire always burning now; the warmth brought out the last vestige of odour of the flowers with which his room was banked. He did not know what time it was; long since he had allowed his clock to run down – it had seemed a foolish measurer of time in regard to the stupendous things that were happening to Oleron; but he knew it was late. He took the *Romilly* manuscript and knelt before the fire.

But he had not finished removing the fastening that held the sheets together before he suddenly gave a start, turned his head over his shoulder, and listened intently. The sound he had heard had not been loud – it had been, indeed, no more than a tap, twice or thrice repeated – but it had filled Oleron with alarm. His face grew dark as it came again.

He heard a voice outside on his landing.

'Paul! . . . Paul! . . . '

It was Elsie's voice.

'Paul! . . . I know you're in . . . I want to see you . . . '

He cursed her under his breath, but kept perfectly still. He did not intend to admit her.

'Paul! . . . You're in trouble . . . I believe you're in danger . . . at least come to the door! . . . '

Oleron smothered a low laugh. It somehow amused him that she, in such danger herself, should talk to him of *his* danger! . . . Well, if she was, serve her right; she knew, or said she knew, all about it . . .

'Paul! . . . Paul! . . . '

'*Paul*! . . . *Paul*! . . . ' He mimicked her under his breath.

'Oh, Paul, it's *horrible*! . . . '

Horrible, was it? thought Oleron. Then let her get away . . .

'I only want to help you, Paul . . . I didn't promise not to come if you needed me . . . '

He was impervious to the pitiful sob that interrupted the low cry. The devil take the woman! Should he shout to her to go away and not come back? No: let her call and knock and sob. She had a gift for sobbing; she mustn't think her sobs would move him. They irritated him, so that he set his teeth and shook his fist at her, but that was all. Let her sob.

'*Paul*! . . . *Paul*! . . . '

With his teeth hard set, he dropped the first page of *Romilly* into the fire. Then he began to drop the rest in, sheet by sheet.

For many minutes the calling behind his door continued; then suddenly it ceased. He heard the sound of feet slowly descending the stairs. He listened for the noise of a fall or a cry or the crash of a piece of the handrail of the upper landing; but none of these things came. She was spared. Apparently her rival suffered her to crawl abject and beaten away. Oleron heard the passing of her steps under his window; then she was gone.

He dropped the last page into the fire, and then, with a low laugh rose. He looked fondly round his room.

'Lucky to get away like that,' he remarked. 'She wouldn't have got away if I'd given her as much as a word or a look! What devils these women are! . . . But no; I oughtn't to say that; one of 'em showed forbearance . . . '

Who showed forbearance? And what was forborne? Ah, Oleron knew! . . . Contempt, no doubt, had been at the bottom of it, but that didn't matter: the pestering creature had been allowed to go un-harmed. Yes, she was lucky; Oleron hoped she knew it . . .

And now, now, now for his reward!

Oleron crossed the room. All his doors were open; his eyes shone as he placed himself within that of his bedroom.

Fool that he had been, not to think of destroying the manuscript sooner! . . .

How, in a houseful of shadows, should he know his own Shadow? How, in a houseful of noises, distinguish the summons he felt to be at hand? Ah, trust him! He would know! The place was full of a jugglery of dim lights. The blind at his elbow that allowed the light of a street lamp to struggle vaguely through – the glimpse of greeny blue moonlight seen through the distant kitchen door – the sulky glow of the fire under the black ashes of the burnt manuscript – the glimmering of the tulips and the moon-daisies and narcissi in the bowls and jugs and jars – these did not so trick and bewilder his eyes that he would not know his Own! It was he, not she, who had been delaying the shadowy Bridal; he hung his head for a moment in mute acknowledgment; then he bent his eyes on the deceiving, puzzling gloom again. He would have called her name had he known it – but now he would not ask her to share even a name with the other . . .

His own face, within the frame of the door, glimmered white as the narcissi in the darkness . . .

A shadow, light as fleece, seemed to take shape in the kitchen (the time had been when Oleron would have said that a cloud had passed over the unseen moon). The low illumination on the blind at his elbow grew dimmer (the time had been when Oleron would have concluded that the lamplighter going his rounds had turned low the flame of the lamp). The fire settled, letting down the black and charred papers; a flower fell from a bowl, and lay indistinct upon the floor; all was still; and then a stray draught moved through the old house, passing before Oleron's face . . .

Suddenly, inclining his head, he withdrew a little from the door-jamb. The wandering draught caused the door to move a little on its hinges. Oleron trembled violently, stood for a moment longer, and then, putting his hand out to the knob, softly drew the door to, sat down on the nearest chair, and waited, as a man might await the calling of his name that should summon him to some weighty, high and privy Audience . . .

II

One knows not whether there can be human compassion for anaemia of the soul. When the pitch of Life is dropped, and the spirit is so put over and reversed that that only is horrible which before was sweet and worldly and of the day, the human relation disappears. The sane soul turns appalled away, lest not merely itself, but sanity should suffer. We are not gods. We cannot drive out devils. We must see selfishly to it that devils do not enter into ourselves.

And this we must do even though Love so transfuse us that we may well deem our nature to be half divine. We shall but speak of honour and duty in vain. The letter dropped within the dark door will lie unregarded, or, if regarded for a brief instant between two unspeakable lapses, left and forgotten again. The telegram will be undelivered, nor will the whistling messenger (wiselier guided than he knows to whistle) be conscious as he walks away of the drawn blind that is pushed aside an inch by a finger and then fearfully replaced again. No: let the miserable wrestle with his own shadows; let him, if indeed he be so mad, clip and strain and enfold and couch the succubus; but let him do so in a house into which not an air of Heaven penetrates, nor a bright finger of the sun pierces the filthy twilight. The lost must remain lost. Humanity has other business to attend to.

For the handwriting of the two letters that Oleron, stealing noise-lessly one June day into his kitchen to rid his sitting-room of an armful of fetid and decaying flowers, had seen on the floor within his door, had had no more meaning for him than if it had belonged to some dim and faraway dream. And at the beating of the telegraph-boy upon the door, within a few feet of the bed where he lay, he had gnashed his teeth and stopped his ears. He had pictured the lad standing there, just beyond his partition, among packets of provisions and bundles of dead and dying flowers. For his outer landing was littered with these. Oleron had feared to open his door to take them in. After a week, the errand lads had reported that there must be some mistake about the order, and had left no more. Inside, in the red twilight, the old flowers turned brown and fell and decayed where they lay.

Gradually his power was draining away. The Abomination fastened on Oleron's power. The steady sapping sometimes left him for many hours of prostration gazing vacantly up at his red-tinged ceiling, idly suffering such fancies as came of themselves to have their way with him. Even the strongest of his memories had no more than a precarious hold upon his attention. Sometimes a flitting half-memory, of a novel to be written, a novel it was important that he should write, tantalised him for a space before vanishing again; and sometimes whole novels, perfect, splendid, established to endure, rose magically before him. And sometimes the memories were ab-surdly remote and trivial, of garrets he had inhabited and lodgings that had sheltered him, and so forth. Oleron had known a good deal about such things in his time, but all that was now past. He had at last found a place which he did not intend to leave until they fetched him out – a place that some might have thought a little on the green-sick side, that others might have considered to be a little too redolent of long-dead and morbid things for a living man to be mewed up in, but ah, so irresistible, with such an authority of its own, with such an associate of its own, and a place of such delights when once a man had ceased to struggle against its inexorable will! A novel? Somebody

ought to write a novel about a place like that! There must be lots
to write about in a place like that if one could but get to the bottom
of it! It had probably already been painted, by a man called Madley
who had lived there . . . but Oleron had not known this Madley –
had a strong feeling that he wouldn't have liked him – would rather
he had lived somewhere else – really couldn't stand the fellow –
hated him Madley, in fact. (Aha! that was a joke!). He seriously
doubted whether the man had led the life he ought; Oleron was
in two minds sometimes whether he wouldn't tell that long-nosed
guardian of the public morals across the way about him; but probably
he knew, and had made his praying hullabaloos for him also. That
was his line. Why, Oleron himself had had a dust-up with him about
something or other . . . some girl or other . . . Elsie Bengough her
name was, he remembered . . .

Oleron had moments of deep uneasiness about this Elsie Bengough.
Or rather, he was not so much uneasy about her as restless about the
things she did. Chief of these was the way in which she persisted in
thrusting herself into his thoughts; and, whenever he was quick
enough, he sent her packing the moment she made her appearance
there. The truth was that she was not merely a bore; she had always
been that; it had now come to the pitch when her very presence in his
fancy was inimical to the full enjoyment of certain experiences . . .
She had no tact; really ought to have known that people are not at
home to the thoughts of everybody all the time; ought in mere
politeness to have allowed him certain seasons quite to himself; and
was monstrously ignorant of things if she did not know, as she
appeared not to know, that there were certain special hours when a
man's veins ran with fire and daring and power, in which . . . well, in
which he had a reasonable right to treat folk as he had treated that
prying Barrett – to shut them out completely . . . But no: up she
popped, the thought of her, and ruined all. Bright towering fabrics,
by the side of which even those perfect, magical novels of which he
dreamed were dun and grey, vanished utterly at her intrusion. It was
as if a fog should suddenly quench some fair-beaming star, as if at the
threshold of some golden portal prepared for Oleron a pit should
suddenly gape, as if a bat-like shadow should turn the growing dawn
to mirk and darkness again . . . Therefore, Oleron strove to stifle
even the nascent thought of her.

Nevertheless, there came an occasion on which this woman Bengough absolutely refused to be suppressed. Oleron could not have
told exactly when this happened; he only knew by the glimmer of the

street lamp on his blind that it was some time during the night, and that for some time she had not presented herself.

He had no warning, none, of her coming; she just came – was there. Strive as he would, he could not shake off the thought of her nor the image of her face. She haunted him.

But for her to come at that moment of all moments! . . . Really, it was past belief! How she could endure it, Oleron could not conceive! Actually, to look on, as it were, at the triumph of a Rival . . . Good God! It was monstrous! Tact – reticence – he had never credited her with an overwhelming amount of either: but he had never attributed mere – oh, there was no word for it! Monstrous – monstrous! Did she intend thenceforward . . . Good God! to look on! . . .

Oleron felt the blood rush up to the roots of his hair with anger against her.

'Damnation take her!' he choked . . .

But the next moment his heat and resentment had changed to a cold sweat of cowering fear. Panic-stricken, he strove to comprehend what he had done. For though he knew not what, he knew he had done something, something fatal, irreparable, blasting. Anger he had felt, but not *this* blaze of ire that suddenly flooded the twilight of his consciousness with a white infernal light. *That* appalling flash was not his – not his *that* open rift of bright and searing Hell – not his, not his! His had been the hand of a child, preparing a puny blow; but what was *this other* horrific hand that was drawn back to strike in the same place? Had *he* set that in motion? Had *he* provided the spark that had touched off the whole accumulated power of that formidable and relentless place? He did not know. He only knew that that poor igniting particle in himself was blown out, that – Oh, impossible! – a clinging kiss (how else to express it?) had changed on his very lips to a gnashing and a removal, and that for very pity of the awful odds he must cry out to her against whom he had lately raged to guard herself . . . guard herself . . .

'*Look out!*' he shrieked aloud . . .

The revulsion was instant. As if a cold slow billow had broken over him, he came to to find that he was lying in his bed, that the mist and horror that had for so long enwrapped him had departed, that he was Paul Oleron, and that he was sick, naked, helpless, and unutterably abandoned and alone. His faculties, though weak, answered at last to his calls upon them; and he knew that it must have been a hideous nightmare that had left him sweating and shaking thus.

Yes, he was himself, Paul Oleron, a tired novelist, already past the summit of his best work, and slipping downhill again empty-handed from it all. He had struck short in his life's aim. He had tried too much, had over-estimated his strength, and was a failure, a failure . . .

It all came to him in the single word, enwrapped and complete; it needed no sequential thought; he was a failure. He had missed . . .

And he had missed not one happiness, but two. He had missed the ease of this world, which men love, and he had missed also that other shining prize for which men forgo ease, the snatching and holding and triumphant bearing up aloft of which is the only justification of the mad adventurer who hazards the enterprise. And there was no second attempt. Fate has no morrow. Oleron's morrow must be to sit down to profitless, ill-done, unrequired work again, and so on the morrow after that, and the morrow after that, and as many morrows as there might be . . .

He lay there, weakly yet sanely considering it . . .

And since the whole attempt had failed, it was hardly worth while to consider whether a little might not be saved from the general wreck. No good would ever come of that half-finished novel. He had intended that it should appear in the autumn; was under contract that it should appear; no matter; it was better to pay forfeit to his publishers than to waste what days were left. He was spent; age was not far off; and paths of wisdom and sadness were the properest for the remainder of the journey . . .

If only he had chosen the wife, the child, the faithful friend at the fireside, and let them follow an *ignis fatuus* – that list! . . .

In the meantime it began to puzzle him exceedingly that he should be so weak, that his room should smell so overpoweringly of decaying vegetable matter, and that his hand, chancing to stray to his face in the darkness, should encounter a beard.

'Most extraordinary!' he began to mutter to himself. 'Have I been ill? Am I ill now? And if so, why have they left me alone? . . . Extraordinary! . . . '

He thought he heard a sound from the kitchen or bathroom. He rose a little on his pillow, and listened . . . Ah! He was not alone, then! It certainly would have been extraordinary if they had left him ill and alone – Alone? Oh no. He would be looked after. He wouldn't be left, ill, to shift for himself. If everybody else had forsaken him, he could trust Elsie Bengough, the dearest chum he had, for that . . . bless her faithful heart!

But suddenly a short, stifled, spluttering cry rang sharply out.
'*Paul!*'

It came from the kitchen.

And in the same moment it flashed upon Oleron, he knew not
how, that two, three, five, he knew not how many minutes before,
another sound, unmarked at the time but suddenly transfixing his
attention now, had striven to reach his intelligence. This sound had
been the slight touch of metal on metal – just such a sound as Oleron
made when he put his key into the lock.

'Hallo! . . . Who's that?' he called sharply from his bed.

He had no answer.

He called again. 'Hallo! . . . Who's there? . . . Who is it?'

This time he was sure he heard noises, soft and heavy, in the
kitchen.

'This is a queer thing altogether,' he muttered. 'By Jove, I'm
as weak as a kitten too . . . Hallo, there! Somebody called, didn't
they? . . . Elsie! Is that you? . . . '

Then he began to knock with his hand on the wall at the side of
his bed.

'Elsie! . . . Elsie! . . . You called, didn't you? . . . Please come here,
whoever it is! . . . '

There was a sound as of a closing door, and then silence. Oleron
began to get rather alarmed.

'It may be a nurse,' he muttered; 'Elsie'd have to get me a nurse, of
course. She'd sit with me as long as she could spare the time, brave
lass, and she'd get a nurse for the rest . . . But it was awfully like her
voice . . . Elsie, or whoever it is! . . . I can't make this out at all. I must
go and see what's the matter . . . '

He put one leg out of bed. Feeling its feebleness, he reached with
his hand for the additional support of the wall . . .

But before putting out the other leg he stopped and considered,
picking at his new-found beard. He was suddenly wondering whether
he *dared* go into the kitchen. It was such a frightfully long way; no
man knew what horror might not leap and huddle on his shoulders
if he went so far; when a man has an overmastering impulse to get
back into bed he ought to take heed of the warning and obey it.
Besides, why should he go? What was there to go for? If it was that
Bengough creature again, let her look after herself; Oleron was not
going to have things cramp themselves on his defenceless back for
the sake of such a spoilsport as *she*! . . . If she was in, let her let herself

out again, and the sooner the better for her! Oleron simply couldn't be bothered. He had his work to do. On the morrow, he must set about the writing of a novel with a heroine so winsome, capricious, adorable, jealous, wicked, beautiful, inflaming, and altogether evil, that men should stand amazed. She was coming over him now; he knew by the alteration of the very air of the room when she was near him; and that soft thrill of bliss that had begun to stir in him never came unless she was beckoning, beckoning . . .

He let go the wall and fell back into bed again as – oh, unthinkable! – the other half of that kiss that a gnash had interrupted was placed (how else convey it?) on his lips, robbing him of very breath . . .

12

In the bright June sunlight a crowd filled the square, and looked up at the windows of the old house with the antique insurance marks in its walls of red brick and the agents' notice-boards hanging like wooden choppers over the paling. Two constables stood at the broken gate of the narrow entrance-alley, keeping folk back. The women kept to the outskirts of the throng, moving now and then as if to see the drawn red blinds of the old house from a new angle, and talking in whispers. The children were in the houses, behind closed doors.

A long-nosed man had a little group about him, and he was telling some story over and over again; and another man, little and fat and wide-eyed, sought to capture the long-nosed man's audience with some relation in which a key figured.

' . . . and it was revealed to me that there'd been something that very afternoon,' the long-nosed man was saying. 'I was standing there, where Constable Saunders is – or rather, I was passing about my business, when they came out. There was no deceiving me, oh, no deceiving *me*! *I* saw her face . . . '

'What was it like, Mr Barrett?' a man asked.

'It was like hers whom our Lord said to, "Woman, doth any man accuse thee?" – white as paper, and no mistake! Don't tell *me*! . . . And so I walks straight across to Mrs Barrett, and "Jane," I says, "this must stop, and stop at once; we are commanded to avoid evil," I says, "and it must come to an end now; let him get help elsewhere."

'And she says to me, "John," she says, "it's four-and-sixpence a week" – them was her words.

' "Jane," I says, "if it was forty-six thousand pounds it should stop...
and from that day to this she hasn't set foot inside that gate.'

There was a short silence: then, 'Did Mrs Barrett ever . . . *see*
anythink, like?' somebody vaguely enquired.

Barrett turned austerely on the speaker. 'What Mrs Barrett saw
and Mrs Barrett didn't see shall not pass these lips; even as it is
written, keep thy tongue from speaking evil,' he said.

Another man spoke.

'He was pretty near canned up in the Waggon and Horses that
night, weren't he, Jim?'

'Yes, 'e 'adn't 'alf copped it . . . '

'Not standing treat much, neither; he was in the bar, all on his
own . . . '

'So 'e was; we talked about it . . . '

The fat, scared-eyed man made another attempt.

'She got the key off of me – she 'ad the number of it – she come
into my shop of a Tuesday evening . . . '

Nobody heeded him.

'Shut your heads,' a heavy labourer commented gruffly, 'she hasn't
been found yet. 'Ere's the inspectors; we shall know more in a bit.'

Two inspectors had come up and were talking to the constables
who guarded the gate. The little fat man ran eagerly forward, saying
that she had bought the key of him. 'I remember the number, because
of it's being three one's and three three's – 111333!' he exclaimed
excitedly.

An inspector put him aside.

'Nobody's been in?' he asked of one of the constables.

'No, sir.'

'Then you, Brackley, come with us; you, Smith, keep the gate.
There's a squad on its way.'

The two inspectors and the constable passed down the alley and
entered the house. They mounted the wide carved staircase.

'This don't look as if he'd been out much lately,' one of the
inspectors muttered as he kicked aside a litter of dead leaves and
paper that lay outside Oleron's door. 'I don't think we need knock –
break a pane, Brackley.'

The door had two glazed panels; there was a sound of shattered
glass; and Brackley put his hand through the hole his elbow had
made and drew back the latch.

'Faugh!' . . . choked one of the inspectors as they entered. 'Let
some light and air in, quick. It stinks like a hearse – '

THE BECKONING FAIR ONE

The assembly out in the square saw the red blinds go up and the windows of the old house flung open.

'That's better,' said one of the inspectors, putting his head out of a window and drawing a deep breath . . . 'That seems to be the bedroom in there; will you go in, Simms, while I go over the rest? . . . '

They had drawn up the bedroom blind also, and the waxy-white, emaciated man on the bed had made a blinker of his hand against the torturing flood of brightness. Nor could he believe that his hearing was not playing tricks with him, for there were two police-men in his room, bending over him and asking where 'she' was. He shook his head.

'This woman Bengough . . . goes by the name of Miss Elsie Bengough . . . d'ye hear? Where is she? . . . No good, Brackley; get him up; be careful with him; I'll just shove *my* head out of the window, I think . . . '

The other inspector had been through Oleron's study and had found nothing, and was now in the kitchen, kicking aside an ankle-deep mass of vegetable refuse that cumbered the floor. The kitchen window had no blind, and was over-shadowed by the blank end of the house across the alley. The kitchen appeared to be empty.

But the inspector, kicking aside the dead flowers, noticed that a shuffling track that was not of his making had been swept to a cupboard in the corner. In the upper part of the door of the cupboard was a square panel that looked as if it slid on runners. The door itself was closed.

The inspector advanced, put out his hand to the little knob, and slid the hatch along its groove.

Then he took an involuntary step back again.

Framed in the aperture, and falling forward a little before it jammed again in its frame, was something that resembled a large lumpy pudding, done up in a pudding-bag of faded browny red frieze.

'Ah!' said the inspector.

To close the hatch again he would have had to thrust that pudding back with his hand; and somehow he did not quite like the idea of touching it. Instead, he turned the handle of the cupboard itself. There was weight behind it, so much weight that, after opening the door three or four inches and peering inside, he had to put his shoulder to it in order to close it again. In closing it he left sticking out, a few inches from the floor, a triangle of black and white check skirt.

He went into the small hall.

'All right!' he called.

They had got Oleron into his clothes. He still used his hands as blinkers, and his brain was very confused. A number of things were happening that he couldn't understand. He couldn't understand the extraordinary mess of dead flowers there seemed to be everywhere; he couldn't understand why there should be police officers in his room; he couldn't understand why one of these should be sent for a four-wheeler and a stretcher; and he couldn't understand what heavy article they seemed to be moving about in the kitchen – his kitchen . . .

'What's the matter?' he muttered sleepily . . .

Then he heard a murmur in the square, and the stopping of a four-wheeler outside. A police officer was at his elbow again, and Oleron wondered why, when he whispered something to him, he should run off a string of words – something about 'used in evidence against you.' They had lifted him to his feet, and were assisting him towards the door . . .

No, Oleron couldn't understand it at all.

They got him down the stairs and along the alley. Oleron was aware of confused angry shoutings; he gathered that a number of people wanted to lynch somebody or other. Then his attention became fixed on a little fat frightened-eyed man who appeared to be making a statement that an officer was taking down in a notebook.

'I'd seen her with him . . . they was often together . . . she came into my shop and said it was for him . . . I thought it was all right . . . 111333 the number was,' the man was saying.

The people seemed to be very angry; many police were keeping them back; but one of the inspectors had a voice that Oleron thought quite kind and friendly. He was telling somebody to get somebody else into the cab before something or other was brought out; and Oleron noticed that a four-wheeler was drawn up at the gate. It appeared that it was himself who was to be put into it; and as they lifted him up he saw that the inspector tried to stand between him and something that stood behind the cab, but was not quick enough to prevent Oleron seeing that this something was a hooded stretcher. The angry voices sounded like a sea; something hard, like a stone, hit the back of the cab; and the inspector followed Oleron in and stood with his back to the window nearer the side where the people were. The door they had put Oleron in at remained open, apparently till the other inspector should come; and through the opening Oleron had a glimpse of the hatchet-like 'To Let' boards among the privet-trees. One of them said that the key was at Number Six . . .

Suddenly the raging of voices was hushed. Along the entrance-alley shuffling steps were heard, and the other inspector appeared at the cab door.

'Right away,' he said to the driver.

He entered, fastened the door after him, and blocked up the second window with his back. Between the two inspectors Oleron slept peacefully. The cab moved down the square, the other vehicle went up the hill. The mortuary lay that way.

Phantas

For, barring all pother,
With this, or the other,
Still Britons are Lords of the Main.
The Chapter of Admirals

I

As Abel Keeling lay on the galleon's deck, held from rolling down it only by his own weight and the sun-blackened hand that lay out-stretched upon the planks, his gaze wandered, but ever returned to the bell that hung, jammed with the dangerous heel-over of the vessel, in the small ornamental belfry immediately abaft the main-mast. The bell was of cast bronze, with half-obliterated bosses upon it that had been the heads of cherubs; but wind and salt spray had given it a thick incrustation of bright, beautiful, lichenous green. It was this colour that Abel Keeling's eyes liked.

For wherever else on the galleon his eyes rested they found only whiteness – the whiteness of extreme eld. There were slightly vary-ing degrees in her whiteness; here she was of a white that glistened like salt-granules, there of a greyish chalky white, and again her whiteness had the yellowish cast of decay; but everywhere it was the mild, disquieting whiteness of materials out of which the life had departed. Her cordage was bleached as old straw is bleached, and half her ropes kept their shape little more firmly than the ash of a string keeps its shape after the fire has passed; her pallid timbers were white and clean as bones found in sand; and even the wild frankincense with which (for lack of tar, at her last touching of land) she had been pitched, had dried to a pale hard gum that sparkled like quartz in her open seams. The sun was yet so pale a buckler of silver through the still white mists that not a cord or timber cast a shadow; and only Abel Keeling's face and hands were black, carked and cinder-black from exposure to his pitiless rays.

The galleon was the *Mary of the Tower*, and she had a frightful list to starboard. So canted was she that her mainyard dipped one of its steel sickles into the glassy water, and, had her foremast remained, or more than the broken stump of her bonaventure mizzen, she must have turned over completely. Many days ago they had stripped the mainyard of its course, and had passed the sail under the *Mary's* bottom, in the hope that it would stop the leak. This it had partly done as long as the galleon had continued to glide one way; then, without coming about, she had begun to glide the other, the ropes had parted, and she had dragged the sail after her, leaving a broad tarnish on the silver sea.

For it was broadside that the galleon glided, almost imperceptibly, ever sucking down. She glided as if a loadstone drew her, and, at first, Abel Keeling had thought it was a loadstone, pulling at her iron, drawing her through the pearly mists that lay like face-cloths to the water and hid at a short distance the tarnish left by the sail. But later he had known that it was no loadstone drawing at her iron. The motion was due – must be due – to the absolute deadness of the calm in that silent, sinister, three-miles-broad waterway. With the eye of his mind he saw that loadstone now as he lay against a gun-truck, all but toppling down the deck. Soon that would happen again which had happened for five days past. He would hear again the chattering of monkeys and the screaming of parrots, the mat of green and yellow weeds would creep in towards the *Mary* over the quicksilver sea, once more the sheer wall of rock would rise, and the men would run . . .

But no; the men would not run this time to drop the fenders. There were no men left to do so, unless Bligh was still alive. Perhaps Bligh was still alive. He had walked half-way down the quarter-deck steps a little before the sudden nightfall of the day before, had then fallen and lain for a minute (dead, Abel Keeling had supposed, watching him from his place by the gun-truck), and had then got up again and tottered forward to the forecastle, his tall figure swaying and his long arms waving. Abel Keeling had not seen him since. Most likely, he had died in the forecastle during the night. If he had not been dead he would have come aft again for water . . .

At the remembrance of the water Abel Keeling lifted his head. The strands of lean muscle about his emaciated mouth worked, and he made a little pressure of his sun-blackened hand on the deck, as if to verify its steepness and his own balance. The mainmast was some seven or eight yards away . . . He put one stiff leg under him and began, seated as he was, to make shuffling movements down the slope.

To the mainmast, near the belfry, was affixed his contrivance for catching water. It consisted of a collar of rope set lower at one side than at the other (but that had been before the mast had steeved so many degrees away from the zenith), and tallowed beneath. The mists lingered later in that gully of a strait than they did on the open ocean, and the collar of rope served as a collector for the dews that condensed on the mast. The drops fell into a small earthen pipkin placed on the deck beneath it.

Abel Keeling reached the pipkin and looked into it. It was nearly a third full of fresh water. Good. If Bligh, the mate, was dead, so much the more water for Abel Keeling, master of the *Mary of the Tower*. He dipped two fingers into the pipkin and put them into his mouth. This he did several times. He did not dare to raise the pipkin to his black and broken lips for dread of a remembered agony, he could not have told how many days ago, when a devil had whispered to him, and he had gulped down the contents of the pipkin in the morning, and for the rest of the day had gone waterless . . . Again he moistened his fingers and sucked them; then he lay sprawling against the mast, idly watching the drops of water as they fell.

It was odd how the drops formed. Slowly they collected at the edge of the tallowed collar, trembled in their fullness for an instant, and fell, another beginning the process instantly. It amused Abel Keeling to watch them. Why (he wondered) were all the drops the same size? What cause and compulsion did they obey that they never varied, and what frail tenuity held the little globules intact? It must be due to some Cause . . . He remembered that the aromatic gum of the wild frankincense with which they had parcelled the seams had hung on the buckets in great sluggish gouts, obedient to a different compulsion; oil was different again, and so were juices and balsams. Only quicksilver (perhaps the heavy and motionless sea put him in mind of quicksilver) seemed obedient to no law . . . Why was it so?

Bligh, of course, would have had his explanation: it was the Hand of God. That sufficed for Bligh, who had gone forward the evening before, and whom Abel Keeling now seemed vaguely and as at a distance to remember as the deep-voiced fanatic who had sung his hymns as, man by man, he had committed the bodies of the ship's company to the deep. Bligh was that sort of man; accepted things

without question; was content to take things as they were and be
ready with the fenders when the wall of rock rose out of the opal-
escent mists. Bligh, too, like the waterdrops, had his Law, that was
his and nobody else's . . .

There floated down from some rotten rope up aloft a flake of
scurf, that settled in the pipkin. Abel Keeling watched it dully as it
settled towards the pipkin's rim. When presently he again dipped
his fingers into the vessel the water ran into a little vortex, drawing
the flake with it. The water settled again; and again the minute flake
determined towards the rim and adhered there, as if the rim had
power to draw it . . .

It was exactly so that the galleon was gliding towards the wall of
rock, the yellow and green weeds, and the monkeys and parrots. Put
out into mid-water again (while there had been men to put her out)
she had glided to the other wall. One force drew the chip in the
pipkin and the ship over the tranced sea. It was the Hand of God,
said Bligh . . .

Abel Keeling, his mind now noting minute things and now clouded
with torpor, did not at first hear a voice that was quakingly lifted up
over by the forecastle – a voice that drew nearer, to an accompaniment of swirling water.

> O Thou, that Jonas in the fish
>   Three days didst keep from pain,
> Which was a figure of Thy death
>   And rising up again –

It was Bligh, singing one of his hymns:

> O Thou, that Noah keptst from flood
>   And Abram, day by day,
> As he along through Egypt passed
>   Didst guide him in the way –

The voice ceased, leaving the pious period uncompleted. Bligh was
alive, at any rate . . . Abel Keeling resumed his fitful musing.

Yes, that was the Law of Bligh's life, to call things the Hand of
God; but Abel Keeling's Law was different; no better, no worse, only
different. The Hand of God, that drew chips and galleons, must
work by some method; and Abel Keeling's eyes were dully on the
pipkin again as if he sought the method there . . .

Then conscious thought left him for a space, and when he resumed
it was without obvious connection.

Oars, of course, were the thing. With oars, men could laugh at calms. Oars, that only pinnaces and galliasses now used, had had their advantages. But oars (which was to say a method, for you could say if you liked that the Hand of God grasped the oar-loom, as the Breath of God filled the sail) – oars were antiquated, belonged to the past, and meant a throwing-over of all that was good and new and a return to fine lines, a battle-formation abreast to give effect to the shock of the ram, and a day or two at sea and then to port again for provisions. Oars . . . no. Abel Keeling was one of the new men, the men who swore by the line-ahead, the broadside fire of sakers and demi-cannon, and weeks and months without a landfall. Perhaps one day the wits of such men as he would devise a craft, not oar-driven (because oars could not penetrate into the remote seas of the world) – not sail-driven (because men who trusted to sails found themselves in an airless, three-mile strait, suspended motionless between cloud and water, ever gliding to a wall of rock) – but a ship . . . a ship . . .

> To Noah and his sons with him
>   God spake, and thus said He:
> A covenant set I up with you
>   And your posterity –

It was Bligh again, wandering somewhere in the waist. Abel Keeling's mind was once more a blank. Then slowly, slowly, as the water drops collected on the collar of rope, his thought took shape again.

A galliasse? No, not a galliasse. The galliasse made shift to be two things, and was neither. This ship, that the hand of man should one day make for the Hand of God to manage, should be a ship that should take and conserve the force of the wind, take it and store it as she stored her victuals; at rest when she wished, going ahead when she wished; turning the forces both of calm and storm against themselves. For, of course, her force must be wind – stored wind – a bag of the winds, as the children's tale had it – wind probably directed upon the water astern, driving it away and urging forward the ship, acting by reaction. She would have a wind-chamber, into which wind would be pumped with pumps . . . Bligh would call that equally the Hand of God, this driving-force of the ship of the future that Abel Keeling dimly foreshadowed as he lay between the mainmast and the belfry, turning his eyes now and then from ashy white timbers to the vivid green bronze-rust of the bell above him . . .

Bligh's face, liver-coloured with the sun and ravaged from inwards by the faith that consumed him, appeared at the head of the quarter-deck steps. His voice beat uncontrolledly out.

> And in the earth here is no place
>   Of refuge to be found,
> Nor in the deep and water-course
>   That passeth under ground –

2

Bligh's eyes were lidded, as if in contemplation of his inner ecstasy. His head was thrown back, and his brows worked up and down tormentedly. His wide mouth remained open as his hymn was suddenly interrupted on the long-drawn note. From somewhere in the shimmering mists the note was taken up, and there drummed and rang and reverberated through the strait a windy, hoarse, and dismal bellow, alarming and sustained. A tremor rang through Bligh. Moving like a sightless man, he stumbled forward from the head of the quarter-deck steps, and Abel Keeling was aware of his gaunt figure behind him, taller for the steepness of the deck. As that vast empty sound died away, Bligh laughed in his mania.

'Lord, hath the grave's wide mouth a tongue to praise Thee? Lo, again – '

Again the cavernous sound possessed the air, louder and nearer. Through it came another sound, a slow throb, throb – throb, throb – Again the sounds ceased.

'Even Leviathan lifteth up his voice in praise!' Bligh sobbed.

Abel Keeling did not raise his head. There had returned to him the memory of that day when, before the morning mists had lifted from the strait, he had emptied the pipkin of the water that was the allowance until night should fall again. During that agony of thirst he had seen shapes and heard sounds with other than his mortal eyes and ears, and even in the moments that had alternated with his lightness, when he had known these to be hallucinations, they had come again. He had heard the bells on a Sunday in his own Kentish home, the calling of children at play, the unconcerned singing of men at their daily labour, and the laughter and gossip of the women as they had spread the linen on the hedge or distributed bread upon the platters. These voices had rung in his brain, interrupted now and then by the groans of Bligh and of two other men who had been alive then. Some of the voices he had heard had been silent on earth this

many a long year, but Abel Keeling, thirst-tortured, had heard them,
even as he was now hearing that vacant moaning with the intermittent throbbing that filled the strait with alarm . . .

'Praise Him, praise Him, praise Him!' Bligh was calling deliriously.

Then a bell seemed to sound in Abel Keeling's ears, and, as if
something in the mechanism of his brain had slipped, another picture
rose in his fancy – the scene when the *Mary of the Tower* had put out,
to a bravery of swinging bells and shrill fifes and valiant trumpets.
She had not been a leper-white galleon then. The scroll-work on her
prow had twinkled with gilding; her belfry and stern-galleries and
elaborate lanterns had flashed in the sun with gold; and her fighting-
tops and the war-pavesse about her waist had been gay with painted
coats and scutcheons. To her sails had been stitched gaudy ramping
lions of scarlet saye, and from her mainyard, now dipping in the
water, had hung the broad two-tailed pennant with the Virgin and
Child embroidered upon it . . .

Then suddenly a voice about him seemed to be saying, '*And a half-
seven – and a half-seven –* ' and in a twink the picture in Abel Keeling's
brain changed again. He was at home again, instructing his son,
young Abel, in the casting of the lead from the skiff they had pulled
out of the harbour.

'*And a half-seven!*' the boy seemed to be calling.

Abel Keeling's blackened lips muttered: 'Excellently well cast,
Abel, excellently well cast!'

'*And a half-seven – and a half-seven – seven – seven –* '

'Ah,' Abel Keeling murmured, 'that last was not a clear cast – give
me the line – thus it should go . . . ay, so . . . Soon you shall sail the
seas with me in the *Mary of the Tower*. You are already perfect in the
stars and the motions of the planets; tomorrow I will instruct you in
the use of the backstaff . . . '

For a minute or two he continued to mutter; then he dozed. When
again he came to semi-consciousness it was once more to the sound
of bells, at first faint, then louder, and finally becoming a noisy
clamour immediately above his head. It was Bligh. Bligh, in a fresh
attack of delirium, had seized the bell-lanyard and was ringing the
bell insanely. The cord broke in his fingers, but he thrust at the bell
with his hand, and again called aloud.

'Upon an harp and an instrument of ten strings . . . let Heaven and
Earth praise Thy Name! . . . '

He continued to call aloud, and to beat on the bronze-rusted bell.

'*Ship ahoy! What ship's that?*'

One would have said that a veritable hail had come out of the mists; but Abel Keeling knew those hails that came out of the mists. They came from ships which were not there. 'Ay, ay, keep a good look-out, and have a care to your lode-manage,' he muttered again to his son . . .

But, as sometimes a sleeper sits up in his dream, or rises from his couch and walks, so all of a sudden Abel Keeling found himself on his hands and knees on the deck, looking back over his shoulder. In some deep-seated region of his consciousness he was dimly aware that the cant of the deck had become more perilous, but his brain received the intelligence and forgot it again. He was looking out into the bright and baffling mists. The buckler of the sun was of a more ardent silver; the sea below it was lost in brilliant evaporation; and between them, suspended in the haze, no more substantial than the vague darknesses that float before dazzled eyes, a pyramidal phantom-shape hung. Abel Keeling passed his hand over his eyes, but when he removed it the shape was still there, gliding slowly towards the *Mary*'s quarter. Its form changed as he watched it. The spirit-grey shape that had been a pyramid seemed to dissolve into four upright members, slightly graduated in tallness, that nearest the *Mary*'s stern the tallest and that to the left the lowest. It might have been the shadow of the gigantic set of reed-pipes on which that vacant mournful note had been sounded.

And as he looked, with fooled eyes, again his ears became fooled.

'*Ahoy there! What ship's that? Are you a ship? . . . Here, give me that trumpet –* ' Then a metallic barking. '*Ahoy there! What the devil are you? Didn't you ring a bell? Ring it again, or blow a blast or something, and go dead slow!*'

All this came, as it were, indistinctly, and through a sort of high singing in Abel Keeling's own ears. Then he fancied a short bewildered laugh, followed by a colloquy from somewhere between sea and sky.

'*Here, Ward, just pinch me, will you? Tell me what you see there. I want to know if I'm awake.*'

'*See where?*'

'*There, on the starboard bow. (Stop that ventilating fan; I can't hear myself think.) See anything? Don't tell me it's that damned Dutchman – don't pitch me that old Vanderdecken tale – give me an easy one first, something about a sea-serpent . . . You did hear that bell, didn't you?*'

'*Shut up a minute – listen –* '

Again Bligh's voice was lifted up.

> This is the cov'nant that I make:
> From henceforth nevermore
> Will I again the world destroy
> With water, as before.

Bligh's voice died away again in Abel Keeling's ears.

'*Oh – my – fat – Aunt – Julia!*' the voice that seemed to come from between sea and sky sounded again. Then it spoke more loudly. '*I say*,' it began with careful politeness, '*if you are a ship, do you mind telling us where the masquerade is to be? Our wireless is out of order, and we hadn't heard of it . . . Oh, you do see it, Ward, don't you? . . . Please, please tell us what the hell you are!*'

Again Abel Keeling had moved as a sleepwalker moves. He had raised himself up by the belfry timbers, and Bligh had sunk in a heap on the deck. Abel Keeling's movement overturned the pipkin, which raced the little trickle of its contents down the deck and lodged where the still and brimming sea made, as it were, a chain with the carved balustrade of the quarter-deck – one link a still gleaming edge, then a dark baluster, and then another gleaming link. For one moment only Abel Keeling found himself noticing that that which had driven Bligh aft had been the rising of the water in the waist as the galleon settled by the head – the waist was now entirely submerged; then once more he was absorbed in his dream, its voices, and its shape in the mist, which had again taken the form of a pyramid before his eyeballs.

'*Of course*,' a voice seemed to be complaining anew, and still through that confused dinning in Abel Keeling's ears, '*we can't turn a four-inch on it . . . And, of course, Ward, I don't believe in 'em. D'you hear, Ward? I don't believe in 'em, I say . . . Shall we call down to old A. B.? This might interest His Scientific Skippership . . .* '

'*Oh, lower a boat and pull out to it – into it – over it – through it –* '

'*Look at our chaps crowded on the barbette yonder. They've seen it. Better not give an order you know won't be obeyed . . .* '

Abel Keeling, cramped against the antique belfry, had begun to find his dream interesting. For, though he did not know her build, that mirage was the shape of a ship. No doubt it was projected from his brooding on ships of half an hour before; and that was odd . . . But perhaps, after all, it was not very odd. He knew that she did not really exist; only the appearance of her existed; but things had to exist like that before they really existed. Before the *Mary of the Tower* had existed she had been a shape in some man's imagination; before that, some dreamer had dreamed the form of a ship with oars; and before that, far away in the dawn and infancy of the world, some seer had seen in a vision the raft before man had ventured to push out over the water on his two planks. And since this shape that rode before Abel Keeling's eyes was a shape in his, Abel Keeling's dream, he, Abel Keeling, was the master of it. His own brooding brain had contrived her, and she was launched upon the illimitable ocean of his own mind . . .

> And I will not unmindful be
>   Of this, My covenant, passed
> Twixt Me and you and every flesh
>   Whiles that the world should last,

sang Bligh, rapt . . .

But as a dreamer, even in his dream, will scratch upon the wall by his couch some key or word to put him in mind of his vision on the morrow when it has left him, so Abel Keeling found himself seeking some sign to be a proof to those to whom no vision is vouchsafed. Even Bligh sought that – could not be silent in his bliss, but lay on the deck there, uttering great passionate Amens and praising his Maker, as he said, upon an harp and an instrument of ten strings. So with Abel Keeling. It would be the Amen of his life to have praised God, not upon a harp, but upon a ship that should carry her own power, that should store wind or its equivalent as she stored her victuals, that should be something wrested from the chaos of uninvention and ordered and disciplined and subordinated to Abel Keeling's will . . . And there she was, that ship-shaped thing of spirit-grey, with the four pipes that resembled a phantom organ now broadside and of equal length. And the ghost-crew of that ship were speaking again . . .

The interrupted silver chain by the quarterdeck balustrade had now become continuous, and the balusters made a herring-bone over their own motionless reflections. The spilt water from the pipkin had dried, and the pipkin was not to be seen. Abel Keeling stood beside the mast, erect as God made man to go. With his leathery hand he smote upon the bell. He waited for the space of a minute, and then cried:

'Ahoy! . . . Ship ahoy! . . . What ship's that?'

3

We are not conscious in a dream that we are playing a game the beginning and end of which are in ourselves. In this dream of Abel Keeling's a voice replied.

'*Hallo, it's found its tongue . . . Ahoy there! What are you?*'

Loudly and in a clear voice Abel Keeling called: 'Are you a ship?'

With a nervous giggle the answer came:

'*We are a ship, aren't we, Ward? I hardly feel sure . . . Yes, of course, we're a ship. No question about us. The question is what the dickens you are.*'

Not all the words these voices used were intelligible to Abel Keeling, and he knew not what it was in the tone of these last words that reminded him of the honour due to the *Mary of the Tower*. Blister-white and at the end of her life as she was, Abel Keeling was still jealous of her dignity; the voice had a youngish ring; and it was not fitting that young chins should be wagged about his galleon. He spoke curtly.

'You that spoke – are you the master of that ship?'

'*Officer of the watch,*' the words floated back; '*the captain's below.*'

'Then send for him. It is with masters that masters hold speech,' Abel Keeling replied.

He could see the two shapes, flat and without relief, standing on a high narrow structure with rails. One of them gave a low whistle, and seemed to be fanning his face; but the other rumbled something into a sort of funnel. Presently the two shapes became three. There was a murmuring, as of a consultation, and then suddenly a new voice spoke. At its thrill and tone a sudden tremor ran through Abel Keeling's frame. He wondered what response it was that that voice found in the forgotten recesses of his memory . . .

'*Ahoy*' seemed to call this new yet faintly remembered voice. '*What's all this about? Listen. We're His Majesty's destroyer* Seapink, *out of Devonport last October, and nothing particular the matter with us. Now who are you?*'

'The *Mary of the Tower*, out of the Port of Rye on the day of Saint Anne, and only two men – '

A gasp interrupted him.

'*Out of WHERE?*' that voice that so strangely moved Abel Keeling said unsteadily, while Bligh broke into groans of renewed rapture.

'Out of the Port of Rye, in the County of Sussex . . . nay, give ear, else I cannot make you hear me while this man's spirit and flesh wrestle so together! . . . Ahoy! Are you gone?' For the voices had become a low murmur, and the ship-shape had faded before Abel Keeling's eyes. Again and again he called. He wished to be informed of the disposition and economy of the wind-chamber . . .

'The wind-chamber!' he called, in an agony lest the knowledge almost within his grasp should be lost. 'I would know about the wind-chamber . . . '

Like an echo, there came back the words, uncomprehendingly uttered, *'The wind-chamber? . . . '*

' . . . that driveth the vessel – perchance 'tis not wind – a steel bow that is bent also conserveth force – the force you store, to move at will through calm and storm . . . '

'Can you make out what it's driving at?'

'Oh, we shall all wake up in a minute . . . '

'Quiet, I have it; the engines; it wants to know about our engines. It'll be wanting to see our papers presently. Rye Port! . . . Well, no harm in humouring it; let's see what it can make of this. Ahoy there!' came the voice to Abel Keeling, a little more strongly, as if a shifting wind carried it, and speaking faster and faster as it went on. *'Not wind, but steam; d'you hear? Steam, steam. Steam, in eight Yarrow water-tube boilers. S-t-e-a-m, steam. Got it? And we've twin-screw triple expansion engines, indicated horse-power four thousand, and we can do 430 revolutions per minute; savvy? Is there anything your phantomhood would like to know about our armament? . . . '*

Abel Keeling was muttering fretfully to himself. It annoyed him that words in his own vision should have no meaning for him. How did words come to him in a dream that he had no knowledge of when wide awake? The *Seapink* – that was the name of this ship; but a pink was long and narrow, low-carged and square-built aft . . .

'And as for our armament,' the voice with the tones that so profoundly troubled Abel Keeling's memory continued, *'we've two revolving Whitehead torpedo-tubes, three six-pounders on the upper deck, and that's a twelve-pounder forward there by the conning-tower. I forgot to mention that we're nickel steel, with a coal capacity of sixty tons in most damnably placed bunkers, and that thirty and a quarter knots is about our top. Care to come aboard?'*

But the voice was speaking still more rapidly and feverishly, as if to fill a silence with no matter what, and the shape that was uttering it was straining forward anxiously over the rail.

'Ugh! But I'm glad this happened in the daylight,' another voice was muttering.

'I wish I was sure it was happening at all . . . Poor old spook!'

'*I suppose it would keep its feet if her deck was quite vertical. Think she'll go down, or just melt?*'

'*Kind of go down . . . without wash . . .* '

'*Listen – here's the other one now –* '

For Bligh was singing again.

> For, Lord, Thou know'st our nature such
>   If we great things obtain,
> And in the getting of the same
>   Do feel no grief or pain,

> 'We little do esteem thereof;
>   But, hardly brought to pass,
> A thousand times we do esteem
>   More than the other was.

'*But oh, look – look – look at the other!* . . . *Oh, I say, wasn't he a grand old boy! Look!*'

For, transfiguring Abel Keeling's form as a prophet's form is transfigured in the instant of his rapture, flooding his brain with the white eureka-light of perfect knowledge, that for which he and his dream had been at a standstill had come. He knew her, this ship of the future, as if God's Finger had bitten her lines into his brain. He knew her as those already sinking into the grave know things, miraculously, completely, accepting Life's impossibilities with a nodded 'Of course'. From the ardent mouths of her eight furnaces to the last drip from her lubricators, from her bed-plates to the breeches of her quick-firers, he knew her – read her gauges, thumbed her bearings, gave the ranges from her range-finders, and lived the life he lived who was in command of her. And he would not forget on the morrow, as he had forgotten on many morrows, for at last he had seen the water about his feet, and knew that there would be no morrow for him in this world . . .

And even in that moment, with but a sand or two to run in his glass, indomitable, insatiable, dreaming dream on dream, he could not die until he knew more. He had two questions to ask, and a master-question; and but a moment remained. Sharply his voice rang out.

'Ho, there! . . . This ancient ship, the *Mary of the Tower*, cannot steam thirty and a quarter knots, but yet she can sail the waters. What more does your ship? Can she soar above them, as the fowls of the air soar?'

'*Lord, he thinks we're an aeroplane! . . . No, she can't . . .*'

'And can you dive, even as the fishes of the deep?'

'*No . . . Those are submarines . . . we aren't a submarine . . .*'

But Abel Keeling waited for no more. He gave an exulting chuckle.

'Oho, oho – thirty knots, and but on the face of the waters – no more than that? Oho! . . . Now *my* ship, the ship I see as a mother sees full-grown the child she has but conceived – *my* ship, I say – oho! – *my* ship shall . . . Below there – trip that gun!'

The cry came suddenly and alertly, as a muffled sound came from below and an ominous tremor shook the galleon.

'*By Jove, her guns are breaking loose below – that's her finish –*'

'Trip that gun, and double-breech the others!' Abel Keeling's voice rang out, as if there had been any to obey him. He had braced himself within the belfry frame; and then in the middle of the next order his voice suddenly failed him. His ship-shape, that for the moment he had forgotten, rode once more before his eyes. This was the end, and his master-question, apprehension for the answer to which was now torturing his face and well-nigh bursting his heart, was still unasked.

'Ho – he that spoke with me – the master,' he cried in a voice that ran high, 'is he there?'

'*Yes, yes!*' came the other voice across the water, sick with suspense. '*Oh, be quick!*'

There was a moment in which hoarse cries from many voices, a heavy thud and rumble on wood, and a crash of timbers and a gurgle and a splash were indescribably mingled; the gun under which Abel Keeling had lain had snapped her rotten breechings and plunged down the deck, carrying Bligh's unconscious form with it. The deck came up vertical, and for one instant longer Abel Keeling clung to the belfry.

'I cannot see your face,' he screamed, 'but meseems your voice is a voice I know. What is your name?'

In a torn sob the answer came across the water:

'*Keeling – Abel Keeling . . . Oh, my God!*'

And Abel Keeling's cry of triumph, that mounted to a victorious 'Huzza!' was lost in the downward plunge of the *Mary of the Tower*, that left the strait empty save for the sun's fiery blaze and the last smoke-like evaporation of the mists.

Rooum

For all I ever knew to the contrary, it was his own name; and something about him, name or man or both, always put me in mind, I can't tell you how, of negroes. As regards the name, I dare say it was something huggermugger in the mere sound – something that I classed, for no particular reason, with the dark and ignorant sort of words, such as 'Obi' and 'Hoodoo'. I only know that after I learned that his name was Rooum, I couldn't for the life of me have thought of him as being called anything else.

The first impression that you got of his head was that it was a patchwork of black and white – black bushy hair and short white beard, or else the other way about. As a matter of fact, both hair and beard were piebald, so that if you saw him in the gloom a dim patch of white showed down one side of his head, and dark tufts cropped up here and there in his beard. His eyebrows alone were entirely black, with a little sprouting of hair almost joining them. And perhaps his skin helped to make me think of negroes, for it was very dark, of the dark brown that always seems to have more than a hint of green behind it. His forehead was low, and scored across with deep horizontal furrows.

We never knew when he was going to turn up on a job. We might not have seen him for weeks, but his face was always as likely as not to appear over the edge of a crane-platform just when that marvellous mechanical intuition of his was badly needed. He wasn't certificated. He wasn't even trained, as the rest of us understood training; and he scoffed at the drawing-office, and laughed outright at logarithms and our laborious methods of getting out quantities. But he could set sheers and tackle in a way that made the rest of us look silly. I remember once how, through the parting of a chain, a sixty-foot girder had come down and lay under a ruck of other stuff, as the bottom chip lies under a pile of spellikins – a hopeless-looking smash. Myself, I'm certificated twice or three times over; but I can only assure you that I wanted to kick myself when, after I'd spent a day and a sleepless night over the job, I saw the game of tit-tat-toe that Rooum made of it in an hour or two. Certificated or not, a man isn't a fool who can do that sort of thing. And he was one of these fellows, too, who can 'find water' – tell you where water is and what amount of getting it is likely to take, by just walking over the place. We aren't certificated up to that yet.

He was offered good money to stick to us – to stick to our firm – but he always shook his black-and-white piebald head. He'd never be able to keep the bargain if he were to make it, he told us quite fairly. I know there are these chaps who can't endure to be clocked to their work with a patent time-clock in the morning and released of an evening with a whistle – and it's one of the things no master can ever understand. So Rooum came and went erratically, showing up maybe in Leeds or Liverpool, perhaps next on Plymouth breakwater, and once he turned up in an out-of-the-way place in Glamorganshire just when I was wondering what had become of him.

The way I got to know him (got to know him, I mean, more than just to nod) was that he tacked himself on to me one night down Vauxhall way, where we were setting up some small plant or other. We had knocked off for the day, and I was walking in the direction of the bridge when he came up. We walked along together; and we had not gone far before it appeared that his reason for joining me was that he wanted to know 'what a molecule was'.

I stared at him a bit.

'What do you want to know that for?' I said. 'What does a chap like you, who can do it all backwards, want with molecules?'

Oh, he just wanted to know, he said.

So, on the way across the bridge, I gave it him more or less from the book – molecular theory and all the rest of it. But, from the childish questions he put, it was plain that he hadn't got the hang of it at all. 'Did the molecular theory allow things to pass through one another?' he wanted to know; '*Could* things pass through one another?' and a lot of ridiculous things like that. I gave it up.

'You're a genius in your own way, Rooum,' I said finally; 'you know these things without the books we plodders have to depend on. If I'd luck like that, I think I should be content with it.'

But he didn't seem satisfied, though he dropped the matter for that time. But I had his acquaintance, which was more than most of us had. He asked me, rather timidly, if I'd lend him a book or two. I did so, but they didn't seem to contain what he wanted to know, and he soon returned them, without remark.

Now you'd expect a fellow to be specially sensitive, one way or another, who can tell when there's water a hundred feet beneath him; and as you know, the big men are squabbling yet about this water-finding business. But, somehow, the water-finding puzzled me less than it did that Rooum should be extraordinarily sensitive to something far commoner and easier to understand – ordinary echoes. He couldn't stand echoes. He'd go a mile round rather than pass a place that he knew had an echo; and if he came on one by chance, sometimes he'd hurry through as quick as he could, and sometimes he'd loiter and listen very intently. I rather joked about this at first, till I found it really distressed him; then, of course, I pretended not to notice. We're all cranky somewhere, and for that matter, I can't touch a spider myself.

For the remarkable thing that overtook Rooum – (that, by the way, is an odd way to put it, as you'll see presently; but the words came that way into my head, so let them stand) – for the remarkable thing that overtook Rooum, I don't think I can begin better than with the first time, or very soon after the first time, that I noticed this peculiarity about the echoes.

It was early on a particularly dismal November evening, and this time we were somewhere out south-east London way, just beyond what they are pleased to call the building-line – you know these districts of wretched trees and grimy fields and market-gardens that are about the same to real country that a slum is to a town. It rained that night; rain was the most appropriate weather for the brickfields and sewage-farms and yards of old carts and railway-sleepers we were passing. The rain shone on the black hand-bag that Rooum always carried; and I sucked at the dottle of a pipe that it was too much trouble to fill and light again. We were walking in the direction of Lewisham (I think it would be), and were still a little way from that eruption of red-brick houses that . . . but you've doubtless seen them.

You know how, when they're laying out new roads, they lay down the narrow strip of kerb first, with neither setts on the one hand nor flagstones on the other? We had come upon one of these. (I had noticed how, as we had come a few minutes before under a tall hollow-ringing railway arch, Rooum had all at once stopped talking – it was the echo, of course, that bothered him.) The unmade road to which we had come had headless lamp-standards at intervals, and ramparts of grey road-metal ready for use; and save for the strip of kerb, it was a broth of mud and stiff clay. A red light or two showed where the road-barriers were – they were laying the mains; a green railway light showed on an embankment; and the Lewisham lamps made a rusty glare through the rain. Rooum went first, walking along the narrow strip of kerb.

The lamp-standards were a little difficult to see, and when I heard Rooum stop suddenly and draw in his breath sharply, I thought he had walked into one of them.

'Hurt yourself?' I said.

He walked on without replying; but half a dozen yards farther on he stopped again. He was listening again. He waited for me to come up.

'I say,' he said, in an odd sort of voice, 'go a yard or two ahead, will you?'

'What's the matter?' I asked, as I passed ahead. He didn't answer.

Well, I hadn't been leading for more than a minute before he wanted to change again. He was breathing very quick and short.

'Why, what ails you?' I demanded, stopping.

'It's all right . . . You're not playing any tricks, are you? . . . '

I saw him pass his hand over his brow.

'Come, get on,' I said shortly; and we didn't speak again till we struck the pavement with the lighted lamps. Then I happened to glance at him.

'Here,' I said brusquely, taking him by the sleeve, 'you're not well. We'll call somewhere and get a drink.'

'Yes,' he said, again wiping his brow. 'I say . . . did you hear?'

'Hear what?'

'Ah, you didn't . . . and, of course, you didn't feel anything . . . '

'Come, you're shaking.'

When presently we came to a brightly lighted public-house or hotel, I saw that he was shaking even worse than I had thought. The shirt-sleeved barman noticed it too, and watched us curiously. I made Rooum sit down, and got him some brandy.

'What was the matter?' I asked, as I held the glass to his lips.

But I could get nothing out of him except that it was 'All right – all right', with his head twitching over his shoulder almost as if he had a touch of the dance. He began to come round a little. He wasn't the kind of man you'd press for explanations, and presently we set out again. He walked with me as far as my lodgings, refused to come in, but for all that lingered at the gate as if loath to leave. I watched him turn the corner in the rain.

We came home together again the next evening, but by a different way, quite half a mile longer. He had waited for me a little pertinaciously. It seemed he wanted to talk about molecules again.

Well, when a man of his age – he'd be near fifty – begins to ask questions, he's rather worse than a child who wants to know where Heaven is or some such thing – for you can't put him off as you can the child. Somewhere or other he'd picked up the word 'osmosis', and seemed to have some glimmering of its meaning. He dropped the molecules, and began to ask me about osmosis.

'It means, doesn't it,' he demanded, 'that liquids will work their way into one another – through a bladder or something? Say a thick fluid and a thin: you'll find some of the thick in the thin, and the thin in the thick?'

'Yes. The thick into the thin is ex-osmosis, and the other end-osmosis. That takes place more quickly. But I don't know a deal about it.'

'Does it ever take place with solids?' he next asked.

What was he driving at? I thought; but replied: 'I believe that what is commonly called "adhesion" is something of the sort, under another name.'

'A good deal of this bookwork seems to be finding a dozen names for the same thing,' he grunted; and continued to ask his questions.

But what it was he really wanted to know I couldn't for the life of me make out.

Well, he was due any time now to disappear again, having worked quite six weeks in one place; and he disappeared. He disappeared for a good many weeks. I think it would be about February before I saw or heard of him again.

It was February weather, anyway, and in an echoing enough place that I found him – the subway of one of the Metropolitan stations. He'd probably forgotten the echoes when he'd taken the train; but, of course, the railway folk won't let a man who happens to dislike echoes go wandering across the metals where he likes.

He was twenty yards ahead when I saw him. I recognised him by his patched head and black hand-bag. I ran along the subway after him.

It was very curious. He'd been walking close to the white-tiled wall, and I saw him suddenly stop; but he didn't turn. He didn't even turn when I pulled up, close behind him; he put out one hand to the wall, as if to steady himself. But, the moment I touched his shoulder, he just dropped – just dropped, half on his knees against the white tiling. The face he turned round and up to me was transfixed with fright.

There were half a hundred people about – a train was just in – and it isn't a difficult matter in London to get a crowd for much less than a man crouching terrified against a wall, looking over his shoulder as

Rooum looked, at another man almost as terrified. I felt somebody's hand on my own arm. Evidently somebody thought I'd knocked Rooum down.

The terror went slowly from his face. He stumbled to his feet. I shook myself free of the man who held me and stepped up to Rooum.

'What the devil's all this about?' I demanded, roughly enough.

'It's all right . . . it's all right . . . ' he stammered.

'Heavens, man, you shouldn't play tricks like that!'

'No . . . no . . . but for the love of God don't do it again! . . . '

'We'll not explain here,' I said, still in a good deal of a huff; and the small crowd melted away – disappointed, I dare say, that it wasn't a fight.

'Now,' I said, when we were outside in the crowded street, 'you might let me know what all this is about, and what it is that for the love of God I'm not to do again.'

He was half apologetic, but at the same time half blustering, as if I had committed some sort of an outrage.

'A senseless thing like that!' he mumbled to himself. 'But there: you didn't know . . . You *don't* know, do you? . . . I tell you, d'you hear, *you're not to run at all when I'm about*! You're a nice fellow and all that, and get your quantities somewhere near right, if you do go a long way round to do it – but I'll not answer for myself if you run, d'you hear? . . . Putting your hand on a man's shoulder like that, just when . . . '

'Certainly I might have spoken,' I agreed, a little stiffly.

'Of course, you ought to have spoken! Just you see you don't do it again. It's monstrous!'

I put a curt question.

'Are you sure you're quite right in your head, Rooum?'

'Ah,' he cried, 'don't you think I just fancy it, my lad! Nothing so easy! I thought you guessed that other time, on the new road . . . it's as plain as a pikestaff . . . no, no, no! *I* shall be telling *you* something about molecules one of these days!'

We walked for a time in silence.

Suddenly he asked: 'What are you doing now?'

'I myself, do you mean? Oh, the firm. A railway job, past Pinner. But we've a big contract coming on in the West End soon they might want you for. They call it "alterations", but it's one of these big shop-rebuildings.'

'I'll come along.'

'Oh, it isn't for a month or two yet.'

'I don't mean that. I mean I'll come along to Pinner with you now, tonight, or whenever you go.'

'Oh!' I said.

I don't know that I specially wanted him. It's a little wearing, the company of a chap like that. You never know what he's going to let you in for next. But, as this didn't seem to occur to him, I didn't say anything. If he really liked catching the last train down, a three-mile walk, and then sharing a double-bedded room at a poor sort of alehouse (which was my own programme), he was welcome. We walked a little farther; then I told him the time of the train and left him.

He turned up at Euston, a little after twelve. We went down together. It was getting on for one when we left the station at the other end, and then we began the tramp across the Weald to the inn. A little to my surprise (for I had begun to expect unaccountable behaviour from him) we reached the inn without Rooum having dodged about changing places with me, or having fallen cowering under a gorse-bush, or anything of that kind. Our talk, too, was about work, not molecules and osmosis.

The inn was only a roadside beerhouse – I have forgotten its name – and all its sleeping accomodation was the one double-bedded room. Over the head of my own bed the ceiling was cut away, following the roof-line; and the wallpaper was perfectly shocking – faded bouquets that made Vs and As, interlacing everywhere. The other bed was made up, and lay across the room.

I think I only spoke once while we were making ready for bed, and that was when Rooum took from his black hand-bag a brush and a torn nightgown.

'That's what you always carry about, is it?' I remarked; and Rooum grunted something: Yes . . . never knew where you'd be next . . . no harm, was it? We tumbled into bed.

But, for all the lateness of the hour, I wasn't sleepy; so from my own bag I took a book, set the candle on the end of the mantel, and began to read. Mark you, I don't say I was much better informed for the reading I did, for I was watching the Vs on the wallpaper mostly – that, and wondering what was wrong with the man in the other bed who had fallen down at a touch in the subway. He was already asleep.

Now I don't know whether I can make the next clear to you. I'm quite certain he was sound asleep, so that it wasn't just the fact that he spoke. Even that is a little unpleasant, I always think, any sort of sleep-talking; but it's a very queer sort of sensation when a man actually answers a question that's put to him, knowing nothing whatever about it in the morning. Perhaps I ought not to have put that question; having put it, I did the next best thing afterwards, as you'll see in a moment . . . but let me tell you.

He'd been asleep perhaps an hour, and I woolgathering about the wallpaper, when suddenly, in a far more clear and loud voice than he ever used when awake, he said: '*What the devil is it prevents me seeing him, then?*'

That startled me, rather, for the second time that evening; and I really think I had spoken before I had fully realised what was happening.

'From seeing whom?' I said, sitting up in bed.

'Whom? . . . You're not attending. The fellow I'm telling you about, who runs after me,' he answered – answered perfectly plainly.

I could see his head there on the pillow, black and white, and his eyes were closed. He made a slight movement with his arm, but that did not wake him. Then it came to me, with a sort of start, what was happening. I slipped half out of bed. Would he – would he? – answer another question? . . . I risked it, breathlessly:

'Have you any idea who he is?'

Well, that too he answered.

'Who he is? The Runner? . . . Don't be silly. *Who else should it be?*'

With every nerve in me tingling, I tried again.

'What happens, then, when he catches you?'

This time, I really don't know whether his words were an answer or not; they were these:

'To hear him catching you up . . . and then padding away ahead again! All right, all right . . . but I guess it's weakening *him* a bit, too . . .'

Without noticing it, I had got out of bed, and had advanced quite to the middle of the floor.

'What did you say his name was?' I breathed.

But that was a dead failure. He muttered brokenly for a moment, gave a deep troubled sigh, and then began to snore loudly and regularly.

I made my way back to bed; but I assure you that before I did so I filled my basin with water, dipped my face into it, and then set the candlestick afloat in it, leaving the candle burning. I thought I'd like to have a light . . . It had burned down by morning. Rooum, I remember, remarked on the silly practice of reading in bed.

Well, it was a pretty kind of obsession for a man to have, wasn't it? Somebody running after him all the time, and then . . . running on ahead? And, of course, on a broad pavement there would be plenty of room for this running gentleman to run round; but on an eight- or nine-inch kerb, such as that of the new road out Lewisham way . . . but perhaps he was a jumping gentleman too, and could jump over a man's head. You'd think he'd have to get past some way, wouldn't you? . . . I remember vaguely wondering whether the name of that Runner was not Conscience; but Conscience isn't a matter of molecules and osmosis . . .

One thing, however, was clear; I'd got to tell Rooum what I'd learned: for you can't get hold of a fellow's secrets in ways like that. I lost no time about it. I told him, in fact, soon after we'd left the inn the next morning – told him how he'd answered in his sleep.

And – what do you think of this? – he seemed to think I ought to have guessed it! *Guessed* a monstrous thing like that!

'You're less clever than I thought, with your books and that, if you didn't,' he grunted.

'But . . . Good God, man!'

'Queer, isn't it? But you don't know the queerest . . . '

He pondered for a moment, and then suddenly put his lips to my ear.

'I'll tell you,' he whispered. '*It gets harder every time*! . . . At first, he just slipped through: a bit of a catch at my heart, like when you nod off to sleep in a chair and jerk up awake again; and away he went. But now it's getting grinding, sluggish; and the pain . . . You'd notice, that night on the road, the little check it gave me; that's past long since; and last night, when I'd just braced myself up stiff to meet it, and you tapped me on the shoulder . . . ' He passed the back of his hand over his brow.

'I tell you,' he continued, 'it's an agony each time. I could scream at the thought of it. It's oftener, too, now, and he's getting stronger. The end-osmosis is getting to be ex-osmosis – is that right? Just let me tell you one more thing – '

But I'd had enough. I'd asked questions the night before, but now – well, I knew quite as much as, and more than, I wanted.

'Stop, please,' I said. 'You're either off your head, or worse. Let's call it the first. Don't tell me any more, please.'

'Frightened, what? Well, I don't blame you. But what would *you* do?'

'I should see a doctor; I'm only an engineer,' I replied.

'Doctors? . . . Bah!' he said, and spat.

I hope you see how the matter stood with Rooum. What do you make of it? Could you have believed it – *do* you believe it? . . . He'd made a nearish guess when he'd said that much of our knowledge is giving names to things we know nothing about; only rule-of-thumb Physics thinks everything's explained in the Manual; and you've always got to remember one thing: You can call it Force or what you like, but it's a certainty that things, solid things of wood and iron and stone, would explode, just go off in a puff into space, if it wasn't for something just as inexplicable as that that Rooum said he felt in his own person. And if you can swallow that, it's a relatively small matter whether Rooum's light-footed Familiar slipped through him unperceived, or had to struggle through obstinately. You see now why I said that 'a queer thing overtook Rooum'.

More: I saw it. This thing, that outrages reason – I saw it happen. That is to say, I saw its effects, and it was in broad daylight, on an ordinary afternoon, in the middle of Oxford Street, of all places. There wasn't a shadow of doubt about it. People were pressing and jostling about him, and suddenly I saw him turn his head and listen, as I'd seen him before. I tell you, an icy creeping ran all over my skin. I fancied I felt it approaching too, nearer and nearer . . . The next moment he had made a sort of gathering of himself, as if against a gust. He stumbled and thrust – thrust with his body. He swayed, physically, as a tree sways in a wind; he clutched my arm and gave a loud scream. Then, after seconds – minutes – I don't know how long – he was free again.

And for the colour of his face when by and by I glanced at it . . . well, I once saw a swarthy Italian fall under a sunstroke, and *his* face was much the same colour that Rooum's negro face had gone; a cloudy, whitish green.

'Well – you've seen it – what do you think of it?' he gasped presently, turning a ghastly grin on me.

But it was night before the full horror of it had soaked into me.

Soon after that he disappeared again. I wasn't sorry.

* * *

Our big contract in the West End came on. It was a time-contract, with all manner of penalty clauses if we didn't get through; and I assure you that we were busy. I myself was far too busy to think of Rooum.

It's a shop now, the place we were working at, or rather one of these huge weldings of fifty shops where you can buy anything; and if you'd seen us there ... but perhaps you did see us, for people stood up on the tops of omnibuses as they passed, to look over the mud-splashed hoarding into the great excavation we'd made. It was a sight. Staging rose on staging, tier on tier, with interminable ladders all over the steel structure. Three or four squat Otis lifts crouched like iron turtles on top, and a lattice-crane on a towering three-cornered platform rose a hundred and twenty feet into the air. At one end of the vast quarry was a demolished house, showing flues and fireplaces and a score of thicknesses of old wallpaper; and at night – they might well have stood up on the tops of the buses! A dozen great spluttering violet arc-lights half-blinded you; down below were the watchmen's fires; overhead, the riveters had their fire-baskets; and in odd corners naphtha-lights guttered and flared. And the steel rang with the riveters' hammers, and the crane-chains rattled and clashed ... There's not much doubt in *my* mind, it's the engineers who are the architects nowadays. The chaps who think they're the architects are only a sort of paperhangers, who hang brick and terra-cotta on our work and clap a pinnacle or two on top – but never mind that. There we were, sweating and clanging and navvying, till the day shift came to relieve us.

And I ought to say that fifty feet above our great gap, and from end to end across it, there ran a travelling crane on a skeleton line, with platform, engine, and wooden cab all compact in one.

It happened that they had pitched in as one of the foremen some fellow or other, a friend of the firm's, a rank duffer, who pestered me incessantly with his questions. I did half his work and all my own, and it hadn't improved my temper much. On this night that I'm telling about, he'd been playing the fool with his questions as if a time-contract was a sort of summer holiday; and he'd filled me up to that point that I really can't say just when it was that Rooum put in an appearance again. I think I had heard somebody mention his name, but I'd paid no attention.

Well, our Johnnie Fresh came up to me for the twentieth time that night, this time wanting to know something about the overhead crane. At that I fairly lost my temper.

'What ails the crane?' I cried. 'It's doing its work, isn't it? Isn't everybody doing their work except you? Why can't you ask Hopkins? Isn't Hopkins there?'

'I don't know,' he said.

'Then,' I snapped, 'in that particular I'm as ignorant as you, and I hope it's the only one.'

But he grabbed my arm.

'Look at it now!' he cried, pointing; and I looked up.

Either Hopkins or somebody was dangerously exceeding the speed-limit. The thing was flying along its thirty yards of rail as fast as a tram, and the heavy fall-blocks swung like a ponderous kite-tail, thirty feet below. As I watched, the engine brought up within a yard of the end of the way, the blocks crashed like a ram into the broken house end, fetching down plaster and brick, and then the mechanism was reversed. The crane set off at a tear back.

'Who in Hell . . . ' I began; but it wasn't a time to talk. '*Hi*!' I yelled, and made a spring for a ladder.

The others had noticed it, too, for there were shouts all over the place. By that time I was halfway up the second stage. Again the crane tore past, with the massive tackle sweeping behind it, and again I heard the crash at the other end. Whoever had the handling of it was managing it skilfully, for there was barely a foot to spare when it turned again.

On the fourth platform, at the end of the way, I found Hopkins. He was white, and seemed to be counting on his fingers.

'What's the matter here?' I cried.

'It's Rooum,' he answered. 'I hadn't stepped out of the cab, not a minute, when I heard the lever go. He's running somebody down, he says; he'll run the whole shoot down in a minute – look! . . . '

The crane was coming back again. Half out of the cab I could see Rooum's mottled hair and beard. His brow was ribbed like a gridiron, and as he ripped past one of the arcs his face shone like porcelain with the sweat that bathed it.

'Now . . . you! . . . *Now*, damn you! . . . ' he was shouting.

'Get ready to board him when he reverses!' I shouted to Hopkins.

Just how we scrambled on I don't know. I got one arm over the lifting-gear (which, of course, wasn't going), and heard Hopkins on the other footplate. Rooum put the brakes down and reversed; again came the thud of the fall-blocks; and we were speeding back again over the gulf of misty orange light. The stagings were thronged with gaping men.

'Ready? Now!' I cried to Hopkins; and we sprang into the cab.

Hopkins hit Rooum's wrist with a spanner. Then he seized the lever, jammed the brake down and tripped Rooum, all, as it seemed, in one movement. I fell on top of Rooum. The crane came to a standstill half-way down the line. I held Rooum panting.

But either Rooum was stronger than I, or else he took me very much unawares. All at once he twisted clear from my grasp and stumbled on his knees to the rear door of the cab. He threw up one elbow, and staggered to his feet as I made another clutch at him.

'Keep still, you fool!' I bawled. 'Hit him over the head, Hopkins!'

Rooum screamed in a high voice.

'Run him down – cut him up with the wheels – down, you! – down, I say! – Oh, my God! . . . *Ha*!'

He sprang clear out from the crane door, well-nigh taking me with him.

I told you it was a skeleton line, two rails and a tie or two. He'd actually jumped to the right-hand rail. And he was running along it – running along that iron tightrope, out over that well of light and watching men. Hopkins had started the travelling-gear, as if with some insane idea of catching him; but there was only one possible end to it. He'd gone fully a dozen yards, while I watched, horribly fascinated; and then I saw the turn of his head . . .

He didn't meet it this time; he sprang to the other rail, as if to evade it . . .

Even at the take-off he missed. As far as I could see, he made no attempt to save himself with his hands. He just went down out of the field of my vision. There was an awful silence; then, from far below . . .

* * *

They weren't the men on the lower stages who moved first. The men above went a little way down, and then they too stopped. Presently two of them descended, but by a distant way. They returned, with two bottles of brandy, and there was a hasty consultation. Two men drank the brandy off there and then – getting on for a pint of brandy apiece; then they went down, drunk.

I, Hopkins tells me, had got down on my knees in the crane cab, and was jabbering away cheerfully to myself. When I asked him what I said, he hesitated, and then said: 'Oh, you don't want to know that, sir,' and I haven't asked him since.

What do *you* make of it?

Benlian

It would be different if you had known Benlian. It would be different if you had had even that glimpse of him that I had the very first time I saw him, standing on the little wooden landing at the top of the flight of steps outside my studio door. I say 'studio'; but really it was just a sort of loft looking out over the timber-yard, and I used it as a studio. The real studio, the big one, was at the other end of the yard, and that was Benlian's.

Scarcely anybody ever came there. I wondered many a time if the timber-merchant was dead or had lost his memory and forgotten all about his business; for his stacks of floorboards, set criss-crosswise to season (you know how they pile them up) were grimy with soot, and nobody ever disturbed the rows of scaffold-poles that stood like palisades along the walls. The entrance was from the street, through a door in a billposter's hoarding; and on the river not far away the steamboats hooted, and, in windy weather, the floorboards hummed to keep them company.

I suppose some of these real, regular artists wouldn't have called me an artist at all; for I only painted miniatures, and it was trade-work at that, copied from photographs and so on. Not that I wasn't jolly good at it, and punctual too (lots of these high-flown artists have simply no idea of punctuality); and the loft was cheap, and suited me very well. But, of course, a sculptor wants a big place on the ground floor; it's slow work that, with blocks of stone and marble that cost you twenty pounds every time you lift them; so Benlian had the studio. His name was on a plate on the door, but I'd never seen him till this time I'm telling you of.

I was working that evening at one of the prettiest little things I'd ever done: a girl's head on ivory, that I'd stippled up just like . . . oh, you'd never have thought it was done by hand at all. The daylight had gone, but I knew that 'Prussian' would be about the colour for the eyes and the bunch of flowers at her breast, and I wanted to finish.

I was working at my little table, with a shade over my eyes; and I jumped a bit when somebody knocked at the door – not having heard anybody come up the steps, and not having many visitors anyway. (Letters were always put into the box in the yard door.)

When I opened the door, there he stood on the platform; and I gave a bit of a start, having come straight from my ivory, you see. He was one of these very tall, gaunt chaps, that make us little fellows feel even smaller than we are; and I wondered at first where his eyes were, they were set so deep in the dark caves on either side of his nose. Like a skull, his head was; I could fancy his teeth curving round inside his cheeks; and his zygomatics stuck up under his skin like razorbacks (but if you're not one of us artists you'll not understand that). A bit of smoky, greenish sky showed behind him; and then, as his eyes moved in their big pits, one of them caught the light of my lamp and flashed like a well of lustre.

He spoke abruptly, in a deep, shaky sort of voice.

'I want you to photograph me in the morning,' he said. I supposed he'd seen my printing-frames out on the window-sash some time or other.

'Come in,' I said. 'But I'm afraid, if it's a miniature you want, that I'm retained – my firm retains me – you'd have to do it through them. But come in, and I'll show you the kind of thing I do – though you ought to have come in the daylight . . . '

He came in. He was wearing a long, grey dressing-gown that came right down to his heels and made him look something like a Noah's-ark figure. Seen in the light, his face seemed more ghastly bony still; and as he glanced for a moment at my little ivory he made a sound of contempt – I know it was contempt. I thought it rather cheek, coming into my place and –

He turned his cavernous eyeholes on me.

'I don't want anything of that sort. I want you to photograph me. I'll be here at ten in the morning.'

So, just to show him that I wasn't to be treated that way, I said, quite shortly, 'I can't. I've an appointment at ten o'clock.'

'What's that?' he said – he'd one of these rich deep voices that always sound consumptive.

'Take that thing off your eyes, and look at me,' he ordered.

Well, I was awfully indignant.

'If you think I'm going to be told to do things like this – ' I began.

'Take that thing off,' he just ordered again.

I've got to remember, of course, that you didn't know Benlian.

I didn't then. And for a chap just to stalk into a fellow's place, and tell him to photograph him, and order him about . . . but you'll see in a minute. I took the shade off my eyes, just to show him that *I* could browbeat a bit too.

I used to have a tall strip of looking-glass leaning against my wall; for though I didn't use models much, it's awfully useful to go to Nature for odd bits now and then, and I've sketched myself in that glass, oh, hundreds of times! We must have been standing in front of it, for all at once I saw the eyes at the bottom of his pits looking rigidly over my shoulder. Without moving his eyes from the glass, and scarcely moving his lips, he muttered: 'Get me a pair of gloves, get me a pair of gloves.'

It was a funny thing to ask for; but I got him a pair of my gloves from a drawer. His hands were shaking so that he could hardly get them on, and there was a little glistening of sweat on his face, that looked like the salt that dries on you when you've been bathing in the sea. Then I turned, to see what it was that he was looking so earnestly and profoundly at in the mirror. I saw nothing except just the pair of us, he with my gloves on.

He stepped aside, and slowly drew the gloves off. I think *I* could have bullied *him* just then. He turned to me.

'Did that look all right to you?' he asked.

'Why, my dear chap, whatever ails you?' I cried.

'I suppose,' he went on, 'you couldn't photograph me tonight – now?'

I could have done, with magnesium, but I hadn't a scrap in the place. I told him so. He was looking round my studio. He saw my camera standing in a corner.

'Ah!' he said.

He made a stride towards it. He unscrewed the lens, brought it to the lamp, and peered attentively through it, now into the air, now at his sleeve and hand, as if looking for a flaw in it. Then he replaced it, and pulled up the collar of his dressing-gown as if he was cold.

'Well, another night of it,' he muttered; 'but,' he added, facing suddenly round on me, 'if your appointment was to meet your God Himself, you must photograph me at ten tomorrow morning!'

'All right,' I said, giving in (for he seemed horribly ill). 'Draw up to the stove and have a drink of something and a smoke.'

'I neither drink nor smoke,' he replied, moving towards the door.

'Sit down and have a chat, then,' I urged; for I always like to be decent with fellows, and it was a lonely sort of place, that yard.

He shook his head.

'Be ready by ten o'clock in the morning,' he said; and he passed down my stairs and crossed the yard to his studio without even having said 'Good night'.

Well, he was at my door again at ten o'clock in the morning, and I photographed him. I made three exposures; but the plates were some that I'd had in the place for some time, and they'd gone off and fogged in the developing.

'I'm awfully sorry,' I said; 'but I'm going out this afternoon, and will get some more, and we'll have another shot in the morning.'

One after the other, he was holding the negatives up to the light and examining them. Presently he put them down quietly, leaning them methodically up against the edge of the developing-bath.

'Never mind. It doesn't matter. Thank you,' he said; and left me.

After that, I didn't see him for weeks; but at nights I could see the light of his roof-window, shining through the wreathing river-mists, and sometimes I heard him moving about, and the muffled knock-knocking of his hammer on marble.

2

Of course I did see him again, or I shouldn't be telling you all this. He came to my door, just as he had done before, and at about the same time in the evening. He hadn't come to be photographed this time, but for all that it was something about a camera – something he wanted to know. He'd brought two books with him, big books, printed in German. They were on Light, he said, and Physics (or else it was Psychics – I always get those two words wrong). They were full of diagrams and equations and figures; and, of course, it was all miles above my head.

He talked a lot about 'hyper-space', whatever that is; and at first I nodded, as if I knew all about it. But he very soon saw that I didn't, and he came down to my level again. What he'd come to ask me was this: did I know anything, of my own experience, about things 'photographing through'? (You know the kind of thing: a name that's been painted out on a board, say, comes up in the plate.)

Well, as it happened, I *had* once photographed a drawing for a fellow, and the easel I had stood it on had come up through the picture; and I knew by the way Benlian nodded that that was the kind of thing he meant.

'More,' he said.

I told him I'd once seen a photograph of a man with a bowler hat on, and the shape of his crown had showed through the hat.

'Yes, yes,' he said, musing; and then he asked: 'Have you ever heard of things not photographing at all?'

But I couldn't tell him anything about that; and off he started again, about Light and Physics and so on. Then, as soon as I could get a word in, I said, 'But, of course, the camera isn't Art.' (Some of my miniatures, you understand, were jolly nice little things.)

'No – no,' he murmured absently; and then abruptly he said: 'Eh? What's that? And what the devil do *you* know about it?'

'Well,' said I, in a dignified sort of way, 'considering that for ten years I've been – '

'Chut! . . . Hold your tongue,' he said, turning away.

There he was, talking to me again, just as if I'd asked him in to bully me. But you've got to be decent to a fellow when he's in your own place; and by and by I asked him, but in a cold, off-hand sort of way, how his own work was going on. He turned to me again.

'Would you like to see it?' he asked.

'*Aha*!' thought I, 'he's got to a sticking-point with his work! It's all very well,' I thought, 'for you to sniff at my miniatures, my friend, but we all get stale on our work sometimes, and the fresh eye, even of a miniature-painter . . . '

'I shall be glad if I can be of any help to you,' I answered, still a bit huffish, but bearing no malice.

'Then come,' he said.

We descended and crossed the timber-yard, and he held his door open for me to pass in.

It was an enormous great place, his studio, and all full of mist; and the gallery that was his bedroom was up a little staircase at the farther end. In the middle of the floor was a tall structure of scaffolding, with a stage or two to stand on; and I could see the dim ghostly marble figure in the gloom. It had been jacked up on a heavy base; and as it would have taken three or four men to put it into position, and scarcely a stranger had entered the yard since I had been there, I knew that the figure must have stood for a long time. Sculpture's weary, slow work.

Benlian was pottering about with a taper at the end of a long rod; and suddenly the overhead gas-ring burst into light. I placed myself before the statue – to criticise, you know.

Well, it didn't seem to me that he needed to have turned up his nose at my ivories, for I didn't think much of his statue – except that it was a great, lumping, extraordinary piece of work. It had an out-stretched arm that, I remember thinking, was absolutely misshapen – disproportioned, big enough for a giant, ridiculously out of drawing. And as I looked at the thing this way and that, I knew that his eyes in their deep cellars never left my face for a moment.

'It's a god,' he said by and by.

Then I began to tell him about that monstrous arm; but he cut me very short.

'I say it's a god,' he interrupted, looking at me as if he would have eaten me. 'Even you, child as you are, have seen the gods men have made for themselves before this. Half-gods they've made, all good or all evil (and then they've called them the Devil). This is *my* god – the god of good and of evil also.'

'Er – I see,' I said, rather taken aback (but quite sure he was off his head for all that). Then I looked at the arm again; a child could have seen how wrong it was . . .

But suddenly, to my amazement, he took me by the shoulders and turned me away.

'That'll do,' he said curtly. 'I didn't ask you to come in here with a view to learning anything from you. I wanted to see how it struck you. I shall send for you again – and again – '

Then he began to jabber, half to himself.

'Bah!' he muttered. ' "Is that all?" they ask before a stupendous thing. Show them the ocean, the heavens, infinity, and they ask, "Is that all?" If they saw their God face to face they'd ask it! . . . There's only one Cause, that works now in good and now in evil, but show It to them and they put their heads on one side and begin to appraise and patronise It! . . . I tell you, what's seen at a glance flies away at a glance. Gods come slowly over you, but presently, ah! they begin to grip you, and at the end there's no fleeing from them! You'll tell me more about my statue by and by! . . . What was that you said?' he demanded, facing swiftly round on me. 'That arm? Ah, yes; but we'll see what you say about that arm six months from now! Yes, the arm . . . Now be off!' he ordered me. 'I'll send for you again when I want you!'

He thrust me out.

'An asylum, Mr Benlian,' I thought as I crossed the yard, 'is the place for you!' You see, I didn't know him then, and that he wasn't to be judged as an ordinary man is. Just you wait till you see . . .

And straight away, I found myself vowing that I'd have nothing more to do with him. I found myself resolving that, as if I were making up my mind not to smoke or drink – and (I don't know why) with a similar sense that I was depriving myself of something. But, somehow, I forgot, and within a month he'd been in several times to see me, and once or twice had fetched me in to see his statue.

In two months I was in an extraordinary state of mind about him. I was familiar with him in a way, but at the same time I didn't know one scrap more about him. Because I'm a fool (oh, yes, I know quite well, now, what I am) you'll think I'm talking folly if I even begin to tell you what sort of a man he was. I don't mean just his knowledge (though I think he knew everything – sciences, languages, and all that) for it was far more than that. Somehow, when he was there, he had me all restless and uneasy; and when he wasn't there I was (there's only the one word for it) jealous – as jealous as if he'd been a girl! Even yet I can't make it out . . .

And he knew how unsettled he'd got me; and I'll tell you how I found that out.

Straight out one night, when he was sitting up in my place, he asked me: 'Do you like me, Pudgie?' (I forgot to say that I'd told him they used to call me Pudgie at home, because I was little and fat; it was odd, the number of things I told him that I wouldn't have told anybody else.)

'Do you like me, Pudgie?' he said.

As for my answer, I don't know how it spurted out. I was much more surprised than he was, for I really didn't intend it. It was for all the world as if somebody else was talking with my mouth.

'*I loathe and adore you!*' it came; and then I looked round, awfully startled to hear myself saying that.

But he didn't look at me. He only nodded.

'Yes. Of good and evil too – ' he muttered to himself. And then all of a sudden he got up and went out.

I didn't sleep for ever so long after that, thinking how odd it was I should have said that.

Well (to get on), after that something I couldn't account for began to come over me sometimes as I worked. It began to come over me, without any warning, that he was thinking of me down there across the yard. I used to *know* (this must sound awfully silly to you) that he was down yonder, thinking of me and doing something to me. And one night I was so sure that it wasn't fancy that I jumped straight up from my work, and I'm not quite sure what happened then, until I found myself in his studio, just as if I'd walked there in my sleep.

And he seemed to be waiting for me, for there was a chair by his own, in front of the statue.

'What is it, Benlian?' I burst out.

'Ah!' he said . . . 'Well, it's about that arm, Pudgie; I want you to tell me about the arm. Does it look so strange as it did?'

'No,' I said.

'I thought it wouldn't,' he observed. 'But I haven't touched it, Pudgie – '

So I stayed the evening there.

But you must not think he was always doing that thing – whatever it was – to me. On the other hand, I sometimes felt the oddest sort of release (I don't know how else to put it) . . . like when, on one of these muggy, earthy-smelling days, when everything's melancholy, the wind freshens up suddenly and you breathe again. And that (I'm trying to take it in order, you see, so that it will be plain to you) brings me to the time I found out that *he* did that too, and knew when he was doing it.

I'd gone into his place one night to have a look at his statue. It was surprising what a lot I was finding out about that statue. It was still all out of proportion (that is to say, I knew it must be – remembered I'd thought so – though it didn't annoy me now quite so much. I suppose I'd lost *my* fresh eye by that time). Somehow, too, my own miniatures had begun to look a bit kiddish; they made me impatient; and that's horrible, to be discontented with things that once seemed jolly good to you.

Well, he'd been looking at me in the hungriest sort of way, and I looking at the statue, when all at once that feeling of release and lightness came over me. The first I knew of it was that I found myself thinking of some rather important letters my firm had written to me, wanting to know when a job I was doing was going to be finished. I thought myself it was time I got it finished; I thought I'd better set about it at once; and I sat suddenly up in my chair, as if I'd just come out of a sleep. And, looking at the statue, I saw it as it had seemed at first – all misshapen and out of drawing.

The very next moment, as I was rising, I sat down again as suddenly as if somebody had pulled me back.

Now a chap doesn't like to be changed about like that; so, without looking at Benlian, I muttered a bit testily, 'Don't, Benlian!'

Then I heard him get up and knock his chair away. He was standing behind me.

'Pudgie,' he said, in a moved sort of voice, 'I'm no good to you. Get out of this. Get out – '

'No, no, Benlian!' I pleaded.

'Get out, do you hear, and don't come again! Go and live somewhere else – go away from London – don't let me know where
you go – '

'Oh, what have I done?' I asked unhappily; and he was muttering
again.

'Perhaps it would be better for me too,' he muttered; and then he
added, 'Come, bundle out!'

So home I went, and finished my ivory for the firm; but I can't tell
you how friendless and unhappy I felt.

Now I used to know in those days a little girl – a nice, warm-
hearted little thing, just friendly you know, who used to come to
me sometimes in another place I lived at and mend for me and so
on. It was an awful long time since I'd seen her; but she found me
out one night – came to that yard, walked straight in, went straight
to my linen-bag, and began to look over my things to see what
wanted mending, just as she used to. I don't mind confessing that I
was a bit sweet on her at one time; and it made me feel awfully
mean, the way she came in, without asking any questions, and took
up my mending.

So she sat doing my things, and I sat at my work, glad of a bit of
company; and she chatted as she worked, just jolly and gentle and not
at all reproaching me.

But as suddenly as a shot, right in the middle of it all, I found
myself wondering about Benlian again. And I wasn't only wondering; somehow I was horribly uneasy about him. It came to me
that he might be ill or something. And all the fun of her having
come to see me was gone. I found myself doing all sorts of stupid
things to my work, and glancing at my watch that was lying on the
table before me.

At last I couldn't stand it any longer. I got up.

'Daisy,' I said, 'I've got to go out now.'

She seemed surprised.

'Oh, why didn't you tell me I'd been keeping you!' she said, getting
up at once.

I muttered that I was awfully sorry . . .

I packed her off. I closed the door in the hoarding behind her.
Then I walked straight across the yard to Benlian's.

He was lying on a couch, not doing anything.

'I know I ought to have come sooner, Benlian,' I said, 'but I had
somebody with me.'

'Yes,' he said, looking hard at me; and I got a bit red.

'She's awfully nice,' I stammered; 'but you never bother with girls, and you don't drink or smoke – '

'No,' he said.

'Well,' I continued, 'you ought to have a little relaxation; you're knocking yourself up.' And, indeed, he looked awfully ill.

But he shook his head.

'A man's only a definite amount of force in him, Pudgie,' he said, 'and if he spends it in one way he goes short in another. Mine goes – there.' He glanced at the statue. 'I rarely sleep now,' he added.

'Then you ought to see a doctor,' I said, a bit alarmed. (I'd felt sure he was ill.)

'No, no, Pudgie. My force is all going there – all but the minimum that can't be helped, you know . . . You've heard artists talk about "putting their soul into their work", Pudgie?'

'Don't rub it in about my rotten miniatures, Benlian,' I asked him.

'You've heard them say that; but they're charlatans, professional artists, all, Pudgie. They haven't got any souls bigger than a sixpence to put into it . . . You know, Pudgie, that Force and Matter are the same thing – that it's decided nowadays that you can't define matter otherwise than as "a point of Force"?'

'Yes,' I found myself saying eagerly, as if I'd heard it dozens of times before.

'So that if they could put their souls into it, it would be just as easy for them to put their *bodies* into it? . . . '

I had drawn very close to him, and again – it was not fancy – I felt as if somebody, not me, was using my mouth. A flash of comprehension seemed to come into my brain.

'*Not that, Benlian?*' I cried breathlessly.

He nodded three or four times, and whispered. I really don't know why we both whispered.

'*Really that, Benlian?*' I whispered again.

'Shall I show you? . . . I tried my hardest not to, you know . . . ' he still whispered.

'Yes, show me!' I replied in a suppressed voice.

'Don't breathe a sound then! I keep them up there . . . '

He put his finger to his lips as if we had been two conspirators; then he tiptoed across the studio and went up to his bedroom in the gallery. Presently he tiptoed down again, with some rolled-up papers in his hand. They were photographs, and we stooped together over a little table. His hand shook with excitement.

'You remember this?' he whispered, showing me a rough print.

It was one of the prints from the fogged plates that I'd taken after that first night.

'Come closer to me if you feel frightened, Pudgie,' he said. 'You said they were old plates, Pudgie. No no; the plates were all right; it's *I* who am wrong!'

'Of course,' I said. It seemed so natural.

'This one,' he said, taking up one that was numbered '1', 'is a plain photograph, in the flesh, before it started; *you* know! Now look at this, and this – '

He spread them before me, all in order.

'2' was a little fogged, as if a novice had taken it; on '3' a sort of cloudy veil partly obliterated the face; '4' was still further smudged and lost; and '5' was a figure with gloved hands held up, as a man holds his hands up when he is covered by a gun. The face of this one was completely blotted out.

And it didn't seem in the least horrible to me, for I kept on murmuring, 'Of course, of course.'

Then Benlian rubbed his hands and smiled at me. 'I'm making good progress, am I not?' he said.

'Splendid!' I breathed.

'Better than you know, too,' he chuckled, 'for you're not properly under yet. But you will be, Pudgie, you will be – '

'Yes, yes! . . . Will it be long, Benlian?'

'No,' he replied, 'not if I can keep from eating and sleeping and thinking of other things than the statue – and if you don't disturb me by having girls about the place, Pudgie.'

'I'm awfully sorry,' I said contritely.

'All right, all right; ssh! . . . This, you know, Pudgie, is my own studio; I bought it; I bought it purposely to make my statue, my god. I'm passing nicely into it; and when I'm quite passed – *quite* passed, Pudgie – you can have the key and come in when you like.'

'Oh, thanks awfully,' I murmured gratefully.

He nudged me.

'What would they think of it, Pudgie – those of the exhibitions and academies, who say "their souls are in their work"? What would the cacklers think of it, Pudgie?'

'Aren't they fools!' I chuckled.

'And I shall have *one* worshipper, shan't I, Pudgie?'

'Rather!' I replied. 'Isn't it splendid! . . . Oh, need I go back just yet?'

'Yes, you must go now; but I'll send for you again very soon . . . You know I tried to do without you, Pudge; I tried for thirteen days, and it nearly killed me! That's past. I shan't try again. Now off you trot, my Pudgie – '

I winked at him knowingly, and came skipping and dancing across the yard.

3

It's just silly – that's what it is – to say that something of a man doesn't go into his work.

Why, even those wretched little ivories of mine, the thick-headed fellows who paid for them knew my touch in them, and once spotted it instantly when I tried to slip in another chap's who was hard up. Benlian used to say that a man went about spreading himself over everything he came in contact with – diffusing some sort of influence (as far as I could make it out); and the mistake was, he said, that we went through the world just wasting it instead of directing it. And if Benlian didn't understand all about those things, I should jolly well like to know who does! A chap with a great abounding will and brain like him, it's only natural he should be able to pass himself on, to a statue or anything else, when he really tried – did without food and talk and sleep in order to save himself up for it!

'A man can't both *do* and *be*,' I remember he said to me once. 'He's so much force, no more, and he can either make himself with it or something else. If he tries to do both, he does both imperfectly. I'm going to do *one* perfect thing.' Oh, he was a queer chap! Fancy, a fellow making a thing like that statue, out of himself, and then wanting somebody to adore him!

And I hadn't the faintest conception of how much I did adore him till yet again, as he had done before, he seemed to – you know – to take himself away from me again, leaving me all alone, and so wretched! . . . And I was angry at the same time, for he'd promised me he wouldn't do it again . . . (This was one night, I don't remember when.)

I ran to my landing and shouted down into the yard.

'Benlian! Benlian!'

There was a light in his studio, and I heard a muffled shout come back.

'Keep away – keep away – keep away!'

He was struggling – I knew he was struggling as I stood there on my landing – struggling to let me go. And I could only run and throw myself on my bed and sob, while he tried to set me free, who didn't want to be set free . . . he was having a terrific struggle, all alone there . . .

(He told me afterwards that he *had* to eat something now and then and to sleep a little, and that weakened him – strengthened him – strengthened his body and weakened the passing, you know.)

But the next day it was all right again. I was Benlian's again. And I wondered, when I remembered his struggle, whether a dying man had ever fought for life as hard as Benlian was fighting to get away from it and pass himself.

The next time after that that he fetched me – called me – whatever you like to name it – I burst into his studio like a bullet. He was sunk in a big chair, gaunt as a mummy now, and all the life in him seemed to burn in the bottom of his deep eye-sockets. At the sight of him I fiddled with my knuckles and giggled.

'You *are* going it, Benlian!' I said.

'Am I not?' he replied, in a voice that was scarcely a breath.

'You *meant* me to bring the camera and magnesium, didn't you?' (I had snatched them up when I felt his call, and had brought them.)

'Yes. Go ahead.'

So I placed the camera before him, made all ready, and took the magnesium ribbon in a pair of pincers.

'Are you ready?' I said; and lighted the ribbon.

The studio seemed to leap with the blinding glare. The ribbon spat and spluttered. I snapped the shutter, and the fumes drifted away and hung in clouds in the roof.

'You'll have to walk me about soon, Pudgie, and bang me with bladders, as they do the opium-patients,' he said sleepily.

'Let me take one of the statue now,' I said eagerly.

But he put up his hand.

'No, no. *That's* too much like testing our god. Faith's the food they feed gods on, Pudgie. We'll let the S.P.R. people photograph it when it's all over,' he said. 'Now get it developed.'

I developed the plate. The obliteration now seemed complete.

But Benlian seemed dissatisfied.

'There's something wrong somewhere,' he said. 'It isn't so perfect as that yet – I can feel within me it isn't. It's merely that your camera isn't strong enough to find me, Pudgie.'

'I'll get another in the morning,' I cried.

'No,' he answered. 'I know something better than that. Have a cab here by ten o'clock in the morning, and we'll go somewhere.'

By half-past ten the next morning we had driven to a large hospital, and had gone down a lot of steps and along corridors to a basement room. There was a stretcher couch in the middle of the room, and all manner of queer appliances, frames of ground glass, tubes of glass blown into extraordinary shapes, a dynamo, and a lot of other things all about. A couple of doctors were there too, and Benlian was talking to them.

'We'll try my hand first,' Benlian said by and by.

He advanced to the couch, and put his hand under one of the frames of ground glass. One of the doctors did something in a corner. A harsh crackling filled the room, and an unearthly, fluorescent light shot and flooded across the frame where Benlian's hand was. The two doctors looked, and then started back. One of them gave a cry. He was sickly white.

'Put me on the couch,' said Benlian.

I and the doctor who was not ill lifted him on the canvas stretcher. The green-gleaming frame of fluctuating light was passed over the whole of his body. Then the doctor ran to a telephone and called a colleague . . .

We spent the morning there, with dozens of doctors coming and going. Then we left. All the way home in the cab Benlian chuckled to himself.

'That scared 'em, Pudgie!' he chuckled. 'A man they can't x-ray – that scared 'em! We must put that down in the diary – '

'Wasn't it ripping!' I chuckled back.

He kept a sort of diary or record. He gave it to me afterwards, but they've borrowed it. It was as big as a ledger, and immensely valuable, I'm sure; they oughtn't to borrow valuable things like that and not return them. The laughing that Benlian and I have had over that diary! It fooled them all – the clever x-ray men, the artists of the academies, everybody! Written on the fly-leaf was '*To My Pudgie*'. I shall publish it when I get it back again.

Benlian had now got frightfully weak; it's awfully hard work, passing yourself. And he had to take a little milk now and then or he'd have died before he had quite finished. I didn't bother with miniatures any longer, and when angry letters came from my employers we just put them into the fire, Benlian and I, and we laughed – that is to say, I laughed, but Benlian only smiled, being too weak to laugh really. He'd lots of money, so that was all right; and I slept in his studio, to be there for the passing.

And that wouldn't be very long now, I thought; and I was always looking at the statue. Things like that (in case you don't know) have to be done gradually, and I supposed he was busy filling up the inside of it and hadn't got to the outside yet – for the statue was much the same to look at. But, reckoning off his sips of milk and snatches of sleep, he was making splendid progress, and the figure must be getting very full now. I was awfully excited, it was getting so near . . .

And then somebody came bothering and nearly spoiling all. It's odd, but I really forget exactly what it was. I only know there was a funeral, and people were sobbing and looking at me, and somebody said I was callous, but somebody else said, 'No, look at him,' and that it was just the other way about. And I think I remember, now, that it wasn't in London, for I was in a train; but after the funeral I dodged them, and found myself back at Euston again. They followed me, but I shook them off. I locked my own studio up, and lay as quiet as a mouse in Benlian's place when they came hammering at the door . . .

And now I must come to what you'll called the finish – though it's awfully stupid to call things like that 'finishes'.

I'd slipped into my own studio one night – I forget what for; and I'd gone quietly, for I knew they were following me, those people, and would catch me if they could. It was a thick, misty night, and the light came streaming up through Benlian's roof window, with the shadows of the window-divisions losing themselves like dark rays in the fog. A lot of hooting was going on down the river, steamers and barges . . . Oh, I know what I'd come into my studio for! It was for those negatives. Benlian wanted them for the diary, so that it could be seen there wasn't any fake about the prints. For he'd said he would make a final spurt that evening and get the job finished. It had taken a long time, but I'll bet *you* couldn't have passed *yourself* any quicker.

When I got back he was sitting in the chair he'd hardly left for weeks, and the diary was on the table by his side. I'd taken all the scaffolding down from the statue, and he was ready to begin. He had to waste one last bit of strength to explain to me, but I drew as close as I could, so that he wouldn't lose much.

'Now, Pudgie,' I just heard him say, 'you've behaved splendidly, and you'll be quite still up to the finish, won't you?'

I nodded.

'And you mustn't expect the statue to come down and walk about, or anything like that,' he continued. '*Those* aren't the really wonderful things. And no doubt people will tell you it hasn't changed; but you'll know better! It's much more wonderful that I should be there than that they should be able to prove it, isn't it? . . . And, of course, I don't know exactly how it will happen, for I've never done this before . . . You have the letter for the S.P.R.? They can photograph it if they want . . . By the way, you don't think the same of my statue as you did at first, do you?'

'Oh, it's wonderful!' I breathed.

'And even if, like the God of the others, it doesn't vouchsafe a special sign and wonder, it's Benlian, for all that?'

'Oh, do be quick, Benlian! I can't bear another minute!'

Then, for the last time, he turned his great eaten-out eyes on me. '*I seal you mine, Pudgie!*' he said.

Then his eyes fastened themselves on the statue.

I waited for a quarter of an hour, scarcely breathing. Benlian's breath came in little flutters, many seconds apart. He had a little clock on the table. Twenty minutes passed, and half an hour. I was a little disappointed, really, that the statue wasn't going to move; but Benlian knew best, and it was filling quietly up with him instead. Then I thought of those zigzag bunches of lightning they draw on the electric-belt advertisements, and I was rather glad after all that the statue *wasn't* going to move. It would have been a little cheap, that . . . vulgar, in a sense . . . He was breathing a little more sharply now, as if in pain, but his eyes never moved. A dog was howling somewhere, and I hoped that the hooting of the tugs wouldn't disturb Benlian . . .

Nearly an hour had passed when, all of a sudden, I pushed my chair farther away and cowered back, gnawing my fingers, very frightened. Benlian had suddenly moved. He'd set himself forward in his chair, and he seemed to be strangling. His mouth was wide open, and he began to make long harsh '*Aaaaah-aaaah's!*' I shouldn't have thought passing yourself was such agony . . .

And then I gave a scream – for he seemed to be thrusting himself back in his chair again, as if he'd changed his mind and didn't want to pass himself at all. But just you ask anybody: when you get yourself just over half-way passed, the other's dragged out of you, and you can't help yourself. His '*Aaaaah*'s became so loud and horrid that I shut my eyes and stopped my ears . . . Minutes that lasted; and then there came a high dinning that I couldn't shut out, and all at once the floor shook with a heavy thump. When all was still again I opened my eyes.

His chair had overturned, and he lay in a heap beside it.

I called 'Benlian!' but he didn't answer . . .

He'd passed beautifully; quite dead. I looked up at the statue. It was just as Benlian had said – it didn't open its eyes, nor speak, nor anything like that. Don't you believe chaps who tell you that statues that have been passed into do that; they don't.

But instead, in a blaze and flash and shock, I knew now for the first time what a glorious thing that statue was! Have you ever seen anything for the first time like that? If you have, you never see very much afterwards, you know. The rest's all piffle after that. It was like coming out of fog and darkness into a split in the open heavens, my statue was so transfigured; and I'll bet if you'd been there you'd have clapped your hands, as I did, and chucked the tablecloth over the Benlian on the floor till they should come to cart that empty shell away, and patted the statue's foot and cried: '*Is it all right, Benlian?*'

I did this; and then I rushed excitedly out into the street, to call somebody to see how glorious it was . . .

They've brought me here for a holiday, and I'm to go back to the studio in two or three days. But they've said that before, and I think it's caddish of fellows not to keep their word – and not to return a valuable diary too! But there isn't a peephole in my room, as there is in some of them (the Emperor of Brazil told me that); and Benlian knows I haven't forsaken him, for they take me a message every day to the studio, and Benlian always answers that it's '*all right*, and I'm to stay where I am for a bit.' So as long as he knows, I don't mind so much. But it is a bit rotten hanging on here, especially when the doctors themselves admit how reasonable it all is . . . Still, if Benlian says it's '*all right* . . . '

The Ascending Dream

To dream that you are ascending steps denotes danger. –
Popular Belief

A few ages ago, on a sunny sea-shore, a young man was building a boat. It was early morning, and grey vapours still dappled the sea, so that now the horizon could be seen, a thin silver thread, and again all was lost beyond the line of glittering surf, no farther away than the young man could have thrown a stone. The surf broke on shining dove-grey sands; then innumerable white boulders strewed the beach; then these became great rocks that formed a talus, and thence the cliffs rose sheer, hundreds of feet, with a thousand sea-birds wheeling and crying about their ledges.

The young man had made a little clearance among the boulders, and on the patch of sand lay his tools and appliances – a flint axe, various other sharpened stones, a few poles and branches for levers and rollers, and, most important of all, the hearth that held his handful of fire. He was a smallish but comely young man, with dark and watchful and brilliant eyes and long black hair. About his middle he wore a skin tied with twisted sinews, and the strips of hide that shod him patterned the sands as he moved.

His boat was a log that he had claimed from the sea. Many tides had tossed it about, now within swimming-distance, now a speck far away, before a higher tide than usual had lifted it to where he could get at it with his levers and rollers. He hoped he had not offended the sea in thus snatching its log from it. He knew the sea as a creature capable of being offended, but he had long ardently wished for just such a log. Only at certain carefully chosen times could he swim unaided to the little island of rock hidden in the mists, and he wished to be able to go there at all times. There were delectable fish to be caught there, much superior to those in the pools among the white boulders. And perhaps the fish were not all he coveted. Beyond the rock nothing could be seen from the shore even in clear weather, but there must be something – perhaps more desirable fish still – perhaps another island – perhaps a better home for himself and his than his present one, the crevice high up in the cliffs where the sea-birds floated and screamed.

And so, with the assistance of certain gods he knew, the young man was earnestly fashioning his boat.

He made much of these gods, since he found that by propitiation they could be made to serve him. He was propitiating two of the most powerful of them that morning, the one that watched and winked at him from his hearth on the sand, and that other one, that stirred his long hair, ruffled the line of surf, and carried the smoke of his fire away over the white boulders. Otherwise the fire would never have consented to be placed in the log's hollow, nor would the wind have driven it as he wished it to be driven. He had his poles and rollers in readiness to alter the log's direction should the caprices of these powers change. By the favour of a third god, who lived in the head of his flint axe, he chipped out the charred wood. The other gods, in the levers and rollers, he allowed to slumber until he wanted them.

At the edge of the cleared patch a young woman also sat. She was sewing a garment of skins, but she gave an occasional glance towards the three naked children down by the water's edge, and from time to time left her needle sticking in her work in order to put more sticks on the fire. She, too, wore a single skin, with a chain of bright shells about her neck, threaded on a plait of her own hair. This still hung in wet points from her tumbling with the children in the surf, and one strand of it encircled her upper arm like an armlet. So lustrous was her skin that it dimly reflected surrounding objects, the gleam of a sunburst through the mists softly lighting a shoulder, the whiteness of a near boulder dimly lurking in a glossy thigh. One breast, too, polished as the head of the young man's axe, gave back the sky overhead.

The young man wished the young woman would look up from her stitching. He knew that at the least unusual movement among the children down by the surf she would have been on her feet, but he, hardly his own length away from her, could not attract her eyes. But he remembered that she had always been like that, even in the tribe before he had brought her away. Many times his head had turned to watch her, in glade or at cave-mouth, but her head had never turned, though she had wanted to turn it never so much. When he wanted to do a thing he did it, but when she wanted a thing done she had some sort of a magic that made him do it for her.

But just once in a while this magic failed her. For example, she did not wish him to make his boat. When he had spoken of superior fish at all times instead of only occasionally, she had said she hated fish, and, the last time he had swum out for them, had refused them, and had cooked one of the common cliff-top animals for herself instead.

As for his wish to know what lay behind the island, that he had never mentioned to her.

So he furtively watched her, divided between his work and his desire to sit down by her, take her stitching from her, put his head in the skin about her knees, and tell her of something that troubled him.

The thing that troubled him was a dream that he had had; and he had had it, the same dream, not once, but many times. It had to do with their cranny in the cliff, high up where the sea-birds wheeled. His eyes sought the way up there as he idly moved the embers this way and that in the hollow of his log. As far as the talus of boulders the white stones made a narrow path. Then the path wound in and out among the great rocks. But where the talus ended and the sheer ascent began, an almost imperceptible snail's track rose up the cliff's face. It zigzagged, made use of the ledges, took in a crannied bush here or a short hand-rope of plaited fibre there, but always rose, until it came to the last flight, which had been cut out with the young man's own axe. Then it ended. A stone at the mouth of that eyrie made the entrance secure against the wild beasts. Inside was their litter, their skins, their fish-hooks and axes, and their winter store of food.

Suddenly the young man came and sat down by the young woman's side. He took her sewing from her, and began to fringe out the damp hair across her shoulders. She made no movement. Then he began to rub the sand from her bare feet. Still she made no response. Then he gave a little tug to her hair that turned her eyes towards him.

The instant her eyes met his they became alive, alert and anxious.

For dumb people still talk, and deaf people still hear, very much as these two conversed – with all their senses save the lacking one. They had very few names for things. He had hardly a name for her. She was the Comfort-thing, but so contrary that she could be ill with good fish, the Soft-to-the-Touch-thing, but so perverse that she could thrive on rank berries when she had a mind. What need, indeed, had they of names, with one god winking and watching them restlessly from the hearth, and another playing about their bodies and entering their nostrils, and another creeping in at their ears from the line of glittering surf? Even the names they knew they avoided for fear of mischief. The stairs to their eyrie were the Climbing-things (since a man might slip on them), the smooth-worn stump of bush was the Holding-thing (since it might break), and the dream was the Night-thing (since it filled the heart with bodings unknown to the day). Thus their tongues faltered, but their fingers streamed intelligence. Currents of meaning, quicker than light on water, ran back and forth between their eyes. And a few numerals, spaces and times illuminated the rest.

So he told her what had happened so many times while she had slept on the litter by his side.

He was always (in his dream) ascending that snail-track to their home. But whereas, many warm weathers ago, he had stood upon the lower portions of it, since then he had stood higher and higher with each recurrence of the dream. On the night when the cliff-fall had carried away his observation-tree, he had stood on the ledge where they had seen the half-swallowed fish carry the bird back again into the water. On that other night, when the wild cat had scratched at their rock, he had reached the niche where the cliff-god had dislodged the stone that had so narrowly missed her head. Sometime after that he had begun to keep a rough tally, as he did for the births of his children and the days when it was possible to swim out to the rock. Now his tally had begun to frighten him. He not only knew where he stood (in his dream) now, but where he would stand the next time.

Once or twice she interrupted him. This was to know how many steps remained yet to mount.

'The wolves – that time – over there,' he said.

She remembered. There had been fifty or sixty wolves that time, where he pointed – fifty or sixty steps still to climb.

And again: 'As the fish on the stick.'

That, too, was plain. There were perhaps a score of the split and salted fish on the stick in their cliff-larder.

Then, as at another point he made a light gesture with both hands, she started.

Ten fingers! Ten! Only ten left!

But apparently even that had been some time ago. There came a point in his story where his bright eyes, following the smoke that flattened out over the shining sands, rested on the children at play. She clutched his arm, and up shot three of her fingers in a swift question.

But he shook his head. Fewer than three –

There are only two numbers fewer than three. Which of these it was appeared when, with a quick movement, he took her into his arms.

She herself was his numeral – the symbol that only a single step now remained between him and the top.

Then, his narration over, their eyes severed, and he continued to sit with his head in the soft scallop between her arm and breast.

As for her, she sat looking blankly before her, her foreknowledge come true. He had offended the sea-god, who was doubtless a kinsman of the god of the Night-thing. Dully she asked him how frequently the Night-thing visited him.

He told her: sometimes in one moon, sometimes in the darkness between the old moon and the new one, sometimes as often as between a sun and the next sun. She had a shiver, and then she pointed abruptly to the boat.

'That,' she said.

But she felt his head shake obstinately under her arm. He would not have it that it was the boat.

'That,' she said again. 'His.' And she pointed to the sea, now a sheet of undimmed silver, with a cloudlet of birds about the island-rock in the middle of it. 'How much time, that?' Her eyes indicated the boat.

'Two, three suns. Then plenty of fish. Enough.'

And he sprang lightly to his feet.

But this time it was she who seized him, clasping him by the knees. Her face was piteously upturned.

'No – no – ' she implored him, her hands about his ankles.

Her arms, her eyes, every particle of her, told him how well he was with her, how little need there was to go elsewhere; but his eyes shone as he put her hands away and lifted her to her feet. By the smoking boat he enfolded her, the Comfort-thing, the Thing-to-which-he-Turned, but that he would leave in order to see what lay behind the island.

That was several ages ago; and for suns and for moons, and for warm weathers a-many, first a young woman with three children, then a woman not young with three tall sons, and then an old woman without sons, who lived between two white boulders of the talus because she could no longer climb the ladder where the sea-birds quarrelled and screamed, looked out over the sea, her eyes seeking a speck that never appeared.

2

A few centuries ago a young man stood against a diamond-paned window, poring over a map. One window-bay looked back upon the flagged terrace of the house, but the rest of it was turned to where the park-land dropped, gentle stage by gentle stage, first to meadow, then to pasture, then to sandhills grey with sea-lavender and thyme, and so to the wrinkled silken cloth of the sea. The closet in which the young man stood was his private apartment, and a homely litter filled it, of boots, old hawk-jesses, farm-books, powder-horns and bullet-moulds, and, on the oak table, the lady's light crossbow he had been repairing. Over the stone mantelpiece hung his father's sword and morion, and on the shelf below it was a small mariner's compass.

He was a tallish young man, with close-cropped dark hair and a beard so slight that it would hardly have been a beard at all but for the razor's careful shaping of it. His head was in dark outline against the window, except for the flat of his brow, which, catching the light as far as the temple, gave his nose an appearance of prominence which properly it had not. His walk through the orchards and coppices had left a few spring-time sheddings on the shoulders of his every-day velvet doublet, and there were traces of garden-mould on his hose.

Across the lawn outside, under a clustered yew, sat the lady for whom he had been mending the crossbow. She was his neighbour, and they were betrothed. Her land, which she would hold in her own right when her mother died, more than doubled his, with holt, chase, mansion, and fifty farms to boot. And she was more than desirable had she not had fifty pence. Half a score of goodly young men were her humble suitors, and would have been glad to see the back of this young man's cropped head and lissom shoulders. She sat at her broidery-frame, and he would have been a backward man at his verse who had not written somewhat in praise of her hands, that passed the needle in and out.

The map that the young man studied he had ridden expressly to Bristol to procure. Riding home again with his treasure in his wallet, he had mused upon the things told him by the old pilot from whom he had procured it. Men had arrived at the East by going West! By the Azores and the old Atlantis of Plato, they had reached the New Found Land, whence to Cipangu and the Chinese Ocean, according to the map, was but a step. The old pilot had spoken of firedrakes and sirens, and had himself seen the dolphins and whales and the fishes that flew.

The young man left the window, fetched the small mariner's compass from the mantelpiece, and placed it over the star-like compass delineated on the map. It seemed to give the map a different meaning to place his own compass there. Then, north of the trembling needle, he read, '*Here men say the mariner's compass faileth.*' West of that was written, '*Land Unknown*', and south of that again, '*Land Unknown*', and the magic rest itself must be all but unknown, so few had ventured there.

But what fame to be even the fourth or fifth to venture! What service even to follow! And what rich profit for himself, did he need it, lay through that gateway of the Azores!

All that day he had spent among his orchards and gardens, giving directions. The day before had been passed among his horses and hawks. The day before that he had ridden after the deer – it was then that the accident had happened to the crossbow. And in the intervals he had sat at his mistress's feet, or talked with her mother. This was his life, and he showed diligence in it. He knew that his men said of him that not even his father had been so good a master as he.

Perhaps not; but – the young man glanced at his father's sword and morion again. Elsewhere in the house were other swords and harness, handed down by his line, that reached back older than the yew-tree, back into the unrecorded mists. Doubtless these forbears of his had not always had the praise of their hinds; but had they no other praise? Had they lived in vain because there were gaps in their fences and blight on their fruit-walls? Were these things all? Must a man go on year after year, planting, farming, keeping accounts, and rubbing his hands as his rent-roll grew? Were men to say to him, when he was old, no more than that he had been a careful husbandman?

Questions such as these had troubled him ever since that visit to Bristol. Ah, those ships, those disturbing ships! They had lain there by the quay as it were asleep, breathing lightly to the tides that lifted them; but what must they be awake – lifeless things, yet living by every pulse and sense of a hundred men, undying things, since when one hundred passed another hundred took their places? Ah, the queenliness of them! He had descended into their dark depths, he had ascended into their tops; and at night, in his bed in the inn, he had dreamed of them.

And he had not ceased to dream of them since. Once a month, once a week, or oftener, a certain dream had come back to him, always the same, yet each time slightly different. He had dreamed he stood on a ship's ladder of tarred rope, looking aloft. And at first he had stood just above the chains, no more than a drop to the deck; and then he had stood higher, a dangerous drop; and then he had mounted higher still, beyond all thought of dropping. That was all he remembered of his dream – that slender, narrowing ladder he was for ever mounting, with the manhole through the topcastle floor above his head, that sooner or later he knew he must enter.

Suddenly, seeing that the tambour-frame beneath the yew stood deserted, the young man folded his map. He had something on his mind that caused him to walk slowly, and he walked more slowly still as he left the closet, passed along the sunny-shafted corridor, and sought the terrace.

She was approaching, with her mastiff by her side. She had a small and imperious face, the hand beneath the ivy-green sleeve had dimples where its knuckles should have been; and her white ruff enclosed her proud neck as if it had been the corolla of an arum-lily

He took her by one of the dimpled hands, and without speaking led her to the terrace-end, where a stone seat stood, not far from the window of his own cabinet. Her ivy-green gown seemed a continuation of the ivy of the wall, which as richly enhanced her young face as if it had been one of the dark backgrounds of the portraits in the house. She sat down, and the mastiff dropped heavily and lazily at her feet.

He had resolved to tell her of his determination without further delay. He loved her; he knew that she did not go a-begging; and if she would not wait, so much the worse. He must entreat her to wait. As for her begging him to stay, that small face was not that of a beggar of anything.

As if she had known without telling why he had brought her there, she was the first to speak.

'So do you go, or do you stay, Edmund?' she asked him.

He answered less promptly. 'If I go I shall come back.'

'Nay, but plain speaking. If I am to wait I must know for how long. I cannot be endlessly plagued with suitors.'

In spite of his anxiety, he smiled. 'That you will be, if they are of my mind about you.'

'And what is your mind, if a maid may ask?' she rejoined. 'At Christmas you would marry. Half way to Easter you would marry, not a woman, but a ship. At Easter, blessed be Ovid! the ship had turned into a woman again. And now it is, "If I go I shall come back." This is some chameleon of a mind!'

It was true; but that was before his dream had taken possession of him. It was the dream, that hitherto he had concealed, that he had resolved to tell her now.

He began to do so.

As he talked he held her dimpled hand. This was well, for her face, proud as a star, would be the last of her sweet assembly to betray her. What her face did not do the fingers that rested in his did. He felt their quick tremor, that told him truer of her thoughts than the voice in which she presently interrupted him.

'Between the ship and the lady one hardly knows where to have you,' she said lightly. 'Do you take your ship by the hand, or have I shrouds – shrouds, marry! – the tarry kind, I would say, not the kind it's early enough to think of yet!'

He shook his head. Her tongue might jest, but the hand in his did not.

'Then if you are climbing your mistress thus, what kisses has she for you in the topcastle?' she rallied him again. 'In truth I should like to see your ship, tarry bower and all!'

Again he shook his head, kissing her hand.

'Oh, but my mastiff will tell me as much as this hand-licking will do! Come, I will be your soothsayer. You stood first at the hem of her petticoat, her deck I should say. Then, God help us! you had her by the waist-ribbon. When has she promised the other favour?'

At his reply her face almost followed the example of her hands.

'When I have had the dream once more,' he said in a low voice.

Suddenly she put her laughing all away. 'Nay, but Edmund, this is foolishness,' she said falteringly. 'Let us walk. A dream is but a dream.'

But he drew her back by the soft hand. It had rested upon his knee, where the garden-stains were, but, remembering certain verses he had written to that hand, he removed it from the soilure and placed it against his breast. It seemed to clutch softly at his heart.

He had not thought to feel her tremble thus. Could it be that she would stoop – beg him to stay?

'And so,' he said, 'I can plant trees and grow old watching them, or I can do this other. But if I stay I might not live, and to go is not to die, sweetheart.'

This it was that brought her starry pride down like a meteor – the secret thought that he might plant, not trees, but children, and grow old with them growing about him to continue his line. A catch came in the throat with the white ruff. She turned to him eyes in which tears trembled. They broke down her cheeks.

'Ah, Edmund, if you must go, then go; but think of me here! I love only you, but the days will pass, and I shall not forget, but only to remember, always only to remember, is bootless. I shall remember your face, but other faces will be nearer. I shall remember your voice, but other voices will be at my ear, perhaps saying words that you have said. My mother will die and I shall be alone. Then they will come, the others, with their gifts and their suits, and who knows, but I shall yield? . . . And as for that,' she raised her eyes with hatred to the sea, 'what trees will you plant there, or what crops sow, or what fruits gather, or horses ride, or music hear, or lips kiss? – Edmund, Edmund! Go if you must – but stay – stay with me – stay! – '

Her fingers, snatching at the points of his doublet, wove a net of points and fingers, as if to hold him. And his virgin beard moved about her hair. But his eyes were on the silky, seductive sea. Far away, appearing from behind a near thorn, a moth-like shape could be seen. It did not seem to move when he watched for its moving, but slowly, slowly it crept away from the hawthorntwig. It was a ship – westward bound.

And so another young man, as the saying is, sold a farm and went to sea; and another young woman remained alone to manage her estate, and to promise her clustering suitors that she would choose among them when her tapestry was finished, and to pick her work out again at night, and to lose her mother, and to grow old herself, but never too old to read, though with failing eyes, the verses he had left her –

> Ah, hadde I *but* an Indies gained –
> You *but* an Orient given –
> Againste your breste I hadde remained
> Nor dreamed another heaven!
> But in such huge excess you give
> When you youre selfe bestowe
> That, sweetlie-gorged, the more I have
> The hungrier I doe growe.
>
> Turne o'er those flowers youre fingers thridde;
> Their silken rootes appeare
> Alle thrummes and knottes, the whiche are hidde
> Beneath, for meaner care.
> The Vaunte of Honour's yours alone,
> Not worthienesse nor debte,
> But skyewarde trumpets vainlie blowne,
> A crested burgonet,

That askes the arrowe, claims the stroke,
And hides the wounde awaye,
As you the thrummes and endes doe cloke
Beneathe youre tambour-traye,
And bringes you nothinge back againe,
Nothinge againe but this –
A dint that iron broke in twaine,
But softe as is youre kisse.

3

A few years ago, in the marble court of the Ralli Hotel, a young man and a young woman were having tea. They sat in a corner a little apart, but had a clear view of the avenue between the tables, where couples hesitated and one-stepped and jazzed to the cacophony of an Ethiopian band. The court was cool as an aquarium; its lighting, too, partly masked behind sconces and cornices and partly 'borrowed' by means of cunningly-contrived glass, suggested some luxurious and artificial tank into which neither white daylight nor electric glitter penetrated; and its jazzing fishes and the water-flora seated at its tables were London's loveliest women.

The head-waiter himself had brought them tea, for Riccardo seldom left Reggie Asshe to underlings. For 'doing him' as well as even the Ralli can do a wealthy young man, Riccardo received gifts in due season of pheasants, trout, hothouse fruit, and, more than all, an occasional whisper, not to be spread about for fear of spoiling the market. As a result of these whispers Riccardo backed, or refrained from backing, one of Reggie's horses. And as Reggie knew about horses as well as owning them, Riccardo was well on the way to managing an hotel of his own.

Reggie Asshe was six-and-twenty. St James's Street booted and spatted him, Sackville Street made his coats and Savile Row his trousers, Piccadilly provided his hats, and the parting of his dark hair had been fixed by his club barber with as much care as if it had been Ordnance-datum. His hat, cane and gloves were in the cloakroom, his Rolls-Royce outside in Pall Mall. The car could take him to his aeroplane-hangar in thirty-five minutes. He had done it, at night, when the roads were empty, in twenty-and-a-half.

The girl by his side was pouting under her coral-coloured bucket hat with the tiny threaded flowers about it. She seemed, as she would have expressed it, 'fed'. The toe of one pink jujube of a shoe fretted against the table leg, and her ice was untouched before her. His eyes were quick and humorous as he rallied her, but there was more of purpose than of humour about his mouth, which, when he spoke, hardly seemed to open sufficiently to let the words out.

'But the prize, dear kid – look at the per-rize!' he was saying, as if he had not most of the prizes the world could offer without lifting a finger. 'Ten thousand isn't to be sneezed at these days, believe *me*!' He pronounced the last word as if it had been French. 'A Bradbury's gone before you can say goodbye to it, and here's you turning up your nose at three-and-sixpenny ices! Now don't go upsetting the works,' he continued, as the pink jujube made another movement that slightly shook the table. 'Looks bad in the afternoon – Riccardo'll be telling you to take more soda with it. Cigarette?'

But the girl was not to be put off so. She was stretching her gloves into a hard narrow strip between her fingers. One of the fingers wore an engagement ring.

'You know the money's nothing at all to do with it,' she broke out. 'You'll soon have spent nearly as much as that on the beastly thing. How much did the machine cost you for a start?'

'Dunno,' he replied indifferently. 'Haven't got the bill in yet. I hate flying other people's busses.'

'You flew them all right – before,' she answered in a failing voice.

'Not across the Atlantic, dear child,' he replied with a sudden compression of his mouth.

She was thinking of that 'before' of which she had spoken, when he had flown aeroplanes not his own. She was only two-and-twenty, but many a two-and-twenty knew, a year or two ago, what she knew – knew what it was to stand, suddenly white, gazing at the unopened telegram, which, when opened, was merely from a boot or dressmaker, and not the thing so sickeningly feared. Events had taught England's women to keep their hearts and expressions well in hand. Tenderness was a dangerous thing when there were only a few hours or a few days for a theatre or two, a lunch or two, a dance, a Medical Board, and back to the inferno again. No good 'asking for it'. Orders were orders, and England's women, a few years ago, did not make them any harder than they were.

But nobody had given him orders about this, his latest adventure. He was doing it to please himself. Even the reasons he did condescend to give were camouflage. He didn't want the prize. He didn't want a comfortable billet with a commercial company. He didn't want to write a book or to lecture about it, and as for the services to science and civilisation they made all the chat about, he wouldn't have missed a dinner or a theatre for either. He just wanted to do it because he jolly well wanted to do it.

And as for letting 'those other blokes' get in first – the Americans – she knew that he would be the first to grasp the hand of the sportsman who beat him.

He sprang to his feet as an old general in mufti made his way through the jazzing couples towards them. The general shook him warmly by the hand, but made a gesture of refusal of the chair Asshe placed for him.

'No, I mustn't stop. I'm with some people over there. You're getting away any time now, aren't you?'

'Yes, sir, with any luck. Off to Ireland tonight.'

'Everything all right?'

'I think so, sir. Don't see why I shouldn't do it, bar accidents.'

'Well, I know you don't mind an old Moses like me envying you young Joshuas a bit. We've done what we could. I hope they won't mob you out of sheer joy when you get to the other side. *Au revoir*, Asshe – best of luck – '

And the old general, sighing a little, but thanking his God he had been allowed to live to see what he had seen, was lost among the dancing couples again.

But the interruption had broken the current of Asshe's thoughts. He sat down again. He was dropping his fiancée presently and going on to dine with some men, and this was their goodbye. It was rather rotten to rag her. He glanced at her as she sat moodily stretching the gloves.

He hoped for her sake that he should be able to do it; anything else he could have given her would merely have meant writing out a cheque. It was largely swank on her account that had made him lavish money on his aeroplane, care on his preparations. His tail was well-up, so was his navigator's, the weather was ideal, and so forth . . . still, it was the Atlantic and its leagues he was pitting himself against, and he knew far too much to make light of them. The chances remained against him. And it would no more have occurred to him to tell her of a certain dream he had had than to have discussed petrol-tanks that leaked in the air or the precise effects of a direct hit.

This dream, that would rather have put the wind up her, had been curious in its way. It had begun many months ago, with his dreaming that he was out for the height-record; and at first he seemed to remember that his altimeter had stood at something like eight thousand metres. He would have thought nothing of this dream had it not presently occurred again, this time with the altimeter at eight thousand five hundred. Then it had come again, and again after that, with the reading each time higher than the last. The record was something over 30,000 feet, and he now stood pretty close to that figure. He had refused to admit even to himself that the beastly dream was becoming something of a nightmare, but he hoped it would keep off till he got away on his flight, as it left him rather a rag the morning after.

And if, as he fancied he had heard somewhere, these ascending dreams were unlucky, all the more reason she should know nothing about it.

'Do smoke or something,' he said presently. 'No hurry – we've half an hour yet.'

As she took the cigarette she lifted her troubled eyes to his.

'Can't I come over to Ireland tonight with you? Nancy Burrowes would come with me – I could ring her up from here – '

'No-can-do, darling,' he replied promptly. 'I shouldn't have any time to spare, and you'd only be in the way. You be practising the "Conquering Hero", and then when I come back you can start buying your ter-rousseau.'

'Can't I see you at the station tonight?'

'Wouldn't do. Might be blotto. I say, what about a couple of Martinis now?'

Again the gloves were stretched, again the pink jujube of a shoe poked at the table. More than ever he was glad he had not told her of that dream. He could see that she was full up to the back teeth already.

Then, quite openly, he took her hand, lightly dandling the fingers that lay limp over the arm of her chair. He bent over her.

'Little boots full of sand, darling, eh? I tell you it'll be quite all right. You do your little God-talks every night – you know – make Reggie a good boy and let him fly the Atlantic – and I say, don't forget to have a bit on *Eclair* – what a jape if I could pull off the Cup and the Atlantic too! Where's Riccardo? We'll drink to it . . . Riccardo, two Martinis, and then the bill – '

He scrawled his name on the back of the bill, and put the little glass into her hand.

'Good 'ealth – say good 'ealth – stiff lip now,' he said, touching the glasses.

Obediently she said it after him; and then suddenly she put the glass down on the table and flung her gloves after it. She rose, and without a word held out her hands to him. For England's women had learned that too – that when you live on the edge of a volcano the only thing to do is to dance. You can't alter the volcano – you can make yourself and everybody about you miserable – so why not make the most of life while it lasts? Her 'little God-talks' would fill her heart no less that those small pink jujubes of her feet moved to the cacophony of the Ethiopians' banging and blaring. Whether she ever saw him again or not, at any rate she had him now

He, too, had sprung laughing to his feet.

'Esker noo jazz?' he said blithely.

'Yes, old thing – come on,' she said hurriedly.

And hand in hand they chasséd towards the space where the dancers turned and pointed and poised.

And so, not an age or two ago, nor a century or two ago, but as it might have been yesterday, another young man went off the deep end, leaving another young woman to pester the Admiralty, and to look haggardly down the lists, and to ache for wireless-messages that never came, until the rolling months told her that all was useless and that she waited in vain.

There is no dream that has not been dreamed before.

And another young man will be dreaming the same dream to-morrow.

The Honey in the Wall

Qu'es la morso
Que nous forço
De bela vers ta cremour
Se lou mètre
Dóu celèstre
Noun t'a facho pèr l'amour?

Frédéric Mistral: A Ève

I

They found it in the fragment of Norman wall just across the grass-court – twenty pounds weight and more of it, the labour of the bees of none of them knew how many years. It was packed away in a cavity as long as a man's arm, and in order to get at it they had to fetch a ladder, to hack down the masses of ivy, and to clear away the grass and valerian and wallflower from the wall-top. Clot after clot it was taken out, unsightly lumps, black as pitch, caked and crusted with earth and scurf and bits of mortar. But the housekeeper cut and scalded the outer grime away, and there was enough of the stored sweetness of long-vanished flowers to fill the row of waiting jars.

Then they gathered up and burnt the ivy and the wallflowers, but left the gap in the wall for people to see whence the honey had been taken.

The Abbey guests had waved to Gervaise to come and see, but she had remained where she stood, in the window-recess of the little picture-gallery, looking down on them. It was one of the days when she wondered what they were doing with guests in the house at all. Guests! Who were they to have guests? As if, in the pass to which things had come, they, she and her mother, could afford to entertain! Oh yes, things might look very well on the surface. The Abbey made a stately showing there on its rounded hill, with its farmlands about it (but farmed by somebody else), its grass-courts between the stubs of its Norman towers, the ruins of its refectory walls, the twisted chimney stacks and stepped gables of the house proper, and, for timber, oaks that were a county's glory, making hillocks upon the hill behind. People passing in Ford cars or on bicycles or afoot turned to look at its widespread magnificence.

But sometimes a car drew up at the great gates and somebody descended from it who was not a guest. They were hardly guests, those people who came by appointment from Spinks' or Christies' or somewhere else in King Street or Pall Mall. And it was Gervaise who received these strangers. Sometimes she spent whole days with them – estate agents, cataloguers, valuers, photographers, minions of one sort and another. She talked to them civilly when she could. When she could not she fell back on her mother's unvarying plaint. 'Spread the rest out a bit – don't take it all from one room – leave it as nearly the same to look at as you can – but you must, you must find the money!'

The money, Gervaise reflected bitterly as she stood in the little picture-gallery! Money for what? For accumulated debts, running expenses, repairs? For nightmare taxation, the overdraft at the bank, interest on mortgages, first, second and third? Pah! little as she knew about these things, she knew that it would take a staff of lawyers and accountants, and something in the nature of a Consolidation Act, before the problem could be as much as touched! And it was no good talking to her mother. Her mother always made such aimless haste to agree with everything she said.

'Yes, darling, I know, I know!' Lady Harow would murmur, moving the patience-cards on the little padded table or putting another jig of the large dissected puzzle into its place. 'It's too dreadful! But we've shut up all the north and west parts, and even the billiard-room when there isn't anybody here. We only live in one teeny corner of it. There used to be twelve gardeners when you were a tot and now there's only one, and the Giles boy. You do so much your-self, darling, that you are – '

Yet, with the vines choking under the glass, and the jungles called gardens untouched since the beginning of the war, and wood and iron perishing for want of paint, and half a dozen of the houses' eyes put out where windows had mysteriously broken themselves – with at least one chimney stack unsafe, and cattle straying on the lawns, and the remaining domestics to pay and feed, and those appalling letters of threat or demand – in the face of all this her mother still had guests!

'Yes, darling, I know, I know! It's terrible! But it's only Freddy and Philip and darling Pam! They perfectly understand! Why, Pamela says she won't come if she isn't allowed to do her own room, and it's so long since we've seen dear Philip – '

And now Pamela and Philip and Freddy and the rest were waving up to her from the court below, calling her to come and see the honey they had found in the wall.

Gervaise turned abruptly away. It seemed to her that in a very little while they might be glad of that honey as mere food.

2

It was only a small gallery in which she stood, three diamonded windows long and not more than half a dozen strides across. (The other pictures were – that is to say they had been – at the place in Ireland.) It was on a side of the house far removed from the occupied quarters, and, except for the pictures, was bareness itself. Its carved stone fireplace was yawning and empty, and the single piece of furniture the apartment contained, a shallow sofa, was covered with a holland dust-sheet, that hid its contours and trailed on the floor. The mantelpiece had nothing on it but a broken keyhole-plate and an empty box that had held kitchen matches. Thank goodness, in that clean country there was little dust.

But the walls facing the diamonded windows showed ravages worse than dust. They were hung with a crimson rep material, and on them the results of her mother's 'spacing out' showed indeed. When you move an object that has stood for a long time on grass, you get a patch of dead and de-chlorophylled white; but ah, the wounds, crimson and recent, where the hatchet had fallen on that gallery! . . . Gervaise had done what she could, but a smaller picture cannot be made to cover the space of a larger one. Here it was a flap of a wound shaped like a carpenter's square. A corresponding carpenter's square, but in reverse, showed a little farther along. And between the two the four Raeburns had hung.

Raeburns! Four of them, no fewer! That small gallery had once been as rich as that!

And now the wall showed no more than a couple of tedious Zoffanys, a Sir Peter on either side of them, a hurried gathering-together of anything in a frame from a cabinet or corridor, and those cruel-looking carpenter's squares, like red incisions for a graft. These were all – these and the 'Artist Unknown', the full length Lady Jane, that hung in the very middle of the wall.

Gervaise stood indifferently before the Zoffanys and the Sir Peters. They were trite, without poignancy, mere occupiers of that once-glorious space. But she was never quite calm in the presence of the

Lady Jane. That always came near, a little too near, as if Gervaise herself had not skipped very many stages in the direct line of her blood. Brown and blackened like sodden winter leaves it was, and, like those same leaves skeletonised, minutely varnish-cracked from top to bottom and from side to side of its frame. Wintry, too – wintry as the family fortunes – were the rigid galloons of cramped bodice and stuffed sleeves, their gold now no more than dying flowers on a December wall. Yet two features, yellowed like old harpsichord keys, still stood palely out. These were the lace-cuffed, taper-fingered hands, one of them holding a tiny valentine of a handkerchief; and the second feature was the face in its angular card-castle of linen. The picture was unglazed, and these portions of it came forward. But they did not come, so to speak, equally forward. So much had vanished beyond recall. If ever there had been pink on those cheeks or living glint on those bony brows, not a trace now remained. All had gone with the fugitive pigment. And at the same time the lashless eyes had darkened to round balls of bitumen black. It was as if the paint had changed chemically and simultaneously in two directions, the one a blanching away to nothing, the other to the night that had swallowed up the 'Artist Unknown' and his sitter alike.

Gervaise was twenty-six, and, if pride of bearing be a sin, in Sheol already. And her beauty but thrust her down deeper. The rough country skirt above the flat-heeled brogues, the knitted leaf-brown jumper, showed the hips and shoulder-lines and breasts of that woman-form that has been padded and veiled, compressed and overlaid through the ages, but that remains today, as it will still be tomorrow, the same that Adam, waking, saw. The shapeless felt hat framed the resentful dark eyes and the scornful mouth, scornful of the whole dying place about her, scornful of itself that it should betray that it cared . . . all this in the light of the gallery so even and secondary that it filled every corner like the air itself; without a shadow even under the sheeted couch, without a shadow even where the decorated fire-back disappeared behind the wall. For it was the borrowed, honey-coloured light reflected from the Norman wall across the grass-court. No flashing, no dazzling; only the equable light on those walls of red rep, their scars, the thin line where Gervaise's soles met the floor, and every hair and lash of the lovely turbulent face distinct within the hollow of the shabby felt hat –

It was another of the days when she hated the Lady Jane. She hated her for her fixity, her achieved unchangingness, the mockery in her jet-black following eyes. Change – she! What had *she* known, living

in the times before these? Had she been in Gervaise's place, Gervaise
in hers! It is all very well not to change when nothing changes about
you, but it is another matter when strangers come from King Street
or Pall Mall, gash your walls, pay you money that you must immediately pay out again, and then depart! Gervaise knew very well that
other pictures would have to follow the Raeburns. The solitary Sir
Joshua downstairs would have to go. The moving little thing in her
own sitting-room, that somebody with spectacles and a magnifying-
glass had said was not a Watteau, would have to go. Perhaps the
Zoffanys and the Sir Peters would go too.

But the Lady Jane would stay. Dealers did not commonly pay large
sums of money for 'Artists Unknown'.

And Gervaise believed very little in the woman herself either.
Strait-waistcoated enough she might look up on the wall there, with
those tapering fingers holding the handkerchief and the unshaded
eyes dark-dead in a white-dead face – virtuous enough if you could
trust the look of her – but Gervaise didn't. In spite of that card-castle
of a headdress and the trussed-up breasts and the mouth a mere black
brush-thread where the red had been, Gervaise wouldn't have trusted
her an inch. She didn't believe in the shape of those handkerchief-
dropping fingers. She didn't believe that the foot in that bodkin-case
of a shoe had never pushed at a door it should not have pushed at. She
didn't believe that those pitchy eyes had never softly glanced, though
they only stared now. Great-great-great-Somebody the Lady Jane
mustn't tell Gervaise that . . . True, she might have had her head
chopped off for it. But then she had not had her head chopped off. She
had been circumspect in her day. And in any case she had not had to
stand by while they photographed and valued, nor to listen, in library
or muniment-room, to their flat voices saying: 'Any special feature?
Charles the First? Priest's Hole, what? Anything a bit out o' the
common – that's what gets the nibbles – '

That was what got the nibbles from these millionaires from White-
chapel and this option-chivalry of Palestine –

Yes, things had been simpler for the woman on the wall there,
whom Gervaise sometimes hated and never, never believed in –

'Gervaise! Gervaise!'

Again they were calling her from the grass-court below.

But she kept away from the window in order that they might think
she was no longer in the gallery. For Freddy Lampeter had called
too, and there were times when Freddy Lampeter troubled her more
than all her troubles put together.

3

They were not to be seen when she returned to the inhabited portion of the house. Only her mother was there, with her soft grey hair piled high as a guardsman's bearskin over her finely-tooled features, smiling at the large jigsaw-puzzle that at present resembled a map of Iceland in its shallow box.

'I thought you'd gone out with the others,' she smiled, looking up. Then, looking down again, but still smiling, she added, 'Would you draw the blind just one inch, darling?'

'Jane will have to go,' said Gervaise abruptly, returning from the adjustment of the blind.

'Jane go!' Lady Harow echoed in mildest surprise, but this time without looking up from the puzzle. 'But you can't possibly get rid of another servant – and the Wyburghs coming next week – '

'I don't mean Jane the housemaid. I mean the portrait.'

'Oh! . . . But never mind about it now. You look tired. Go out and have a good blow. I think they said they were going past Giles's.'

'I'd better write about it now. I do hope they don't send that young man with the spots again.'

'Sweetheart,' Lady Harow murmured to the puzzle, 'do take a short rest from things! You'll wear yourself out. Did you see the honey? Such a mass! They brought it in for me to look at. There should be enough to last the winter.'

The beautiful lips were pursed. 'I don't think I shall be here for the winter, mother.'

'What? Not Switzerland, my own! Those foolish Swiss! They got across with the French during the war – so unwise of them, with all these German places one can't possibly go to – I've been reading about it – '

'Switzerland!' The tone was too tired to be impatient. 'Shall I never make you see, mother?'

'But I do see, darling! *Must* we sell more pictures? Is there nothing else? There seem to be cabinets and cabinets full of things – or the trees – '

'I think the Lady Jane.'

'But, my sweet – is she valuable?'

The words seemed to slip out of themselves, yet not without a certain impact of concentration.

'I really don't know! They can have her for nothing if they'll only take her away!'

Lady Harow's arched brows rose to the springing of her tower of hair.

'My precious! . . . Now you know this is only one of your moody-moodies, and they're so bad for you! Now do run away and have a blow. I think they said past Giles's. Do you see a piece anywhere with a little bit out like this?'

Gervaise's mother turned to the puzzle again.

Gervaise went out, but only to enter the house again a few minutes later by another way. She passed to her own small sitting-room – the room she still retained, with a key thank heaven, to turn in the door when things got too much for her. But she did not sit down. From a drawer she took a large cluster of other keys, ringed and tabbed, and lettered and numbered. Then, passing out again, she locked the door of her room behind her.

She knew that what her mother called her 'moodies' were not good for her. But Lady Harow's unvarying prescription – to go out and have a blow – never did any good. On the other hand, by precipitating matters, a ramble through the vast house often did. When a thing cannot be avoided it is best to face it and get it over.

She had always felt the house to be much more hers than her mother's. Switzerland, the Riviera, London, Normandy, Scotland – this had been her mother's itinerary as long as the family fortunes had stood the expense; but Gervaise had always been dragged unwillingly at her heels, and her heart had always lifted again at the first glimpse of the Abbey on its rounded hill. The house was as much a part of her as her bones were. And – though not lately – she had had dreams about its labyrinthine windings. Maze enough it was as it stood in its actuality, with its hundreds of real doors, its dozens of real passages, its solid staircases. These things were the house itself. But in her dreams all had been strangely and adventurously enlarged. The very fabric of the Abbey had been a theme on which the oddest variations had been played. She had crept (in her dreams) through gullet-like apertures low down in walls, always remembering that this was not the first time she had passed through them, always knowing they would issue into some other chamber, which also she would remember the moment she saw it. She had found herself (in her dreams) in sheeted rooms (and, dreaming or waking, one set of rooms or another always was sheeted) – bedroom after bedroom with furniture piled on the stripped beds, sitting-rooms turned into lumber-rooms, through dream-known doors into chambers completely empty . . . and so (when the moment of waking came) through yet another door of baize or leather, into a staircase all at once part of the daily world again with maids moving about, ordinary hats and crops and sticks on the stands, and a bright square of grassy court, where puppies rolled and mats lay out in the sun.

And besides being thus shiftingly mapped, the place had been peopled too. The curious thing was that between the mapping and the peopling was a certain correspondence. Just as those chambers had been – what shall one say? – darkly expected, recognised the moment they were seen, and another getting ready to be recognised after that, so the people were imminently familiar. Awake, she could not remember one of them. Until the very moment of dream-meeting she did not quite remember them. But once met they were centuries old and known. She was not in the least afraid of these guessed-at people of her dreams. Curiously, the vanishing of their fringes when her eyes opened again gave her far more fear.

But the last dream, either of people or place, was some time ago. She had had other things to think about. Especially she had Freddy Lampeter to think about.

She thought of Freddy as she stood in a preposterous apartment that extended over half a dozen rooms below. It was a ballroom, with three chandeliers like breaking crystal rockets. Sofas were dwarfed by the walls they stood against, and a long row of southward windows looked out over hills of softly-rolling arable, farmed to their tops. And the scorn died away out of her face. She forgot for a moment the secret of that Abbey on its rounded hill – the weight of its taxation, its looming foreclosures, the ways and means of its maintenance. She knew that it might end by overwhelming her. But she forgot that in the thought of Freddy Lampeter.

She had no illusions about him. She was aware that he was a butterfly here, there and everywhere, passing from this house to that, his name now lightly linked with one girl's name, now as lightly with that of another. Oh, Gervaise could guess his kind – she was no fool! And, to be fair to him, it was not all his doing. They ran after him, could not leave him alone. But for some restraining quality in her that they apparently had not, Gervaise would have run after him too. She didn't like to think how often she had been on the point of it. That was why at those times she had answered him curtly or not at all. Obviously it was his gift. She saw through him clearly. But she was not at the beck of a finger.

And yet, when she had seen through him, and shown him that she saw through him, there he would be at her side again, always as if by some happy accident, murmuring smilingly and understandingly, as if everybody but they two were puppets in an amusing show and he and she privately commenting behind the scenes of it all. Yes, it was his gift. Half the girls she knew probably had their share of it. But somehow even the sharing made the thought of it none the less sweet.

Tall mirrors behind her reflected the showery chandeliers and the arable across the smooth valley. Turning, she saw herself in one of them, and advanced to meet herself.

Those others – Blanche Chayter, for example? Blanche had her forthright attractions, open and declared and made the most of; but had Gervaise not beauty too? That body of hers in the rough skirt and leaf-brown jumper, was it not a Toledo blade for suppleness and temper? The arrogant face within the shabby hat, was it inferior in loveliness to Blanche's? And what treasure, disordered it might be, the bitter with the sweet, the dross with the gold, the honey caked with mortar and scurf and chaff; did not her tumultuous heart contain? Standing before the mirror she asked herself this.

But she turned away from the mirror again and walked with quickened pace out of the ballroom. Too well she knew the answer to her own question. The honey was there, but it was walled up, and it was she herself who was unable to release it. She could give of her care, her brain, the labour of her body, but not of her inmost heart. It had always been so. Others might laugh through their lives, cease from thinking, or never have begun. They might turn their backs upon burdens, leaving anybody to shoulder them who cared. They might be all open honeybags, for Freddy or somebody else to sip. But not she. She was different. Why?

Entering a corridor that turned away from the smiling sweep to the south, she saw them in the distance, trooping down the hill from Giles's.

4

They had been what they called 'Maying', though the month was July and the time afternoon. That meant that they had straggled in twos and threes across the fields, picking flowers, throwing stones, running short races, hindering Giles's men at their work, dropping sixpences into the money-boxes of the Giles's children. They were still laughing at these things when Gervaise entered the drawing-room.

'Do pull yourself together, Pamela – this is merely absurd!' somebody admonished a buttercup-haired girl, who had laughed herself into semi-hysterical tears and was still unable to stop.

'Deplorable! Don't take any notice of her!'

'Pamela!'

'Really, Pam!' they scolded the uncontrolled girl.

Freddy Lampeter was watching indulgently from among cushions. His small dark head was against the sunny window-opening, and the spare spread of his shoulders was emphasised by the position of his arms along the couch-back. The light hid the little healed wound at the left corner of his mouth – the little pucker that always made Gervaise think of him as two men, the one whose letters came at wide intervals from places where things of that kind were to be picked up, the other who might have lounged among cushions all his life. His soft voice too always seemed the softer for the scar, and it was with an irony that she took no trouble to hide that Gervaise made herself his handmaid.

But on this occasion it was he who waited upon her. One of the girls turned as Gervaise entered.

'Here she comes! Gervaise, where have you been? Freddy, don't be so abominably lazy – get up and get her some tea – '

Freddy Lampeter rose. He brought her the tea. He was taller than she, who was herself tall, and he stood bending a little over her, smiling the fixed smile of the scar. When he spoke his lips hardly moved. This, too, seemed to give whatever he said its own privacy.

'Why didn't you come down?' he said in her ear.

She merely made a gesture – she didn't know –

'Haven't you been out?' he asked.

'No.'

'I'd have stayed behind if I'd known,' he remarked. These were the things she hated him to say. How did he know that she would have liked him to stay behind? And if he did know it, was it not a thing he would have done better to keep to himself?

'Where did you go?' she asked coldly.

'Don't ask me. Pamela took charge. Look at her – she hasn't finished yet – '

And indeed Pamela's laughter was of the inordinate kind that sometimes seizes the young in church. She called across to Freddy.

'Isn't it *anybody's* birthday?' she implored. 'Oh, I do so want it to be a birthday! *Do* have been born today, Freddy!'

Freddy Lampeter sent her a smile, but did not move from Gervaise's side.

'Let her alone, she'll run down,' he remarked to Gervaise, and again it was as if he and she were apart, commenting on the spectacle of the overstrained girl.

Then suddenly he addressed her on her own account.

'What were you doing in the picture-gallery?' he asked her.

Her reply was as briefly informative as she could make it.

'I'm going to sell the Lady Jane.'

He expostulated softly. 'Oh! must you?'

'It isn't a question of "must". I needn't if it comes to that.'

'Then why sell her?'

Were her private reasons any of his business? She had turned to the verandah, but he moved with her. After them floated Pamela's voice. 'Oh, do let's all dress up tonight!' Gervaise and Freddy Lampeter stood outside, at the top of the flagged steps that descended to the lawn.

'Is she by one of the big men?' he broke silence after a minute.

'Who?' she asked, as if she had forgotten what they had been talking about.

'The Lady Jane.'

'No.'

'Then – ' Apparently he would not let it alone. He meant why, in need such as hers, and with a Sir Joshua still in the house, sell 'Artists Unknown' for a negligible sum?

'You know we are selling pictures,' she said as they moved together a little way along the lawn.

'Raeburns – yes,' was his half-heard reply.

Then suddenly he employed the gift that disturbed her most of all. He walked by her side in complete silence.

Of their encounters it was these unprepared-for ones that always troubled her the most. Give her but a little time in which to take hold of herself; and she could always contrive to strip him of some of his wonderfulness. Nay, with a little preparation, she could dissect him, reduce him to quite ordinary components. That voice of his, she could steel herself against its pitch and quality; such-and-such things he said in it – she could sift his meanings through and through, run them through her fingers like sand. And it was always heartsease to her to analyse him in this way and to find nothing whatever at the bottom . . . But that was only possible when she spent some hours with him. Away from him, all was to do again. Though she scattered him as Lady Harow might have scattered her jigsaw map of Iceland, he always reassembled, to trouble her as profoundly as ever at their next impromptu meeting.

Therefore, as with the oppression of the house itself; better face it and get it over. She cared little at these times what thrusts she gave him; it was even prudent to be a little rough. He wanted to know her real reason for selling the Lady Jane. She would not have told him even if she could. So she allowed her silence to match his.

An iron fence crossed the park, with a gate in a semicircular opening that only allowed their passage one at a time. It closed with a clash behind them, and they climbed the hill among the grazing cattle. In silence they still mounted. From the unseen lower road came the light pattering of a quick-stepping horse in a rubber-tyred trap. An oak half as big as the world hid the Abbey from their view.

Then, as they rose higher and ever higher, the Abbey was seen again, a roof-view, with oblique peeps into its towers, and the valerian and the wallflowers marking the plan of its crumbling walls.

When at last he spoke he did so without lifting his amused eyes from the ground. He returned to the charge again.

'I wonder why you want to sell the Lady Jane,' he repeated.

She felt that his finger-tips were on her nerves; he was experimenting with her. She gave him the coldest of glances.

'You seem to have that picture on your mind,' she said.

'Oh, I don't call mine a mind,' he laughed softly.

She knew that if she was to free herself from him now was the time. She faced him haughtily.

'Do you really suppose that I don't know perfectly well what you mean?' she asked him.

He looked quickly up. 'What do I mean?' he asked with curiosity.

'You aren't wondering about the Lady Jane at all. You're wondering about me, and I'd much rather you didn't.'

He knew that that was not true, but she now wanted to have him like her mother's puzzle, all scattered into little pieces. She wanted him handable, without that tormenting glamour, powerless over her. She had come out with him for that very purpose.

But he merely acquiesced, with an appearance of gravity even.

'I do often wonder about you, Gervaise. You know that.'

Thereupon she laughed. 'Oh, yes, I know! I know quite well how often that is! You wonder about me when you happen to remember me!'

He made no sign of resentment. He seemed to be examining himself.

'Well, you may be right,' he said at last. 'And anyway, I'm not putting in for extra leave.'

And that also she knew in him – the modestly picturesque attitude with which he could admit a fault. He meant that he would be off in October, perhaps to get another of those little puckers in the flesh from an Afghan bullet or a knife. He was reminding her how perilously he lived.

But if he hoped by this to get under her guard, again he failed.

'You're going on to the Chaytors, aren't you?' she abruptly challenged him.

'Yes. I promised Blanche. Why don't you come? She'd love to have you,' was his reply.

'Has she said so?'

'Why,' he said, suddenly stopping, 'you haven't had a row, have you?'

For answer she laughed again. Blanche ask her! If Blanche had said that she wanted Gervaise in the house, Gervaise did not believe her. On that rounded hill, with the mountainous oaks behind them and the Abbey laid out in plan below, an invisible Blanche Chaytor stood between Freddy Lampeter and Gervaise Harow. Gervaise knew it by his very readiness with her name; much better to be ready than to wait to be accused. Once more she laughed. He was actually helping in his own dismembering now, by laying bare his processes. And oh the immediate comfort she found in it! Already she had faced the obsession of him, was half-way through with it, and felt her approaching liberation. What (she wondered) must it be to be married to a man like that! To find no ease in him save in his imperfections, no love but when he was not there! Let Blanche have him! By and by Blanche would know as much as Gervaise knew!

The blessedness, once more, to have laid the ghost of him!

Her lips relaxed into a sudden smile. In her moment of triumph she could not help saying what she did say, gaily, her eyes almost thanking him for his share of it.

'All right, Freddy! It isn't as if I minded, you know! Friends as much as you like, but you know I have your measure!'

And he, as they descended again, said not another word.

5

Gervaise was blythe. She and Lady Harow were the first down from dressing, and she stood behind her mother's chair. Not one look, word or thought did she want of Freddy Lampeter now. Was not that quietude within her breast more to be desired than that storm-upon-a-storm they called love?

'What was darling Pamela laughing at this afternoon?' Lady Harow asked, her fingers delicately over the puzzle.

'How should I know, mother? I wasn't there.'

'Of course not. How forgetful of me. How much did they say the honey weighed?'

'I haven't seen the honey, either,' Gervaise answered. 'How do I look tonight, mother?'

For Freddy Lampeter's express benefit she had made of her arms a gratuitous and dazzling insult. Now that she no longer feared him he should have something to look at! Bare to the pits, they issued from the low frock of sooty black, rousing like a trumpet-flourish. Let Blanche match them if she could! The ringlessness of her finger, too, was meant to mock him. A smile played about her lips as she put out her hand to the map.

'Wait, mother – this piece goes in here – then this – then all that patch will fit in – '

She pushed a little islet of wood to the mainland. She laughed a delighted laugh as she did so. It was almost as if, having dismembered Freddy, she could put him together again or not, just as she chose.

But the white arm was swiftly withdrawn again. Absent-mindedly Lady Harow had touched it with her lips as it had reached over her shoulder to the puzzle. Gervaise's smile vanished. She did not know why she had not wanted her mother to kiss her arm.

'Listen – I think I hear them,' she said in an altered voice.

It was Pamela and Evelyn, with Freddy Lampeter and another man at their heels.

They assembled in the hall about the aperitif-tray, eight or ten of them, gay to the eye as a battle of flowers, noisy as a nest of young birds. One of them was busy with a shaker, and Pamela's lush, formless little mouth munched cocktail cherries. About her buttercup temples was a wreath of minute flowers, and she steadied herself against Freddy Lampeter's shoulder as she eased the ribbon of a satin slipper. Gervaise had advanced, and had taken the small glass somebody proffered her. She drained it without a glance at Freddy. She stood near a high wainscot the top of which formed a ledge. Lesson number one for Freddy! Indifferently the arrogant arm reached up. She placed the glass upon the ledge. Pamela could have walked under that up-stretched limb without disturbing a hair of her yellow head.

It was long since Lady Harow had taken the head of the Abbey table. That was Gervaise's place, and on the previous evening Freddy Lampeter had sat at her right hand. But this night another guest, arrived hardly an hour before, sat in that seat. It happened that to

Sir Walter more than an ordinary measure of consideration was
due. Moreover, white-haired as he was, it amused Gervaise to think
that he was at least a whole man, and not, like the younger man he
had displaced, a thing of scattered bits, permitted for decency's sake
to keep the appearance of wholeness. For it was part of her tyranny
that nobody else should see how stripped Freddy was. Pamela, for
example, her hair almost brushing Freddy's shoulder a few places
down the table, knew nothing of it. It was quite enough that Freddy
himself knew.

'But how dare you show your face here without Auntie, Uncle
Watty!' Gervaise was saying to Sir Walter. He was not really an
uncle. He was her godfather. But she never called him anything but
'Uncle Watty'.

The old man shook his head.

'Ah, my dear, we're both a little bit on in years for your sort of
party,' he replied. 'I shall sit with your mother while you dance. Is it
to be dancing?'

Pamela's high little bosom was thrust half-way across Freddy
Lampeter as she interposed.

'Did Sir Walter say dancing? Oh, but we aren't going to dance!
We're going to dress up and play hide-and-seek all over the house –
we may, mayn't we, Lady Harow?'

'Of course, darling,' Lady Harow gave vague and sweet permission.
'Has Sir Walter been told about the honey that was found, Gervaise?'

They took coffee in the hall. The firelight (Lady Harow liked a fire
even in July) gave the wainscot a richer patina and flushed the frocks
of the girls like a flower-bed seen at sunset. And as they stood,
Gervaise took occasion to give Freddy Lampeter lesson number two.
The aperitif-glass still stood on the wainscot ledge where she had set
it down. A tiptoe maid was reaching for it. And now she saw that
Freddy was watching her. Once more she lifted that arm that a man
might have run a mile to see. She handed the glass to the maid, who
retired. The next moment he was at her side, and, for the first time
since their walk that afternoon, speaking to her.

'Rather like the princess in the story, what?' the private voice was
saying.

With her head back, she looked along her lashes at him.

'What story?'

'Oh, a very old one; don't you know it?'

'No. But it's nice to be called a princess,' she remarked off-
handedly.

The ironical little pit at the corner of his mouth seemed to deepen. His voice was the voice of the Freddy Lampeter who might have lain among cushions all his life.

'It was their bridal-night, and the lamp in the chamber had to be put out. He was already in her arms. She couldn't let him go, even for that moment. "Love, it would seem an age," she whispered to him; and – Freddy's eyes rested for a moment on the long white arm, and then seemed to make a track across the hall to the staircase at the further end of it – and so she stretched out her arm. And it stretched away from her, out and out, till it reached the lamp. It snuffed the wick. And then it was round him again. Didn't you know it?'

Low as he had spoken, Pamela must have heard, for she gave a little shriek.

'Oh, Freddy, how *frrrrrightful*! He married a ghost woman! Do let's be ghosts tonight!'

But Gervaise had turned away.

Was it quite so well with her as she had thought?

6

The table with the puzzle had been brought into the hall, and over it Sir Walter and Lady Harow talked. Sir Walter, too, had his gift, of a great simplicity of heart, so that even his learning sat as lightly on him as a garment. He had grown up with these owners of the Abbey. He had taken Gervaise, a puckered pink mite, from her mother's arms. He had seen her, a little anemone of flesh, in her bath. There was nothing he might not say to this family, so different a man would he have been had he said anything he should not have said.

'Gervaise is tired out,' he was saying to Lady Harow.

'The darling child has so much to do!' Gervaise's mother answered serenely.

'Does she do everything?'

'Everything! So wonderfully!'

'Does she happen to be in love?'

'In love? Gervaise?' said Lady Harow mildly. 'She's more like a man than a woman. She always was. And I'm sure she would never leave the Abbey.'

'But she says you may have to?'

'That's when she looks on the black side. It passes off. A good blow and she's all right again.'

Sir Walter mused. He understood Lady Harow, but he loved Gervaise. Where Gervaise went, there his love was as the air about her.

'I don't think she's in love – ' Lady Harow's sentence tailed away.

'Will you lend her to me for a little while?'

'Oh, you'd never persuade her!'

Sir Walter, too, doubted it. He knew the vanity of that magnificence, the Abbey on its rounded hill, and Gervaise had grown to her task of being its sole prop.

'I might try,' he said.

'I think I shall be visiting in Ayrshire this autumn,' Lady Harow remarked; and she added, as another piece of the puzzle dropped into its place, 'There! The last one took me three weeks, but I really believe I shall finish this in a week!'

As she spoke Gervaise entered the hall.

7

Ordinarily they played billiards or bridge after dinner, or danced; but no distant click of balls nor strumming of the piano had accompanied Sir Walter's talk with Lady Harow. Indeed not a sound had been heard since, half an hour and more ago, the party had swept as if before a gale up the staircase that branched off to galleries to right and left. Pamela and another girl, waltzing together across the hall, had tried to waltz up the staircase also; and 'Darling Pamela – always in such high spirits!' Lady Harow had smiled as the two girls had come down in a flower-like huddle half way up. Now Gervaise entered alone, crossing the hall on her way to her own sitting-room.

'What are they doing now, darling?' her mother asked. 'They want the doors unlocked. I'm going for my keys.' 'But surely it will be very dark!' The lighting-system of the Abbey was ancient, the lamps half a day's work, and family and guests lighted themselves to their rooms with the candles that stood in a long row on the table under the newel-post.

'The far side will have the moon,' Gervaise replied.

But before proceeding to get the keys she paused once more before the puzzle table. The map of Iceland was now a sizeable continent, and growing apace as the number of unused jigs diminished. As Gervaise looked her mouth became compressed, and there was a gloom of doubt in her eyes. Yet the lips were not still for all their compression, and neither were the fingers of the hand nearest

Sir Walter. Next to him at dinner she had been gay. She was so no longer.

'I've been asking your mother if you could come away with me,' Sir Walter said.

She made a brave effort to shake off the growing mood.

'Now? With the house full of people?' she laughed.

'Yes, if that were possible,' he answered simply.

'But it isn't possible! And besides, why should I?'

'For a change, my dear,' he replied.

She laughed again, but now after quite a different fashion. Change! What else was her life but change – change, yet at the same time foredoomed unalterableness, either or both? To change her scene would not change Gervaise; and what could stop the onrushing changes of the Abbey itself? All this was in her breast; but aloud she merely said, 'Is Uncle Watty just a little bit fond of me, mother, do you think?' and she moved away.

And on her return through the hall she did not stop, but brightly waved the cluster of keys and ran upstairs.

For the convenience of the servants, the occupied bedrooms lay together. A single corridor turning a right-angle contained them all, first those of the girls, then those of the men, with Freddy Lampeter's at the corner. Only Gervaise's own room lay apart, down a different passage altogether.

She sought the guest-rooms. The first three into which she looked were lighted but empty. She only heard voices as she approached the turn of the corridor. Apparently they had all flocked to Pamela's room.

It was a theatrical glimpse that Gervaise saw as she pushed at the door, of girls stepping out of this, slipping that over their heads, shaking out their hair, trying on cavalier hats, sashing themselves with impromptu borrowings. One of them, catching sight of Gervaise's face, held up a shawl that glistened like a wall of Aladdin's cave.

'Come along and dress, Gervaise, we've kept this for you!' she cried.

But Gervaise shook her head. First there were the dozens of doors to unlock. She waved to the half-dressed girls and shut them in. No sound came from the men's quarters as she passed. Only under one door was a crack of light, and somewhere the odour of a Turkish cigarette. Gervaise set out on her journey.

She had provided herself with an electric torch, the beam of which flitted mysteriously over floorboards and skirtings. Certain doors she passed by; they were not essential to the escapade. But elsewhere the light of the torch rested for a moment on locks and fastenings, there was a jingling as she chose the key, and she passed on, leaving the door open behind her. Door after door she opened. High up in the wall of one passage a sort of clerestory of glazing glimmered palely, but this was not yet the moon's quarter of the heavens. One door which she found open she closed again. It led to the servants' rooms. It occurred to her that it might be as well to warn the servants of the game about to be played.

Then, at a point where she could travel no farther in a straight line, but must turn sharply to the left, she opened the door of a corner chamber and saw the astounding moon.

She stopped short and drew a deep breath; that rising moon compelled her. It seemed almost near at hand, within a bird-flight, hardly to be believed to be the same that in another hour or two would be riding small and high in the sky. It bulged over the hill, orange and enormous. Such was its solid rotundity that the perspective of its volcano-scape could be traced over its retreating round. It made a glow a quarter of the heavens wide about it, and its effulgence seemed to dye the earth, as the foot of the rainbow tints field and tree and hill. The apartment in which Gervaise stood was a mere plastered cell in the honeycomb of the house, never used; but that hanging bullseye out in space pencilled with shadow every tiniest accident of its walls, and sent Gervaise's own shadow streaming across the floor and then doubling like a piece of dark folded paper a yard up the skirting.

And thereafter, as she passed along the moonlit wing, leaving door after door wide open behind her, sometimes two rooms, sometimes three, were as curiously patterned with light and dark as if the eye had peered down the shining barrel of a gun.

8

Already she would have given a good deal to have been excused her part of the harlequinade; but what was the good of moping? Pamela's way was the sensible way – to laugh till the tears came into the eyes, dress up, have a fling! Here were the moon-flooded rooms, and the doors stood open. Romp through them, then, and let cares take care of themselves!

But one does not become a Pamela on quite such easy terms as that. One is perhaps less a Pamela than ever when one has to tell one's self these things. Gervaise, reaching the ballroom with the chandeliers and the mirrors in which she had gazed at herself that afternoon, knew that she could no more be Pamela than Pamela she. We are born ourselves, die ourselves, and are nothing but ourselves in the space between.

Honey of the richest, but locked up in the interior of a wall!

But at least one can always take one set of clothes off and put others on. For the matter of that, if this whim was her guests' choice, she herself must most conspicuously dress up and be one of them. Her round of the doors had taken some time. She was still far from her own room. Their fantastic game of 'Puss-in-the-corner' might already have begun. She had better hasten.

With the beam of the torch wavering like a will-o'-the-wisp about her feet she hurried in the direction of her own room.

She did not intend to wear the shawl they had kept for her, that looked like a wall of Aladdin's cave. She had had a gayer inspiration. At some time or other in the past, she had forgotten for what tableau or amateur performance, she had made herself a gown, not (to be sure) very accurately the Lady Jane's of the picture in the little gallery, but near enough, the slightness of the occasion taken into account, to pass muster as a representation. She had long since forgotten all about this costume. She had no idea where it was, supposing her still to have it; and things lost in that rambling Abbey were best looked for by daylight. But she remembered it now. Pamela, little mayfly that she was of moist mouth, satiny textures and artless sprawls, got her effects after a fashion, but there was more of dateless beauty in one of Gervaise's Pheidian arms than in the whole of Pamela's putting-together. So – the Lady Jane be it.

And if Freddy Lampeter's inquisitiveness about the picture really *had* been an experimenting with Gervaise herself; and if she *should* happen to surprise him in moonlit chamber or dark corridor, that would be lesson number three for him.

Her luck stood by her. In an oaken room of cupboards, by the light of the electric torch, she put her hand upon the costume straight away. Then, seeking her own room, by fire and lamplight mingled, she looked in the glass, first at those arms of hers that issued from the sooty black, and then at the stuffed and quilted sleeves of the tableau-dress. And her thought must have pleased her, for she smiled. From what she knew of Freddy, arms that he did not see might well be more interesting to him than those displayed in their beauty before his eyes. She had taken care that he should see them from armpit to finger-tip once that evening. Let him make what he could of the Lady Jane and her padding now!

But as she still stood in the sooty black with the firelight warm on the ceiling and her image in the tilted glass sloping towards her as if to fall upon her, again she paused. Her arms? What was that story about arms he had whispered so privately into her ear? Who was this princess of his tale, who could not spare her lover from his warm place by her side, no, not for the mere moment it would have taken to put out a light? What eternity in an instant was this he had hinted at? What this urgency of passion, this ghost-woman's arm long enough to have gone nine times round him? Had he meant her and himself? And had he actually had the effrontery to tell her so?

As if she had been dealt a blow, all at once she knew why she had paused at her mother's puzzle-table on her way through the hall. She knew why her compressed lips had quivered and her hands had not been still. He was *not* dismembered. He was whole once more, with the old, easy, scoffing, familiar power over her. All was to begin anew. Once more she was to know those perturbed moments of meeting, the pain at her pent heart, the flushings, the exhausting resolve, his re-demolishing. The two or three hours in which she had been rid of him were over, and when next they met it would be she who would have to beware, not he.

Well, if it was so, so it was, and there was an end of it. That cramping bodice and those bolstered sleeves would serve as well as anything else for their next encounter. Off with the black, then, and on with them! She was far too late already.

Twenty minutes later there issued from her room a living Lady Jane, with the hues of the coursing blood in her cheeks and the glint of life on her brows. In one hand she carried the morsel of a handkerchief; in the other the torch.

But with her hand on the closing door she paused. The glow of the firelight lay on the disorder of garments within. She was oddly conscious of parting from them, of going out into some strange world strangely attired. Her eyes rested lingeringly on those usual clothes. Should she close the door or leave it open?

She took a couple of paces away.

But suddenly she turned again and re-entered the room. From the inside of the door she took the key and reinserted it on the outside. The sound of the closing door echoed along the corridor. She turned the key, tucked it somewhere in her waist, and sought the others.

9

All in the house was quiet; but that was of the essence of the escapade – to steal noiselessly upon one another and suddenly to startle the air with a spoken name. Gervaise could imagine Pamela's shriek should she happen to be stolen upon and named after such a fashion. But the chances were that by this time they were all at the other side of the house. The passages along which Gervaise moved showed only an occasional lamp burning, and those clerestory windows dim grey in the wall. They would have to grope to find one another here. But away over there, with the moonlight flooding the chambers, it would be flashing indeed, strange, and a little heart-quickening. To imagine yourself alone and yet to know that you might not be alone – to pause with an arrested gesture almost as if you feared your own presence – and then, perhaps, as children leap out of their ambushes, to see one of them, startlingly attired, spring forward with outspread arms into that torrent of moonlight, calling aloud a name . . . that was the game they played that July night in that Abbey upon its rounded hill.

It had been arranged that no door found open was to be closed again; and, by those she had unlocked half an hour ago, Gervaise set out over the same ground once more. But no gleam of electric torch accompanied her now. The torch was hidden in her hand. She knew the Abbey's windings as well by night as by day, as well asleep as awake. Only once she thought she heard a rustle. With her fingers still closed over the torch she pressed the button. Her hand became a little pink fairy, hovering all by itself in the darkness. The rustle turned out to be nothing. She released the button, and the fairy vanished.

She reached the corner chamber from which she had first seen the moon, but already its aspect had changed. That bulging orange ball was now a mere round of brilliance with even its volcano-scape hardly discernible. It changed the colour of things, greened the tinsel of Gervaise's garments, turned the reds and browns of bodice and stuffed sleeves to black; and her face within the dormer-shaped structure of linen was lost to the bridge of her nose in shadow. And, forgetting all about the game, she thought again of the lovely place, so proudly awaiting its end. She supposed somebody would buy it, some preposterously rich person or some public body; but how little of it their money would buy! Hardly the mere stones of it, for the busy brains of the wilful hearts of her race were the very mortar in which they were set! Hardly a yard of its ground or an oak of its hill, for an older allegiance would remain in the air, the very winds whisper their loyalty to the exiled stock! Probably it would be turned into a hospital or a hydro. It didn't matter. Gervaise would not be there to see.

Musing, she had left the moonlit rooms behind her and was approaching the ballroom again. All was still strangely quiet, and she stopped, wondering whether it would not be best to go back to the starting-point yet again.

But even as she stood irresolute, their nocturnal adventure took a swift stride forward. Recently – within a few minutes at most – somebody had passed that way smoking a Turkish cigarette.

Gervaise could have given no reason for knowing that that cigarette was Freddy Lampeter's. Other men in the house smoked Turkish cigarettes, not to mention the girls. She merely *knew* that this cigarette was Freddy's. She knew it all in a moment, just as certainly as she knew something else, namely, that Pamela was with him. Indeed the wonder was, not that she knew it, but that she had not known it sooner. Now that she came to think of it, he had hardly been parted from Pamela the whole afternoon. He had watched her in those fits of laughter at teatime; he had sat next to her at dinner; it had been his shoulder on which she had leaned to tie the ribbon of her slipper. How Freddy would be dressed Gervaise did not know. Probably he would have cast something casually over his evening clothes, a pierrot's voluminous garment, say, or the traditional Mephistopheles cloak and hood. Pamela, Gervaise remembered, was to have been a *paysanne* of sorts, with a short, striped petticoat over her bare legs and a gaudy scarf clipping her buttercup head and depending in streamers below.

None of them knew of the impulse that had led Gervaise herself to dress as the Lady Jane.

Ahead of her stretched the dim perspective of the ballroom; but between her and it lay two ante-chambers. It was in the doorway of the first and larger of these that Gervaise stood. The smaller one, that immediately preceding the ballroom, was only smaller by reason of a comparatively modern alteration. Somebody, Gervaise's father or grandfather probably, had had the idea of turning it into a buffet or service-room for occasions on which the ballroom was used, and, as the domestic offices lay immediately below, this had been no great task. The panelled wall had been moved some three or four feet forward, the floor behind it had been cut through and a wooden staircase had been fitted in. To this stairhead one of the panels, now a door, gave access. The apartment had no furniture except a heavy Jacobean table.

Well, if in a game that depended on vigilance and stealth, Freddy Lampeter chose to leave a breast-high scent of Turkish tobacco behind him, that was his look-out. Keeping away from the middle line of the doors, Gervaise furtively advanced. She crossed the first of the two rooms, which was empty. Empty, too, was the smaller room, with the Jacobean table in it. But from the ballroom itself there came a subdued murmur, and Gervaise peeped cautiously round the upright of the door.

They stood midway down the room, under one of the glimmering chandeliers, and the sounds Gervaise had heard had been his half-vouchsafed tones, and something sudden and as suddenly checked from Pamela.

And Gervaise had guessed his dress rightly. He was wearing the garb you will find in any costumier's wardrobe though there be but a couple there. The close-fitting hood of a Mephistopheles enclosed his small head, and the long crimson cape draped the spare spread of his shoulders and fell to his heels.

But what Pamela wore could not be seen. She was completely enfolded in his cloak, strained to his breast. Her small mask was all that was visible of her. It resembled the petal of some other flower, windlodged in the heart of a dark poppy.

So he had not been able to refrain, even from poor weak-headed little Pamela!

It was like him, too, to have chosen his position skilfully, as it were with an eye for the surrounding country. From whichever end of the gallery they might be spied there was escape in the other direction. True they could be seen, but fourteen or fifteen yards away, and not a word of their murmuring would be distinguishable. Gervaise, as a matter of fact, saw them twice over – once directly, and once in one of the mirrors before which she herself had stood that afternoon. She saw his head bend closer over Pamela's.

But those who see in a mirror can also be seen in a mirror. Suddenly a clear shrill shriek seemed to find the very note of the chandelier overhead. With no more volition than if she had been asleep, Gervaise had moved away from the upright of the door, and now stood flamed in the ballroom entrance – the Lady Jane herself stepped down from the picture-gallery wall, and as motionless as she.

But the shriek was quenched almost before the chandelier had ceased to ring. His arms within the cloak had made a swift gathering movement, and the folds of the poppy closed completely over the alien petal. He was looking straight at Gervaise. He feared nothing. But Pamela was not to be allowed to see.

Prompt and admirable as ever (Gervaise reflected bitterly) – trust him! Even with that foolish little heart beating against his own he could still act instantaneously! Ghosts of the Lady Jane for him? It took more than a woman in a tableau-costume to shake those nerves! He was smiling the fixed smile of the scar within the oval of the crimson casque. And Gervaise scornfully waited for him to speak, disclose himself; acknowledge that he was out of the game.

But he did no such thing. Not only was he smiling that immovable smile; he was coming towards her, with Pamela, still unseen and unseeing, shepherded along blindfold in the cloak. He was within a few yards of her, nearer, coming on without a falter –

All at once terror took Gervaise. No ghost could have been more affrighting than that steady, silent, smiling oncoming. There was only one bolt-hole – the service-stairs –

The dim, empty vista of the rooms showed again through the doorway where the Lady Jane had stood.

She did not know how her fingers found the catch of the door-panel. She could not stop to pick up the torch that fell from her hand and rolled against the Jacobean table. She closed the door again behind her. She shivered at the dark stair-head, with only the partition of oak between herself and them.

What would he do next? Be sure he would do something! He, too, knew of that little recess in which she crouched. He had only to pick up the torch she had dropped, fling open the panel, blaze the light into her face –

She waited, unable to move.

Then from the other side of the panel came Pamela's scarcely-heard quaver.

'Oh! Oh! Take me where it's light!'

Gervaise did not hear his soft laugh, but she could guess at it.

'It was – it was one of them, wasn't it?' came Pamela's piteous voice again.

Then his quiet, undisturbed tones – 'What? Who?'

'When you covered my face up – in the glass – '

'I don't know what you mean. Whatever made you shriek like that?'

'Oh, oh – ' Pamela sobbed.

Then, after an interval of time of which Gervaise took no account, and quietened by heaven knew what consolation, the sobbing grew gradually less and less.

Open the door, he? He had found a more damnable way!

And suddenly there came from Pamela a sharp, 'No, Freddy – no, no – '

The rest might just as well have been shouted.

'But you promised – '

'No, no – that was this afternoon – '

Gervaise heard his smothered, masterful laugh. 'A bit late to change your mind now, isn't it?'

The next thing that Gervaise knew was that she was leaning against the door at the bottom of the stairway, where the arch gave on the courtyard.

10

The pressure in her lungs gave her pain, as if she breathed only with the last cells of them. And as with her lungs, so with the rest of her. Emotions and sensations (but not yet thoughts) rushed upon her and mobbed her. Before one could be identified the next had swallowed it up.

What had happened? Where was everybody? Why (for the irrelevant things jostled with the relevant), why hadn't the servants locked this lower door? Why was she dressed in those clothes? Hadn't she been carrying a torch? What had she done with the key of her sitting-room?

'Oh, not all at once – one at a time, one at a time!' she wanted to cry, but could not because of the painful breath.

Then with so deep an expiration was she rid of its excess that but for the support of the archway she must have fallen.

Ah! that was better!

By and by it began to come back in images less disordered. It began with that trace of Turkish tobacco that she had known to be his. From that starting-point the rest fell into proper sequence. She saw them again under the crystal shower of the chandelier. She saw Pamela's weak upturned little mask. He had seemed to hold it as some conjurer or ventriloquist might have held a property-mask, he the wizard, she the puppet, to play her part in the little illusion and then back with Blanche and the others into the trick-box again.

'What is the matter with darling Pam?' Lady Harow had asked that afternoon. Well might she ask! Ask *him* what was the matter with her! He had had all the afternoon in which to perfect himself in it, and should know!

And presto! Even as Gervaise had watched, with a pass of his clever fingers the mask had vanished, and the *prestidigitateur* had advanced, with mocking eyes steadily fixed on her own.

Yet why had she not stood her ground? Why had she stood, dumb, and rooted there when she might have sprung forward and claimed the forfeit?

Had she been the guilty one, he the innocent?

She seemed to hear Pamela's voice again – '*No, no, Freddy, that was this afternoon*' – and then his soft masterful laugh –

They were still up there, with her torch lying on the floor to show where she had passed –

Gervaise stumbled out of the arch, out into the open court. Wildly she looked about her. Across the court, under a moon-gilded chimney-stack, was the latticed window of her own ground-floor sitting-room. She must escape quickly. She must lock herself up, be alone with herself.

She ran into the house.

But one other thing she had forgotten. Her sitting-room door was locked, and the key that she drew from the stiff-busked waist of the tableau-dress was that of her bedroom door. As if in some way he had been to blame for this mischance, the thought of him swept over her again.

Oh, devilish, devilish! Yes, doubly devilish, for surely a devil ought not to disguise himself as a devil! As an angel of light if you like; one allows a devil that; but to disguise himself merely as what he was!

Devilish too would be the skill with which he would presently be setting himself right with Gervaise. She could almost hear the low privy words in advance, for her ear only, as if she and he understood and the others were a mere spectacle.

'Poor Pam! Jumpy little thing! Of course *I* saw in a moment who it was. Pity you couldn't see yourself as you stood in the doorway there – really awfully effective – I confess you startled me for a second or so. But I had a feeling it might upset her. So I just covered her face up. I found that red rig of mine in one of the cupboards. What I don't understand is *your* bolting like that!'

And again (oh, you couldn't say that Gervaise did not understand her Freddy!): 'I suppose you dodged down those back-stairs? I nearly

opened the door, but thought perhaps better not. That would have
scared her worse than ever. And I say, Gervaise – I don't think I'd say
anything to her if I were you – she thinks it was all her fancy – best let
well alone, don't you think?'

A soft '*Oh*!' broke from Gervaise as she struck at the air with one
lace-cuffed fist.

In order to get to her bedroom she must cross the hall again. She
found it empty, but lighted; evidently her mother and Sir Walter
had gone to bed. But the half-completed puzzle still stood where
they had left it in its tray before the hearth, where the logs streamed
up the chimney in amethyst flames. Gervaise stopped suddenly in
her flight.

Whole again, was he, and lord over her once more? Ah, no! Not
so! She would see to that!

The lace-cuffed fist descended in the middle of the puzzle. The
fretwork fountain leaped into the air and fell again in a hundred
fragments. She plunged her hands among the wooden jigs, scattered
them, crushed them together, drove them this way and that.

And now a double handful into the heart of the amethyst there!

See them spit and flame and crackle!

That was the place for devils!

For a moment she watched the yellow flare that lighted the farthest corners of the hall. Then, with a stifled cry she ran upstairs.

11

'Gervaise! Gervaise!' they called to her as she sped past them. Their
game was over, and they were trooping down the staircase again, a
motley rabble of squires in beaver hats, men in Dutch trousers,
Philip in something frilly and satiny and green, girls in silver bells
and cockle-shells, girls in velvet gowns.

'It was Gervaise, wasn't it?'

'Wherever can she have been all this time?'

'And what's become of Freddy and Pam?'

A bright-eyed girl put her finger to her lips and made her eyes
brighter still. They laughed. Hilda was only seventeen, the youngest
of the party.

'But what *was* Gervaise supposed to be?' somebody else interposed.

'I know! Don't you remember those tableaux, Philip, when she got
herself up as one of the pictures?'

'Yes. The Lady Jane.'

'Then she was going to frighten us, all on her own! Brrr! I shall creep into your bed, Evelyn!'

'Shall you, indeed!' said Evelyn with a toss, and there was another laugh.

They made merry, discussed their escapade, told who had found. Men in beavers, men in turbans and sashes, got themselves whiskey-and-soda. Then, 'Bedtime – off you go,' they ordered the girls, and silver bells and cockleshells took their candles, waved good-nights, and moved off chattering upstairs. The men gathered about the table of glasses and syphons and cigarettes, helping themselves to nightcaps.

'Hallo, what's been happening here?' one of them suddenly asked.

It was what remained of Lady Harow's puzzle.

'Why, it's all over the place.'

'Well, we may as well pick it up.'

But in the hearth charred pieces were found, and more and more charred pieces.

'That seems to have gone west all right,' a squire in a beaver hat remarked; and they turned to other matters.

'Whose idiotic idea was this rag, anyway?'

'Pamela's, wasn't it?'

'It would be.'

'But did nobody see Gervaise?'

Nobody had.

'Well, mine's Bedfordshire. You fellows going to stay up all night?'

They finished their drinks and yawned.

'Do we turn out here, or are the servants still up?'

'Better leave a night-light in case.'

'Pity about Lady Harow's jig.'

'Well, 'night, everybody.'

They sought their candles and filed up the stairs. Philip's green frilled ankles were the last to go. On the table under the newel-post the night-light burned. Except for that, the glow of the dying fire, and the little gleams that came and went along the guests' wing, the Abbey on its rounded hill was in darkness.

12

Gervaise had heard their calling as she had fled past them, but she was not their hostess now. They must make shift to put themselves to bed without help from her. Usually they flocked in a body into her room, perched themselves on the edge of her bed, brushed their hair, chattered, laughed, made free with her toilet things, and remained until she shooed them out. But tonight she could not have endured their prattle. She had long since began to weary of it. She did not intend to go near her own room at all until they should have settled down for the night. She turned away in another direction, avoiding the corridors by which she had passed a few hours before.

It was immeasurably more than a question of Freddy Lampeter now, a thousand times more than the Abbey itself, with its crushing burden of maintenance and mortgages and debt. She had now to face the whole range of her own nature and its widest extremes, from her ecstasies if she had any, down to the last of her bodily hungers. And especially she must face that strange midway lack which, when all that she asked was to be allowed to give, kept her for ever inhibited and immured.

Only to be allowed to give, only to offer herself; like a box of alabaster, to be broken open and have her treasure spilt in sweetness! Was it too much to ask, with the rest of the world intent upon nothing but getting? Why should she be mistress of so many gifts and not of the final gift of giving? Is there *no* escape from that draconian law that is written in the blood of every individual heart that beats, that what we are we are, and so we must remain till the end? Oh, we seem free as the winds that blow! From our cradles to our graves we move in the illusion of liberty. We establish ourselves upon our fellows, do as they do, think their thoughts, and become indistinguishable from them. And then, lo, of a sudden there comes to us an hour. The unsharable thing has found us out in the midst of the multitude. One voice only reaches us in our isolation, the voice of our forgotten, nay, of our unlearned selves. For an hour, face to face with the void, we lie upon a bed that is only an anticipation of the bed of death itself.

And so it was with Gervaise. She must find an outlet for her generosities, her charities, her passionate love, her mere physical cravings, or break down. She must brave the angel with the sword, and force her way out of the Eden that had become her Hell. If prayer would save her she must pray. If it would not, better to sin with humanity than to die of heart-hunger in their midst.

She stood in a narrow, plastered passage with dim lancet-windows on her right hand. It led by the northern circuit of the house to the muniment-room, whence, by another passage, the picture-gallery could be reached. And it may have been that already she was on the threshold of one of those *nuits blanches* of hers, in which the ancient place itself played so fantastic a part. She knew where she was, but knew it as it were with an added sense. That old feeling of timeless familiarity with every winding of the house had begun to enwrap her. She knew that she had stood in that same passage before, not merely many times – the visitations were not to be counted in that way – but immemorially. This experience, whatever it was, was only a repeated former experience, the times between were inessential interruptions. She was seeking now what she had always sought, only with an added and immense urgency. It had nothing to do with the muniment-room – she wasn't selling anything, consulting any plan, verifying any title. It was not the picture-gallery – there was nothing there but scars on the dull red walls and a wintry old woman whose clothes she appeared to be wearing at that moment. What she sought she did not know – *but she was going to know in a moment*. She did not quite remember its magic name – *but that name was imminently in her ears*. And when the thing for which she was looking did come, it would be one of those always-known things, that the day kept under lock and key, but the night like a thief unpicked again. Why not? Was she one of the farm-animals, to be yoked to her diurnal task and given nothing but her portion of nightly straw at the end of it? This was her own hour, when she was released from responsibility. Whatever beckoned was implicitly to be followed. There was not a riddling door in the whole of that dream-haunted Abbey but sooner or later would open upon its own reply . . .

Suddenly and confidently, she put out her hand. She had a little thrill of joy as her fingers encountered what she had known they would encounter – a door in the plaster wall. She had no key for it, but out of some remembered knowledge of the day it seemed to communicate its own secret. She had only to put her fingers under a ledge, to lift and push gently with her shoulder, and open it would come. She pushed and lifted, and the door stood open.

The muniment-room. The slight increase of light told her that. It was a small octagonal room, with a roof-lantern that looked directly to the zenith; but the moon that peeped down on her was but a leaden moon now. Cobwebs, dust, dead leaves, the droppings and deposits of the years since the lantern had last been cleaned, besmirched its brightness. About her stood the dim array of chests, strapped and ironbound like church-doors, nail-studded chests, chests of peeling leather, coffers of wood, boxes of japanned tin, piled up against the walls, scattered over the floor. Old calf bindings looked through wire lattices, and in corners maps and plans stood rolled up like stovepipes.

But these were all. There was no revelation. Whatever she sought was not in the muniment-room.

But as she stood under the lantern, spectral in the stiff linen head-dress, one lace-cuffed hand resting on the table, all at once a light tremor took her. It was as if for the first time some insecurity menaced her suspended state. Her moving fingers had touched a piece of paper that lay like a dead moth on the dusty table. And in the same moment there broke in on her consciousness the distant memory of a voice, flat and jarring and without modulation. The piece of paper was one on which she had made notes the last time she had been there. The voice was the remembered voice of some estate-agent's young man or other, perhaps the one with the spots whom she had hoped they would not send again.

'*Quaint – I won't deny as it's quaint –* ' that voice that set her teeth on edge seemed to be saying, ' *– but a fancy property in a manner of speaking – not every buyer's money – now what about "Or near offer"?*'

Her agitation increased. Those people again! Even in the quiet night they must force themselves upon her, with their trade-cards and their orders-to-view and their notebooks and their pencils behind their ears!

She looked wildly about her, and suddenly, with a swift spring, was at the second door of the room.

It had a modern spring-lock, and, with her hand on the little milled knob, she opened the door just sufficiently widely to allow the slipping through of her body. Then, with a bang that resounded along the passage, she drew the door violently to again. She stood, panting and listening, almost as if she expected to hear an impris-oned young man beating upon the panels.

Those odious associations! *Those* unwanted presences! Then, as the echoes of the slammed door died away and no further sound came, she gave a deep 'Ah!'

But it had been touch-and-go, that!

13

To tell the truth it had been very much worse. That tranced solitude of hers had been threatened, if not actually invaded. And if one set of people could break in on her by mere force of memory like that, so could others. What others?

No need to look far! Almost anybody Gervaise could have named seemed to have this power over her. It was not for her, their hostess, to comment on these guests who slept under the Abbey roofs that July night. Pride forbade that she should whisper even to herself that they had outstayed their welcome. They might remain for months for all the sign that Gervaise would make. And she admitted that after all they were there at her mother's invitation.

But what was the good of talking to her mother? Her mother always made such haste to agree.

'I know, darling, I know! But it's *only* Philip and darling Pamela – it's ages since we've seen dear Philip, and Pamela will do her own room. You look tired, sweetheart – do run out and have a blow – '

No, no, they must not come near her! These unconscionable guests were not the people she had set out in the stillness of the night to find! She was looking for those older, more deeply-known friends of hers, the loving, understanding people, the helpful ones, who knew without telling what was in her heart and could draw it out, all the stored sweetness of her life, like wild honey found in the heart of a wall. Any others were only the weary day all over again. What she must now have, and quickly, was just the boon of mere rest. She wanted a hand laid without passion on her hair, the kiss of peace on her lids, a quiet breast on which to forget. Rest from night-wandering for her tired body, rest for her bruised spirit! Any seat into which she could sink would do for the first; as for the second, can there, except in Hell, exist such a thing as an unappeasable need? No, no, no! If God is not mocked, neither does He mock. To seek is to find! To hunger *is* to be satisfied at the last!

Heavily she stumbled along the black passage, wearily she pushed at the door at the farther end of it. She stood at the top of the three shallow steps at the gallery's end. She descended them, and dragged her feet to the embrasure of the nearest of the diamond-paned windows. She had reached the breaking-point. She sank into the window-seat, while the Jane of the canvas looked down on her from the wall.

Time she supposed, would use her so too. A year or two longer of beauty, a year or two more after that, and nobody would remember as much of her as her name. That inanimate thing on the wall would immeasurably outlive her; her portrait had never been painted.

Foolish, ever to have thought she could sell that Artist Unknown! Love her or hate her, the tie between them was indissoluble . . . Gervaise envied her her starkness. At any rate trouble was over now for her . . .

Across the grasscourt the wallflower and valerian lay velvety-black along the top of the Norman wall. At the wall's foot a single glow-worm burned in the grass, like a broken-off crumb of the unseen moon. Somewhere in the July night a hunted thing began to scream in agony. The screaming persisted intermittently for a time, and then ceased. But Gervaise heard nothing of it. With the linen-dressed head fallen on one gallooned shoulder, she slept.

That is to say she must have slept; for how else could she awake? She supposed she must call it an awakening, yet never before had she awoke after so strange a fashion. The chamber was a warm clear dusk, and somehow differently placed with regard to herself. She saw all its altered angles, not from the floor-level, but from above. She saw the thick dust on the upper edge of the portrait of the Lady Jane and the fastenings that secured the picture to the wall. The sheeted couch and the mantelpiece with the box of kitchen matches upon it seemed some yards below her. She felt light, free, and suddenly laughing to herself with tenderness and happy tears.

No need to look further for her peace. Here, in this unlocated, so oddly uplifted place, she had found it.

Nevertheless her eyes did range further. Past the sheeted couch, past the matchbox on the mantelpiece, she saw a huddled and widely-staring figure in tableau-garments in the corner of the window-seat. If that figure on which she looked down breathed, its breathing would not have stirred a feather; if an artery pulsed, then the pulse of the Lady Jane on the wall might equally have stirred. Gervaise knew that she had left that empty tenement of herself. She, the ecstatic one, was sublimated from that poor shell of thwarted desires. Unless she chose to re-enter it, that Gervaise in the mummer's dress was dead.

And why return? Why fear to gaze at the last upon one's own elements, these made pure, the others cast aside? There had been no pain. It had been the gentlest of subtractions, as if from some white beam a hue had been withdrawn, or as if some super-imposition, imperfectly coinciding, made the double image. Gervaise yearned divinely over that untenanted body in the window-seat that also was Gervaise. She put out her arms to that her lifeless sister, showering down on her an unimaginable love.

'Sleep, sleep, poor tired thing!' she silently cried. 'Sleep, for I have taken from you the honey that was in your breast! I flow with it, it gushes from me out of the Seven Wounds with which my heart was pierced! See, I put out my breast to you like the pelican! Eat of me,

feed on me, poor girl with the locked and hungry heart! For I am
your angel, who was kept from you for a time and times and half-a-
time, but bring you comfort now!'

So she rained it down, the thing that passes understanding, showers
of gentleness and pity, gifts of honey and oil and wine, Samarias
of love.

But all at once she felt a pang. The body in the window had made
a feeble movement. The gallery too seemed to have shifted again,
so that she no longer saw the dust on the picture's top, nor the
cracks of its varnish. She was sinking, being summoned back, re-
entering . . . A fleece that crossed the moon dimmed the clear
obscurity of the chamber. The old hangings took on a sombrer red.
New and recent gashes appeared on them. The figure in the window seat seemed to be looking for that other half of her, drawing
gropingly nearer . . .

Then came a moment rather than endure which death itself might
have been preferred. Her heart gave a horrible bound, and she was
back, on her feet, numbed and tingling, her hands fumbling about
her sleeves, headdress, busk.

What had happened?

Where had she been?

She did not remember. Neither did she know what she was doing
there in the picture-gallery at all. Her brows were knitted, as she
tried to remember.

They had been playing some kind of a game, but that had been
hours ago. And she had taken it into her head to dress as the Lady
Jane. Again her hands went to her head, as if to make sure. Yes, it was
so. She looked up at the picture on the wall, and there rushed back
on her the mood of the afternoon.

How she hated the woman, with her pitch-black unsheltered eyes
and mocking bony look! Never tell Gervaise that *she* had never had
her fling in her day. Gervaise did not know where she had this
knowledge from, but she would have taken her oath that all had not
been denial in *that* handkerchief-dropping lady's story! She had
been Sir Everard's lady; that had been her room with the antique
black four-poster between the two gilt French chairs; but – foolish
Sir Everard, if he had not watched her comings and goings! The
Abbey was large, and it was not difficult to push at the wrong door!
(Look like that as much as you please, Jane, but don't tell these
things to those whose descent is from your own body!) There
had been somebody, somebody to ask her private and disturbing

questions, and to choose delicately among her nerves until he had found the exquisite innermost one of all, and then to twang out its piercing note!

And probably he had not even pretended to be faithful to her, this lover who had exchanged glances with those pitchy eyes behind Sir Everard's back! Gervaise knew these gallants! Fear them in the field, but dread them exceedingly in the bower! To look at them one would think they had lain among cushions all their life! They went from house to house, from love to love –

Gervaise began to tremble violently.

Yes, from love to love – Blanche Chayter, a dozen others, even weak hysterical little Pamela –

Pamela, dressed as a *paysanne*, in wooden shoes and bare legs –

It all came back to Gervaise again – those two standing under the dim chandelier, he a bloody Mephistophelian red, like those gashes on the walls, her face seen for a moment against the poppy's heart and then swiftly covered up –

In vivid cinema-flashes it broke over her, shock on shock, sometimes in sequence, sometimes not –

His mocking story about the princess with the arm – Gervaise's own hands feverishly gathering up her mother's puzzle and casting it on the fire – his talk with her on the hill that afternoon –

'*Friends as much as you like, Freddy, but I have your measure –* ' they were her own words –

She had *not* his measure – she never would have his measure – he had hers –

Friends! What friendship could there be with a man whom she despised when he was not there, but to whose lifted finger she fell again the moment he made his reappearance?

And what had all that rant been of quiet breasts to lean on, kisses that weren't kisses placed on eyes, cool guardian hands placed on hair such as Gervaise Harow's? Was that a woman's business? Even wretched little Pamela had known better than that! True, she had begun by refusing, as a woman may well do –

'*No, no, Freddy – that was this afternoon –* '

Then his soft masterful laugh: '*Isn't it a bit too late now? –* '

She seemed to be at the head of the dark service-stairs again, listening to words beyond the panel that no doubt had been intended for her to hear –

Quiet breasts? . . . She laughed aloud. No, no! Breasts not *quite* so quiet! Hands a little *less* spiritual in their errands! Kisses an hour long, and not on the eyes either, but kisses that made shapeless the mouth, that satisfied, at least until the next one! –

Again her hands flew to her head, this time in a frenzy of energy.

Though she hated him she would love him! Loving him she would still hate him! But not for another hour would she go without!

In each of her fingers a devil sprang to life. There followed the linen head-gear to the floor a second garment, and a third. Her voice came in broken, suppressed, disordered interjections.

'Arms? He shall see, he shall see! . . . No, mother, you're not to kiss my arm . . . That was this afternoon, was it, Pamela? Too late now? Wait, Freddy! . . . And then perhaps I shan't hate you quite so much, Jane . . . "*And she stretched out her arm quite across the bedroom and the light was put out . . .*" My feet will be dusty . . . And then you can go, Freddy. I shall have finished with you. I shan't want ever to see you again . . . Now these – '

Off they came. She showed white as a peeled wand in the transparent darkness. Her rich hair made a wavy heraldic mantling where not a single piece of armour was. Then approaching the sofa, she passed the holland dust-sheet about her, while the Lady Jane watched ironically from the wall.

Past where the turned-down lamp stood in the angle of the guests' corridor there stole a barefooted sheet-wrapped figure that paused listening, now at one door, now at the next. At the door where the corridor turned it listened a little longer before putting its hand to the knob. All seemed to be still within. With infinite precaution she turned the knob. The door was not even locked. She slipped in and softly closed it again.

A man's suitcase lay on the stand at the bed's foot, a man's toilet-things strewed the table. But the morning moonlight that came in at the window showed no man's dressing-gown. It lay across an un-pressed pillow and an empty bed.

She stood still for a moment before opening the door again and drawing it to behind her. She had not even the key of her own room; that lay by a tumble of masquerade garments at the other side of the house, on the picture-gallery floor.

And why should she have taken his key from the lock and fastened his own door against him? Would that have been any help? What help – when from behind the door on the opposite side of the corridor there stole the scent of a freshly-lighted Turkish cigarette?

The Rosewood Door

I am a little world made cunningly
Of elements, and an angelic sprite;
But black sin hath betrayed to endless night
My world's both parts, and O, both parts must die!

Donne

I

The house was of moderate age, mid-Georgian perhaps; it certainly
did not date back to Charles, or anything like it. But its owners
were amateurs in houses up to their fairly comfortable means, and
Mr James in particular, if he happened to be passing a demolition
that looked interesting, would instantly make for the door in the
hoarding, risk the falling débris, and potter about on the look-out
for a bargain. In this way he had acquired, from an old house in
Soho, the Adam mantelpiece that beautified one end of his long
drawing-room. At a Bloomsbury rebuilding he had picked up a very
beautiful cistern of old English lead, with neoclassic figures upon it,
and this, mounted on a stone plinth, stood in the pond of his lily
garden and had been converted into a fountain. In one place he had
found a piece of inlaid pavement, in another a pair of gates of
wrought iron; but it was in Chelsea, at the breaking-up of an old
Caroline house, that he came upon the rosewood door.

The demolition was in the preliminary stage that always provided Mr James with his happiest hunting, and he happened to be
passing the place during the workmen's dinner-hour. The house
stood open, and past the contractors' boards at the gate Mr James
looked clear along the passage and through to the garden at the
back. The rosewood door had been dismounted and leaned against
the passage wall in full view, and something uncommon about it
had already caught Mr James's quick eye. He lost no time, for on
these trespasses of his he was occasionally approached and politely
asked what his business was. He walked up the paved path and
entered the house.

The unusual thing about the door he saw to be its slight curve, as if it had come from the wall of a circular room; but hardly less singular was its beauty. It was gracefully panelled, the lower part in tall linen-folds, and its proportions were exquisite. Even its solid brass hinges were tooled like the backs of slender volumes of poems, and Mr James noted with a pang the care with which it had been unhinged and taken down. Evidently somebody else knew its value too. Mr James looked along the passage for a curved wall. Then he began to roam over the house.

He found little else of interest. The house was historic in a middling sort of way, but as he went over its empty rooms, from attics to cellars, he found no trace of a curved wall. Possibly he had been anticipated by a century or two, and the door's history included an older house still. He reached the hall again and approached the door anew. His fingers touched its mouldings lovingly. He did not know exactly where in his own house he should put it, but the first thing to do was to make sure of it. He would cheerfully pay twenty pounds for it. And at that moment a pleasant young foreman entered, and Mr James fell into conversation with him.

The door? the foreman said. But it was curved! Now if it had been a flat one – not that it wasn't a pretty enough piece of work . . . He spoke almost in disparagement of the door's most singular beauty, and Mr James wished that the foreman had had the selling of it. He asked which room the door had come from, and the foreman scratched his head under his cap. That was odd now. He hadn't noticed. It would be Bill or Burkie who had taken it down, Bill probably. Sold? No, it wasn't sold, not that he knew of. They had only started on the job that morning. If the gentleman was a dealer and cared to make an offer for the lead –

After another covetous glance at the door Mr James left. At the gate he made a note of the contractors' address, and looked at his watch. It occurred to him that workmen began work earlier and had their midday meal earlier than the clerks in the offices, and there might be time to catch some responsible person before he went out. The address was quite near, in Pimlico, and the bus at the corner would pass the door. Mr James hastened to the bus, and five minutes later descended again.

He bought the door, for ten pounds – half the price he had been prepared to give. But as the firm would have accepted five pounds for a quick-sale-and-be-done-with-it, both sides were content. On his way back to the old Caroline house Mr James stopped at a furniture removers'. Here again all went smoothly; nothing, in fact, ever went so smoothly as the buying of that door. The firm had a packer actually doing nothing at that moment, and if it wasn't a long job . . . No, it was only to pack up a door, Mr James said, and he took the packer and his packing materials along with him. The door was carefully sewn up in sacking, with even the spare screws tied up separately, and Mr James gave a card. The thing was to be delivered at that address, he said, and despatched it was, that very afternoon. At four o'clock on the following afternoon it was lifted from the van at its destination, Mr James's home, which was some forty miles out of London, but whether south, north, east or west does not particularly matter and need not be told.

The house stood in about seven acres, and had a fanlighted window over the middle door of its façade with two rows of flat-sashed windows extending to left and right. It had been photographed in *Country Life*, a complete file of the bound volumes of which periodical, together with books on Landscape Gardening, Armour, Domestic Architecture and Italian Fountains, formed a good portion of the library – the second door on the right as you went in by the fanlighted door, level with the foot of the wide shallow staircase; and the room had tall windows that gave on the lily garden at the back. It was into the library that the rosewood door was carried, and there unpacked by Mr James himself, in the presence of the family.

They were unanimous in their praise of it and truly, by the time Mr James had finished with it and the mess of sacking and news-paper and cleansing-materials had been removed, it deserved all they said. Its flat curve was sufficient to allow it to stand up of itself and it had been placed facing the light, with the family and one guest gathered in a dark group against the window. It gave back the group from its depths, and the tall library windows also, and the garden outside, and the sky over the trees. The white bearskin rug at its foot met its own reflection, and the beautiful object did all this while remaining itself, true to every delicate level of its moulds and panels.

'What an adorable thing, James!' said Miss Virginia. 'What did you say you paid for it?'

'Ten pounds,' said Mr James, with modest satisfaction.

'Absurd! And was there anything else?'

'Nothing worth bringing away.'

'Can anyone guess at its date?'

'The house was Georgian, but I shouldn't be surprised if this was older.'

'The linen-folds suggest Tudor.'

'It may be.'

'It takes the light like a – like a – '

'Like a breastplate – '

'Like a curved decorated shield – '

'The question is where are we to put it?'

And that remained the question until Agatha Croft made a laughing suggestion. She was the single guest, and she had the gift of being frequently in the house, but she came each time as if a personage came, so that it counted almost as a sort of merit in the one who had had the happy thought to ask her.

'You'll most certainly have to have a door-warming!' she laughed. 'And in that case there's only one place for it, and that is to make it the door of the room of the constant guest!'

'Capital!' they applauded as they turned to one another. 'It always *is* her room, and the door will look straight down the stairs – quite the chosen spot of the house!'

'It seems almost a pity to have to put a lock on it.'

'Oh, I can't sleep behind a door without a lock!' laughed Agatha.

'A lintel and posts could be made to fit it – '

'Then need we say anything more? James must put it in hand at once!'

'It shall be put in hand tomorrow,' said James, and at that moment a gong sounded through the house and they departed to their several rooms to dress.

There was a smile on Agatha's face as she ascended the broad shallow stairs. They were dear and kind, these friends of hers, but oh, how old-maidish! All this excitement about a door! The smile broke into a contralto laugh. James, she sometimes thought, was the most spinsterish of them all. She remembered him over the Adam fireplace. He had fussed about it like a hen with only one chicken. Agatha herself sometimes caught a trace of their dainty amateurism; it is difficult to be often in a house and not to share the thoughts and interests of the people of that house. But Agatha sometimes turned round on it all. When all was said, wood and marble were not flesh and blood. She was in her room and half-way out of her clothes as she mused thus. She had taken her bath an hour before, to leave the room free for Virginia, and on her quilt a maid had left out her evening frock of Malmaison pink. She was a statelily-made creature, as if some special earnestness of intention had gone to her moulding, and there was a responsibility about her grey eyes, which nevertheless could dance with mirth. Wood! Marble! . . . She wanted something more in touch with reality than all that. Men had asked her to marry them, but she had shaken her head. She was six-and-twenty, but she could wait. She never doubted that the thing for which she waited would come. It might not be a happy thing, but at least it would be hers, gay or tragic or both. And him she would marry. They would move in this world, but they would also move in a world shared with none. It would be a fulfilment, an appointment made from the ends of known space and time, and faithfully kept. Never – and the grey eyes twinkled again – would he be the kind of man who 'carried' a proportion or a contour in his eye, as a woman 'carries' the colour of a ribbon she wishes to match.

And then came the impulsive contralto laugh.

'And what does all *that* mean?' she jested with herself. 'It means, my girl, that in the end you will do as other girls do – take what's offered you. And if you go on long enough nothing will be offered you, and there you'll be, left on the shelf like one of James's vases!'

She finished her hairdressing and approached the door of her room. It was of white glossy-painted wood, and she stood for a moment in the Malmaison pink before it.

Then she thought of James and his fortunate find again. She wondered whether they would really put it up in the place she had so laughingly suggested.

The second gong rang, and she opened the door and passed down.

2

Mr James went specially to the East End of London and chose the rosewood for the posts and lintel himself. He would have given another ten pounds for the members that had originally supported it in the old house in Chelsea, but he had seen none. In any case the workmanship must be of the best, and he went to a famous firm about it. The local carpenter removed the old door with its frame, and the local builder made good the broken wall again. The new frame was put up, and the rosewood door was carefully carried upstairs as if it had been a sick person. The family was slightly unhappy when the job was finished. There was nothing now to occupy them. But they went frequently out of the house and re-entered slowly, for the pleasure of seeing the door gradually reveal itself as they mounted the broad shallow stairs. All this took nearly a month, and Agatha had long since departed.

'But she must come and see it at the earliest moment,' Miss Virginia said. 'It was her idea to put it there.'

'And didn't she say something about a door-warming?' Mr James laughed.

'Why not? It's nearly a year since we gave a house-party.'

'What do you think, Arthur?'

'I think it a capital idea.'

The proposed party was discussed.

They dearly liked to show their house. With a little shifting about among themselves they could sleep half-a-dozen guests. Also after a measured fashion they danced, for, as Mr James said, to behave as if you were young was to be young, and for that matter they knew young people too.

'There are the Radcliffes, and of course Humphrey Paton – '

'Of course Humphrey – '

'They would drive over and go back again. But we should have to find beds for the Trevors and the Owens.'

'I could go in with James, if James has no pronounced objection.'

'Brother, I should be honoured.'

'There would be no need for Virginia to move at all.'

'And Agatha would go where she always goes.'

So, a week later, the invitations had been sent out and accepted, and the house was in a stir.

The time was early June, and the weather perfect. The cuckoo called all day long, and Miss Virginia's bowls were already full of Lady Hillingdons and Frau Karls. Outside the library windows the lily leaves trembled to the plashing of the lead fountain, and in the house maids in dust-caps moved furniture about – for the long drawing-room with the Adam mantelpiece was to be cleared for dancing. Some of the guests might remain for several days, but those living in the neighbourhood would come for dinner and the dance only, driving back at daybreak.

The preparations went forward apace. The dance was to be on a Friday, and on the Thursday afternoon Agatha Croft arrived, met at the station and driven by Mr James. Under the fanlighted door Miss Virginia kissed her, and Mr James himself carried her two suitcases upstairs. Before the new rosewood door he paused, his eyes expectantly on her face.

Agatha had fallen back, duly admiring the door. – 'Oh! then you did put it where I suggested!'

'Exactly where you said. *And* complete with lock. Let it welcome you,' said Mr James. And he opened the door and entered with the suitcases.

Later in the day other guests arrived, and dinner that evening was a merry one. They sat long over it, since the drawing-room had been cleared of all save its chairs and sofas, and the Adam fireplace and the clear showering chandelier reigned as its two beauties. Everybody had been shown what they called Agatha's door, and Mr James told again the story of the young foreman who had thought it a demerit that it was curved – 'as I once heard a man say of a most glorious twisted Elizabethan chimney-stack that it had been built on the twist because the builder hadn't known how to build a plain one,' he chuckled. They gathered afterwards in the library, but those who had come the longer distances began to talk of going to bed. 'We shall be late enough tomorrow night,' they laughed. 'Pray let us not breakfast at cockcrow, Virginia!' As a matter of fact there was to be no set breakfast. The meal would be taken in the rooms, and they might spend the morning in bed or get up, just as they pleased.

'So sleep well, and we shall all meet at luncheon tomorrow,' they said; and by half-past ten there was only one light upstairs, the light behind the rosewood door, where Agatha Croft lay reading in bed.

The maid who tapped at half-past eight the next morning got no reply. She tapped again and entered. Agatha was not there. But as the maid advanced to draw the curtains and let in the morning light she saw her below in the lily garden, standing by the stone margin of the pond, apparently deep in thought. She hoped that Miss Croft would look up and see her, that she might be spared the trouble of going round, but Agatha did not look up. A few minutes later the maid sought her and told her that her breakfast-tray was ready in her room. Agatha started at the sound of her voice.

'What did you say?' she asked, and the maid, who knew her well enough, said later that Miss Croft seemed 'all come-over like'.

'Your tray is ready in your room, Miss,' the maid said again.

'Ah yes. My tray . . . Is Miss Virginia down yet?'

'I think she's getting up, Miss. Did you wish to see her?'

'It doesn't matter. I shall be seeing her presently. It looks like being another lovely day.'

But an hour later the same maid, going into Miss Croft's room again, found the breakfast-tray untouched.

'Virginia!'

It was Agatha's voice. She was still idling in the lily garden, but through the open library window she had seen Virginia inside.

'Are you too busy to come out for a moment?'

'Of course not, darling;' and Miss Virginia stepped out. She was a pinky little lady, not the best person in the world to take a trouble to, by reason of the very excess of her solicitude and affection. She fussed and petted and comforted when the troubled person would have been better left alone. Agatha was plainly troubled, and Virginia was in a flutter already as she asked her what was the matter.

'I suppose I may take it that there isn't anybody about this house addicted to practical joking?' Agatha demanded without preface.

'My *dear* Agatha! What can you mean.'

'The Trevors? Or those people I haven't met before?'

'Darling! Haven't you slept well? If you haven't you won't be fit for tonight. I thought you looked a little run down when you arrived. You are up too early. Let me take you up to your room again.'

Agatha's eyes went up to the windows of the room she had left, which was immediately above the library. Then she said, 'Somebody came into my room last night.'

'My *dear*!' Virginia was staring at her. 'How can that be? Who would come into your room? Not the maids. Surely none of us. Not the Trevors. And as for the Owens, they're among the nicest people we know!'

'An armed man came into my room some time during the night,' said Agatha.

Even in making light of a thing Miss Virginia overdid the laughing off. She gave a high little laugh now, at which Agatha frowned momentarily.

'I see! I see so plainly! This comes of having dinner late. Or else you've been dreaming. Now put yourself in my hands. You shall take ten grains of aspirin and I will tuck you in myself, and put a screen round you, and nobody shall come near you. Or shall I ring up Doctor Benn?'

'Come up to the room,' said Agatha, and up in the room she went straight to the head of her bed.

'I was lying, with my head there, reading,' she said. 'There is the book, that little pocket edition. I read till a little after eleven, and then switched the light off. I don't know what time it was next, but I suddenly sat up wide awake. And that door opened' – she pointed with an abrupt gesture – 'and a man came in.'

'Agatha!' Miss Virginia shrieked.

'He stood with his back against the door. He seemed to fit into the curve of it. You would have thought he was bending the door with his back.'

'*Agatha!*'

'And he had a drawn sword in his hand.'

'Agatha! What are you saying?'

'I know. I know what it sounds like. That's why I'm telling you. And of course if it *was* one of the Mr Owens he knows all about it without telling.'

'But didn't you see his face?'

'No.'

'And weren't you terrified?'

'I was startled for a moment, but I wasn't terrified. In fact the moment I saw his eyes I wasn't frightened at all.'

'Then you did see his eyes?'

'Yes. They were looking at me – for me – I don't quite know – he seemed to want something – '

'And what did he do then?'

Agatha closed her own eyes for a moment. Her lip trembled. Then she opened her eyes again.

'I don't know. Except that I wasn't in the least frightened. I think I may have shut my eyes. When I opened them again he had gone.'

Miss Virginia seemed a little recovered. She put her arm about Agatha. – 'Darling, I think you closed your eyes for more than a moment,' she said sweetly. 'Of course it was all a dream.'

'Shall I show you I was not dreaming?'

'It could only have been a dream.'

For answer Agatha crossed the room. She opened the door of the hanging cupboard. From the cupboard she took out a straight bright sword with a chape across its simple basket-hilt.

'He left that behind him when he went out,' she said.

3

It was well that the guests were breakfasting in their rooms, for Miss Virginia was not the kind of woman to keep tidings so startling to herself. She stared at the weapon in Agatha's hand; then she stared at Agatha, as if she wondered whether she had gone suddenly out of her head. She laughed, in pure bewilderment.

'But Agatha! This is inconceivable! As head of the family James must be told at once!'

'I'd much rather he were not,' said Agatha quickly.

'But he *must* be told! If somebody is playing a joke – '

'I don't know what made me say that. That's a mistake. Nobody's playing a joke,' and she said this slowly.

'But you thought it might be one of the Mr Owens – '

Agatha shook her head. – 'I humbly beg the pardon of both the Mr Owens. Of course they wouldn't dream of such a thing. I can't imagine what made me say that.'

'Well, James will know what to do.'

Agatha stared. – 'How, to do?'

'I mean his judgment is always so sound.'

Agatha was looking at the sword again, down the length of its blade. – 'I'm sorry to be such a nuisance,' she said, and added, looking suddenly up, 'Tell James if you like. It doesn't matter. Perhaps I'd better put this away for the present.'

She crossed to the wardrobe again and replaced the sword, closing the wardrobe door.

It was in the library that not only James was told, but the assembled brothers also, for in such a matter the family was held to be one and indivisible, and Agatha had hardly said twenty words before Mr James put up his hand and asked her to wait till the others had been sent for. Then she began all over again. With one or two slight corrections from Virginia she repeated her story. She stood just within the library door, to illustrate how the man had stood. Mr James had taken his place at the writing-table, and his finger-tips were joined together. In his earlier days he had read a little law, and there was that in his manner that gave them all confidence in his ability to clear up the matter out of hand.

'So even the new lock didn't keep him out?' he smiled.

'Even the new lock didn't keep him out,' Agatha answered.

'Well, as everything seems to turn on the sword,' Mr James observed, 'suppose that interesting exhibit is produced?' And they had to wait till Mr Arthur fetched it, carrying it concealed in an old Burberry because of the servants. It was placed on the library table before Mr James, like the mace upon the table in Parliament.

'And now may I question you, Agatha?' he asked kindly.

'Please do.'

'Won't you sit down?'

'I will in a moment.'

There was silence in the library as Mr James began.

'In the first place you say you did not see this visitor's face – '

'Except his eyes – '

'Except his eyes. How was he dressed?'

Agatha seemed suddenly uncertain. – 'I hardly know,' she confessed. 'I wasn't thinking of his clothes. They seemed to belong to him as clothes do belong to people. There was a sort of soldier look about him, but I don't think he was in uniform of any kind.'

Mr James nodded approval. – 'Association of ideas with the sword. We will take it that he was not in uniform. If you had described his armour, let us say, your answer would have had far less evidential value.'

'A mere adumbration of things seen on the stage,' Mr Arthur put in.

'The Royal Academy has much to answer for too,' Mr Henry observed.

'Next,' Mr James continued, 'you tell us you were reading in bed. You switched your light off. By what light did you see this person of the sword?'

At this unexpected question Agatha was suddenly nonplussed. Her fingers went to her lips, her eyes were on the floor. She knitted her brows.

'You didn't switch your light on again?'

She looked up for a moment. – 'I don't remember doing so.'

'Was it by ordinary electric light? Romantic moonlight? What sort of light?'

'I don't know.'

'There's never been a hint of a ghost in this house,' said Miss Virginia tremulously.

'Let us put off the unknown till we have thoroughly explored the known,' said Mr James tolerantly. 'It is always possible that Agatha switched on the light without knowing it. Let us turn for a moment to the sword. You, Arthur, had once a few stray pieces, I believe. If I remember rightly you exchanged them.'

'I exchanged them for the rose-pink set,' Mr Arthur nodded.

'All of them?'

'All of them. I can show you the catalogue.'

'No sword was left over?'

'That you may take as certain.'

'And there has never been any other sword in the house?'

'I don't think this family makes mistakes about things of that kind,' said Mr Arthur with a satisfied little laugh.

'So it comes to this – that we are now in possession of a sword that came mysteriously into the house in the small hours of the morning. We're agreed that it is a sword?' he added quizzically, his fingers hovering over it.

'Perhaps it will vanish again the same way it came.'

'That of course would simplify our little investigation,' Mr James agreed.

Suddenly Agatha spoke. She spoke as if out of a deep musing.

'I'm so sorry, but there's one thing I forgot to say. He had a brown sort of look, very brown, as if he had been out in all weathers. And his head was of a rather steep and handsome shape.'

Mr James gave her a shrewd glance. – 'Ah! So he did not wear a hat?'

'Oh no!'

'You said dark eyes?'

'Wonderful eyes, dark and bright.'

'And a brown weathered face. The gentleman appears to be assembling himself.'

'But you told me at first you thought it might be one of the Mr Owens!' said Virginia almost reproachfully. 'Why, they're as fair as butter!'

Agatha made no reply.

'As a King's Armourer *manqué*, what date would you give that sword, Arthur?' Mr James next asked.

Mr Arthur approached the table. Then he crossed the room and reached down the armour book. Agatha's grey eyes watched his every movement resentfully. She suddenly hated him to touch that sword. She wished she was anywhere else. She wished she had said nothing about it all, even to Virginia. What good had it done? These people were pleasant and well-meaning, but she knew already that they couldn't help in this. Why wouldn't they leave the sword alone? . . . Again the faint smile rose to her lips. At any rate there *was* the sword. But for that they would have said she had been dreaming. Oh, why wouldn't somebody come in and break up this comic, important little court of inquiry, with its talk of 'evidential values' and its probing and futile questions? She wanted to laugh at them all. What did it matter that already there were discrepancies in her tale? If something she surmised was right there might be more discrepancies before long. Why couldn't they leave the sword alone?

Then somebody laughed for her. It was a voice in the passage beyond the library door.

'Where is everybody? Is there nobody to say good-morning to?'

The other guests were astir. The hosts looked at one another. The rest would have to be left to a more convenient time. The court rose.

But Agatha had done one emphatic thing almost before she was aware. Mr Arthur had taken the sword again and was putting it away in a sliding tray where photographs and folios were kept. She could not bear the sight of it in that slight and lace-white hand. She started forward, and on her face was her best smile.

'May I have my sword?' she asked.

Mr Arthur turned, also smiling. – 'Her sword, she says, James!'

'Well, it certainly isn't our sword!'

'Then may our Agatha have it?'

But Agatha had already taken it. Concealing it as well as she was able, half under her arm and half down her thigh, she ran out of the library, up to the room with the rosewood door, and closed the door behind her.

She was breathing quickly, but not with the quick run upstairs. She was excited at what was passing within herself. Downstairs they had baited and bothered her. Twice and thrice they had caught her out. Her tale had varied even at its first repetition, so that Virginia had raised her brows and corrected her. She had first said that she would not know her visitor again – then that she might – and now she knew that she infallibly would. She would know him by his marvellous eyes. She would know him by other things, that seemed to add themselves, one after another, as if out of the shadows into the glad incredible day. She had placed the sword on the quilted bed; she stretched herself beside it. It was *The Tempest* that she had been reading the night before, and the thin volume was still on her bedside table. She opened it at the lines and read:

'*And like this insubstantial pageant faded Leave not a wrack behind –*'

Oh, was Shakespeare always right, and was never a wrack left behind?

'*We are such stuff as dreams are made on –*'

Oh, could not our little life, just for once, be rounded, not with a sleep, but with a waking?

She continued to read, the book in her left hand, the fingers of her right hand tapping lightly on the sword's hilt.

Suddenly she dropped the book and looked round the room. She had slept in it dozens of times, but now she looked at it as if she had never seen it before. Here was the bed, there the wardrobe, there the dressing-table, there the glimpse of the lily-garden below. One thing only was new in it – the rosewood door. She raised herself on her elbow, looking at the door. She slid from the bed and advanced towards it with the sword still in her hand. Softly and richly red the door took the light of the window in its shallow decorated curve. All of a sudden she found herself passionately longing to know where the door had come from.

4

Only the inner ring of the family knew about the sword, but late that afternoon there happened something that filled the whole house-party with an almost awed delight. Miss Virginia was at the hall-telephone, and Henry and both the Owen men ran up as her explosive cry broke from her.

'*No!* – '

'What is it Virginia?' they cried.

'*Hush*! . . . When? . . . *Here*? Here *now*? . . . Oh, my dear, I always knew it! I was always sure that God had preserved him!'

'Virginia! What is it?' For other of the guests had come up, and Virginia's pinky face was as if tapers of thankfulness burned behind it.

'Tonight? Oh, at *once*! This *afternoon*! . . . Oh, my dear, my dear!'

Then she turned.

'Barty!' she said faintly.

'*What*!'

'He's alive! He's home! He's coming here tonight!'

'Barty Paton!'

'Yes . . . Oh, get me some eau-de-Cologne somebody – I feel as if I should faint – '

'Run upstairs for my salts, Sibyl – '

'No, it doesn't matter – ' Miss Virginia was laughing and crying both at once.

'Who is he? Anything to the other young Paton?' Charles Owen asked.

'Yes. Humphrey's brother. He was four years older than Humphrey. He was posted missing in '16. They have that place at Wychelm, about a dozen miles away.'

'By – Jove! What they must have felt!'

'Since 1916!'

'The waking of the dead!'

'By – *Jove*!'

And the more they thought of it the greater their wonder became. Agatha alone was not there, knew nothing of the resurrection. She was in her room, lying half-undressed under her quilt, in a profound sleep. The tea-gong had not wakened her, Virginia's push at the door and peep in did not waken her. Softly Virginia closed the door again. She met James on her way down the stairs.

'Agatha's fast asleep,' she whispered.

'I should let her sleep. That was certainly a most extraordinary circumstance she told us this morning. Is Agatha prone to – er – these experiences?'

'Most unusual I should say.'

'In any case she couldn't look a sword into existence. I confess myself puzzled.'

'What I'm most puzzled at is the way it seems to get added to as it goes on,' Miss Virginia opined. 'She said nothing to me about the man's being brown, nor having wonderful eyes, nor the shape of his head. And yet she's the most truthful person.'

'It is just possible that Arthur is mistaken, and that there *has* been a sword in the house all the time.'

'But how did it get into Agatha's room? She says she picked it up from the floor.'

'Agatha *is* truthful, I concur – ' said Mr James doubtfully.

'You surely don't disbelieve her, James! What earthly motive could she have for bringing a sword into the house and making up this story about it?'

'And I carried her cases up myself,' mused Mr James.

'Well, I shall let her sleep till it's time to dress.'

'I wish she'd sleep that sword out of existence again,' Mr James complained, for the thing was beginning to worry him.

'Well, if it was all a dream it would be as easy to dream it out as in;' and Virginia passed down the stairs, and her brother up and along to his own room.

With a stretch that refreshed every inch of her Agatha woke towards seven o'clock. Ah-h-h! *that* had been a sleep! Such a sleep was a thing to remember! She looked at her little travelling-clock. Only two-and-a-half hours! It seemed like a great space of life! Historic things might have happened in that mere portion of an afternoon! She sprang from the bed and ran to the tall wardrobe glass. She was frockless, slipperless, and she knew that her shoulders and back were magnificent, and rejoiced. Were they not worth taking care of? They were a trust, a debt, a promise. Already in her heart she exulted in the ratification. She reached for her bathrobe. She opened the rosewood door and peeped out – for it was the single defect of her room that it opened on the stairs. She passed to the bathroom. No frock had been laid out for her; evidently orders had been given that she was not to be disturbed; but she would choose her frock herself. Not the Malmaison pink . . . she ran over her frocks as she bathed. The golden velvet. Gold for gladness and the rising of the sun. Also gold for the golden voice in which she sang. She returned to her room and got out the frock. She heard the noise of an arriving car, but made no haste. The others would be in their rooms, also dressing, and some dinner-guest had arrived a little early, that was all. She thought she heard Humphrey Paton's voice. Humphrey admired her and hung about her and would not leave her alone, but she could never make herself golden for Humphrey. 'If there was a spare me you could have it,' she had told him, 'but I've only one, and I'm keeping it.' Humphrey had said he would ask her again. He might ask her again that night. It would make no difference. Sibyl Trevor was head over ears in love with him too. Why didn't Sibyl ask *him*? She was modern enough. Agatha was not modern. She wasn't anything. She was just Agatha – dressed in gold and passing out by the rosewood door that gleamed as richly red as her heart.

She reached the foot of the stairs. The before-dinner tray was always carried to the library, and Agatha put her hand on the rounded bottom of the handrail that curled like a shell. It encountered another hand there. Gazing, she saw that it was a brown and weathered hand. She was looking down into a pair of eyes – a man's eyes. The eyes looked up back into hers. She knew that in that moment her true life began. The miraculous thing was upon her.

5

At dinner that night Agatha Croft sat far away from Barty Paton. Humphrey Paton was on her one hand, Mr James on the other. Mr James seemed for some reason specially to take charge of her, but Humphrey's charge seemed even more special. As if, even if he had ever had a chance, there remained a hope for him now! She knew that with the other there would be neither asking nor offering; it was as it was, a sealed and perfect circle. Amazing! She did not even remember to have heard that there was a missing brother. And at the thought that these people had claims of priority over her own she laughed. Priority! Thenceforward there was neither first nor last, but only that sealed and perfect circle. Hearing her soft laugh Mr James's fears were confirmed in him. Something had happened to Agatha. A strange Agatha had come into the house. She had dreams about tall, brown, soldierly-looking men, and produced swords from nowhere. Agatha, of whom they had all been so fond!

Dinner ended. This tall young man so extraordinarily risen from the dead had not yet been introduced to Agatha The band in the drawing-room was tuning up. Suddenly she saw across the room the daring eyes in the steep handsome head fixed powerfully on her own. Straightway they asked the question, and she smiled and nodded the answer. She walked out of the room. Two minutes later he had joined her. This was where their hands had first encountered, on the scroll of the rail at the foot of the stairs.

'How brown you are!' she said, and thought the beginning perfect.

'Yes, I'm rather brown. Don't you like me brown?' he asked.

She laughed, as she had always known that one day she would laugh. – 'Well, I don't think I should have liked you pale. Where have you been?'

'Oh, don't begin that!' he too laughed. 'For the last twenty-four hours I've been doing nothing but tell people where I've been! Where *haven't* I been?'

'You know perfectly well I didn't mean that.'

'Are you staying here, in this house?'

'Yes.'

'Have they still got that lily-garden?'

'Yes.'

'Then come and take a turn in it.'

'Ought we to, straight away like this? So many people want to talk to you!'

'I want to talk to you.'

'We mustn't be long,' she said.

They went out by the library window. The music was loud at the other side of the house, but became softer as they closed the door behind them.

'What is your name?' he asked her.

'Couldn't you have known that too? Agatha.'

'Agatha.' He repeated it, and it sounded like a vow on his tongue. 'Mine's Barty.'

'I did know that.'

'Why did you put your hand in mine on the stair-rail there?'

'I think it was you who put yours in mine.'

'Give it to me now.'

She placed it in his.

'Now turn to me.'

'Oh, I am turned!'

'And now – '

That too she did, her mouth on his, the golden velvet gathered to his black and white.

'Now tell me when we can be married,' he ordered her.

She said, whenever he liked, and he mused.

'Of course you realise I'm a most infernal nuisance?' he said.

'Why, love?'

'Well, Humphrey for one thing.'

'He's told you?'

'He told me I should be meeting the girl he wanted to marry.'

'*You* ought to know how little hope I gave him!'

'Still, it makes rather a mess of things, my turning up. I see that already. They'd got everything nicely settled. Things were running smoothly. Then up I pop, and there isn't any place for me.'

'Isn't there?' Her laugh was as musical as the fountain among the lilies. 'See – try – '

And again they kissed, for a minute as still as the classic figures on the leaden bowl.

'All of which,' she said releasing herself, 'is manifestly absurd. You *must* come in.'

'Will you promise to come out again a little later?'

'Yes. But not with you. Come now.'

It was with Humphrey that she knew she must come into the garden later, but at present she could hardly spare him a thought. It was part of Barty's riches that they were precious with the griefs of others. He was not dancing; his dancing was eleven years old now; and what did it matter to her who her own feet danced with when her heart danced so for him? She hardly knew who her partners were. Where Barty stood conspicuous by the Adam mantelpiece was a constant group, that was added to and taken away from, but remained; and her eyes met his every time she passed. Then Barty himself left the group. She saw him in another part of the room, talking to James. And she would have taken any wager that they were talking about herself.

It was some minutes later that James came up to her. There was a harassed look on his face. Poor James, she thought. She was giving him rather a day of it!

'Are you dancing this dance, Agatha?' he asked.

Poor dear! Why should she tease him? – 'No. I'm talking it out with you,' she answered.

'Shall we go into the library?'

'Unless somebody's proposing there,' she laughed.

They found the library empty. Mr James did not so much begin as flounder helplessly into it. All his judgmaticalness seemed to have left him.

'This is an extraordinary announcement that has just been made to me – extraordinary! Incomprehensible!'

'What, James?' (And yet why should she play with him? Why not proclaim it in a loud voice to the world?) 'That I've just promised a man I'll marry him?'

'A man you never set eyes on till an hour or two ago! Extraordinary! Incomprehensible!'

'I'm not pretending it's exactly usual,' Agatha admitted, 'but then one's marriage isn't.'

'But there's measure – degree – suitability – '

'Oh no!' she interposed quickly. 'There's complete suitability, and there's the other thing, but I don't know of any degrees.'

'Unsound, unsound – a leap in the dark is always to be deplored – '

'Oh, but one *knows*! And I could never have married Humphrey.' (For James's heart had always been set on the Humphrey affair.)

'Humphrey's was always the steadier nature of the two.'

'But surely, dear James, you aren't trying to persuade me to change my mind!' she laughed at him.

'Only to common prudence, my child – not that I ever credited Barty with much – '

'I grant you he has a sort of neck-or-nothing look.'

'Neck-or-nothing! – Then there are all these adjustments that will have to be made – his death was never legally presumed, but naturally steps had to be taken on reasonably plain assumptions – '

'Do you mean to say they aren't glad to have him back?' (Because if *that* was so Humphrey's shrift would be short indeed!)

Mr James looked shocked. As if everybody wasn't overjoyed to see Barty back!

'Agatha,' he said, 'forgive my saying that there's something strange in your manner all day. Virginia's noticed it, Arthur's noticed it, we've all noticed it.'

A little of the irradiation seemed to leave Agatha. Her voice dropped a little. – 'You mean about this morning?' she said.

'We cannot pretend that the occurrence is yet explained.'

She knitted her brows. – 'It looks as if Barty and I were both nuisances,' she said slowly

'To go back for a moment to this morning, you will admit – may I say, the slight inconsistencies – '

'I know,' said Agatha.

'I suppose you couldn't unknowingly – subconsciously – I am at a loss for a word – in any way have brought that weapon into the house?'

Agatha's face suddenly cleared. – 'Oh no. I found it where I said I found it. And in *that* case – ' she added with decision.

'In that case what?'

'It comes to this, that Barty and I are both nuisances, and the sooner we stop being nuisances separately the better.'

'You mean that you are announcing the engagement?'

'There isn't going to be any engagement. We're going to be married immediately, and I'm going to speak to Humphrey now,' she replied.

6

The first rejoicings over, the everyday effects of the return of a young man from the dead have to be considered. They have specially to be considered when that young man is the elder of two brothers, and from childhood has been the dominating character. And the particularity with which they must be considered becomes extreme when the absentee's first act, and within a few hours of his return, is to carry off the young woman the other hopes to make his wife.

It began about the car. There were two cars, but one was only a Ford runabout, mostly used for short errands to the village, while the other was a magnificent Hispano-Suiza. Without asking anybody Barty took the Hispano-Suiza the very next morning, and did not return with it till late at night. He had been used to doing these things, and merely resumed his habits. On the following day he was starting up the car when Humphrey entered the garage.

'If you're taking that out do you think you could manage to be back by midday?' he asked. 'I rather want to run up to town this afternoon.'

'Can't you take the train?' Barty asked. 'I did rather want her for the day. Get Thompson to take you in the Ford to the twelve-thirty, there's a good chap.'

'Of course if this is going to be a daily business – ' said Humphrey with a shrug.

And there it was in a nutshell. There was every likelihood of its being a daily business. For various reasons a marriage within a couple of days had been found to be impracticable, but the master-reason of all was that by refusing to remain quietly in his coffin Barty had undoubtedly upset everything. Nobody dared say that he wasn't wanted, but things had gone much more comfortably without him. He even wore his brother's clothes until he could get some of his own, and how he was to be provided with money was still undetermined.

Fifty pounds had been put into his pocket to be going on with. But fifty pounds was not enough to marry on.

'You can have the Ford as a present if it's any good to you,' said the wretched Humphrey.

'Thanks,' Barty answered, stretching his sinewy frame as if to keep it in exercise. He almost added that he would see them all at the devil before Agatha set foot in a Ford, but instead he placed his hand on his brother's shoulder, for he was a reasonable sort of young man as long as he had things his own way. 'I know how you must feel, old chap,' he said. 'It's devilish rough on you, and don't think I don't sympathise. But she wouldn't have had you at any price, if you don't mind my putting it in that way, so where was the harm in my having a go? I'm hanged if I'd ask *you* to take *your* girl round the country in a Ford!'

'She'd have had me but for you. James says so.'

'James is just an old housemaid. *She* doesn't say so!'

'My feelings don't seem to count for very much.'

'I'm dashed sorry. I truly am. But I didn't cut you out. I won't say I'd have stood off in any case, but I'd have given you decent notice.'

'I hope you'll give me notice when you bring her over here. I'll take care to be out of the way.'

'Come, be a man about it,' said Barty, slightly contemptuously; and he started up the car.

The twelve miles of road between the two houses could be covered in about a quarter of an hour. People standing back in the hedges heard the roar, saw the flash of coach-work; and then stood looking into the dust when it had gone. No Fords for Barty! Then, pulling up at the fanlighted door, he descended – an unhesitating, hard-trained fellow wearing his brother's clothes and shaved with his brother's razor, brown as a gipsy, with a steep cropped head and eyes that flashed with daring. 'Where today, love?' he would say, bathing her with a look that brought all inner beauty to the surface as the sun brings out the perfume of a flower; and if she said the pinewoods the pinewoods it was, and if she had said the skies he would have attempted it. Their food was packed in a basket, and they would run the car a quarter of a mile into the wood and leave it there, while they walked or sat. And they talked gloriously, of nothing but themselves and the wondrous thing that had descended upon them.

'Oh, how heavenly to have waited!' she would murmur to him.

And sometimes he did not talk to her quite as he talked to everybody else, in the speech of the day, but after a dateless fashion, quite proper in a man who announced himself through a rosewood door before setting his firm, real lips on hers.

'But it was such an age!'

'How heavenly now that it was such an age!'

'I have always known and loved you!'

'How can you always have known and loved me?'

'Perhaps not so – nor so – nor so – ' The so's were crushed on her lips.

'Barty!'

'Spirit!' he breathed.

'It's all one with us – '

'Then what should I kill if you betrayed me?'

'Could you dream that I betrayed you?'

What did they mean? They knew what they meant: and it was because she knew what he meant that she never asked him what everybody else asked him, when he yawned and stretched that warrior frame of his and replied, 'Oh, all over the place – Central Africa, Nubia, Abyssinia, the Desert – ' If fragments of this did come out from time to time it was more when he spoke to others in her presence than to herself. For his wanderings in search of her had been in Abyssinias of time, not of earthly locality; through Deserts of years his longings had come to hers, as his body had now come to his father's house. They had known it separately before. Now they knew it together.

She too had one thing, and only one thing, that she kept from him. It was the episode of the sword. She tried not to think of the sword. She even feared that he might divine the thought in her mind, and that some nameless ill might befall if the sword came between. Also she had a more immediate reason.

For just as her account to Virginia had varied, so his accounts of these dual wanderings of his, of the body and of that other, varied.

She noted this, but she was not a Mr James, to place her fingertips together and talk of evidential values. What did it matter? If he had said that such and such a thing had happened at such and such a time and place, and later said it had happened somewhere else, it was all queer together, and he lied as innocently as she. However he had come to stay now, and she sometimes flung her arms about him, not out of passion, but for reassurance of his solid substance.

'Love,' he said to her one day suddenly as they lay side by side under the still pines, 'why *should* we get married?'

'Why?' she echoed, and then she laughed. 'Are you going to send me back to Humphrey?'

'I mean,' he went on, 'here we are, you and I. And as far as we can make out we've always been so. There's something about it – I don't know – somehow it doesn't seem to fit in with a church – '

She put her hand into his powerful brown one and spoke slowly.

'Dear, I am yours, now, in any place, at any moment. With ceremony or without. Here we are, in a lonely pine-wood. But I should like the ceremony.'

'The devil of it is this, you see,' said this lover who sometimes spoke with an angel's speech, as when he had called her 'Spirit!' and sometimes otherwise. 'I mean about getting a job of some sort. I don't mean Humphrey's actually making a stink or anything, but I was away the dickens of a time, and he was cock of the walk, and it's only natural. Then I blow in and pinch his girl, at any rate he thinks so' – he looked profoundly at her – 'but *you* know I didn't pinch his girl . . . you with those stars of eyes that come and go!'

'Barty! What are you saying?' she cried startled.

'Saying?' He gave a little laugh. 'I'm saying we've got to live on something, and I don't want to crab old Humphrey, nor upset the old folks either for that matter. In fact if it wasn't for you I think I should push off again.'

She looked at him with the last simplicity. – 'I am yours to do what you like with, my love,' she said.

'We were going to get married straight away. It's a damnable nuisance. Everything's hanging fire.'

'I'll do without a church, Barty.'

'Eh? No, no! I was a low-lived scoundrel to say that! It comes of living abroad, where they don't bring you early-morning tea and ring gongs for dinner and send you a writ if you don't pay your bills. We'll manage somehow. All I meant about the church was – hanged if I know quite what I meant!'

Why not now? Why not take it as it came? Was he not right? What had this sweet dark mystery of theirs to do with the church after all? The church looked with disfavour on apparitions that came through rosewood doors in the middle of the night. It called such things heathen and evil, and put them away into outer darkness. If Barty went away into the outer darkness again he must take her with him. If he could not take her with him then something else he must take with him, to be his remembrancer when perils beset him, so that he went about with a naked sword in his hand. The wood was still, the birds songless. The hand that had taken hers on the stair-rail was in her's now. Resolutely she drew it about her. She felt its firm closing on her.

'We are all alone, Barty,' she whispered.

As she spoke the barking of a dog was heard, not thirty yards away, and a man's voice that called.

She put Barty's arm away, rose abruptly, and shook herself free of the needles.

'Shall we go?' she said.

Her mind was made up. They must be married at once. She *had* preferred a church, and the church might be right in calling these things heathen and evil. If the church was right, then perhaps it had a remedy and a purge.

7

She went herself to the Faculty Office to get the licence. She went blithely, for the skies were smiling again. The house with the fan-lighted door was to be shut up; Mr James wanted to see certain Loire châteaux again; and suddenly one evening Virginia had exclaimed, 'James! What idiots we all are!'

'On any particular point my dear?' Mr James had asked.

'Why shouldn't Agatha and Barty have this house while we're away?'

'For a honeymoon?'

'Why not? The servants will be here on board-wages.'

'Odd nobody thought of it.'

'Why not?'

'But we want the car – '

'Trust Barty to get hold of a car if he wants one – '

'I hope Agatha won't go bringing any more swords into the place,' had been Mr James's comment: and a telegram had been telephoned that same evening.

With the licence in her pocket Agatha mounted a bus that went down Ludgate Hill. On one other point she was going, if she could, to set her mind at rest. James had given her two addresses. One was in an old street in Chelsea, the other quite near it, a contractors' place in Pimlico. She wanted to learn all she could about the rosewood door.

Why she wanted this she would have found it difficult to explain. She had so often slept in that room, and nobody had ever come into it as long as the familiar glossy-painted white door had remained there. But the moment they put in an unfamiliar door of rosewood things begin to happen. On her very first night there Barty came in with a bright sword in his hand, and eyes as bright as the sword as they had sought her own. He had not been since, for there had been no reason for his coming again *that* way; the very next evening he had walked into the house the proper way – in that hard-trained, solid, brown flesh of his. What had all this to do with the door? Might he not equally have come in by any other door? 'Agatha's door' they had jestingly called it. But she knew that it was his door, not hers. And Barty was to enter by it once more. He would spend his bridal-night behind it.

'Sloane Square.'

She got off the bus. She had looked at the street plan, and had found that the street she wanted was a bare ten minutes away. She set out on foot, and found the place Mr James had described to her. His description was quite accurate, for there was nothing there. There was merely a gap in the street, and a board that announced an Eligible Site for sale.

So that was that. She turned away and sought the other address.

At the other address they received so beautiful a lady with bowings and chair-placings. Indeed she was so beautiful that more heads turned to look at her in the street than did not. That was Barty's doing. Sometimes she could almost look at herself in the glass, say to herself 'You're a little tired-looking under the eyes this morning, my girl,' think of Barty, and find her eyes those of the lovely name he had called them – the eyes that came and went. She could feel as it were a gushing outward at the thought of him. And was she not thinking of him now? Trying in some way to keep him? To save him? . . . They asked her to sit down, and pressed about her, and got out their letter-books and files.

Yes (they said), that was a job of theirs. Who had been in charge of it? Here it was; young Merritt; see if he's in. There entered a pleasant-mannered young foreman. He was told to tell the lady all she wanted to know.

But Merritt's all was little. Yes he did remember a gentleman coming in to look at a door, a thinnish, greyish sort of gentleman, who had asked if there were any curved walls in the house and which room the door had come from. And Merritt hadn't been able to say. Burkie might know, or Bill –

But Burkie and Bill were on a job and could not be called in.

'What was the date of the house?' Agatha asked.

Well, now, the dates of houses had more to do with them that built them than them that broke them up, but they might say about Charles the First. Or Second. Or George. Wasn't the gentleman satisfied with the door?

And as Agatha could not tell them how infinite was her own satisfaction with it, she left.

She went next to her furnished lodgings. She and Barty might presently have to go into furnished lodgings, but not these; she felt a little about them as Barty had felt about the Ford. Barty would have to get a job. She herself might have to get a job. You can wait alone indefinitely on a shadowy, spiritual inheritance, a few hospitable friends and a hundred pounds a year; you can even get married on them; but what about the years to come? She wondered, she wondered . . .

That night she was taken to the theatre by some sketchy person, who of course proposed marriage to her. This pleased her, because it was yet another gift to Barty. On the following day she was to see Barty again. He was coming up to town in the Hispano-Suiza, and they would lunch at a teashop if she had her way, at the Hyde Park if he had his. Then in the afternoon he was going to drive her back . . . He duly appeared, and they lunched at the Hyde Park. They did not drive straight back to their hosts of the house with the fanlighted door, but made an excursion into the pinewoods again. They visited the very spot where she had offered herself. And now the licence was in her bag, and it was to be in a church after all. She was glad.

'Agatha is looking *most* radiant this evening!' Miss Virginia admired, late that night after Barty had departed. Their trunks were packed and they were off shortly before midday on the following day. They had wisely deferred their choice of a wedding-present, saying that they would wait and see what was most needed.

'She is expected to be making rather a special effort at being beautiful,' Mr Arthur said with a twinkle.

'You will consider the house absolutely your own, darling?'

'Servants, everything – except, alas, the car, which we *must* take – '

'You dearest, kindest things!' said Agatha, her heart full, and shortly after they all went to bed.

From tomorrow morning on, when they would depart, and until after the wedding, there was now one house closed to Barty, and that was the house where she was. And as she sought her room that night it occurred to her quite suddenly, so that her heart gave a momentary flutter, that the man whom she was about to marry had never seen the rosewood door she had just closed behind her. The dining-room and the drawing-room and the library of the house he knew, but he had never set foot in its upper part; indeed he had spent almost more days in the pinewoods with her than he had hours in the house all told. There was nothing strange about this. There was nothing strange about the door, except that the people who might have known seemed to know so remarkably little about it. Except for a book-entry that had been shown her the whole transaction might have been purely legendary. Then she put out her light and forgot about the door. A woman whose wedding is to be in two day's time has other things than doors to think about.

Or at least she should have had plenty to think about; curiously, she had not. Nor apparently had he. Normally he would have been saying goodbye as a bachelor to his friends, she would have been surrounded by busy chattering girls. But he had no friends, and by midday tomorrow her own friends would be on their way to France. What would happen after their return was dark and uncertain. Furnished rooms perhaps, or Barty might want to wander again and take her with him. She had no idea how he had lived during his wanderings, but wildly enough she had little doubt. But she cared nothing about how he had lived in the past. There lodged in his body a spirit special to her own. Lacking a word for the implied lineage of love between them they spoke as it as 'it'. For 'it' she had waited, and 'it' had brought them together in the end. Whatever happened 'it' would have been, and having been was a thing that all eternity could not cancel.

By midday the next day the car was ready, the luggage loaded up, and Mr James was looking at his watch.

'Time we were off,' he said.

'Goodbye, my darling, and every, every happiness!' said Virginia kissing her.

'We all wish you more than we can tell you,' James said.

'We must all kiss Agatha.'

They kissed her, beginning with James and ending with Virginia again, and the car moved away.

Agatha returned to the house. A great solitude seemed suddenly to have fallen upon it; she had not realised how comfortable and livable a thing the gentle spinsterishness of these hosts of hers could be. She went from room to room. The whole house seemed to have come to pieces. Its fanlight was its own, and possibly its shining stair-rail, but, without James as its purchaser and proprietor, the Adam mantelpiece showed out suddenly as a borrowed thing. It was as borrowed as Barty's clothes, as borrowed as their bridal-bed. The chandeliers seemed to be twinkling at some older memory; and the leaden cistern on its plinth chattered softly that it had never been meant for a fountain at all. She wished Barty would come. He could at least take her out in the car. As a matter of fact he was taking her to see his people that afternoon. Three times already she had been there, and had been glad each time that Humphrey had had the consideration to be somewhere else. She was looking out of one of the front landing windows, hoping Humphrey would do the same today, when she heard the tearing note of the electric horn and saw the rush of the car up the drive. She ran down, seizing a hat and coat as she went, and hardly knowing why she ran. Barty had thrown down his cap and was advancing along the hall.

'Have they gone?' he demanded.

'More than two hours ago.'

'Hang. I should have liked to see them. I tried to get away, but they kept me.'

'I'm just ready. I was waiting for you.'

'There's no hurry, is there?'

But at something in his kiss she moved out to the steps.

'And as I'm mistress now I suppose I'd better close the door,' she said.

He stared a little, but 'Oh, all right,' he said, and fetched his cap and put it on again.

Clear of the outer gates she had to ask him not to drive so quickly, for the hedges were swimming past in a blur of grey-green.

'Oh, we may as well get there and get it over,' he said. '*How* I loathe it all!'

'All what?'

'Oh, all this infernal talk about things that don't matter! As long as we've something to eat and a roof over our heads – '

'We've a very nice roof over our heads, at any rate for a few weeks – '

'All this talk about permanent arrangements! How can we tell? There may be an earthquake for all we know! As if there wasn't enough for everybody!'

Her heart sank. – 'Do you mean Humphrey?' she asked. 'Oh – all this putting things in black-and-white as they call it – '

He took a bend in a manner that brought her heart back again and into her mouth, and they drove on in silence.

She saw. There was not much doubt about who was master of the house they were approaching. It was Barty. Barty was behind everything. It was Barty who, magnificently, would not hear for a moment of Humphrey's dispossession, but it was also Barty who would turn round on his brother with bright scorn and ask him whether *he* would have made a fuss about a few beggarly hundreds or whatever it was! She knew that in Humphrey's place he would have behaved exactly as he wanted Humphrey to behave now; he hated money; and yet, even when he was saying that he didn't see himself squatting down on a few score of acres and dozing out his days there, there still remained that in his eyes that Agatha shared with none, not even with the mother who had borne him.

The reverberations of the family discussion seemed still to linger in the dark-walled study where old Mr Paton retired after meals to slumber and Humphrey administered for him. Mrs Paton was there too, frail and twice aged, once by her son's vanishing from the world, and again by the destroying joy of the first days of his return. Agatha shook hands with Humphrey, who seemed bent on showing himself reasonable before his outrageous and unreasonable brother. Apparently there had been a breathing-space, for Humphrey returned to the matter.

'Well, now that we've all had time to think,' he said, 'is it too much to ask that we should at least know where we are?'

'Not at all, my dear fellow,' Barty replied, his hands behind his head as he lay back in a long chair. 'I thought I'd explained that.'

'You made a great deal of fun of people who ventured to have opinions different from your own, if that's an explanation,' Humphrey replied.

'I've told you I'm trying to get some sort of a job. You know useful people and I don't, or at least you ought to. I've made absolutely no difficulty about things as I found them.'

'Except that we're merely to be your bankers. We're prepared to be your bankers. But we should like to know to what extent.'

'Do you mean how many meals a day I eat and how many suits of clothes I want a year?'

'Barty, it's impossible to talk to you. I should have thought that in the circumstances – ' poor Humphrey checked himself.

Agatha's eyes were beseechingly on old Mrs Paton's. Barty's mother rose shakily. She reached for Agatha's arm.

'Come and see my dahlias, Agatha.'

She was as much under Barty's domination as the rest, and had as little to set against it as they, but she was his mother, and this was the girl he was going to marry. A single glance at Agatha had told her how it was with her; her son would be able to do little wrong in the eyes of one so much in love as *that*! Well, well. People had to find out these things for themselves. Her experience told her that it was better not to know what was ahead. Thinking Barty dead had in some ways been better than having him back like this – not better that he should *be* dead, but better that she should have thought so. It had indeed been a question whether she would survive his return. His going away again she would not survive. Her hope of Agatha was that at last her arms might keep him.

'It is very difficult for them both,' she complained shakily to the dahlias. 'Don't forget how difficult it is for Humphrey too.'

Agatha sighed. – 'I'm the cause of the trouble.' But she knew that it was not true, and that something that was neither herself nor Barty was the cause of the trouble.

'You won't expect more of him than he can give you, will you?'

'No,' said Agatha in a low voice.

'He's headlong, he's passionate. And remember that doesn't last. It burns itself out. He might even leave you again.'

'I know. I'm prepared for it. We all have to take chances, and this is mine.'

'I hope you aren't making a promise to yourself that you won't be able to keep,' said the tired old mother.

'Is it true,' Agatha asked very slowly, as a young woman to one with all her years behind her, 'that if people had a second chance they would do exactly the same again?'

'I cannot tell, my dear – I have seen too much trouble to be able to tell you that.'

'Because,' said Agatha as she passed her arms about the old lady and looked down into her eyes, 'I do see what Barty is. He is tyrannous. He is so wilful himself that he laughs away the wills of others without hearing what they have to say, and you can't laugh away people's wills like that. I don't think I shall be happy with him for more than a very little while. I'm not sure I shall be happy at all. I think I had my chance of happiness with him, and it's already past. But if Barty were to come to me again, as he did before, and I knew all this and a thousand times more, I know I should do the same thing again.'

'I hope you may be right, my dear.'

'Oh, I may not be happy – but I'm right!'

And they went on, almost as if it were some other person's affair, to talk of the wedding.

They had tea, she and Mr and Mrs Paton; and not long after Barty sought her. He was ready to take her back. She knew that his idea was to come in with her and she was as resolved that he should not. She had taken another resolve too, of which he should hear presently.

'I'm ready,' she said.

He drove her back at even greater speed. One would have said that he was pressed for time, in some desperate strait. Before the fan-lighted door he vaulted from the car and waited for her to produce her key. She stood with the key in her hand.

'Good night, Barty,' she said.

'Open the door.'

'When you've gone, dear love.'

'Do you mean I'm not to come in?'

'You can't possibly come in, Barty. You see that.'

Suddenly he laughed. – 'Well, I suppose it's all of a piece. I've had a day of conventions, with Humphrey and now this. But of course you're right, sweetheart. There are the servants. I quite see.'

'There's another thing I want to ask you,' she said.

'What's that, dearest?'

'I want you not to come tomorrow at all. I'll meet you the morning after, at the church.'

'Not see you tomorrow at all!' he repeated, dumbfounded.

'Not again until we meet in the church.'

'Heart of mine, something's the matter. What is it? Tell me,' he urged.

'Only that I love you, Barty.'

'Come for a turn in the lily-garden, where I first kissed you.'

'Not now, Barty. I want to go in. And I want you to go home.'

'Don't you even want to know what I fixed up with Humphrey?'

'Later. Please, Barty – '

She turned up her face.

A few minutes later he was on his way back, but he drove as slowly as if the road had been newly tarred and he wished to save the Hispano-Suiza's bodywork from splash.

8

It was what she had told his mother – that she was not sure she had not had her chance of happiness with him, and it had passed now for ever. There was one nook of the pinewood that she wished to visit again, alone, and it would not matter this time if a man did come past with a dog and a gun. On the day after that she would be his wife, and they would come here to this house together, but in a sense closer and dearer than she could have expressed she felt that that other should have been her bridal, that no church had assisted at. Oh, with what a pain she loved him, and how exquisitely unendurable that pain would be were that afternoon in the pine wood to be *really* all! But why should it be all? Was he not coming here, into this room, by the very door he had first entered at?

She was lying in bed with the reading lamp on. There was a thin volume there; it was *The Tempest*, and it lay open at a page. Her eyes caught the words.

'And like this insubstantial pageant faded Leave not a wrack behind – '

They were the very words she had been reading that other night, an hour or two before he had come in –

She had seen only his eyes then, and a dim brownness and tallness, and the vague steep shape of his head –

But since then he had drunk her very soul at her lips –

There was another door he had yet to enter for the first time, a door that had never been entered –

And she remembered that he had come with a sword.

She could not truthfully have said that she was not frightened now.

She was frightened with a fright for which she could give no reason, for those were not reasons, that a builder's man didn't know which room an old door had come from, that James could not date it, that she had jestingly suggested that it should be fitted to her room and they had agreed. That door admitted too much strangeness. It had let one mystical fulfilment in, but it might let in a doom too. It did not even look as still as a door should, softly shining there beyond the electric lamp, for a flat door is a door at rest, but one that is shaped like

a bow suggests spring and compression and power. And she had seen
Barty with his back in it, a sword in his hand, looking for her

Her decision came to her swift as a flash. He and she must not
occupy this room. Barty must not even enter it. He must not as
much as . . . ah! But that was impossible! There the door was, the
most conspicuous thing in the house, the thing one's eyes rested on
a third of the way up the stairs. He could not help but see it. Wild
ideas of covering it up with a curtain, of taking it down altogether
and putting up the quiet white one again rushed through her head.
But she couldn't go moving other people's doors about like that. At
all events they would change to another room. Almost frantically
she ran over the rooms available. Not Virginia's room of course;
there could be no bridal there. Nor yet the room James had shared
with Arthur. In fact not any of their rooms. Any old room would do,
a maid's room, a box-room, an attic. But not the room with the
rosewood door. The servants would think it odd, but she couldn't
help that . . .

She fell asleep still passing the rooms of the house in review.

The next morning she put as bold a face on it as she could, sought
the housekeeper, and gave her first directions as temporary mistress of
the house. She wished her things moved to another room, she said.

Mrs Bradley beamed fatly and comprehendingly. Agatha was a
favourite with them, and the whole of Mrs Bradley's staff was
as excited about the wedding as if they had been getting married
themselves.

'To be sure!' Mrs Bradley said. 'If it was me I should feel just the
same!'

Agatha gave her a startled look.

'Not that your room isn't a nice one, and over the garden too,' Mrs
Bradley went on. 'But when a room's always been Miss Agatha's room,
and Miss Agatha isn't going to be Miss Agatha herself many hours
longer, as you might say – '

'Oh! I see.'

'And me can hardly get a hand's turn done, with all the maids in
such a stir about it – '

'I can never understand why everybody's so good to me,' said
Agatha wistfully.

'Ah! That's people's different natures, Miss Agatha. Some calls forth
liking and some the other thing. Which room were you thinking of?'

'Not any of the family rooms.'

'If you could spare the time to walk round – '

Agatha and Mrs Bradley walked round together, but Agatha already knew the portion of the house she wanted. It was the portion as far away as possible from the rosewood door. This left her the choice of the two ends of the house. But the upper room of one end was a sort of museum workshop, where they polished and repaired things and put away objects when their eyes grew temporarily tired of them, and that left only one room, dimity-papered, carpetless, and with a large brass bedstead without as much as a piece of felt over the bare springs of its box-mattress. Mrs Bradley was turning away.

But 'This will do beautifully,' Agatha said.

'Miss Agatha! I should be ashamed!'

'It's beautifully light. (And it hasn't got quite such a mad-looking sort of door,' she added to herself.)

'But not a curtain or anything! Whatever should I say to Miss Virginia?'

Agatha laughed. – 'Say I wanted it because it looks towards Mr Paton's home,' she said.

'And what would Mr Barty think, and the best of everything *never* any too good for him!' Mrs Bradley protested.

'Well, he's supposed to be getting the best of everything in me . . . I should like this room, please Mrs Bradley, if it could be got ready in time.'

'It could be got ready. No bother about that. But it hasn't even a light to read in bed by without getting up to turn it off.'

Agatha's reply was repeated afterwards by Mrs Bradley to Mr Crooks, the butler, a sedate and family-sort of man, but as fond of his chuckle as here or there a one.

'So she looked at me with those beautiful eyes of hers, like pools, they were so full of what was to come, and she put her cheek so close to mine that I declare I could feel the blush warm on it, and she smiled and said, "Did *you* read in bed, Mrs Bradley?" and there it was. Ah, he's a lucky one, is Mr Barty, it's to be hoped he knows it!'

True to his promise, Barty kept away, and that afternoon she took the longest walk she had taken for years. It was six miles as the crow flies to a certain spot in the pinewoods, but she was happy in having no car, since to walk made it in some sort a pilgrimage. But perhaps pilgrimage was not the word, for pilgrimages have to do with churches, and it was to a place where she had offered to set the church aside that she was going that afternoon. She reached it, a part of the wood so seldom visited that hardly from one year's end to the next would a man with a dog and a gun pass by. She cast herself down on the dry fragrant needles, in the same spot where she had lain with him. She felt herself taking his strong brown hand again and drawing it about her body. Tomorrow it was to be so in reality. Through one door he had come, but there was to be no such door for him to go out by. Cunningly she had changed the room. Even Barty would find it difficult to escape again through *that* ordinary machine-made door with dimity wallpaper about it! She would have him fixed, found, clenched happily down. All the space and time he would need thenceforward until death he would find in her heart. The Licence she had obtained at the Faculty Office was usable anywhere, but she had had to make a declaration that one of the parties had lived for the space of fifteen days previously in the parish of the church where the marriage was to take place, and she had smiled in signing it. Barty had actually lived for fifteen days in one parish! Therefore they were to be married in the church near his home. Only Barty, herself, his parents, and old Doctor Benn, whom James had entrusted with the duty of giving her away, were to be present. Then, Barty's idea was, a dash up to town in the car, a jolly matinée somewhere, and back to the house that was their temporary home.

She lay long in the pinewood, musing, musing. The world, she thought, had been very kind to her. She had friends, a hundred or so a year, and now that shadowy bequest that had brooded over her all her days was to be inherited in reality and light. She looked about her for the last time. Her sacrifice had not been accepted, but it was in this spot that she had made it, so that earth had no other place like it. She put her face down to the needles. She kissed them. Then she rose and set her face the way she had come.

On her return Mrs Bradley met her.

'Would you like to see what we've done, Miss Agatha?' she said, and up they went to the room at the end of the wing.

If the best of everything was none too good for Mr Barty, neither was it for Miss Agatha. A carpet of violent crimson, unearthed from heaven knew where, covered the floor. Long curtains of stiffly-starched lace, looped back with broad blue ribbons, fell from the window-poles to the floor. A primrose-yellow quilt covered the bed, and over the head of it hung an engraving of 'The Light of the World'. There were other pictures too, and china ornaments on the mantelpiece.

'And it was a pleasure to do it,' Mrs Bradley declared, 'for there's some odd-fangled things about this house, what with Mr Arthur's

Chinese ladies with knobs sticking out all over their heads and I'm sure I don't know what! The Hunt' – she had picked up the family habit of speech – 'is a little present from myself. The Sadler' – she pointed – 'is from Mr Crookes. And the ornaments' – she pointed again – 'are a lend from Annie; she has them against when *her* happy day comes along, which we hope won't be long first, for she's a good girl and deserves it.'

Whatever gift she should receive from Virginia and James could never mean more than the warm-heartedness that had gone to the making ready of the room. Not for anything would she have removed an ornament or taken a ribbon from a curtain.

'You dear, kind things,' she said. 'But I shall sleep in the other room tonight.'

'To be sure. It makes a difference, like,' said Mrs Bradley, understanding to the end. 'Your things are all laid out, and we'll carry them over tomorrow.'

That night Agatha slept for the last time but one in the room with the rosewood door.

9

The wedding was curiously of a piece with the rest – the still and relaxed house, the uncertainty of the future, the atmosphere of un-reality in which she seemed to move. It should have been something to remember, and yet she remembered little of it afterwards; it even seemed insignificant. She was hardly aware of Doctor Benn's arm on which she leaned, little more aware of Barty's parents, of Barty himself. As the vicar spoke the words, in a low, almost conversational voice, she found her thoughts wandering to the pinewoods. Even when Barty put a ring upon her finger it was the same, and when she rose from kneeling and came out of the church again, it was as if she were still waiting for something to happen, and somebody said to her, 'That's all.'

No more real was the run up to London, nor the lunch at which she drank champagne. After lunch they went on to a theatre some-where, but except that she sat in a stall, watching the quietly intent face of a woman who played the fiddle in the orchestra, she did not remember very much. People were laughing, and there was a confusion of lights and colour and music. The woman who played the fiddle was earning her living. Agatha supposed she would have to do something about a living too. Barty, by her side, was laughing from time to time; he seemed to be enjoying himself. She felt the new ring on her finger. Assuredly it was real. Barty had placed it there, and in a church, so that was all right too . . . And then Barty was standing up, stiff and soldierly by her side. The conductor had turned round, and they were playing God Save the King. She watched the woman fiddler go out, with the fiddle under her arm. She and Barty went out. He told her to wait, for he had left the car a street away, and she waited, looking at photographs. He came back, and she got into the car. There were cars, buses, taxis, lorries, vans. Barty impetuously seized openings, braked as suddenly. Then came a long wide road, and the car leaped forward. She knew when they were clearing London by the open spaces with factories dotted here and there.

'Ah!' said Barty, as they reached hedges and fields and trees. 'I think we can let her out a bit now – '

Mrs Bradley and the servants were gathered about the front door of the house. Barty was wearing his own clothes now, though they were paid for by somebody else, and other people's servants welcomed him into a house not his own. None the less he who had no house picked her up and carried her over the threshold of it. Mrs Bradley was still at her congratulations. She had had a fire put into their room, because of its not having been used lately as well as being more welcoming like; and Barty had taken the car round to the garage. Agatha wished the way back from London had been longer. It was only seven o'clock, the sun high in the sky; he might have taken her out in the car again. But dinner would be in an hour, and that might take an hour, and then it would be nine. Was nine too early for bride and bridegroom to seek their chamber?

Then she felt herself trembling. At the head of the stairs was the rosewood door. She had locked it with the new lock and put away the key, and she knew that presently he would be seeing it twenty times a day, passing it constantly as long as they were in the house; but that made no difference. An impulse to head him off from it took her – right away from it. He was in the garage, putting the car to bed. There was a secondary staircase to their room, used by the servants, and the way to it was through the back parts of the house . . . Already she was on her way, hurrying to the garage.

He was just closing the double doors. She tried to make her voice sound natural.

'Ah, there you are! Don't you want to see your room?'

'Time to change presently. Have they sent my things over?'

'Yes. They're upstairs. Come and I'll show you. There's a short way without going round – '

She took him by the hand and led him quickly across the paved yard.

He made no remark on the way by which he was entering. They passed a row of sculleries, and found themselves on a bare, light wooden staircase. This led to a carpeted landing at the top, and there was their room. She pushed at its door, and they entered. He closed the door behind her and looked round.

His evening clothes, together with her evening frock, were laid out on the primrose-yellow eiderdown, but it was not at these he was looking. He was looking at the ornaments on the mantelpiece, the starched and ribboned curtains, the crimson jam of the carpet, the Hunt and the Marcus Stones. Suddenly he broke into a peal of laughter.

'Great heavens, Aggie, you don't mean you've been put in here!' he exploded.

She felt that she must play her part boldly and skilfully. She laughed too, and clasped both her hands on his sleeve.

'Of course not, darling. I've been using another room' – and she looked the implication of the pronoun deeply at him. 'But if you only knew the pleasure it gave them' – and she told him how there was not a servant in the house but had contributed something to the room out of sheer goodness of heart.

He was not listening; he was looking at her as if his eyes were his ears too. He was looking at her as he had looked at her that first time at the foot of the stairs. His arm was passed about her.

'Any old room will do to kiss you in,' he muttered.

They kissed as they stood, while the Marcus Stones looked down from the paper walls.

'All the same,' he said presently, 'I should have thought that in a house like this – '

Her cunning deepened. She became a hypocrite. She made herself disappointed, hurt.

'And it was *my* choice – I didn't want to take Virginia's room or James's – I wanted *this* one – '

She won. He took her into his arms again. – 'My love, my love!' he breathed.

She could not take him down again by the way she had brought him. A few minutes later they sought the main passage. Her heart gave a sudden bound as, at the stairhead that looked down into the hall, he paused before the rosewood door.

'That's an odd piece of work,' he said. 'I don't remember to have seen one like that before.'

They passed down.

But in the drawing-room, as he stood before the Adam mantel-piece, he returned to the subject of their room. – 'I thought they'd made us free of the whole place,' he said.

She laughed nervously. – 'Really, Barty, I should have thought that with me – '

'Yes, but I don't take you about in Fords as long as there's a decent car.'

'Do you love me very much? Because I've been wondering Barty – '

'What?'

'Suppose we didn't stay here for our honeymoon after all. Suppose we went somewhere else? I have a little money – '

'Oh, the place is right enough. I like it. Though' – he laughed as the dressing-gong boomed – 'I think it might have run to a dressing-room – '

He was shown the men's bathroom, she sought the other. Again at the head of the stairs he paused before the door. – 'How long have we before dinner?' he asked.

'Half an hour.'

'Better be getting a move on then,' he said.

She was out of her bath before him, and, hurrying to their room, she made haste into her frock. She knew what he was thinking, that it was odd that they should bury themselves in a disused portion of the house like this, and so it was; her choice had been a stupid one after all. If only they could go away altogether . . . She made the more haste. She was ready when he appeared, in his dressing-gown.

'I'll wait downstairs,' she smiled as she passed; and she closed the door on him and descended to the drawing-room.

He was not down by the time the second gong sounded. In the dining-room the maid and the butler waited. She walked out into the hall and looked up the stairs. There she saw him. He was trying the handle of the rosewood door.

10

Dinner was over, coffee had been brought into the library, and they were alone. They stood by the tall windows, he with his arm about her, looking out into the lily-garden. It was a heavenly August evening, with the light beginning to fade. As if by some tacit and blissful understanding their lips did not now kiss. For minutes they had not spoken.

'It will be a short night,' he said softly.

He might have meant that it would be light by half-past three.

'Do you remember – out there?' His nod was towards the leaden fountain.

'Yes.'

'I hadn't even to ask you if you would. You simply came to me.'

'You came to me. I was there all the time.'

'It has been wonderful.'

She was mute.

The water plashed on the lily-leaves, the sky became smoky gold. Without a word they passed out into the garden. They stood where they had formerly stood, facing one another, her right hand in his left hand, her left hand in his right. They looked long at one another.

'Do you know what I should like?' he asked.

'What, beloved?' she asked faintly.

'It was here that we kissed first, by this fountain. Your voice made music like the fountain. I hadn't even to ask you; I only said "when?" and you said "When you like". It is now.'

'Now is for ever. Husband, shall we go to our room?'

'No.'

'No?'

'No. Not to that room. I want to be by the fountain, where we kissed. I want to hear it with your breathing in the night. I do not want that other room. I want the room over this, and the garden, and the fountain, and you.'

Her knees had almost failed her; he felt the sudden slackness of her hands.

'Come with me,' he said.

'Barty,' she said suddenly in a voice that shook, 'go and start up the car. I want to go to London.'

'It is too late to go to London,' he answered, and she did not know what it was in his voice that made it almost the voice of a stranger.

'I want to go away. I don't want to stay in this house. I will go with you anywhere. I will go with you into the pinewoods. The needles shall be your couch all night. And tomorrow we will go away. I cannot stay in this house. I will wander – wander anywhere with you – '

'I want to stay.'

'Get the car, get the car – '

'Come into the house, Agatha.'

'No, no, no, no, no – ' She tried to drag her hands away.

'Come into the house.'

All at once she obeyed him. She did come into the house. But entering the library, it was only to cross to the door. She stood with her back to it, as she had stood on the morning when the family had questioned her about the sword. Her arms were spread across it.

'Barty,' she said slowly, 'you cannot pass me.'

'I would not pass you,' he answered; and it was not the phrase of the Barty who spoke the easy slang of the hour. 'I would not pass you. I would have you come with me, and now.'

'Love, love, love, not to that room!' broke from her, and she could have slain herself for the last two words.

His bright eyes danced. – '*Ah!*'

'Not through that door!' Again it seemed to come from her of itself.

'Ah! the door! And why not the door?'

'Barty!' She flung out her arms to him, and again her right hand was in his left hand, and the hand on which a woman wears a ring in the hand in which a man holds a sword. 'Loved and dearly loved, take me away! All my days I will love you – I will be your slave – there shall be nothing you ask that shall not be done on the instant – but do not ask me this!'

'That I should not enter the room I choose?'

'That you should not enter *that* room, by *that* door!'

His reply was to draw her powerfully away from the library door and to march past her.

She made a little start forward, and then stopped. She stopped because he too had stopped. He had stopped, suddenly irresolute, where the stair-rail made its shell-like turn. She saw him put up his hand, as if he felt for something, and then he took a halting step forward, not up the stairs, but in the direction of the drawing-room. With her fingers on her lips she stole after him. She looked down the long room with the chandeliers and the Adam fireplace at the end.

He was standing with his back to her, over by the fire-place, and his head moved slightly, as if he was looking for something. Strong and soldierly his black-jacketed back looked, patterned against the dim white – for the light by which she saw all this was merely the familiarity of her own eyes with the falling evening, and to have switched a light on for a moment and then off again would have been to see nothing at all. But looking up the stairs the upper portion of the house held a little more of the day. She walked down the drawing-room to him.

'Barty, Barty – dearest, dearest – '

He spoke. – 'Ah! Is that you, love?'

'This is our wedding-night. I am waiting for you.'

'Is our chamber ready?'

Ah! But she had the key of *that* chamber safely put away! She had taken him into her arms. She whispered. – 'I am waiting, Barty – waiting – '

'I am ready.'

Enfolded, they passed down the drawing-room and out into the hall. Still enfolded they slowly mounted the stairs. They stood before the door. After all what did it matter? Had he not tried it before dinner and found it locked? And had she not the key?

Nevertheless he stopped. His hand, as she saw by the dim edge of his cuff, was fumbling over the door. He muttered something inaudible. Afraid to use force, still she sought to draw him gently away. He muttered again.

'It is in my mind – it is in my mind – ' she heard him say, like a man who tries to remember . . .

Ah!

She had almost shrieked. In the name of God, what was that? That sound within the door itself, as if a mouse crept? Something was yielding. Where a moment before a linen-fold had been a vertical strip of twilight appeared. It widened as with a creaking noise the panel slid aside. His fingers had found it.

The opening was wide enough to have stooped and entered sideways by, but he did not stoop and enter sideways. Instead he put a hand of today through that opening centuries old and slipped back the modern catch that had been fitted. The door opened, and the linen-folds creaked back into their place again.

II

He was where he had wished to be, with the smell of lilies and the sound of the plashing fountain and with her; but where, and when? Space? Time? Space and time are too much for human love. There is no love in a void. God is great, but He must make Himself little to our hearts, close in our flesh in a bridal bed; if we love otherwise it is not He who penetrates us, but another. But who then? Who was her Barty? A demon-lover, and she the woman who wailed? No, no, no, no, no! He was Barty, whose people lived not a dozen miles away! He was Barty, who that day had put a ring on her finger and promised to worship her with his body! It was all a mistake that he been missing in that body for eleven years! What did that matter, since he was here, in the chamber of his own choosing, and on his wedding-night?

The room had still a little light, enough to see by. There was the wardrobe, there the bedside table, there the bed she had slept in last night. But he was so brown, so nearly the colour of that rosy door, that except for his eyes and the white shape of his evening shirt she saw him as she had seen him first, blurred and dim. But the eyes were brilliant and roving, and he spoke in a stern voice.

'I have been long away. I was not expected back. You have been constant?' he said.

Appalled, she found no voice.

'Our fathers locked their women up, with a girdle,' he went on. 'There is one in my family. My younger brother has it, as he has all else. But you I girdled with your promise only. Now I have come back. Have you been constant?'

'Barty – !' came faintly from her.

'He may have the rest, my brother. I give it to him. But you I give to no man.'

'Barty! You have me, you have me! Hold me, hold me!' she cried, terrified.

'I was away too long,' he muttered again. 'Perhaps I ought not to have come back.'

'What is this frightful thing you are saying? You were missing at Guillemont, in 1916!'

He spoke quickly. – 'At what place?'

'At Guillemont. Or Thiepval. You didn't always say exactly the same.'

She felt that he shook his head.

'I know no Guillemont nor Thiepval. They have a French sound. Edge Hill I knew. We were on the top there, but we went down, because of the Banbury men behind us. We went down against the traitor Essex, and Rupert cut them up. And Chalgrove knew me, and Naseby! . . . Who fought at those French places?'

'Barty! Barty! You were at the war! *This* war! The war they called The Great War!'

'Then let them not call it The Great War in my hearing!' he said curtly. 'It is much that they call it The Great Rebellion! Does a king make war on a rebel subject?'

'Dear God, what is he saying?' she asked.

'And *then* I was missing!' Barty's voice rang out. 'They passed their Act. Oblivion and Pardon they called it, but I was not there. I missed my Oblivion and Pardon! . . . I was at Tunis with Blake. Carthage is there – Carthage is there – Carthage – Car – Car . . . I pray you pardon me. There has been much fighting in the world – '

'Love, love, love!' was all she could say, for she too knew what was to come. He was remembering farther back still.

'Stay a moment – I was with The Lion at Acre, but Carthage – '

The Great War! The Rebellion! The Crusades!

'Was it there the Switzers fought, they with the swords a half taller than themselves? But 'tis no weapon. All is wind and flash. Give me the short sword and the run-in! . . . Was't you who said Carthage?'

Then he gave a little cry of satisfaction.

'Ah! It comes! What said Scipio? "*Delenda est.*" But that was Cato's doing. For a hundred and twenty years they fought, and Hasdrubal's wife spat upon him, and cast herself and her children into the flames – there has been much fighting – much, much fighting – '

She could endure no more. At least there could be light. She sprang to the switch at the side of the rosewood door, and the room broke into light.

For a moment she thought she had done the right thing, for he blinked and then stood looking at his own clothes. He was precisely as he had been at dinner, but no frown such as *this* had bitten into his face at dinner.

'What sorcery was that?' he demanded harshly. She had fallen back.

'What chamber is this? Its door I know, but what are these other furnishings? And how came that light from nowhere? Answer me!' he said.

Had she the courage? Dared she throw herself on that strange and haunted breast?

Oh, if it only needed *courage* – if *courage* would avail –

But he put her back, repeating his first question of all.

'Have you been constant?'

She was at peace now, for she knew that it was upon her. She smiled.

'Oh, have I not!'

'I held you, not with a girdle, but with your word. I knew my brother loved you. He had my inheritance, but I thought nought of that. I was long away, and a word is only a word. Thought you I was dead?'

'I always knew you would come.'

'You bear a Saint's name. Have you been a Saint?'

Saintly she looked as she stood there, smiling, waiting. – 'It should have ended that day in the pinewood, Barty,' she said.

He was looking round the room again; he took a stride across it. With a swift movement he flung open the wardrobe door, as if he expected to find a man inside. He found no man, but he found something else. It was the sword. He took it in his hand. He looked at it long, steadfastly, rememberingly.

'It is a sorcery,' he muttered. '*That* is the door of my chamber. *This* is my sword. But all else is strange . . . Is it *not* strange?' he demanded in a tone that made her heart glad, for it could not be long now.

'Thrust quickly, Barty,' she said.

'Why would you not open that door? You had the key. Why had I to open it myself, the secret way?'

The secret way? Ah, more secret than he knew!

'I will tell you why. He was here. My brother was here. You sought to gain time, that he might escape by the window and the garden . . . Have you anything to say?' he loudly challenged her.

'Yes, beloved. It was always my fear that you would get there before me,' she replied.

'Will you pray?'

'I have prayed.'

'You are very beautiful,' he said, looking at the bosom as bare as that of the Saint whose name she shared. 'I am loth to mar that. You may choose another way, so it be tonight.'

'No, this way; we will lose no time – '

'Then – *hai*!'

Her swimming eyes saw his face become a sudden blur of brown, and the brightness of his own eyes was the last thing to leave her as she sank.

12

Barty's memory is clear up to a point. He remembers that he wanted to change rooms, he says, for they had put him into one that hadn't even a dressing-room and was miles from the bathroom. And he remembers seeing a room with a rosewood door, but he doesn't suppose the door had anything to do with it. Certainly he fell into a violent trembling when they showed him the door, but there might easily have been another explanation of that. He loved her, he says, and it was their wedding-night. They had been going to bed. And somehow – how he can't explain – he managed to open the door, and that is all he knows about it. As for the sword, he *might* have had a service-pattern one, for ceremonial, but they hadn't used swords much in The Great War. He knows nothing whatever about the one they showed him.

Of course they can't allow that kind of man his freedom, but he will probably get it in another way soon, for he was always of a roving disposition, and frets under restraint. Probably his wanderings about Africa – or wherever it was – had not done him any good. He has a little patch of garden, in which he works, and last summer he got quite remarkably brown. People go to see him, but Mr James never. Mr James is to be pitied, because, although nobody locks him up, he has a bee in his bonnet too. It is about a sword. He cannot even go into a museum where there are swords, and strangers are sometimes warned not to mention swords in his presence.

But they may talk as much as they like about rosewood doors.

The Accident

I

The street had not changed so much but that, little by little, its influence had come over Romarin again; and as the clock a street or two away had struck seven he had stood, his hands folded on his stick, first curious, then expectant, and finally, as the sound had died away, oddly satisfied in his memory. The clock had a peculiar chime, a rather elaborate one, ending inconclusively on the dominant and followed after an unusually long interval by the stroke of the hour itself. Not until its last vibration had become too subtle for his ear had Romarin resumed the occupation that the pealing of the hour had interrupted.

It was an occupation that especially tended to abstraction of mind – the noting in detail of the little things of the street that he had forgotten with such completeness that they awakened only tardy responses in his memory now that his eyes rested on them again. The shape of a doorknocker, the grouping of an old chimney-stack, the crack, still there, in a flagstone – somewhere deep in the past these things had associations; but they lay very deep, and the disturbing of them gave Romarin a curious, desolate feeling, as of returning to things he had long out-grown.

But, as he continued to stare at the objects, the sluggish memories roused more and more; and for each bit of the old that reasserted itself scores of yards of the new seemed to disappear. New shopfrontages went; a wall, brought up flush where formerly a recess had been, became the recess once more; the intermittent electric sign at the street's end, that wrote in green and crimson the name of a whiskey across a lamp-lit façade, ceased to worry his eyes; and the unfamiliar new front of the little restaurant he was passing and repassing took on its old and well-known aspect again.

Seven o'clock. He had thought, in dismissing his hansom, that it had been later. His appointment was not until a quarter past. But he decided against entering the restaurant and waiting inside; seeing who his guest was, it would be better to wait at the door. By the light of the restaurant window he corrected his watch, and then sauntered a few yards along the street, to where men were moving flats of scenery from a back door of the new theatre into a sort of tumbril. The theatre was twenty years old, but to Romarin it was 'the new theatre'. There had been no theatre there in his day.

In his day! . . . His day had been twice twenty years before. Forty years before, that street, that quarter, had been bound up in his life. He had not, forty years ago, been the famous painter, honoured, decorated, taken by the arm by monarchs; he had been a student, wild and raw as any, with that tranquil and urbane philosophy that had made his success still in abeyance within him. As his eyes had rested on the doorknocker next to the restaurant a smile had crossed his face. How had *that* door-knocker come to be left by the old crowd that had wrenched off so many others? By what accident had *that* survived, to bring back all the old life now so oddly? He stood, again smiling, his hands folded on his stick. A Crown Prince had given him that stick, and had had it engraved, 'To my Friend, Romarin'.

'You oughtn't to be here, you know,' he said to the door-knocker. 'If I didn't get you, Marsden ought to have done so . . . '

It was Marsden whom Romarin had come to meet – Marsden, of whom he had thought with such odd persistency lately. Marsden was the only man in the world between whom and himself lay as much as the shadow of an enmity; and even that faint shadow was now passing. One does not guard, for forty years, animosities that take their rise in quick outbreaks of the young blood; and, now that Romarin came to think of it, he hadn't really hated Marsden for more than a few months. It had been within those very doors (Romarin was passing the restaurant again) that there had been that quick blow, about a girl, and the tables had been pushed hastily back, and he and Marsden had fought, while the other fellows had kept the waiters away . . . And Romarin was now sixty-four, and Marsden must be a year older, and the girl – who knew? – probably dead long ago . . . Yes, time heals these things, thank God; and Romarin had felt a genuine flush of pleasure when Marsden had accepted his invitation to dinner.

But – Romarin looked at his watch again – it was rather like Marsden to be late. Marsden had always been like that – had come and gone pretty much as he had pleased, regardless of inconvenience to others. But, doubtless, he had had to walk. If all reports were true, Marsden had not made very much of his life in the way of worldly success, and Romarin, sorry to hear it, had wished he could give him a leg-up.

Even a good man cannot do much when the current of his life sets against him in a tide of persistent ill-luck, and Romarin, honoured and successful, yet knew that he had been one of the lucky ones . . .

But it was just like Marsden to be late, for all that.

At first Romarin did not recognise him when he turned the corner of the street and walked towards him. He hadn't made up his mind beforehand exactly how he had expected Marsden to look, but he was conscious that he didn't look it. It was not the short stubble of grey beard, so short that it seemed to hesitate between beard and unshavenness; it was not the figure nor carriage – clothes alter that, and the clothes of the man who was advancing to meet Romarin were, to put it bluntly, shabby; nor was it . . . but Romarin did not know what it was in the advancing figure that for the moment found no response in his memory. He was already within half a dozen yards of the men who were moving the scenery from the theatre into the tumbril, and one of the workmen put up his hand as the edge of a fresh 'wing' appeared . . .

But at the sound of his voice the same thing happened that had happened when the clock had struck seven. Romarin found himself suddenly expectant, attentive, and then again curiously satisfied in his memory. Marsden's voice at least had not changed; it was as in the old days – a little envious, sarcastic, accepting lower interpretations somewhat willingly, somewhat grudging of better ones. It completed the taking back of Romarin that the chiming of the clock, the doorknocker, the grouping of the chimney-stack and the crack in the flagstone had begun.

'Well, my distinguished Academician, my – '

Marsden's voice sounded across the group of scene-shifters . . .

''*Alf* a mo, *if* you please, guv'nor,' said another voice . . .

For a moment the painted 'wing' shut them off from one another.

*   *   *

In that moment Romarin's accident befell him. If its essential nature is related in arbitrary terms, it is that there are no other terms to relate it in. It is a decoded cipher, which can be restored to its cryptic form as Romarin subsequently restored it.

*   *   *

As the painter took Marsden's arm and entered the restaurant, he noticed that while the outside of the place still retained traces of the old, its inside was entirely new. Its cheap glittering wall-mirrors, that gave a false impression of the actual size of the place, its Loves and Shepherdesses painted in the style of the carts of the vendors of ice-cream, its hat-racks and its four-bladed propeller that set the air slowly in motion at the farther end of the room, might all have been matched in a dozen similar establishments within hail of a cab-whistle. Its gelatine-written menu-cards announced that one might dine there *à la carte* or *table d'hôte* for two shillings. Neither the cooking nor the service had influenced Romarin in his choice of a place to dine at.

He made a gesture to the waiter who advanced to help him on with his coat that Marsden was to be assisted first; but Marsden, with a grunted 'All right', had already helped himself. A glimpse of the interior of the coat told Romarin why Marsden kept waiters at arm's-length. A little twinge of compunction took him that his own over-coat should be fur-collared and lined with silk.

They sat down at a corner table not far from the slowly moving four-bladed propeller.

'Now we can talk,' Romarin said. 'I'm glad, glad to see you again, Marsden.'

It was a peculiarly vicious face that he saw, corrugated about the brows, and with stiff iron-grey hair untrimmed about the ears. It shocked Romarin a little; he had hardly looked to see certain things so accentuated by the passage of time. Romarin's own brow was high and bald and benign, and his beard was like a broad shield of silver.

'You're glad, are you?' said Marsden, as they sat down facing one another. 'Well, I'm glad – to be seen with you. It'll revive my credit a bit. There's a fellow across there has recognised you already by your photographs in the papers . . . I assume I may . . . ?'

He made a little upward movement of his hand. It was a gin and bitters Marsden assumed he might have. Romarin ordered it; he himself did not take one. Marsden tossed down the *apéritif* at one gulp; then he reached for his roll, pulled it to pieces, and – Romarin remembered how in the old days Marsden had always eaten bread like that – began to throw bullets of bread into his mouth. Formerly this habit had irritated Romarin intensely; now . . . well, well, Life uses some of us better than others. Small blame to these if they throw up the struggle. Marsden, poor devil . . . but the arrival of the soup interrupted Romarin's meditation. He consulted the violet-written card, ordered the succeeding courses, and the two men ate for some minutes in silence.

'Well,' said Romarin presently, pushing away his plate and wiping his white moustache, 'are you still a Romanticist, Marsden?'

Marsden, who had tucked his napkin between two of the buttons of his frayed waistcoat, looked suspiciously across the glass with the dregs of the gin and bitters that he had half raised to his lips.

'Eh?' he said. 'I say, Romarin, don't let's go grave-digging among memories merely for the sake of making conversation. Yours may be pleasant, but I'm not in the habit of wasting much time over mine. Might as well be making new ones . . . I'll drink whiskey and soda.'

It was brought, a large one; and Marsden, nodding, took a deep gulp. 'Health,' he said.

'Thanks,' said Romarin – instantly noting that the monosyllable, which matched the other's in curtness, was not at all the reply he had intended. 'Thank you – yours,' he amended; and a short pause followed, in which fish was brought.

This was not what Romarin had hoped for. He had desired to be reconciled with Marsden, not merely to be allowed to pay for his dinner. Yet if Marsden did not wish to talk it was difficult not to defer to his wish. It was true that he had asked if Marsden was still a Romanticist largely for the sake of something to say; but Marsden's prompt pointing out of this was not encouraging. Now that he came to think of it, he had never known precisely what Marsden had meant by the word 'Romance' he had so frequently taken into his mouth; he only knew that this creed of Romanticism, whatever it was, had been worn rather challengingly, a chip on the shoulder, to be knocked off at some peril or other. And it had seemed to Romarin a little futile in the violence with which it had been maintained . . . But that was neither here nor there. The point was, that the conversation had begun not very happily, and must be mended at once if at all. To mend it, Romarin leaned across the table.

'Be as friendly as I am, Marsden,' he said. 'I think – pardon me – that if our positions were reversed, and I saw in you the sincere desire to help that I have, I'd take it in the right way.'

Again Marsden looked suspiciously at him. 'To help? How to help?' he demanded.

'That's what I should like *you* to tell *me*. But I suppose (for example) you still work?'

'Oh, my work!' Marsden made a little gesture of contempt. 'Try again, Romarin.'

'You don't do any? . . . Come, I'm no bad friend to my friends, and you'll find me – especially so.'

But Marsden put up his hand.

'Not quite so quickly,' he said. 'Let's see what you mean by help first. Do you really mean that you want me to borrow money from you? That's help as I understand it nowadays.'

'Then you've changed,' said Romarin – wondering, however, in his secret heart whether Marsden had changed very much in that respect after all.

Marsden gave a short honk of a laugh.

'You didn't suppose I *hadn't* changed, did you?' Then he leaned suddenly forward. 'This is rather a mistake, Romarin – rather a mistake,' he said.

'What is?'

'This – our meeting again. Quite a mistake.'

Romarin sighed. 'I had hoped not,' he said.

Marsden leaned forward again, with another gesture Romarin remembered very well – dinner knife in hand, edge and palm upwards, punctuating and expounding with the point.

'I tell you, it's a mistake,' he said, knife and hand balanced. 'You can't reopen things like this. You don't really *want* to reopen them; you only want to reopen certain of them; you want to pick and choose among things, to approve and disapprove. There must have been somewhere or other something in me you didn't altogether dislike – I can't for the life of me think what it was, by the way; and you want to lay stress on that and to sink the rest. Well, you can't. I won't let you. I'll not submit my life to you like that. If you want to go into things, all right; but it must be all or none. And I'd like another drink.'

He put the knife down with a little clap as Romarin beckoned to the waiter.

There was distress on Romarin's face. He was not conscious of having adopted a superior attitude. But again he told himself that he must make allowances. Men who don't come off in Life's struggle are apt to be touchy, and he was, after all, the same old Marsden, the man with whom he desired to be at peace.

'Are you quite fair to me?' he asked presently, in a low voice.

Again the knife was taken up and its point advanced.

'Yes, I am,' said Marsden in a slightly raised voice; and he indicated with the knife the mirror at the end of the table. 'You know you've done well, and I, to all appearances, haven't; you can't look at that glass and not know it. But I've followed the line of my development too, no less logically than you. My life's been mine, and I'm not going to apologise for it to a single breathing creature. More, I'm proud of it. At least, there's been singleness of intention about it. So I think I'm strictly fair in pointing that out when you talk about helping me.'

'Perhaps so, perhaps so,' Romarin agreed a little sadly. 'It's your tone more than anything else that makes things a little difficult. Believe me, I've no end in my mind except pure friendliness.'

'No-o-o,' said Marsden – a long 'no' that seemed to deliberate, to examine, and finally to admit. 'No. I believe that. And you usually get what you set out for. Oh yes. I've watched your rise – I've made a point of watching it. It's been a bit at a time, but you've got there. You're that sort. It's on your forehead – your destiny.'

Romarin smiled.

'Hallo, that's new, isn't it?' he said. 'It wasn't your habit to talk much about destiny, if I remember rightly. Let me see; wasn't this more your style – "will, passion, laughs-at-impossibilities and says", et cetera – and so forth? Wasn't that it? With always the suspicion not far away that you did things more from theoretical conviction than real impulse after all?'

A dispassionate observer would have judged that the words went somewhere near home. Marsden was scraping together with the edge of his knife the crumbs of his broken roll. He scraped them into a little square, and then trimmed the corners. Not until the little pile was shaped to his liking did he look surlily up.

'Let it rest, Romarin,' he said curtly. 'Drop it,' he added. 'Let it alone. If I begin to talk like that, too, we shall only cut one another up. Clink glasses – there – and let it alone.'

Mechanically Romarin clinked; but his bald brow was perplexed.

' "Cut one another up?" ' he repeated.

'Yes. Let it alone.'

' "Cut one another up?" ' he repeated once more. 'You puzzle me entirely.'

'Well, perhaps I'm altogether wrong. I only wanted to warn you that I've dared a good many things in my time. Now drop it.'

Romarin had fine brown eyes, under Oriental arched brows. Again they noted the singularly vicious look of the man opposite. They were full of mistrust and curiosity, and he stroked his silver beard.

'Drop it?' he said slowly . . . 'No, let's go on. I want to hear more of this.'

'I'd much rather have another drink in peace and quietness . . . Waiter!'

Either leaned back in his chair, surveying the other. 'You're a perverse devil still,' was Romarin's thought. Marsden's, apparently, was
of nothing but the whiskey and soda the waiter had gone to fetch.

*   *   *

Romarin was inclined to look askance at a man who could follow up
a gin and bitters with three or four whiskeys and soda without
turning a hair. It argued the seasoned cask. Marsden had bidden the
waiter leave the bottle and the syphon on the table, and was already
mixing himself another stiff peg.

'Well,' he said, 'since you will have it so – to the old days.'

'To the old days,' said Romarin, watching him gulp it down.

'Queer, looking back across all that time at 'em, isn't it? How do
you feel about it?'

'In a mixed kind of way, I think; the usual thing: pleasure and
regret mingled.'

'Oh, you have regrets, have you?'

'For certain things, yes. Not, let me say, my turn-up with you,
Marsden,' he laughed. 'That's why I chose the old place – ' he gave a
glance round at its glittering newness. 'Do you happen to remember
what all that was about? I've only the vaguest idea.'

Marsden gave him a long look. 'That all?' he asked.

'Oh, I remember in a sort of way. That "Romantic" soap-bubble of
yours was really at the bottom of it, I suspect. Tell me,' he smiled,
'did you really suppose Life could be lived on those mad lines you
used to lay down?'

'My life,' said Marsden calmly, 'has been.'

'Not literally.'

'Literally.'

'You mean to say that you haven't outgrown *that*?'

'I hope not.'

Romarin had thrown up his handsome head. 'Well, well!' he murmured incredulously.

'Why "well, well"?' Marsden demanded . . . 'But, of course, you
never did and never will know what I meant.'

'By Romance? . . . No, I can't say that I did; but as I conceived it, it
was something that began in appetite and ended in diabetes.'

'Not philosophic, eh?' Marsden enquired, picking up a chicken bone.

'Highly unphilosophic,' said Romarin, shaking his head.

'Hm!' grunted Marsden, stripping the bone . . . 'Well, I grant it
pays in a different way.'

'It does pay, then?' Romarin asked.

'Oh yes, it pays.'

The restaurant had filled up. It was one frequented by young artists, musicians, journalists and the clingers to the rather frayed fringes of the Arts. From time to time heads were turned to look at Romarin's portly and handsome figure, which the Press, the Regent Street photographic establishments, and the Academy Supplements had made well known. The plump young Frenchwoman within the glazed cash office near the door, at whom Marsden had several times glanced in a way at which Romarin had frowned, was aware of the honour done the restaurant; and several times the blond-bearded proprietor had advanced and enquired with concern whether the dinner and the service was to the liking of m'sieu.

And the eyes that were turned to Romarin plainly wondered who the scallawag dining with him might be.

Since Romarin had chosen that their conversation should be of the old days, and without picking and choosing, Marsden was quite willing that it should be so. Again he was casting the bullets of bread into his mouth, and again Romarin was conscious of irritation. Marsden, too, noticed it; but in awaiting the *rôti* he still continued to roll and bolt the pellets, washing them down with gulps of whiskey and soda.

'Oh yes, it paid,' he resumed. 'Not in that way, of course – ' he indicated the head, quickly turned away again, of an aureoled youngster with a large bunch of black satin tie, ' – not in admiration of that sort, but in other ways – '

'Tell me about it.'

'Certainly, if you want it. But you're my host. Won't you let me hear your side of it all first?'

'But I thought you said you knew that – had followed my career?'

'So I have. It's not your list of honours and degrees; let me see, what are you? R.A., D.C.L., Doctor of Literature, whatever that means, and Professor of this, that, and the other, and not at the end of it yet. I know all that. I don't say you haven't earned it; I admire your painting; but it's not that. I want to know what it *feels* like to be up there where you are.'

It was a childish question, and Romarin felt foolish in trying to answer it. Such things were the things the adoring aureoled youngster a table or two away would have liked to ask. Romarin recognised in Marsden the old craving for sensation; it was part of the theoretical creed Marsden had made for himself, of doing things, not for their own sakes, but in order that he might have done them. Of course, it had appeared to a fellow like that, that Romarin himself had always had a calculated end in view; he had not; Marsden merely measured Romarin's peck out of his own bushel. It had been Marsden who, in self-consciously seeking his own life, had lost it, and Romarin was more than a little inclined to suspect that the vehemence with which he protested that he had not lost it was precisely the measure of the loss.

But he essayed it – essayed to give Marsden a *résumé* of his career. He told him of the stroke of sheer luck that had been the foundation of it all, the falling ill of another painter who had turned over certain commissions to him. He told him of his poor but happy marriage, and of the windfall, not large, but timely, that had come to his wife. He told him of fortunate acquaintanceships happily cultivated, of his first important commission, of the fresco that had procured for him his Associateship, of his sale to the Chantrey, and of his quietly remunerative Visitorships and his work on Boards and Committees.

And as he talked, Marsden drew his empty glass to him, moistened his finger with a little spilt liquid, and began to run the finger round the rim of the glass. They had done that formerly, a whole roomful of them, producing, when each had found the note of his instrument, a high, thin, intolerable singing. To this singing Romarin strove to tell his tale.

But that thin and bat-like note silenced him. He ended lamely, with some empty generalisation on success.

'Ah, but success in what?' Marsden demanded, interrupting his playing on the glass for a moment.

'In your aim, whatever it may be.'

'Ah!' said Marsden, resuming his performance.

Romarin had sought in his recital to minimise differences in circumstances; but Marsden seemed bent on aggravating them. He had the miserable advantage of the man who has nothing to lose. And bit by bit, Romarin had begun to realise that he was going considerably more than halfway to meet this old enemy of his, and that amity seemed as far on as ever. In his heart he began to feel the foreknowledge that their meeting could have no conclusion. He hated the man, the look of his face and the sound of his voice, as much as ever.

The proprietor approached with profoundest apology in his attitude. M'sieu would pardon him, but the noise of the glass . . . it was annoying . . . another m'sieu had made complaint . . .

'Eh? . . . ' cried Marsden. 'Oh, that! Certainly! It can be put to a much better purpose.'

He refilled the glass.

The liquor had begun to tell on him. A quarter of the quantity would have made a clean-living man incapably drunk, but it had only made Marsden's eyes bright. He gave a sarcastic laugh.

'And is that all?' he asked.

Romarin replied shortly that that was all.

'You've missed out the R.A., and the D.C.L.'

'Then let me add that I'm a Doctor of Civil Law and a full Member of the Royal Academy,' said Romarin, almost at the end of his patience. 'And now, since you don't think much of it, may I hear your own account?'

'Oh, by all means. I don't know, however, that – ' he broke off to throw a glance at a woman who had just entered the restaurant – a divesting glance that caused Romarin to redden to his crown and drop his eyes. 'I was going to say that you may think as little of my history as I do of yours. Supple woman that; when the rather scraggy blonde does take it into her head to be a devil she's the worst kind there is . . . '

Without apology Romarin looked at his watch.

'All right,' said Marsden, smiling, 'for what *I've* got out of life, then. But I warn you, it's entirely discreditable.'

Romarin did not doubt it.

'But it's mine, and I boast of it. I've done – barring receiving honours and degrees – everything – everything! If there's anything I haven't done, tell me and lend me a sovereign, and I'll go and do it.'

'You haven't told the story.'

'That's so. Here goes then . . . Well, you know, unless you've forgotten, how I began . . . '

Fruit and nutshells and nutcrackers lay on the table between them, and at the end of it, shielded from draughts by the menu cards, the coffee apparatus simmered over its elusive blue flame. Romarin was taking the rind from a pear with a table-knife, and Marsden had declined port in favour of a small golden liqueur of brandy. Every seat in the restaurant was now occupied, and the proprietor himself had brought his finest cigarettes and cigars. The waiter poured out the coffee, and departed with the apparatus in one hand and his napkin in the other.

Marsden was already well into his tale . . .

The frightful unction with which he told it appalled Romarin. It was as he had said – there was nothing he had not done and did not exult in with a sickening exultation. It had, indeed, ended in diabetes. In the pitiful hunting down of sensation to the last inch he had been fiendishly ingenious and utterly unimaginative. His unholy curiosity had spared nothing, his unnatural appetite had known no truth. It was grinning sin. The details of it simply cannot be told . . .

And his vanity in it all was prodigious. Romarin was pale as he listened. What! in order that *this* malignant growth in Society's breast should be able to say 'I know', had sanctities been profaned, sweet conventions assailed, purity blackened, soundness infected, and all that was bright and of the day been sunk in the quagmire that this creature of the night had called – yes, still called – by the gentle name of Romance? Yes, so it had been. Not only had men and women suffered dishonour, but manhood and womanhood and the clean institutions by which alone the creature was suffered to exist had been brought to shame. And what was he to look at when it was all done? . . .

'Romance – Beauty – the Beauty of things as they are!' he croaked.

If faces in the restaurant were now turned to Romarin, it was the horror on Romarin's own face that drew them. He drew out his handkerchief and mopped his brow.

'But,' he stammered presently, 'you are speaking of generalities – horrible theories – things diabolically conceivable to be done – '

'What?' cried Marsden, checked for a moment in his horrible triumph. 'No, by God! I've done 'em, done 'em! Don't you understand? If you don't, question me! . . . '

'*No, no!*' cried Romarin.

'But I say yes! You came for this, and you shall have it! I tried to stop you, but you wanted it, and by God you shall have it! You think your life's been full and mine empty? Ha ha! . . . Romance! I had the conviction of it, and I've had the courage too! I haven't told you a tenth of it! What would you like? Chamber-windows when Love was hot? The killing of a man who stood in my way? (I've fought a duel, and killed.) The squeezing of the juice out of life like *that*?' He pointed to Romarin's plate; Romarin had been eating grapes. 'Did you find me saying I'd do a thing and then drawing back from it when we – ' he made a quick gesture of both hands towards the middle of the restaurant floor.

'When we fought – ?'

'Yes, when we fought, here! . . . Oh no, oh no! I've lived, I tell you, every moment! Not a title, not a degree, but I've lived such a life as you never dreamed of – !'

'Thank God – '

But suddenly Marsden's voice, which had risen, dropped again. He began to shake with interior chuckles. They were the old, old chuckles, and they filled Romarin with a hatred hardly to be borne. The sound of the animal's voice had begun it, and his every word, look, movement, gesture, since they had entered the restaurant, had added to it. And he was now chuckling, chuckling, shaking with chuckles, as if some monstrous tit-bit still remained to be told. Already Romarin had tossed aside his napkin, beckoned to the waiter, and said, 'M'sieu dines with me . . . '

'Ho ho ho ho!' came the drunken sounds. 'It's a long time since m'sieu dined here with his old friend Romarin! Do you remember the last time? Do you remember it? *Pif, pan*! Two smacks across the table, Romarin – oh, you got it in very well! – and then, *brrrrr*! quick! Back with the tables – all the fellows round – Farquharson for me and Smith for you, and then to it, Romarin! . . . And you really don't remember what it was all about? . . . '

Romarin had remembered. His face was not the face of the philosophic master of Life now.

'You said she shouldn't – little Pattie Hines you know – you said she shouldn't – '

Romarin sprang half from his chair, and brought his fist down on the table.

'And by Heaven, she didn't! At least that's one thing you haven't done!'

Marsden too had risen unsteadily.

'Oho, oho? You think that?'

A wild thought flashed across Romarin's brain.

'You mean – ?'

'I mean? . . . Oho, oho! Yes, I mean! She did, Romarin . . . '

The mirrors, mistily seen through the smoke of half a hundred cigars and cigarettes, the Loves and Shepherdesses of the garish walls, the diners starting up in their places, all suddenly seemed to swing round in a great half-circle before Romarin's eyes. The next moment, feeling as if he stood on something on which he found it difficult to keep his balance, he had caught up the table-knife with which he had peeled the pear and had struck at the side of Marsden's neck. The rounded blade snapped, but he struck again with the broken edge, and left the knife where it entered. The table appeared uptilted almost vertical; over it Marsden's head disappeared; it was followed by a shower of glass, cigars, artificial flowers and the table-cloth at which he clutched; and the dirty American cloth of the table top was left bare.

*   *   *

But the edge behind which Marsden's face had disappeared remained vertical. A group of scene-shifters were moving a flat of scenery from a theatre into a tumbril-like cart . . .

And Romarin knew that, past, present, and future, he had seen it all in an instant, and that Marsden stood behind that painted wing.

And he knew, too, that he had only to wait until that flat passed and to take Marsden's arm and enter the restaurant, *and it would be so.* A drowning man is said to see all in one unmeasurable instant of time; a year-long dream is but, they say, an instantaneous arrangement in the moment of waking of the molecules we associate with ideas; and the past of history and the future of prophecy are folded up in the mystic moment we call the present . . .

It would come true . . .

For one moment Romarin stood; the next, he had turned and run for his life.

At the corner of the street he collided with a loafer, and only the wall saved them from going down. Feverishly Romarin plunged his hand into his pocket and brought out a handful of silver. He crammed it into the loafer's hand.

'Here – quick – take it!' he gasped. 'There's a man there, by that restaurant door – he's waiting for Mr Romarin – tell him – tell him – tell him Mr Romarin's had an accident – '

And he dashed away, leaving the man looking at the silver in his palm.

Io

As the young man put his hand to the uppermost of the four brass bell-knobs to the right of the fanlighted door he paused, withdrew the hand again, and then pulled at the lowest knob. The sawing of bell-wire answered him, and he waited for a moment, uncertain whether the bell had rung, before pulling again. Then there came from the basement a single cracked stroke; the head of a maid appeared in the whitewashed area below; and the head was withdrawn as apparently the maid recognised him. Steps were heard along the hall; the door was opened; and the maid stood aside to let him enter, the apron with which she had slipped the latch still crumpled in her greasy hand.

'Sorry, Daisy,' the young man apologised, 'but I didn't want to bring her down all those stairs. How is she? Has she been out today?'

The maid replied that the person spoken of had been out; and the young man walked along the wide carpeted passage.

It was cumbered like an antique-shop with alabaster busts on pedestals, dusty palms in faience vases, and trophies of spears and shields and assegais. At the foot of the stairs was a rustling *portière* of strung beads, and beyond it the carpet was continued up the broad, easy flight, secured at each step by a brass rod. Where the stairs made a turn, the fading light of the December afternoon, made still dimmer by a window of decalcomanied glass, shone on a cloudy green aquarium with sallow goldfish, a number of cacti on a shabby console table, and a large and dirty white sheepskin rug. Passing along a short landing, the young man began the ascent of the second flight. This also was carpeted, but with a carpet that had done duty in some dining- or bed-room before being cut up into strips of the width of the narrow space between the wall and the handrail. Then, as he still mounted, the young man's feet sounded loud on oilcloth; and when he finally paused and knocked at a door it was on a small landing of naked boards beneath the cold gleam of the skylight above the well of the stairs.

'Come in,' a girl's voice called.

The room he entered had a low sagging ceiling on which shone a low glow of firelight, making colder still the patch of eastern sky beyond the roofs and the cowls and hoods of chimneys framed by the square of the single window. The glow on the ceiling was reflected dully in the old dark mirror over the mantelpiece. An open door in the farther corner, hampered with skirts and blouses, allowed a glimpse of the girl's bedroom.

The young man set the paper bag he carried down on the littered round table and advanced to the girl who sat in an old wicker chair before the fire. The girl did not turn her head as he kissed her cheek, and he looked down at something that had muffled the sound of his steps as he had approached her.

'Hallo, that's new, isn't it, Bessie? Where did that come from?' he asked cheerfully.

The middle of the floor was covered with a common jute matting, but on the hearth was a magnificent leopard-skin rug.

'Mrs Hepburn sent it up. There was a draught from under the door. It's much warmer for my feet.'

'Very kind of Mrs Hepburn. Well, how are you feeling today, old girl?'

'Better, thanks, Ed.'

'That's the style. You'll be yourself again soon. Daisy says you've been out today?'

'Yes, I went for a walk. But not far; I went to the Museum and then sat down. You're early, aren't you?'

He turned away to get a chair, from which he had to move a mass of tissue-paper patterns and buckram linings. He brought it to the rug.

'Yes. I stopped last night late to cash up for Vedder, so he's staying tonight. Turn and turn about. Well, tell us all about it, Bess.'

Their faces were red in the firelight. Hers had the prettiness that the first glance almost exhausts, the prettiness, amazing in its quantity, that one sees for a moment under the light of the street lamps when shops and offices close for the day. She was short-nosed, pulpy-mouthed and faunish-eyed, and only the rather remarkable smallness of the head on the splendid thick throat saved her from ordinariness. He, too, might have been seen in his thousands at the close of any day, hurrying home to Catford or Walham Green or Tufnell Park to tea and an evening with a girl or in a billiard-room, or else dining cheaply 'up West' preparatory to smoking cigarettes from yellow packets in the upper circle of a music-hall. Four inches of white up-and-down collar encased his neck; and as he lifted his trousers at the knee to clear his purple socks, the pair of paper covers showed, that had protected his cuffs during the day at the office. He removed them, crumpled them up and threw them on the fire; and the momentary addition to the light of the upper chamber showed how curd-white was that superb neck of hers and how moody and tired her eyes.

From his face only one would have guessed, and guessed wrongly, that his preferences were for billiard-rooms and music-halls. His conversation showed them to be otherwise. It was of Polytechnic classes that he spoke, and of the course of lectures in English literature that had just begun. And, as if somebody had asserted that the pursuit of such studies was not compatible with a certain measure of physical development also, he announced that he was not sure that he should not devote, say, half an evening a week, on Wednesdays, to training in the gymnasium.

'*Mens sana in corpore sano*, Bessie,' he said; 'a sound mind in a sound body, you know. That's tremendously important, especially when a fellow spends the day in a stuffy office. Yes, I think I shall give it half Wednesdays, from eight-thirty to nine-thirty; sends you home in a glow. But I was going to tell you about the Literature Class. The second lecture's tonight. The first was splendid, all about the languages of Europe and Asia – what they call the Indo-Germanic languages, you know. Aryans. I can't tell you exactly without my notes, but the Hindoos and Persians, I think it was, they crossed the Himalaya Mountains and spread westward somehow, as far as Europe. That was the way it all began. It was splendid, the way the lecturer put it. English is a Germanic language, you know. Then came the Celts. I wish I'd brought my notes. I see you've been reading; let's look – '

A book lay on her knees, its back warped by the heat of the fire. He took it and opened it.

'Ah, Keats! Glad you like Keats, Bessie. We needn't be great readers, but it's important that what we do read should be all right. I don't know him, not really know him, that is. But he's quite all right – A I in fact. And he's an example of what I've always maintained, that knowledge should be brought within the reach of all. It just shows. He was the son of a livery-stable keeper, you know, so what he'd have been if he'd really had chances, been to universities and so on, there's no knowing. But, of course, it's more from the historical standpoint that I'm studying these things. Let's have a look – '

He opened the book where a hairpin between the leaves marked a place. The firelight glowed on the page, and he read, monotonously and inelastically.

> And as I sat, over the light blue hills
> There came a noise of revellers; the rills
> Into the wide stream came of purple hue –
>   'Twas Bacchus and his crew!
> The earnest trumpet spake, and silver thrills
> From kissing cymbals made a merry din –
>   'Twas Bacchus and his kin!
> Like to a moving vintage down they came,
> Crowned with green leaves, and faces all on flame
> All madly dancing through the pleasant valley
>   To scare thee, Melancholy!

It was the wondrous passage from *Endymion*, of the descent of the wild inspired rabble into India. Ed plucked for a moment at his lower lip, and then, with a 'Hm! What's it all about, Bessie?' continued.

> Within his car, aloft, young Bacchus stood,
> Trifling his ivy-dart, in dancing mood,
>   With sidelong laughing;
> And little rills of crimson wine imbrued
> His plump white arms and shoulders, enough white
>   For Venus' pearly bite;
> And near him rode Silenus on his ass,
> Pelted with flowers as he on did pass,
>   Tipsily quaffing.

'Hm! I see. Mythology. That's made up of tales, and myths, you know. Like Odin and Thor and those, only those were Scandinavian Mythology. So it would be absurd to take it too seriously. But I think, in a way, things like that do harm. You see,' he explained, 'the more beautiful they are the more harm they might do. We ought always to show virtue and vice in their true colours, and if you look at it from that point of view this is just drunkenness. That's rotten; destroys your body and intellect; as I heard a chap say once, it's an insult to the beasts to call it beastly. I joined the Blue Ribbon when I was fourteen and I haven't been sorry for it yet. No. Now there's Vedder; he "went off on a bend", as he calls it, last night, and even he says this morning it wasn't worth it. But let's read on.'

Again he read, with unresilient movement.

> I saw Osirian Egypt kneel adown
>   Before the vine-wreath crown!
> I saw parched Abyssinia rouse and sing
>   To the silver cymbals' ring!
> I saw the whelming vintage hotly pierce
>   Old Tartary the fierce! . . .
> Great Brahma from his mystic heaven groans.

'Hm! He was a Buddhist god, Brahma was; mythology again. As I say, if you take it seriously, it's just glorifying intoxication. – But I say; I can hardly see. Better light the lamp. We'll have tea first, then read. No, you sit still; I'll get it ready; I know where things are – '

He rose, crossed to a little cupboard with a sink in it, filled the kettle at the tap, and brought it to the fire. Then he struck a match and lighted the lamp.

The cheap glass shade was of a foolish corolla shape, clear glass below, shading to pink, and deepening to red at the crimped edge. It gave a false warmth to the spaces of the room above the level of the mantelpiece, and Ed's figure, as he turned the regulator, looked from the waist upwards as if he stood within that portion of a spectrum screen that deepens to the band of red. The bright concentric circles that spread in rings of red on the ceiling were more dimly reduplicated in the old mirror over the mantelpiece; and the wintry eastern light beyond the chimney-hoods seemed suddenly almost to die out.

Bessie, her white neck below the level of the lamp-shade, had taken up the book again; but she was not reading. She was looking over it at the upper part of the grate. Presently she spoke. 'I was looking at some of those things this afternoon, at the Museum.'

He was clearing from the table more buckram linings and patterns of paper, numbers of *Myra's Journal* and *The Delineator*. Already on his way to the cupboard he had put aside a red-bodiced dressmaker's 'shape' of wood and wire. 'What things?' he asked.

'Those you were reading about. Greek, aren't they?'

'Oh, the Greek room! . . . But those people, Bacchus and those, weren't people in the ordinary sense. Gods and goddesses, most of 'em; Bacchus was a god. That's what mythology means. I wish sometimes our course took in Greek literature, but it's a dead language after all. German's more good in modern life. It would be nice to know everything, but one has to select, you know. Hallo, I clean forgot; I brought you some grapes, Bessie; here they are, in this bag; we'll have 'em after tea, what?'

'But,' she said again after a pause, still looking at the grate, 'they had their priests and priestesses, and followers and people, hadn't they? It was their things I was looking at – combs and brooches and hairpins, and things to cut their nails with. They're all in a glass case there. And they had safety-pins, exactly like ours.'

'Oh, they were a civilised people,' said Ed cheerfully. 'It all gives you an idea. I only hope you didn't tire yourself out. You'll soon be all right, of course, but you have to be careful yet. We'll have a clean tablecloth, shall we?'

She had been seriously ill; her life had been despaired of; and somehow the young Polytechnic student seemed anxious to assure her that she was now all right again, or soon would be. They were to be married 'as soon as things brightened up a bit', and he was very much in love with her. He watched her head and neck as he continued to lay the table, and then, as he crossed once more to the cupboard, he put his hand lightly in passing on her hair.

She gave so quick a start that he too started. She must have been very deep in her reverie to have been so taken by surprise.

'I say, Bessie, don't jump like that!' he cried with involuntary quickness. Indeed, had his hand been red-hot, or ice-cold, or taloned, she could not have turned a more startled, even frightened, face to him.

'It was your touching me,' she muttered, resuming her gazing into the grate.

He stood looking anxiously down on her. It would have been better not to discuss her state, and he knew it; but in his anxiety he forgot it.

'That jumpiness is the effect of your illness, you know. I shall be glad when it's all over. It's made you so odd.'

She was not pleased that he should speak of her 'oddness'. For that matter, she, too, found him 'odd' – at any rate, found it difficult to realise that he was as he always had been. He had begun to irritate her a little. His club-footed reading of the verses had irritated her, and she had tried hard to hide from him that his cocksure opinions and the tone in which they were pronounced jarred on her. It was not that she was 'better' than he, 'knew' any more than he did, didn't (she supposed) love him still the same; these moods, that dated from her illness, had nothing to do with those things; she reproached herself sometimes that she was subject to such doldrums.

'It's all right, Ed, but please don't touch me just now,' she said.

He was in the act of leaning over her chair, but he saw her shrink, and refrained.

'Poor old girl!' he said sympathetically. 'What's the matter?'

'I don't know. It's awfully stupid of me to be like this, but I can't help it. I shall be better soon if you leave me alone.'

'Nothing's happened, has it?'

'Only those silly dreams I told you about.'

'Bother the dreams!' muttered the Polytechnic student.

During her illness she had had dreams, and had come to herself at intervals to find Ed or the doctor, Mrs Hepburn or her aunt, bending over her. These kind, solicitous faces had been no more than a glimpse, and then she had gone off into the dreams again. The curious thing had been that the dreams had seemed to be her vivid waking life, and the other things – the anxious faces, the details of her dingy bedroom, the thermometer under her tongue – had been the dream. And, though she had come back to actuality, the dreams had never quite vanished. She could remember no more of them than that they had seemed to hold a high singing and jocundity, issuing from some region of haze and golden light; and they seemed to hover, ever on the point of being recaptured, yet ever eluding all her mental efforts. She was living now between reality and a vision.

She had fewer words than sensations, and it was a little pitiful to hear her vainly striving to make clear what she meant.

'It's so queer,' she said. 'It's like being on the edge of something – a sort of tiptoe – I can't describe it. Sometimes I could almost touch it with my hand, and then it goes away, but never *quite* away. It's like something just past the corner of my eye, over my shoulder, and I sit very still sometimes, trying to take it off its guard. But the moment I move my head it moves too – like this – '

Again he gave a quick start at the suddenness of her action. Very stealthily her faunish eyes had stolen sideways, and then she had swiftly turned her head.

'Here, I say, don't, Bessie!' he cried nervously. 'You look awfully uncanny when you do that! You're brooding,' he continued, 'that's what you're doing, brooding. You're getting into a low state. You want bucking up. I don't think I shall go to the Polytec. tonight; I shall stay and cheer you up. You know, I really don't think you're making an effort, darling.'

His last words seemed to strike her. They seemed to fit in with something of which she too was conscious. 'Not making an effort . . . '

she wondered how he knew that. She felt in some vague way that it was important that she *should* make an effort.

For, while her dream ever evaded her, and yet never ceased to call her with such a voice as he who reads on a magic page of the calling of elves hears stilly in his brain, yet somehow behind the seduction was another and a sterner voice. There was warning as well as fascination. Beyond that edge at which she strained on tiptoe, mingled with the jocund calls to Hasten, Hasten, were deeper calls that bade her Beware. They puzzled her. Beware of what? Of what danger? And to whom? . . .

'How do you mean, I'm not making an effort, Ed?' she asked slowly, again looking into the fire, where the kettle now made a gnat-like singing.

'Why, an effort to get all right again. To be as you used to be – as, of course, you will be soon.'

'As I *used* to be?' The words came with a little check in her breathing.

'Yes, before all this. To be yourself, you know.'

'Myself?'

'All jolly, and without these jerks and jumps. I wish you could get away. A fortnight by the sea would do you all the good in the world.'

She knew not what it was in the words 'the sea' that caused her suddenly to breathe more deeply. The sea! . . . It was as if, by the mere uttering of them, he had touched some secret spring, brought to fulfilment some spell. What had he meant by speaking of the sea? . . . A fortnight before, had somebody spoken to her of the sea it would have been the sea of Margate, of Brighton, of Southend, that, supplying the image that a word calls up as if by conjuration, she would have seen before her; and what other image could she supply, could she possibly supply, now? . . . Yet she did, or almost did, supply one. What new experience had she had, or what old, old one had been released in her? With that confused, joyous dinning just beyond the range of physical hearing there had suddenly mingled a new illusion of sound – a vague, vast pash and rustle, silky and harsh both at once, its tireless voice holding meanings of stillness and solitude compared with which the silence that is mere absence of sound was vacancy. It was part of her dream, invisible, intangible, inaudible, yet there. As if he had been an enchanter, it had come into being at the word upon his lips. Had he other such words? Had he the Master Word that – (ah, she knew what the Master Word would do!) – would make the Vision the Reality and the Reality the Vision?

Deep within her she felt something – her soul, herself, she knew not what – thrill and turn over and settle again . . .

'The sea,' she repeated in a low voice.

'Yes, that's what you want to set you up – rather! Do you remember that fortnight at Littlehampton, you and me and your Aunt? Jolly that was! I like Littlehampton. It isn't flash like Brighton, and Margate's always so beastly crowded. And do you remember that afternoon by the windmill? I did love you that afternoon, Bessie!' . . .

He continued to talk, but she was not listening. She was wondering why the words 'the sea' were somehow part of it all – the pins and brooches of the Museum, the book on her knees, the dream. She remembered a game of hide-and-seek she had played as a child, in which cries of 'Warm, warm, warmer!' had announced the approach to the hidden object. Oh, she was getting warm – positively hot . . .

He had ceased to talk, and was watching her. Perhaps it was the thought of how he had loved her that afternoon by the windmill that had brought him close to her chair again. She was aware of his nearness, and closed her eyes for a moment as if she dreaded something. Then she said quickly, 'Is tea nearly ready, Ed?' and, as he turned to the table, took up the book again.

She felt that even to touch that book brought her 'warmer'. It fell open at a page. She did not hear the clatter Ed made at the table, nor yet the babble his words had evoked, of the pierrots and banjos and minstrels of Margate and Littlehampton. It was to hear a gladder, wilder tumult that she sat once more so still, so achingly listening . . .

> The earnest trumpet spake, and silver thrills
> From kissing cymbals made a merry din –

The words seemed to move on the page. In her eyes another light than the firelight seemed to play. Her breast rose, and in her thick white throat a little inarticulate sound twanged.

'Eh? Did you speak, Bessie?' Ed asked, stopping in his buttering of bread.

'Eh? . . . No.'

In answering, her head had turned for a moment, and she had seen him. Suddenly it struck her with force: what a shaving of a man he was! Desk-chested, weak-necked, conscious of his little 'important' lip and chin – yes, he needed a Polytechnic gymnastic course! Then she remarked how once, at Margate, she had seen him in the distance, as in a hired baggy bathing-dress he had bathed from a machine, in muddy water, one of a hundred others, all rather cold, flinging a polo

ball about and shouting stridently. 'A sound mind in a sound body!' ...
He was rather vain of his neat shoes, too, and doubtless stunted his
feet; and she had seen the little spot on his neck caused by the chafing
of his collar-stud . . . No, she did not want him to touch her, just now
at any rate. His touch would be too like a betrayal of another touch ...
somewhere, sometime, somehow . . . in that tantalising dream that
refused to allow itself either to be fully remembered or quite forgotten. What was that dream? *What* was it? . . .

She continued to gaze into the fire.

Of a sudden she sprang to her feet with a choked cry of almost
animal fury. The fool *had* touched her. Carried away doubtless by
the memory of that afternoon by the windmill, he had, in passing
once more to the kettle, crept softly behind her and put a swift
burning kiss on the side of her neck.

Then he had retreated before her, stumbling against the table and
causing the cups and saucers to jingle.

The basket-chair tilted up, but righted itself again.

'I told you – I told you – ' she choked, her stockish figure shaking
with rage, 'I told you – you – '

He put up his elbow as if to ward off a blow.

'You touch me – *you*! – *you*!' the words broke from her.

He had put himself farther round the table. He stammered.

'Here – dash it all, Bessie – what is the matter?'

'*You* touch me!'

'All right,' he said sullenly. 'I won't touch you again – no fear. I
didn't know you were such a firebrand. All right, drop it now. I won't
again. Good Lord!'

Slowly the white fist she had drawn back sank to her side again.

'All right now,' he continued to grumble resentfully. 'You needn't
take on so. It's said – I won't touch you again.' Then, as if he
remembered that after all she was ill and must be humoured, he
began, while her bosom still rose and fell rapidly, to talk with an
assumption that nothing much had happened. 'Come, sit down again,
Bessie. The tea's in the pot and I'll have it ready in a couple of jiffs.
What a ridiculous little girl you are, to take on like that! . . . And I
say, listen! That's a muffin-bell, and there's a grand fire for toast!
You sit down while I run out and get 'em. Give me your key, so I can
let myself in again – '

He took her key from her bag, caught up his hat, and hastened out.

But she did not sit down again. She was no calmer for his quick
disappearance. In that moment when he had recoiled from her she

10

had had the expression of some handsome and angered snake, its hood puffed, ready to strike. She stood dazed; one would have supposed that that ill-advised kiss of his had indeed been the Master Word she sought, the Word she felt approaching, the Word to which the objects of the Museum, the book, that rustle of a sea she had never seen, had been but the ever 'warming' stages. Some merest trifle stood between her and those elfin cries, between her and that thin golden mist in which faintly seen shapes seemed to move – shapes almost of tossed arms, waving, brandishing objects strangely all but familiar. That roaring of the sea was *not* the rushing of her own blood in her ears, that rosy flush *not* the artificial glow of the cheap red lampshade. The shapes were almost as plain as if she saw them in some clear but black mirror, the sounds almost as audible as if she heard them through some not very thick muffling . . .

'Quick – the book,' she muttered.

But even as she stretched out her hand for it, again came that solemn sound of warning. As if something sought to stay it, she had deliberately to thrust her hand forward. Again the high dinning calls of 'Hasten! Hasten!' were mingled with that deeper 'Beware!' She knew in her soul that, once over that terrible edge, the Dream would become the Reality and the Reality the Dream. She knew nothing of the fluidity of the thing called Personality – not a thing at all, but a state, a balance, a relation, a resultant of forces so delicately in equilibrium that a touch, and – *pff*! – the horror of Formlessness rushed over all.

As she hesitated a new light appeared in the chamber. Within the frame of the small square window, beyond the ragged line of the chimney-cowls, an edge of orange brightness showed. She leaned forward. It was the full moon, rusty and bloated and flattened by the earth-mist.

The next moment her hand had clutched at the book.

'Whence came ye, merry damsels! Whence came ye
 So many, and so many, and such glee?
 Why have ye left your bowers desolate,
     Your lutes, and gentler fate?'
'We follow Bacchus, Bacchus on the wing
     A-conquering!
 Bacchus, young Bacchus! Good or ill betide
 We dance before him thorough kingdoms wide!
 Come hither, Lady fair, and joinèd be
     To our wild minstrelsy!'

There was an instant in which darkness seemed to blot out all else; then it rolled aside, and in a blaze of brightness was gone. It was gone, and she stood face to face with her Dream, that for two thousand years had slumbered in the blood of her and her line. She stood, with mouth agape and eyes that hailed, her thick throat full of suppressed clamour. The other was the Dream now, and *these*! . . . they came down, mad and noisy and bright – Maenades, Thyades, satyrs, fauns – naked, in hides of beasts, ungirded, dishevelled, wreathed and garlanded, dancing, singing, shouting. The thudding of their hooves shook the ground, and the clash of their timbrels and the rustling of their thyrsi filled the air. They brandished frontal bones, the dismembered quarters of kids and goats; they struck the bronze cantharus, they tossed the silver obba up aloft. Down a cleft of rocks and woods they came, trooping to a wide seashore with the red of the sunset behind them. She saw the evening light on the sleek and dappled hides, the gilded ivory and rich brown of their legs and shoulders, the white of inner arms held up on high, their wide red mouths, the quivering of the twin flesh-gouts on the necks of the leaping fauns. And, shutting out the glimpse of sky at the head of the deep ravine, the god himself descended, with his car full of drunken girls who slept with the serpents coiled about them.

Shouting and moaning and frenzied, leaping upon one another with libidinous laughter and beating one another with the half-stripped thyrsi, they poured down to the yellow sands and the anem-onied pools of the shore. They raced to the water, that gleamed pale as nacre in the deepening twilight in the eye of the evening star. They ran along its edge over their images in the wet sands, calling their lost companion.

'Hasten, hasten!' they cried; and one of them, a young man with a torso noble as the dawn and shoulder-lines strong as those of the eternal hills, ran here and there calling her name.

'Louder, louder!' she called back in an ecstasy.

Something dropped and tinkled against the fender. It was one of her hairpins. One side of her hair was in a loose tumble; she threw up the small head on the superb thick neck.

'Louder! – I cannot hear! Once more – '

The throwing up of her head that had brought down the rest of her hair had given her a glimpse of herself in the glass over the mantelpiece. For the last time that formidable 'Beware!' sounded like thunder in her ears; the next moment she had snapped with her fingers the ribbon that was cutting into her throbbing throat. He with the torso and those shoulders was seeking her . . . how should he know her in that dreary garret, in those joyless habiliments? He would as soon known his own in that crimson-bodiced, wire-framed dummy by the window yonder! . . .

Her fingers clutched at the tawdry mercerised silk of her blouse. There was a rip, and her arms and throat were free. She panted as she tugged at something that gave with a short 'click-click', as of steel fastenings; something fell against the fender . . . These also . . . She tore at them, and kicked them as they lay about her feet as leaves lie about the trunk of a tree in autumn . . .

'*Ah!*'

And as she stood there, as if within the screen of a spectrum that deepened to the band of red, her eyes fell on the leopard-skin at her feet. She caught it up, and in doing so saw purple grapes – purple grapes that issued from the mouth of a paper bag on the table. With the dappled pelt about her she sprang forward. The juice spurted through them into the mass of her loosened hair. Down her body there was a spilth of seeds and pulp. She cried hoarsely aloud.

'Once more – oh, answer me! Tell me my name!'

Ed's steps were heard on the oil-clothed portion of the staircase.

'My name – oh, my name!' she cried in an agony of suspense . . . 'Oh, they will not wait for me! They have lighted the torches – they run up and down the shore with torches – oh, cannot you see me? . . . '

Suddenly she dashed to the chair on which the litter of linings and tissue-paper lay. She caught up a double handful and crammed them on the fire. They caught and flared. There was a call upon the stairs, and the sound of somebody mounting in haste.

'Once – once only – my name!'

The soul of the Bacchante rioted, struggled to escape from her eyes. Then as the door was flung open, she heard, and gave a terrifying shout of recognition.

'I hear – I almost hear – but once more . . . IO! *Io, Io, Io!*'

Ed, in the doorway, stood for one moment agape; the next, ignorant of the full purport of his own words – ignorant that though man may come westwards he may yet bring his worship with him – ignorant that to make the Dream the Reality and the Reality the Dream is Heaven's dreadfullest favour – and ignorant that, that Edge once crossed, there is no return to the sanity and sweetness and light

that are only seen clearly in the moment when they are lost for ever –
he had dashed down the stairs crying in a voice hoarse and high with
terror.

'She's mad! She's mad!'

The Painted Face

I

How Mrs Van Necker had come to be in charge of the party of girls can be told in a very few words. Say that you were travelling Europe with your daughter, and business or some other reason called you home. You might then have to bring the girl back with you. But you looked round, and there was Mrs Van Necker, with a daughter of her own, ready for a consideration to undertake the responsibility till your return. She knew her Mediterranean; she still preserved a good presence; and her frank admission that her job was no sinecure gave you confidence. Here (you said) is a woman who knows that young girls are a handful, and lays her plans accordingly. So you said goodbye to your child, and went about your business with a mind at rest.

In this way it had come about that the two English girls had been handed over to Mrs Van Necker in Rome, and a third, an American art-student, in Naples. With her own daughter Mollie that brought her party up to four, all between sixteen and nineteen years old, and she was to pick up a fifth girl in Palermo on her way to Northern Africa. To Palermo the party had made with all speed, descending at the hotel exactly two hours before the departure of the Tunis boat.

Mrs Van Necker was privately a little elated. She knew Umberto Francavilla by repute as an immensely rich Sicilian, the financial power behind at least a quarter of the casinos and hotels along a ten-thousand-miles littoral. The future was not always without anxiety for Margaret Van Necker. With the daughter of such a man knitted to her by kindness and obligation the outlook would be considerably rosier.

She was known at the Palermo hotel, and she and her four charges were shown to a tea-table. She ordered tea, and then herself disappeared for ten minutes or so. When she returned not an eyelash was out of place, and the silvery lock of hair that somehow made her a pretty as well as a responsible woman, lay flat exactly where she wished it to lie.

There were not more than a dozen people in the hotel lounge, and a glance had told Mrs Van Necker which couple were father and daughter on the point of leavetaking. They sat half hidden behind an oleander in the farthest corner of the room, and on the table in front of Umberto Francavilla stood an untouched drink, in which the ice had melted to a wafer. They were hand-in-hand, and Mrs Van Necker's eyes took in the father's externals first – the early-bald head with the unwrinkled brow, the severe black morning-coat, and his sad, clever, unsmiling dark eyes. The sadness of parting, Mrs Van Necker reflected. A cheerful demeanour for that. After all the girl was to rejoin him in two or three weeks' time in Algiers. So smiles and reassurances for Signor Umberto. She caught a little of what he was saying as she bore in her pale sweet-pea colours down the room.

' – not this time, little heart. You have been with me too much. It is not good for you to be alone in hotels while I am occupied all day, also there are people I do not wish you to see. You must be more with girls of your own age. They know me at the Tunisia Palace. You will be looked after. So go, little one, and do not forget to pray every night to Santa Rosalia – '

Then the unsmiling eyes saw Mrs Van Necker's manicured hand with the new glove dangling from the wrist, and he was on his feet.

'You are Signor Francavilla? I am Margaret Van Necker. And this, I suppose – ' she smiled at the young girl, who stood up.

Umberto Francavilla presented his daughter Xena, and fetched another chair.

It did not take Mrs Van Necker three minutes to decide that she couldn't bear the man. She might as well have smiled at the tub that held the oleander as at him. Perhaps that was how he had become a financial power – by listening, and looking measuringly into people's eyes like that, and not saying a word. His attitude to his daughter she set down as mawkish. A separation would take them out of themselves and each other and be good for them both. And she had heard him say that he wished Xena to be with girls of her own age.

'That's my brood over there,' she said pleasantly, with a nod across the room. 'The one with the teapot is my daughter Mollie, Xena. The girls on each side of her are Cicely and Daphne Bruce-Harries. They are English. You have been in England, Signor Francavilla?'

'I have been in many places.'

'Then perhaps you have met General Bruce-Harries?'

Instead of answering her question he said abruptly, 'Have you a car?'

Mrs Van Necker was obliged to say that for the moment she had no car.

'Then I will have one sent. You will be so good as to ask two days from now at the Tunisia Palace Hotel. It is there that I wish you to go, not to the other one, which I built. If you go to Sfax I should stay at the Hotel de France. At Sousse the Grand is the best. At the hotels or elsewhere you have only to say that this is my daughter.'

Mrs Van Necker liked him less and less. He talked to her as if she were an untravelled person. She was to use his daughter's name. In one breath he commended the child to Santa Rosalia, and in the next put her over Mrs Van Necker's own head as the member of the party for whom most would be done. She glanced again at the bearer of a name so potent. The child could hardly be seventeen yet, but she wore a perfectly mouth-watering Lanvin frock, over calves that perhaps swelled a shade unusually from her slender ankles, as if she had taken lessons in professional dancing. Her pale blue Canterbury-bell of a hat was pulled so far down that Mrs Van Necker suspected there were tears to hide. Cars despatched to Tunis because of her, as casually as if they were picture-postcards! It slightly overpowered Mrs Van Necker. But she rose and spoke gaily.

'Shall I leave you two? Or would Xena like to be introduced to the others now? Not that there's any hurry for half an hour – '

'Go to them, little one. I shall see you at the boat,' said Umberto Francavilla, and Mrs Van Necker felt the words not so much as a permission to his daughter as a dismissal of herself as a tiresome woman.

'We're all going to be *so* happy,' she said with her hand possessively on the young girl's shoulder as they crossed the room; but what she was really thinking was, 'Casinos! Well, he has that hard sort of look. But Santa Rosalia! I shouldn't have thought that! Anyway except for this child with her frocks and cars he's a woman-hater, not much doubt about that! . . . Molly – Daffy – Cicely – Amalia this is Xena. And her father's having a car sent over for us.'

The two English girls were of the half-pretty, half-plain, out-to-marry kind, both with eyebrows so light that they might as well not have had any. The taller of them said, 'How lovely! What sort?'

In a shy, yet strong and musical little voice, the girl murmured the names of Isotta, Lancia, Rolls; whereupon the one who had poured out tea broke in explosively.

'Oh, what a *nice* girl to join our party! But why doesn't your father send us over in his steam yacht?'

Timidly the girl lifted a pair of eyes as blue as her hat. She had not been crying.

'Shall I go and ask him?' she said.

'*What*! he *has* one! I was only – '

'Come, come, as if we shouldn't all be fond of Xena for her own sake!' Mrs Van Necker smiled, with her hand again on Xena's shoulder.

'Is it Zena like Zena Dare?'

'You spell it with an X, don't you, Xena?'

'What's her other name?'

'Francavilla.'

'I shall call her Frankie.'

'Is that her father over there?'

Mollie Van Necker was busy with a puff and a mirror. – 'I like men of that age; they always smell so nice of bath-salts,' she remarked.

'Mollie!'

'Well, don't you smell men as they pass?'

'We hate to call you vulgar, Mollie – '

'All bath-salts and lovely cigarettes – '

'They have to be bowed down with years before they can afford those things,' the younger English girl observed.

'Well, I suppose we can't have everything – '

'*I* shall do it like tennis-service, a jolly good smash if it comes off, and one left if it doesn't – '

Mrs Van Necker's voice was heard – 'Hadn't somebody better be seeing about a taxi?'

The Sicilian child had taken a step to where she could see beyond the revolving doors. She returned, and spoke unspoken-to for the first time. – 'That's my father's car waiting for us,' she said.

'However many cars *has* her father?'

'I think about eight,' the shy, earnest voice replied. 'He keeps them in different places. He travels a great deal.'

'Eight – cars! – '

'And oh, what a handsome chauffeur! What's his name, Frankie?'

'Ruggiero,' said the child in the Lanvin frock.

'Is he the one we're going to have in Tunis?'

'I don't know. I could ask father.'

'Doesn't she speak good English!'

'Just like any of us!'

'Xena speaks five languages, besides having been at school in England,' Mrs Van Necker informed them.

'And isn't that a lovely frock she has on!'

'And that hat to match her eyes – '

'Well, don't let's talk *at* her like this – '

'Suppose we consider the ice broken – '

The chatter continued.

Umberto Francavilla still sat in the far corner, bald and dark-suited, as if the oleander above him had been tied up with a mourning-streamer of black. It was the first time he had been separated from his daughter, and he had not come to his resolution without many prayers to the Saint. For this hotel-lord, who provided glittering halls for the amusement of others and looked on with contempt, was also a man of a deep and superstitious piety. Wherever he was and on whatever business, September always found him back in Palermo, carrying his candle in the procession. Had not the Saint prospered him? Had anything he had undertaken in her name failed him? And had he not still need of her grace for other enterprises? Therefore he saw to it that his daughter's prayers were added to his own. When she had been no more than a lisping child her '*O cara Verginella Rosalia*' had never failed to bring the tears to his eyes. He disliked and mistrusted women. For even the small part they played in his life (which the Saint forgive him) he despised himself. In a year or two his daughter – but it was no good thinking of that. It was best she should go. She would be safe in the keeping of that overdone woman with the gummed-down hair. The girls seemed like other girls, and he was terrified of them, but that too would be good for Xena. So let her go. And sweet Rosalia protect her.

His daughter approached him. She did not sit down.

'They're going in a few minutes, father,' she said wistfully.

Yes, he knew with sorrow that the moment was drawing near.

'Are you coming with us?'

'First sit down for a minute.'

She did so, leaning slightly towards him, as if they had been lovers.

He found no words; with so much to say, how begin? Enough that he felt the air about them to be a sacred and a prayerful thing at that moment. But it would have been less than natural had Xena not felt some flutter of excitement. This was not like going to school in

England. That Xena who had been in England had been a head-and-a-half smaller than herself. Sometimes that seemed a remote Xena, of whom she had dreamed. On Saints' days she had always dressed in simple white down to her heels. A prim little bouquet and chaplet had been her only adornment. But now she was to be a young woman among young women, flattered for her frocks, her hats, her command of cars. Only a few moments ago Mollie Van Necker, with a '*Do* let us see what's in your bag!' had grabbed the bag and opened it, and had exclaimed at finding there no face-powder, no eyebrow-pencil, no stick for the lips. 'However do you manage!' Mollie had laughed, and Xena had admired Mollie's full bosom and the lips that already men looked at. She felt that she had ever So many things to learn.

Suddenly her father spoke.

'Take your hat off for me, little one.'

Her hands went to the blue Canterbury-bell and removed it. She sat a little back, looking at her father, he at her.

With the removal of the hat the anomaly instantly appeared. Ordinarily the Sicilian woman is slight and dark and vivacious, with a beauty she cannot let alone. She may wear that modest chaplet on Saints' Days, but let carnival come and she claps a white wig on that dusky hair, and the rest is powdered and pomped out in palest pinks and lightest blues. Even the young men put on sham whiskers of burnt cork, confessing a Spanish strain. And thus far this child of seventeen was Sicilian. Sicilian was the cool honeysuckle brown tint, that, unlike the English sunburn, probably did not vary over her whole young body. The smoky helmet of uncropped and not very long hair, sudden on the low brow, was Sicilian too. But the rest? Those broad temples, their breadth accentuated by the setting of the eyes, as if a hand on either cheek drew them apart? That tapering pointed chin? And above all the eyes themselves? Whence did *they* come? . . . There is a Sicilian blue. Noble families vaunt it. But it is not *that* blue. Xena's eyes were blue as the waters of Sidi-Bou-Said. They had a morning blue, and a blue as if a wind passed over them and ruffled them. And the mouth beneath was a Punic rose, with that serious faintly-hovering smile that always has in it more of tragedy than of mirth. Light blue eyes and grave undying smile, seen it may be across a flower-barrow in a Smyrna street or over a glove-counter in Athens – they are only varyingly submerged, and sometimes come up to within an inch of the surface of the centuries' flood. And hotels were not the only things about the Mid-World sea that Umberto Francavilla knew. His sad eyes were attentively on the young face.

'No, not your mother – ' his lips were murmuring. 'And she had no lover but me – '

'What, father?'

He shook his head. She did not catch his muttering.

'Nor was her mother's mother so. And it may be forgotten again in her daughter. If she has one. If she has one . . . Say once again *"O cara Verginella Rosalia"*, little one – '

And under the oleander the young girl in the Paris frock, piously closing those ancient eyes of freshest blue, placed her hands together, dipped her knee dutifully under the table, and repeated, in the musical voice that had always moved him so: '*O cara Verginella Rosalia, elevatissima Sposa di Cristo, Voi a guisa d'immacolata colomba, che teme macchiarsi l'intatto candore dello sue penne –* '

And she added, '*Gloria al Padre . . . Amen.*'

An hour later she stood on the boat's upper deck, looking out over the stern as the shipping slid slowly by. Among the small knot of people at the quay-head her father was still to be seen, his fluttering handkerchief a white speck, his head a tiny egg. The mountains shut in the town behind, and on her right as she looked back rose Pellegrino, grey, stony and precipitous, the Saint's chapel not to be seen on his clouded top. Past shipping and factories and lighthouse the steamer slipped, and Umberto Francavilla was no more to be seen.

But as the boat rounded the headland and skirted the sheer cliff the skies broke. From between ragged clouds there poured a glory of sun. It picked out every wrinkle of Pellegrino's brow, pencilling his visage with a tracery of light. And highest of all the Saint's huge effigy stood, with her ruins about her and the halo above her head. Xena, on a deck so far below, tried to realise how often she had been up there, and placed tapers in the grotto-chapel, held her breath at the thought of the miracle that had been wrought there. She crossed herself; and, as she did so, as suddenly as it had come, the glory of sun went out. Before her was the grey sea, with Ustica a cloudlet far away. The air was chill.

She felt a little cold. Turning, she went below in search of her new companions.

2

Twin-cabins had been booked on the port side, Mrs Van Necker
sharing one of them with the art-student who had been put into her
charge at Naples. As for the other two cabins, so far they appeared to
be anybody's. Xena had been given a bunk opposite Mollie Van
Necker's, but the other girls were so in and out, Mollie herself was so
in and out, that sometimes they all got jammed together in the
narrow passage that rose and sank again on a gentle swell.

'Out, all of you, and give me air!' Mollie cried. 'I want to see
Xena's things!'

But they all wanted to see Xena's things, and one at least of her
trunks had to be opened straightaway.

'How beautifully she packs!' Cicely Bruce-Harries admired, looking at the tray of clothing, as neat as a box of paints that has never
been used.

In the very smallest things Xena had always been scrupulously
truthful. It was wrong to take to oneself the praise due to somebody
else.

'My maid did that,' she shyly confessed. 'She's a very good maid,
but father didn't think I'd need to bring one away.'

'Her maid! . . . Never mind, I'll be your maid.' And Mollie Van
Necker, who appeared to be good-natured before everything else,
took out the costly garments one by one, tucking them under her
chin with one thigh extended in order to admire their draping upon
herself. 'And her father's a widower! *And* I always liked them not too
young!'

Xena knew what Mollie meant. She did not look upon her father as
old. She considered it carefully.

'I don't think father would ever marry again,' she said, and then
shrank from the laughter she had caused.

'I know I'm going to *love* her! She takes everything so seriously!'

'Perfectly literally – '

'Mollie wasn't *really* thinking of marrying your father, Frankie!'
the elder of the English sisters informed her.

'Oh, wasn't she!' This from Mollie. 'Give her a quarter of a
chance – '

'Shut up, Mollie . . . and oh, just *look* at this embroidery and then
think of ours!' And the English girl with even less eyebrow than the
other held up a garment that seemed to be sown with mignonette,
and, like mignonette closely examined, broke up into minute glows.

'And it isn't a trousseau, mind you. It's just one of the rags she wears.' Mollie Van Necker, with a sniff of disdain affected to cast the rag from her.

Xena spoke again. – 'I haven't started a trousseau yet. I've always been with father.'

Again they talked at her, past her, about her.

'*Isn't* she a pet!'

'And I was once like that!'

'That you never were!'

'And speaking all those languages! What chances I'd make for myself in five languages!'

'You don't do badly in one.'

'Well, I'm open about it, that's all the difference. – Xena, have you ever had a cocktail?'

'Oh, yes!' said Xena promptly, glad to be back in the conversation instead of being the subject of it. 'Often! I've always been about with father, and I've often had them with him and his friends.'

'Well, we're going to have one presently'; and the chatter moved to other things.

'I suppose Dear Mamma will do the usual?'

'Oh, *she* prepares for the worst the moment she sets foot on a train-ferry!'

'And always sends her apologies, as if it had never happened before!'

'Please remember it's my sainted Mamma you're talking about – '

'The way *you* talk about your sainted Mamma sometimes!'

'Well, thank God, if I'm lovesick I'm not seasick!'

Xena seemed a little startled that God should be thanked for a thing like that, but after all why not? She had never been seasick, but it must be very unpleasant. As for Mrs Van Necker being sainted, she was sure they oughtn't to say those things.

'Is anybody going to change? Or shall we go in as we are?'

'For dinner? You bet I am!' said Mollie. 'Trains aren't worth it, but boats *are*.'

Half an hour later, over the cocktails, the prediction about Mrs Van Necker came true. The bearer of the message was the American art-student, Amalia Sherren. She was turned eighteen and the oldest of them, Cicely Bruce-Harries coming next, then Mollie, then Daphne. There was something about Amalia that gave an impression of impoverishment – not of circumstances, since, though she was careless about her dress, she still had money to travel – not of physique, though she was inconspicuous and as unlike the plump and vascular Mollie as she could well be – but a hunger of the eyes for colour, a craving of the heart and brain for the things of others, their passion, their vitality, their secret sacred things. She had been closeted with Mrs Van Necker, and so far Xena had hardly seen her. Amalia exclaimed at the sight of the frock into which Xena had changed.

'If that isn't just a won-derful colour!'

The frock was of a curious terracotta scarlet. It was sleeveless, and it showed the honeysuckle brown arms that, like her calves, had a smooth but distinct play of muscle. Amalia was looking Xena up and down.

'It's two shades off the colour of a gladiolus. And I guess you've exercised a lot. Degas draws legs like yours,' she said.

'Father brought it from Paris,' Xena faltered. Now Amalia was beginning to talk about her

'And it makes your eyes the colour of a spirit-flame. I guess I could just sit and look at you for a month.'

And the hueless eyes really looked as if they were going to do so.

The sudden clanging of the steward's bell summoned the passengers to dinner.

The boat was to touch at Trápani, so that this meal was served early. The sun was still at half-height, and his golden shafts burned through the portholes of the dining-saloon and wavered slowly over the floor to the swaying of the ship. They turned the black boots of the waiters to gold, and napery and flowers stood out in vivid relief against spaces of darkness in which the shapes of diners were floatingly divined rather than seen. Once in a while the torrent of gold died out entirely, leaving only the mild chains and clusters of the incandescents. A far less attractive group of girls would have sufficed to let loose a pleasant contagion on the air.

'He's looking at you again, Mollie,' the younger girl without eyebrows whispered.

Mollie's eyes were on her plate. 'Do you suppose I don't know?' she said. 'I think he's rather nice with his little fluffy moustache.'

And then the girl who had said that Xena's eyes were the colour of spirit-flames spoke.

'He isn't looking at Mollie. He's looking at Xena.'

A sudden wave of misery broke over Xena. It had come back to her all at once – the strangeness, the loneliness, the thought of her father. How she loved and missed him already! She knew that the talk of these girls was all about young men, but what young man

could ever take her father's place? Young men had never seemed
quite real to her. She hated being looked at by them; like Amalia they
always looked at her legs. She wanted to be like the Saint who bore
both the rose and the lily in her name, and for the love of Jesus had
turned her back on her father's palace and had chosen to live a virgin,
praying on her knees in a grotto. She wondered when her father
intended that this probation of being away from him and in the
company of girls of her own age should come to an end. When she
was twenty perhaps –

And she was only just turned seventeen –

Three years –

All at once she got up from the table, shaking her napkin to the
floor. She knew they were staring at her, but she took no notice. The
golden light flooded the calves beneath the scarlet frock as she
hurried to the door. She ran up the shallow brassbound stairs and out
on to the boat-deck. She wanted to be all by herself for a few
minutes.

What business had that girl to say that she had eyes like spirit-
flames and dancer's legs? If it was true that was all the more reason
she shouldn't say it. Uncomfortable things are more uncomfortable
than ever when they are true. Xena knew she looked like that. Sometimes it almost made her wish she hadn't a body. Bodies were only a
trouble and a burden. One would be happier with only a soul, like
Rosalia. Then one could say one's prayers and be at rest in the love
of Jesus . . .

All at once something seemed to be happening to the ship.

It was merely the fetch-round they were making, with their wake
a vast half-circle behind them. Trápani was in sight, a long low
sun-flushed coastline with two churches roofed with pale green
copper, and an ashen cobweb of masts behind. The four occulting
lights were already winking over the pale water, and the men of
the round-bellied boats let down the long lateens and took to the
stern-oars as they gained the shelter of the mole. Not far from
where Xena stood a rattling and commotion had broken out. Steam
had been got on the donkey-engine, and they were to drop cattle
and take up mules. She had seen the score or so of shaggy unhappy
beasts in the well, roped together and lurching. One of them
was so roped that its muzzle was jammed between the lower rail
and the deck, and she had wished she could unfasten it. Animals
were among her spiritual troubles. She thought it terrible that
they should suffer. First people were kind to them, and then they

killed them. In the Old Testament they had even sacrificed them. Abraham had been going to sacrifice Isaac, his own son, but had found a ram instead and had sacrificed that. And now her father was not going to be with her to answer her questions or else to turn her thoughts to something else. She wondered whether they had loosed that poor cow yet, and walked slowly forward as the custom-houses and the ash-wood of ships' masts drew nearer over the clear green of the water.

On the pontoon below the mules waited, pressed together, ears twitching, with an occasional snatch of yellow teeth and a smothered kick. After all mules were very bad-tempered. A young man was in charge of them who looked as bad-tempered as they, and he wore spats, and a soft silk collar and a smart hat. A mule had slipped and wasn't able to get on to its feet again, and the young man was beating it over the nose with a stick. Probably this was his last job of the day, and some girl was waiting for him, and he was in a hurry. He would take her to a cinema or for a walk, the way Xena knew they did. The ways of young men and girls were even more puzzling than people's ways with animals.

She continued to watch the beasts in the slings, twirling helplessly round in the air, till with a scrape against the fenders they found their feet again on the mule-fouled pontoon.

Suddenly she heard a voice behind her. It was Amalia come to bother her again. Her strained eyes were thirstily drinking in the faded greens and oranges of the lateen-boats and the flush that dyed the roofs along the quay.

'That would paint,' she said, 'but I know what I'd like to paint better.'

'What?' Xena asked.

'You.' And again she looked at Xena as if she was going to look for a month.

'I don't think I want to be painted, thank you,' said Xena politely.

'I guess you're a study,' Amalia went on, as if Xena hadn't spoken.

'I'd rather not be studied, please.'

Amalia gave a little laugh that seemed as parsimonious as everything else about her.

'They won't let us steal from people, but we can help ourselves to the way they look, I guess, and if they don't like it they'd better wear a veil,' she replied as she walked away.

At the other side of the boat the sea was a glare of copper, as if molten under its own giving-off of rusty smoke. Xena stood there.

The rattle of the donkey-engine had ceased. A hoarse blast shook the ship, as if deep lungs spoke without a throat; it rolled away over the wide waters, and was silent again. Indigo invaded the copper even as Xena watched. The occulting lights looked more staringly about them, other lights burned like steady rubies. She almost started back from the rail as, soundless as a ghost, a long lateen-yard passed not six feet away. Another trouble was now on Xena's mind. She considered it as Trápani's lights moved again and the ship slid out backwards into the night.

She shared a cabin with Mollie. Except in church, and to her father, she had never yet said her prayers to the Saint with anybody else in the room. Perhaps if she went down now she would have the cabin to herself. Somehow she wanted Mollie there less than anybody.

Nor was Mollie there. She was quite otherwise occupied. It was in the shadow of the after deckhouse that Xena came upon the huddle of two figures. As well as could be distinguished in the gloom one of them wore a red képi and black riding-boots. The silver slipper against the boots was the slipper of Mollie Van Necker.

Xena hurried below.

What had happened? Xena's hand was at her breast. She knew that as the screw throbbed and the water rushed past she was drawing every moment farther away from the known and familiar things and nearer to things unknown. Neither of the two she had just seen had known that Xena was there, so startled and still had she stood for perhaps five seconds, so silently had she glided away. So what had happened? To Xena? Nothing. The young French officer hadn't been kissing Xena; it was Mollie he had been kissing, and Xena was almost frightened that by accident she had seen it. She didn't think she would be able to look Mollie in the face tomorrow. She wished either that Mollie hadn't or that she had not seen. She wished that something, something she couldn't describe, was all over. She wished she was off this boat and in Tunis. There, in a new place, she would put out of her mind what she had seen – Mollie's lips crushed motionless against a man's. She must forget that the very first thing she did. She knew that that wasn't what her father had put her among girls of her own age for. It was something she could never, never tell him, and it was her first secret from him.

Yet he must have had a reason for sending her away. The night air seemed different already. She was sure that tomorrow was going to bring something *really* new, the thing that Umberto had meant. She ought to get up early, say her morning prayer, and see tomorrow before anybody was about. She ought to see its sunrise, all by herself. Mollie hadn't come down to the cabin yet, but Xena didn't know how long it took to be kissed, and she might be down at any moment. She had had a strange and exciting day, and was very sleepy. Perhaps for once the Saint would forgive her if she said one of the quite short prayers. Quickly she undressed and knelt down.

But the prayer would not come. She said the words, but she was thinking all the time of other things. She was thinking of Mollie, being kissed behind the deckhouse. She was thinking of Amalia Sherren, who said she had Degas legs and spirit-flame eyes. She could not even fix her thoughts on her father, perhaps praying for her at that moment. It was wicked not to give the whole of one's attention to the Saint, but she couldn't help it. She rose from her knees, switched off the light, and got into her bunk.

The last thought she remembered before she slept was that she must see the sunrise tomorrow morning.

Mollie was still a humped and slumbering shape in the opposite bunk when, at half-past six, Xena woke. Her first thought was about the sunrise. Had she missed it after all? She slipped out of bed and peeped out of the curtained port. No, she was in time, but only just; she would have to say her prayers later. Her dressing-gown was a royal purple-and-silver wrap; she put it on and thrust her feet into slippers. Softly she opened the door and stole out. She mounted to the deserted boat-deck.

The sea was cold and inky, but, as if a hurricane had taken a vast pink cloud and scattered it in rags abroad, the east was a flowering campion-field. Beyond one of the ship's boats distant slaty mountains rose, stretching away southward until they piled themselves up to the two-horned mass of Bou-Kornine, the ancient Hill of Baal. To starboard a white town straggled along a low green hill. It unfolded itself like a white flower, passed, and another white town succeeded it, with half a league of greeny-white bathing-cabins. In the far distance airy wireless-masts rose, and there drew nearer a lighthouse, with an eye red and sodden from watching all night. It was the Goulette, the entrance of the eight-miles-long canal, a waterway running through the sea itself; a vast pale sunny lake on either side of it, on which hundreds of white flamingoes rested. Past the salt-workings, past the hydroplane-station, at a snail's pace the boat crept along the dead-straight perspective, followed by its crawling backwash. The dark cloven mountain loomed nearer. Ahead lay Tunis, all white, split through by a straight green avenue. And as if somebody had told her, already Xena knew that another mirage of water lay beyond the town.

For she was standing there in that royal wrap of purple-and-silver, perplexed, and ever so slightly frightened. What was the matter with the wide and free and lovely place? It wasn't as if she had expected it to be like the harbour at home. She had been to lots of places with her father and knew how different places were. But even the difference here was different. It didn't *look* as if it had a Saint watching over it, as the effigy on Pellegrino's top watches over Palermo. God had made it, as He had made everything; but it didn't quite look as if it was in the Bible. And of course she wasn't frightened really. That was silly, as if she had been still a little girl. It was more like Christian taking off the Burden of Sin, she felt so released, only it was some other burden, not sin, because though she had done lots of little sins she hadn't done any big ones. Soon the fright would be *quite* past, and then – she knew it already – it was going to be lovely –

And once more she was aware of Amalia Sherren standing by her side.

Amalia was fully dressed in a walking-suit, ready to go ashore. If she was a painter of course she would want to see the sunrise too. She was looking at Xena's purple-and-silver wrap.

'You ought to go ashore in that,' she said casually.

'Oh, but I couldn't!' said Xena, shocked at the thought of going ashore in a dressing-gown.

Amalia was looking at the pale sunny waters, looking into Xena's eyes.

'And I guess I'm not wondering any more,' she said.

'Wondering what?'

'See the sun on that whitey-brown sand? You're that colour when you take that peignoir off. And you could dip a cup into that water and make a pair of eyes for yourself. I guess most folk would be scared to death at the half of what *you* know, Xena Francavilla!'

Xena stared at her for a moment. Then, with a cry that might have been joy or pain or both, she fled, with the purple-and-silver fluttering about her strong bare brown calves, the colour of the salty sand.

3

The green split through the white town is the Avenue Jules Ferry, and a quadruple row of trees runs up it. They are not the heavy plantains nor the catalpas, that meet overhead and make a tunnel of darkness; they are the tall ficus-tree, small-leaved like a birch, for ever a-tremble, translucently sifting through a clear and honeyed sun. Soft and distinct in the sweet impartial light they pass and re-pass – Frenchmen, Arabs, Jews, negroes, Greeks – crape-veiled Mahommedan women and typists and midinettes from Marseilles and Paris – between stalls banked with flowers. Half way up its length the Avenue is crossed by another, with clanging trams and two cafés that face one another. One of these has a terrace, raised some five feet above the pavement.

At a little before midday that day there approached this terrace a lightly-built English boy of twenty-two or thereabouts, whom you would have guessed at a glance to be just down from his University and taking a breather before plunging into life. His trousers were carefully creased, his socks gay, and his feet must have been still warm from the chamois-friction that had polished his brown (but not English-made) shoes. From the terrace above him a thoughtful-looking man of middle age called his name from behind a three-days-old *Times*.

'Good morning, Arden.'

The youth looked up – 'Good morning, Mr Thorne,' he smiled. 'Are you – '

But the question remained unfinished and unanswered. A clanging tram had drawn up, apparently hiding something that young Verney Arden wished to see. He stepped from the pavement, but seemed to change his mind at the sight of a smart, florid woman with a recently freshened-up look about her. She was accompanied by a young girl in a blue hat. The tram had shut out the little picture for a moment; when it moved on again neither the smart woman nor the blue hat was to be seen.

Apparently the English youth forgot all about his friend on the café terrace. He stood for a moment, and then suddenly turned towards his hotel, which was the Tunisia Palace, not a minute's walk away. Pushing through the swing doors he called the concierge, and asked him whether Signor Umberto Francavilla had arrived at the hotel. At the mere sound of the spellbinding name the concièrge inclined his body.

'*Non*, *m'sieur*. It is mademoiselle who arrived this morning.'

'Who's she with?'

'There are five young ladies, in the charge of a Madame – Mrs – ' he consulted his list, ' – Mrs Van Necker.'

'American?' (The lady had looked American.)

A shrug. – '*Ameliorée*.'

'Are they lunching here today?'

'*Oui m'sieur*. A table is being made ready now.'

'*Merci*.'

Past the hotel bookstall and up the stairs the young man passed to make himself beautiful.

In his room, where his belongings were as neatly set out as himself, he marched straight to his glass. Yes, he thought he would do. His grey summer-weight suit was hardly three weeks out of England, his Winchester tie was knotted as ex-prefects should knot their ties. His soft grey silk shirt and collar were all right, and his sheeny brown hair had been cut only yesterday.

Yes, a scrub and a polish-up and he thought he might do –

These externals were all it occurred to him to look at. As long as he hadn't cross-eyes or a wart or anything like that to worry about, why should a fellow waste time looking at his own face? There it was, and he couldn't alter it. A pretty girl's face, now, or the face of some fellow he liked –

And there in fact it was, looking at him from the glass – a face a thought too trusting and truth-believing for the job in life he had taken on. It was a face that ought to have had money behind it, and more even than money, love, and the flowery things of life. If you had told him that life might let him down he would have given a boyishly-cynical and altogether delightful laugh. As if with his daily experience he didn't know *that*! Anyway there was no time to go into these things now. He looked at himself again. For a moment he even entertained the wild idea of shaving again today, having already done so yesterday. Then he threw off his coat and filled his basin.

Love and the deep-end – he supposed that would come one of these days. It wasn't that yet – he almost added thank God. But when a fellow knocked about the Levant as much as young Verney Arden did, an exile from home and sometimes writing a letter to a girl in England just to remember that there *were* girls – well, these things mean rather more to a fellow like that than they do to other fellows. They had asked him after Winchester whether he would have the University or this, and he had chosen this, but it wasn't turning out exactly as he had thought it would. And it had really been her father's acquaintance that he had made in Cairo now more than three months ago. The daughter had been merely in the offing, so to speak. And while he hoped he wasn't trying to keep something alive because it was still faintly fragrant and pleasurable, there *had* been that sweet, baby-like look about little Xena Francavilla that always made a fellow feel a bit of a rotter, whether he had been up to anything or whether he hadn't.

Anyway she did that, and now, once more, the most unlikely thing in the world had happened, and here she was. A pity her father wasn't with her. He might have made up to the party then. But five girls with a duenna was another matter. People might even make a point of not intruding on a bevy like that. The only thing to do was to wait and see.

Descending again, he paused at the glass panes of the dining-room for a peep at the table that had been made ready for them. There it stood in the middle of the room, picking itself out from the surrounding tables like a bride among her maids. Ice-bucket, flowers, glass – that came from being called Francavilla! The table in the farthest corner that he and Mr Thorne shared seemed a poor relation by comparison. And he had better be sitting there in good time, to see them come in.

He moved to the bar, for the aperitif he had not had with Mr Thorne at the café with the raised terrace.

Some twenty minutes later, just as Verney Arden had taken his seat at the table in the corner, there were sudden bowings and scrapings at the door. The *maître-d'-hôtel*'s arms shot out like a policeman's in traffic, a lane was formed. They entered, the *Americaine ameliorée* leading, Xena hidden behind her shoulder, a glimpse of blue hat only, and the others following behind.

And 'Oh, dash,' muttered Verney Arden, for Mr Thorne too had entered, and was following in the party's wake down the room.

It wasn't that Mr Thorne wasn't quite a decent sort, in spite of the sometimes boring interest he seemed to take in Verney, his job, and everything about him. Verney didn't know what Mr Thorne did; he seemed comfortably off. But he wished he had been somewhere else today. He wanted to look at the party in the middle of the room, and at Xena Francavilla. Just a hint of that silly, nice, tender Cairo feeling had come over him again. Now he would have to talk to Mr Thorne, who would certainly begin with his usual well-meant question – how he had got on that morning.

Mr Thorne drew up the opposite chair. 'I thought you were calling at the café,' he said in his rather nice, hesitating voice.

'I beg your . . . oh!' Verney had completely forgotten. 'I'm sorry, Sir. I suddenly remembered something.'

'Well,' said Mr Thorne, reaching for his roll, ' – how are things this morning? Had a good slant of French?'

'Oh – much as usual – '

Mr Thorne broke his roll with deliberation.

'Much as usual, eh? Well, well, everything comes in time. I still think that was a wise choice of yours in many ways. A University is a little world. You see a much bigger one. How many thousands of miles have you travelled in the last six months?'

'Quite a lot. Athens. Cairo. Syria. Cyprus. And now here and on to Algiers and Gib.' (Why had Xena placed herself where he could only see the back of her hat?)

'Well, you'll write a book about it one of these days,' said Mr Thorne, taking a sardine.

Verney Arden could have written that book now, but it wouldn't have been the kind of book Mr Thorne meant. Had he had a good slant of French! Nobody knew better than he how rotten his French was, but let Mr Thorne put in a few months drumming the Levant, trying to found commercial agencies that nobody wanted! He'd know the difference between the French you bought in a shop with and the other French you tried to do business in then! What? With the fellow you were talking to knowing perfectly well what you meant, but letting you flounder and run down and ditch yourself; and never once helping you out. A book? . . . *'Notes for Chapter on Selling Things in the French you learn in English Public Schools*; Greenway's Bottled Products, *Adoptez-les* – take them on; *Agence Unique* – Sole Representative this side of Cap Bon' . . . And that other Chapter, on that ghastly taxi-load of samples he was so rottenly sensitive about, thrusting them out of sight in *consignes* and garages whenever he could, just as he did with that third suitcase, the one with the 'literature' in it –

If only he could have chucked business! If only he could have found himself in a place like the places those yachting fellows had talked about in Athens, where drummers and their Products had never been heard of; and wine cost a penny a bottle, and there was a quail for your dinner wherever you kicked over a stone!

His eyes travelled down the room. He knew most of the people there – old General Lorimer travelling for his health, his wife and daughter with their morning's shopping beside them on the floor; the Dean and his wife; the stiff and solitary young German with the book; the saturnine fellow who never had a meal without receiving a telegram; cactus-like old Lady Lyle in her white wool shawl, her French companion in black

And there in the middle, bright as the flower-stalls under the ficus-trees, the newest arrivals – Xena sitting with her back to him without a notion that he was in the room; that other girl who couldn't keep her eyes in the boat; the two English girls (he wondered who they were); that queer-looking young woman without any colour who looked as if she lived on ice-water; the brightly-dressed American chaperone –

Suddenly, to his measureless astonishment, he saw that the American chaperone, whom he had seen once in the street an hour ago, and who hadn't seen him at all, was giving him a most express smile and bow across the room.

There must be some mistake –

But there was no mistake. A moment later a waiter came up to him. Mrs Van Necker sent Mr Verney Arden her compliments, and would like the pleasure of meeting him, and would he take coffee with them in the garden after luncheon?

4

Mr Thorne was talking amiably on, but Verney Arden did not hear him. That side of the room was of a semi-clear glass, that varied faintly in colour, and it gave on the garden outside. Through it mazy sunspots of brightness and shadowy nodding palms showed. They had left the dining-room, Mrs Van Necker throwing him another backward smile, as if to say 'Presently', but they had not reappeared outside yet. The girl who couldn't keep her eyes in the boat had glanced his way too as she had gone out. But Xena had not so much as turned. She hadn't even looked round at the closing door.

Of course it was Xena's doing. It could only be Xena. But why hadn't she looked? It was O.K. and perfectly in order that the invitation should come through Mrs Van Necker, but surely she might have looked! She was shy, of course. He remembered her shyness in Cairo. But she hadn't been too shy to get Mrs Van Necker to send the message.

He sat looking through the tinted glass, watching the mazy sun-spots that dissolved into the cool greenness of the palms.

Suddenly they appeared, a muslined variegated patch, with Xena's blue hat swimming faintly in it. Rabat, the scarlet-fezzed negro, was dimly to be seen in the doorway behind them. Verney Arden pulled himself together. Anyway Xena would have to look at him in a moment or two. With a good-morning to Mr Thorne he rose. He walked down the room, through the adjoining lounge. As he approached the door where Rabat busied himself among the pip-kins on his copper table he heard a voice say 'Here comes your friend, Xena – '

What happened after that he could never afterwards quite remember in its proper order.

Presumably Xena would be the first to speak, introducing him in her shy moving little voice to Mrs Van Necker. Thereupon (he supposed) Mrs Van Necker would introduce him to the others. It couldn't very well be any other way. But all that had nothing to do with what really happened. In the dining-room Xena had not looked at him. She had come in behind Mrs Van Necker not looking at him. She had kept her head turned during the whole of lunch. And she had gone out without looking round.

Yet she had known all the time he was there.

Now she looked at him. Nothing more, nothing less. Her eyes met his in a slow lifting look.

Mrs Van Necker was talking, pronouncing names – 'My daughter Mollie – Miss Cicely and Daphne Bruce-Harries – '

Still, as she stood under a palm, Xena's eyes were on his, three parts as if they would have run away, but the fourth holding bravely on. The palm threw a shadow over the blue hat, so that the light from the sunspots on the ground made the eyes under the hat's brim the lighter blue of the two.

And he knew now why she hadn't looked at him in the hotel. Looks like *that* are no looks to let loose across dining-rooms, or to shoot, blue and bottomless, from the edge of a closing door!

' – Miss Amalia Sherren – Amalia's a painter – '

He had wondered whether he was still a little in love with her. Still! What was that word 'still', that implied a continuance, not a beginning? He was not *still* in love with her. He was in love with her. Wherever she had got it, it came from her, was her, and if there was anything in him worth saving and keeping it was his own no longer.

And the world continued to exist and function as usual – the little knot of guides and hawkers gathered about the gate they were not allowed to enter, a carpet-seller passing, somebody closing sun-shutters across the street, people sitting at other tables, Rabat approaching to know which coffee they would have –

'Well, now that everybody knows who everybody is let's all be comfortable – '

It had all taken just as long as it had taken to pronounce a few names –

And that (he told himself) was that.

Presently he found himself listening to Mrs Van Necker, replying to her.

'Signor Francavilla saw us off at Palermo.'

'How is Signor Francavilla?'

'Naturally just a little,' – Mrs Van Necker dropped her voice a little as she glanced towards Xena – 'but of course it's the first time – '

'I saw him last in Cairo.'

'Yes, Xena told me. Have you been in Tunis long?'

'A little more than a fortnight.'

'Then you'll be able to tell us everything there is to see.' More surprising still, he could actually turn to the girl on his right and talk to her.

'If your name's Bruce-Harries I knew a fellow of that name at Eton.'

'Oh, he knows Ronnie, Daffy! Were you at Eton?'

'No. Winchester. But I caught-and-bowled him one match. But I say – you mustn't think I'm a gentleman of leisure – I'm here in this part of the world as a sort of boxwallah really – '

Followed talk of Ronnie, of Eton, of the match.

Something told Verney Arden that he must now look at Xena less than at any of them. He must keep as it were to the environs of her, her garments, her little dangling foot, the green shade in which she sat. She was leaning back in a green wooden chair, with her head a little on one side and one hand along the chair's arm. And at the hand he did look. He had noticed her hands in Cairo. If he had been asked to put her whole meekness into one image it would have been an image with knees bent, eyes trustingly lifted, and the two little soft palms together. But now the fingers on the chair were moving ever so minutely, patiently rather than impatiently, and it was as if her eyes shut themselves up with their own happy thoughts now that his

own had run, leapt, flown to their bold yet bashful appeal. For hers
had done the calling. 'I want somebody to love me,' had been their
message. 'I'm not a little girl now, but a grown-up person with girls
of my own age, and they're loved, and I want to be loved. And I want
somebody for me to love too. I've only just learnt about it, but I feel
I want that more than anything. I didn't mind so much when father
was there, but it's dreadful having nobody, and I don't know anybody
but you yet.' This, from those Easter-cards of eyes he had seen in
Cairo, blue as the robes of the little images they place in niches in the
walls! Sweet, shy, yet adventurous little heart! He had heard that
girls 'shot up' quicker than boys, but had she glowed and deepened
into this in three short months? Two years – a year even – he could
have understood that. But this –

'I think we ought all to get tinted glasses,' Mrs Van Necker was
saying lazily. 'The sun is so glaring in the afternoons.'

Nearly half an hour had passed, and they had had coffee. Her
daughter laughed.

'Oh, we know all about *you*, mother! Do you know what mother's
going to do, Mr Arden?'

Astounding, Verney Arden thought, that this should be a girl too,
with eyes so different!

'She'll go upstairs, and take the Guide Book with her, and she'll
read it for nearly five minutes, and then – ' Mollie made the unlady-
like sound of a snore. 'The question is what are we all going to do?'

'I'm going to unpack my painting-things,' said Amalia Sherren.

There was a suppressed colloquy a little apart, of which Mollie
Van Necker was the centre. It ended in a shocked exclamation from
Cicely Bruce-Harries.

'Mollie! You *aren't*!'

'I am!'

'But you've only seen him once!'

'Then I shall have seen him twice.'

'Hallo, where Xena's off?'

For Xena had got up from the wooden chair. She approached Mrs
Van Necker.

'I think Verney and I would like to go for a walk,' she said, with
the same mixture of diffidence and resolution as before. 'May we,
please?'

Mrs Van Necker's manicured finger tips were delicately at her
mouth. – 'Child! In the heat of the afternoon!'

'I like the heat. Will you come, Verney?'

'May I take her?' Verney asked, his heart beating fast.

Of the battle between yawn and finger tips the yawn won. – 'When you say it in that English voice of yours – and you know Umberto Francavilla better than I do' – Mrs Van Necker replied.

'I shan't be five minutes, Verney,' said Xena; and she walked past Rabat and his tray and disappeared into the hotel.

Verney! When had she used that name before? Still a little bewildered, he turned to Mrs Van Necker.

'It's awfully good of you. What time would you like her brought back?'

To his surprise, another person answered him. He had not yet spoken to the ice-water-looking girl who had said she was going to unpack her paintbox. It was this girl who spoke, from behind his chair.

'Girls like Xena used sometimes to go out and not come back at all, I guess,' she said.

The fair-haired boy looked round and up at her. But he thought it best to turn it off as a joke.

'Oh, we aren't going to elope!' he laughed.

'No, I guess *you're* to be trusted,' Amalia replied, looking at him as she had looked at Xena.

Because it had been no part of his upbringing to talk from a chair while one of the opposite sex stood, Verney Arden had arisen. 'One of the opposite sex,' he couldn't help thinking, rather described this girl.

'Are you afraid somebody'll take her from me?' he asked, smiling.

'A man wouldn't, maybe. But I've heard of their gods getting a hold of people and not letting them go.'

'I – I'm sorry – I don't quite understand – '

'I guess I don't travel to see the things I can see at home,' the girl replied as she turned away.

In front of Rabat's red fez and sooty face Xena's blue hat appeared. 'Are you ready, Verney?' she called softly.

5

He was bursting with questions, quite apart from the sweet, secular confession itself; what had she said about him to Mrs Van Necker? Why had she, who had never before called him anything, suddenly called him Verney? That heavenly look she had given him had been no practised look; it had been touchingly the other way; where had she found it? And what in the name of goodness had the painter-girl meant about gods who took people and didn't bring them back?

But he had only to gaze at the sunshiny little feet moving by his own to forget everything else.

She wore shoes so slight that they were hardly more than pods for those little peas, her toes. Her stockings too were filmy, so that the busy tendons showed through them. The honey-coloured skirt flowed like windy corn as her knees knocked against it. And because it had all nothing to do with Greenway's Bottled Products it didn't matter what nonsensical loveliness he let his mind give way to. The pavements were full of other feet, varnished boots, high heels, shuffling heelless slippers, dusty brown feet with nothing on them at all. His own boots had been bought in Malta, for he couldn't send to England every time he wanted a pair of boots, and he was just a young fellow on the move, trying to do business in schoolboy French. But he told himself that those little feet had come all the way from Cairo, all the way from Palermo, all the way from wherever they had been, to walk beside his own. Darling little pilgrim pair! And then suddenly she gave the first laugh he had ever heard her give.

'What long strides you take!' she said. 'Nearly twice mine!'

'Not twice – '

He shortened his, she lengthened hers. Both laughing, they made for a few moments grotesque timing along the pavement.

'Where shall we go?' he asked, as the feet fell into their natural irregularity again.

There were the *souks*, the Avenue, the Belvedere, the quays. They could walk, or take one of the low-hung *carosses*. Or they could seek the shade of a café. It was Ramadan. Devout Mahommedans who would not break their fast by as much as a cup of coffee until six o'clock sat grave and silent behind screens and awnings. The African sun seemed to burn away the colour from the tops of the ficus-trees, imprisoning it in that gentle glow within. Watercarts sprinkled the streets, Renault cars picked up and dropped their passengers. It was at the sight of one of these that she suddenly spoke again.

'The car ought to be here tomorrow,' she said, as if out of her thoughts.

'What car?'

'Oh, I haven't told you. Father's sending us a car.'

'You girls?'

'I shall let the others use it,' she said with a little air of magnanimity that also struck him as new.

They walked on, he watching the feet again that popped in and out.

They were approaching the Porte de France, not far from the entrance of the *souks*, and all at once he knew where he would take her. He would take her to Hayoun's. His job made him known here and there in the bazaar quarter, and Hayoun was a good fellow. He had refused the agency Verney had asked him to take up, but Verney wished that some of the Frenchmen he knew were half as decent about it as Hayoun. Hayoun understood, and would give him coffee as a friend, and not as a guide-tout who, in Xena, had brought a possible customer.

'This way,' he said, and led her under the arch and across the busy *Place*.

They entered a crowded, vaulted ruelle, arcaded with painted wooden pillars and lighted by piercings overhead. In dark niches men tapped with little hammers, filed, incised, polished objects of brass. Slow-moving Arabs in hooded burnous jostled bare-legged porters with sacking on their backs, and half-naked figures slept under the bulks. All was a throng of lights and hues and noise and the odour of attar . . . and all at once, as somebody pushed him close to her, it came over him that he wanted nothing so much on earth as to see again that look she had given him in the garden, that soft wide-templed look, blue as artichoke flowers, blue as the piercings of the vault over their heads that let in the African sky.

But it was another blue that suddenly caught his eye. It was the horizon-blue of a young French officer in black riding-boots and a red képi. He was absorbed in lighting a cigarette at a match that a girl with her back turned to Verney shielded between her palms. The girl did not turn, but the officer, engaged as he was, nevertheless moved his eyes sideways. They rested on Xena's face in a way that Verney suddenly loathed. It was a familiar look, almost as if he claimed to know her. He hurried Xena past. He was glad that she had noticed neither officer nor look.

Hayoun's bazaar was round by a green-shuttered door up another cobbled and vault-roofed alley. It was only a tiny shop, just big enough for Hayoun himself; a broad low divan, a desk, an assortment of bric-a-brac, and the carpets on the walls. His principal stock of carpets was kept in the room at the back. Hayoun himself, enormously fat, red-fezzed and in a choke-collared black frock coat, greeted his English acquaintance with a friendly smile. He bowed as Verney presented Xena.

'*Ça marche toujours*?' he asked the youth, his clever eyes twinkling.

Verney made a face. – 'No, I can still take lessons from you, Hayoun. You give a thing away and they buy it. They eat my dinners and that's all.'

Hayoun chuckled as he moved a burnous from the divan and invited them to sit down.

'Everything comes with the years,' he said. '*La jeunesse* – ah! It has better things to do than sell carpets and copper dishes. You will see – '

He disappeared to prepare coffee.

As Verney Arden sat down by Xena's side on the divan the strangeness of it all came over him once more. It was too strange; it was unreal. In Cairo she had glanced back at her father if she had left his side for a few moments. She had run to him again the instant the excursion was over. Now she called him Verney, asked him to take her out for a walk, and told him with her eyes that she wanted him to love her. All this could *not* have come to pass in three short months. And yet it most evidently had come to pass.

'Well, tell me about since I saw you. Where have you been?' he asked.

'I've been at home,' she replied, almost shyly again.

'At home in Palermo?'

'Yes.'

'All the time?'

'Except for little journeys,' she answered, the eyes dropped.

'And you only left there yesterday?'

'Yes.' And suddenly she turned the blue gaze on him, not with the look of the garden this time, but anxiously, as if she thought he understood, but was not quite sure. 'But I know what you mean,' she added.

'What do I mean, Xena?'

'You mean I'm different, don't you?'

'You are different.'

'Don't you like me different?' she said in a low voice.

'Oh, I – ' but he checked himself. There would be time for that by and by. 'I mean why do *you* say you're different? Other people notice of course, but one doesn't strike oneself as being different.'

'I *think* it began on that boat,' she said reflectively.

'What began on the boat? The difference?'

'Yes. It hasn't been like this ever since Cairo. I'm certain it only began yesterday.'

He would have loved to hear her say that it had begun with her first sight of him, whatever it was, but she hadn't said that.

'Tell me all about it,' he begged her.

She spoke slowly, conscientiously. – 'I don't think I can tell you quite *all* about it, Verney, because that wouldn't be fair; you can't tell other people's secrets, can you?'

'Then tell me as much as you can tell me.'

'I was going to. I want to. I want to get all that part finished. – Is there another lake here, besides the one we came in at?' she suddenly asked.

'Here in Tunis? Yes. There's Es Sedjoumi, just beyond.'

'I thought there was. And I knew the mountain too, as if I'd dreamed about it sometime. I knew the mountain best of all. And then Amalia came up and said my legs were like the sand and I'd got my eyes out of the sea, and I was frightened at first.'

'Is Amalia the girl who paints?'

'Yes.'

'Are – are you frightened now?'

The look of uttermost candour was on him again. – 'Oh no. It's beautiful now,' she replied.

It might be beautiful, but somehow he found it a little intimidating. But he had better hear her account of it.

'You've never been in Tunis before?'

'No.'

'You say something began on the boat, and then comes something you'd rather not tell me, and that other girl said something, and you thought there was another lake. What comes after that, Xena?'

'Nothing till I got off the boat.'

'And then what?'

'I don't know yet.'

'You don't know – yet?'

Her lids were dropped again. The musical voice too was lowered. She must be very careful not to tell him a story. 'Well, I think I know in a *way*,' she answered softly.

'Is that all you can tell me?'

'It's all I can tell you *so* far, Verney.'

Verney Arden was not himself given to remembering lakes and mountains he had never seen before. Neither did he use 'so far's with quite that tranquil confidence that more was to come. Amalia Sherren's last words became more puzzling than ever.

'What did that girl who paints mean when she said that?' he demanded.

'That about my legs and eyes?'

'No. About people going out and sometimes not coming back.'

No sooner had it escaped him than he could have kicked himself. Ass! She hadn't been there, and hadn't heard. She had been making herself ready in the hotel. Amalia might even not have said it had she been there.

'Did she say that?' Xena asked, without surprise.

'Never mind.'

'Because I think that's quite *possible*,' Xena went on with deep gravity. 'You see there *was* that feeling I had, just like Christian having his Burden of Sin taken off. Only of course this wasn't sin. I don't quite know what sort of a burden it was, except that we're all sinners, aren't we? So it must have been a burden of another kind. Amalia's very clever. She knows things that other people don't. She says I know things that other people don't too.'

At that moment Hayoun entered with the coffee-tray, and no more could be said about Amalia and people having their burdens taken off.

If that ice-water woman was trying to frighten this child with her talk about knowing things that other people didn't (Verney thought) she ought to have a straight talking-to. Still, he himself had rubbed shoulders with a good many people and types during the past six months, and it was astonishing how even six months in the Levant made a fellow less cocksure about things. He had sometimes thought that if *he* had lived (for example) under a volcano and a long time ago, *he* might have been inclined to put a giant or a devil or a something there. Still, he was C. of E. A fellow had to be something, and in England he had been C. of E. But Hayoun, talking to Xena in Arabic there, wasn't, and other people had their beliefs too. They were in the middle of the Ancient world, and important things had happened here before England had been heard of. '*Ex Africâ* – ' he finished the tag.

'But we are impolite,' Hayoun said suddenly in French.

He meant that Verney did not understand Arabic, and the talk passed to French again.

Xena was gazing about Hayoun's shop, at the sound-deadening carpets on the walls, at his bric-à-brac, at the semi-transparent mat of plaited grass that fell half across the doorway, at the shelf of blue and green pots high on the wall. And as she looked the mat was drawn aside, and a young Arab head was thrust in. The lad said something to Hayoun in Arabic, who excused himself and rose. It was business, he said, and promising that he would not be long he waddled to the door. His bulk darkened the entrance for a moment; then the alfa-mat rustled back, and Verney and Xena were left together.

There was a long silence. Then, 'You were saying about Amalia,' he resumed.

But apparently Xena didn't want to talk about Amalia any more. It was as if something that puzzled him was already plain to herself.

'I wish I could tell you everything,' she said wistfully, 'but I can't, can I, if it drags other people in?'

Still (she thought) he might guess, even if she didn't say that about Mollie. She no longer wished she hadn't seen Mollie being kissed. She was glad she had seen. At first it had made her unable to think of her father or say her prayers properly, but it had brought other things instead, and each one of them was becoming lovelier than the last. There was even one little joke she had all to herself – for she knew that she had been very mischievous not to look at Verney in the dining-room. She knew that he must wonder about that – why she hadn't looked herself; but had told Mrs Van Necker that there in the corner was a friend of her father's and she wanted to give him a surprise, and might he be asked to coffee? For he didn't know that she had seen him first. But she had. She had seen him as she had come into the hotel, by the glass panes of the dining-room, looking in, though only the waiters were there. She had known him in a moment and of course it wasn't like Cairo now. And she had gone up to her room, and had thought very quickly, and it had come to her suddenly what to do. On the boat Mollie had known that she was being looked at without lifting her eyes from her plate. At first Xena had wondered how she did it, as if it had been a conjuring-trick. But all at once, making up her mind in her room, she had somehow known, and it was true, because it had worked instantly, looking at Verney like that under the palm. Now she could do something she hadn't known about before. What a lot she had learned in twenty-four hours! Why should people go in procession to a wet grotto, where once a miracle had been done, when there were miracles of one's very own, like this, to do?

And if she could do all this she could also please herself whether she did it or not. That was a thing she would have to be very conscientious about. She wanted to be good, and not to let first one man kiss her and then another, as she knew from their talk Mollie did. How clean and pretty Verney looked by the side of his fat Mahommedan friend! He had a nice small head, and looked as if he could run lightly, and swim, and catch a horse and ride it. He seemed part of this new thing, that for a moment had frightened her, but after that had grown more beautiful with each hour that passed. So far she had only shown him her eyes; she herself didn't know what she could do with her lips, the way Mollie did. She wished she hadn't drunk this heavy, sweet, thrice-pounded, thrice-boiled coffee. She would rather have had her mouth as scented as flowers, as fresh as fruit, for the kiss she knew he was going to have as soon as she had made up her mind.

She had only to look at him in the new way and she knew he would *have* to kiss her.

What he saw was a strong, straight-backed figure sitting with knees pressed close together, loins taut, hands on the divan at her sides. In a blue hat and a Lanvin frock, she sat strangely as Egyptian figures sit, to whom time is nothing, so certain are they of the end.

And he too knew that she had only to raise those lids and his life thenceforward was a sealed-up thing. His fate would be hers, whatever that was. He could not alter it, he would not attempt to alter it. He saw the lids quiver. They lifted. Straightway he dropped on his knees before her.

'I love you, I love you,' he said.

He had taken the young hands. The clear eyes looked down on his face.

'Do you, Verney?' the fresh voice said.

'Do you love me?'

As well as of the wish to love and be loved, the eyes were full of sweet scruples and truth-speaking too.

'I *think* I do, Verney dear. I *like* you to love me. I think I should like loving somebody too.'

'Oh, love me!'

'Even in Cairo I thought your hair was nice, but it isn't any good talking about Cairo now, is it?'

'I've thought of you ever since then – '

'Have you? Then perhaps now you may kiss me,' said the daughter of Umberto Francavilla.

He drew her head down. The two heads lay together on Hayoun's divan, his fair head, the tossed blue hat. And his soul passed to that unravished Punic rose of her mouth.

6

'So the gods didn't get her after all,' Mrs Van Necker jested.

They were back in the hotel lounge, which they had to themselves. It was not yet the dressing-hour, and chatter of the afternoon was being exchanged. Amalia Sherren was turning over the pages of a sketch book, but in her right hand a stump of pencil was palmed, ready for use. The two Bruce-Harries girls were scribbling picture-postcards at a writing-table, and Verney Arden had dutifully returned Xena to Mrs Van Necker.

'How far did you get in the guide book, mother?' her daughter asked lazily from the depths of a low chair, where she lay with legs crossed and hands clasped behind her head.

'Now you're all laughing,' said Mrs Van Necker, but with the air of one about to turn the laugh. 'You think I didn't read any, but just to show you you're wrong I'm going to tell you the most romantic thing.'

'Oh, do tell us, mother. I'm dying for a romance.'

'It's about the Greek ship that's in the Museum here. I expect *you* know all about it.' The last words were to Verney.

'No.'

'Then listen. A ship went down off this coast nearly two thousand years ago. It stayed there till 1907, and then one day the men found it as they were diving for sponges. Or rather they found what it had been loaded with, marbles and terracottas and bronzes. And they got them up, and they're all in the Museum here. I've been telling Amalia about it while you were out. We're going tomorrow.'

But she showed them the cover of the guide book with its account of that most wondrous of salvages, the *fouilles sousmarines* of Mahdia.

'But these ancient names are very confusing,' she chattered on. 'Sometimes its Ceres and sometimes it's Demeter, and among these things there's a Hermes that seems to be a Dionysos too, and it's by somebody called – I forget his name, but anyway tell me *now* I was asleep!'

'No, mother gets the marks this time,' her daughter conceded.

'Nearly two thousand years ago, in the First Century, and there these wonderful things have been till nearly up to the Great War!'

'That,' Amalia remarked as she turned the pages of the sketch book, 'ought to interest Xena.'

'It ought to interest anybody,' Mrs Van Necker declared.

'And gods can take their own time, I guess,' said Amalia.

From over by the writing-table the voices of the Bruce-Harries sisters were raised.

'*I* like them. They always look so wicked and good-tempered. And there's one here that's the image of her.'

'Let me look.' Daphne leaned over. 'Oh, isn't it! We ought to make her up as one sometime!'

'With that crimpy bandeau thing that makes them look as if butter wouldn't melt in their mouths – '

'And those draperies – where's the one with the draperies?'

Mrs Van Necker turned. – 'What are you two talking about?'

They brought her over a postcard. It was one of three busts side by side, and one of them was a wide-templed young woman.

'Isn't that exactly like Frankie? Even to her ears being a bit higher than anybody else's – '

Amalia muttered to the sketch book. – 'So they are. Hats don't show ears much nowadays.'

'Amalia ought to draw her.'

'All blowy draperies – '

'When they had any – they seem to have worn them a bit off and on – '

'Well, it isn't for the modern girl to talk,' Mollie remarked tolerantly.

'It certainly isn't for you to talk, the way you're sitting now – '

Amalia closed the sketch book. 'I'll wait till you've put that make-up on her; then I'll sketch her,' she said as she turned away.

Xena had not spoken since she had come in. She now felt herself a very important person, and it pleased her that they should talk about her like that, because it was her due. Of course she wasn't going to tell any of them she had been kissed. She hadn't told about Mollie being kissed. But they might guess if they liked. She wasn't sure Amalia didn't guess; Amalia was so clever. But even if they all guessed she belonged to herself. And it might be rather fun to let them dress her up as they suggested. Not with just a white frock and a posy and a chaplet, but with draperies like the postcard, and those other things one saw pictures of on vases – long sticks with leaves on them and fir-cones on the end, and things to clap in your hands, and a harp made of the skull of an animal. But she felt that all this ought to be on an occasion of some kind. In Sicily it was just before Lent. They put the white wigs on and made up their eyes, and the young men had whiskers of burnt cork. Verney would look funny with his fair brown hair and whiskers of burnt cork. She had seen one procession all decorated motor cars, full of white-wigged girls who threw flowers, and one car she had particularly liked. They had made it into a sea-horse, with an enormous papier maché head over the bonnet and a vast cockleshell for its tail, and it had puffed out a bright spume of confetti as it had passed along. And they used scents too. Hayoun's shop had been all scenty with amber, and she felt all scenty still, perhaps dispersing it, as tobacco-flowers give off those faint tracts that you can't smell if you get too close to the flower itself. She didn't care if they did smell her. Verney loved her, and it was lovely being loved, and she was honestly going to try to love Verney too. Then it would be more than just two people loving separately. She didn't quite know how it would be more, but it would, like the two halves of something that aren't any good by themselves. And though she didn't think she would drink aperitifs any more, or smoke, because she wanted to smell nice for Verney, there would always be that once a year, like the carnival, when they got out the sticks with the green leaves, and danced about and had wine.

And she didn't see how Verney *could* feel more scenty and glowy than she did, but if he loved her more than she loved him she supposed it was so.

'Time to get ready for dinner,' Mrs Van Necker remarked, rising.

In his tidy room Verney Arden sat down on the edge of his bed. He knew that there was now no hope in life for him except to kiss her so till the hour came for him to die. Life was unthinkable without her as its sun and centre. And only this morning she had been a faintly-moving memory, no more! He now had one immediate, practical question to ask himself. What was he going to do about it?

But he couldn't come to earth quite so suddenly as that. He couldn't face it, yet, that she was the child of immense wealth, he an impecunious drummer with a taxi-load of samples and a suitcase full of 'literature'. It was still all mixed up with bright fragments of the afternoon – his love under the palm, her sunny feet by his side, Hayoun, the alfa-mat across the doorway, the kiss. Hateful that there should be jobs to do! What was this civilisation that put this burden first of all? What were these Arabs, Frenchmen, negroes, Jews, himself, all doing? Passing a few coins or a few soiled notes to one another and then taking them back again. Buying clothes, wearing them out; eating, fasting; walking the same pavements to the same offices, casting up the same ledgers at the end of the day. No, he couldn't face all that yet. Better the thought of that sunny island in the blue, of the next kiss. When was that to be? And the next? And all the others?

He hoped that Mr Thorne would not be too chatty at dinner that evening.

Mr Thorne was not. Apparently it had struck Mr Thorne that some paragraph in the afternoon paper, a paragraph of no importance, might interest Verney, and he passed him the paper across the table, with his finger on the part he was to read. When Verney had read the paragraph and put the paper down again he saw that Mr Thorne was deep in a little book. That seemed to excuse him. If Mr Thorne would rather read than talk, so would he. He propped up the paper, and pretended to be reading it till the end of the meal.

A young man who has been introduced to a party of five girls, and only wants one of them, nevertheless has uses for the others. It would obviously be sowing the good seed, for example, to cultivate Mollie Van Necker. The two English girls he was less sure about. But it was neither Mollie nor a Bruce-Harries with whom he spent the later part of that evening. He spent it with Amalia Sherren.

The lounge or drawing-room was half full of the hotel residents. In their accustomed corner General Lorimer and his party played bridge. The Dean was buried behind a Church newspaper, and his wife was busy with her fancy-work. The two English girls sat each on a hassock at the feet of old Lady Lyle, with whom they had discovered common acquaintance, and Mollie Van Necker was at a writing-table, apparently replying to a very long and closely-written letter, with a much-stamped envelope, over which she pored from time to time. Her mother and Xena were in the curve of a corner sofa, and Mrs Van Necker appeared to be making much of her young charge, questioning, nodding, smiling, occasionally patting her hand. Amalia had brought down half a dozen sketch books this time, and sat on a central sofa that commanded the door to the hall and dining-room.

There was no escape from her watery glance of invitation, even had her first words not been what they were.

'You might be asked over later, but you won't yet,' she said, scarcely moving her lips. Her voice, like the rest of her, seemed to lack emphasis. '*She's* finding out all about father, I guess. You may as well sit here and watch her and look at my sketches.'

Verney Arden sat abruptly down on the sofa by her side.

She drew well, with an almost uncanny simplification, that brought meanings down to a few heavily-charged lines. This trip to the Old World was the first adventure of her life, and her sketch books

held the fruits of it. But Amalia's sketch books were the last thing
Verney Arden was thinking about. Amalia had seen – about himself
and Xena. Possibly the whole hotel would see presently. Perhaps
that was why Mr Thorne had read the book. Vaguely he asked
Amalia why she didn't 'finish' her sketches, and Amalia shut the
book in her hand.

'They're as finished as they're going to be,' she answered. 'I guess
that seeing a thing's all there is *to* it. There isn't much to do after
that.'

'I've sometimes wished I could draw,' he said at random.

'Then learn to see,' she answered, he thought rather rudely. And
suddenly she asked him, 'You've been in a good many places, haven't
you?'

'A good many this last six months.'

'Around this old Mediterranean?'

'By the time I've finished I shall have done most of it.'

Almost the most startling thing about Amalia's next words was the
ordinary conversational tone in which she said them.

'Then wouldn't *you* say these gods of theirs are just about as good
a proposition as the next?'

He stared. – 'What do you mean?'

'I should think it took all sorts of gods to make *this* corner of the
world. If you've been to all those places you ought to know more
about it than I do.' And she added, 'I guess I'm one of those religious
people who hasn't got any particular belief; but when a type jumps
straight up at you and hits you in the eye after all those stretches of
time – ' she shrugged her shoulders, which were thin.

He thought for a moment. – 'I wish I knew what you meant, Miss
Sherren.'

'You'd better call me Amalia like other folk. And when you're
through with your British beating about the bush – '

'Why did you say I shouldn't be asked over there?' His eyebrows
indicated the corner where Xena and Mrs Van Necker sat. 'What
made you think I wanted to be asked over there?'

'When did you see her last?' Amalia asked in return.

'In Cairo, three months ago.'

'I never set eyes on her till yesterday.'

'Well?'

'But I saw her yesterday with her father. You'd have thought she
was being sent to a convent instead of on a trip. She just sat there in
a corner holding his hand. She couldn't even say Bo to a goose like

Margaret Van Necker. And look at them now. Which of them's going to be the goods before the curtain goes down, should you say?'

He made no reply. Amalia went on.

'Her father's Umberto Francavilla. They bring out all the incense and let off all the fire-crackers when she comes in. There's a car coming for her from Constantine tomorrow. She's so rich she could travel around this little old Sea for nothing – we have them like that in the States too. And who's Margaret Van Necker? She's just a lazy old thing that likes to travel around and have a good time. She never left her cabin in the boat – I know because I was with her. Maybe people do lie down in the afternoons here, but she would if nobody else did. And off goes Mollie this afternoon with a Frenchman she picked up on the boat, and off you go with Xena Francavilla. Well – what about it?'

There seemed all the more about it that she did not once lift her eyes from the sketch book in her hand. She continued to turn its pages.

'Then I saw her yesterday morning as the boat came in. She'd gotten on a wonderful purple peignoir with silver appliqué. That peignoir was like her – it belonged right here. That's from Paris, that green frock she's wearing now. But she's as much Paris as these African sheep you can't tell from the goats . . . Say, that's good, I guess, about the sheep and the goats. It hits it just about middle. It isn't her that puzzles me. It's you.'

'Why me?'

'To see what you're going to do.'

'What's all this got to do with Mediterranean gods?'

'She knows,' Amalia replied. 'She's sizing it up while Momma Van Necker's talking. Look.'

Indeed Xena did not appear to be listening to the florid, *fardée* woman by her side. She was not even looking at Verney. She sat in the curve of the sofa gazing straight in front of her, under a fillet of green ribbon that further accentuated her temporal breadth. Amalia had glanced up and down again.

'I guess nobody looks all that saintly without there being a bit of sediment left over somewhere,' she said. 'Momma Van's up against it in baby-eyes there. Don't you bother about me. I'm an artist, and they're all clean crazy. It would take a philosophy to explain me. But as for you' – she turned her wan look on him as she closed the sketch book – 'well, brother, I guess you're headed for about as plumb-gorgeous an adventure as anybody need want. Now go to her if you like.'

But he did not gó to her. He sat looking at the carpet for a moment. Then he rose and walked thoughtfully out of the room.

He wondered what he ought to do. He could stay on here. On the other hand there was something to be said for packing up and getting on to Algiers and Gib.

7

By mid-morning the next day the car from Constantine had not arrived. A telephone-call was put through by the *direction*. The reply was that the car had left Constantine on the previous afternoon. Mrs Van Necker and her brood were gathered by the hotel bookstall.

'Well, there's plenty to see, and it's a heavenly morning,' she said. 'What about that Museum place? Is our young man coming, Xena?'

But the concierge informed them that Verney Arden had gone out more than an hour ago.

'Well, don't let's waste any more of this beautiful morning. We can squeeze three apiece into those little horse-carriages.'

The carosses were just across the road. Into two of them the party climbed, Mrs Van Necker and the English girls into the first, Amalia, Mollie and Xena following.

There were unwonted signs that Xena had got up out of the wrong side of the bed. The blue eyes looked moodily at the gay and multitudinous life about her. The carriage was driven by a brown young *gaillard* of a Frenchman, who seemed to have a greeting for quite half the people who thronged the pavements – his friends the Arabs in burnous, his friends the Chasseurs d'Afrique, his friends the red-coated soldiers of the Bey, and above all for his friends the Jewish women in the high curved balconies, who dressed, undressed, and waved their hands in return to the salute of his flourishing whip. He used the whip rather a lot, and the soft-hearted Mollie asked Xena to tell him not to flog the horses so. Xena made no reply, and Mollie asked her again.

'He isn't hurting them,' said Xena.

'He is – look, he's doing it again.'

'It's all noise, and we're late, and we shan't get there,' said Xena.

For reply Mollie leaned forward and herself took the whip from the hands of the much-friended young man, who immediately fell into the sulks. The unwhipped horses dropped straightway to a crawl.

'Now you see,' said Xena, pushing out her lips.

Mollie laughed and gave Xena's arm a little push.

'Just because he can't give you every moment of his time!' she scolded softly.

'It isn't that at all!' said Xena with a little shake of her body.

'Anyway that's why I think it's always such a good plan to have two,' Mollie answered, her eyes on the crowded pavements.

They issued by the Bab Bou Saadoun and passed under the Viaduct.

Xena was still naughty when they arrived at the plateau that forms the courtyard of the Musée Alaoui. Mrs Van Necker had been waiting for nearly a quarter of an hour, and wanted to know where they had been. Half the morning had gone – they had only about an hour and a quarter to see everything there was

'All right, mother,' said the peace-loving Mollie as she led her into the vestibule. 'Nobody but you and Amalia wants to see the stupid things anyway – '

And she looked from the frigid plinths and slabs and potsherds to the only human thing in sight – the grave white-bearded Arab attendant.

'So why not just see the Greek things you're so mad about and let's get back into the world again?' Mollie suggested.

By leaving the ground-floor alone there was plenty of time. They mounted the bleak staircase, and Mrs Van Necker sailed ahead, guide book in hand.

Xena still felt as if she wanted to put out her tongue at somebody. She wore a red hat and a sheeny half-open coat of coloured blazer-like stripes, and at her breast was a bunch of violets she had bought on the pavement opposite the hotel. She had put the frock on because it was different from the one Verney had seen her in yesterday, and now he had gone out early. He had sat for half an hour last night with Amalia Sherren too, looking at her sketches, and then had suddenly got up and walked out without a word. And worst of all, Mollie had made a joke about it. She had said that he couldn't give her every minute of his time, and that that was why she liked to have two. What business was it of Mollie's? She had her own French officer. Nothing seemed to be going right. She wished she was somewhere else. This bare place with its cold top-lighting was like being in a vault. She didn't want to be with the others. She wanted to be by herself. She fancied she heard Mollie's compassionate whisper to Cicely Bruce-Harries as she turned away.

'Her first boy – '

She passed through several rooms, all empty save for the attendants. She wondered the attendants did not die, waiting about in a place like that all day. They were dressed exactly like Hayoun, who had given them coffee in his carpet-shop, in a tight-necked frock coat and red fez. It was beastly of Verney to have sat talking to Amalia, and then to go out this morning without seeing her. She hadn't thought he would behave like that. But all the time she knew she was being very naughty, and that she ought to forgive Verney. Nobody would *really* fall in love with Amalia. He had his work to do. Perhaps he simply hadn't come up because of Mrs Van Necker, asking her all those questions about her father, and his yacht, and how many houses he had, and making her feel all fussy and fretful. She wanted to love Verney. It had been lovely, sitting there in Hayoun's little shop, ever so prim on the edge of his divan, waiting for him to kiss her. No wonder people thought such a lot about kissing. It made everything simple and beautiful. And to hear him say that he had loved her even in Cairo when all that she had noticed of him was that he had nice hair –

She almost felt his arms drawing her down to the sofa again, her face side by side with his, his lips –

And then she saw the object looking at her.

Before her was the portal of another Salle, and it stood facing her just past the opening. It was looking at her from under a frontlet that seemed to be fruits, with eyes full of an infinite sadness and beauty. She took a step towards it.

It was the Hermes of Boethos, and strictly speaking it is not a statue at all. It is a six-foot *stylè* or terminal in greenish bronze, a pedestal with a braided and bearded head on it, archaic and grave. The whole is no more than an empty shell, with a large portion of the lower part missing entirely, and to look at it disturbs. It is the eyes. The eyes of English sculpture are commonly dotted or incised, to give a look of spurious life, but these eyes are not eyes at all. They are holes in a mask. Only at a little distance do they look at one with that expression of profundity and unutterable grief. Boethos, they say, was a Chalcedonian. He lived three centuries before Christ. And he made and signed this thing before which stood a blue-eyed girl in a red hat and sheeny blazer-striped coat, with a bunch of violets at her breast.

She took a step nearer, and suddenly the eyes ceased to look. How can holes look without living eyes behind them? And what eyes look after a two-thousand-years immersion in the sea?

For it was the Dionysos that the Mahdia sponge-fishers had found, and it mourned its own lost eyes.

Trembling, Xena looked at the imbricated fruits of the statue's brow, at the plaited abacus of a beard. A vague deep sense of contrition had

come over her, as if she had been to blame for something and deserved
to be scolded. And as she gazed into the sea-eaten holes she thought
she knew why she was to be blamed. She had been a naughty girl and
a truant. This poor god who had looked so sorrowfully at her through
the doorway had reproached her because she had left him, and had
been elsewhere when she should have been amongst his girls, the girls
who came with the sticks rustling with leaves, and pomegranates, and
the jingling sistra and the instruments made of animals' bones. She
felt that she ought to have been there when they had brought the
garlanded kid for the offering, watching the priest with his knife and
basin, and glad that a holy thing was being done. She ought to have
been there among the noble virgins with the little golden baskets,
when the ceremony of anointing had been performed and the sacred
rites with the unseen symbols. She ought to have been there with
those other girls of his, who had stained their faces with bruised
berries, and there had been antics and dancing and wine.

But she had been somewhere else, a long way off, and he wasn't even
angry with her, but only very, very sad.

The strong calves seemed a little unsteady as she took a faltering
step forward. The hand as brown as the baked sea-sand moved
to the bunch of violets at her breast. And the next moment the violets
fell to the floor. She gave a little stifled cry and covered her face with
her hands. She knew now – all, all of her knew – that the hour of her
ordeal had come. And it was well that the Salle was empty, for she fell
suddenly on her knees before the Dionysos, praying. But not to the
Dionysos. That was the terrible thing – that her soul should be fought
for like this, as two men might fight for a woman's body. With her
hands over her eyes to shut out the sad and beautiful god, she was
praying to Santa Rosalia, the Virgin of Pellegrino's grotto.

It was all the fault of this darkly-brilliant. All the pious lessons she
had been taught seemed somehow to have fallen away from her the
moment she had set foot off the boat. Before she had been an hour in
the place she had made bold forward eyes at a young man, not even
waiting for him to begin, but making him begin, just like a horrid
girl. In the same way she had put all the blame of the kissing on
him, just sitting still there on Hayoun's sofa with her lids dropped,
knowing all the time what he was going to do. She was not a scrap
better than those prancing creatures into whose eyes this thing of
bronze had laughed.

Here she caught her breath and pressed the hands more tightly
over her eyes.

'*Gloriosissima Vergine ed elevatissima Sposa di Christi –* ' she prayed.

For all that it was lovely being loved, and she was going to try to love him too –

And it was beastly of Amalia to take him away like that, and as for Mollie Van Necker

'*Bella Pellegrina Angioletlo di celeste amore,*' – she prayed – as for Mollie Van Necker, it was disgusting of her to talk about having two boys when Xena only wanted Verney – she and her pitying 'Her first boy – '

'*Dall' alto seggio di gloria che vi meritaste per tanta purità –* ' she prayed.

Besides, girls got old, like Mrs Van Necker. They hadn't as much time before them as men. Unless one made up one's mind never to look at a young man at all one had to learn their ways without showing too much of one's own. Of course girls had the advantage in some ways. They could get themselves kissed by just dropping their eyes. But they did get old, and everybody wanted youth and joy and beauty, and they worshipped the god who gave it to them. While it was very wrong, one could still understand those girls who came with their dribbles of flowers and the berry-juice trickling down their faces, all capering and playing antics, trying to make the god laugh, making sure he didn't overlook them –

All at once she remembered that she was on her knees in a public place and that anybody might come in at any moment. She uncovered her eyes and looked up. High above her towered the bronze abacus of beard. and, glancing past the broken hole in the statue's pedestal, she saw that she was being watched by Amalia Sherren.

At least she thought she was being watched; she couldn't be sure, because Amalia was in the room beyond, and when Xena looked again she was pretending to examine one of the four *cratères* in marble that occupied each a corner of the apartment. On its plinth it stood half as tall again as she, and its flanged and beaded rim overhung Amalia like an eaves, and round its bowl a faun supported a drunken Silenus and satyrs and maenads chased one another.

8

If Amalia had seen her she made no sign as Xena walked up. She just went on looking at the vase.

'It's a copy,' she said. 'It's the Borghese Vase, I saw it in Rome. There's another in the Louvre.' And she added, 'I guess those people made the most of life.'

'These on the vase?'

'They enjoyed it in Pompeii too. Even more than the Greeks I should say. I could spend six months in that Naples Museum. And I've got to go back to the United States.'

'Don't you want to go back to the United States?'

For reply Amalia said, 'Have you seen these?' and led her to a glass-fronted case in the middle of the room. In it were the poor scraps of planking of the ancient ship herself. In other cases were her anchors, her trenails, her nails of bronze.

'*That* was before Christopher Columbus,' said Amalia with a detached air.

Looking at the exhibits Xena felt a little as she had felt before the Dionysos. One fragment under flat glass was one of the vessel's lamps, a morsel of terracotta with the wick still in it. It seemed so sad, so forlorn, so useless now. Tears came into Xena's eyes. One of the tears fell on the glass.

'I'm terribly, terribly sorry,' she gulped.

'What for?' Amalia asked.

'I don't know. I expect they were drowned. It's dreadfully sad. I don't think I can bear it. Let's go.'

The only way out of the Mahdia Rooms is by way of the Salle of the Dionysos. Therefore, as nobody had passed Xena as she had knelt before the god, but praying to the Saint, Amalia must have been in the inner room all the time. Both girls paused as they approached the god now. A complication of strapwork forms the back of the statue's head, and down its right side a band of bronze ends in a finger-like curl near another emblem. Xena saw Amalia pass round to the statue's front and stoop to pick something up. It was the bunch of violets she had dropped.

'Somebody seems to have dropped these,' Amalia remarked.

Xena was still thinking how terribly, terribly sorry she felt for the poor drowned sailors.

'Looks like they were meant for an offering. They'll get swept up there. I don't suppose that old fellow ever expected to see violets again. Well, they're his, I guess – '

And she pushed the scented bunch into the curl of bronze near which Xena had prayed.

At the entrance of the Mahdia Rooms they met the rest of the party coming in, but nothing would have dragged Xena back. She wanted to be out of the Museum altogether. She did not even tell the others she was going. She descended the staircase

alone and sought the waiting carosse. And there she sat until
the others should come down, thinking all the time of those poor,
poor sailors.

For the return journey they arranged themselves differently, Xena
and Amalia sitting one on either side of Mrs Van Necker. The pack
of carts and donkeys and people in the streets were almost impass-
able; they went at no more than a walking-pace; merchants sat under
their sagging awnings; children played almost under the wheels of
the carosse; the swing-boats of a fair rose in twos and threes, with the
mushroom dome of a mosque behind; but Xena still thought of the
sailors. They were going back to the hotel for lunch; she didn't want
any lunch. Still thinking of the sailors she drew in her breath, so that
Mrs Van Necker turned.

'What's the matter Xena?'

'I've got rather a headache,' Xena murmured.

'Aspirin,' said Mrs Van Necker.

They were approaching the Porte de France.

'I don't think I want any lunch. I think I'll get out and walk,' said
Xena.

'Child! As if I could have you walking about Tunis alone!'

'We're nearly there. Stop him, please.'

Mrs Van Necker thought for a moment. After all, nothing could
happen to her at midday in the principal street of the town. And
three in a small carriage was rather a crush

But while she was thinking Xena had stopped the driver herself
and got out.

She watched Mrs Van Necker settle herself more comfortably, and
then slowly followed the carosse down the boulevard.

She had no headache, but for all that a bathe with toilet-water and
perhaps a shampoo might be refreshing. A hairdresser's shop adjoined
the hotel, with a ladies' saloon upstairs. She could go through the
ground floor from the street without entering the hotel. She quickened her pace a little. She turned the corner by the terraced café; she
reached the shop door and pushed. As she did so somebody inside
made haste to assist her. A pair of heels clicked, a pair of spurs
jingled. It was Mollie's young cavalry officer, freshly barbered and
smelling of essences. It had not occurred to her that the ground floor
was the men's part of the shop. A couple of towelled men sat before
basins, one on them quite old and bald.

That he had spoken to Mollie on the boat and kissed her behind
the deckhouse seemed no reason why he should claim to know Xena

too, but in a tone that Xena thought quite nice and respectful he murmured a '*Bonjour, mademoiselle.*'

'*Bonjour, monsieur.*'

'*Je vous ai vu sur le bâteau?*'

'*Oui, monsieur.*'

'*Mademoiselle* your friend, have you lost her?'

'No, she is in the hotel, *monsieur.*'

'*Vous dansez ce soir?*'

'I don't think they dance in this hotel,' murmured Xena, quite aware that he was trying to detain her.

'But they dance at the Majestic. There is even dancing elsewhere,' the officer smiled.

'*Pardon, monsieur – on m'attend – bonjour, monsieur.*'

'*Bonjour, mademoiselle.*'

And with another click and a salute he opened the interior door for her and closed it again behind her.

Hot, blushing and annoyed, she sought the ladies' saloon upstairs. At that hour she had it to herself. Her hat was removed and her smoky hair deftly taken down.

What a strange morning it had been, she thought as her cheeks grew cooler. First her being so naughty and cross, and then trying to say her prayers in a public museum before a god of bronze, and then her being so sorry about the poor sailors! It had been the most extraordinary morning of her whole life. *Why* had she felt so contrite when those mournful eyes that weren't eyes at all had looked at her? And – this came to her the more powerfully that it came tardily – what an astonishing thing for Amalia to have done! On a glass shelf before her as she sat were coloured bottles of toilet preparations, creamy, pale green, with little coloured capsules round their stoppers and tied up with coloured ribbons. One had a chocolate-coloured ribbon, another a purple one. Bronze and violets . . . *What* a strange thing for Amalia to have done! To tuck a bunch of violets into that curl of bronze! And to have said that *he* never expected to see violets any more! Of course he hadn't. He might as well as have expected his poor eyes back. And they had really been her violets, Xena's violets, that Amalia had given.

And if Amalia *had* been watching her from the inner room she would think it was to the Dionysos that Xena had been praying –

Wicked as it might be, it was more wicked to tell a lie about it. Xena knew now that she hadn't really been praying to the Saint at all. Or if she had the Saint had taken no notice. If they really were struggling for the soul of a little girl like Xena she was sure the Saint hadn't won. And now that for the first time in her life she came to think of it, she wasn't quite sure what a Saint was. It wasn't God – not the Big God. If it was a lesser god, why didn't they call it a lesser god? Why didn't they speak of Saint Venus and Saint Mars and dear little Baby-Saint Cupid, and the goddess Rosalia and the god Giovanni? At least the gods gave you something to look at. There were Flora's flowers, Ceres' grain, Olympus' Mount and the mountain here. But meekness and resignation and hope were ever so much harder. Xena was sure they were too hard for her. All her life she had tried, and it all seemed very unsatisfactory. She would have to make up her mind about it somehow or else be very unhappy.

Brush-brush, sweep-sweep: the feeling under the man's hands was as if he brushed away a lot of things she wanted to get rid of. Under the glass shelf of bottles was a mirror, and she lifted her eyes to it. They met the other eyes, vaguely saw the shape of the white-jacketed hairdresser. And looking at herself she suddenly thought she would *like* Amalia to paint her. Amalia was very clever. Xena had been a little afraid of her at first, but she wasn't now. Amalia *understood*. 'I guess that old fellow never expected to see violets any more.' Amalia too had been sorry for the poor neglected god, and had given him something to comfort him all alone and unworshipped in the Museum there.

Yes, at first she hadn't wanted Amalia to study her, but now she would ask her to paint her. And suddenly her eyes met those of the barber in the glass. She spoke without the least premeditation, and had said it almost before she was aware.

'I think I'll have it cut off,' she said.

The barber seemed surprised, but 'Mademoiselle would like it bobbed? Shingled?' he asked.

'Yes. Shingled.'

And suddenly she laughed for fun.

How astonished they would be to see what she had done while they were sitting at lunch! She could see Mrs Van Necker's face, Mollie's, the faces of the English girls. But she knew that Amalia would put her head critically on one side and Say, 'Well, I guess that's just right.' Amalia and her 'I guesses!' But it was true. Amalia *did* guess. And Amalia should paint her.

The hairdresser had moved away. He returned with scissors and comb. He was pausing, deliberating, considering the processes of his art.

'*Coupez*,' she said.

It was quite a loud, harsh noise, and there was something cruddley and thrilling about it. Flakes fell to the floor; there; that was gone! Another slow crunch, another lock fell. How suddenly cool it felt! She had wanted that coolness. She had been bothering herself too much, about Saints and such matters. What did Saints do with their hair? Nuns, she knew, had it cut or shaved off but Saints were so wimpled and wrapped up that you couldn't tell. But Verney would be pleased. Indeed it would be queer (she thought with a delicious little pushing-out of her mouth) if she couldn't please Verney, whatever she chose to do with herself! She would be all eyes for his first glance at her, would miss not a jot of his surprise and delight. Now for the shampoo.

Twenty minutes later she stood examining herself between two mirrors. She thought it lovely. It didn't make her look in the least boyish, but more than ever a girl. She thought that everybody would be sure to like it. She would have it parted on the right side. She sat down in the chair again for the final brushing. She must compose herself to walk into the hotel in a natural way, as if nothing had happened. Would they notice it at once? With her hat on?

She put on her hat, gave the number of her room, and walked out.

The communicating way into the hotel led to the bookstall where the guide books and picture-postcards were sold. A man stood there buying a newspaper. She saw that it was the middle-aged man who sat at the corner table with Verney. And of course it had been fearful cheek of Mollie's young officer to speak to her like that in the barber's shop, because he was a man, but girls could speak first if they liked, and could stop whenever they liked, and pass without speaking the next time if they wanted. It was part of their power, and Verney's *vis-à-vis* would do for the first, to see whether he noticed her shingle with her hat on.

Mr Thorne heard a musical little voice in his ear. – 'Good morning.'

'Good – ah – good morning, good morning. You are Miss Francavilla, are you not?'

'Yes.'

She knew that Mr Thorne was admiring her, but she didn't think he had noticed about the shingle.

'I missed you at lunch. I always miss the people who aren't there. I had lunch by myself too,' he said.

From the way he said it she was almost sure he had noticed about her and Verney.

'And I think – I heard somebody say – that the concièrge has news for you.'

'What?' Xena asked quickly, though it was hardly likely that the concièrge had news for her about Verney.

'I think it's something about a car,' said Mr Thorne.

'Oh! . . . '

She ran across to the concierge's desk.

'Has a car come for me?' she demanded.

A deep bow. – '*Oui, mademoiselle.*'

'Where is it?'

'I will fetch the chauffeur instantly.'

'No, I will go to him.'

'François!' The concierge's voice and arm were raised. 'Conduct mademoiselle to the garage.'

9

A handsome young Moor, dressed from head to foot in a white livery, stood in the courtyard, looking on while two of the garage attendants were busy with a hose on the wheels of an enormous car. It was a magnificent Itala, with a nobly-rounded and streamlined black body and two spare wheels in a leather valise. It seemed part of Francavilla's power that some of it descended to his chauffeur too, so that others performed the menial work for him. Xena walked up to him.

'What is your name?' she asked.

His manner was not that of the obsequious staff of the hotel. She had asked his name, and he told it. – 'Achmed.'

'I am Miss Francavilla. What made you late?'

'There were many camels on the road, many goats. Also the Signor's telegram was delayed,' he replied.

'Have you made arrangements for yourself?'

'*Oui, madame.*'

'You will take your orders from me, and from an American lady, Mrs Van Necker.'

'*Oui, madame.*'

'How soon will the car be ready?'

'In half an hour, madame. It is only dust.'

Xena returned to the hotel.

The car had come; good. Nominally she had placed it at Mrs Van Necker's disposal, but she would have it herself just as often as she wanted it, and she knew where she would make Verney drive her first. She would make him drive her to that mountain with the two horns that she had so strangely seemed to know the other morning from the boat. Why wasn't he here to take her today? They could have been there in half an hour. But perhaps that wouldn't have left enough time for the mountain itself. Still, he ought to have been there. Bother his old business. If he was going to let his business interfere with their plans like this it was going to be very dull. To kiss her and tell her he loved her one day, and the very next day not to come near her at all! And where had the others got to? They hadn't seen her new crop yet.

With a sudden wish to see it again herself, she ran up to her room. She threw off the red hat, and stood before the tall glass with her small mirror in her hand. Oh, she was glad she had had it done! Now what frock should she wear that evening that Verney hadn't seen before?

She began to open drawers. She spread the frocks on the bed, and stood looking at them. Suddenly she thought that she had never seen such a dull lot of frocks in her life. The other girls had admired and coveted those! She herself had liked, chosen and worn those nursery things! Oh, if she had only been in Paris! But surely Tunis could provide something to be going on with. There down in the courtyard was the car. She would go at once. Mollie and the others could have those dowdy old things on the bed.

With another admiring look at the clean-lined nape she put on the red hat again and ran downstairs.

That afternoon there went the round of the Tunis shops, driven by a handsome young man in a white livery, a resplendent Itala car, big enough inside for half a dozen blue-eyed girls in red hats to have lolled in its cream upholstery. That is to say Xena wore the red hat as far as the first shop. She came out of the shop again with a small dull-gold toque on her head, with a bird-of-paradise feather tucked into the front of it. The red hat was pinned up in paper, and a cardboard carton accompanied it. She passed to the next shop, and the next, and Achmed and the car waited outside while, inside, Xena said that her name was Francavilla. Before looking-glasses, with looking-glasses to right and left of her, she put garments off and on, choosing, refusing, examining again, tossing aside. Life up to now had been a fast and a penance. That was all over. Verney should see. If he had loved her before he should love her a hundred times more now. When he saw her tonight that would teach him to stay away all day again. And tomorrow he should take her out in the car.

At last with a happy sigh she cried enough. There was no longer room for six Xenas in the Itala. Two might perhaps have been got in; the rest of the space was occupied with her purchases.

As she entered the hotel again the concièrge handed her a letter. It was addressed in her father's hand. Giving orders that her things were to be taken to her room she took the letter into the lounge. She opened it and read.

BELOVED LITTLE HEART,

I watched your boat till it was quite round the headland, and then went back to the hotel. It was very lonely, little one, but I know it is for the best. I have much business, but that does not prevent my thinking ceaselessly of you. I sometimes think I should like to give up business and be only with you, but that could not be for ever either, since one day you will wish to leave your father and trust your happiness to somebody else. That I shall have to bear as best I can. Only your happiness matters. I pray nightly for you, and know that you pray for me too. I often hear your voice again saying '*O cara Rosalia*'. I trust the car has arrived, and that amid new scenes you do not forget your father. Rosalia guard you, little one, and good night.

UMBERTO

She sat with the letter slackly in her hand, not looking at it. The blue eyes were on the writing-tables, on Rabat's coffee-table at the door, on the palms of the garden outside. If somebody had told her a few minutes before that she was going to have a letter she would instantly have thought of Verney. She would have thought he had sent her a little note to say how dreadfully he had missed her all day. Now that the letter was from her father, and all these new things had happened, she knew it was very important that she should be very truthful with herself about it. Of course she couldn't go on being with her father all the time. She hadn't quite made up her mind yet, but if she did come to love Verney as much as he loved her she would marry him, and of course she wouldn't want her father too. So though she was awfully fond of him, and it was nice of him to have written to say how fond he was of her, except for that that part of the letter didn't really mean very much. *He* hadn't wanted *his* parents about the place all the time when he wanted to kiss somebody else. Young people were more important than old

ones. Old people had had their lives, but the young ones still had
everything to come. She was very sorry he was lonely, but Rosalia
would cheer him up by and by. Xena would write to him tomorrow.
She would tell him – she hardly knew yet what she would tell him.
That the car had arrived. That they had had a smooth crossing.
That at Trápani they had dropped cattle and taken up mules. That
she was very well – but not that she didn't much care for Mrs
Van Necker, because that might worry him, and besides, he might
come for her and take her away from Verney. As for telling him
anything else, she would hardly know where to begin. Oh, and
perhaps she would ask him for some more money. She could get
most things she wanted by merely pronouncing her name, but it
might be as well to have a little in hand. Then her love. Should
she say 'kisses' too? As she had always done? She must think about
that. Perhaps if she said 'tons of kisses' that would be all right,
because it would be merely an extravagant expression, not meaning
real kisses at all.

And soon it would be time for her to put that new frock on.

Mollie Van Necker came tapping at Xena's door as Xena made
ready for dinner that night, but Xena asked her what she wanted,
and when Mollie said 'Oh, only a chat,' sent her away. She wanted it
to come as a surprise to them all. It was going to, too! She had
had her bath, and made her choice among the new frocks. She
would have liked her maid there, but she thought she could put it
on herself. Between the glasses she looked at her back. She had
seen Mollie's back, and in spite of Mollie's dark colouring it was
wonderfully smooth and white. Her own was of the soft, pale, all-
over honeysuckle brown. And she didn't want to tell herself stories
even about her own back. For some things she preferred Mollie's.
Her own seemed to have too many muscles or something. But
Mollie's back got white suddenly, whereas nobody would have
dreamed from the even tone of Xena's neck that she had only got
shingled that very day.

She put on new shoes, new stockings. From her head to her foot
there was not a thing upon her that had not been new in some shop
that afternoon. And there came down to dinner a Xena so transfigured that people asked one another with their eyes whether Mrs
Van Necker had gone wrong in her head to allow it. She was bare to
the buds of her breasts. The cool muscular back was displayed half
way down. And the rest of her was as if she had gummed herself and
then rolled in a field of hyacinths. The newly-shorn head glistened

like an ash-bud, and she had lengthened her eyes ever so slightly at the corners with two touches of a pencil.

'Oh! Xena!' was all that Mollie Van Necker could gasp. And there watched her from the corner table a stripling in a dinner-jacket from whose own eyes looked out a soul that seemed to hold all the trouble of the world.

Dinner ended. The astonished guests sought the lounge, the palm-garden, the music-hall next door. It was by the book-stall where she had spoken to Mr Thorne that Xena Francavilla summoned Verney Arden to her with her eyes.

'Can you drive an Itala car?' she asked.

He seemed unable to find his voice.

'Because I want you to drive me to the mountain tomorrow. I will meet you here at ten o'clock. Good night.'

And she was off with her head high, leaving him standing there.

10

'I call it *frightfully* bad taste!' Cicely Bruce-Harries declared.

'Cicely! It's a *lovely* frock!' Mollie pleaded.

'I don't mean the frock. I mean that our fathers aren't all million-aires. And I don't want her old clothes.'

'But remember she isn't English,' Daphne joined forces with Mollie.

'I don't think mother would like you to have that striped jacket and hat.'

'I shan't tell mother where I got them.'

'And of course we know who it's all for.'

'Well, why not?' said Mollie defiantly. 'I think he's ever so nice.'

'Far too good for her,' Cicely answered. 'And as for her car, a carosse will do for me, thanks.'

'Well, you wouldn't have had a ride tomorrow anyway, because she's bagged it for herself.' (All this, by the way, was late that same night, in the bedroom that the Bruce-Harries sisters shared.)

'Well, *I* hope they enjoy themselves, and I think you're all very bad-tempered, and *I'm* going to bed.'

And off Mollie went, to fondle once more the frocks that Xena had given her.

Mrs Van Necker had every right to feel aggrieved. A shy, tongue-tied little Xena had been handed over to her, who in no time at all had taken the reins into her own hands in the most extraordinary

way. Mrs Van Necker had made certain money-arrangements
with Umberto Francavilla. They were not altogether detrimental to
herself. But what was she to do about it when her charge went off in
a car, turned shops upside-down, and came back and put on a frock
that set the whole hotel talking? The position was delicate. She could
go the extreme length of sending Xena back to her father, but short
of that she had very little choice. And since a disregarded chaperone
is in an impossible position, the tactful thing to do was to shut her
eyes and let Xena wear what frocks she would. If the Dean's wife and
old Lady Lyle chose to look disapproval, let them.

Nevertheless at a quarter to ten next morning there seemed a
likelihood that there would be no trip to the mountain that day after
all. Mollie Van Necker came upon a troubled Verney Arden standing irresolutely by the table of time-tables and booklets of steamers
and hotels. She spoke mysteriously.

'Is it all off?' she asked.

'I don't care if it is off,' the unhappy young man replied. 'Why?'

'It's the car this time. Don't say I told you, but mother says that car
is going to make life very difficult for her.'

The boy made no reply.

'*Much* the best way,' the experienced Mollie went on, 'would have
been for us all to go somewhere together and then to split off when
we got there. Then there isn't any fuss. Mother's quite easy if only
you humour her a bit. Xena doesn't know the right way.'

'Is there a row?' he asked wretchedly; but he was unanswered, for
at that moment Mrs Van Necker came up.

'Xena tells me you've been so good as to offer to drive her this
morning,' she said with a quite successful smile. 'Well, everybody
seems to have the day mapped out. Amalia's off sketching, of course,
and Lady Lyle's kindly asked Cicely and Daffy to go to Carthage
with her. So that only leaves you and me, Mollie.'

'It only leaves you,' her daughter answered promptly. 'I've – oh, a
hundred things to do.'

'Then as I appear to be a person of no particular importance – '
said Mrs Van Necker graciously.

In the courtyard some minutes later Achmed had the car softly
running. Xena was looking at Verney in a way that made his heart
sink.

'Because if you don't want to come you needn't,' she was saying.
'But I've said I'm going and I'm going, even if I have to go by myself.
Achmed – ' She motioned the chauffeur to the wheel.

Verney had slept little. All the day before he had not seen her, and he had come down to dinner to find that she had cut her hair and was publishing her beauty in a frock that showed a back like the breaking day. And she was looking at him now with almost cold eyes, and telling him that if he didn't wish to come he needn't.

And as he looked back at her Amalia Sherren's words returned to him. 'Well, brother, I guess *you're* headed for about as plumb-gorgeous an adventure as a man could want.'

Achmed was already at the wheel. At the arch stood a garage-attendant looking to see if the way into the street was clear. And she stood there waiting for him to say Yes or No.

Suddenly he held the door open for her. She got in, and he after her. There was the soft knock of a gear and the car glided forward.

Ten minutes later they were speeding past the *salines* on the road to Hammam-el-Lif.

The plate-glass windows were half lowered, and air moved pleas-antly in the upper spaces of the creamy car. Achmed's neck, brown against his white livery, never moved. Xena was sitting almost as she had sat when she had waited for him to kiss her, but she was not waiting to be kissed now. She had had her hair cut off for him, had worn a frock the night before for him, and so far he had not opened his mouth about either. They were rushing through a world of morning beauty. Across the *salines* the sea sparkled like pale sapphires, and on the other side was a wilderness of bosky verdure. Achmed was no dawdling driver. He had been rebuked once for tardiness, and didn't intend that it should happen again. From the centre of Tunis to the little *plage* of Hammam-el-Lif is perhaps sixteen kilometres. There seemed every chance that it would be covered in as many minutes. Xena was wonder-ing whether she should take her hat off. It was the lightest of hats. It might have been made of the iridescent flaking that lines an oyster-shell. She hardly knew she had it on. Still, this morning air on her nape –

Then suddenly, almost violently, she clutched Verney's arm.

'Stop him, stop him!'

Startled, he had turned.

'Stop him! Achmed! Back – back there to where the tramline branches off – '

And with both hands she drummed on the pane before her until the car came to a standstill.

'Back – back to there – ' She pointed.

The car slid slowly back. They were at a little roadside tramway-cabin where the line swung off to the right in the direction of a clump of pineapple palms. Without being told Achmed had descended and was holding the door open. The door was on Xena's side of the car. She was wearing another of yesterday's new frocks, a white taffeta that the sun outlined upon her like a thistledown of light. She was looking towards the cluster of pineapple palms a couple of hundred yards away, and there had come into her eyes the look that Amalia had said was like spirit-flame. Verney had got out of the car after her.

But her hands made a little agitated movement to keep him away. She was breathing quickly.

'You stay here,' she panted. 'You are not to follow. I shall be a quarter of an hour.'

'Where are you going?'

The hand moved him back as if his touch would have contaminated her. She spoke a few rapid words in Arabic to Achmed. Then she was speeding off along the branch-line, with the sunlight playing about her.

Verney had no Arabic. French would have to do. He turned to the chauffeur.

'What is it? Where's she gone? What made her stop the car all at once like that?'

Achmed turned his handsome head and replied in English. – 'Sir?'

'Where's she gone?'

Achmed's brown eyes were expressionless. – 'She will not be long,' he said. 'It is Friday.'

'What do you mean?'

'We are at Sidi Fathallah.'

'What's that?'

'We wait here. We are men. Men do not visit the Rock on Fridays.'

'What rock?'

'You do not know the Rock of Sidi Fathallah?'

'No.'

'El-Lif was a holy man. It is his Rock. Three times the woman slides down it. It is polished like marble with their sliding. You may see for yourself, but not on Fridays. That is the day they slide. She has gone to slide. It is before they marry. So they are purified, and they shall not be barren.'

Slowly Verney Arden got back into the car.

Of colour, only the weathering of his travels remained in his face. What world was this he was in? Achmed had said it in English, Verney Arden's own tongue. He had said, in English, that here, at the branching-off of a twentieth-century tramline, was a holy place with a Rock, down which women about to be married slid, and that the Rock was polished like marble. Naturally Achmed had said it reluctantly and in the fewest possible words, as a gentleman should who leaves the women to their own private affairs. He had said she wouldn't be long. It was merely her purification. She would then marry. Probably Achmed did not even trouble to ask himself whom she would marry. Presumably she would marry this young Englishman. Perhaps Achmed's own wives, if he had any, had been to the Rock too. Achmed knew.

And Xena, who had never been that way in her life before, had also known, and had known that Friday was the day, and had stopped the car, and had spoken excitedly to Achmed in Arabic, and had fled as if to an appointment.

A blackness seemed to rise before Verney Arden's eyes. He had covered three quarters of the Levant, and no longer laughed at strange things because they were different. He remembered her arrival in Tunis as she had described it to him in Hayoun's shop. She had felt that she had known those wide sunny morning waters and that two-horned mountain that rose with its pines ahead. And at first she had been frightened, but that had soon passed, and after that it had been beautiful. All day yesterday he hadn't seen her and didn't know where she had been. Had she made yet another new and astounding discovery? Had Amalia, with her talk of gods who got hold of people, been at it again? What purification could this little dove need? He wished he could shut his thoughts as he shut his eyes. He wished he had been like Achmed. Achmed's face was not the face of a man who questions. It was the face of a man who accepts. If women must slide down rocks they must do so; no man knew anything about these things. The wise man did not enquire. They made themselves ready to marry. What did a man want more?

Verney Arden had no idea what time passed before, lifting his eyes again, he saw her reappear by the palms. She came forward, the sunlight tangled itself in the frock again. She reached the car, and as she took her place by his side again he saw that the frock had an earthy stain.

'*Roulez*,' she said.

The car gathered speed again.

The boskage became patched with open spaces, with here and there women and children among the shaggy-black sheep that Amalia had said resembled goats. Across blue jacaranda-trees the pine-clad mountain seemed to be rushing in a steep slope towards them. On the left the sapphire glittered more palely over the shallows, and Hammam-el-Lif swung into sight, with its bathing-boxes and plage. A sunny wall shut it out, and the car came to a standstill. Achmed stood gravely at the door, white against the white of a green-shuttered café. She had to rouse him.

'We're here, Verney,' she said, and he hardly knew the voice that had told him less than an hour ago that he might either come or stay away. It had a new sweet gravity and self-importance. A child speaks so who is told on its birthday that from getting up to going to bed again it shall be the most important person of all. And there seemed too a desire to make amends, for she turned to Achmed.

'We shall be ever so long up in the mountain, and Mrs Van Necker might want you,' she said. 'Tell her I hope she'll go somewhere nice and enjoy herself. If you're back here by five it will do.'

Achmed saluted and got back into the car. It turned by the corner of the green-shuttered café, moved forward again, and became a dark speck on the white road.

'You see,' she said in a serious voice as she and Verney turned away, 'I've been very naughty. I don't mean I said anything naughty, but I felt naughty, and people can always tell the difference, can't they? First it was about the frock. She said it was too old for me, and of course I'm going to wear what frocks I like now, but I meant to annoy her and I did. Then there was the car, but I've sent that back to her. And I've given Mollie three frocks, and anyway she's getting old and won't be important much longer – '

He was watching her feet again, as he had watched them in the Avenue Jules Ferry. One slender foot, the other, the first again, the other – he sought in the rhythm a composure for the wild tossing of his thoughts. For he could no longer doubt. Bit by bit, almost imponderably it had come, so that a dozen times during the night he had dismissed it as a fantasy and had remembered only that first kiss. But who had told her about Sidi Fathallah and its Rock? Why had she stopped the car, knowing that Friday was the day, and that the Rock waited for her beyond the clump of palms? There was only one answer. She had *always* known. Out of a remembered dark her feet had sought the Rock, and had run to it even along a twentieth-century tramline. Her youth was written on an ancient page. It was written in characters of impermanence, and the permanence lay beneath. Something he blenched to guess at *had* happened to the fleeting superficies, and the old legend stood forth. The child of Cairo had gone. He knew that the child of Palermo had gone too. But a child compact of the sweetnesses of all the ages walked on those borrowed feet by his side.

Sweetness? She did not cease to prattle out of that new sanctity of her purification as they ascended the beaten paths, past finger-posts that showed others the way but had nothing to tell her. It was of Mollie and Amalia and the Bruce-Harries sisters that she prattled, with little laughs alternating with little earnestnesses, while the wind and the sun played with the white frock with the stain of earth on it.

'I think both Mollie and Amalia have been very great influences in forming my character,' she said. 'Those two more than anybody I know. Amalia's cleverer than Mollie, but I think I like Mollie the best. Of course I haven't mixed much with girls of my own age since I left school. And I haven't mixed very much with Cicely and Daphne yet. I've mixed more with the other two. Mollie's kind. I can't quite make up my mind whether Amalia's really kind or not. Do you like her?'

'I hardly know her.'

'But you were talking to her the other night on the sofa when she showed you her sketches.'

'Yes.'

Then she laughed. – 'Shall I tell you something, Verney? You will laugh!'

'I shan't laugh.'

'Well, I was jealous. I was dreadfully jealous. I wanted you by me. Because I've quite decided, Verney. At first I thought I mightn't be able to love you, and I didn't want to promise till I was sure. But now I know. I shall love you for ever and ever. But Mrs Van Necker was sitting there instead asking me all sorts of questions about father, and it rather annoyed me just for the moment, but I've thought about it since, and I don't think she's very well-off because she has to look after us girls for a living. But I was jealous, and it was worse yesterday, because I didn't see you all day, and I went to the Museum instead. Where were you?'

He himself felt a thousand years old. But across whatever gulf, he must answer her.

'I was wretched. I don't know where I went. I just walked about. I walked about all day. I didn't do any work at all.'

'What is your work, Verney? Isn't it funny that I haven't an idea?'

'It isn't work. It's only an experiment. They pay my expenses. Even then my people had to put up some sort of a premium.'

'What's a premium?'

'Oh . . . '

In and out went the feet they had made play with in the Avenue Jules Ferry, she lengthening her step, he shortening his, that they might walk together. But she forgot her question.

'And do you know another thing I'm going to do? I'm going to get Amalia to paint me,' she said. 'At first I hated her to study me, but that was while we were still on the boat, before it all happened. Now I shall get her to paint me. Can you guess what for, Verney?'

'Oh, God, what's happened to us both!' he almost groaned aloud.

'Can't you guess? Then I'll tell you. It will be a present from me to you. I haven't ever given you a present, and you haven't ever given me one. But of course there's heaps of time now. And – ' for a moment she turned on him a look like the flash of a king-fisher, but made a little laughing face and shook her head – 'but I shan't tell you that yet. You'll have to wait till we get to the top. And do you know I went shopping yesterday? I spent such a lot of money! The frock I have on now is some of it. So is my hat. I like frocks and hats.'

He was wondering how he had ever dared to kiss those lips, old with such a youth, young with all those mysterious years behind. That had been before the knowledge had come to him. Would the strangeness pass for him also? Was he too presently going to find it beautiful? Before his eyes she had slipped back to ancient things; was he going to slip too? He, a young man of today, with his truck-load of samples and that third suitcase at the hotel? Did he care if he did? Did it matter? Did anything matter except that island of his dreams, where no thought need be given to the morrow, but the fruit came to the mouth fresh and unasked as the kiss, and there were rivers alike of water and love for body and soul to bathe? But he had undergone no purification yet. Perhaps he was not yet worthy. And suddenly, with an 'Oh, look!' she drew a deep breath.

The wonders of the mountain were beginning to unfold. From the path up which they were walking there rose glade after glade of rosy-lilac waves of nodding flowers, chaste purple, the lovely little cyclamen in its countless multitudes. Among it the hawthorn broke into sunny spray, loading the air with its scent. So near was beauty brought that the sun on a swelling bud pushed the glimmering immensities of blue back, merging sky and sea into one. Heavenly hill, with its pines to the north, its arid crags to the south, and the gulfs of flowers far below! The path wound round the contour, discovering ravine after ravine of delight. Some were green with grass, with silver links of water at the bottom, some were dry and bouldered and waterless; and he knew that by his side walked a creature wrapped about in an innocence so perfect that it was old knowledge too. No such knowledge had come to her from that rocky chapel on Monte Pellegrino. That chapel's Sinai was fierce with lightnings and voices of awe. But here on Baal's beautiful Hill were flowers and fragrance. Pat-pat, in and out, went the little feet under the earth-stained frock, over cyclamen and geranium, coltsfoot and myrtle and thyme, with sudden bursts of mimosa and yellow broom. And ever she talked, pouring out her purified heart.

'I worried till I nearly cried about whether I should be able to love you properly,' she poured it out to him. 'Because if I hadn't liked you a bit I oughtn't to have let you kiss me, ought I? But how do people *know*? I mean you might kiss somebody and even after that not truly love them, but you couldn't love them without kissing them to see, could you? I mean *could* you?'

'Oh my God, how I love you!' broke in a tortured groan from him. For another fear had taken him now, driving out the other cowardice. It was that most beautiful of lovers' fears, that fear of the very beauty itself, the fear that brings tears to the eyes because of the dread of haplessness and mischance. Her loveliness seemed to prepare a way for itself, marching down upon him like an army with banners. It trampled him, but now he would rather be trampled by her than taken to any other bosom on earth. He flung out his hands. He could not wait another moment for his kiss.

But she looked at him with that crystal-clear earnestness, and her lips shaped a whispered 'No.'

'We mustn't till we get up to the top,' she told him.

'But you do love me? You have said you love me? Two days ago I could have done without you, but if you don't love me now I don't know what I shall do – '

'I know we mustn't till we get up to the top – ' she persisted softly.

'Because for two nights I don't know whether it's been heaven or hell – '

'Poor boy!' she smiled her fondness at him. 'But it won't be long now, and then we can get married. I had a letter from father last night. He says he watched the boat quite out of sight and then went back to the hotel. And he says I couldn't have stayed with him for ever. He knows I shall have to get married sometime. And at first I was going to tease you, and tell you that he would never let me marry anybody who wasn't *tremendously* rich. But if he didn't say "Yes", we'd just get married as we are, and then he'd have to do something.'

'Darling!' he chokingly thanked her; for he no longer feared to marry her. The centuries' sport as she was, left over from an older time and cast up again today, his only fear now was that he might even yet miss her.

They walked on in silence. They were now nearing the northern summit, and the last stage of the climb seemed to come almost suddenly. A narrow path led to a crest, half rocks, half thymy turf. She was a few yards ahead, walking lightly, her cheeks ever so faintly flushed. And after a few more minutes she stopped and turned. Her feet were on the carpet of lavender and thyme, and nothing on the whole mountain was nearer heaven than her head.

And what a heaven! The sun was south, fiery-towering in the blue, dwarfing the noontide shadow of every stone and bush and flower. She stood there gulls-winged against the light, betrayed, undone, in that gossamer frock with the enbrowned stain. The oyster-shell hat rimmed her head with iridescence, her face was in shadow; but her head might have been roofless, so did the sky seem to shine straight down on her and out again through her eyes. She was looking north over the sea.

Slowly he climbed up after her and saw what she saw.

The near mountain fell away in a fringe of pine-tops, of which the needled sprigs were drawn against a sun-white Tunis as if with a brush. Hot and pale the salines glittered, held within the thin arms of La Goulette. Thereafter towns became mere toy-like straggles on that vastness of blue. From the west, sweeping through the whole of the north, and lost to view in the east, sky and sea were confounded. Here for a score of leagues the sea was faintly bluer, then for another twenty leagues it showed a paler band. Sidi Bou Said and Carthage, Porto Farina and the hills of Bizerta's crest seemed evanescent things, Zembra and Zembretta mere puffs upon it, that might melt away and leave no trace. And Xena's eyes drank in the colour as if they had been Amalia's own. They drank it in and gave it out again, as if she and it had been one element, she a lent thing, a hostage held awhile by the firm-footed earth. And there was deep happiness in the eyes, because she was purified. Now that she had reached the mountain-top, she loved, knowing what love meant. She knew why Amalia had given the god the violets. Poor thing, he ought to be given violets. Those other girls who had come with green leaves and berry-stained faces had always given him violets, and Xena knew why. It meant that she too would have a little baby of her very own, with ten little toes to take into her hand and pretend to gobble up with her mouth, and two naughty little eyes to shake her shingled head at. She knew all those things now because her heart was pure. And Verney must be getting impatient.

He was indeed one ardent flush of love; if she loved him too, how should he not have taken the flame? Nothing could come between them now. She was alone with him on the mountain, with only the blue and the fiery-towering sun to be their witness. So they were kind to him now, thenceforward he served whatever gods she served. He was only waiting for one thing, and that was till her eyes should look away from the sea again and into his own, as the deeper. It happened. She turned the eyes to him.

'Darling – ' she said, and this time her voice did tremble.

'My love – my sweet love that's sent me – '

'I was only a little girl when you saw me before,' she faltered, 'but now I'm not a little girl any more – '

'I don't care what you are, nor where you have come from, nor where you are going to – I only know I love you – '

'Kiss me now, please, Verney – '

Glowingly he pressed to her. He put both his hands under the nacred hat. They were on her shingled nape as he bent her head back and approached his lips to hers.

And at that moment, a mile away in the mountain behind them, there was a dull explosion, as if a gun had gone off. It echoed and died away again.

But the two mouths had not met.

For she had started violently in his arms, and had given a swift look back over her shoulder. That way looked south, where the mountains frowned. Leaden bright under the torrid sun rose the ragged skyline of Djebel Recas and the menacing mass of Zaghouan. The air might have been made of sand-flies, it seemed so to hop and dance over their pale shapes: and in between lay Bou Kornine's other horn, across a stony saddle-shaped sag.

'What was that?' she asked in a faint voice. Her lips were parted, and the young cheeks seemed to have dropped.

'I know they quarry farther south. It was only a blasting-charge, darling,' he said in a shaky voice. He still held her.

'No, no – it wasn't that – and I seem to remember – that they used to quarry here – wait – keep so – '

They waited, but no other sound came. The scattered men, if it was a blast, had come together again.

And suddenly she struggled free. 'No – no – ' she panted. 'It's this way – '

Running quickly ahead she began to descend the slope. The crest on which they stood seemed to rise up behind them. Carthage, Sidi Bou Said and the sea disappeared.

They were in a rock bowl, that seemed filled with the silence of the suddenly shut-off airs. Its stones gave off an increased heat, and the flowers were sparser. Many wild pigeons flew overhead. The rough irregular slopes might have been arranged as an amphitheatre for the staging of some primal drama on sunny, arid Zaghouan. Burnt patches seemed the skins of lions, spread for the watchers to recline on. He was frightened of the solitude and silence of the place, of the threat of that fiery blue overhead.

'Love, let's go back,' he besought her, taking her hand. But she only muttered. – 'No, it is this way – it is somewhere here – ' She drew her hand away.

'Darling, let's go.'

But she only muttered again. – 'The Rock was there, and this is here, and there *were* quarries – '

'What is here?'

'There used to be a temple,' she replied.

With a face as altered as the mountain itself, he stood watching her while she wandered vainly about. Sometimes she returned to him, but when she did not he followed her at a little distance. Round and round she went, over an area of nearly a quarter of a mile; then, finding a patch of stone and a tamarisk bush, she crouched down, curling herself up. Her face was blank. She was looking at him apparently without seeing him. He crossed to her and knelt down beside her.

'Come away, dear love, back where the flowers are,' he begged her.

'It used to be here,' she said, on the brink of tears. He sought to pass his arm about her, but she put the arm rebukefully away.

'We mustn't do that here, Verney,' she said. 'They would be angry. This is a very holy place.'

'It is Bou Kornine, only just outside Tunis,' he faltered.

'Yes. It is Bou Kornine. I saw it from the ship. But what have they done with the temple?'

'What do you want the temple for?'

'To make my sacrifice.'

'What sacrifice?'

But her spirit seemed to have to go a long way for the answer, and then it came back without one.

'I forget, and I ought not to forget,' she said unhappily.

'Oh, let me kiss you, and kiss this dreadful thing away!' he cried in sudden dread.

This time surprise, expostulation almost, were in the look she turned on him.

'But you *have* kissed me, Verney,' she said, as if he ought to have known better than that.

'And I'm going to kiss you again, now, and then take you away.'

'*Here?*' The eyes looked the unthinkableness of it. 'Something very, *very* dreadful would happen if you did,' she assured him without anger.

'But we're going to be married – you have said you loved me – we were up there in the sun, among the scents and flowers, and you were going to kiss me – '

She put her hand quickly to her breast. She closed her eyes. She opened them again, and a forlornness the like of which he had never seen brimmed from them.

'I'm afraid you must go now,' she said in a hurried little voice. 'I want to make my sacrifice.'

'I can't leave you here, in this ghastly spot.'

'You must please go. You must go now.'

'I will not go.'

And he seized her.

Like a panther she was on her feet. There was a baleful blaze in the blue eyes, and in her hand was a stone. Her voice broke with indignation at his blasphemy.

'What? When I tell you that I want to make my sacrifice? You say you will not go? You *will* not?' The stone was raised to strike him down.

His head fell. He waited. Best so now, perhaps; let her strike him down. If she wished to make her sacrifice he had no more business here than he had at the Rock. How were her gods his gods if he refused her this?

'Are you going?' Her voice was utterly unrecognisable.

He lifted his defeated eyes.

'I will go. I will wait for you down there.'

The lead they mine in Zaghouan was not heavier than his heart as he turned brokenly away.

That night, in his neat room at the Tunisia Palace, Verney Arden had a dream. He dreamed that he was a junior boy at Winchester again, answering to call-over on St Catherine's Hill. Archie Hemingway, his great chum was there, who had gone on to Merton before Verney had been offered this job in the Levant. He and Verney had had tremendous confidences together that they had never shared with anybody, and had sometimes told one another about the girls they hoped to marry. Verney had hardly thought of Archie for months, but there Archie was, bursting into his room with his face all radiant, and though Verney didn't catch her name he knew that Archie was telling him about the most wonderful girl in all the world. 'I've told her all about you, and she's dying to meet you,' Archie said, and he brought the girl . . . and it wasn't St Catherine's Hill now, but the bright cricket-field where Verney had caught-and-bowled Ronnie Bruce-Harries, and all the fellows' pretty sisters were there, and Verney had the ball in his hand. And Archie looked a perfect ass for happiness, and he knew by the girl's face that Archie had told her what chums they were, and her eyes wished Verney luck too. And Verney laughed, and said he mustn't think of that just now, because he was going on to bowl, and she took the ball from him. And suddenly her eyes blazed, and the ball became a stone in her hand, and Verney gave a loud cry that woke him.

But he went to sleep again, if it could be called sleep, and Mr Thorne was telling him what a wise choice he had made in coming to the Mediterranean instead of going on to College. But Hayoun said No, because there were better things for young people to do than go sell carpets and brass bowls. They ought to go up into the mountain and gather flowers, Hayoun said, and gaze at one another, drawing ever nearer and nearer, till they kissed. And he was drawing nearer and nearer to Xena, with his hands on the nape under her hat, and she was full of sanctification and gladness, and then came a fearful bang that woke him again. But it was only the door of another room . . . or else the door of the Itala as he and Achmed waited for her to come down again. Not that he could possibly ride back with her after that, but he must make sure she did come down, or what would Mrs Van Necker think?

So down she came again for the twentieth time since he had gone to bed, and he was glad he had stood behind the green-shuttered café out of sight, for she had got straight into the car without asking for him and had driven off. That in some ways had been the worst of all – that she should think he had brought her out and left her to find her way back alone. Alone? Who was now more alone than he, unless it was herself? Why should morning come at all? That he might sell Greenway's Bottled Products here in Tunis? In Constantine? In Algiers? In Gib.? '*Adoptez-les*: take them on? *Agence Unique*: Sole Representative?' Why?

Waking again to see what time it was he found that he had omitted to wind up his watch, which had stopped.

But it was no more at a standstill than his heart.

11

'I don't blame the girls. I blame that woman.'

'Her own daughter spends her afternoons outside the *Cercle Militaire* with a young officer.'

'Some of the frocks that Francavilla girl wears really verge on an outrage – '

'No mother I expect – '

'And far too much money – '

'I suppose that other girl's all right, sketching all day by herself?'

'Well, if it were any of *my* business – '

Thus the older folk of the hotel had begun to talk, notably old Lady Lyle and the Dean. Lady Lyle had taken the two Bruce-Harries girls much under her own rather scaly wing. The Dean was of the opinion that a properly-couched letter from one of his cloth to Xena's father might be of help in the circumstances.

Some days had passed, and various things had happened, important or unimportant as one chose to regard them. It was hardly a matter for the *Va-et-Vient* column of the *Petit Tunisien*, for example, that Mr Verney Arden had left the Tunisia Palace Hotel *en route* for Algiers and Gibraltar; but Mr Thorne missed him very much, and asked Miss Amalia Sherren one evening whether he had really gone or was still hanging about somewhere.

Amalia spoke quickly. 'Have you seen him?'

'No – no – '

'Don't you think he's best right away now?'

'Perhaps, perhaps. If it's a question of best. It might be best. But he mightn't be able to do it.'

'No, I guess starting things is easier than stopping them,' Amalia said as she walked with hung head away.

In the meantime the girls discussed Xena in Mollie's bedroom.

'I'm worried about her. She isn't herself,' said Mollie anxiously.

'What *is* herself, that's what I should like to know,' Cicely Bruce-Harries replied with a lifting of her eyebrowless ridges. 'When you remember how scared she was if you as much as looked at her – '

'She hadn't seen him all the day before, because we were all in the Museum together and in the afternoon she was buying those frocks.'

'And then they had that day together, and he went off the very next morning.'

'I don't care, I think she's a pet.'

'Yes, because she lent you the car for *your* young man.'

'Anyway I've stopped calling her Frankie.'

'Yes, and if *I* were *you*, Mollie – '

But Mrs Van Necker entered, and the advice remained ungiven.

Indeed Xena now looked the more forlorn because of those very frocks. One puts on a beautiful frock out of gladness; but Xena sat of an evening by Mrs Van Necker's side, looking straight before her for minutes on end, without a tear, but so wistful and dismayed that one imagined tears would have been a relief. Apparently Mr Thorne thought so, for sometimes he watched her over his newspaper, or his little book, as he had watched Verney Arden. And one night Amalia showed Mr Thorne her sketches, as she had shown them to Verney, and sometimes they did not turn over a page for minutes, but their lips went on moving all the time. Then Mr Thorne's lips only were moving, and Amalia was looking almost as straight in front of her as Xena did.

Amalia was now out all day, taking her midday meal with her and not returning till the evening. She came back very tired. And seeing Amalia setting out from the hotel one morning Xena stopped her.

'Where are you going today?' she asked in a dull voice.

'Oh, not far. Only as far as the Belvedere.'

'How do you go?'

'I take the tram.'

'I'll drive you if you like.'

'It's hardly worth it.'

'I should like to drive you, Amalia, and I should like to come with you.'

'All right,' said Amalia. 'You'll have to walk a bit at the other end.'

'I don't mind,' said Xena, and walked slowly away to find Achmed.

The sketch that Amalia was making that morning was of a ruined Moorish pavilion not far from the Koubba, and she pointed it out to Xena as the car approached it – a torrent of crimson bougainvillea a quarter of a mile away, dripping down broken white marble, with a sea-green copper roof that was almost incandescent against the deep blue of the sky. They left the car at the park gates and walked up the slope towards the ruin.

But Xena gave its brilliance hardly a glance. Inside it she threw herself down on the grass among the hawk-weed and marigold and nibbled grass. Amalia got out her sketching tackle and was soon at work. Xena did not speak. She continued to chew grass after grass, spitting the little bits from the tip of her tongue as she had done when she was a little girl. Amalia had her work as a reason for her silence. Nevertheless it was Amalia who, after nearly half an hour, spoke first. Without turning her head or otherwise interrupting herself, and speaking exactly as she had spoken over the sketch-books, she said without preface:

'Xena, you're not to quarrel with Mollie.'

Xena took her time about replying. – 'I haven't quarrelled with Mollie,' she answered in a toneless voice.

'No, but you're going to.'

Xena did not reply.

'Are you going to that dance tomorrow night?' Amalia was asked.

'What dance?'

'At the *Café de la Garoun.*'

'I don't know where the *Café de la Garoun* is.'

'No, but I guess Captain Lemoine does.'

Xena was silent once more. Amalia sat on her camp-stool with brush poised and head back and a little on one side.

'It seems kinder mean to lend Mollie a car one day and then to steal him yourself the next,' she remarked.

A little gulp broke from Xena – 'I'm not trying to steal him!'

'No?' said Amalia laconically.

'I don't tell stories, and I'm not trying to steal him.'

'All the better. But I guess I've enough to answer for as it is, and this is to let you know right now that I'm quitting.' And Amalia stopped painting for a moment, that Xena might know that she meant it.

At that a fount of piteous tears rushed to Xena's eyes. She sat half up among the marigolds, her fingers working like things that did not share the life of the rest of her. It was terrible to hear a cry so tragic break from one so young.

'*Don't* leave me, Amalia! Don't leave me! It gets dark, and I'm frightened, and it's terribly, terribly lonely!'

Amalia nodded. – 'I guess it's lonely. That's why you spell yourself with an X. You're the unknown quantity all right.'

But Xena had come to her over the grass on her hands and knees. The working fingers clutched Amalia's skirt.

'But you don't know!' she cried. '*You* only know that *first* little bit! I haven't told you! I haven't told anybody! There wasn't anybody to tell but you, because the others wouldn't understand – ' And suddenly breaking down with her face in her hands she moaned, 'Oh, how I wish I could die!'

Amalia put down her brush. – 'Xena Francavilla,' she said, 'it's a good thing I haven't any nerves to speak of. What do you mean, you haven't told me? I guess you've told me enough to last *my* time out!'

'But I don't think I ever *quite* died,' Xena went unlisteningly on. 'Something didn't go back. Do you know where I went the other day?'

Amalia's muttering was almost inaudible. – 'I guess we can't always quit just when we'd like.'

'I went up the mountain with Verney,' she went on, suddenly as freely as a child that unburdens itself. 'And there was a place on the way, and I stopped there first of all to purify myself; and Verney waited in the car, because men aren't allowed there, so he waited with Achmed in the car. So I came back, and we got there, and sent Achmed away, and started to go up the mountain. And I'd been trying ever so long to love Verney, and it wouldn't come, but the moment I was purified it came, and oh, I can't tell you how lovely it was, as long as we were among all the flowers! And I knew all about *that*, Amalia, I mean about having little babies, and somebody to kiss you always, because I was purified. And Verney and I were looking at one another, on the top of the mountain, and he'd put his hands under my hat, where I had my hair cut off; and he was just going to kiss me, and his face came close, and I was waiting for him to kiss me when that noise came.'

'What noise?'

'He said it was some men blasting, but I knew almost for certain what it was, and he didn't kiss me after all, and my heart will always be broken because of that!'

'Go on,' said Amalia in a queer voice.

'So when I heard the noise I knew what it was, and we went to the other part of the mountain, where it was all rocky and frightening, and everything begins to get rather mixed up after that. I was looking for something, and Verney wouldn't go away when I told him, but wanted to kiss me, and I forget a lot here, but I know I was very angry, because of course he couldn't kiss me there, and I was going to kill him with a stone. So he went away, and he hadn't been gone very long before everything got dark. And there were tremendous noises going on, like when they move heavy things about behind the curtain at a theatre, only these were a million times heavier, and I can't tell you how pitch-dark it was. And tremendous big soft voices were talking all the time, about what place they should make next, because they were making all the places and things; it was the world they were making, you know, and they'd got as far as Africa. And I was lying there waiting, because they were making the big things first, and I was only a little girl after all.'

'Xena Francavilla!'

'So I lay there waiting till it came to my turn, and they were moving about, making things all the time, and they came nearer, and one of them said, "What shall we do with this?" And one said "Kill it", but another said "No, I think I could love that", and they talked about me, and then they decided to gamble for me. And the knocking went on all the time in the darkness, and the big deep voices counting as they gambled for me. And then somebody said "She's his", and another voice said "Yes, she's mine", and all at once everything smelt cold and salty, and I fell and hurt myself and made a mark here – '

And she pulled down the crêpe-de-chine and showed, purply-faint between her breasts, a triple sign, at which Amalia looked attentively.

'Poseidon,' she muttered, in a voice that Xena did not hear. 'That's his trident.'

'So long as I belonged to somebody and wasn't going to be killed I didn't mind,' Xena went on. 'He was rough, but very good-tempered in between, and he said that by and by when all the things were made and he'd a little time, he'd make me somebody all to myself, to love always, because I like that best. But they weren't all good-tempered, because every now and then a quarrel broke out about who the things they were making belonged to. And a very long time seemed to go by, and one day another quarrel broke out, and I knew it was all about me.'

'Xena Francavilla!'

She looked soberly up from Amalia's knee and nodded.

'It was, because one of them said I'd drowned some of his sailors. And my one stood up for me, but the others shouted him down, and they said I should have to be tried. So they tried me, and asked me what I wanted most. I was frightened, but I said that most of all I wanted to love somebody and be loved by them. And they told me because I'd drowned those sailors and made all their girls very unhappy I shouldn't ever have that, and the punishment was that I should just be going to love people, and then something would happen and they would be taken away, like Verney.'

Amalia's voice was a whisper. – 'And has it been so? All the time?'

Xena gave a deep sigh – 'I expect so.'

'And they –'

'I'm allowed to kiss them once, not loving them frightfully, but then when I begin to love them frightfully they're taken away. And I don't think that's fair, because it's punishing them too. But' – her voice dropped to a whisper and she looked mysteriously – 'I've thought of something about that!'

'I guess you would.'

'You'd have to help me though.'

'You stray little thing, I guess I helped to lose you.'

Xena put her hands to Amalia's neck, drew her ear down close, and whispered. Then she nodded once or twice. Amalia started.

'Wherever did you hear that?'

'I think in the mountain, but I'm not sure. But it's true, and ever so old. Then of course it thinks it's another person, and it can't find it's way back, and I've thought about it for three whole days, and I've decided that would be the best.'

This time Amalia did not even exclaim 'Xena Francavilla!'

'And of course you'd have to be careful not to wake me, or it would know the trick after that.'

'The trick! Sakes!' Amalia breathed.

'And I can't do it myself, because I know, and it would know what I was doing.'

Slowly Amalia took up her brush again. The purple bougainvillea she had put on in a rich raw mass, and she wanted lemon-yellow for the copper-green that burned so vividly against the blue. Xena's hand went to the tube in Amalia's fingers.

'Do, please, Amalia,' she pleaded.

Amalia began to paint busily. Besides the green and the purple and the deep African blue there were arabesques of coloured porcelain inside the ruin, lost in shadow, with a dazzling white marble column cutting straight across them. With an unsteady hand Amalia went on painting. Not to disturb her, Xena crept quietly back to her place among the hawk-weed and marigolds again. At any rate Amalia knew all about it now, and that it would be the same the next time, and the next, and always something would happen, and each time she would have to begin all over again. It had tired her to tell Amalia all this. The grass had a nice burnt smell. She wondered how Amalia could go on working as hard as that.

Five minutes later Amalia, looking round, saw that Xena was fast asleep.

To have her face disguised while she slept, so that the soul, returning from its flight abroad, should not recognise its habitation, but should remain shut out for ever!

Amalia began to paint still more feverishly. She knew that she herself had sinned. Out of an idle itch she had experimented with a soul, and a soul that gods had gambled for in that ancient darkness of the making of the world. She had not intended that that soul should pass the experiment on to another, but that too was a consequence she had incurred. What should she do? Give the tossed spirit rest the way she said, and then do something about herself? What world did this morsel of spindrift that called itself Xena Francavilla live in anyway? Who should say it was killing? Whoever before had killed with a few touches of water-colour and a sable brush? There she slept, her face in the pavilion's shadow and one arm stretched out on the sunny grass. Amalia could dodge Achmed, leave the park by another way, take the tram back to the hotel, and with a little veronal her own amends and peace would be made too.

Softly she put down her work and approached the sleeping Xena. She bent over her. The paintbox was within reach of her hand.

But she remembered that water-colour is wet. At the first touch of the cold brush Xena would start and wake, and the spirit would be nimbly home again.

Slowly she turned away from the sleeping girl, took up her sketch again, and went on painting.

Xena woke with a yawn and a drowsy limpid look. She stretched herself.

'What time is it? How long have I been asleep?'

'Not long. About a quarter of an hour.'

'Have you nearly finished your sketch?'

'Not yet.'

'Then I think I shall go back to the hotel. If you'll tell me what time I'll send the car.'

'It doesn't matter. The walk will do me good,' said Amalia with a brush between her teeth.

Xena walked down the sunny slope in the direction of the car, and Amalia went on painting.

12

There walked about Tunis – for though he had left his hotel he had not found strength to leave the town – a young man of two-and-twenty whose breast no longer contained a heart. He wasn't quite sure what had become of his heart; sometimes he thought he had left it up a mountain, and sometimes that a stone, lifted to break his head, had somehow got into his bosom instead. His funds were low, but there was a certain consolation in the thought that it didn't really matter whether he made a living or not. People may go short in the Levant, but they can always beg. Much more than the making of a living was the remembered dream of an island, for his desolation was simple and complete, and the dream had vanished too.

He had taken a bedroom in a cheap *pension*, but he was seldom to be found there. He called at no offices, never mentioned Greenway's Bottled Products. He had not even left an address for his letters. What should he want letters for? A man with no desire in life has little use for letters. Let them think he had perished. All that mattered of him had in fact perished. What, if not dead, is a young man without a heart?

Yet he was incapable of leaving Tunis. He would probably have stayed inertly on even if she had no longer been there. And while the quays saw his face, drawn like that of a middle-aged man, and the native quarters and the waste and pasture-land towards Carthage, he knew there was one danger-zone he was best away from. This was the neighbourhood of the Tunisia Palace Hotel.

Yet while avoiding the danger he toyed with it. There was, for example, the question of hours. The terraced café was certainly better avoided during the busy time of the day. Sitting there he might see her pass at any moment. But the evening was different. Negligently chaperoned as he knew her to be, he had not yet known her to go out in the evening. At the same time there was always the remote chance that something might bring her abroad, and therein lay the fascination. For two nights, alone and without a heart, he had sat on the café's terrace. On the third night he sat there again, with a cup of coffee in front of him that he had ordered because he had had to order something. The few salted wafers he had eaten at a counter could hardly be called dinner. He hated to think he had a stomach when he hadn't a heart.

Opposite him the flickering bats played among the telegraph-wires, and the tall electric standards made muslin of the ficus-tree. The awning of the café opposite was a shadow-show of moving shapes. To his right was the glow of the music-hall, beyond that the hotel. Fez and bowler, burnous and black veil, passed within a few feet of him without knowing they passed a young man who no longer had a heart. To have got up and sought his shabby pension would have required more effort than he felt capable of. He would get up when they closed the cafe. That was long enough yet.

He continued to watch the bats, the shadow-shapes on the awning opposite, and the green muslin of the ficus-trees.

And he thought, as he had thought ever since, of the loveliness of one side of that fatal mountain, of the horror of the other. Why hadn't he kissed her at first, on Bou Kornine's hither horn, when she had looked at him with that infinity of blue shining back from her eyes? Why had he delayed until they had got to a place where his answer was a lifted stone? Now – oh! how gladly he would have died there among the cyclamen and the thyme, her smile the last thing he saw! But he had to go on living, without a heart.

Why go on living, when it was so easy to do the other thing? Was it that some destiny he shared with her was not even yet complete? He didn't know, and he didn't much care. At the last perhaps that was why he was sitting there, dinner-less and with an untouched cup of coffee in front of him. Achmed would have sat so. Strokes of destiny are things that have to be waited for.

He had not to wait long. Even as he was thinking it he saw the shape of her shingled head mingled with the shadows of the café opposite.

And there passed with her an officer in a uniform of horizon-blue.

He was on his feet. *That* fellow! Once, twice, he had seen that same officer with Mollie Van Necker. And he was the same fellow who, that first afternoon of all, had looked in that hateful way at Xena in the souks, even while Mollie had been giving him a light for his cigarette.

Verney hadn't paid for his coffee. With his eyes strained on the opposite corner he was calling loudly to the waiter to make haste. Damn the waiter! Damn the coffee! He couldn't stop there waiting to pay for a few centimes-worth of coffee!

'*M'sieu*'?'

It was the waiter. Verney crammed a couple of notes into his hand and dashed away.

Damnation! He had lost them! Captain Lemoine was not the only officer in that uniform in Tunis, and except for her uncovered and shingled head he had had no time to see what Xena wore. He dashed in under the ficus-tree. Up or down there was no sign of them. Then he remembered that a short street ran back in the other direction. He doubled back and looked down its dark length.

He wasn't sure – there seemed to be figures at the other end. He ran.

He reached a corner where the street was crossed by another. It was they. Facing him a little to the left, in vertical crimson lights against a background of blackness, were the words '*Café de la Garoun*'.

She, who had never gone out in the evenings, now being taken there!

Already they were entering. They disappeared from his view. And they must have booked their table in advance and walked straight in, for they were not to be seen the next moment, when Verney Arden stood in the low-lighted doorway with notes in his hand. A manager was looking him up and down with apologetic regret.

'*Pardon* – ' the eyes were deferential but firm, ' – *monsieur* is not suitably dressed – '

'I have friends who have just gone in – '

Parfait – but it was a rule of the establishment –

'*Monsieur le Capitaine* – ' he expostulated.

'*Ah ça*! But *Monsieur le Capitaine* was in uniform –

'It is important – it is very important – '

The manager spoke soothingly. 'People do not come to the *Café de la Garoun* and leave immediately, *monsieur*. You are no doubt staying at the Majestic, at the Tunisia Palace. Both are quite near. The night is yet early – '

It was true. He had forgotten that there was plenty of time.

Already he was hurrying back to his *pension* to change.

That fellow! The gummy look he had given her in the *souks* even while another girl was lighting a cigarette for him – oh, he was a bad piece of work, that fellow! And as he hurried towards his *pension* Verney Arden knew very well what had happened to himself. His torpid heart had come back into his breast and was waking up again.

His lodging was over a bakery in the Rue d'Espagne. And just when he felt, without knowing why, that every instant was of importance, lucklessness dogged him again. He had either forgotten or lost his key. An electric standard stood opposite his door, and the street was empty. He knocked. He knocked again, more loudly, and called '*Madame*! *Ouvrez*!' He knocked until a gendarme came up. He explained. Both knocked, and the gendarme raised the voice of authority. At last a glimmer of light appeared. Shuffling feet were heard descending. The door opened, and an aged beldame in a brown blanket showed her single tooth to the light and covered the gendarme with screams of abuse. But Verney did not hear her. He had pushed past her and was running up to his room.

Lucklessness still clung to his heels. At the Tunisia Palace he had always laid his own things neatly out in readiness beforehand; but here they were all bundled together in a strapped trunk. The room had no electric light, and he set a match to the two *bougies*, but the lamp in the street gave more light than both. He flung the trunk on his bed and began to tug at his straps. He had left the Tunisia Palace in too much agitation to pack methodically, and he didn't know where anything was. Out his suitcases had to come too, and by the time he had cast half his possessions on the floor he knew less than ever where anything was. And as he hunted and kicked aside and swore there ran ever through his head the thought that she was with him, that bad piece of work, and that he had taken her to a night-club.

Half by candlelight, half by the light of the standards outside, he dressed. He looked at his watch. The *Café de la Garoun* was less than ten minutes' walk away, but it was just over an hour since he had been refused admission. His handkerchief – there. His money – there. And this time his key –

But no, he couldn't begin to look for his key in that litter that filled the room. If it came to the worst and later he found himself locked out he could walk about till morning –

He dashed down the stairs again, came out into the Rue d'Espagne, and made haste to the establishment with the vertical sign in red.

They bowed a welcome to his transformed appearance. From the farther end of a short corridor came sounds of music. He had never been in the place before, but apparently the ballroom was at the end. He pushed at double doors and there it was, a large oblong room with a floor that was sunk a foot or so like a shallow swimming-bath. Surrounding this, where the dressing-rooms of the swimming-bath might have been, were interrupted bays, with three or four supper-tables in each. The room was lighted from above in the usual way, and some thirty or forty couples were already dancing. There were many watchers, and half-way down on the left was a table apparently of a different character from the others. Over-hatted professional partners sat there, or left their wraps and encumbrances when they danced.

But he did not see Xena.

And yet, as his eyes became accustomed to the lights and the stir of dancers in the well, he vaguely saw somebody with Xena's shingled head. Across the room, over the dancers' heads, the watchers were clustered more densely, culminating towards the middle in a group of pale blue. Some seven or eight officers made a party there, with ladies. But the girl who resembled Xena was not of their party. She sat in front, with another officer, and there was champagne in a bucket on the table between them. And this girl who resembled Xena appeared to be wearing only a single garment, and a scanty one at that. The officer was smearing her over with his eyes, and his frizzed moustache was close to her nape as he poured her out more champagne.

Then she lifted her eyes, and across the room they met Verney's.

It *was* Xena.

Had the whole French Army stood between, those eyes would have brought him to her side. Jostled by the moving dancers, as a spun top moves the little wooden toys about, he made his way across the dancing-floor.

Only then, while he was still in the well, did the monstrous falsity of his position flash upon him.

Why had he come? And now that he was here what was he going to do?

And he saw now what the frock was. Actually it was the usual two
or three garments, but so close was their mimicry of herself that she
appeared merely to have tossed a shawl of many-coloured sequins
sparsely sewn on black lace about herself; in her own bathroom.
Even the professional dancing-partners glanced at her and pushed
out their lips, and there were bursts of laughter from the group
of officers behind, not perhaps at her, but only too obviously at
something of which she had been the original cause.

But her eyes met Verney's again, and with a leap that was pure
anguish his heart broke once more to life and suffering in his breast.
Never, never had he seen her eyes so. He had seen that first look of
all, when they had supplicated him to love her, and she would love
him if love between them was to be. He had seen them when he had
kissed her in Hayoun's shop, full of a strange waiting and wonder.
He had seen them childish and petulant, when she had told him
that if he didn't want to come to the mountain she would go by
herself. He had seen them at that mountain's top, shining with that
light of uttermost readiness, calling him to kiss her and not to cease
kissing her till death. And he had seen them fixed on his own with
an infernal light, while her hand had held aloft a stone. But *this*
profundity of pellucid grief! *This* basic and immemorial look, as if
all the other looks were mere variants, and to this she must return!
She seemed, in that lewd fraud of a frock, to be bidding him a
sorrowful and endless goodbye. He could not bear it. He was out of
the well and by her side.

'Darling!' broke from that newly-found heart, strong now to endure
a thousand years of pain again. 'What is it?'

She did not speak. She only looked.

'What's the matter?'

'It's – it's only seeing you,' she gasped.

'Yes, I'm here, love. We're both here. Sit quite still and don't think
for a minute. I'll – I'll try to think.'

'I'm here with Captain Lemoine.' And then she began to use words
he didn't understand. 'I ought to be sorry for him too. But I don't
think it hurts them all the same way. That's why I picked him, and
not what Amalia thinks. And if I promise him, I don't mean really
saying yes, but just nodding, perhaps I shan't have to give him even
one, and then yours will be the last one of all, Verney.'

'The last what?'

He hardly heard her reply. – 'I mean that time in the carpet-shop.'

She continued to gaze straight before her.

There was no third chair, even had Verney Arden been asked to sit down. Captain Lemoine sat there with his head thrown back, so that Verney could see through the frizz of his brown moustache. He gave no sign that he had heard his name spoken.

Then Verney thought he saw a way out. He spoke low and rapidly.

'Look here. I can't take you away. That would be worse than ever. Mrs Van Necker ought to be here. But I saw Mr Thorne over there. Will you let him take you back to the hotel?'

Slowly but steadfastly she shook her head. – 'No. I have to stay here now. Because I've thought of a plan. It's almost *sure* to be all right if I'm very, very careful.'

'I wish you'd – '

Suddenly Captain Lemoine turned his head slightly towards Verney. After all there does come a moment when an intruder who hasn't been asked to sit down has stayed long enough.

'*Vous parlez français, monsieur?*'

'*Oui, monsieur.*'

'*Vous êtes seul ici?*'

'*Oui, monsieur.*'

'*Moi-vous voyez – *'

And with a shrug of the blue shoulders up went the moustache into the air again.

Verney Arden had one crumb of satisfaction. He had suffered much at the hands of Frenchmen who understood his French best when he invited them to dinner. At any rate Captain Lemoine spoke no English.

Then suddenly he was conscious of suppressed sounds of mirth behind him. A voice said '*Monsieur*', and he turned. A stout major with a jovial face had ceremoniously set a gilt rout-chair for him within a yard or so of Xena's table, and two ladies of the party were whispering behind their hands with their smiling eyes on him.

It took him some moments to realise what was happening. Then he thought he saw. Captain Lemoine did not appear to be too popular with his brother-officers. The comedy of Captain Lemoine with a half-undressed girl and a young Englishman who was plainly told to go and yet remained was too good to miss. Probably they had laughed at his ill-breeding in remaining so long; now they were receiving him with open arms and pressing him to remain. The fat major with the jovial face had even put a glass of champagne into his hand; that too was part of it – to see on which table he would set it down. He wondered whether they would have done so had they seen Xena's eyes. But Xena had her back to them, and her eyes were on his own again.

He bowed to the fat major, put the glass of champagne on the floor, and sat down.

Several minutes passed, during which Captain Lemoine evidently thought the position over. Then Xena spoke.

'Verney – ' she faltered.

'Love?' (Would he ever say 'Love' to her again?)

'If you please, I want you to forgive me.'

'About sending me away from the mountain, my darling?'

'No. I mean for having looked at you that day in the garden. It *had* to be that day, because of everything that had happened, and you were the only person I knew. Will you forgive me?'

'No,' he murmured slowly. 'When I've nothing else to thank the world for I shall still thank you for that.'

'And he'll hardly feel it. He won't feel it like you. Mollie knows he's half a dozen girls, and it isn't what Amalia thought. It isn't even like those poor sailors who got drowned.'

'What sailors, heart's love?'

'I haven't time to tell you now. Amalia knows. I've got to smile at him now. Then he'll take it all off; and it'll be over. I hope another little girl like me won't get it next time, and perhaps it will get lost altogether, and *you* couldn't kiss me any more, if we were ever so alone, but you can look at me just once – '

Slowly she turned on him the long blue farewell.

Suddenly the whole room was transformed. The ceiling lights went out. The shallow sides of the dancing-well were of greenish glass; they became flooded with light. It gleamed on the calves of the dancers, who danced in a sea of light. Across the tumult of dark heads only the matches and cigarettes of the other side of the room could be seen. Verney had turned his head for a moment. When he turned it again she was not there. She and Captain Lemoine had left the table and had joined the dancers.

He sat there, mechanically counting how many times the strongly-sprung calves, the honeysuckle shape, the flimsy sequined shawl came round. He sat as he had sat at the café, with that dull feeling that though he had finished he had one final act to perform. He heard a woman's compassionate murmur behind him, '*Non, non, c'est trop cruel* – ' but if she meant him she was quite mistaken. The cruel thing would have been to go back to Greenway's Bottled Products again.

The dance ended and the lights went up again. Xena and Captain Lemoine returned to the table. His face was flushed with exult-ation. Aha, Captain Lemoine knew his sex! Obviously he had had his promise. Give him the promise and it would be an odd thing if the kiss didn't follow! And with the kiss would come that more-than-a-kiss that he hoped for. He poured Xena out more champagne. He swallowed a glass at a gulp himself. Then he turned insolently to Verney.

'*Vous vous amusez, monsieur?*'

And because Verney Arden had not yet talked with Amalia, and did not understand that though Captain Lemoine might get the kiss he would get no more, nor that twice, nor as much as that if Xena was to be believed, he frowningly watched Xena drink the champagne. It was the last of the bottle, but Captain Lemoine, perfect host, had evidently given orders, for another bottle was on the table instantly.

'*Vous vous amusez, monsieur?*' the officer again asked the uninvited young man.

Verney Arden attempted a shrug.

'It is a pity I do not speak English,' said the Frenchman in French.

'I answer *mademoiselle* in the same language she speaks to me in,' Verney coldly replied.

'Still, if you wish to dance, you also, there are ladies over there – '

'I do not wish to dance.'

'Only to sit?'

'For the moment only to sit,' said Verney, withdrawing his chair one farther neutral inch.

'Perhaps to see that Mademoiselle behaves herself?'

Xena sat like a half-stripped penitent with her eyes upon the ground.

'To see that you give her no more champagne,' said Verney Arden suddenly, with his eyes on the bottle.

'It is perhaps permitted to offer a cigarette?' the Frenchman mocked, producing his case and proffering it to Xena.

After that it could only be a matter of moments. Captain Le-moine's hand was on the bottle.

'*Mademoiselle* – '

Verney sprang up. She was his love, his life, what remained of it. But for fatality he and she might have been speeding together to her father now. Her eyes might bid him goodbye, but he would *not* let her go. His voice was raised.

'*Monsieur*, this lady is promised to me.'

'Truly, *monsieur*?' came the ironical reply.

'We are engaged to be married – '

'*Permettez, mademoiselle* – '

'You shall not – '

Captain Lemoine looked haughtily at Verney. – '*Vous êtes commis voyageur, monsieur*? You have the manners of one.'

And he filled Xena's glass.

At least he attempted to fill it. He half-filled it. What came next was swift as three rapier-passes.

'I know her father – '

'*Mon Dieu*, but I – '

'Have it, then – '

Xena's glass was half-full no longer. Its contents were running down Captain Lemoine's face.

The officers behind had leapt to their feet. Hands seized Verney, other hands held back the insulted officer. There was a swift pushing-back of chairs, the tottering of a table, cries, commotion. Verney was struggling violently, but only because he was being borne moment by moment farther away from Xena.

'Go back to the hotel!' he panted. 'Go back to the hotel!' he shouted over their heads when he could no longer see her. Two cloaked and sworded gendarmes appeared.

'*C'est inutile, monsieur* – '

Then a reassuring English voice spoke.

'Go with them quietly. I will look after her. Then I'll come to you if I can.'

Turning, Verney saw Mr Thorne.

'You'll take her yourself; sir?' he panted.

'She shall be back at the hotel in ten minutes.'

Without further resistance Verney Arden suffered himself to be led away.

13

In a French Protectorate, where prestige is of importance, young commercial travellers do not publicly insult French officers. But neither do French officers carry off and take to the *Café de la Garoun* first one, and then another, of a party of young girls in the charge of a professional chaperon. As the youth was leaving the country in any case the simplest way out was that his departure should be a little hastened.

Verney Arden, after a day and a half of incarceration during which
the only visits he received were visits from magistrates, officials, and
the jovial major, now sternness itself, was released. Somebody threw
him a raincoat to put over his crumpled evening clothes, and he had
no hat. He had twenty-four hours in which to pack up and be off.

He had gone in at midnight. He came out again at noon of the
next day but one. The only young-looking thing about him was
that after two days in a cell he hardly yet required to be shaved.
And as his place of confinement was nowhere near the sea-front,
he was unaware that almost at the same moment as that of his
release, there alighted on the hydroplane lake, with a gash of green
and white half a furlong long, a seaplane. A boat put out to the
seaplane. It brought ashore the silk-hatted, morning-coated figure
of Umberto Francavilla.

Verney thought of taking a taxi, because of the noticeable way in
which he was dressed. In the street into which he had been bundled
there was no taxi, and he walked in search of one. But as he walked
he saw his own black evening trousers under the fawn-coloured
raincoat and his varnished shoes that moved in and out. They
reminded him of another pair of feet, that had lengthened their step
to his, he shortening his own to them. Taxis passed him, but he
continued to walk. He wanted to know two things. He wanted to
know whether Mr Thorne had got her safely back to the hotel. And
he wanted to know what it was that Amalia knew that Xena had not
had time to tell him.

Forgetting all about his clothes, he was approaching the Tunisia
Palace Hotel. But he was approaching it in the opposite direction
from his accustomed one, and on the hotel side of the pavement.
Thus he did not see what he would have seen from across the way –
that the only un-blinded windows of the hotel's frontage were the
glazed panes of the double entrance-doors. These doors opened as
he was about to mount the steps. There came out of them the very
man he wanted to see.

Without speaking Mr Thorne took him by the arm and led him
away.

'Did you take her back?' were the young man's first words.

'Yes. Yes, yes. They wouldn't let me see you, but I did my best with
the Consulate. You have twenty-four hours, I believe.'

'That swine was trying to make her drunk.' For a day and a half
he had been saying this to himself; but it still had power to make
him hot.

'Yes. Yes. Walk a little this way.'

But instead of walking, at something in Mr Thorne's tone Verney suddenly stopped and looked at Mr Thorne.

'What's the matter?' he asked quickly.

'My boy – '

Mr Thorne had not wanted it to come so quickly. They had barely turned the corner. They were passing the other cafe, and it had round iron tables and iron chairs painted to resemble wicker. One of these rang like a drum to Verney's elbow as he sat suddenly down. The face he turned to Mr Thorne was stark.

'She's dead,' he said.

Mr Thorne took off his glasses and polished them.

'You're telling me she's dead.'

Mr Thorne made no reply.

For nearly five minutes neither spoke. Then the young man thought he could bear it.

'Tell me,' he said almost inaudibly.

'You know without telling,' Mr Thorne replied.

'I mean – I mean how it happened.'

'I think I will let Amalia tell you that. Amalia took charge of everything. She sent for her father. He only arrived half an hour ago.'

'Was it – that same night?'

'Yes. But it was as you would have wished – painless, peaceful, happy – happy – '

It was not Verney, but Mr Thorne who broke down. He covered his face with his hands and sobbed as Verney had never sobbed. Verney wished he wouldn't. She wasn't *his* Xena. Presently Mr Thorne was a little better.

'Forgive me,' he said, wiping his wet glasses. 'Sometimes young people do not quite know how much they are to those who aren't young any longer. Death is better than a living loneliness. I am very fond of you, Verney, and I hope you will come and see me when you get back to England. And now perhaps you would like to be alone. You cannot go to the hotel just yet. Her father is there. And you haven't much time. I will speak to Amalia. If I'm not intruding I should like to speak to him too. What are you doing this afternoon?'

'Nothing.'

'You have your packing to do.'

'Eh?'

'And in any case you cannot go about dressed like that. Come and see me at three o'clock. I shall have seen Amalia by then.'

Mr Thorne moved away in the direction of the blinded hotel.

His packing. Yes, that would pass the time. His samples might remain where they were. At last he would be rid of that suitcase of 'literature' too. And of course he couldn't go about in those clothes. It was time he was getting a move on.

He dragged himself up and walked shufflingly towards the Rue d'Espagne.

No attempt had been made to straighten up his room, and his things were as he had left them; he noticed that both *bougies* had guttered down; and concluded he must have left them burning. He looked at the gaping trunk on the bed, at the disorder everywhere. All these things were to be packed. Well, they could wait. He must find his day-suit first. That, being the most immediate, was the most important thing. The next most important thing was a piece of paper in his pocket, that would speed him indeed. On no account must he lose that. It directed him what trains to take, what towns to go through, what officials to report to on the way. Messages would go over the wires before him, saying that he was to be expected; messages would flash back, saying that his papers were stamped and he was off on the next stage. That document, his English passport and the clothes he was looking for – and, oh! yes, his remaining money – those were the things he mustn't lose. He looked at his watch. Once more it had stopped. But it must be two hours or more yet before he could see Mr Thorne.

Slowly he extricated his garments from the litter. He had been in too much of a hurry to fold and press them, but he couldn't be bothered now. But he would shave because he was to see Amalia. A shave and a clean collar.

And to whom ought he to return that raincoat?

He got out of his evening clothes, drew on his English-made, summer-weight, grey flannel trousers, and prepared to shave.

The station was not far away, and an hour later found him there, not to take his ticket or comply with formalities, but to kill time and because he wanted something to eat. He ate several sandwiches, drank a couple of bocks, and felt better. He thought he could listen to Amalia now. He knew it was odd that he shouldn't be thinking more than he did of Xena, and Xena dead. Had Mr Thorne actually *said* she was dead? No he hadn't. It was Verney himself who had said that, and Mr Thorne simply hadn't said she wasn't. Anyway it didn't matter. It wasn't even funny that he, Verney, should have known. He had known before. She had looked a long, blue goodbye at him, and then the lights had gone out, and she had danced with that fellow who had got the wine down his face. Verney was sorry to have made a scene in public, not because he had got his own marching-orders for it, but because he hated scenes. He looked at the buffet clock, and set and wound up his watch. A fellow couldn't get along without the time. Especially a fellow with trains to catch and a paper in his pocket that made it advisable he should catch them.

And now – soon – for Amalia.

But he thought he wouldn't go inside the hotel after all. There were all the people he knew there – old General Lorimer, Lady Lyle, the Dean. They would know that he had been 'Vine-streeted', and the garden would be empty at that hour of the afternoon. Rabat would send up word to Mr Thorne that he was waiting there. Yes, the garden, where she had given him that first look. The garden, where she had sat in a hat less blue than her eyes, under a palm.

And there at three o'clock he was, waiting for Mr Thorne to descend.

But Amalia came instead. She sat down by his side without greeting.

'How's Signor Francavilla?' he asked. He felt singularly composed and in hand.

'He's up there.'

He looked the next question.

'She's just lying on her bed. She's to be taken to Monte Pellegrino. I don't know how he's fixed it, but he can fix most things, and I've been doing the fixing this last day and a half.'

'The last I heard was that Mr Thorne brought her home.'

'Are you feeling all right if I tell you, brother? Because I guess I'm through with experimenting on my fellow-creatures.'

'I'm all right.'

'She told me about you and her up on that mountain. Then she told me what happened after you left.'

'What did happen?'

'What I said happen. They knew their own when they saw it, and they got hold of her.'

'I didn't see her after that till I saw her going along to the Café with that Frenchman. He tried to made her drunk.'

'I guess you were mad-jealous too.'

'I loved her, Amalia.' He could just say it.

'Steady, brother . . . Well, you've no cause to worry about *him*. Nor any other man. You're the first and the last this trip on earth, if that's any comfort to you. Now I'm just going to tell you . . . '

Amalia told him. Amalia went on talking. The sunspots crept under the palm, the guides and hawkers hung lazily about the gate, Rabat's copper tray gleamed unattended in the doorway.

'And I guess that Frenchman did just what she wanted him to do,' Amalia continued. 'He gave her just enough to turn the corner. How much did she have?'

'I don't know. Things happened, and I got there late.'

'Did he give her a cigarette too?'

'I don't remember. Yes, I believe he did. But she didn't smoke it, because it was just then – '

'She brought the cigarette away. I found it in her bag. It was *ambrée*-doped. She didn't carry doped cigarettes. I guess she figured the champagne would be enough without it, but there it was if she wanted it. She knew a strange lot. Did I tell you about her asking me to paint her face?'

'To paint her face? What for?'

'To paint it when she was asleep. Your soul's off somewhere then, and it comes back, and it's like finding the number of your room changed, and it doesn't know where it is, and doesn't get in again. I guess she'd lugged that old soul round long enough and anybody could have it for her. And you can't do it yourself; because your soul's watching, and it isn't going to be fooled.'

For the first time his voice shook. – 'Is that – '

'It sure is. Seems to me she was just intoxicated enough to do it without knowing she was doing it. The only thing is, had she made up her mind to do it?'

He remembered that last, blue goodbye. –

'She had,' he choked.

'Old Man Thorne saw her to her door. He saw her go in. But she came out again. She couldn't borrow my paint-box for fear of putting me wise. And she couldn't get Mollie's face-things because of waking Mollie. But there's a barber-shop downstairs that you can get into from the hotel. There's a ladies' saloon. I guess as long as the street door's all right they don't bother much about the inside one. Anyway she got in, and got hold of a box of make-up and took it to her room.'

'And she painted herself?'

'Without some of those folk came down from the mountain to help her. She was found painted in the morning.'

'Who found her?'

'They couldn't wake her, but she hadn't locked her door, and Momma Van Necker walked in. After that – well, I guess I was the head of the family. I got through to Umberto. Nobody else dared. Momma Van Necker didn't. She ran out of the hotel at eleven o'clock that morning, and nobody knows where she is. Lady Lyle's taken over Cicely and Daphne, and – I guess I'll have Mollie till we hear she's been found.'

'Did – did you see her?'

'I did, and it would have been a smart soul that had known *that* for its face. She'd made no mistake about it. She'd taken the blue-black and put it right round her eyes like thick goggles. Then she'd taken the red and striped herself like one of these Punic masks, all grinning. And her mouth was just a wob of carmine-stick.'

That flower of a mouth, those skyey eyes! He groaned. God, if only he could have painted *his* face!

'So as long as Momma Van had seen I guessed there was no need for anybody else to, so I tidied her up and sent for Umberto. What time is it?'

'Nearly half-past three.'

'At half-past three Umberto won't be in the room. He'll be out for ten minutes.'

He trembled. – 'You mean I can – ?'

'Nobody'll stop you. Old Man Thorne and I fixed it for you.'

Then he broke down. She had called him brother –

'Sister – ' he sobbed, his face buried on her thin shoulder.

So, leaving the garden, he did go into the hotel after all. And even with her eyes open she had not been more innocently beautiful. "Blessed are the pure in heart, for they shall see God." Her hands were crossed over Umberto's own crucifix. Below, Amalia had told him, the bruise of the mountain had gone, and over those dancer's knees were placed the flowers of the Saint who bore both the rose and the lily in her name. Umberto, with all his Casinos, had never heard of gods who gambled for souls nor of ships lost two thousand years ago. But (to show how little we know of people even when we sit at the same table with them) Mr Thorne had, or, three days later with Xena gone and the sun shining in at the windows of the Tunisia Palace Hotel once more, he would not have written the following. It was written on the Tunisia Palace notepaper, and he gave it to

Amalia, who was still awaiting news of Mrs Van Necker. He didn't
want a copy, he said. He had it by heart.

> Hands bright as foam i' the sun, yet fickle as spray –
> Eyes of the sea, yet haunted with who that drowned? –
> Siren-songed lips that cast a ship away –
> Her 'wildering rest of metamorphoses, crowned
> With wreath of rainbowed spume, and spirit-bound –
> He was the wind that down the unnumbered years
> Passed o'er her tossing; nor needed he to feign
> His soul went down in the wave, from whence his prayers
> Like the Morgana rise in the air again,
> Element questioning element, all in vain.
>
> Alpheus in him still Arethusa chases;
> Her sighs are Syrinx in the whiskered reeds;
> And innocent lovers with their old, new faces
> 'Plain for each other 'cross the new, old creeds.

The Out Sister

I

Tall cactus and prickly-pear guarded the convent's approach, but the outer doors stood half open. Jennie Fairfax had already been there once that day, and she passed into the forecourt, leaving the doors as she had found them. A delicious cool light filled the place, which was also a well of odours, of the stocks and violets and cherry-pie of the parterres, the jasmine and japonica that straggled up the plaster arcades. And there, facing her at the cloister's end, was the Saracenic doorway she had come to draw.

How still it was! From the stirrings of the little town outside she might almost have passed into another world. And though only that morning she had received permission to come it would be as well to let them know she was here. The door had a bellrod of Sicilian wrought-iron. Jennie put out her hand to its little filigreed knob and pulled.

There answered her a clanging so harsh and near at hand that she fell back, a little startled. The little shower of almond-petals that came down might have done so because of the disturbance of the air. And as she waited she was suddenly a little less sure about her permission to come. *Had* the Sister said that afternoon, or had she meant some other day?

For the echoes of the bell died away and nobody came, and as tomorrow was the beginning of Lent she might have intruded on some hour of meditation and repose. In any case she dared not ring again. But once more her eyes rested on the lovely doorway. It was like a delicate brooch set in the wall's plaster breast, a brooch of carved sandstone inlaid with tesserae of black lava. A great Ali Baba jar of baked earth stood beside it, big enough for a man to have hidden in if any man had got so far; certainly he would have got no farther, for in the upper portion of the door was a small curtained grille, and underneath it, in church letters on a brass plate, the word '*Clausura*'.

As Jennie turned slowly away her suspicion that she had made a mistake became a certainty, for from somewhere aloft a smaller bell spoke. Its eight or ten notes seemed so routine-like as almost to be perfunctory, and could only mean service. At the same moment the air moved to the tremor of an organ. Somewhere the thin voices of women rose. And just as she was giving it up the door with the grille was opened very quietly and the Sister of that morning stood there, her finger half way to her lips in caution and her eyes turned in the direction of the singing. Jennie had not noticed before how very, very beautiful she must once have been.

Jennie Fairfax wasted few thoughts on her own looks. She supposed she was pretty on some days, was quite sure she was plain on others. She would be putting on other clothes that evening, but for the moment she was dressed in her short tweed skirt and crisscross golf-stockings, and she didn't see why the Sister should gaze so attentively at the hair that slipped from under her shapeless little hat like a golden wash from a sluice. Then she thought she guessed. Under the close band of linen above the Sister's brows there would be no hair. Her hair – from the way she looked it had quite likely been golden too – had been one of her sacrifices. Rigid in her black and white the only speck of gold about her now was the little finger-worn crucifix at her waist. And suddenly one wide sleeve was raised. Her hand was motioning Jennie to stay where she was. She disappeared and returned in a few moments with a rush-bottomed chair. She placed it by the Ali Baba jar and walked to the outer doors. She stood there for a minute looking away past the cactus and prickly-pear; then she closed the doors and walked slowly back. As she passed Jennie her eyes smiled. The organ in the chapel swelled and the voices of the nuns were raised in unison. Jennie drew in a deep breath of the odorous air and began to busy herself with her drawing-materials. The door with 'Clausura' on it closed behind the Sister, to watch who was left while the others prayed.

But Jennie had now little desire to draw. Even drawing seemed too secular an occupation for the peace of this place. She took a step back to look at the beautiful door from another angle and as she did so an almond-leaf floated down, turning as it fell, and lay lightly for a moment on her hand. Over a parterre a couple of butterflies were at play, and though they were of milky blue there seemed no reason why they should remind Jennie of the Sister's eyes as they had looked into her own in passing. But they did remind her of them. She hardly knew how to put it, but there had been something not quite settled about them, something not quite in one place; indeed as she had lingered at the outer doors looking past the cactus there had been an almost escaping look in them, as if they took a flight back into the world she had left. Then Jennie, her pencil in her idle hand, ceased to hear the drowsy murmur of worship in the chapel. It would never, never have done to have confessed it to these holy women, but – she yawned a little, for she had been up very late the night before – oh, the fun it had been at the Teatro Margherita, just the four of them, herself and her brother and his two friends!

It was as flimsy as an eggbox, the Teatro Margherita, with its little stuck-on decorations of papier-maché and fibrous plaster and its sprinkling of booths everywhere. They had had one of the upper boxes, and all round that tier, coming into view a little to her left, the same posters had run without a break that one saw everywhere in the town, corsets-stockings-shoes-corsets-stockings-shoes, all the way from one corner of the stage and back again to the other. And down in the stalls little supper-tables had been set out, and bars in the wings with mineral-waters and champagne and confectionery and ices, and as the evening had worn on the whole Teatro had become a maze of paper streamers and puff-balls and confetti, as if a kitten had been turned loose into a workbox of coloured silks. And little stencilled goats and fauns and donkeys had capered in front of the Grand Tier boxes –

Here Jennie Fairfax felt very much shocked at herself that she should be thinking of such things in a place like this; but it was like a fit of giggles in church, not to be stopped and so best got over, and on her thoughts raced.

– and every box had been gay with the ladies from the afternoon's procession of cars, the Sea Horse car with Neptune and the Nymphs, the Almond car all pink branches and pink-frocked girls, the Pompadour car pale blue and scattering violets, the harem car, the others, and every girl powdered to her eyes and with a pale wig pulled over the sooty poll nature had given her –

And of course Jennie, whose fairness was all her own, had been the target for half the confetti and streamers within reach. Young zouaves, young bull-fighters, young brigands had signalled up to her box for dances, and her brother had heaped her lap with more and more streamers and confetti, for in the tier beneath them the Mayor of the town had risen and was making gracious speeches as he bestowed prizes for this coiffure or that.

'Turn the charms on, Jennie,' her brother had urged her. 'Make a pass at the Mayor . . . By Jove, you've hooked him! Look, he's bowing to you – '

And sure enough within five minutes there had arrived at Box Number Six a flat, beribboned parcel, with his Worship's compliments.

'Chocolates,' her brother had guessed, untying the ribbons.

But not so. The astute Mayor did not throw away his compliments like that, for he was the town's barber too, and Jennie, who ought to have been thinking of pious little emblems with '*Al. S. Cuore di Gesù*' on them, tittered again as she remembered the Mayor's offering – the trade-cards of his profession, telling how in all Sicily he was without rival for undulations, perms, tinting, shampooing and the other branches of his art.

But all at once the organ-music had stopped. Shuffling footsteps were heard and the voices of the nuns raised on secular matters once more. And suddenly Jennie's heart jumped right up into her mouth. Heavens, what was this on her drawing-block? Her sketch of the door already finished, and she with no memory of having set down a single line of it? How long had she been there? An hour? Longer? And how had she come to leave out one little detail that surely should have been put in – the little brass plate with '*Clausura*' on it? She had omitted it entirely, and she was not sure that in some other ways her sketch was not a little as if her drawing-mistress had taken up the pencil while she was thinking of something else and, bending over her – but all at once she covered the drawing away out of sight. The Sister must have come out by some other door, for all at once she stood by her side again. And when Jennie could think of no better way of covering her confusion than by asking her what the convent was called, she thought the Italian syllables lovely on the Sister's faded lips.

'*Santa Maria di Gesù.*'

'Are – are there very many Sisters here?'

'Twenty-two. But only sixteen are choir-Sisters. I am Sister Maddalena, one of the out-Sisters. I sell the lace and the embroidery in the little kiosk over there. I wonder if you know you have something in your hair. May I take it off for you?'

Again the wide sleeve fell from the slender hand, and from Jennie's fair hair she picked a single piece of confetti, a souvenir of the Teatro and the evening before. And when next she spoke, if Jennie had not known she was a Sister she would never have guessed it from her tone.

'One always finds bits of it about, weeks, months afterwards,' she smiled. 'Even at the laundry they do not always get it out. Are there many people staying at the San Carmelito?'

'The San Carmelito? How did you know I was staying there?'

The Sister seemed to speak as much to the bit of confetti in her hand as to Jennie. 'I thought perhaps – but never mind. It is a very long time since I was there. At one time I had a friend – ' her voice died away.

'Anyway, there will be plenty of people there tonight. It's the Gala, you know,' said Jennie.

'Yes,' said the Sister with dropped head. 'Tomorrow is Ash Wednesday. For forty days Our Lord fasted.' Then, lifting her head again and speaking more lightly, 'But on Shrove Tuesday one first confesses and then makes merry too. What is at the San Carmelito tonight?'

It was to be an Egyptian Revel, and they had Tutenkhamened the walls, and the table-lamps were little silk pyramids, and the *chef* had made a vast mummy of layers of chocolate and spongecake and ice. As Jennie described it all Sister Maddalena listened; then suddenly she let the scrap of confetti fall from her hand and her fingers folded themselves about the little gold crucifix at her waist. She spoke with downcast lids, and meekly and dutifully enough, but somehow Jennie didn't feel a bit at her ease.

'We have our little feast tonight, too. We are to have almonds and cakes, we who see one another every day, and the Reverend Mother will play the *Pastorale* to us on the harmonium.'

Then suddenly Jennie knew what it was that lurked in the Sister's eyes. It was truancy. And her heart suddenly flowed over with sympathy. The *Pastorale* played by the Reverend Mother! To this Sister, still beautiful, who had known the revelry of the San Carmelito! And it wasn't as if she was *quite* a nun. She was an out-Sister, who sold things to visitors, and no doubt heard lots of gossip of the world outside. Jennie glanced over one shoulder, as if somebody might have been behind them, and then whispered conspiratorially.

'Oh, would it matter? Nobody would know! Couldn't you, just for once? I don't mean to dance of course, but just to look on? Couldn't you tell them somebody was taken ill and you were sent for?'

But Sister Maddalena shook her head. It was against all rules. 'I am not allowed to minister. I am only the out-Sister who sells the lace. But do one little thing for me. I will pray for us both afterwards. My hair was once exactly like yours. Take your hat off. I want to see it.

Jennie's hands flew to her hat. Out gushed the pent-up gold, with yet more confetti in it. The tumbled locks were close to the cere-clothed brow, and Jennie thought it perfectly dreadful that that other hair had once been golden too.

'Oh, do, *do*! You say you can pray afterwards – '

But the hand that had been straying over Jennie's head, whether in benediction or caress, trembled and paused suddenly. From behind the grille a light sound had come, and Jennie saw the dropping of a corner of the curtain. Sister Maddalena must have heard it, too, for with a noiseless flutter she was half way across the court, making for the office where the lace was sold. The cloister door opened, and there stood there a grim-faced nun with a large iron key in her hand. She gave a quick glance in the direction of Jennie's drawing-things.

'Since the signorina has finished – ' she said abruptly, in a tone that made Jennie feel that she had been trespassing after all.

So it was not the Sister with the straying eyes who locked the outer gates behind Jennie that afternoon. They were locked by the sub-Prioress, and nobody would have accused the sub-Prioress of linger-ing there to look at the world beyond them.

2

No sooner was Jennie out of the place than she asked herself whether it had been wicked of her to tempt the poor out-Sister like that. Evidently it had, or the Sister would not have said that about praying for them both afterwards. But she couldn't help thinking the Sister had begun it, wanting to know what they were doing at the San Carmelito and stroking her hair and telling her her own hair had once been the same. It might help her to collect her thoughts if she took a walk through the town before returning to see what the others were doing.

It was a clear greenish dusk as she turned into the short principal street. Lights burned in the depths of the lace-shops, turning their white interiors into chapels, and that reminded Jennie that she ought to have dropped something into the convent's box. But she could do so tomorrow, and if she happened to see Sister Maddalena tomorrow she would be able to tell her all about tonight's Gala. In the mean-time there were other Eve-of-Lent Balls as well as that at the San Carmelito, and the street was crowded with young men and young women who had got into fancy dress already. Then Jennie began to hasten her steps a little, for they were beginning to throw not new clean confetti, but handfuls they swept up from the ground, and even as she was thinking this – swish – somebody threw a handful of it into her face, so that she spluttered. Now her hair would certainly have to be done again. She was standing exactly opposite the shop of his Worship the barber, but she peeped in and saw that a dozen other girls were waiting already, and passed on. Perhaps they wouldn't be quite so busy at the hotel, where one usually made one's appointment. From a side-street she turned into the almond-grown alley that descended the slope.

The huge rambling place had at one time been a monastery, and already the arriving cars were parking themselves in the cloisters. Young men lounged by Italas and Isottos, bold, over-barbered young men, and it was fairly certain that many of them were not the owners of the cars they drove. In from Catania and Messina they had come, and the multiplicity of their lights flashed and wavered in the plate-glass with which the cloister arches had been filled in. Visitors at the San Carmelito slept in vaulted cubicles of plaster furnished by firms from Naples and London and Paris, and it took one a couple of days to learn one's way about the interminable arcaded, red-carpeted corridors. Jennie's own bedroom sometimes seemed half a mile away, in a different set of buildings altogether.

But before going to her bedroom she wanted to find her brother, and with her sketching-materials still under her arm she sought the cocktail-bar. Alan was not there, but other young men were, and a young woman with a chrysanthemum wig and a powdered back who also happened to be a young man, and she hurried out again. A couple of empty card-rooms led to the supper-room, and in the supper-room they were laying the tables and finishing the decorations. Hawk-headed profiles draped the walls, cotton lotuses swathed the tubs. The white-coated carvers wore the tall head-dresses of Pharaohs, and there on its waggon lay the five-foot mummy, ready for dissection into strata of cream and chocolate and sponge.

It was as she was passing out of the supper-room that a hurrying waiter bumped into her, knocking her sketching-things from her hand. He was one broken heart of apologies as he picked them up again, dusted them with his napkin and, bowing double, returned them to her. But unaccountable things were happening to Jennie Fairfax that day. She had felt queer and flighty ever since she had set foot in that convent court. The top sheet of paper had come loose from the block, and she was staring at it as if her eyes would drop out. She turned it over, and then looked at the block itself. Already she had forgotten to put on the Saracenic door the little brass plate with '*Clausura*' on it. Now she had forgotten far, far more than that. Nowhere on the paper was there to be found as much as a single line.

More than a little frightened now, she hurried up to the corridor at the far end of which her bedroom lay. Half way along it she broke into a run. She slammed her heavy oak door behind her and sat down on the edge of her bed. She was quite, quite sure that she had not lost that sketch on her way back to the hotel. Picking at one corner of the block with her thumb she began to peel off sheet after sheet. Nowhere was there a trace of a drawing. She was positive now that she had not done a drawing. But a drawing, done by somebody, had been there, and now the paper was as spotless as the linen band over Sister Maddalena's airy, flyaway eyes.

From the moment she became matter-of-fact about it all the more frightened she grew. Those eyes of the Sister's? At some time or other she *must* have escaped, or how should she know so much about the San Carmelito and its doings, ask how many visitors were there, what the Gala was to be? Because she had once had 'a friend' there? How old was she? When had she taken her vows? How long ago was it since this place had ceased to be a monastery and had become an hotel? In Jennie's time? And how long had it stood an empty ruin before then? She looked at the door, at the ceiling. The one was ancient and pointed and Gothic, the other low and groined and centuries old. In this cell, with a plank and a jug of water and a crucifix, Brother after Brother had fasted and prayed and groaned to be delivered from the torments of the flesh, while a bare half mile away Sister after Sister had done the same. Jennie couldn't bear it any longer. Who *was* this Sister who smiled into Jennie's eyes, so that drawings left bits out of themselves, and did and undid themselves, who had wanted to see Jennie's hair and had played with a bit of confetti she picked from it? Why was she not admitted a full Sister, but only allowed 'out' at given times to sell the lace and the trinkets? And how – Jennie had only just remembered this – had she been noiselessly half way across a courtyard and then nowhere to be seen in the time it takes to drop a corner of curtain before a peephole? Claustrophobia did they call this dread of shut doors and shackles and vows and a cerecloth frontlet where the golden hair had been? Had she rebelled, and sinned, and caused a Brother to sin too? And had Jennie herself sinned in asking her if, just for once, she couldn't, because nobody would ever know? But at any rate she had shaken her head and said she couldn't come, and as for Jennie herself, she knew what she was going to do. She was going to forget all about everything and dance all night. She was going to dance till she dropped. Alan would dance with her, and Pat and Phil, and if these were not enough there were the young men from Catania and Messina. And now she must get her hair seen to and have her bath. Shutting the Gothic door behind her she hurried back to the main part of the building where the hairdressing rooms were.

But they were busier in the hotel's hairdressing-rooms than they were in the shop of his Worship the barber. The assistants, too, had their own plans for the evening, and were getting through their work as fast as they could with their working-jackets over their fancy costumes and the heads of half of them wigged already. One of them, dressed as a shuffle of playing-cards with a spotted dice-cube perched on her head, knew Jennie by sight, and came tripping up to her.

'*Gesù*, the rush! It is all these nobodies from Catania and the clients of the other hotels! But quickly, before others hear of it – there is a little cabinet at the end empty. The signorina will excuse that it is perhaps not very tidy, but it is better to seize it quickly. Then two, three little minutes while I finish my present client – after that I myself will attend to the signorina – ' and with a bright little nod she was off with her knaves and deuces fluttering about her calves.

The little closet at the end was really no more than a storeroom where reserves of linen and other hotel accessories were kept. The young woman bustled in again, swathed Jennie in towels, but was again called and bustled out again. Jennie, in an uncomfortable chair, sat at a small kitchen table on which was an ordinary bedroom basin with a few bottles and brushes, a couple of hand-mirrors, and a borrowed hot-air machine joined up to the nearest plug. And as she waited again her thoughts began to rise as it were of themselves, a little way above her head. As a matter of fact her hair had been done for the Teatro yesterday. Should she hurry and have her bath and make shift with it? But no, that lout in the street had thrown the grimy confetti all over it; if only there had been a proper glass to look at herself in! Then she wondered whether the Mother Superior had begun the *Pastorale* on the harmonium yet and whether Sister Maddalena was listening with downdropped lids. Poor darling, what a life for her! Jennie half wished now she *had* come, if only for half an hour; she could have found her a cloak or something and put her in some dark corner where she couldn't be seen. Anyway, tomorrow, when Jennie went to put a few *lire* into the convent box, she would find out exactly what had happened about that sketch, and why Sister Maddalena had skipped so swiftly and guiltily away when she had heard the sub-Prioress at the curtain, leaving Jennie feeling all worked-up and queer.

And suddenly Jennie was conscious of light hands that moved about her head and shook out and loosened and caressed her hair. After a minute or two they began to brush, and the brushes on the cheap table had seemed quite ordinary ones, but never before had any brush stroked her hair like that. Such strokes, light as falling olive-leaves, took people's headaches and troubles away, and Jennie closed her eyes, it was so exquisite to feel that one was being touched by somebody else exactly as one would have touched oneself. She wondered what the shampoo-perfume was that stole so drowsily about her. There seemed to be a little bit of this and a little bit of that in it, lovely, fragrant bits – stocks, violets, jasmine, cherry-pie –

She came to with a start and a catch of her breath. Where was she? It took her some moments to realise; then she saw the bedroom basin, the bottles, the two handglasses. She picked up first one of these and then the other. How heavenly, to have one's hair done like that while one slept! She sprang to her feet, throwing off the towels, and at that moment there appeared at the door of the cubicle a girl with a spotted cube of cardboard on her head and wavy playing-cards that descended half way to her dancing-shoes. Vivaciously she closed the door behind her.

'See, *this* time I lock it – not a soul shall call me again – *now* I am ready for the signorina – '

Jennie stared. 'But if you mean my hair, it's done!'

'Done! By whom?'

'I do not know. Find out the name of the girl. Send her to me in the morning. My room is 121.'

'Assuredly I will find out. It will be Bice, or perhaps Fiammetta. But excuse' – for Jennie was moving to the door – 'the signorina is leaving something behind – '

She held the something up. It was a finger-worn gold crucifix that dangled at the end of a thin broken chain.

Jennie looked at it. When at last she spoke her voice was little more than a breath.

'You found that – *here*?'

'*Si* – in the towel – '

'Tell me – yes, yes, I am perfectly well – do you know the convent of *Santa Maria di Gesù*?'

'But who does not?'

'Do you know – the out-Sister – who sells the lace there?'

'The old Sister Lucia, with her sticks and her ear-trumpet?'

'*She* sells the lace?'

'Since before I was born, signorina.'

'And Sister – Sister Maddalena?'

'Sister Maddalena? Sister Maddalena? I do not know the name. But it would be easy to find out.'

But Jennie had turned her back. 'It doesn't matter. Perhaps I have the name wrong. But send me the girl who did my hair. My room is 121.'

But she knew that no Bice or Fiammetta would come to her room in the morning. Neither would it be any good to ask at the convent kiosk for the Sister Maddalena who sold the lace. Now that she came to think of it, had she actually *been* to sketch the door in the convent court that afternoon, or had she only *intended* to go?

But as she slowly made her way to the bathroom the bit of thin chain was twisted round one of her fingers, and the worn old crucifix lay hidden in the palm of her hand.

'John Gladwin Says . . . '

If we are to believe John Gladwin, the oncoming car made no attempt to avoid him, but held straight on. It held on at top speed, he says, for the first he saw of it was the sudden blinding gold of the afternoon sun on its screen, almost on top of him. He was not woolgathering or thinking of anything else at the time, and he had been for years a teetotaller. As for there not being any other car there at all, he naturally scouts the idea, for if there had been no other car why should he have made that violent and instinctive swerve? He did swerve; something hurtled past him; into the hedge and through it he and his car plunged; and where a moment before the white secondary road had run straight as a ruler for miles, he found himself on soft green, still at the wheel, his screen unbroken, his engine still running.

He says that his first thought was this – people ought not to drive like that. All was quiet on the road behind him, but the fellow could hardly be out of sight yet. John Gladwin came to life. He climbed as quickly as he was able out of the car and pushed through the hole he had made in the hedge.

Properly speaking he had not come through the hedge at all. He had broken through a thin part of it, a gap, thinly tangled over, and his car had come to rest on an old grass-grown track beyond. He looked first down the long white road. There was no sign of any other car, and no other roads ran into it. Then he looked at his own wheel-marks in the dust, and they rather scared him. Heavens! What a mercy he had been crawling along! It would be just as well to report a lunatic who drove like that.

But what was there to report, except that golden flash, gone in a moment, the empty road, and his own tracks in the dust? He scrambled back through the broken hedge and climbed into the car again. At any rate he was alive.

Something had happened to the car none the less. The lever would not go into reverse. Again and again he tried; it went with ease into the other speeds, but not into the one that would take him out backwards again into the road he had left. He got out and set his shoulder to the car, but that was a younger man's job, and the car remained immovable. Then he looked ahead, and thought he saw the best thing to do.

Old Harkness Bottom he knew the region to be called, and from the pocket of the car he fetched out the map. It was an old map, mounted on linen, in tatters with much use, but it told him what he wanted to know. Harkness itself – New Harkness the older people still called it – lay away over the hill and out of sight, and New Harkness was almost a bustling sort of place. A tarred main road ran through it, with traffic at all hours, and it had red and yellow petrol-pumps, and a church already old as new churches go, with its shrine and flowers at the lych-gate and its tablet with the names of seven Harkness lads inside. But nobody ever went near Old Harkness. Something had happened about the price of corn, and its very stones had been carted away to make the new village.

But there was probably a way through and out again beyond, and John Gladwin, unable to go back, decided to go forward.

On the left of the green lane along which he bumped rose a rough slope covered with ragwort and thistles, and on his right he brushed another hedge so closely that clusters of berries, vivid and rank, scarlet and bright green and glossy black all on the same bunch, broke off and fell into the car, with strippings of deadly-nightshade and fat-fruited bryony. Swish, snap, rip; it was far from being a new car, and a loose mudguard rattled and the headlamps vibrated with the jolting. For half a mile or so he drove, winding now to the left and now to the right. And then suddenly he came upon a whole world of palest pinkish-silver.

It rose steeply round three sides of a deep dell, the seeding willow-herb, deadly-soft, wreathed, billowing, with here and there a maple of a gold so vibrant that the eye was almost sensible of a twang. A week or two before it must have been a dyer's vat of the flagrant purple; now the very air was thickened with the fleece of its pro-creation. And down in the bottom, in the only patch the weed had not invaded, stood a church.

John Gladwin would hardly have known it was a church, he says, if it had not been for the tombstones. There were perhaps a score of these, lying and leaning at all angles, and some of them were not stones at all, but nameboards of ancient wood with finials sticking up at the ends like prick-ears, John Gladwin says. As for the church – well, there it was, what remained of it, that wrecked and ivied hum-mock in the middle of the field. The gap into the field had no gate.

John Gladwin imagines he must have stopped his engine, for this pink and silver bowl in the hills was filled with an immense quiet. He got out of the car. Picking his way among the tombstones he pushed through coarse grass to the ruin.

The stone-movers had been there too, John Gladwin says, for half of the broken buttress over which he clambered had gone; but that ragged 'V' against the sky where the belfry had been had probably fallen down of itself. He could only just force his way in for brambles and tangled rose, and a mountain-ash filled the chancel, its berries already turning red. The whole church was not more than fifteen strides long. A greenish semi-darkness filled it, says John Gladwin. And all over brooded that stillness, not of peace (he says), but of the desolation of things lost to the world. He started when, with a harsh beating of wings, a thrush flew out of the chancel where the mountain-ash was. But he jumped nearly a foot into the air when, loud and immediately above his head, there clanged out the single stroke of a bell.

Of course he knew there was no bell. The nearest bell was the thin-noted bell of New Harkness Church, away over the hill, and anyway its sound would have passed unheard overhead. Nevertheless John Gladwin looked up. And naturally he saw only the ragged 'V' where once a bell had been. And then the note came again, urgent and earnest, as if it summoned somebody to make haste. John Gladwin, suddenly remembering that he was in a church, took off his hat.

The bell that wasn't there rang a third time, and he bent his knee and crossed himself. As he did so he heard his name spoken behind him.

Now the most astounding statement of a number that John Gladwin makes is that of a sudden all this seemed reasonable and natural and right. Indubitably there had been a bell in that crumbling 'V' above his head. It had had its own voice, earnest and urgent and compelling. But in another moment he had forgotten all about the bell, he says. What was a bell by the side of the voice that had called him by his name? It was a young voice, of a lingering sweetness, that finished each syllable exquisitely, and had always moved John Gladwin past telling. It took him back more than thirty years – and already John Gladwin was fifty-eight years old when he says all this happened. And then the voice spoke his name again.

'John!'

This time he did not turn round, as a minute or two before he had looked up at that startling ringing of the bell. What, he asks, is the good of turning round to see something that is as much you as your heart itself? Instead he replied to the voice, and his own tones shook with a still passion of tenderness.

'Emily!'

'So you were able to come?'

'I was not able to stay away.'

'You rode over on Grey Boy?'

'Yes, most loved.'

'I have his piece of sugar. It is in my muff.'

'How beautiful you are!'

'Am I?'

'Have you no kiss for me?'

And the voice said, 'Hush – we are in a church.'

She had always been like that, John says, sweet and circumspect, decorous and right, so that those other moments, when there had been no need of circumspection, had been by contrast unutterably full. And when a love like that has been it still is, and dies only with the heart it has visited. So in that sense I should say that every word John Gladwin says is to be believed. He was in a church with her once more, with Grey Boy contentedly cropping in the adjoining pasture. Not the leprous silver of the willow-herb disgraced the hill outside, but the corn whispering in the sun, with the horseless reaper left where it was until Monday morning. He was less aware of the hymn book they shared than of her hand so near to his own; and he wore a cravat, and she an adorable little bonnet with ribbands, and a flounced skirt with a waterfall behind. And John Gladwin says it didn't seem to be any particular Sunday. The Sundays seemed to run together, he says, as snowy Christmases run together in our memories, and sunny summers, and indistinguishable daisy-fields, that somehow seem the same daisies year after year.

But there came suddenly a Sunday that did stand out from the rest. As plainly as he had heard the bell he heard the parson's voice again, pronouncing his name with hers who sat there in the square pew so consciously glowing by his side.

'I publish the Banns of Marriage – '

There was a rustle in the mountain-ash that filled the chancel; the thrush had returned. Through a fissure where the ivy had forced the stones apart two butterflies could be seen at play. Morsels of fleece settled on John Gladwin's new black arm-band, and something stirred among the thigh-deep nettles. But to John Gladwin it was her voice again. Thrice the Banns had been proclaimed, and none had known of any let or impediment.

'So now you can hardly run away!' the voice laughed.

'Away! Where, away from you, when you are everywhere?'

'So that's what you mean when you say I'm the world to you!'

'You are both worlds, the bread I eat and the prayers I say.'

'Listen to him, Grey Boy! Did ever you hear such a man?'

'We are not in a church now, love. Have you no kiss for me?'

And the remembered kiss was as fresh to John Gladwin as on the day it had been given.

At this point John Gladwin admits to a certain confusion as to what was really happening. His actual surroundings, he says, stood out clearly enough before his eyes. Looking up he saw the gap where the bell had been. Looking out of the breach by which he had entered he saw the spilth of silver seed, the raw gold of the maples, his car not a hundred yards away. But in some other way he cannot explain the things he saw were doubled with other things, just as by mechanical ingenuity pictures are imposed on pictures and made to come and go. It was, he says, as if one looked at a half-obliterated sketch and saw brightly through it, drawing nearer and nearer, a golden-hued irradiation behind.

Unfortunately, to question him too closely is to confuse him and make him give different answers. He acknowledges, for example, that he is not a Harkness man and that his Banns were never called in Old Harkness Church. It was in a church two hundred miles away that they were published. But Holy Church, he says, is one no matter where the location of its fabric, and wedding-bells are the same whether they be a merry peal or a single blithe note.

For it was his marriage, he says, that that vanished bell next gave tongue to. Not nettles and brambles, but guests filled the church, the friends of the bride on the one side, those of the groom on the other. The gilded pipes of the little organ reared themselves among the berries of the mountain-ash. The fissure where the butterflies played healed itself; and there floated into its place the placid white marble tablet of Henry Gladwin, Justice of the Peace, benefactor of the church, and owner of acres long before things had happened about the price of corn. The altar was raised again, a roof of oak shut out the September sky, John Gladwin says. And she came in on her father's arm and was brought to where he waited for her. She wore her great-grandmother's lace, and never, the village declared, had bride looked lovelier.

And John Gladwin thinks that as he stood there, as one might say in two churches at once, he saw something no man has seen before – two faces also at once, not as one sees them in some old album, with the gradations of the years coming, coming calmly and imperceptibly in between, but vividly and violently contrasted, the unwrinkled face side by side with the wrinkled one, the veined hand by the flower-smooth one, and nothing to account for the fading and change. And one face was shrouded in lavendered lace, and the other had lain now for a week in another shroud. The two faces looked together at him, different yet the same, as his love had been different yet the same. She had neither utterly died nor utterly grown old. Something as inalienable as her name had persisted throughout – Emily.

So she said 'I will' that day, and there was a hush, because they were in a church.

John Gladwin says that he saw himself too. He saw himself in a pouting grey cravat and beautiful tubular trousers, and he was straight-backed then and strong-limbed, and could if need be walk his thirty miles in a day instead of being glad of a coughing old two-seater to trundle him about. But he did not see himself twice over, side by side, as he had seen her, for what was there to look at in the John Gladwin who stood that afternoon among the brambles that choked Old Harkness Church, friendless, alone and very tired? Life was a thing to look back on, not forward to, and now, in this curious experience of his, he had nothing but thanks for that mad driver who, dashing past him with a flash of gold, had pushed him through the hedge and into the old lane. He heard the organ in the mountain-ash again and the words joined in of themselves – 'The voice that breathed o'er Eden that earliest wedding day'. He saw the throng at the sunny church-door, saw the waiting carriages and the coloured favours of the horses, the showers of rice, an old shoe. He says he turned himself about in Old Harkness Church and actually saw these things, and not merely his own old two-seater waiting for him beyond the overturned tombstones. If they were not there, he says, he saw them none the less.

But some richness of light had passed away from the golden maples, a tarnish had come over the silver of the shedding weed. One could hardly have imagined a greater stillness than before, and yet the pause and hush seemed intensified, John said, as he suddenly remem-bered a pause and hush in his life before. Here again he admits to a certain amount of confusion. He was no longer in a church, but in his own office or study, where he kept his guns and account-books and received his rent from his tenants, regaling them in the cleared barn afterwards with beef and beer. He had taken off his boots, quite unnecessarily, since his walking about could not possibly have been heard, and sometimes his brown hands were clasped before him and sometimes they touched grain-samples or farm-plans, or his magnifying-glass, or a strap, or some other of the objects that littered the room. He was waiting with tense nerves for news from upstairs, news of Emily.

It was brought to him, less by the doctor's words than by his cheerful face. The child was a boy, and all was well. John Gladwin pulled his boots on again and put his hand to the little porcelain bell-knob by the side of the mantelpiece. Wine and glasses were brought – and then, without warning he says, he was back in the church again. He was standing by the font, and when the priest said 'Name this child' John Gladwin answered 'George', and by that name he was baptized in the Name of the Father and of the Son and of the Holy Ghost.

And a year and a half later it happened again, and the name this time was William.

John Gladwin says quite frankly that he is by no means certain as to what came next. As the light had died out of the maples so the pictures had become a little less distinct, a little more run together. Perhaps that was because on the whole his life had been a peaceful and eventless one. He had brought up his two sons in the fear of the Lord. On Sundays, in the square pew, and while they were yet quite small, he had had to tell them to hush, because they were in a church, and as they grew older, and those things began to happen about the price of corn, and the lads shot up to the height of their mother's waist, and then to her breast, churchgoing lads they remained, as was right in the successors of that Henry Gladwin whose tablet in white marble looked down on the pew from the fissure where the butterflies were no longer at play.

John had not noticed the departure of the butterflies; butterflies go everywhere; and neither had he noticed the further sombring of the maples nor the change of light that turned the pink of the willow-herb silver to a whitey-brown. He was still, he supposed, half in the church two hundred miles away, and the Sabbaths ran together as the snowy Christmases had run together and the hot summers and the daisied fields and the birthdays of the boys. He was troubled about the boys, he says. The price of corn was becoming less and less what it should have been. The marble Henry Gladwin, gazing stead-fastly from the wall into the square pew, might presently find one of the boys missing. Probably it would be George, the elder one. He spoke of Canada and South Africa. And it might be a good thing, for it was not right that John Gladwin's labourers only should bear the brunt of a period of agricultural depression. John talked with Emily about it.

'But you have an offer for the shooting, John.'

'Which I shall take, but it is only delaying matters for another year. It is no remedy.'

'George only wants to go because he thinks it may ease matters.'

'George is not the only one who is going.'

'And then I suppose William will want to go after him.' John Gladwin vows that he heard all this again, in the broken church in Old Harkness Bottom.

'We must do what we can. And if you're going to read let me get you your glasses.'

But as things chanced it was neither Canada nor South Africa that took George and William. If John Gladwin is to be believed, that vanished bell against the now unnaturally-hued sky spoke loudly once again. And, knowing now what was happening, he did not jump a foot into the air this time. Quietly he sank to his knees among the nettles.

'Let them go,' he said with bowed head. 'I will go too. We shall all be needed.'

'John!' he says her voice rang sharply out. 'They cannot take them! They did not bear them! They are mine!'

'They will go laughing. You will not be able to keep them.'

'But I shall be alone!'

'There is nursing. There is cooking. I will find you something to do.'

And again, says John Gladwin, the bell rang warningly out, as if to summon the women as well as the men.

But in the end neither did he find anything for her to do nor yet anything for himself. They wanted captains of twenty-five, not forty-five, they said, and he must wait his turn. Youngest and best first, and go George and William did. Shortly after, John Gladwin, seizing an occasion, sold his land two hundred miles away and brought his wife south and settled her in a small house not far from Harkness, and himself became a special constable since that was all they seemed able to find him to do.

And now, though he was on his knees, he was not in a place that at all resembled a church, but in some dim twilight of mud and flashes and roaring and death, that naturally he could not see clearly because he had never been there. An occasional 'Pretty hectic' was all he got out of the letters of his sons, varied once in a while with a jest about its healthiness. The light through the brambles and the mountain-ash became of a more sullen green. The wall-tablet of Henry Glad-win, John says, dissolved away and another slid relentlessly into its place. This one was of oak, with names upon it in gold, and there was one exactly like it in New Harkness Church as well as where John Gladwin knelt. Even the names were the same:

George Gladwin
William Gladwin

They were the first two of the seven. The names only survived. What had become of the rest of them neither John Gladwin nor anybody else knew.

A low muttering filled the air. It was the first rumble of the storm. There was a pale flash like the flash of a shell in daylight, and if John Gladwin wanted to get home before it came he had best put his hood up and begone. But he remained where he was, so still that the very field mice might have approached him. Then the muttering was no longer a muttering. Suddenly the heavens cracked and pealed harshly above his head. A chill gust filled the air with fleece, and a bright flash showed every leaf and berry of the ash. But between it and the crash that followed John Gladwin says he heard another voice, the voice of the white-haired New Harkness vicar, who had put the names of John Gladwin's sons in gold on the wall.

'We bring nothing into this world, and it is certain that we can carry nothing out . . . The Lord gave and the Lord hath taken away; blessed be the name of the Lord . . . We therefore commit her body to the ground . . . Not to be sorry, as men without hope . . . '

Three days before the words had been spoken, and John Gladwin says he heard their very vibrations still.

'Amen,' he said with bowed head, and rose as the first great drop struck his bare crown like a falling pebble.

He was hardly out of the church when the rain crashed down. Every broken tombstone was hidden in a mist and spray of it. The maples were not to be seen, the craven silver of the weed seemed to cower under its thrashing. Rivers coursed between the old graves, and at the gap where the wedding-carriage had stood, with favours on the horses and flowers in the lamps – it was only John Gladwin's car that stood there, twanging like a drum and spouting out valances of water.

Soaked to his spine, John Gladwin bent over the starting-handle. The engine broke into a rattle. He climbed into the sodden seat and sat for a moment wondering whether he should turn round or go forward. He decided to go forward. A gate might close the old track at its other end, but he would risk it. The other would be miles round to where he wanted to be – standing before a gold-lettered name-board, standing before a mound of earth three days old.

And John Gladwin says, and stands to it, that it was to the tolling of the bell of Old Harkness Church heard above the shout of the rain that he swayed and splashed in the car round the churchyard and skirted the beaten-down silver of the weeds.

First, he says, he found roofless buildings, then a solitary inhabited farm, and then a straggle of cottages along a cart-track, but ever getting nearer to the known world. Then, almost suddenly because of the rain, he saw the tree-line of the tarred main road. At the crest the shower ceased as suddenly as if an invisible hand had turned it off at the main. Swiftly the clouds packed themselves away behind him and ahead there flashed on his eyes a dazzle of gold. It glittered on the still-showering branches, it made prisms in the air, and as John Gladwin swung out of the lane into the tarred road he saw nothing but a glow of molten light. He says it was like looking into the middle of the Sun Himself.

And the manner of his going out of Old Harkness Bottom was as the manner of his entering it. I think myself that Death did not ride on a Pale Horse that afternoon, but took a trip in a Golden Car. John Gladwin was driving slowly; at his time of life he never did anything else. He never saw what rushed towards him (he says), but only the effulgent road. And this time it was too late to swerve. It was just where the red and yellow petrol-pumps stood, backed by their sheet-iron advertisements. New Harkness Church with its shrine and lych-gate was a bare hundred yards away. John Gladwin thinks, and says, that it was the same car as before. The noise of the smash was heard by a Bentley more than a mile away.

The Bentley came up and drew to a standstill. It had come from that direction, but it had met no other car. And it was the Bentley that took John Gladwin to the cottage hospital, with a broken back.

I myself have never been to Old Harkness Bottom, and have only John Gladwin's word for it that there is a church there at all. We go to see him where he lies. He lies on a white bedstead, with a white-uniformed nurse to make things easy for the remaining time, which we, like himself, hope won't be too long. And he tells us these things with the dreadful candour of a man about to die.

But sometimes, with the screen at his feet and the chart over his head, without regard to where he is, in a red-roofed cottage hospital with white woodwork and a privet hedge round it, he breaks off with a gesture. His fingers go to his lips and his eyes steal round. He is in Old Harkness Bottom again, and for all I know his boys are being naughty once more.

'Hush!' he reproaches them in a whisper. 'We are in a church!'

Hic Jacet

A Tale of Artistic Conscience

INTRODUCTION

As I lighted my guests down the stairs of my Chelsea lodgings, turned up the hall gas that they might see the steps at the front door, and shook hands with them, I bade them good night the more heartily that I was glad to see their backs. Lest this should seem but an inhospitable confession, let me state, first, that they had invited themselves, dropping in in ones and twos until seven or eight of them had assembled in my garret, and, secondly, that I was rather extraordinarily curious to know why, at close on midnight, the one I knew least well of all had seen fit to remain after the others had taken their departure. To these two considerations I must add a third, namely, that I had become tardily conscious that, if Andriaovsky had not lingered of himself, I should certainly have asked him to do so.

It was to nothing more than a glance, swift and momentary, directed by Andriaovsky to myself while the others had talked, that I traced this desire to see more of the little Polish painter; but a glance derives its import from the circumstance under which it is given. That rapid turning of his eyes in my direction an hour before had held a hundred questions, implications, criticisms, incredulities, condemnations. It had been one of those uncovenanted gestures that hold the promise of the treasures of an eternal friendship. I wondered as I turned down the gas again and remounted the stairs what personal message and reproach in it had lumped me in with the others; and by the time I had reached my own door again a phrase had fitted itself in my mind to that quick, ironical turning of Andriaovsky's eyes: '*Et tu, Brute*! ... '

He was standing where I had left him, his small shabby figure in the attitude of a diminutive colossus on my hearthrug. About him were the recently vacated chairs, solemnly and ridiculously suggestive of still continuing the high and choice conversation that had lately finished. The same fancy had evidently taken Andriaovsky, for he was turning from chair to chair, his head a little on one side, mischievously and aggravatingly smiling. As one of them, the deep wicker chair that Jamison had occupied, suddenly gave a little creak of itself, as wicker will when released from a strain, his smile broadened to a grin. I had been on the point of sitting down in that chair, but I changed my mind and took another.

'That's right,' said Andriaovsky, in that wonderful English which he had picked up in less than three years, 'don't sit in the wisdom-seat; you might profane it.'

I knew what he meant. I felt for my pipe and slowly filled it, not replying. Then, slowly wagging his head from side to side, with his eyes humorously and banteringly on mine, he uttered the very words I had mentally associated with that glance of his.

'*Et tu, Brute!*' he said, wagging away, so that with each wag the lenses of his spectacles caught the light of the lamp on the table.

I too smiled as I felt for a match.

'It *was* rather much, wasn't it?' I said.

But he suddenly stopped his wagging, and held up a not very clean forefinger. His whole face was altogether too confoundedly intelligent.

'Oh no, you don't!' he said peremptorily. 'No getting out of it like that the moment they've turned their backs! No running – what is it? – no running with the hare and hunting with the hounds! *You* helped, you know!'

I confess I fidgeted a little.

'But hang it all, what could I do? They were in my place,' I broke out.

He chuckled, enjoying my discomfiture. Then his eyes fell on those absurd and solemn chairs again.

'Look at 'em – the Art Shades in conference!' he chuckled. 'That rush-seated one, it was talking half an hour ago about "Scherzos in Silver and Grey"! . . . Nice, fresh green stuff!'

To shut him up I told him that he would find cigarettes and tobacco on the table.

' "Scherzos in Silver and Grey"!' he chuckled again as he took a cigarette . . .

All this, perhaps, needs some explanation. It had been the usual thing, usual in those days, twenty years ago – smarming about Art and the Arts and so forth. They – 'we', as apparently Andriaovsky had lingered behind for the purpose of reminding me – had perhaps talked a little more soaringly than the ordinary, that was all. There had been Jamison in the wicker chair, full to the lips and running over with the Colour Suggestions of the late Edward Calvert; Gibbs, in a pulpy state of adoration of the less legitimate side of the painting of Watts; and Magnani, who had advanced that an Essential Oneness underlies all the Arts, and had triumphantly proved his thesis by analogy with the Law of the Co-relation of Forces. A book called *Music and Morals* had appeared about that time, and on it they – we – had risen to regions of kite-high lunacy about Colour Symphonies, orgies of formless colour thrown on a magic-lantern screen – *vieux jeu* enough at this time of day. A young newspaper man, too, had made mental notes of our adjectives, for use in his weekly (I nearly spelt it 'weakly') half-column of Art Criticism; and – and here was Andriaovsky, grinning at the chairs, and mimicking it all with diabolical glee.

' "Scherzos in Silver and Grey" – "Word Pastels" – "Lyrics in Stone"!' he chuckled. 'And what was it the fat fellow said? "A Siren Song in Marble"! Phew! . . . Well, I'll get along. I shall just be in time to get a pint of bitter to wash it all down if I'm quick . . . Bah!' he broke out suddenly. 'Good men build up Form and Forms – keep the Arts each after its kind – raise up the dikes so that we shan't all be swept away by night and nothingness – and these rats come nosing and burrowing and undermining it all! . . . *Et tu, Brute!*'

'Well, when you've finished rubbing it in – ' I grunted.

'As if *you* didn't know better! . . . Is that your way of getting back on 'em, now that you've chucked drawing and gone in for writing books? Phew! . . . Well, I'll go and get my pint of beer – '

But he didn't go for his pint of beer. Instead, he began to prowl about my room, pryingly, nosingly, touching things here and there. I watched him as he passed from one thing to another. He was very little, and very, very shabby. His trousers were frayed, and the sole of one of his boots flapped distressingly. His old bowler hat – he had not thought it necessary to wait until he got outside before thrusting it on the back of his head – was so limp in substance that I verily believed that had he run incautiously downstairs he would have found when he got to the bottom that its crown had sunk in of its own weight. In spite of his remark about the pint of beer, I doubt if he had the price of one in his pocket.

'What's this, Brutus – a concertina?' he suddenly asked, stopping before the collapsible case in which I kept my rather old dress suit.

I told him what it was, and he hoisted up his shoulders.

'And these things?' he asked, moving to something else.

They were a pair of boot-trees of which I had permitted myself the economy. I remember they cost me four shillings in the old Brompton Road.

'And that's your bath, I suppose . . . Dumb-bells too . . . And – *oh, good Lord*! . . . '

He had picked up, and dropped again as if it had been hot, somebody or other's card with the date of a 'day' written across the corner of it . . .

As I helped him on with his overcoat he made no secret of the condition of its armholes and lining. I don't for one moment suppose that the garment was his. I took a candle to light him down as soon as it should please him to depart.

'Well, so long, and joy to you on the high road to success,' he said with another grin for which I could have bundled him down the stairs . . .

In later days I never looked to Andriaovsky for tact; but I stared at him for his lack of it that night. And as I stared I noticed for the first time the broad and low pylon of his forehead, his handsome mouth and chin, and the fire and wit and scorn that smouldered behind his cheap spectacles. I looked again; and his smallness, his malice, his pathetic little braggings about his poverty, seemed all to disappear. He had strolled back to my hearthrug, wishing, I have no doubt now, to be able to exclaim suddenly that it was too late for the pint of beer for which he hadn't the money, and to curse his luck; and the pigmy quality of his colossus-ship had somehow gone.

As I watched him, a neighbouring clock struck the half-hour, and he did even as I had surmised – cursed the closing time of the English public-houses . . .

I lighted him down. For one moment, under the hall gas, he almost dropped his jesting manner.

'You *do* know better, Harrison, you know,' he said. 'But, of course, you're going to be a famous author in almost no time. Oh, *ça se voit*! No garrets for *you*! It was a treat, the way you handled those fellows – really . . . Well don't forget us others when you're up there – I may want you to write my "Life" some day . . . '

I heard the slapping of the loose sole as he shuffled down the path. At the gate he turned for a moment.

'Good night, Brutus,' he called.

When I had mounted to my garret again my eyes fell once more on that ridiculous assemblage of empty chairs, all solemnly talking to

one another. I burst out into a laugh. Then I undressed, put my
jacket on the hanger, took the morrow's boots from the trees and
treed those I had removed, changed the pair of trousers under my
mattress, and went, still laughing at the chairs, to bed.

This was Michael Andriaovsky, the Polish painter, who died four
weeks ago.

I

I knew the reason of Maschka's visit the moment she was announced.
Even in the stressful moments of the funeral she had found time
to whisper to me that she hoped to call upon me at an early date.
I dismissed the amanuensis to whom I was dictating the last story
of the fourth series of *Martin Renard*, gave a few hasty instructions
to my secretary, and told the servant to show Miss Andriaovsky
into the drawing-room, to ask her to be so good as to excuse me for
five minutes, to order tea at once, and then to bring my visitor up
to the library.

A few minutes later she was shown into the room.

She was dressed in the same plainly-cut costume of dead black she
had worn at the funeral, and had pushed up her heavy veil over the
close-fitting cap of black fur that accentuated her Sclavonic appearance. I noticed again with distress the pallor of her face and the
bistred rings that weeks of nursing had put under her dark eyes. I
noticed also her resemblance, in feature and stature, to her brother. I
placed a chair for her; the tea-tray followed her in; and without more
than a murmured greeting she peeled off her gloves and prepared to
preside at the tray.

She had filled the cups, and I had handed her toast, before she
spoke. Then: 'I suppose you know what I've come about,' she said.

I nodded.

'Long, long ago you promised it. Nobody else can do it. The only
question is "when".'

'That's the only question,' I agreed.

'We, naturally,' she continued, after a glance in which her eyes
mutely thanked me for my implied promise, 'are anxious that it
should be as soon as possible; but, of course – I shall quite understand – '

She gave a momentary glance round my library. I helped her out.

'You mean that I'm a very important person nowadays, and that
you're afraid to trespass on my time. Never mind that. I shall find

time for this. But tell me before we go any further exactly how you stand and precisely what it is you expect.'

Briefly she did so. It did not in the least surprise me to learn that her brother had died penniless.

'And if you hadn't undertaken the "Life",' she said, 'he might just as well not have worked in poverty all these years. You can, at least, see to his fame.'

I nodded again gravely, and ruminated for a moment. Then I spoke.

'I can write it, fully and in detail, up to five years ago,' I said. 'You know what happened then. I tried my best to help him, but he never would let me. Tell me, Maschka, why he wouldn't sell me that portrait.'

I knew instantly, from her quick confusion, that her brother had spoken to her about the portrait he had refused to sell me, and had probably told her the reason for his refusal. I watched her as she evaded the question as well as she could.

'You know how – queer – he was about who he sold his things to. And as for those five years in which you saw less of him, Schofield will tell you all you want to know.'

I relinquished the point. 'Who's Schofield?' I asked instead.

'He was a very good friend of Michael's – of both of us. You can talk quite freely to him. I want to say at the beginning that I should like him to be associated with you in this.'

I don't know how I divined on the spot her relation to Schofield, whoever he was. She told me that he too was a painter.

'Michael thought very highly of his things,' she said.

'I don't know them,' I replied.

'You probably wouldn't,' she returned . . .

But I caught the quick drop of her eyes from their brief excursion round my library, and I felt something within me stiffen a little. It did not need Maschka Andriaovsky to remind me that I had not attained my position without – let us say – splitting certain differences; the looseness of the expression can be corrected hereafter. Life consists very largely of compromises. You doubtless know my name, whichever country or hemisphere you happen to live in, as that of the creator of Martin Renard, the famous and popular detective; and I was not at that moment disposed to apologise, either to Maschka or Schofield or anybody else, for having written the stories at the bidding of a gaping public. The moment the public showed that it wanted something better I was prepared to give it. In the meantime, I sat in my very comfortable library, securely shielded from distress by my balance at my banker's.

'Well,' I said after a moment, 'let's see how we stand. And first as to what you're likely to get out of this. It goes without saying, of course, that by writing the "Life" I can get you any amount of "fame" – advertisement, newspaper talk, and all the things that, it struck me, Michael always treated with especial scorn. My name alone, I say, will do that. But for anything else I'm by no means so sure. You see,' I explained, 'it doesn't follow that because I can sell hundreds of thousands of . . . you know what . . . that I can sell anything I've a mind to sign.' I said it, confident that she had not lived all those years with her brother without having learned the axiomatic nature of it. To my discomfiture, she began to talk like a callow student.

'I should have thought that it followed that if you could sell something – ' she hesitated only for a moment, then courageously gave the other stuff its proper adjective, ' – something rotten, you could have sold something good when you had the chance.'

'Then if you thought that you were wrong,' I replied briefly and concisely.

'*Michael* couldn't, of course,' she said, putting Michael out of the question with a little wave of her hand, 'because Michael was – I mean, Michael wasn't a business man. You are.'

'I'm speaking as one,' I replied. 'I don't waste time in giving people what they don't want. That is business. I don't undertake your brother's "Life" as a matter of business, but as an inestimable privilege. I repeat, it doesn't follow that the public will buy it.'

'But – but – ' she stammered, 'the public will buy a *Pill* if they see your name on the testimonial!'

'A Pill – yes,' I said sadly . . . Genius and a Pill were, alas, different things. 'But,' I added more cheerfully, 'you can never tell what the public will do. They *might* buy it – there's no telling except by trying – '

'Well, Schofield thinks they will,' she informed me with decision.

'I dare say he does, if he's an artist. They mostly do,' I replied.

'He doesn't think Michael will ever be popular,' she emphasised the adjective slightly, 'but he does think he has a considerable following if they could only be discovered.'

I sighed. All artists think that. They will accept any compromise except the one that is offered to them . . . I tried to explain to Maschka that in this world we have to stand to the chances of all or nothing.

'You've got to be one thing or the other – I don't know that it matters very much which,' I said. 'There's Michael's way, and there's . . . mine. That's all. However, we'll try it. All you can say to me, and more, I'll say to a publisher for you. But he'll probably wink at me.'

For a moment she was silent. Then she said: 'Schofield rather fancies one publisher.'

'Oh? Who's he?' I asked.

She mentioned a name. If I knew anything at all of business she might as well have offered *The Life of Michael Andriaovsky* to The Religious Tract Society at once . . .

'Hm! . . . And has Mr Schofield any other suggestions?' I enquired.

He had. Several. I saw that Schofield's position would have to be defined before we went any further.

'Hm!' I said again. 'Well, I shall have to rely on Schofield for those five years in which I saw little of Michael; but unless Schofield knows more of publishing than I do, and can enforce a better contract and a larger sum on account than I can, I really think, Maschka, that you'll do better to leave things to me. For one thing, it's only fair to me. My name hasn't much of an artistic value nowadays, but it has a very considerable commercial one, and my worth to publishers isn't as a writer of the Lives of Geniuses.'

I could see she didn't like it; but that couldn't be helped. It had to be so. Then, as we sat for a time in silence over the fire, I noticed again how like her brother she was. She was not, it was true, much like him as he had been on that last visit of mine to him . . . and I sighed as I remembered that visit. The dreadful scene had come back to me . . .

On account, I suppose, of the divergence of our paths, I had not even heard of his illness until almost the finish. Immediately I had hastened to the Hampstead 'Home', only to find him already in the agony. He had not been too far gone to recognise me, however, for he had muttered something brokenly about 'knowing better', that a spasm had interrupted. Besides myself, only Maschka had been there; and I had been thankful for the summons that had called her for a moment out of the room. I had still retained his already cold hand; his brow had worked with that dreadful struggle; and his eyes had been closed.

But suddenly he had opened them, and the next moment had sat up on his pillow. He had striven to draw his hand from mine.

'Who are you?' he had suddenly demanded, not knowing me.

I had come close to him. 'You know me, Andriaovsky – Harrison?' I had asked sorrowfully.

I had been on the point of repeating my name but suddenly, after holding my eyes for a moment with a look the profundity and familiarity of which I cannot express, he had broken into the most ghastly haunting laugh I have ever heard.

'*Harrison?*' the words had broken throatily from him . . . '*Oh yes; I know you!* . . . *You shall very soon know that I know you if . . . if . . .*'

The cough and rattle had come as Maschka had rushed into the room. In ten seconds Andriaovsky had fallen back, dead.

2

That same evening I began to make notes for Andriaovsky's 'Life'. On the following day, the last of the fourth series of the *Martin Renard*s occupied me until I was thankful to get to bed. But thereafter I could call rather more of my time my own, and I began in good earnest to devote myself to the 'Life'.

Maschka had spoken no more than the truth when she had said that of all men living none but I could write that 'Life.' His remaining behind in my Chelsea garret that evening after the others had left had been the beginning of a friendship that, barring that lapse of five years at the end, had been for twenty years one of completest intimacy. Whatever money there might or might not be in the book, I had seen *my* opportunity in it – the opportunity to make it the vehicle for all the aspirations, faiths, enthusiasms, and exaltations we had shared; and I myself did not realise until I began to note them down one tithe of the subtle links and associations that had welded our souls together.

Even the outward and visible signs of these had been wonderful. Setting out from one or other of the score of garrets and cheap lodgings we had in our time inhabited, we had wandered together, day after day, night after night, far down East, where, as we had threaded our way among the barrels of soused herrings and the stalls and barrows of unleavened bread, he had taught me scraps of Hebrew and Polish and Yiddish; up into the bright West, where he could never walk a quarter of a mile without meeting one of his extraordinary acquaintances – furred music-hall managers, hawkers of bootlaces, commercial magnates of his own Faith, touts, crossing-sweepers, painted women; into Soho, where he had names for the

very horses on the cab-ranks and the dogs who slumbered under
the counters of the sellers of French literature; out to the naphtha-
lights and cries of the Saturday night street markets of Islington
and the North End Road; into City churches on wintry afternoons,
into the studios of famous artists full of handsomely dressed women,
into the studios of artists not famous, at the ends of dark and break-
neck corridors; to tea at the suburban homes of barmaids and
chorus girls, to dinner in the stables of a cavalry-barracks, to supper
in cabmen's shelters. He was possessed in some mysterious way
of the passwords to doors in hoardings behind which excavations
were in progress; he knew by name the butchers of the Deptford
yards, the men in the blood-caked clothes, so inured to blood
that they may not with safety to their lives swear at one another;
he took me into an opium-cellar within a stone's-throw of Oxford
Street, and into a roof-chamber to call upon certain friends of
his . . . well, they *said* they were fire extinguishers, so I'd better not
say they were bombs. Up, down; here, there; good report, but more
frequently evil . . . we had known this side of our London as well as
two men may. And our other adventures and peregrinations, not of
the body, but of the spirit . . . but these must be spoken of in their
proper place.

I had arranged with Maschka that Schofield should bring me
the whole of the work Andriaovsky had left behind him; and he
arrived late one afternoon in a fourwheeler, with four great packages
done up in brown paper. I found him to be a big, shaggy-browed,
red-haired, raw-boned Lancashire man of five-and-thirty, given to
confidential demonstrations at the length of a button-shank, quite
unconscious of the gulf between his words and his right to employ
them, and bent on asserting an equality that I did not dispute by a
rather aggressive use of my surname. Andriaovsky had appointed
him his executor, and he had ever the air of suspecting that the
appointment was going to be challenged.

'A'm glad to be associated with ye in this melancholy duty, Harrison,' he said. 'Now we won't waste words. Miss Andriaovsky has
told me precisely how matters stand. I had, as ye know, the honour to
be poor Michael's close friend for a period of five years, and my
knowledge of him is entirely at your disposal.'

I answered that I should be seriously handicapped without it.

'Just so. It is Miss Andriaovsky's desire that we should pull together.
Now, in the firrst place, what is your idea about the forrm the book
should take?'

'In the first place, if you don't mind,' I replied, 'perhaps we'd better run over together the things you've brought. The daylight will be gone soon.'

'Just as ye like, Harrison,' he said, 'just as ye like. It's all the same to me . . .'

I cleared a space about my writing-table at the window, and we turned to the artistic remains of Michael Andriaovsky.

I was astonished, first, at the enormous quantity of the stuff, and next at its utter and complete revelation of the man. In a flash I realised how superb that portion at least of the book was going to be. And Schofield explained that the work he had brought represented but a fraction of the whole that was at our disposal.

'Ye'll know with what foolish generosity poor Michael always gave his things away,' he said. 'Hallard has a grand set; so has Connolly; and from time to time he behaved varry handsomely to myself. Artists of varry considerable talents both Hallard and Connolly are; Michael thought varry highly of their abilities. They express the deepest interest in the shape your worrk will take; and that reminds me. I myself have drafted a rough scenario of the forrm it appeared to me the "Life" might with advantage be cast in. A purely private opinion, ye'll understand, Harrison, which ye'll be entirely at liberty to disregard . . .'

'Well, let's finish with the work first,' I said.

With boards, loose sheets, scraps of paper, notes, studies, canvases stretched and stripped from their stretchers, we paved half the library floor, Schofield keeping up all the time a running fire of 'Grand, grand! A masterpiece! A gem, that, Harrison!' They were all that he said, and presently I ceased to hear his voice. The splendour of the work issued undimmed even from the severe test of Schofield's praise; and I thought again with pride how I, I, was the only man living who could adequately write that 'Life' . . .

'Aren't they grand? Aren't they great?' Schofield chanted monotonously.

'They are,' I replied, coming to a consciousness of his presence again. 'But what's that?'

Secretively he had kept one package until the last. He now removed its wrappings and set it against a chair.

'*There*!' he cried. 'I'll thank ye, Harrison, for your opinion of *that*!'

It was the portrait Andriaovsky had refused to sell me – a portrait of himself.

The portrait was the climax of the display. The Lancastrian still talked; but I, profoundly moved, mechanically gathered up the drawings from the floor and returned them to their proper packages and folios. I was dining at home, alone, that evening, and for form's sake I asked this faithful dog of Andriaovsky's to share my meal; but he excused himself – he was dining with Hallard and Connolly. When the drawings were all put away, all save that portrait, he gave an inquisitive glance round my library. It was the same glance as Maschka had given when she had feared to intrude on my time; but Schofield did these things with a much more heavy hand. He departed, but not before telling me that even my mansion contained such treasures as it had never held before.

That evening, after glancing at Schofield's 'scenario', I carefully folded it up again for return to him, lest when the book should appear he should miss the pleasure of saying that I had had his guidance but had disregarded it; then I sat down at my writing-table and took out the loose notes I had made. I made other jottings, each on a blank sheet for subsequent amplification; and the sheets overspread the large leather-topped table and thrust one another up the standard of the incandescent with the pearly silk shade. The firelight shone low and richly in the dusky spaces of the large apartment; and the thick carpet and the double doors made the place so quiet that I could hear my watch ticking in my pocket.

I worked for an hour; and then, for the purpose of making yet other notes, I rose, crossed the room, and took down the three or four illustrated books to which, in the earlier part of his career, Andriaovsky had put his name. I carried them to the table, and twinkled as I opened the first of them. It was a book of poems, and in making the designs for them Andriaovsky had certainly *not* found for himself. Almost any one of the 'Art Shades', as he had called them, could have done the thing equally well, and I twinkled again. I did not propose to have much mercy on *that*. Already Schofield's words had given birth to a suspicion in my mind – that Andriaovsky, in permitting these fellows, Hallard, Connolly, and the rest, to suppose that he 'thought highly' of them and their work, had been giving play to that malicious humour of his; and they naturally did not see the joke. That joke, too, was between himself, dead, and me, preparing to write his 'Life'. As if he had been there to hear me, I chuckled, and spoke in a low voice.

'You were pulling their legs, Michael, you know. A little rough on them you were. But there's a book here of yours that I'm going to tell the truth about. You and I won't pretend to one another. It's a rotten book, and both you and I know it . . . '

I don't know what it was that caused me suddenly to see just then something that I had been looking at long enough without seeing – that portrait of himself that I had set leaning against the back of a chair at the end of my writing-table. It stood there, just within the soft penumbra of shadow cast by the silk-shaded light. The canvas had been enlarged, the seam of it clumsily sewn by Andriaovsky's own hand; but in that half-light the rough ridge of paint did not show, and I confess that the position and effect of the thing startled me for a moment. Had I cared to play a trick with my fancy I could have imagined the head wagging from side to side, with such rage and fire was it painted. He had had the temerity to dash a reflection across one of the glasses of his spectacles, concealing the eye behind it. The next moment I had given a short laugh.

'So you're there, are you? . . . Well, I know you agree very heartily about that book of poems. Heigho! If I remember rightly, you made more money out of that book than out of the others put together. But I'm going to tell the truth about it. *I* know better, you know . . . '

Chancing, before I turned in that night, to reopen one of his folios, I came across a drawing, there by accident, I don't doubt, that confirmed me in my suspicion that Andriaovsky had had his quiet joke with Schofield, Hallard, Connolly and Co. It was a sketch of Schofield's, imitative, deplorable, a dreadful show-up of incapacity. Well enough 'drawn', in a sense, it was . . . and I remembered how Andriaovsky had ever urged that 'drawing', of itself, did not exist. I winked at the portrait. I saw his point. He himself had no peer, and, rather than invite comparison with stars of the second magnitude, he chose his intimates from among the peddlers of the wares that had the least possible connection with his Art. He, too, had understood that the Compromise must be entirely accepted or totally refused; and while, in the divergence of our paths, he had done the one thing and I the other, we had each done it thoroughly, with vigour, and with persistence, and each could esteem the other, if not as a co-worker, at least as an honour-able and out-and-out opposite.

3

Within a fortnight I was so deep in my task that, in the realest sense, the greater part of my life was in the past. The significance of those extraordinary peregrinations of ours had been in the opportunity they had afforded for a communion of brain and spirit of unusual rarity; and all this determined my work with the accumulated force of its long penning-up. I have spoken of Andriaovsky's contempt for such as had the conception of their work that it was something they 'did' as distinct from something they 'were'; and unless I succeed in making it plain that, not as a mere figure of speech and loose hyperbole, but starkly and literally, Andriaovsky *was* everything he did, my tale will be pointless.

There was not one of the basic facts of life – of Faith, Honour, Truth-speaking, Falsehood, Betrayal, Sin – that he did not turn, not to moral interpretations, as others do, but to the holy purposes of his noble and passionate Art. For any man, Sin is only mortal when it is Sin against that which he knows to be immortally true; and the things Andriaovsky knew to be immortally true were the things that he had gone down into the depths in order to bring forth and place upon his paper or canvas. These things are not for the perusal of many. Unless you love the things that he loved with a fervour comparable in kind, if not in degree, with his own, you may not come near them. 'Truth, "the highest thing a man may keep",' he said, 'cannot be brought down; a man only attains it by proving his right to it'; and I think I need not further state his views on the democratisation of Art. Of any result from the elaborate processes of Art-education he held out no hope whatever. 'It is in a man, or it isn't,' he ever declared; 'if it is, he must bring it out for himself; if it isn't, let him turn to something useful and have done with it.' I need not press the point that in these things he was almost a solitary.

He made of these general despotic principles the fiercest personal applications. I have heard his passionate outbreak of 'Thief! Liar! Fool!' over a drawing when it has seemed to him that a man has not vouched with the safety of his immortal soul for the shapes and lines he has committed to it. I have seen him get into such a rage with the eyes of the artist upon him. I have heard the ice and vinegar of his words when a good man, for money, has consented to modify and emasculate his work; and there lingers in my memory his side of a telephone conversation in which he told a publisher who had suggested that he should do the same thing precisely what he thought of him. And on the other hand, he once walked from Aldgate to Putney Hill, with a loose heel on one of his boots, to see a man of whom he had seen but a single drawing. See him he did, too, in spite of the man's footman, his liveried parlourmaid, and the daunting effect of the electric brougham at the door.

'He's a good man,' he said to me afterwards, ruefully looking at the place where his boot-heel had been. 'You've got to take your good where you find it. I don't care whether he's a rich amateur or skin-and-grief in a garret as long as he's got the stuff in him. Nobody else could have fetched me up from the East End this afternoon . . . So long; see you in a week or so – '

This was the only time I ever knew him break that sacred time in which he celebrated each year the Passover and the Feast of Tabernacles. I doubt whether this observance of the ritual of his Faith was of more essential importance to him than that other philo-sophical religion towards which he sometimes leaned. I have said what his real religion was.

But to the 'Life'.

With these things, and others, as a beginning, I began to add page to page, phase to phase; and, in a time the shortness of which aston-ished myself, I had pretty well covered the whole of the first ten years of our friendship. Maschka called rather less, and Schofield rather more frequently, than I could have wished; and my surmise that he, at least, was in love with her, quickly became a certainty. This was to be seen when they called together.

It was when they came together that something else also became apparent. This was their slightly derisive attitude towards the means by which I had attained my success. It was not the less noticeable that it took the form of compliments on the outward and visible results. Singly I could manage them; together they were inclined to get a little out of hand.

I would have taxed them fairly and squarely with this, singly or together, but for one thing – the beautiful ease with which the 'Life' was proceeding. Never had I felt so completely *en rapport* with my subject. So beautifully was the thing running that I had had the idle fancy of some actual urge from Andriaovsky himself; and each night, before sitting down to work, I set his portrait at my desk's end, as if it had been some kind of an observance. The most beautiful result of all was, that I felt what I had not felt for five years – that I too was not 'doing' my work, but actually living and being it. At times I took up the sheets I had written as ignorant of their contents as if they had proceeded from another pen – so freshly they came to me. And once, I vow, I found, in my own handwriting, a Polish name, that I might (it is true) have subconsciously heard at some time or other, but that stirred no chord in my memory even when I saw it written. Maschka checked and confirmed it afterwards; and I did not tell her by what odd circumstance it had issued from my pen.

The day did come, however, when I found I must have it out with Schofield about this superciliousness I have mentioned. The *Falchion* had just begun to print the third series of my *Martin Renard*; and this had been made the occasion of another of Schofield's ponderous compliments. I acknowledged it with none too much graciousness; and then he said: 'I've na doubt, Harrison, that by this time the famous sleuth-hound of crime has become quite a creature of flesh and blood to ye.'

It was the tone as much as the words that riled me; and I replied that his doubts or the lack of them were a privacy with which I did not wish to meddle. From being merely a bore the fellow was rapidly becoming insolent.

'But I opine he'll get wearisome now and then, and in that case poor Michael's "Life" will come as a grand relaxation,' he next observed.

If I meant to have it out, here was my opportunity.

'I should have thought you'd have traced a closer connection than that between the two things,' I remarked.

He shot a quick glance at me from beneath his shaggy russet brows.

'How so? I see varry little connection,' he said suspiciously.

'There's this connection – that while you speak with some freedom of what I do, you are quite willing to take advantage of it when it serves your turn.'

' "Advantage", Harrison?' he said slowly.

'Of the advertisement *Martin Renard* gives you. I must point out that you condone a thing when you accept the benefit of it. Either you shouldn't have come to me at all, or you should deny yourself the gratification of these slurs.'

'Slurrrrs?' he repeated loweringly.

'Both of you – you and Miss Andriaovsky, or Maschka as I call her, *tout court*. Don't suppose I don't know as well as you do the exact worth of my "sleuth-hound", as you call him. You didn't come to me solely because I knew Andriaovsky well; you came because I've got the ear of the public also; and I tell you plainly that, however much you dislike it, Michael's fame as far as I'm of any use to him, depends on the popularity of *Martin Renard*.'

He shook his big head. 'This is what I feared,' he said.

'More,' I continued, 'you can depend upon it that Michael, wherever he is, knows all about that.'

'Ay, ay,' he said sagely, 'I misdoubt your own artistic soul's only to be saved by the writing of poor Michael's "Life", Harrison.'

'Leave that to me and Michael; we'll settle that. In the meantime, if you don't like it, write and publish the "Life" yourself.'

He bent his brows on me.

'It's precisely what I wanted to do from the varry first,' he said. 'If you'd cared to accept my symposium in the spirit in which it was offered, I cannot see that the "Life" would have suffered. But now, when you're next in need of my services, ye'll mebbe send for me.'

He took up his hat. I assured him, and let him take it in what sense he liked, that I would do so; and he left me.

Not for one single moment did I intend that they should bounce me like that. With or without their sanction and countenance, I intended to write and publish that 'Life'. Schofield – in my own house too – had had the advantage that a poor and ill-dressed man has over one who is not poor and ill-dressed; but my duty first of all was neither to him nor to Maschka, but to my friend.

The worst of it was, however, that I had begun dimly to suspect that the Lancastrian had hit at least one nail on the head. 'Your artistic soul's only to be saved by writing poor Michael's "Life", he had informed me . . . and it was truer than I found it pleasant to believe. Perhaps, after all, my first duty was not to Andriaovsky, but to my-self. I could have kicked myself that the fool had been perspicacious enough to see it, but that did not alter the fact. I saw that in the sense in which Andriaovsky understood Sin, I had sinned . . .

My only defence lay in the magnitude of my sin. I had sinned thoroughly, out-and-out, and with a will. It had been the only respectable way – Andriaovsky's own way when he had cut the company of an Academician to hobnob with a vagabond. I had at least instituted no comparison, lowered no ideal, was innocent of the accursed attitude of facing-both-ways that degrades all lovely and moving things. I was, by a paradox, too black a sinner not to hope for redemption . . .

I fell into a long musing on these things . . .

Had any of the admirers of *Martin Renard* entered the library of his author that night he would have seen an interesting thing. He would have seen the creator of that idol of clerks and messenger-lads and fourth-form boys frankly putting the case before a portrait propped up on a chair. He would have heard that popular author haranguing, pleading, curiously on his defence, turning the thing this way and that.

'If *you'd* gone over, Michael,' that author argued, 'you'd have done precisely the same thing. If I'd stuck it out, we were, after all, of a kind; We've got to be one thing or the other – isn't that so, Andriaovsky? Since I made up my mind, I've faced only one way – only one way. I've kept your ideal and theirs entirely separate and distinct. Not one single beautiful phrase will you find in the *Martin Renard*s; I've cut 'em out, every one. I may have ceased to worship, but I've profaned no temple . . . And think what I *might* have done – what they all do! They deal out the slush, but with an apologetic glance at the Art Shades; *you* know the style! – "Oh, Harrison; he does that detective rubbish, but that's not Harrison; if Harrison liked to drop that he could be a fine artist!" – I *haven't* done that. I *haven't* run with the hare and hunted with the hounds. I *am* just Harrison, who does that detective rubbish! . . . These other chaps, Schofield and Connolly, *they're* the real sinners, Michael – the fellows who can't make up their minds to be one thing or the other ("artists of considerable abilities" – ha! ha!) . . . Of course you know Maschka's going to marry that chap? What'll *they* do, do you think? He'll scrape up a few pounds out of the stew where I find thousands, marry her, and they'll set up a salon and talk the stuff the chairs talked that night, you remember! . . . But you wait until I finish your "Life" . . .'

I laid it all before him, almost as if I sought to propitiate him. I might have been courting his patronage for his own 'Life'. Then, with a start, I came to, to find myself talking nonsense to the portrait that years before Andriaovsky had refused to sell me.

4

The first check I experienced in the hitherto so easy flow of the 'Life' came at the chapter that dealt with Andriaovsky's attitude towards 'professionalism' in Art. He was inflexible on this point; there ought not to be professional artists. When it was pointed out that his position involved a premium upon the rich amateur, he merely replied that riches had nothing to do with the question, and that the starver in the garret was not excused for his poverty's sake from the observance of the implacable conditions. He spoke literally of the 'need' to create, usually in the French term, *besogne*; and he was inclined to regard the imposition of this need on a man rather as a curse laid upon him than as a privilege and a pleasure. But I must not enlarge upon this further than to observe that this portion of his 'Life' which I was approaching coincided in point of time with that period of my own life at which I had been confronted with the alternative of starving for Art's sake or becoming rich by supplying a clamorous trade demand.

It came, this check I have spoken of, one night, as I was in the very middle of a sentence; and though I have cudgelled my brains in seeking how best I can describe it, I am reduced to the simple statement that it was as arresting, as sharp, actual and impossible to resist, as if my hand had been seized and pinned down in its passage across the paper. I can even see again the fragment of the sentence I had written: ' . . . *and the mere contemplation of a betrayal so essential –* ' Then came that abrupt and remarkable stop. It was such an experience as I had formerly known only in nightmare.

I sat there looking blankly and stupidly at my own hand. And not only was my hand arrested, but my brain also had completely ceased to work. For the life of me I could not recall the conclusion of the sentence I had planned a moment before.

I looked at my hand, and looked again; and as I looked I remembered something I had been reading only a few days before – a profoundly unsettling description of an experiment in auto-suggestion. The experiment had consisted of the placing of a hand upon a table, and the laying upon it the conjuration that, the Will notwithstanding, it should not move. And as I watched my own hand, pale on the paper in the pearly light, I knew that, by some consent to the nullification of the Will that did not proceed from the Self I was accustomed to regard as my own, that injunction was already placed upon it. My conscious and deliberate Will was powerless. I could only sit there and wait until whatever inhibition had arrested my writing hand should permit it to move forward again.

It must have been several minutes before such a tingling of the nerves as announces that the blood is once more returning to a cramped member warned me that I was about to be released. Warily I awaited my moment; then I plucked my hand to myself again with a suddenness that caused a little blot of ink to spurt from my fountain-pen on to the surface of the paper. I drew a deep breath. I was free again. And with the freedom came a resolve – that whatever portion of myself had been responsible for this prank should not repeat it if I could possibly prevent it.

But scarcely had I come, as I may say (and not without a little gush of alarm now that it was over), to myself, when I was struck by a thought. It was a queer wild sort of thought. It fetched me out of my chair and set me striding across the library to a lower shelf in the farthest corner. This shelf was the shelf on which I kept my letter-files. I stooped and ran my fingers along the backs of the dusty row. I drew out the file for 1900, and brought it back to my writing-table. My contracts, I ought to say, reposed in a deed-box at my agent's office; but my files contained, in the form of my agent's letters, a sufficient record of my business transactions.

I opened the file concertina-wise, and turned to the section lettered 'R'. I drew out the correspondence that related to the sale of the first series of the *Martin Renard*s. As I did so I glanced at the movable calendar on my table. The date was January 20th.

The file contained no letters for January of any significance whatever.

The thought that had half formed in my brain immediately became nonsense. I replaced the letters in their compartment, and took the file back to its shelf again. For some minutes I paced the library irresolutely; then I decided I would work no more that night. When I gathered together my papers I was careful to place that with the half-finished sentence on the top, so that with the first resting of my eyes upon it on the morrow my memory might haply be refreshed.

I tried again to finish that sentence on the morrow. With certain modifications that I need not particularise here, my experience was the same as on the previous night.

It was the same when I made the attempt on the day after that.

At ten o'clock of the night of the fourth day I completed the sentence without difficulty. I just sat down in my chair and wrote it.

With equal ease I finished the chapter on professional artists.

It was not likely that Schofield would have refrained from telling Maschka of our little difference on our last meeting; and within a week of the date I have just mentioned I learned that she knew all about it. And, as the circumstances of my learning this were in a high degree unusual, I will relate them with such clearness as I am able.

I ought first to say, however, that the selection of the drawings that were to illustrate the book having been made (the drawings for which my own text was to serve as commentary would be the better expression), the superintendence of their production had been left to Schofield. He, Maschka, and I passed the proofs in consultation. The blocks were almost ready; and the reason for their call that evening was to consider the possibility of having all ready for production in the early spring – a possibility which was contingent on the state of advancement of my own share of the book.

That evening I had experienced my second check. (I omit those that had immediately succeeded the first one, as resembling that one so closely in the manner of their coming.) It had not come by any means so completely and definitively as the former one, but it had sufficed to make my progress, both mentally and mechanically, so sluggish and struggling a performance that for the time being I had given up the attempt, and was once more regarding with a sort of perturbed stupor my hand that held the pen. Andriaovsky's portrait stood in its usual place, on the chair at the end of my writing-table; but I had eyes for nothing but that refractory hand of mine.

Now it is true that during the past weeks I had studied Andria-ovsky's portrait thoroughly enough to be able to call up the vivid mental image of it at will; but that did not entirely account for the changed aspect with which it now presented itself to that uncom-prehended sense within us that makes of these shadows such startling realities. Flashing and life-like as was the presentation on the canvas (mind you, I was not looking at it, but all the time at my own hand), it was dead paint by comparison with that *mental image* which I saw (if I may so use a term of which custom has restricted the meaning to one kind of seeing) as plainly as I ever saw Andriaovsky in his life. I know now that it was by virtue of that essential essence that bound us heart and brain and soul together that I so saw him, eyes glittering, head sardonically wagging, fine mouth shaping phrases of insight and irony. And the strange thing was, that I could not have located this so living image by confining it to any portion of the space within the four walls of my library. It was before me, behind me, within my head, about me, *was me*, invading and possessing the 'me' that sat at the table. At one moment the eyes mockingly invited me to go on with my work; the next, a frown had seated itself on that massive pylon of his forehead; and then suddenly his countenance changed entirely . . . A wave of horror broke over me. He was suddenly as I had seen him that last time in the Hampstead 'Home' – sitting up on his pillow, looking into my eyes with that terrible look of profundity and familiarity, and asking me who I was . . . '*Harrison – ha ha*! . . . *You shall very soon know that I know you, if* . . .'

It is but by the accident of our limited experience that sounds are loud or soft to that inner ear of us; these words were at one and the same time a dreadful thunder and a voice interstellarly inaccessible and withdrawn. They, too, were before, behind, without, and within. And incorporated (I know not how else to express it) with these words were other words, in the English I knew, in the Hebrew in which he had quoted them from the sacred Books of his People, in all languages, in no language save that essential communication of which languages are but the inessential husk and medium – words that told me that though I took the Wings of the Morning and fled into the uttermost parts of the earth, yea, though I made my bed in Hell, I could not escape him . . .

He had kept his word. I *did* know that he knew who and what I was . . .

I cannot tell whether my lips actually shaped the question that even in that moment burst from me.

'But Form – and Forms? It *is* then true that all things are but aspects of One thing? . . . '

'Yes – in death,' the voice seemed to reply.

My next words, I know, were actually spoken aloud.

'Then tell me – tell me – *do you not wish me to write it?*'

Suddenly I leapt out of my chair with a gulping cry. A voice *had* spoken . . .

'Of course we wish you to write it . . . '

For one instant of time my vision seemed to fold on itself like smoke; then it was gone. The face into which I was wildly staring was Maschka's, and behind her stood Schofield. They had been announced, but I had heard nothing of it.

'Were you thinking of *not* writing it?' she demanded, while Schofield scowled at me.

'No – no – ' I stammered, as I got up and tardily placed them chairs.

Schofield did not speak, but he did not remove his eyes from me. Somehow I could not meet them.

'Well,' she said, 'Jack had already told me that you seemed in two minds about it. That's what we've called about – to know definitely what it is you propose to do.'

I saw that she had also called, if necessary, to quarrel. I began to recover a little.

'Did you tell her that?' I demanded of Schofield. 'If you did, you – misinterpreted me.'

In my house, he ignored the fact that I was in the room. He replied to Maschka.

'I understood Mr Harrison to say definitely, and in those words, that if I didn't like the way in which he was writing Michael's "Life"' I might write and publish one myself,' he said.

'I did say that,' I admitted; 'but I never said that whatever *you* did *I* should not go on with mine.'

'Yours!' cried Maschka. 'What right have *you* in my brother's "Life"?'

I quickly told her.

'I have the right to write my recollections of him, and, subject to certain provisions of the Law, to base anything on them I think fit,' I replied.

'But,' she cried aghast, 'there can't be *two* "Lives"! . . . '

'It's news to me that two were contemplated,' I returned. 'The point is, that I can get mine published, and you can't.'

Schofield's harsh voice sounded suddenly – but again to Maschka, not to me.

'Ye might remind Mr Harrison that others have capabilities in business besides himself. Beyond a doubt our sales will be comparatively small, but they'll be to such as have not made the great refusal.'

Think of it! . . . I almost laughed.

'Oh! . . . Been trying it?' I enquired.

He made no reply.

'Well, those who have made the refusal have at least had something to refuse,' I said mildly. Then, realising that this was mere quarrelling, I returned to the point. 'Anyhow, there's no question of refusing to write the "Life". I admit that during the last fortnight I've met with certain difficulties; but the task isn't so easy as perhaps it looks . . . I'm making progress.'

'I suppose,' she said hesitatingly, after a pause, 'that you don't care to show it as far as it is written?'

For a moment I also hesitated. I thought I saw where she was. Thanks to that Lancashire jackanapes, there was division between us; and I had pretty well made up my mind, not only that he thought himself quite capable of writing Andriaovsky's 'Life' himself, but that he had actually made an attempt in that direction. They had come in the suspicion that I was throwing them over, and, though that suspicion was removed, Maschka wished, if there was any throwing over to be done, to do it herself. In a word, she wanted to compare me with Schofield.

'To see it as far as it is written,' I repeated slowly . . . 'Well, you may. That is, *you*, Michael's sister, may. But on the condition that you neither show it to anybody else nor speak of it to anybody else.'

'Ah!' she said . . . 'And only on those conditions?'

'Only on those conditions.'

I saw a quick glance between them. 'Shall we tell him?' it seemed to say . . .

'Including the man Michael's sister is going to marry?' she said abruptly.

My attitude was deeply apologetic, but, 'Including anybody whomsoever,' I answered.

'Then,' she said, rising, 'we won't bother. But will you at least let us know, soon, when we may expect your text?'

'I will let you know,' I replied slowly, 'one week from today.'

On that assurance they left; and when they had gone I crossed once more to the lower shelf that contained my letter-files. I turned up the file for 1900 once more. During their visit I had had an idea.

I ran through the letters, and then replaced them . . .

Yes, I ought to be able to let them know within the week.

5

Against the day when I myself shall come to die, there are in the pigeon-holes of the newspaper libraries certain biographical records that deal roughly with the outward facts of my life; and these, supplemented by documents I shall place in the hands of my executors, will tell the story of how I leaped at a bound into wealth and fame with the publication of *The Cases of Martin Renard*. I will set down as much of that story as has its bearing on my present tale.

Martin Renard was not immediately accepted by the first editor to whom it was offered. It does not suffice that in order to be popular a thing shall be merely good – or bad; it must be bad – or good – in a particular way. For taking the responsibility when they happen to miss that particular way editors are paid their salaries. When they happen to hit it they grow fat on circulation-money: since it becomes me ill to quarrel with the way in which any man earns his money, I content myself with merely stating the fact.

By the time the fourth editor had refused my series I was about at my last gasp. To write the things at all I had had to sink four months in time; and debts, writs and pawnshops were my familiars. I was little better off than Andriaovsky at his very worst. I had read the first of the *Martin Renard*s to him, by the way; the gigantic outburst of mirth with which he had received it had not encouraged me to read him a second. I wrote the others in secret.

I wrote the things in the spring and summer of 1900; and by the last day of September I was confident that I had at last sold them. Except by a flagrant breach of faith, the editor in whose desk they reposed could hardly decline them. As it subsequently happened, I have now nothing but gratitude for him that he did, after all, decline them; for I had a duplicate copy 'on offer' in another quarter.

He declined them, I say; and I was free to possess my soul again among my writs, debts and pawnshops.

But four days later I received the alternative offer. It was from the *Falchion*. The *Falchion*, as you may remember, has since run no less than five complete series of *Martin Renard*s. It bought 'both sides', that is to say, both British and American serial rights. Of the twelve *Martin Renard*s I had written, my wise agent had offered the *Falchion* six only. On his advice I accepted the offer.

Instantaneously with the publication of those six stories came my success. In two continents I was 'home' – home in the hearts of the public. I had my small cheque – it was not much more than a hundred pounds – but 'Wait,' said my agent; 'let's see what we can do with the other six . . . '

Precisely what he did with them only he and I know; but I don't mind saying that £3000 did not buy my first serial rights. Then came second and third rights, and after them the book rights, British, American, and Colonial. Then came the translation rights. In French, my creation is, of course, as in English, *Martin Renard*; in German he is *Martin Fuchs*; and by a similar process you can put him – my translators have put him – into Italian, Swedish, Norwegian, Russian, and three-fourths of the tongues of Europe. And this was the first series only. It was only with the second series that the full splendour of my success appeared. My very imitators grew rich; my agent's income from his comparatively small percentage on my royalties was handsome; and he chuckled and bade me wait for the dramatic rights and the day when the touring companies should get to business . . .

I had 'got there'.

And I remember, sadly enough now, my first resolution when the day came when I was able to survey the situation with anything approaching calm. It was, 'Enough'. For the rest of my days I need not know poverty again. Thenceforward I need not, unless I chose, do any but worthy work. *Martin Renard* had served his purpose handsomely, and I intended to have nothing more to do with him.

Then came that dazzling offer for the second series . . .

I accepted it.

I accepted the third likewise; and I have told you about the fourth . . .

I have tried to kill *Martin Renard*. He was killing me. I have, in the pages of the *Falchion*, actually killed him; but I have had to resuscitate him. I cannot escape from him . . .

I am not setting down one word more of this than bears directly on my tale of Andriaovsky's 'Life'. For those days, when my whole future had hung in the balance, *were the very days covered by that portion of Andriaovsky's life at which I had now arrived.* I had reached, and was hesitating at, our point of divergence. Those checks and releases which I had at first found so unaccountable corresponded with the vicissitudes of the *Martin Renard* negotiations.

The actual dates did not, of course, coincide – I had quickly discovered the falsity of that scent. Neither did the intervals between them, with the exception of those few days in which I had been unable to complete that half-written sentence – the few days immediately prior to my (parallel) acceptance by the *Falchion*. But, by that other reckoning of time, of mental and spiritual experience, *they tallied exactly*. The gambling chances of five years ago meant present stumblings and haltings; the breach of faith of an editor long since meant a present respite; and another week should bring me to that point of my so strangely reduplicated experience that, allowing for the furious mental rate at which I was now living, would make another node with that other point in the more slowly lived past that had marked my acceptance of the offer for the second half-dozen of the *Martin Renard*s.

It had been on this hazardous calculation that I had made my promise to Maschka.

I passed that week in a state of constantly increasing apprehension. True, I worked at the 'Life', even assiduously; but it was plain sailing, mere cataloguing of certain of Andriaovsky's works, a chapter I had deliberately planned *pour mieux sauter* – to enhance the value of the penultimate and final chapters. These were the real crux of the 'Life'. These were what I was reserving myself for. These were to show that only his body was dead, and that his spirit still lived and his work was still being done wherever a man could be found whose soul burned within him with the same divine ardour.

But I was now realising, day by day, hour by hour more clearly, what I was incurring. I was penning nothing less than my own artistic damnation. Self-condemned, indeed, I had been this long time; but I was now making the world a party to the sentence. The crowning of Andriaovsky involved my own annihilation; his 'Life' would be my 'Hic Jacet'. And yet I was prepared, nay, resolved, to write it. I had started, and I would go forward. I would not be spewed with the lukewarm out of the mouth of that Spirit from which proceeds all that is bright and pure and true. The vehemence with which I had rejected its divine bidding should at least be correspondent with my adoration of it. The snivelling claims of the Schofields I spurned. If, as they urged, 'an artist must live', he must live royally or starve with a tight mouth. No complaining . . .

And one other claim I urged in the teeth of this Spirit, which, if it was a human Spirit at all, it could not disregard. Those pigeon-holed obituaries of mine will proclaim to the world, one and all, the virtues of my public life. In spite of my royal earnings, I am not a rich man. I have not accepted wealth without accepting the personal responsibility for it. Sick men and women in more than one hospital lie in wards provided by *Martin Renard* and myself; and I am not dishonoured in my Institution at Poplar. Those vagrant wanderings with Andriaovsky have enabled me to know the poor and those who help the poor. My personal labours in the administration of the Institute are great, for outside the necessary routine I leave little to subordinates. I have declined honours offered to me for my 'services to Literature', and I have never encouraged a youth, of parts or lacking them, to make of Literature a profession. And so on and so forth. All this, and more, you will read when the day comes; and I don't doubt the *Falchion* will publish my memoir in mourning borders . . .

But to resume.

I finished the chapter I have mentioned. Maschka and her fiancé kept punctiliously away. Then, before sitting down to the penultimate chapter, I permitted myself the relaxation of a day in the country.

I can't tell you precisely where I went; I only know it was somewhere in Buckinghamshire, and that, ordering the car to await me a dozen miles farther on, I set out to walk. Nor can I tell you what I saw during that walk; I don't think I saw anything. There was a red wintry disc of a sun, I remember, and a land grey with rime; and that is all. I was entirely occupied with the attempt I was about to make. I think that even then I had the sense of doom, for I know not how otherwise I should have found myself several times making little husbandings of my force, as if conscious that I should need it all. For I was determined, as never in my life have I been determined, to write that 'Life'. And I intended, not to wait to be challenged, but to challenge . . . I met the car, returning in search of me; and I dined at a restaurant, went home to bed, and slept dreamlessly.

On the morrow I deliberately refrained from work until the evening. My challenge to Andriaovsky and the Powers he represented should be boldly delivered at the very gates of their own Hour. Not until half-past eight, with the curtains drawn, the doors locked, and orders given that on no account whatever was I to be disturbed, did I switch on the pearly light, place Andriaovsky's portrait in its now accustomed place, and draw my chair up to my writing-table.

6

But before I could resume the 'Life' at the point at which I had left it, I felt that there were certain preliminaries to be settled. It was not that I wished to sound a parley with any view of coming to terms; I had determined what the terms were to be. As a boxer who leaps from his corner the moment the signal is given, astounding with suddenness his less prompt antagonist, so I should be ready when the moment came. But I wished the issue to be defined. I did not propose to submit the whole of my manhood to the trial. I was merely asserting my right to speak of certain things which, if one chose to exaggerate their importance by a too narrow and exclusive consideration of them, I might conceivably be thought to have betrayed.

I drew a sheet of paper towards me, and formally made out my claim. It occupied not more than a dozen lines, and its nature has already been sufficiently indicated. I put my pen down again, leaned back in my chair, and waited.

I waited, but nothing happened. It seemed that if this was my attempt to justify myself, the plea was certainly not disallowed. But neither had I any sign that it was allowed; and presently it occurred to me that possibly I had couched it in terms too general. Perhaps a more particular claim would meet with a different reception.

During the earlier stages of the book's progress I had many times deliberated on the desirability of a Preface that should state succinctly what I considered to be my qualifications for the task. Though I had finally decided against any such statement, the form of the Preface might nevertheless serve for the present occasion. I took another sheet of paper, headed it 'Preface', and began once more to write.

I covered the page; I covered a second; and half-way down the third I judged my statement to be sufficient. Again I laid down my pen, leaned back, and waited.

The Preface also produced no result whatever.

Again I considered; and then I saw more clearly. It came to me that, both in the first statement and in the Preface, I was merely talking to myself. I was convincing myself, and losing both time and strength in doing so. The Power with which I sought to come to grips was treating my vapourings with high disregard. To be snubbed thus by Headquarters would never, never do . . .

Then I saw more clearly still. It seemed that my *right to challenge* was denied. I was not an adversary, with the rights and honours of an adversary, but a trangressor, whose trangression had already several times been sharply visited, and would be visited once more the moment it was repeated. I might, in a sense, please myself whether I brought myself into Court; but, once there, I was not the arraigner in the box, but the arraigned in the dock.

And I rebelled hotly. Did I sit there, ready for the struggle, only to be told that there could be no struggle? Did that vengeful Angel of the Arts ignore my very existence? . . . By Yea and Nay I swore that he should take notice of me! Once before, a mortal had wrestled a whole night with an angel, and though he had been worsted, it had not been before he had compelled the Angel to reveal himself! And so would I . . .

Challenge, title to challenge, tentatives, preliminaries, I suddenly cast them all aside. We would have it in deeds, not in further words. I opened a drawer, took out the whole of the 'Life' so far written, and began to read. I wanted to grasp once more the plan of it in its entirety.

Page after page, I read on, with deepening attention. Quickly I ran through half of it. Then I began to concentrate myself still more closely. There would come a point at which I should be flush with the stream of it again, again feel the force of its current; I felt myself drawing nearer to that point; when I should reach it I would go ahead without a pause . . .

I read to the end of Chapter Fifteen, the last completed chapter. Then instantly I took my pen and wrote, 'Chapter Sixteen . . . '

I felt the change at the very first word.

I will not retraverse any ground I have covered before. If I have not already made clear my former sensations of the petrefaction of hand and brain, I despair of being able to do so any better now. Suffice it that once more I felt that inhibition, and that once more I was aware of the ubiquitous presence of the image of the dead artist. Once more I heard those voices, near as thunder and yet interstellarly remote, crying that solemn warning, that though I took the Wings of the Morning, made my bed in Hell, or cried aloud upon the darkness to cover me, there was one Spirit from which I could not hope to escape. I felt the slight crawling of my flesh on my bones as I listened.

But there was now a difference. On the former occasion, to hear again those last horrible words of his, '*You shall very soon know I know who you are if* . . . ' had been the signal for the total unnerving of me and for that uncontrollable cry, '*Don't you then want me to write it?*' But now I intended to write it if I could. In order that I might tell him so I was now seeking him out, in what heights or depths I knew not, at what peril to myself I cared not. I cared not, since I now felt that I could not continue to live unless I pressed to the uttermost attempt. And I must repeat, and repeat again, and yet repeat, that in that hour Andriaovsky was immanent about me, in the whole of me, in the last fibre and cell of me, in all my thoughts, from my consciousness that I was sitting there at my own writing-table to my conception of God Himself.

It may seem strange – whether it does so or not will depend on the kind of man you yourself are – that as long as I was content to recognise this immanence of Andriaovsky's enlarged and liberated spirit, *and not to dispute with it*, I found nothing but mildness and benignity in my hazardous experience. More, I felt that, in that clear region to which in my intensified state of consciousness I was lifted, I was able to move (I must trust you to understand the word aright) without restraint, nay, with an amplitude and freedom of movement past setting down, as long as I was satisfied to possess my soul in quiescence. The state itself was inimical neither to my safety nor to my sanity. I was conscious of it as a transposition into another register of the scale of life. And, as in this life we move in ignorance and safety only by accepting the hair-balance of stupendous forces, so now I felt that my safety depended on my observation of the conditions that governed that region of light and clarity and Law.

Of clarity and Law; save in the terms of the great abstractions

I may not speak of it. And that is well-nigh equal to saying that I may not speak of it at all. The hand that would have written of it lay (I never for one moment ceased to be conscious) heavy as stone on a writing-table in some spot quite accidental in my new sense of locality; the tongue that would have spoken of it seemed to slumber in my mouth. And I knew that both dumbness and stillness were proper. Their opposites would have convicted me (the flat and earthly comparison must be allowed) of intrusion into some Place of beauty and serenity for which the soilure of my birth disqualified me.

For beauty and serenity, austerity and benignity and peace, were the conditions of that Place. To other Places belonged the wingy and robed and starry and golden things that made the heavens of other lives than that which I had shared with Andriaovsky; here, white and shapely Truth alone reigned. None questioned, for all knew; none sinned, for sin was already judged and punished in its committal; none demonstrated, for all things were evident; and those eager to justify themselves were permitted no farther than the threshold . . .

And it was to justify, to challenge, to maintain a right, that I was there. I was there to wrestle, if needs be, with the Angel of that Place, to vanquish him or to compel him to reveal himself. I had not been summoned; I had thrust myself there unbidden. There was a moment in which I noticed that my writing-table was a little more than ordinarily removed from me, but very little, not more than if I had been looking over the shoulder of another writer at it; and I saw my chapter heading. At the sight of it something of the egotism that had prompted me to write it stirred in me again; everywhere was Andriaovsky's calm face, priest and Angel himself; and I became conscious that I was trying to write a phrase. I also became conscious that I was being pitifully warned not to do so . . .

Suddenly my whole being was flooded with a frightful pang of pain.

It was not local. It was no more to be located than the other immanences of which I have spoken. It was Pain, pure, essential, dissociated; and with the coming of it that fair Place had grown suddenly horrible and black.

And I knew that the shock came *of my own resistance*, and that it would cease to afflict me the moment I ceased to resist.

I did cease. Instantly the pain passed. But as when a knife is plucked from a wound, so only with its passing did I shriek aloud . . .

For I know not how many minutes I sat in stupefaction. Then, as with earthly pains, that are assuaged with the passing of accidental time, the memory of it softened a little. Blunderingly and only half consciously, I cast about to collect my dispersed force.

For – already I was conscious of it – there still remained one claim that even in thought I had not advanced. I would, were I permitted, still write that 'Life', but, since it was decreed so, I would no longer urge that in writing it I justified myself. So I might but write it, I would embrace my own portion, the portion of doom; yea, though it should be a pressing of the searing-iron to my lips, I would embrace it; my name should not appear. For the mere sake of the man I had loved I would write it, in self-scorn and abasement, humbly craving not to be denied . . .

'*Oh, let me but do for Love of you what a sinful man can!*' I groaned . . .

A moment later I had again striven to do so. So do we all, when we think that out of a poor human Love we can alter the Laws by which our state exists. And with such a hideous anguish as was again mine are we visited . . .

And I knew now what that anguish was. It was the twining of body from spirit that is called the bitterness of Death; for not all of the body are the pangs of that severance. With that terrible sword of impersonal Pain the God of Peace makes sorrowful war that Peace may come again. With its flame He ringed the bastions of Heaven when Satan made assault. Only on the Gorgon-image of that Pain in the shield may weak man look; and its blaze and ire had permeated with deadly nearness the 'everywhere' where I was . . .

'*Oh, not for Love? Not even for Love?*' broke the agonised question from me . . .

The next moment I had ceased, and ceased for ever, to resist. Instantaneously the terrible flashing of that sword became no more than the play of lightning one sees far away in the wide cloudfields on a peaceful summer's twilight. I felt a gentle and overpowering sleep coming over me; and as it folded me about I saw, with the last look of my eyes, my own figure, busily writing at the table.

Had I, then, prevailed? Had Pain so purged me that I was permitted to finish my task? And had my tortured cry, 'Oh, not even for Love?' been heard?

I did not know.

I came to myself to find that my head had fallen on my desk. The light still shone within its pearly shade, and in the penumbra of its shadow the portrait of Andriaovsky occupied its accustomed place. About me were my papers, and my pen lay where it had fallen from my hand.

At first I did not look at my papers. I merely saw that the uppermost of them was written on. But presently I took it up, and looked at it stupidly. Then, with no memory at all of how I had come to write what was upon it, I put it down again.

It was indeed a completion.

But it was not of Andriaovsky's 'Life' that it was the completion. As you may or may not know, Andriaovsky's 'Life' is written by 'his friend John Schofield'. I had been allowed to write, but it was my own condemnation that, in sadness and obedience, in the absence of wrath but also in the absence of mercy, I had written. By the Law I had broken I was broken in my turn. It was the draft for the fifth series of *The Cases of Martin Renard*.

No, not for Love – not even for Love . . .

The Rocker

I

There was little need for the swart gipsies to explain, as they stood knee-deep in the snow round the bailiff of the Abbey Farm, what it was that had sent them. The unbroken whiteness of the uplands told that, and, even as they spoke, there came up the hill the dark figures of the farm men with shovels, on their way to dig out the sheep. In the summer, the bailiff would have been the first to call the gipsies vagabonds and roost-robbers; now . . . they had women with them too.

'The hares and foxes were down four days ago, and the liquid-manure pump's like a snowman,' the bailiff said . . . 'Yes, you can lie in the laithes and welcome – if you can find 'em. Maybe you'll help us find our sheep too – '

The gipsies had done so. Coming back again, they had had some ado to discover the spot where their three caravans made a hummock of white against a broken wall.

The women – they had four women with them – began that afternoon to weave the mats and baskets they hawked from door to door; and in the forenoon of the following day one of them, the black-haired, soft-voiced quean whom the bailiff had heard called Annabel, set her babe in the sling on her back, tucked a bundle of long cane-loops under her oxter, and trudged down between eight-foot walls of snow to the Abbey Farm. She stood in the latticed porch, dark and handsome against the whiteness, and then, advancing, put her head into the great hall-kitchen.

'Has the lady any chairs for the gipsy woman to mend?' she asked in a soft and insinuating voice . . .

They brought her the old chairs; she seated herself on a box in the porch; and there she wove the strips of cane in and out, securing each one with a little wooden peg and a tap of her hammer. The child remained in the sling at her back, taking the breast from time to time over her shoulder; and the silver wedding ring could be seen as she whipped the cane, back and forth.

As she worked, she cast curious glances into the old hall-kitchen. The snow outside cast a pallid, upward light on the heavy ceiling-beams; this was reflected in the polished stone floor; and the children, who at first had shyly stopped their play, seeing the strange woman in the porch – the nearest thing they had seen to gipsies before had been the old itinerant glazier with his frame of glass on his back – resumed it, but still eyed her from time to time. In the ancient walnut chair by the hearth sat the old, old lady who had told them to bring the chairs. Her hair, almost as white as the snow itself, was piled up on her head *à la Marquise*; she was knitting; but now and then she allowed the needle in the little wooden sheath at her waist to lie idle, closed her eyes, and rocked softly in the old walnut chair.

'Ask the woman who is mending the chairs whether she is warm enough there,' the old lady said to one of the children; and the child went to the porch with the message.

'Thank you, little missie – thank you, lady dear – Annabel is quite warm,' said the soft voice; and the child returned to the play.

It was a childish game of funerals at which the children played. The hand of Death, hovering over the dolls, had singled out Flora, the articulations of whose sawdust body were seams and whose boots were painted on her calves of fibrous plaster. For the greater solemnity, the children had made themselves sweeping trains of the garments of their elders, and those with cropped curls had draped their heads with shawls, the fringes of which they had combed out with their fingers to simulate hair – long hair, such as Sabrina, the eldest, had hanging so low down her back that she could almost sit on it. A cylindrical-bodied horse, convertible (when his flat head came out of its socket) into a locomotive, headed the sad *cortège*; then came the defunct Flora; then came Jack, the raffish sailor doll, with other dolls; and the children followed with hushed whisperings.

The youngest of the children passed the high-backed walnut chair in which the old lady sat. She stopped.

'Aunt Rachel – ' she whispered, slowly and gravely opening very wide and closing very tight her eyes.

'Yes, dear?'

'Flora's dead!'

The old lady, when she smiled, did so less with her lips than with her faded cheeks. So sweet was her face that you could not help wondering, when you looked on it, how many men had also looked upon it and loved it. Somehow, you never wondered how many of them had been loved in return.

'I'm so sorry, dear,' Aunt Rachel, who in reality was a great-aunt, said. 'What did she die of this time?'

'She died of . . . Brown Titus . . . 'n now she's going to be buried in a grave as little as her bed.'

'In a what, dear?'

'As little . . . dread . . . as little as my bed . . . you say it, Sabrina.'

'She means, Aunt Rachel,

> Teach me to live that I may dread
> The Grave as little as my bed,

Sabrina, the eldest, interpreted.

'Ah! . . . But won't you play at cheerful things, dears?'

'Yes, we will, presently, Aunt Rachel; gee up, horse! . . . Shall we go and ask the chair-woman if she's warm enough?'

'Do, dears.'

Again the message was taken, and this time it seemed as if Annabel, the gipsy, was not warm enough, for she gathered up her loops of cane and brought the chair she was mending a little way into the hall-kitchen itself. She sat down on the square box they used to cover the sewing machine.

'Thank you, lady dear,' she murmured, lifting her handsome almond eyes to Aunt Rachel. Aunt Rachel did not see the long, furtive, curious glance. Her own eyes were closed, as if she was tired; her cheeks were smiling; one of them had dropped a little to one shoulder, as it might have dropped had she held in her arms a babe; and she was rocking, softly, slowly, the rocker of the chair making a little regular noise on the polished floor.

The gipsy woman beckoned to one of the children.

'Tell the lady, when she wakes, that I will tack a strip of felt to the rocker, and then it will make no noise at all,' said the low and wheedling voice; and the child retired again.

The interment of Flora proceeded . . .

An hour later Flora had taken up the burden of Life again. It was as Angela, the youngest, was chastising her for some offence, that Sabrina, the eldest, looked with wondering eyes on the babe in the gipsy's sling. She approached on tiptoe.

'May I look at it, please?' she asked timidly.

The gipsy set one shoulder forward, and Sabrina put the shawl gently aside, peering at the dusky brown morsel within.

'Sometime, perhaps – if I'm very careful – ' Sabrina ventured diffidently, ' – if I'm *very* careful – may I hold it?'

Before replying, the gipsy once more turned her almond eyes towards Aunt Rachel's chair. Aunt Rachel had been awakened for the conclusion of Flora's funeral, but her eyes were closed again now, and once more her cheek was dropped in that tender suggestive little gesture, and she rocked. But you could see that she was not properly asleep . . . It was, somehow, less to Sabrina, still peering at the babe in the sling, than to Aunt Rachel, apparently asleep, that the gipsy seemed to reply.

'You'll know some day, little missis, that a wean knows its own pair of arms,' her seductive voice came.

And Aunt Rachel heard. She opened her eyes with a start. The little regular noise of the rocker ceased. She turned her head quickly; tremulously she began to knit again; and, as her eyes rested on the sidelong eyes of the gipsy woman, there was an expression in them that almost resembled fright.

2

They began to deck the great hall-kitchen for Christmas, but the snow still lay thick over hill and valley, and the gipsies' caravans remained by the broken wall where the drifts had overtaken them. Though all the chairs were mended, Annabel still came daily to the farm, sat on the box they used to cover the sewing machine, and wove mats. As she wove them, Aunt Rachel knitted, and from time to time fragments of talk passed between the two women. It was always the white-haired lady who spoke first, and Annabel made all sorts of salutes and obeisances with her eyes before replying.

'I have not seen your husband,' Aunt Rachel said to Annabel one day. (The children at the other end of the apartment had converted a chest into an altar, and were solemnising the nuptials of the resurrected Flora and Jack, the raffish sailor-doll.)

Annabel made roving play with her eyes. 'He is up at the caravans, lady dear,' she replied. 'Is there anything Annabel can bid him do?'

'Nothing, thank you,' said Aunt Rachel.

For a minute the gipsy watched Aunt Rachel, and then she got up from the sewing machine box and crossed the floor. She leaned so close towards her that she had to put up a hand to steady the babe at her back.

'Lady dear,' she murmured with irresistible softness, 'your husband died, didn't he?'

On Aunt Rachel's finger was a ring, but it was not a wedding ring. It was a hoop of pearls.

'I have never had a husband,' she said.

The gipsy glanced at the ring. 'Then that is – ?'

'That is a betrothal ring,' Aunt Rachel replied.

'Ah! . . . ' said Annabel.

Then, after a minute, she drew still closer. Her eyes were fixed on Aunt Rachel's, and the insinuating voice was very low.

'Ah! . . . And did *it* die too, lady dear?'

Again came that quick, half-affrighted look into Aunt Rachel's face. Her eyes avoided those of the gipsy, sought them, and avoided them again.

'Did what die?' she asked slowly and guardedly . . .

The child at the gipsy's back did not need suck; nevertheless, Annabel's fingers worked at her bosom, and she moved the sling. As the child settled, Annabel gave Aunt Rachel a long look.

'Why do you rock?' she asked slowly.

Aunt Rachel was trembling. She did not reply. In a voice soft as sliding water the gipsy continued.

'Lady dear, we are a strange folk to you, and even among us there are those who shuffle the pack of cards and read the palm when silver has been put upon it, knowing nothing . . . But some of us *see* – some of us *see*.'

It was more than a minute before Aunt Rachel spoke.

'You are a woman, and you have your babe at your breast now . . . Every woman sees the thing you speak of.'

But the gipsy shook her head. 'You speak of seeing with the heart. I speak of eyes – these eyes.'

Again came a long pause. Aunt Rachel had given a little start, but had become quiet again. When at last she spoke it was in a voice scarcely audible.

'That cannot be. I know what you mean, but it cannot be . . . He died on the eve of his wedding. For my bridal clothes they made me black garments instead. It is long ago, and now I wear neither black nor white, but – ' her hands made a gesture. Aunt Rachel always dressed as if to suit a sorrow that Time had deprived of bitterness, in such a tender and fleecy grey as one sees in the mists that lie like lawn over hedgerow and copse early of a midsummer's morning. 'Therefore,' she resumed, 'your heart may see, but your eyes cannot see that which never was.'

But there came a sudden note of masterfulness into the gipsy's voice.

'With my eyes – *these* eyes,' she repeated, pointing to them.

Aunt Rachel kept her own eyes obstinately on her knitting needles. 'None except I have seen it. It is not to be seen,' she said.

The gipsy sat suddenly erect.

'It is not so. Keep still in your chair,' she ordered, 'and I will tell you when – '

It was a curious thing that followed. As if all the will went out of her, Aunt Rachel sat very still; and presently her hands fluttered and dropped. The gipsy sat with her own hands folded over the mat on her knees. Several minutes passed; then, slowly, once more that sweetest of smiles stole over Aunt Rachel's cheeks. Once more her head dropped. Her hands moved. Noiselessly on the rockers that the gipsy had padded with felt the chair began to rock. Annabel lifted one hand.

'*Dovo se li*' she said. 'It is there.'

Aunt Rachel did not appear to hear her. With that ineffable smile still on her face, she rocked . . .

Then, after some minutes, there crossed her face such a look as visits the face of one who, waking from sleep, strains his faculties to recapture some blissful and vanishing vision . . .

'*Jal* – it is gone,' said the gipsy woman.

Aunt Rachel opened her eyes again. She repeated dully after Annabel: 'It is gone.'

'Ghosts,' the gipsy whispered presently, 'are of the dead. Therefore it must have lived.'

But again Aunt Rachel shook her head. 'It never lived.'

'You were young, and beautiful? . . . '

Still the shake of the head. 'He died on the eve of his wedding. They took my white garments away and gave me black ones. How then could it have lived?'

'Without the kiss, no . . . But sometimes a woman will lie through her life, and at the graveside still will lie . . . Tell me the truth.'

But they were the same words that Aunt Rachel repeated: 'He died on the eve of his wedding; they took away my wedding garments . . . ' From her lips a lie could hardly issue. The gipsy's face became grave . . .

She broke another long silence.

'I believe,' she said at last. 'It is a new kind – but no more wonderful than the other. The other I have seen, now I have seen this also. Tell me, does it come to any other chair?'

'It was his chair; he died in it,' said Aunt Rachel.

'And you – shall you die in it?'

'As God wills.'

'Has . . . *other life* . . . visited it long?'

'Many years; but it is always small; it never grows.'

'To their mothers babes never grow. They remain ever babes . . . None other has ever seen it?'

'Except yourself, none. I sit here; presently it creeps into my arms; it is small and warm; I rock, and then . . . it goes.'

'Would it come to another chair?'

'I cannot tell. I think not. It was his chair.'

Annabel mused. At the other end of the room Flora was now bestowed on Jack, the disreputable sailor. The gipsy's eyes rested on the bridal party . . .

'Yet another might see it – '

'None has.'

'No; but yet . . . The door does not always shut behind us suddenly. Perhaps one who has toddled but a step or two over the threshold might, by looking back, catch a glimpse . . . What is the name of the smallest one?'

'Angela.'

'That means "angel" . . . Look, the doll who died yesterday is now being married . . . It may be that Life has not yet sealed the little one's eyes. Will you let Annabel ask her if she sees what it is you hold in your arms?'

Again the voice was soft and wheedling . . .

'No, Annabel,' said Aunt Rachel faintly.

'Will you rock again?'

Aunt Rachel made no reply.

'Rock . . . ' urged the cajoling voice.

But Aunt Rachel only turned the betrothal ring on her finger. Over at the altar Jack was leering at his new-made bride, past decency; and little Angela held the wooden horse's head, which had parted from its body.

'Rock, and comfort yourself – ' tempted the voice.

Then slowly Aunt Rachel rose from her chair.

'No, Annabel,' she said gently. 'You should not have spoken. When the snow melts you will go, and come no more; why then did you speak? It was mine. It was not meant to be seen by another. I no longer want it. Please go.'

The swarthy woman turned her almond eyes on her once more.

'You cannot live without it,' she said as she also rose . . .

And as Jack and his bride left the church on the reheaded horse, Aunt Rachel walked with hanging head from the apartment.

3

Thenceforward, as day followed day, Aunt Rachel rocked no more; and with the packing and partial melting of the snow the gipsies up at the caravans judged it time to be off about their business. It was on the morning of Christmas Eve that they came down in a body to the Abbey Farm to express their thanks to those who had befriended them; but the bailiff was not there. He and the farm men had ceased work, and were down at the church, practising the carols. Only Aunt Rachel sat, still and knitting, in the black walnut chair; and the children played on the floor.

A night in the toy-box had apparently bred discontent between Jack and Flora – or perhaps they sought to keep their countenances before the world; at any rate, they sat on opposite sides of the room, Jack keeping boon company with the lead soldiers, his spouse reposing, her lead-balanced eyes closed, in the broken clockwork motor-car. With the air of performing some vaguely momentous ritual, the children were kissing one another beneath the bunch of mistletoe that hung from the centre beam. In the intervals of kissing they told one another in whispers that Aunt Rachel was not very well, and Angela woke Flora to tell her that Aunt Rachel had Brown Titus also.

'Stay you here; I will give the lady dear our thanks,' said Annabel to the group of gipsies gathered about the porch; and she entered the great hall-kitchen. She approached the chair in which Aunt Rachel sat.

There was obeisance in the bend of her body, but command in her long almond eyes, as she spoke.

'Lady dear, you must rock or you cannot live.'

Aunt Rachel did not look up from her work.

'Rocking, I should not live long,' she replied.

'We are leaving you.'

'All leave me.'

'Annabel fears she has taken away your comfort.'

'Only for a little while. The door closes behind us, but it opens again.'

'But for that little time, rock – '

Aunt Rachel shook her head.

'No. It is finished. Another has seen . . . Say goodbye to your companions; they are very welcome to what they have had; and God speed you.'

'They thank you, lady dear . . . Will you not forget that Annabel saw, and rock?'

'No more.'

Annabel stooped and kissed the hand that bore the betrothal hoop of pearls. The other hand Aunt Rachel placed for a moment upon the smoky head of the babe in the sling. It trembled as it rested there, but the tremor passed, and Annabel, turning once at the porch, gave her a last look. Then she departed with her companions.

That afternoon, Jack and Flora had shaken down to wedlock as married folk should, and sat together before the board spread with the dolls' tea-things. The pallid light in the great hall-kitchen faded; the candles were lighted; and then the children, first borrowing the stockings of their elders to hang at the bed's foot, were packed off early – for it was the custom to bring them down again at midnight for the carols. Aunt Rachel had their good-night kisses, not as she had them every night, but with the special ceremony of the mistletoe.

Other folk, grown folk, sat with Aunt Rachel that evening; but the old walnut chair did not move upon its rockers. There was merry talk, but Aunt Rachel took no part in it. The board was spread with ale and cheese and spiced loaf for the carol-singers; and the time drew near for their coming.

When at midnight, faintly on the air from the church below, there came the chiming of Christmas morning, all bestirred themselves.

'They'll be here in a few minutes,' they said; 'somebody go and bring the children down;' and within a very little while subdued noises were heard outside, and the lifting of the latch of the yard gate. The children were in their nightgowns, hardly fully awake; a low voice outside was heard giving orders; and then there arose on the night the carol.

'Hush!' they said to the wondering children; 'listen! . . . '

It was the Cherry Tree Carol that rose outside, of how sweet Mary, the Queen of Galilee, besought Joseph to pluck the cherries for her Babe, and Joseph refused; and the voices of the singers, that had begun hesitatingly, grew strong and loud and free.

' . . . and Joseph wouldn't pluck the cherries,' somebody was whispering to the tiny Angela . . .

> Mary said to Cherry Tree,
> 'Bow down to my knee,
> That I may pluck cherries
> For my Babe and me.'

the carollers sang; and 'Now listen, darling', the one who held Angela murmured . . .

The uppermost spray then
        Bowed down to her knee;
'Thus you may see, Joseph,
        These cherries are for me.'

'O, eat your cherries, Mary,
        Give them your Babe now;
O, eat your cherries, Mary,
        That grew upon the bough.'

The little Angela, within the arms that held her, murmured, 'It's the gipsies, isn't it, mother?'

'No, darling. The gipsies have gone. It's the carol-singers, singing because Jesus was born.'

'But, mother . . . it *is* the gipsies, isn't it? . . . 'Cos look . . . '

'Look where?'

'At Aunt Rachel, mother . . . The gipsy woman wouldn't go without her little baby, would she?'

'No, she wouldn't do that.'

'Then has she *lent* it to Aunt Rachel, like I lend my new toys sometimes?'

The mother glanced across at Aunt Rachel, and then gathered the night-gowned figure more closely.

'The darling's only half awake,' she murmured . . . 'Poor Aunt Rachel's sleepy too . . . '

Aunt Rachel, her head dropped, her hands lightly folded as if about some shape that none saw but herself, her face again ineffable with that sweet and peaceful smile, was once more rocking softly in her chair.

Dear Dryad

I

It all began so long ago that even the girl's name is forgotten; but you can still see her type as she moved up the steep oak-wood on that far-off April morning – dense milky skin, hair of raw Pictish red, and light and wary eyes under the whitey-gold glint of her brows. Today, as then, that skin freckles lightly over the bridge of the nose, but scarcely takes the sunburn; and, if a sleeve happens to come apart or a brooch to slip, no vein shows through that thick whiteness.

The brooch that fastened the girl's single woollen garment was of jet, and the garment's blue was neither quite that of the bluebells that dimmed the tangled glades, nor yet the springtime blue of the sky against which the oaks raised their crewelwork of colour. The wide sleeves fell almost to her knee, and the plaited hair that made red runnels down her growing breasts were tied at the tips with little laces of the same skin that covered her feet.

She was not aware that she had climbed up into the oak-wood that long-ago morning to worship. She did not know what worship was – or rather she did not know what it was not to worship. These things were not her concern, but that of those Wisers and Elders of her tribe, who, because it was their business to attend to them, neither drove the burnt-wood share through the earth nor hunted nor fought with the bronze-headed hammers and axes. These Elders themselves seemed to the girl to resemble ancient oaks, mysterious, reverend, apart, white with frost and hoary with the hue of mistletoe. Their lore was rooted in the years as the trees had their deep footing in the hills. She herself, by comparison with them, was no more than a bird that nested for a brief space in their boughs, a passing winged thing, nearly as quickly gone as the arrowy young bracken that thrust up its pale green shoots at her feet.

And yet she was conscious that morning of a knowledge that those ancient ones had not. They knew nothing of those tender preparations within herself, those first makings-ready, of which her mother had warned her. These it was that had brought her up into the high oak-wood.

And not all the oaks, but her own special, dedicated oak, had called her, as already in her short life it had called her twice before.

Naturally she remembered nothing whatever of the first time it had called her. Her mother had undertaken that service for her, carrying her, a tiny bundle rolled up in a cloak. When the cloak had been put aside, the brain within the little red knob had comprehended nothing, the little fixed eyes (darker then) had seen nothing, and the weakly-moving mite of a hand had continued to fumble for the nipple.

So, when she had been not more than a few days old, she had been passed with ceremony over the oak's bough, and had then been borne off in the cloak again.

But her second visit to the oak she remembered quite clearly. Once more her mother had accompanied her, helping her by the hand up the steep slopes, in and out, among the undergrowth that had stood as high as herself. It had been explained to her that this second visit was a Confirmation of the former occasion, and that henceforward she was to know for herself her own oak from other oaks, as her oak would know her from all other maids, and be specially hers. A dozen other maids she knew also had oaks, specially theirs. The world was a place full of hostile and inimical things, particularly (her mother said) for maids, and it was well to have so powerful a friend as an oak for one's protector and refuge and home.

The girl had a feeling that her mother ought to have been with her this morning also, but she no longer knew where her mother was. That was by no means an unusual thing. People, mothers included, did mysteriously come and go, seemed to be here one day and then never seen again. The men who carried the brighthandled weapons often went out and did not come back again, and the cattle, too, came and went. She hardly wondered what had become of her mother. That was the way things were, so what was the good of asking questions?

She knew from tradition the observances her oak required of her. She must give something to the tree, and she must take something from the tree, and if one took and gave something very near and close to either, that too was an excellent thing. One was then (the Wisers and Elders said) part of the tree, as the tree was part of one's self. And, though one died or were carried off, to the tree one would always return.

So, a long time ago, with the sunlight coming and going on the Pictish hair as she climbed, she moved in search of her oak.

She found it in the middle of its own little glade, among thorn and dark holly and the foolish birch that nobody worshipped. It was young and slender, like herself, but, young as it was, already a slip of ivy had grown up since her last visit and had wound itself round its trunk. That must be seen to at once. Oaks must be served if they were to serve you in return,

She did not intend to offer the oak her first blood. Long ago as all this was, it was not so long ago as all that. In those older days still the tree had had to be gashed, and so that it might understand that a friend of flesh was there and not only an enemy of bronze or stone, certain words that the girl did not know had had to be spoken. Now, the gift of a shoestring or a garment or some small possession sufficed. Walking among the oaks you frequently saw these gifts hanging from the branches, and they were never removed or disturbed. Everything else in life might change – mothers be seen no more, the men go out with the bright-handled weapons and never return, the cattle be driven off and the stockaded patch be possessed by strange folk – but the oaks and the offerings always remained.

The girl sat down under the tree and began to loosen the laces that tipped her plaits of hair. The glowing strands fell apart, and a toss of her head brought them all about her like a bush of burning sumach. Another toss flung the bush back again, showing the whole of the round white brow, and then her fingers began to seize wisp after wisp and to prick them violently out. Her brow was drawn with pain and her mouth was awry, but presently she had garnered a small hank. One end of this she took between her teeth, and her fingers moved as she wove a plait. All this time she was unaware that a pair of bright eyes watched her from across the glade. They were the eyes of a dark young man clad in skins. With one hand he put aside the hazels in order to watch the girl, and in the other was the smooth stone he used as a club.

Then, her gift for the oak ready, came the oak's gift to her. She rose, and inserted her fingers round the stem of ivy that was trying to throttle the tree. The branches rustled and waked, a couple of birds flew away, but the stem parted, and the ivy-leaves came down in a glossy shower about her head and shoulders.

Sitting down again, she took a length of the ivy-stem and began to unravel it; for the stem of ivy, as you know, is made up of a close-spiralled twisting of narrow ribbons. These made a loose heap about her, as the shavings curl from the mouth of a carpenter's plane. These also she chose and plaited. Then, her garters made, she drew up her blue garment and fastened them about the swathings that crossed her legs.

Nothing had grown closer to the oak than the ivy, and nothing was received nearer to herself. The end of the garters secured, she drew down her dress again and rose. As she reached upwards with the braid of her own red hair in her hand, suddenly, magnificently, the wide sleeve of blue fell clear away from her arm. She reached, as it were, to the oak's strong shoulder that veinless milk-white bough of herself. She fastened to the tree that twist plucked living from her own head.

Then it was that the young man, who had advanced stealthily half-way across the glade, with a rush was upon her; and at the same moment, from away across the valley at the wood's bottom, there floated a sudden light, uproar and clamour.

She uttered no scream. In that moment of rush and shock it came swiftly upon her what had happened. As that faint harsh clamour from below reached her ears she knew all at once what had become of her mother. An old recollection re-possessed her, of women and children hurriedly rushed with the cattle into the stockade, of men hastily catching up those shiny-handled weapons, and then of a hideous tumult of running and shouting and blows. She seemed again to be fearfully peeping through a chink in the stockade, to see the men of her own tribe forced back, and then a darkness as her mother, rushing to her, had caught her up in a garment. Then a rough scuffle and nothing more – nothing but that final glimpse, of the marauders pouring away over the shoulder of the hill again, driving the cattle before them, fire and smoke all about her, and, dimly through it all, the wild screaming creature flung over a man's shoulder, who had cried out for her babe in vain.

Yes, that (she realised now) was what had happened to her mother.

She could only pant in the young man's close embrace and look up into his sparkling eyes. Because he was causing her pain there was hatred in her look, and she bared her teeth for a moment as he raised his stone in menace. But the gleam died down as the stone did not descend. The wary eyes, pale as silver through her dishevelled mane of red, continued to move from his fierce eyes to the stone and back again.

But not for a moment did she upbraid her oak that it had betrayed her. How should she be betrayed, when this was the way things were? Had they not always been so? Had not her own sire borne off her mother in exactly the same way, and kept her until a stronger had taken her away from him? True, there had been a difference. The girl knew there was a difference, though she could not have explained what it was. Her father had taken his *lodas goch*, his red woman, to be his comfort, to share his meat by day and his litter by night. He had fished and hunted and built for her, and had never beaten her except when she had displeased him. But not so his conqueror. He had carried away a mere toiling-thing, a weaver of the blue cloth, a follower of the wood-yoked oxen, a tender of the little corn-patch. But the girl supposed that that, too, was the way of things. No doubt in time to come it would be her own lot too. It was no good asking of her oak more than her oak could give. Should not oaks, that lived so long in the world, know the way of the world?

So, perhaps, things were not so very much amiss after all – unless this young man should raise the stone again –

She gazed at the stone where it lay in his hand.

A stone! Had he no better weapon than a stone?

He had twisted one hand through the glowing hair and had turned her head down the wood. She turned once to look again at her oak, and his glance followed hers. He saw her offering tied to the bough, and his eyes approved. It was right that she should pay her service in her season. It was a good *lodas goch*, of a whiteness that he liked, and strong and excellently grown. Also within that blue sleeve was the long arm with the hint of russet beneath it to put round him by and by. A very good *lodas goch* indeed, and very well met.

So he drove her down the wood, and at the bottom of it they came to a gap. From the gap she saw it to be as she had already known it would be – fire and smoke from the stockade and the women and cattle being driven away over the shoulder of the hill. Here and there a small skin-clad figure lay stretched out motionless on the hillside, but she knew that no weapons remained with them. Weapons were great riches, greater even than the red cattle and the red women, since with weapons a man could be sure of all the rest. Again she glanced covertly at the stone in the young man's hand. For his own sake and for hers he ought to have a better weapon than that. Other maids might jeer at her, that her man should be armed only with a stone! She knew where an axe was hidden away in a secret place. All would depend on how he used her –

And, provided he did not menace her with the stone again – provided he fed and guarded her properly and pleased her in other ways – well, she might by and by show him where the axe was.

2

The important thing about the oak was that thenceforward it possessed something it had not possessed before. Not the twist of red
Pictish hair – thread by thread the birds stole that to weave into their
nests. Not relief from the strangling ivy – that grew bushy and thick
again as the oak put on the years that packed its heart-wood ever
closer. But something else, some dedication, some bespeaking, some
far-off echo of worship, lingered thereafter hauntingly about its
boughs. It waited, grew great, yet kept as it were a secret as if it
attended some sign peculiarly its own. Away over on the hillside there
rose, not a rude stockade, but a great castle of staring new stone, with
grim machicolations and a drawbridge and a ponderous portcullis.
Steel-capped men-at-arms, men with bows and pikes, tramped where
the men with the polished axes had fought, and the clink of the
armourer's hammers was for ever sounding within its courtyards.

For men still fought for their possessions, and made war for the
possessions of others.

Only, if they would possess a lady, they now went about the
business after a different fashion, as you may read.

Up that part of the hillside where the oaks had been felled to
provide beams for the castle, there moved on an early morning a tall
youth of seventeen. He was of a gay and open countenance and an
exercised carriage, and the things that youth sees still lingered in his
musing blue eyes. His hands were large and brown and strong, and
the throat that carried his small head was supple as a limb. His jacket
and hose were of grass-green silk; at his girdle he wore a pouch and
anlace, and in his hand he carried a paper with writing upon it. He
glanced at this paper from time to time as he walked. But at any
movement from unseen bird or beast he readily forgot the paper.

He had slept little that night, because of thinking upon horses and
armour and courtesy and love; but who or what it was he was in love
with he would have been hard put to it to tell you. True, he would
have answered promptly enough that all his love was for the lady
whose glove had lain all night under his pillow. And perhaps after all,
'love' is not the word. What is the word when a youth lies so,
enriching the soft curtain of the darkness with his fancies as the
ladies of the castle wrought their tapestries, with scenes of jousts
and huntings and fabulous beasts and magical flowers? What is the
enchanted word, when the glove under the pillow is not so much one
lady's glove as all the gloves of all the ladies in the world? And what is

it when you write your verse to the Spirit of Beauty itself, but think you mean La Beale Alys?

La Beale Alys, who was not quite old enough to be this young squire's mother, knew only too well what that wonderful word was. It was the word 'Seventeen'.

For it was but natural that his first lady should be a mature lady, the wife of a grown and proved knight, and merry, half-mothering lady, and his own mother's friend.

There was promise of a hot day, but the sun was still far from its height. Dazzlingly it flashed along the dewy glades, glittered on leaves as if the whole wood had been set with lark-traps. The spell of his verse-making was still upon the stripling, and his lids were a little lowered against the brightness.

Perhaps that was why he remained unaware that La Beale Alys also was abroad, watching him, but taking care to keep within the edge of the clearing lower down the hill.

She was a fresh and comely and bouncing lady, but red and black, red as a rose and black as a raven's wing. There was still time and to spare before one need ask whether she would have been less comely had she been less carefully attired. A mesh of gold twist, with a red stone at each knot, confined her ebon hair. Black too were her brows, with a gold fillet uniting the twin cauls across them. Numerous tiny golden buttons fastened her tight sleeves of russet velvet from knuckle to elbow, and her full robe was gathered up out of the drench of dew, showing little red stones on her slender feet also. She lurked out of sight of the green-clad figure ahead, as if after all she had a mind to turn back.

The straight green back disappeared, and she quickened her steps, making a detour.

The verses in the youth's hand were those he had made during the night, repeating them over and over again, and then rising to write them down by the light of the paling dawn. As he walked he sang them softly to himself, fitting notes to the words as the harper at the castle had taught him. He would have vowed they were about La Beale Alys and about nobody and nothing else. Here, jargon of armour and all, and altered only a little, is the rhyme he had made –

> What need you other harness than your own
>> When cap-à-pie your Beauty is your gear?
> Your whiteness self is all your habergeon,
>> Your helm the basnet of your sable hair,
>> Vambrace your snowy arm, bosom your mam'lière

So do I feign you built in Steadfastness,
　　Castled in Truth and in all Virtue towered,
That lo, I keep for very joyfulness
　　Ardent my vigil, as by you empowered
　　To guard that gentle gear while as you lie embowered!

It cannot be but on some time agone,
　　Whiles I ne saw no face, a faery arm
Rose in a woodland or a fountain lone,
　　Bearing a chrism-white brand whereof the charm,
　　'Use me for ladies all, but keep her most from harm',

Her and our Very Lord, whose blessèd Grail
　　Joseph in duty brought –

Suddenly his song died on his lips. Beyond the wide-spreading oak
under which he stood, he saw La Beale Alys herself approaching.
　　The eyes under the dark brows were modestly downcast, yet it
could hardly be that she had not heard his song. He wondered that
she should appear not to have done so, as also that she should be thus
early abroad and unattended. He could not guess that she had slept
no more than he. Had he guessed it he would have concluded that
she was restless because Sir Sandys, her husband, was away.
　　Then she raised her dark-fringed eyes, and he advanced and bade
her good-morrow, bending diligently over the dimpled knuckles that
issued from the gold-buttoned sleeve. He asked her whether her rest
had been good. In her reply she gave him a name that was not his, but
one of the hundred names her fancy had for him.
　　'Neither good nor ill, since I have not rested, Pleindamour,' she
answered. And with suddenly averted face, she added, 'But you know
not the meaning of that.'
　　He protested. Was he not, by her husband's leave, body and soul at
her command?
　　'Nay, madam, but I do. It were untrue to say that I have not closed
my eyes, but slept I have not.'
　　'No? Then of what were the thoughts that kept you awake?' she
asked him.
　　'Of you, as ever,' was his prompt reply, and he went straight on to
enquire when her husband, Sir Sandys, was due to return.
　　'Sir Sandys!' she replied, with a dropping of her lids again.
　　For La Beale Alys was a little out of suits with the grave and
preoccupied knight who was her husband. A proper enough knight

of his body he was, and of a good head withal, since in his charge were all the engines for the defence of the castle; and as for the good man's worship of herself, she had little fault to find with that either, except that he worshipped somewhat frequently at a distance, when he went forth to buy his pitch and hides and oil and other provender. When he did return, he was for ever exercising his men-at-arms at their stations, or overhauling his catapults and fenders, or giving directions to his builders for the repair of this or that, or poking his nose into masses of clammy mortar, or melting something perchance, or greasing something else, or poring over plans that the artificers had thumbed, or – but La Beale Alys could have talked a whole summer's day about Sir Sandys and his occupations and then not have finished. The good knight had been like that these seven years.

'What song was that you were singing even now?' she suddenly asked him, thus informing him that she had heard his song.

He turned his head quickly as something rustled in a thicket. Then, turning his eyes back to her, he told her that it was a song he had made in her honour.

'Mine?' She gave a little laugh, and her hands made a slight move-ment towards the jet-black hair in its gold tiring. 'What ails your eyes that you should see me thus, Pleindamour? Already I am old!'

He vowed (but his glance was on the thicket again) that nothing ailed his eyes – not one of his hawks saw more keenly than did this same love of his. Her answer was to tease herself and him.

'But this brow is lined! This hair, what know you of the grey that is hidden in it ? A steel cap, pardie! – '

It was only a squirrel in the thicket after all . . . As he turned to her again he would not have it either that brow was wrinkled or her hair grey. Neither in truth were they, for all it pleased her to say so, and this time her look at him went farther than her words.

'My whiteness my harness! And what know *you* of my whiteness? It is tidings to me that I am safest in my smock! By my reasoning a heavier habergeon were not amiss! And I like not much this brick-layer's work of steadfastness. That is a trowelful of Sir Sandys' mortar indeed! We shall be greasing the portcullis chains anon! Castled! Towered! . . . Come, let us have this fortification again, since it is thus you see me – '

She was merry enough, this early-rising lady who counted her grey hairs before they came; but it was a little in despite both of herself and him. She intended no harm (more than a very little), yet she could not leave it alone. It was much on her mind that men, and not women, had invented this stuff of the stone-yard and the armourer's shop that they made their verses of. For herself, she accounted a little mirth in due season as more to the purpose. The day would come when this *damoiseau* would so account it too. He, too, would learn that ladies were made of quite other material. At present he knew as much about them as he knew about unicorns, and it was in order that he might know a little more that she sent him so constantly on boot-less errands, and watched his face when she called him Pleindamour or some other soft name, and secretly thought his verses naught but his running and leaping and catching of horses a great deal.

And it was in order that he might know anything else he wished that she had dropped her glove one day as she had gone into her bower, and had been careful not to look back.

'Many an one in your place – ' she began in a low, tremulous voice.

'Madam?' he asked.

' – would sing again,' she ended unexpectedly, on a laugh that he did not understand.

He did not understand, and neither did he know how already she was busying herself as he began his song over again. Her lips were pursed . . . Her whiteness her gear? He had written truer than he knew! He must needs take the habergeon on trust, yet she could give him some guerdon of it –

With her hands hidden in the ivy that mantled the oak, she was busily stripping away the score of little buttons that fastened the tight-fitting velvet sleeve.

> It cannot be but on some time agone,
>   Whiles I ne saw no face, a faery arm
> Rose in a woodland or a fountain lone,
>   Bearing a chrism-white brand whereof the charm,
>   'Use me for ladies all, but keep her most from harm.'

Suddenly his song ceased under her darkling gaze. He wondered whether she was ailing that she should look so. Her voice was smothered, passionate.

'Yes, I have whiteness for a season or two longer – then all will be too white! And a song about my whiteness contents you! You make a song for my ears when I go hungry! You speak of brassarts and vambraces – ' she broke out. 'Would you know how white? And how white the rest? Look – be you and this oak my witness!'

And somewhat to his surprise, for indeed he thought her ailing, she stripped away the velvet sleeve, showing an arm still as young as any.

You meant mischief, La Beale Alys. You planned this last night in your chamber as you tossed – nay, weeks ago, when you dropped that glove. But you waste your trouble when you call that oak to witness. That is no dark lady's oak, has no help for such as wear raven's-feathers for brows. You never gave it a single hair of your head, nor accepted from it a garter to bind your knee. No vows passed between you and it; that did not change when your race supplanted the red. Therefore seek another oak, La Beale Alys. Every rustling branch of this one, every tingling root, was married to another ages before you were born.

Nor shall it avail you that he praises your arm as in duty bound, nor that he kisses its finger-tips, so that for a moment his hair lies warm upon it. You are in different woods, you and he. Your wood is the everyday wood you see from the castle-walls, the wood that provides timber for joists and food for swine; but his is Brocehaunde. You may see it now if you care to look into his wide and wondering eyes –

For a light breeze stirs in the oak, and he listens and slowly smiles, as if returning some soft and musical echo of laughter within its boughs. Already you are fastening up those little golden buttons again, but he gazes at the place where your arm lately was, as if its image were still there. Across the glade something moves in the bushes; there is a soft scampering across the clearing . . .

All that your eyes are aware of is a hart, startled to find that it is not alone in the wood.

And the oak sees to it that even your verses (if ever they were yours) are taken from you; for suddenly the young man stoops and picks up a twig. With his anlace he shapes and points it.

Then, notching the oak's rough bark, in the place where once a twist of red-gold hair hung, he pins his paper to the bough.

3

After that the oak grew to be so old that, merely because it had lived so long, nobody would have thought of cutting it down. Instead, with wooden props, they shored up two of its arms, so that it resembled Moses when he would see the battle to the end. And still that some-thing, that early thing, that was neither a wisp of hair nor the verses of a dreaming boy, persisted mysteriously about it. On the hillside there now stood a gabled house, built of the stones of the old castle. Of the castle itself only a few butts of old masonry remained, with grasses seeded in the chinks and wild flowers in the crannies.

Then one day, not very long ago, the oak fell. A December tempest brought it down, and it lay there among the broken upstart saplings, epic in its ruin, hollow as an old skull, grey with lichen and the wintry rime, bearded like a Druid with the pale mistletoe, its ancient arms tossed up in agony to the skies.

On the morning of a Christmas Eve a young man and a young woman stood together beside the dying tree. They had come up into the wood to gather holly and mistletoe for the decoration of the gabled house – that is to say, the young woman had come for that purpose. The young man was there because she was there, and he rather thought that had she come on the morning of Christmas Eve for mushrooms or plover's-eggs he would have been there just the same.

But whether or not he wanted to marry the girl he could not for the life of him have told.

Her name was Bronwen, which, in the country that had cradled her and her foebears, means 'white breast'; and the hair that showed under her knitted cap of white wool was a splendour of raw red gold. A few strands of it stirred about the white muffler she had carelessly cast about her throat, and the brows above her pale eyes were of whitey-gold. She wore a jazz blouse of little red and white flames with freakings of black in between, and the boots under her short tweed skirt were laced high, and were the same boots in which she had driven a three-ton W. D. Berna lorry.

And she would have married him any hour of the day he had asked her.

If one could judge by his few mumbled words, the young man appeared to be wondering how the fallen tree was to be disposed of. But his eyes were as often on the girl as on the tree. They were quiet, rather anxious grey eyes, as if he really did not know what to do for the best. He wore an old tweed shooting-jacket, so old that it had had to be reinforced with leather at the wrists; but his breeches and puttees and the collar at his neck were of khaki, and he tapped his thick-rubber-clumped boots with his cane from time to time.

'Wouldn't be easy to get at it with a crosscut,' he muttered. 'And it's hardly worth burning, anyway. Drill it and stick a primer or two in – '

The girl scarcely heard him, for her thoughts were quite other-where. She had known the oak all her life. It had been her mother's favourite sitting-place, and, when it had grown insecure, it had been at her mother's request that the props had been placed under its failing limbs. Bronwen remembered her mother quite well; she even remembered rolling, as a mere baby, on the shabby old manoeuvre-rug that had been spread under the oak. Later, when she had begun to read her fairy-books, she had crept into the tree's cavernous hollow, and had pretended to herself that she lived there and was a dryad. She had always felt that she had some special understanding of what a dryad was. Where she had this conviction from she could not have told.

And now the tree was as good as dead. Too bad that trees had to die like that! Why, they said it was more than a thousand years old! A thousand years! All sorts of dead-and-gone people must have sat under it, and met their best boys there, and quarrelled and kissed and had the time of their lives under its poor old boughs! Really she couldn't help feeling a bit mopey about it. It had been such a pal of an oak. And now it had gone west.

As the driver of a three-ton lorry she would have kept her mouth shut about the oak. As the owner of that hair and of the ancient name that meant 'white breast' she still held her tongue about it. But for all that she had a feeling that she was losing part of herself.

'Anyway your father won't let it lie here,' the young man's voice came as if from a distance. 'Breeds more pests than all the others put together – '

Because his talk of pests and crosscuts and primers jarred on her a little, abruptly she bestirred herself.

'Well, let's do something. The car'll be round to take us to the Proberts' at three, and half the decorations ought to be up by then. You've got the thickest gloves. Will you get the holly if I'll get the mistletoe?'

She cast aside her throat-wrap, scrambled up on to the giant trunk, and began to make her way towards one hoary limb.

The young man watched her. He was still unable to decide what was the best course for her, the best course for him. Girls were the devil of a problem nowadays. Sometimes they scared him half out of his wits with their new crude logic, or what they called their logic. He didn't know that he called it logic at all. Much of it sounded to him like a pert and unfounded *tu quoque*, as if a man's meat were never by any chance a woman's poison. But it came to much the same thing in the end whatever you called it, and he wasn't sure it was good enough to risk marriage on. Not that Bronnie was one of the worst specimens, of course; there were times when he found her quite reasonable. He didn't suppose she would take it as a sex-challenge if he ventured to ask her whether she would mind being married in a church. She might not object to the word 'obey' or to a wedding-ring. But for all that she sometimes had extraordinarily decided views on things. Picked 'em up in the Waacs, he expected. He hadn't wanted her to go into the Waacs. He would have preferred to keep women and war entirely apart. It might have helped the country, but he couldn't see that it had done the girls themselves much good. It had unsettled them, put half-baked ideas into their heads, till they knew what they didn't want, but hadn't much idea of what they did want. And he liked to look up to his women-folk – you know – to keep them a bit apart. What did they want anyway – to be dragged away by the hair, or knocked over the head with a stone?

But he shook off his thoughts. Whatever else she was she made a perfectly topping picture as she stood up there, hanging on to the oak.

Well might he admire. She stood in a forked crutch some seven or eight feet from the ground, and the wintry sun made of the dark ivy and the rimy boughs, the jazz-bloused girl and the myriad intricate shadows of limb on limb, a miraculous dapple of pale colour. By Jove, if he could only have been an artist and painted that! But no artist could have got that burning gold of her hair against the thick creamy white of her nape. Whether he ever married her or not, he would always see her like that – all in the picture, so to speak, perched up in the oak as if she was part of it, for all the world as if she lived there. That was something to have seen anyway . . .

And, having seen it, he turned away in search of holly.

But he had not taken a dozen steps before he heard the sound of a breaking branch, and a thud and a short stifled cry. In an instant he was at her side again.

'What's the matter, Bronnie? . . . Oh, Lord! Are you hurt?'

His eyes went upwards to the branch from which she had slipped. She hardly seemed to know whether she was hurt or not, she trembled so, and he was unaware that for the moment he had her almost in his arms. His hand, supporting her, encountered something cool and soft and firm.

It was her arm, naked from finger nails to shoulder.

On the arm itself there was not a scratch, but the whole of the jazz sleeve fluttered from the bough overhead, ripped clean out from the shoulder as she had sought to save herself.

And suddenly he knew what to do now, as he held her a little way from him and drew a deep breath. He stared at the lovely white thing that clung to his shoulder. Bronwen, his *lodas goch*! He had never dreamed of such loveliness There could hardly be another arm like it in the world, unless it were its fellow, to put round him! Doubts? Questions? Woman old and woman new? A man can but venture – it was always so –

The next moment she was at arm's length no longer, but crushed, that lovely whiteness and all, against his breast.

'Bronnie!' he cried, laughing, and looked into her eyes.

What was the look he saw there? What made it seem so old, though seen by him for the first time? For she seemed both aware of his nearness and yet unutterably far away. Readiness and yielding were in those silvery eyes, but there was something else also. Was it fear lest, having got her, he should not always be able to keep her? Was it a still deeper need, a need of something more even than he could give, some nearer fellowship, worship, identity?

And why did her eyes go upwards so to the torn sleeve fluttering from the bough overhead?

The look only lasted for a moment. Then he was covering the arm with kisses, as much of it as he could reach without letting her go. And she was lifting eyes to him in which were now neither fear nor any other need, but only the readiness.

'If you like, Pearce,' she said.

'But I say, you'll catch cold,' he said by and by. 'I'll get it down and you can fix it up with a pin.'

But she answered rather quickly. 'No, no – leave it there.'

'But it's only the seam that's gone.'

'No, no. Leave it. And I'll get just one sprig of mistletoe. We'll get the rest somewhere else.'

She swathed the white arm in the less-white muffler, and placed in her bosom a bit of mistletoe she had brought down in her fall.

Naturally she had no idea the same thing had ever been done before.

The Real People

I

Just because Aubrey Kneller came to grief there, the little street shall not be given its real name. We will call it Fountney Place. It is in the London Postal District s.w.1, and Harrods' and the Oratory are near its upper end. At the other end a glimpse of pale Belgravia stucco closes its short perspective of hardly more than a couple of hundred yards. No great volume of traffic passes along it; in fact it has that air some women have, whom one does not know, would just a little like to know, yet somehow never takes the trouble to be better acquainted with. Aubrey Kneller had never set foot in it until that May afternoon. Then he yielded to its lure and entered it, noting its shy Hogarth frontages, its bright but modest sunblinds, and the windows of its *couturières* and florists and antique dealers and makers of glossy and expensive boots.

Until that afternoon or thereabouts, Aubrey had not been the kind of man to spy out secrets, of streets or anything else. He had always kept, as one might say, to the Brompton Road of life, well content with its plate-glass frontages and elaborated window-displays. He knew his business, which in a sense was plate-glass too – the writing of books that people wanted and were willing to pay for, and not of those they didn't want and would not have had given. He had the air of a fortunate and well-paid man – faultless suit of navy blue, gold-mounted stick and yellow gloves, and new light-grey Homburg hat. And it was his fate that he wandered into that coy little street instead of sticking to the Brompton Road.

He was vaguely conscious that for some months past he had not been altogether himself. The trouble, if trouble there was, seemed to be about his latest book, *Delia Vane*. There was no doubt that, in one way and another, it had led him the devil of a dance. Even now that it was finished, sealed, registered and handed over the Post Office counter hardly an hour before, he was somehow not rid of it. It still echoed. He half wished he had the manuscript back. A telephone-call to his publishers would bring it back. He couldn't make up his mind about it. It was a risk, in that it was a marked break-away from his former manner. In some way that he could not explain, the thing itself had taken charge, and Aubrey was very uneasy in his mind about it.

For, originally, *Delia Vane* was not to have been the title of his book at all. It was not even to have been about anybody called Delia Vane, nor to have had a character of that name in it. Merely, at an early stage of his work, he had felt the need of some nondescript minor personage, the needy-governess kind, meek, self-effacing, the loving-but-not-loved sort and so forth, to be used as he wanted and shoved into the background again when he had finished with her. And note that it is necessary to speak of this purely imaginary character in Aubrey's book as if in some sort she had had a real and corporal existence.

Precisely such a character, then, had stepped forward from wherever it is that these figments do come from, and had humbly applied, as it were, for the situation. And Aubrey, judging that she would suit very well, had hardly given her a second glance. Out of the ragbag of his mind he had tossed her a skimpy little frock, a pair of thread stockings and resoled shoes. Not for a moment had he dreamed that she would not be as good as gold.

But mark what had followed. One afternoon Aubrey had put aside his work, well content with it, happy to think that it was running on the same smooth lines as the eight or ten books that had preceded it. And he had taken it up again the next morning to find that this foundling, this poor relation, this waif who ought to have thought herself lucky to be in a book at all, had so far forgotten her station in life as to set her cap at his principal male character.

Naturally such a thing was not to be thought of for a moment. In that illimitable little world of a few inches wide that separates an author from the paper he writes on there had been something like a scene. Aubrey was a kindhearted man, reluctant to hurt the feelings even of a puppet in a printed book, but this was rank insubordination, calling for firm action. Later he regretted that he had not been still firmer, even at the expense of some kindness. As it was, he had had her up on the magic carpet, next his blotting-pad, had pointed out her offence to her, and had left the rest to her proper feeling. A tear, as one might say, had trembled on her lashes – the length and curve of which, by the way, he had not hitherto noticed. She had hung her head in contrition. Then, the lecture over, she had vanished whence she had come. The creator must be master of his creatures.

But barely a week afterwards he had had to rap her over the knuckles once more. Again we must suppose that we are watching something that happened in that mysterious little realm that lies between an author and his desk. The following dialogue had, to all intents and purposes, taken place between Aubrey Kneller and this little starveling who ought to have been washing down somebody's front steps.

'But it's so dull there!'

'Dull where?'

'Where we all are till you think of us.'

'I can't help that. It's your proper place. Suppose I hadn't thought of you at all?'

'I shouldn't have minded that so much. I hadn't been out then. I didn't know anything else.'

'Well, I don't want to be hard on you, but you must do as you're told or else get somebody else to think of you,' Aubrey had informed her.

'If I'm not to have any fun why didn't you let me alone?' she had sulked.

'Now that's quite enough. Off you go. I'm busy.'

And off she had trotted, with downhung but mutinous head. When next she had popped up the scene had been almost painful.

'But I want to!' she had flung at him.

'Well, you're not going to, and there's an end of it.'

'Who says?'

'Annie – ' this is solemn warning from Aubrey, ' – now you be a good girl!'

'What's the good of being good if you don't get anything for it?'

'You must be good because it's the proper thing to be. Understand that Pat's far above you in station, and he's going to marry Rosamond. That's what my readers expect, and it's what they're going to have.'

'Rosamond!' (One would have said real contempt, real disdain.) 'She's only a showroom dummy! And you've given her every decent thing there is to wear in the book! That's all she is – clothes and a lot of words by you! You ask Pat!'

'Pat! Do you mean Sir Patrick Archdale?' Aubrey had demanded.

'Yes, if you're going to be pompous about it!'

'Now look here, Annie – '

'I don't think I like that name very much,' she had remarked coolly. 'I shall think of another one.' And then, with sudden coaxing, for when all was said it was in his power to forbid her the book altogether, 'Please, Mr Kneller! Just a tiny little!'

'I've told you no.'

'Then – ' here had come a gleam of temper swift as the flash of a blade, ' – then I shall do just whatever I like and I shan't tell you anything about it! So send me back, there! I'd rather be there than in that mouldy crowd you've written!'

You see the kind of thing that was running in Aubrey Kneller's mind as he strolled along Pountney Place, unaware that anything in particular was lying in wait for him.

2

His eyes rested on a little antique shop with a single Sheraton chair in the window, its price-ticket carefully hidden. Then they fell on a similar window, with nothing in it but a cabinet with a blue jar on the top. And again he was conscious of the prim, quakerish aspect of the whole street. Its shops, small and expensive, were really old Georgian houses, put to their present purpose with hardly any attempt at conversion at all. They had fanlights and rod-bellpulls and old knockers, domestic for all their double life. The Sheraton chair, although for sale, hardly ceased to be part of the furniture of the room within, and the cabinet with the blue jar had only turned its back on the interior for a moment, and would turn round again when it discovered that there was nobody in the street to look at but Aubrey Kneller.

And Aubrey was restless, and in two minds whether he would not telephone for that manuscript back after all.

For he lived in an expensive flat in King Street, St James's, and was fond of such things as first editions, watercolours by Cox, and intaglios in exquisite little nests of trays. He liked his stall at first nights, the quietude of his club, and his luncheons *chez* Bellomo or Jules. And these things run into a certain amount of money. He wanted rather to increase his income than to check the source of it, and he could only increase it by diligent tillage of that Tom Tiddler's Ground, the few inches of space between him and his writing table in which everything in his books happened. If all went well there, money flowed. If anything went amiss it did not flow. In the event of things going very badly indeed, the news would quickly spread that he had lost touch and exhausted his freshness. There were twenty eager young rivals straining every nerve to take his place. Well-to-do as he was, he merely lived on his wits, and must take care to keep them bright and in good running order.

And now a chance-found little nobody whose insignificance appeared in her very name – Annie Thompson – had seriously interfered with his style.

For she had been as good as her word. She had begun to act precisely as she pleased, without consulting him at all. Meek, self-effacing and unloved, she? By no means! He had long since begun to go in dread of her. And at first, fearing that he had been sticking at it too closely, he had tried a change of air. He had gone into the country for a few days, and had almost succeeded in putting her out of his mind, where she ought never to have been at all.

But God only knew what had happened during those few days' absence. How, indeed, could anything happen to his book, and him away? Yet there it was. Whether this upstart wanted Pat for his own sake, or to come between him and Rosamond, or merely to be evens with Aubrey Kneller, maker of all three of them, made not an atom of difference in the result. Simply, behind Aubrey's back, she had dug herself in past dislodging, and Rosamond, with a noble gesture, had stalked clean out of the book. Vain to ask where she had gone. Perhaps she had never really been there. Perhaps she had merely been something Aubrey had thought of a long time ago and had gone on copying ever since because people paid him to do so. It was not even in his power to call his heroine back. That would have been to knock his book on the head once for all. Annie Thompson reigned supreme; and for the unusual reason that she was the only real person it had ever entered his head to describe.

Perhaps you begin to see the grief to which Aubrey Kneller came that afternoon in Pountney Place.

The rest had followed very quickly.

'I've been thinking it over about my name,' Annie Thompson announced one day, her voice thrilling through that mystical little world in which she ruled. 'I've chosen Delia. Delia Vane. You're to call me that. And of course when I marry Pat, I shall be Lady Archdale.'

'Oh,' was all that the unhappy Aubrey had been able to say.

'And you'd better make a note of the book's title too. Aubrey, my dear. That's to be *Delia Vane* too, after me.'

And since she decreed it, so it had come to pass.

One more of these author-and-character colloquies and we can be getting on. The question of Miss Vane's clothes had arisen.

'But there are plenty of clothes in the book,' the wretched Aubrey had demurred. 'There are all Rosamond's.'

'Rosamond's!' the answer had come back with a little explosion of laughter. 'Do you mean those Jaegers? Do you think I'd be found dead in those? Now don't you bother about making me too pretty, Aubrey. I can do without the peaches-and-cream. But clothes I *must* have. You give me clothes and leave the rest to me. I've pinched one or two things as a matter of fact – on credit, sort-of – look – '

And with one finger she had fished up from her bosom about an inch of some black, cobwebby stuff or other – a black lace chemise.

'I won it,' she had purred. 'Do you like it?'

'I never gave Rosamond that!' the startled Aubrey had cried. 'She'd have blushed to wear such a thing!'

'Course. I tell you I won it. Some blusher, Rosamond; she nearly blushed me out of my book – jam-angel!'

'But look here, Delia,' Aubrey had miserably expostulated. 'What about my public? Don't you see that's the way to get us banned?'

'What's banned?'

'Not stocked at the libraries. What's going to happen to us then?'

When it came to a point of that sort Delia always knew on which side her bread was buttered. She had drawn as it were closer, snuggling up to Aubrey with an affectionate look.

'What a shame to tease the nice old thing!' she had cooed. 'Do you know, Aubrey, I think it's so clever of you to have written Pat and me! I can't think how you do it! How do you think of it all? Is it just genius? Where do you get the ideas? Do they just come? . . . And I will be good. I promise. I'll be as good as Rosamond. And you will get me oodles of readers, won't you – Aubrey – dear?'

But the most curious thing of all was that, even now, with his book finished, Aubrey was never quite sure of the personal appearance of this creature who, from being nobody at all, had ended by thrusting everybody but Pat and herself clean off the stage. Of her caprices, impulses, ingrained selfishness, he was overwhelmingly sure; but of her exterior manifestation – no. Only her voice he sometimes almost heard, fickle and soft. For the rest, she might have been fair or dark, tall or small, blue-eyed or speckled or brown. Her features were composite, picked up here and there, in streets or tubes or restaurants. Often he lingered at shop-windows, in search of clothes that seemed appropriate to his creation.

And suddenly something that looked rather like Delia's style caught his eye on the other side of Pountney Place.

'Hallo, we'll have a look at that,' said the suddenly wide-awake Aubrey; and he crossed the street.

The object that had caught his eye was a hat, half hidden behind the sunblind of one of those so private-looking little shops. It was the only thing in the window, a ruffle of pale green and white, as if a seabird had alighted in a rock-pool. He looked round the awning at it on its slender wooden stand.

At the same moment he was aware that he was being looked at in return.

Now privacy or no privacy, if there is one kind of window into which one may peer without offence, surely it is the window of a shop. And yet those small-paned Pountney Place windows had such an intimate look as well! Nobody peers into intimate interiors. All the same, Aubrey was being watched through the chink of a net half-curtain. He was caught, moreover, in a divided mind. He would have felt singularly foolish if he had had to explain that he had crossed the street to try the effect of a hat upon a person who had no existence, and yet that was the simple truth. So he turned away, walking past the sunblind.

The watcher made a simultaneous movement to the other side of the window.

Now Aubrey Kneller was engaged to be married. He had, therefore, a perfectly good reason for buying a hat if he wished to. And he felt piqued and played with, and in a sense challenged. He stepped back to take a look at the frontage. The sunblind was a new one and bore no name; obviously the shop had not been opened very long. The bricks of that house-shop were old and mellow, its windows flat-sashed, and many-angled zinc chimney-cowls made ragged the skyline over the parapet. Below was a whitewashed area, and four whitened steps rose to the door, which stood open. But the door just within on the right was closed, and bore a brass plate with the words 'Please ring' on it.

As if he had been dared to do so, Aubrey mounted the steps. It must have been a very lightly-poised bell, for Aubrey was hardly aware that his finger had touched it. But from somewhere inside the shop there came a low silver trilling. And after all, a shop is a shop, even if one does have to ring for admittance.

The door opened; but so negligible was the mien of the person who opened it that Aubrey entered with hardly a glance at her.

3

The parlour was all a soft pigeon-grey, with a grey carpet fitted close up to the walls and sheeny grey curtains giving access to the room or rooms behind. Its smell was that of the Burlington Arcade, a public sort of mingling of anybody's powder, sachet, cream. Half a dozen small water-colour carnivals hung on the walls, done with much white, which pervaded their thick impasto like a bloom of cosmetic. The slanting sunblind outside gave the place the cool light of the interior of a marquee. But for the hat in the window, the room was to all appearances a living-room – barring again the tall cheval-glass and a half-unpacked carton, frothing with tissue-paper. Aubrey looked round for the person in charge – for the child who had admitted him could hardly be she.

But he saw nobody else, and she stood there waiting. So he looked at her again.

Only slightly did she seem to detach herself from the prevailing hues of the room. Her complexion seemed as pervaded with white as the carnivals on the walls. Her dress was an indeterminate scrambled-egg of yellow and white, without either intention or design.

'Well, here's a plain-headed piece of goods,' was Aubrey Kneller's first thought.

But the next moment, 'Heavens alive!' he had almost exclaimed out-right. 'What in the name of goodness has she been doing to her mouth?'

It was a blear of greasy crimson. It must have taken half a lipstick to do. Dreadful experiment! One would hardly have supposed that the rawest novice could have made such a hash of it! 'How truly distressing!' was Aubrey's first comment.

But she lifted eyes of the colour of the glass marble one sees in the constricted neck of a soda water bottle, and spoke in a voice that reminded him of something or somebody, though for the life of him he could not remember of what.

'Good afternoon, sir.'

'Good afternoon. May I see the hat in the window?'

'Won't you sit down, please?'

She fetched the hat from the window. He asked her to put it on her head. She did so, placing herself before the cheval-glass. Her cropped string-coloured hair made little cheekpieces over her ears, and her thin arms, bare midway between elbow and shoulder, had a pathetic defencelessness as she adjusted that seabird of a hat. Then she turned, the glassy eyes full of apprehension.

And 'Execrable, execrable!' Aubrey Kneller thought to himself; but, being a kind-hearted man, and unwilling to wound the feelings even of such a snippet as this, 'Charming, charming!' he murmured. 'Quite charming – on you – '

The next moment she had astonished him by saying, in a small timorous voice, 'It is Mr Kneller, isn't it?'

He recovered himself. Ah! So *that* was why she had peeped at him through the curtain! She had seen his photograph in the papers, and had recognised him!

'Yes, my name is Kneller,' he confessed.

'Mr Kneller the author?'

'Yes, I am an author.'

'How wonderful!' she breathed.

He disclaimed the wonderfulness of it, but for a moment she seemed almost to assert herself.

'Oh, but it is! To sit down and make up people! I can't imagine how you do it! I can't think how you begin! How do they come to you? Is it just genius? Are they all people you know? Or what?'

He laughed a little. 'So that was why you peeped through the curtains?'

Once more she was abashed. 'Oh, it was rude! I'm so sorry! But you've no idea how lonely it is in here, with hardly anybody coming in – '

'Do you mean to say you're here all alone?' he asked. Less and less did she seem the sort of person to be carrying on an enterprise that depended on a few specialised articles, stiff prices, and salesmanship of a highly intensive order.

'Oh, no! There's Mathilde. She does the upstairs part. But I look after down here. It's all my idea. Don't you like pictures?'

It was evidently from the pictures that she had got that terrible mess of a mouth. He longed to wipe it clean for her. But for that she might not have been so much amiss. The green and white of the hat did at least repeat those glassy eyes and the pastel white of her matt skin. But those lips – !

'I wonder,' Aubrey said suddenly, 'whether I might say something very personal?'

'What?' she said, frightened again.

'Why have you done that to your lips?'

He could have bitten his tongue off. Dismay rushed into her face, wildly her eyes sought the glass. He saw her reflection tilted in it, the mouth on which he had remarked a shapeless open smear.

'*Oh!*' she wailed. 'And I did so try!'

The next moment she had thrown the hat on a chair and had fled through the curtains at the back of the room.

And with her disappearance it came all at once over Aubrey to wonder what he was doing in that parlour at all. He felt a little confused in his head. He had been walking along Pountney Place. He had crossed the street to look at a hat. And without quite knowing how it had happened he had found himself in this grey, scented place, saying wounding things to this scrap of a child. Why? What business of his was it what she did with her mouth?

'Time I was pushing along,' he muttered to himself.

She came back very quietly. The pigeon-grey curtains hardly seemed to part to admit her. She stood just within them, in an attitude that made him feel ashamed of himself, so crushed and humble was it. The crimson smear was gone.

He felt that it was his duty to speak first. He took a step towards her. He was a big man, and felt his bigness the more by the side of her slightness.

'You know my name,' he said gently. 'May I ask yours?'

He understood her to say that it wasn't quite settled yet.

'I don't mean your business-name. I see your shop's new. The reason I ask is that I want to apologise very humbly for hurting your feelings just now.'

'Is it better now?' she asked faintly.

Indeed there had been no need to bedaub that mouth with paint. It had its own tender appealing charm, a pale carnation, that did not quite close upon the nacre within. Why would girls always be trying to make themselves something they were not! She was standing at attention for his inspection, so close that he could smell the soap or other preparation with which she had cleansed herself. The string-coloured hair was pushed quite back from her brow.

'And now if you will put the hat on again,' he said, his eyes on hers, 'it would give me very great pleasure if you would keep it on.'

She fell back, as if disbelieving her ears. 'What? For myself? To keep?' she gasped.

'If I might be allowed.'

'*Oh!*'

The little stir of blood in her cheeks touched him infinitely. Poor little phantom! More likely than not she did not get enough to eat. Most, most likely; for, now that he looked again, those arms in the cut-off sleeves, though frail, were exquisitely boned. Her lines, sketchily drawn and unfilled-out, had a certain witchery . . . which was precisely the reason why he suddenly placed a spindley gilt chair for her. Aubrey was forty-four, old enough to be her father. Anyway, that clove-pink of a mouth was better a little farther away.

'Tell me about yourself,' he said abruptly. 'Who are your people?'

She hadn't any people.

'What, nobody at all?'

'I'm an orphan,' she sighed.

'How old are you?'

'I – I call myself nearly eighteen.'

'You call yourself! Don't you know?'

'Please don't,' she begged, in a failing voice.

Poor little brat, he thought compassionately! Who was he, to torture her with questions that she couldn't answer? The workhouse, no doubt, or the Foundling Hospital steps. Chance-named according to any matron's will. Better people than she have not always found their birth-certificates easy to come by. The ignominy of it! If it gave her a moment's pleasure he was glad he had offered her the green and white hat.

She began to talk, diffidently, falteringly, every now and again lifting worshipping eyes to him. She talked of that narrow grey-hued parlour in which she spent her days. She talked of the two or three clients who had called, of how so far they had bought nothing, of the people who passed the window. And as she talked an arresting thought fastened itself on Aubrey Kneller.

It had something to do with her voice. It was a voice he had heard somewhere before. It was the voice of somebody he knew a good deal about. The solution was on the tip of his tongue, but still it eluded him. It was tantalising. He couldn't let it alone –

In such cases Aubrey Kneller had a device that frequently, if not always, succeeded. This was to try to forget that he was trying to remember anything at all, to make his mind as complete a blank as he could, and to spell slowly through the alphabet, listeningly, alertly, a letter at a time, with long pauses.

So, as the girl ran on, with gradually gathering courage, 'A,' thought Aubrey Kneller, and paused. Did the thing of which he was in search begin with A? Apparently not.

'B.' Nothing had come of 'A.' What about 'B'? But he had no better success.

'C.' Still nothing. (But what a tender little mouth it was now that it was scrubbed!)

'D.' *Aha*! Found! Why had he not known at once? Had it not been chiming in his head ever since he had handed the manuscript of his book over the Post Office counter?

Her voice was the voice of Delia Vane.

4

Now up to six months ago Aubrey Kneller had never seen why books should give any trouble to the writers of them. His own never had. His Sir Rolands and Sir Guys had flowed smoothly from his fountain-pen, chivalrous and high-minded knights and baronets all. Indeed, he had been not a little pleased with one of his *mots*, which was, that if the writing of books was as toilsome a business as all that the presumption was that the writer had mistaken his job.

But *Delia Vane* had given him nothing but trouble from the very beginning. The final pangs of book-birth had been extreme. And the outcome of his labour had been, not that insignificant Annie Thompson of his first conception, but this other usurper, of whom, though in a sense he was her lord and master, he was secretly afraid.

And now, in that quiet little parlour in Pountney Place, he had already done several totally unexpected things within the short space of a quarter of an hour. He had so far forgotten himself as to remark on what a perfectly strange young woman chose to do with her mouth. On an unaccountable impulse he had given this young person a hat he had intended for his *fiancée*. And – he confessed it to his shame – he had been on the very brink of a desultory little tenderness, in plain words a kiss, that Sir Guy and Sir Roland would never have dreamed of. It was all very bewildering. He hadn't a notion what had happened.

For of course that was sheer nonsense about this child's voice. How could her voice resemble the voice of Delia, who had never possessed a voice? Other fantastic similarities there might be. The girl in the scrambled-egg frock was evidently a sort of Annie Thompson, in so far as she had any individuality at all. He had never been able to visualise this intruder very clearly. And Aubrey Kneller had not become a successful author by wasting his time over such unusual speculations.

Yet nothing comes out of nothing, not even a character in a book. He had not yet forgotten those pangs of the bringing forth of *Delia Vane*. There *had* been those quarrelsome scenes between this impudent newcomer and his proper heroine, Rosamond. Something

had happened that had never happened to Aubrey before. And
this shop-assistant's voice was the very voice of the Delia of his
imagining.

Aubrey was conscious of passing through three distinct stages. The
first of these was to tell himself that he was not very well. His book
had taken more out of him than he had supposed, and indeed, in
mere bulk, it was nearly double the length of any of his former books.
A stiff brandy-and-soda would have done him good . . . and at that
thought he gave a little jump, for never in his life had he drunk
brandy-and-soda at that hour of the afternoon.

The second stage was that he found himself gazing furtively at the
girl's mouth again. She had sat down in the chair he had placed for
her, and he was guiltily aware that he was wishing that he had not
placed it quite so far away from his own. She was sitting in an attitude
of patient stillness, with her hands folded in her lap. The lids had
dropped over the colourless eyes. The light, troubled little sigh that
she gave was the living echo of Annie Thompson in the days when
she had promised to be good.

The third phase had a certain slyness about it. Aubrey had thought
of a way of bringing those chairs closer together that the tenderest
conscience could not have found fault with. Several times, in his
books, Sir Guy or Sir Somebody Else had taken forlorn little orphans
under their wing, had sheltered and clothed them and had them
educated, all in a spirit of purest benevolence. It was as if the lordly
mansion should pat the thatched roof of the cottage at the park gates.
Honi soit qui mal y pense. As long as Aubrey moved his chair strictly in
this spirit –

But he was not to do so. From somewhere upstairs there came a
shrill call.

'*Marie-e-e-e!*'

Swiftly the girl sprang to her feet. She spoke in a hurried whisper:
'It's only Mathilde – I'll see what she wants – I shan't be a minute – '

She was off, a vanishing sprite of yellow and white.

With her disappearance Aubrey seemed again to come to himself.
He passed his hand over his brow. It all seemed dreamy; he had an
idea that he had been mixing up people who had no existence with
those who had. What had those figments, Annie Thompson and
Delia Vane, to do with his *fiancée*, Helen Boyd, whom he was to meet
at Rumpelmayers' at four? And what was this about a voice? The
only voice he heard was the sound of a neighbouring clock, striking
four already.

He sprang to his feet. If she wasn't back in a moment he must walk out of the place.

But he had given her a hat, and hadn't paid for it.

He was about to call when she appeared; and oh, how very much more she was in the picture now! For she had changed her frock. She was dressed for the street, in shabby black, with a dusty black velvet tam dragged over the cheek-pieces of her hair. Merely a little milliner's run-about, like a thousand others, sent out with a parcel and her 'bus fare in her pocket! He had her placed – yes, even to the parcel, for she crossed to the carton with the tissue-paper, put the lid on it, and began to tie the package with a narrow green-and-white band that she spun from a wooden reel.

Then once again the sound of her voice gave him that secret thrill.

'What did I do with my gloves?'

'Are these they?'

'Oh, thank you . . . I'm ready now.'

Observe, she did not say, 'I've got to go out; will you pay for the hat now or leave an address?' She merely announced that she was ready, as if he had called for the purpose of taking her out. And Aubrey Kneller, known novelist, was in some sort a public man. Not that it really mattered, of course. Still, to be seen in broad daylight in the company of a *midinette* with a bandbox over her arm – that apparently was her innocent idea –

'I must be getting along, too,' he said, he hoped not too pointedly.

She must have been extremely sensitive. Immediately there happened the same thing that had happened when he had commented on the overpainted mouth. She winced. She shivered forlornly. She seemed to become sizes smaller.

And could he, with that other piteous 'Oh!' still in his memory, say to her, 'I mustn't be seen with you; it's one thing to be on the point of kissing you in a private room, but I shall have to cut you in the street; perhaps I'll look in another day and kiss you when nobody can see us?'

He couldn't. He heard the passing of a taxi. He stepped to the door and hailed it with his stick.

'Which way are you going? Can I drop you anywhere?' he said.

Half a minute later they were speeding along Pountney Place, with the bandbox between them, half on her knees, half on his.

5

Helen Boyd waited in Rumpelmayers' with her Academy catalogue on her knee. She was not sorry to sit down, for, besides the Academy, she had done several miles of shopping, and the mile in London and the mile over the mountains at home were not the same thing. Neither was she impatient. It was quite amusing sitting there, watching the people who came in, went out or passed up and down St James's Street. He was late, but she was sure he had said Rumpelmayers' at four, and even if there had been a mistake there was always the flat in King Street, not three minutes' walk away.

She was not in the least embarrassed that the young man who also waited in the outer shop apparently found the view in her direction as pleasant as that in any other. She was quite capable of going up to him and saying, 'Do you mind turning your chair so that it faces another way?' So her cool, interested eyes continued to look past the cakes and candied fruits in the window, the young man continued to look at her, and Aubrey Kneller continued to be late.

She thought her engagement to Aubrey such an excellent thing for Aubrey himself. She was the practical one; he had to have the artistic temperament. His temperament reminded Helen of a muslin bag, through which he strained things, and out came the most extraordinary results. He had strained Helen herself that way, and out had come a Rosamond or a Margaret or a Phyllis. And of course she managed him. When he came to stay with them in the country she had everything just-so for him – sprayed the roses in her prettiest frock (but didn't tell him that she used somebody's soapy bath-water for the purpose), wore her prettiest shoes for him (and said nothing about her sloshy old gum-boots that hung upside-down in the potting-shed with hay in the toes of them to dry). He made quite a lot of money by his trade, and Helen, at twenty-six, was some years past thinking that money didn't matter, even in love.

The pertinacity of the young man was getting more amusing every moment. He was trying to – what was the expression? – to 'get off' with her. How funny men were! So single in their aims! He was doing his utmost to make her look at him! He had a vacant, likeable sort of face, dissipated perhaps, but with the right sort of come-from. She didn't think she would tell Aubrey what this young man was trying to do. He was inclined to take such things a little fussily. He himself seemed to have a blind spot as far as women were concerned, and his attitude to them never gave Helen a moment's anxiety. A little lacking in devil? That didn't matter. Helen would find devil enough for two.

She put up her catalogue again, but immediately dropped it as a taxi drew up at the door. At last! She gave a quick glance at her wrist-watch, not in the least crossly, but just to know the time. Then, with a slight start, she looked up in time to see Aubrey lifting his Homburg hat to somebody. The taxi moved away, and Aubrey entered Rumpelmayers'.

'Hallo, Kneller,' said the young man whose eyes had made the overtures to Helen; and Aubrey gave him a brief nod as he advanced to Helen. He was a bustle of insincere apologies; he, too, looked at his watch.

'So sorry – more than five minutes late – I make it twenty-three minutes to five – '

'I was a little early,' Helen remarked.

Nevertheless she was perfectly sure that Aubrey *had* said four o'clock, and not half-past. 'Who was that?' she asked, as they passed into the inner room.

'That chap? Oh, his flat's on the same landing as mine. I some-times wonder whether my telephone belongs to me or to him. His name's Upwester. He's a peer of sorts.'

'I didn't mean that young man. I meant who were you speaking to in the taxi.'

'Oh!' Aubrey gave an easy laugh. 'Oh! Now I'm going to say something that sounds silly. I haven't the least idea who it was!'

She thought it sounded particularly silly. But 'Do you mean somebody was taken ill and you picked them up?' she asked with concern.

'No, no, no,' he reassured her. 'I was shopping. She was in a great hurry. She didn't ask me. I offered it. A very great hurry, and she looked very tired, and it was the only taxi – you surely don't mind a casual little thing like that, darling?'

'Of course not!' The blue eyes under the duckling-yellow brows were wide open. 'And you look tired yourself, dearest!'

'Yes. That beastly book. Took rather a lot out of me. Anyway it's finished with now.'

'Here comes your neighbour.'

Upwester had entered with the lady for whom he had been waiting. A glance at her sufficed to set Aubrey wondering whether she was the 'Bee' on the Museum Exchange with whom Upwester communicated so frequently. Had Aubrey been on such merry terms with a lady as

Upwester seemed to be with this one, he would have preferred to have a telephone of his own.

'Rather a sad face, don't you think?' Helen was saying.

Sad? Upwester? No, Aubrey couldn't see that. Judging from things he had heard, Upwester's flat was no abode of sadness.

'I mean a sort of lost-child expression,' said Helen.

'I dare say,' Aubrey answered off-handedly. 'Upwester's life and mine run on different lines.'

It was nearly true. So, hitherto, they had.

6

He had just told Helen that his book was off his hands; but as he sat there, with a bright smile on his face, automatically talking, he was conscious of another disquieting little parallel that up to that moment he had not remembered. It was this.

The Pat of his book – that Sir Patrick Archdale who originally was to have married Rosamond in the last chapter – this *preux chevalier* had been sent by Aubrey, his master, with a large bunch of roses as a gift to Rosamond. The compliment with which he was to have presented them had cost Aubrey quite a lot of thought. But Pat, the mere creature, had demurred at the words put into his mouth; that is to say, Aubrey had written the elaborate little phrase and had then struck it out again. Pat's voice had sounded almost audibly in his mind.

'But look here, my dear old tin of fruit,' Pat had protested, almost contemptuously, 'nobody talks like that nowadays! Why don't you give us a chance? Why can't you let us run our own show?'

'And keep Rosamond waiting?' Aubrey had taken up his part in this little drama of which the stage was only a few inches wide.

'Heaps of time. I'm not meeting her till four-thirty.'

'What's that? I told you four o'clock.'

'Oh, we've altered that!' Pat had replied.

A character after an author's time-table, carefully worked out with regard to every exigency of the plot!

'You've *what*?' Aubrey had gasped.

'Changed it. We can look after ourselves. She can have her roses, but I'm damned if I'm going to make that silly speech about them!'

The next day the sub-plot of the book had thickened even more menacingly. Aubrey, sitting with Helen in Rumpelmayers', remembered a certain alternative draft that had, as authors say, 'written itself', almost without his co-operation. He had promptly discarded it, but in the end had had to restore it again. Merely as an experiment, he had written something like this:

Pat. I bought you a bunch of roses, darling, but they dropped with the heat.

Rosamond. Wouldn't they have picked up in water, my loved one?

Pat. Oh, I wouldn't give you a dud lot like that!

Rosamond. Ever thinking of me! Ah, that flowers, so fair today, so faded tomorrow, should be the symbol of the love of unchanging hearts!

Pat. Eh? Oh, rather! Quite! And I say, am I a bit late? I honestly thought it was four-thirty! Sorry and all that. I had to see a man.

At this point Aubrey Kneller, sitting in Rumpelmayers' tea-shop, blushed suddenly and violently. He remembered the gesture with which he had crumpled up that tentative draft and thrown it into the wastepaper basket. He remembered how he had once more rubbed (as it were) his magic ring, and the genie of Archdale had once more appeared. He remembered what had next passed.

'Now look here, Archdale, I want to talk to you,' he had said severely.

'Start her up, old thing.'

'Who's this man you say made you late for Rosamond?'

'Feller I know.'

'Is he in the book?'

'Do you mean the telephone-book?'

'Is he in *my* book, *Delia Vane*?'

'Shouldn't think so.'

'Then where did you pick him up?'

'Barged into him one day in the Premier Lounge.'

'Where's that?'

'Dover Street, of course.'

'I know the Bath Club in Dover Street, and Browns' and Batts' and the Sesame. I never heard of any Premier Lounge.'

'West side, near the bottom. You can get your hair cut there.'

'Didn't I tell you to go straight to Rosamond?'

'They kept me waiting in the flower-shop.'

'Pat, that's untrue. I don't believe you bought those flowers.'

'Then go and ask 'em in the shop. They're down on your account anyway.'

'Then what became of them?'

Then Pat, with a snort that had startled even his creator, had replied: 'Well, if you damn-well want to know, I gave 'em to Miss

Thompson! She's the only bit of fun there is in your whole blighted book – *haw, haw, haw, haw!*'

Aubrey's throat was dry. He drank some more of Rumpelmayers' excellent tea, which went the wrong way, so that he coughed. And all at once he was afraid.

For what had Pat done that he himself had not been guilty of, and all within an hour and a half? Pat had given Rosamond's roses to somebody else; but had not Aubrey given another woman Helen's hat? Pat had shuffled and lied; but what else had he done to Helen? Pat was trying, as he would have expressed it, to 'shake' Rosamond; but had not Aubrey for some time past doubted whether Helen was quite the proper mate for a writer of books?

And worst of all, had there not been that exciting, disgraceful little scene in the taxi hardly half an hour before?

For he *had* kissed that little Pountney Place stranger in the black dusty velvet tam. He had kissed her as they turned into Pont Street, and again after that, and again after that. And he had told the driver not to hurry. It was then that the ingenious idea had occurred to him that he might pretend to Helen that he had thought their appointment to be for half-past four. He had told her how pretty her mouth was when she didn't do anything to it, and had kissed it again. Her pallid little face had flushed and glowed. They had sat hand in hand, and he had promised to send people to her shop, and had told her that if ever she was in trouble she must come to him. In a word, he had done almost everything that Sir Rupert or Sir Guy would have nobly condemned.

'And now that you've got a new hat you can chuck that old thing away,' he had told her.

'Oh, I couldn't wear the new one all the time!' she had answered.

'You girls are all alike!' he had laughed. 'Give you one thing and you want something else! Well, I suppose we shall have to see what can be done – '

And he reddened again, with something nearer even than betrayed honour, when he remembered that if he had only had the sense to stop the taxi a few yards up the street Helen need have known nothing at all about it.

A couple of tables away Upwester and his companion were laughing, with now and then a glance in Aubrey's direction. A little farther along the wall an electric fan spun, almost invisible in its light cage. It was one of those fans that, besides spinning, moved slowly from side to side. It caught Aubrey's eye. He found something fascinating in its regular movement – a turn to the right, a pause, and then back again to the left. It was as if a shining face stared mildly, now at Upwester and his friend, now at Aubrey and Helen. Its expression changed too. Now, two glistening sectors would stand for a moment still, point to point; then they would flutter and flow and become a single golden spoke. This, too, would pulse and pale, and then dissolve suddenly into a blank.

'*Haw, haw, haw, haw! Haw, haw, haw, haw!*'

Half the heads in the room turned. It was Upwester's raucous laugh. He was laughing helplessly – '*Haw, haw, haw, haw!*' – and his companion was trying to quieten him.

Aubrey had sprung to his feet. That was twice that afternoon the same thing had happened! He shook with excitement. Again a voice, straight out of a book! The other time it had been the girl in the butter-and-eggs frock who had spoken with Delia's voice; now this was the authentic laugh of Pat Archdale when, in that experimental draft, he had told Aubrey that this new governess creature was the only bit of fun in his whole benighted book!

'*Haw, haw, haw, haw!*' roared Upwester again, while the faces of strangers also smiled politely, that somebody should be enjoying himself so. From Upwester to Aubrey turned the fan, from Aubrey to Upwester. It seemed to be beamingly introducing them to one another: 'Sir Patrick Archdale – Mr Kneller – Sir Patrick Archdale – Mr Kneller – '

'*No, no, no!*' Aubrey wanted to cry. 'His name's Upwester – Lord Upwester – he's the flat next to mine, just along the street there – !'

'Miss Marie Somebody – Miss Delia Vane – Miss Marie Somebody – Miss Delia Vane – ' seemed to come from the unresting fan.

'*No, no, no!*' Aubrey inwardly shrieked.

'Miss Rosamond De Vere – Miss Helen Boyd – Miss Rosamond De Vere – Miss Helen Boyd – Upwester – Archdale – Miss Marie Somebody – Miss Delia Vane – ' the names spun in poor Aubrey's head.

Suddenly, with a laugh almost as loud as Upwester's own, Aubrey, who had been standing up, sat down in his chair again as if he had been poleaxed. Helen was asking him what was the matter. But he only gaped at that fluttering disc of thin brass.

'Not an atom of doubt about it, not an atom of doubt about it, not an atom of doubt about it,' was all that he could mutter, over and over again.

7

Aubrey had planned to get married that autumn. He was in treaty for a house out Rickmansworth way, that should satisfy Helen's need for air, space and a garden and his own convenient nearness to town. Of course he would have to give up his flat in King Street, and sleep at his club when business happened to keep him late.

But it would be a wrench to give up the flat. He liked its situation, almost at the corner of St James's Square. He liked to sit in its wide, many-paned window-bay, to look down on the stately park of cars, and to picture to himself which of them had just set down Sir Ronald at the portals of his club or Sir Ronald at the wide doors of the Embassy. He liked King Street, with its china and cabinets and rare prints and two-hundred-guinea guns. He loved the flat itself – the tiny anteroom where the telephone was, the large airy study adjoining, his bedroom leading from it, his bathroom beyond that again, and the little chamber at the end where Clough, his man, slept. He esteemed and respected Clough, from his plain all-round collar to his silent boots. When Clough brought Aubrey a card on a salver Aubrey was often on the point of placing half-a-crown there instead of picking up the card. And a spot of dust anywhere about the place would have been a spot on Clough's conscience.

But as Aubrey sat in his study late that night the flat seemed somehow all wrong. Not that an article was out of place. The porcelain clock was right to a second – five minutes to one. His books had not been touched, his chairs stood in their proper places, only the flowers had been taken out for the night and placed in the bathroom. He knew that if he went to the telephone there would not be a breath on its glass mouth-piece and that not a peerage or guide would be a fraction out of alignment. To open the door of his bedroom would be like opening a box of confectionery straight from the makers.

Yet something was amiss. It was as if an alteration had taken place in the air, giving things harsher edges than usual. He felt as if he had somebody else's spectacles on, not quite suited to his eyes. Somehow the place would have been better for a little litter – something half-unpacked, say with tissue-paper lying about. A smell, a feminine smell for preference, of powder or burning incense-paper, would have been a change from its tiresome cleanliness. And he was sick of those two Cox water-colours. He wanted to put up something

garish and modern and rather extravagant in their places. And it was
depressingly quiet. It wanted voices, voices of a certain *timbre*. It
wanted whatever it was that rooms did take from their occupants.
Anyway it wanted something.

Suddenly he sat up in his chair, listening. Then he sank back again.
The gates of the lift-cage had clashed on the landing outside, and
Upwester had come home, apparently bringing a number of his
friends with him, for there had been sounds of muffled laughter.

The door of the other flat banged, and Aubrey resumed his
reverie.

No, it wasn't the room; it was he himself who had changed. He
had been changing for months past, imperceptibly and day by
day. With each completed chapter of *Delia Vane* he had changed a
little more, and he didn't think it would make the least bit of
difference now if he did send for the manuscript of his book
back. He had done his work. He could destroy it, but he could
not alter it. Nobody, reading his most famous book, *Loved I Not
Honour More*, would suppose that *Delia Vane* could possibly have
come from the same pen. He knew that he had placed his professional reputation in the gravest jeopardy, and that the odds were
a thousand to one that if Delia had any success at all it would be a
succès de scandale.

Suddenly the door across the corridor opened again. Again the
gale of muffled laughter was heard, and through it Upwester's boist-
erous '*Haw, haw, haw!*' They were gathered outside his own door.
He heard Upwester's words.

'Dig the o' feller out – all in there by himself – *hoi*! Kneller! Show
a leg! Want you to come to my party! Come into the body o' the
kirk! Come and 'joy yourself!'

A drumming on Aubrey's door accompanied the invitation.

Aubrey had half-risen from his chair. Often as he had been made
aware of Upwester's nocturnal revels he had never been asked to take
part in them before. Had he been asked he would certainly have
refused, for he did not approve of this figure who had sometimes shot
up the lift-shaft at dawn, with a large metal motor-spirit advertisement reverberating in his arms as a trophy and a cloakroom-ticket still
stuck in the band of his opera-hat. But tonight was different. He was
weary to death being alone. It was rather decent of Upwester to have
asked him. Why not go in for an hour?

As he opened his door there was a clap of laughter, at which the
very cars parked in the Square might have shied. It took Aubrey a

moment to realise what had happened. Then he saw the joke. The peer had been standing on his hands with his feet against the upper panels of the door, and he lurched in full-length, feet first.

'*Haw, haw, haw*! *Haw, haw, haw*!' he laughed as he lay on the ground.

'Sssh – don't wake my man!' Aubrey begged, his fingers on his lips.

The nobleman picked himself up. 'Bring him in, Bee,' he cried, hospitably. 'Let him come to the party – 'snames Kneller – 'snauthor – lets me use his telephone – bring him in – come on, Kneller – '

He seized Aubrey by the waist and pulled his door to behind him.

8

So *this* was the place where his neighbour turned night into day and broke Aubrey's rest with the liquid howls of his water-whistle! As a first impression of Upwester's flat, Aubrey was put in mind of a visit he had once paid to Madame Tussaud's. There, figures that he had taken for dummies had suddenly moved a hand or a head, but had been dummies after all; and others, that he had taken to be dummies also, had smiled at Aubrey and walked away. So it was here. The room was almost as dim as a photographer's dark-room, dyed deep by the rosy silk-shaded lights. He hardly knew whether a thing was animate or inanimate till it moved, and even then he might have been mistaken. He couldn't count them, but he had the feeling that there were quite a lot of people about him. Here and there the sudden glow of a cigarette would momentarily light up a face, which would then go out again. A soft huddle of colour at the end of a divan might have been a heap of cushions, until it stirred and resolved itself into a lady, curled up in the least possible compass, and nursing an unslippered foot in one hand. What looked like a piece of tapestry over the mantelpiece *might* have been a sheet-iron advertisement of a motor spirit, and standing near a door was a figure that Aubrey supposed to be Upwester's servant, until a struck match showed it to be a stuffed brown bear holding out a tray. He hadn't a notion who anybody was. The mingled smell of cigarettes and perfume was subtly exciting. His host was introducing him, genially and at large.

'Here he comes. 'Swellknown author. Forgotten what his books are, but dam' good; must read 'em, everybody. This is Kathleen. Give him a cigarette, somebody; they're on the bear. Think you

know Bee, Kneller; she's always using his telephone; dashed good of
him. Writes books. Not much of a reading man myself, but dashed
proud all same. Hoi, Sylvie, come and say how-d'ye-do to friend of
mine, Mr Kneller. Writes hics. Beats me where he gets his ideas
from; couldn't write a hic to save my life. Give him a drink. Have a
drink, Aubrey, ol' man.'

The drink was brought to Aubrey by a young person in a calyx
of flimsy skirt held up by a pair of ribbon braces. A large woolly
Bonzo pup nestled in one soft white arm, and she asked Aubrey
if she hadn't met him at the Saturn Club. A young man seated
on the bear's pedestal was making soft terrier-like yelps on that
whistle that Aubrey knew so well, and he broke off to ask how long
the kippers were going to be. Aubrey suddenly smelt the kippers.
Apparently they were cooking in Upwester's bedroom, for the
door opened, showing a bright glimpse. The bedroom was the
counterpart of Aubrey's own, but of course placed the other way
round, which, nevertheless, surprised Aubrey a little. It had been
turned to the purpose of a ladies' cloak-room, for piled high on
the bed were wraps and furs and cloaks and stoles. On the small
bedside table stood a chafing-dish, over which a tall fair-haired
youth busied himself with a fork. As the kippers were cooked, two
at a time, a young woman set them down before the orange pillars
of the electric fire to keep hot. Upwester was introducing Aubrey
all over again.

'Splendid author. Full o' brains. Going to put us all into his book,
large as life. Lots o' copy for him. Put Sylvie in, too – give him
'nother drink – '

That it was 'copy' had occurred to Aubrey too. These merry,
careless, perhaps not quite reputable people, who sipped their sweets
as they came, certainly were a new aspect of life to him. And now
that he was here he intended to enjoy himself. He began to think
that he had misjudged his neighbour and his charming friends. One
was only young once . . . There was a movement among the
cushions where the girl nursed the silk-clad foot, moving her tiny
toes about inside. One large liquid eye looked roguishly at Aubrey.
Aubrey smiled back. He might ask her to make room for him
presently.

'May I help myself, Upwester?' he asked.

'Pleasure – all there is!' cried the peer.

It was a full round Burgundy that Aubrey drank, and he wanted
to ask Upwester where he got it. Sound stuff; a few dozen of

that wouldn't be amiss in his own flat! Capital cigarettes, too; Aubrey made a note of the brand. And a devilish pretty bunch of girls old Upwester had got together, too, by Jove! Why shouldn't Aubrey give a party like this? True, there was Clough. Very good servant Clough was, and knew Aubrey's ways; but whose flat was it, Clough's or Aubrey's? Hang Clough! Clough would have to do as he was told. Aubrey wasn't going to consult Clough about what kind of party he gave. Jolly nice party, and jolly good host, and jolly girls –

The bedroom door opened again, and the tall fair-headed young man who had cooked the kippers marched in with them on a dish. But what was this figure that followed, with plates and what-not piled up on a tray? Eastern, that gold and purple attire? A houri, summoned by the clapping of a caliph's hands? No. Merely Miss Teddy Seymour, of the 'Thalia', dressed in Upwester's silk sleeping-suit. Aubrey found himself clapping rhythmically with the rest as the procession of two made the tour of the room. He laughed, he laughed; and '*Haw, haw, haw, haw, haw, haw!*' sounded Upwester's guffaw.

Never before in his life had Aubrey Kneller eaten kippers at three o'clock in the morning; never before in his life had he been unable to remember how many glasses of Burgundy he had drunk nor what he had drunk when the Burgundy was finished. 'Taste mine,' said the young female with the calyx of skirt, putting her glass, not directly to his lips, but in such a manner that that scented white arm was passed about his neck. Her nape was shingled, and she had a fringe of hair, so that the eyes that sparkled through it should not be too bright to bear.

'I live next door,' Aubrey by and by heard himself saying, first to one young woman, then to another. 'All come – whole lot of us! Bee's coming, 'n Teddy's coming, 'n jolly ol' Upwester – fix night – only next door – 'nother jolly party, what? – '

' 's a top-hole author – been trying to get know him for months, haven't I, my jolly old Hicspeare, what?' Upwester was saying, now here, now there. ''Novelist – I saw him this afternoon – *haw, haw, haw*! Saw him in the tea-shop! Says goodbye to a girl in a taxi 'n meets 'nother one next minute – *haw, haw, haw*! He's a lad. Mus' read his books. Get 'em at Mudie's. Times Booclub. Look at him – got a crush on Sylvie now! Saw him with girl in a taxi – *haw, haw, haw*!'

> Once my face was as fair as a lily,
> But look at the funny thing now!

softly sang the girl with one slipper, holding up a tiny mirror in her hand.

An electric bell was heard to trill.

'Who's that?' Upwester called. 'Bobbie an' Lou, I expect. Let 'em in, somebody – night's young yet – 'sintro duce jolly ol' Kneller to Bobby an' Lou – '

The door of the dark-room opened, a glimmer of white silk muffler became pink, and in came Bobby and Lou.

Aubrey Kneller woke at midday the next day, and immediately went to sleep again. Coming out of his flat sometime during the afternoon he encountered Upwester, also coming out. At the sudden stopping of the lift that took them down together Aubrey's hand went to his aching head, but Upwester had a flower in his buttonhole and looked as if he had just stepped out of a bandbox. 'Morning,' said the peer curtly; and later – for a dog's body could have done all the thinking of which Aubrey was capable that day – later it occurred to Aubrey that Helen had said of Upwester that he had a sad face. Aubrey, by a great effort, might have summoned up a grin of sorts that afternoon after the night before; but neither by word nor look did Upwester refer to the party. Perhaps that was what Helen had meant. It is sad to know beforehand that even if you make a vow you will not keep it. It is sad to vow over and over again, until at last you vow that you will vow no more, but go whither the stream takes you. It is sad, between a sin and the next, fatalistically to shoulder the burden, without either a look behind or a hope to come. All this was in that curt, prohibitive 'Morning' of Upwester's. And Aubrey Kneller's subsequent recollection of these things was part of the grief to which he came – the grief that is knowledge.

9

Aubrey was in the habit of writing to Helen twice a week. He wrote to her what books he had read, what plays or pictures seen, sent her his press-cuttings, told her how matters were progressing about the Rickmansworth house. Her letters to him were full of how the gardens were looking, how the hens were laying, who had been to tea. Never on either side was there as much as a peep into that surging little world of images that lies between a writer and the tip of his pen.

But now he felt that either he must write to Helen straight out of that teeming little world or not write at all. What was the good of writing if the words came, not as a heart beats, but as a clock ticks? One morning he tried to tick off a letter to Helen. He stuck half way through. If he had written what he wanted to write he would have said, 'Of course you see that all this is perfunctory, insincere rubbish. If it were not a Tuesday I don't suppose I should be writing to you at all. I know before you write it what your answer will be. And so we shall go on, and marry, and live the life that is expected from people in our position, and I shall get just a little bit tired of you – and I'm not sure as a matter of fact that I'm not a bit tired of you now.' That was what he would have written, and since it was out of the question to write it he left the empty addressed envelope on his desk and went out for a walk.

He walked across St James's Square and up towards Jermyn Street, and then turned to the right in the direction of Lower Regent Street. And he knew that with every step he took he was telling a lie to himself. His destination did not lie that way at all. He was going to Pountney Place. Yet, despising himself for the subterfuge, he continued the pretence for a little longer. Then, in the middle of the Haymarket, he suddenly stopped. 'Damned if I'm going on humbugging myself like this,' he muttered. A row of taxis waited. He jumped into the first of them.

'Pountney Place,' he said.

'Any number, sir?'

'Yes. No, I mean. The far side. I'll tell you.'

He didn't know the number. He didn't know the name either. Now that he remembered, the new sunblind that had hidden the little Georgian window like an eyelid had not borne a name at all.

That suddenly struck Aubrey as absurd. A business without a name! Why, businesses ought to be given names before they started, not afterwards! There ought to have been months of advance-advertising! And the giving of names to things was Aubrey's peculiar trade. Sitting there in the smooth-running taxi he sought a name for the shop in Pountney Place.

'Delia', of course – with or without the 'Robes' or 'Modes', just as she liked, but obviously 'Delia'. In flowing script, diagonally across the blind. Capital D-e-l – , with his forefinger he wrote the name in the air. And perhaps the final 'a' ending in a scroll. So intent on his flourishes was he that the taxi had almost passed the demure little shop. He alighted, paid off the taxi, mounted the whitened steps, and once more touched the bell under the brass plate.

Again she answered the ring herself. Again she wore the featureless frock of yellow and white. But he saw, or fancied he saw, a notable change in her. That first time he had called he had had the impression that if he took his eyes off her she might in some way elude him. Only that daub of a mouth had made as it were an exaggerated bull's eye for his eyes to rest on. But now her cheeks had a faint diffused flush. Her hair had a softer sheen. The soda-water-bottle eyes glowed more lively, even her frail arms seemed to have acquired a substance. Nor was it that he saw her now in the morning light, whereas before it had been afternoon. Aubrey knew very well what it was. He knew exactly what she was thinking of. She had flushed at the recollection of those kisses in the taxi. She glowed more deeply still.

'Good-morning, sir,' she said, her lids downcast.

He laughed a little – ' "Sir"?'

'Mr Kneller.'

'That's better. Well, how are you?'

'I'm very well, thank you. Won't you sit down?'

'Is Mathilde in?'

'No.'

'Well, what were you thinking of doing about luncheon?'

She told him that she usually had a scone and butter in there.

'A scone and butter? I said lunch!' he laughed.

'I don't eat very much.'

'You don't look as if you did. Well, I hardly mean that perhaps. You look charming. You make me want to kiss you again.'

'Don't, Mr Kneller,' she faltered. 'I've made up my mind to be good.'

'What? Is a kiss such a terrible crime?'

'I oughtn't to have let you.'

He passed his arm about her and tilted up her face. 'No?' he smiled.

'You see I only sell hats, and you're a famous man,' she faltered.

'I never heard that famous men went without kisses. There!' He set his lips to her reluctant ones. 'And there, and there! Now forget all about that scone and butter. I'm going to take you out to lunch.'

There was nothing about his being seen in the company of a *modiste* now. What, was he a snob, that he should deny in public somebody he kissed in private? He rather hoped not! He would not only take her out; he would 'do' her as well as he would have done himself. The Hyde Park Grill was quite near. Aubrey chuckled, rubbed his hands.

'Come, get your things on,' he said. 'We're going to the Hyde Park.'

She fell back almost in terror, her slender fingers pressed into her cheeks. The Hyde Park! Perhaps, passing that establishment in her dusty velvet tam with her bandbox over her arm, she had ventured to lift her eyes to its frontage, but to enter its portals – !

'Oh!' she breathed; and her 'Oh' was the 'Oh' of Annie Thompson when Aubrey Kneller, author, had called that restive little creature of his brain to account.

Jocularly he bustled her. – 'Come, don't stand there saying "Oh!" '

'But – but – I haven't anything to wear!' she said, aghast.

'You've that new hat.'

'But look at me!'

'I am looking at you. Very nice to look at too. You've frocks here in the shop, haven't you? Get one of those. Shoes? Stockings? What's Harrods' just round the corner for? We'll look in there and rig you up. Hurry, now – it's nearly half-past twelve – '

He kissed her till her face was rosy, and then pushed her away.

So it was that two of Aubrey Kneller's acquaintances, strolling into the Hyde Park Grill an hour or so later, saw Aubrey at luncheon with (as they put it) 'something to make you sit up' – something demure but radiant, in a green-and-white hat and frock of dove-grey marocain, with little shoes pressed together under the table as if her feet were saying their prayers, who lifted innocent-looking eyes to Kneller from time to time. One of these acquaintances happened to be Upwester. His fit of next-morning stiffness was apparently over, for as he passed Aubrey's table on his way out he gave Aubrey a comical, questioning little lift of one eyebrow.

10

Helen wrote slowly, putting her pen almost to the paper and then withdrawing it again, and with meditative sidelong glances out of the window from time to time.

DEAREST,
Only a short note today, as I –

'as I what?' she asked herself. Why only a short one today?

– as I haven't been sleeping very well. I think it was worrying about you. Is anything the matter, darling? Because you know you promised to tell me if anything ever was. There was no letter from you on Thursday, and only the merest scrap on Friday, and you've always so much more to write about than I have. Do let me know if anything's wrong. Things here are much as usual. The gardens are looking lovely, and we had forty-six eggs yesterday. All send love, I don't mean all the eggs of course, but the people.

HELEN

'There!' she concluded. 'He *did* say four o'clock, and he knows he did, and I will find out who she was! He's been up to something for months – '

She sealed and stamped her letter, and put it with the others on the tray in the hall.

Clough brought this letter to Aubrey with his early cup of tea. Then, instead of withdrawing, he waited, as if he wished to say something.

'Well?' said Aubrey drowsily.

'Begging your pardon, sir, but I've been thinking things over,' said Clough.

'Oh? Ah! What? What do you say?' Aubrey yawned.

'It isn't the place, sir. The place suits me. I couldn't wish for a better place.'

'What's this? What do you say?' said Aubrey sitting up.

'And I'm not saying you aren't the master, sir – '

'Oh? Then what are you saying?'

'About that party, sir. I should wish to speak to you about it. I suppose those is your orders, sir, and I always have my remedy.'

'Tummy out of order or something this morning, Clough?'

'It's not for me to take liberties, sir, either with his lordship or anybody else. But it's all hours of the day and night likewise. It breaks my rest, besides being sinful of itself. Many's the time you've complained about it yourself, sir. So if it's going to begin here, sir, in this flat that I've always looked on as all that a flat should be – '

'Look here, do you mean that I'm not to give a party?' Aubrey demanded, now wide awake.

'I've never said that, sir. There's parties *and* parties.'

'Perhaps you don't approve of my guests?'

'I doubt if Miss Boyd would, sir.'

'Clough – ' said Aubrey.

'Sir?'

'Nothing. I was only thinking what a priceless undertaker you'd make.'

'*Sir!*' Clough could not believe his ears.

'And take that filthy wash away and get me a brandy-and-soda.'

Aubrey was astonished at himself. A month or two ago he would not have dreamed of using such words to Clough. There had been times when they had been more like cronies than master and man. Especially they had united in deploring the goings-on in the flat across the way. Yet here was Aubrey, not only ticking his faithful servitor off, but doing so with a relish such as he had seldom known.

Clough drew himself up. 'I should wish to give notice at once, sir,' he said austerely.

'Righty-oh, Clough. But get the brandy-and-soda first.'

'I should wish to give notice, sir,' Clough went on zealously, 'for your own good – yes, for your own good, sir! It is written in the Book whithersoever these things leads, and you're going the way you shouldn't go, Mr Kneller! That young female that's begun to come up here – '

'Don't be very long with the drink, Clough.'

'If convenient, might we say a week today, sir?'

'What, for the drink?'

'For my notice, sir.'

'Capital.' Clough had reached the door. 'Er – Clough!' said Aubrey, and Clough turned.

'Sir?'

'Go to hell.'

The door closed behind Clough.

Aubrey lay back on his pillow, chuckling softly. Long-nosed old snuffler! Aubrey wondered what scales had been over his eyes that he should even have taken on a fellow like that – him and his elastic-sided whiskers and pussyfoot boots! Anyway the scales had fallen now, thank the lord, and Aubrey had a keen and exhilarating sense that he saw things as they really were. The idea of his man-servant going through his list of guests was the funniest thing he had heard for a long time; he shook with laughter at it. Then, as he sat up again with a sigh of contentment, wondering if it would startle Clough still further if he threw a boot at the door, his eyes fell on Helen's letter. He opened it, gave it two flutters, back and forth, took in all there was in it, and laughed again.

Not sleeping very well, she! She had the nerve to tell him that! True, he had never seen Helen asleep, but if a dormouse slept more soundly he'd eat his pillow! A hundred-to-eight she just curled herself up and went off like a squirrel! So like these people who heard the clock strike once and then vowed they had never closed their eyes all night! And what was all this about there being something the matter with him? What should be the matter with him? He felt lighter and jollier than he had ever felt in his life! He could laugh at anything; above all he could laugh at himself. Lord, what a blind, blinkered life he had led! Those books of his filled from cover to cover with gestures and doings absolutely like nothing on earth! Those duds, those sticks, those mutts, Sir Hugh and Sir Guy and Sir Wilfred! Those posing wax dummies out of Swan and Edgar's window, his Phyllises and Rosamonds and Joans! Not a breath of life in a single one of them – barring that one little skivvy in a shabby black frock, and re-soled shoes, who had begun as Annie Thompson, and had grown – and grown – and grown –

Aubrey was in the middle of a luxurious yawn when this particular thought occurred to him. The yawn was suddenly cut in two. He had remembered the noble gesture with which Rosamond had gathered her skirts about her and had stalked out of his book. She had taken herself off rather than be published between the same covers as this little grasper who had commandeered nine-tenths of the book. There had been too many parallel possibilities already for another of them to be ignored. What, then, of Helen? As Rosamond had disappeared from his book, was Helen going to disappear from his life? Was *that* the meaning of her letter?

He picked up the letter again, and re-read it in the light of this new intelligence. By Jove, he was right! Unerringly he seemed to read between the lines, with brilliant clearness to divine her thought. He had been late that day at Rumpelmayers', and *had* pretended that he had made a mistake in the time. She *had* seen him alight at the door and lift his hat. From that moment on she *had* smelt a rat, and had resolved to know who his companion was. It all explained itself to Aubrey as he lay there in bed.

And then what? Aubrey's own growing intimacy with Upwester – Marie (or, as he had taken it into his head to call her, Delia) lunching and teaing with him whenever she could make the opportunity – Clough dismissing himself rather than countenance this total reversal of his master's life and habits – what did it all mean? People spoke of characters 'living' in a book. Certain of these nonexistent people had undoubtedly more vitality than most of the so-called 'real' people about them. To have written a real book cannot possibly be without its reaction on the book's writer. And what does it matter whether people in a book come to life or life comes to them? Life and fiction at the last interfuse, as the glitters come and go on a ventilating fan that turns on a wall. Already Upwester was what Sir Patrick Archdale should have been. Rosamond, the type of Helen, had left the stage. The little milliner he called Delia now occupied it exclusively. Physically and mentally she had bloomed since that first day in Pountney Place when the crimson daub on her mouth had seemed the only solid thing about her. She was acquiring an air and aplomb with marvellous rapidity. From stage to stage she had formed and built herself up, and now looked like becoming a piece of witchery indeed!

Witchery? Indeed, yes! Aubrey now felt that he had known her poutings and tempers and cajoleries for years! If she took it into her head that she wanted anything, that thing she would have, by whatever means. She would promise or refuse, keep her word or break it, kiss him or not kiss him, but always to the same end – her own. Already her frocks and furs and other what-nots had cost Aubrey something like two hundred pounds. And he liked spending the money on her. At any rate this was life, and what was two hundred pounds compared with life? Hang the money! This was not Helen, with her files and receipts and housekeeping accounts, the corn and meal on one side of them and the eggs balancing them on the other! Aubrey wanted a change from all that. Helen's letters frankly bored him. She met plenty of other eligible young men at her tennis-parties and so forth. Young Haverford, for example, would make an admirable husband for her. And from the very beginning, had not she and Aubrey always had the arrangement that if either of them ever thought differently about things the whole question was to be freely discussed?

Helen's letter meant that there would soon be a breach. She did not know, but Aubrey knew, that no power on earth could now prevent it. And he lay there in bed, thinking it all over, and light-heartedly humming a tune.

11

Aubrey's investments were nicely-settled ones, unspeculative, of the safe kind that left his mind free for other matters. Unless a tempting profit was to be taken he rarely thought of disturbing them. But one day not long after all this he rang up his broker and told him to sell a considerable block of stuff and to remit the proceeds to him. His current balance at the bank was never very large considering the comfortable way in which he lived.

Delia of course was at the bottom of it. She had come to Aubrey at his flat one morning in tears. The principal backer of the business in Pountney Place had announced that he must withdraw his support. Her distress moved Aubrey strangely as she asked him, her small gloved hands working at his lapels, whether he knew anybody who would take over the obligation.

Aubrey asked her this and that. He was no fool about money. He wanted details. But it was the wrong moment. It would drive her to distraction (she said) to have to go into all that now. He looked carefully at her, from her newest shoes to the little chocolate caramel of a hat on her head. The little anguished face that peeped through her furs was once more a pallor of white. Her eyes, frightened at the prospect of being thrown on her own resources again, seemed almost as he had first seen them – of the colour of the glass marble in the neck of a soda-water bottle.

'You must, you must!' she could only moan, the little hands clasped hard together. 'Oh, I'm frightened, I'm frightened, I'm frightened!'

The only words in which he could have expressed his concern were that she seemed to be slipping back – back into the colourlessness of the little saleswoman who had first opened the door to him in Pountney Place. And a queer sense of urgency was strong upon him. If she, who had driven everything else out of his mind, went back, then he too would be helpless and alone. The thought filled him also with sudden dread. Not in order to comfort her, but for his own sake, he wanted to take her into his arms and to cover her face and neck and hair with kisses. She was standing at his desk with her hands before her face. He stepped forward.

But she pushed him almost violently back.

'Oh, do leave me alone for once! That's all you think of! Here am I at my wits' end – I don't want to be kissed! I wish you'd never kissed me! You took me out of all that beastly life – you let me see something else – '

'Come, darling, come! The skies haven't fallen yet! We shall find something to do about it. These things have to be examined, you know.'

She broke into anger. 'Yes, and while you're examining them, as you call it, ruin's staring me in the face! You needn't bother. I shall go to somebody else! I don't care where I go. I shall go to that friend of yours in the other flat! I must know where I stand, and I must know today!'

'But be reasonable, darling! Of course I'll help you! But who are your backers? Where are your books? Who are your auditors? I must know these things!'

But she was now furious. Her hand struck the edge of the table.

'You see me in this state and ask me all those things! And you expect me to believe that you love me! What do I know about books? I come to you for help and you simply want to kiss me and make me do sums! Oh, I'm going!' She took a stride to the door.

Her hand was on the knob. She was going to somebody else, perhaps to Upwester. He, too, sprang forward.

'Little goose!' he said softly, patting her shoulder.

'Oh, it's all very well for you!' she stormed. 'You buy me a few things and think that's the end of it! You think more of your money than you do of me – '

'Delia!' he cried, hurt.

'You do! You waste money on things I could do without, just because you like me to look smart when I'm with you – it's all you – just who you're seen with – but as soon as *I* want it for something important – '

'Oh, hush, darling! You know I'll do anything for you!'

'Yes, if I'll kiss you!' she cried unrestrainedly. 'That's what you think of me!'

'I think you're lovely and wonderful!'

'Lovely and in the gutter! We know what that means!' she said scornfully.

'What *is* all this about the gutter? Who mentioned the gutter?' he said, his arms outspread.

'Oh, I'm tired of talking! I'm off!' she cried.

Off – off to Upwester or somebody else! Suddenly he could not endure the thought of it. Lose her – now! He loved her, loved her! He might be a fool. He knew that she was petulant, avaricious, not to be trusted a yard, given to these outbursts of unbridled anger. He knew all this from his book. But he always forgot it all again the moment she crept into his arms, sobbing and penitent, making herself small against him, and then, in the very middle of her tears, looking up at him with a smile and the tiniest little movement of her carnation lips. He had to kiss them then. He must kiss them now. The money side of the matter could be settled later.

'As if there was any need for all this!' he comforted her. 'I promise. Now come and sit down quietly by me.'

He led her to the sofa, where she sat down as if all her strings had been cut. He gathered her to his breast. She gave an exhausted sigh.

'Oh, I feel *so* lonely!'

'Poor little love!'

'Keep your arms round me for a bit.'

'Did you think I was going to take them away?'

'Hold me close,' she murmured brokenly. 'I'm sure if she understood everything she wouldn't mind.'

'She? Who?' said Aubrey, a little startled.

'The girl you're engaged to. *Would* she mind, do you think, if she knew?'

'She wouldn't have to,' said Aubrey grimly.

'Promise me you'll tell her, though. I should hate to do anything behind her back.'

Something, some echo out of that strange little world into which authors peep, seemed to awake in Aubrey's ears. A deep sense of inevitableness came over him; he had the memory of it all before. So it was appointed, so it must be, and the next step was already taken. He put her a little away from him and looked at her gravely.

'But didn't I tell you that was all off?'

'What, Aubrey?' she asked.

'About Miss Boyd. She's written to me breaking it off. Surely I told you!'

She gave a low cry of self-accusation. 'Oh, that's me!'

'You?' he said gently. 'It's nothing to do with you. At least, it's only this to do with you, that ever since I saw you I've known you've been the woman I dreamed of all along!'

'Oh, oh, what have I done!' she moaned. Then she sprang to her feet. 'Oh, Aubrey, I must go! Forget me, forget me! Forget everything about me! Never mind the business; I shall find somebody else. If I don't it doesn't matter. Let me go. Goodbye!'

But he was on his knees before her, his arms about her slender middle. He smelt the perfume of her clothing; he buried his face in it. Though it took every penny he had to keep her she should not go now. They could live there, in that King Street flat. It didn't matter where they lived, so long as it was together.

'Oh, Delia, Delia – marry me, marry me, marry me!' he cried in anguish.

Only a mirror saw that infinitesimally small gleam of triumph in her eyes. It was gone before his own eyes, brimming with supplication, were lifted up to her. She smiled sadly down on him.

'Do get up, Aubrey. You're spoiling my frock,' she said.

He kissed her knees and rose. He put on a cheerful, masterful manner.

'So that's all right, eh? We'll consider that settled, what?'

'Aubrey!' she reproached him. 'How can we, all in a moment like this? She'd be sure to say I'd taken you from her! Besides, look at you and look at me! No, it wouldn't do. And you mustn't kiss me again. You mustn't see me again. It isn't safe. I've got too fond of you. Aubrey, do help me to forget!'

'No!' he said resolutely. 'I know what I want, and I know what I'm going to have! So that's that!'

'Oh, you rush me off my feet – you don't give me a chance!' she quavered.

But even at lunch, which they took presently at Bellomo's, she still refused to say Yes or No. They had plenty of time, she said. Helen's feelings must be considered first. So she chatted about the food, the lunchers at the neighbouring tables, and how atrociously the manicuriste had done her nails.

12

The banking-account that Aubrey opened for Miss Delia Vane, in that name, was convenient for several reasons. If Aubrey was to finance some portion of the business in Pountney Place he would save a transaction by doing so out-and-out, and he and Delia could settle matters between them afterwards. For her personal expenses, which were not inconsiderable, it was hardly fitting that she should have to run to him every time she wanted a few pounds. And Aubrey himself was not a chartered accountant, but an author, whose royalties had, after all, to be earned, and who must presently be setting about another book unless his fortunes were to experience something like a slump.

He was getting more and more nervous about the book that was to appear in the autumn. It was a good book, but a good book

and good business are not necessarily the same thing. And his
fears grew on him when he took up his old press-cutting books
and read how, in the opinion of the reviewer, his Sir Vivians and
Lord Marmadukes gave not only a true and vivid picture of the
highest type of English gentleman as he is, but provided all that
a happy idealism demanded into the bargain. Aubrey shook his
head. The reviewers might be right about the idealism, if by that
they meant something that resembled nothing on earth; but –
well, what about Upwester, for example. They say authors are
touchy and vain. Aubrey might have been touchy and vain had
somebody else pointed out these things. But the scales had fallen
from Aubrey's eyes, and now, if he wanted a really good cynical,
hearty, wholesome laugh, he picked up his own most successful
book, *Loved I Not Honour More*.

The funny thing was that Upwester, to whom he lent this work,
and who kept it for a fortnight on the bedside table where the kippers
had been cooked, was (as he put it) 'all over it'. He liked it most
enormously – couldn't imagine how Aubrey had done it, nor where
he got his ideas from. There was a certain earnestness in his childish
eyes as he explained all this to Aubrey.

'You see, dear old bran-bag,' he confided to Aubrey, helping himself to a whiskey-and-soda from the cupboard that had not been
locked since Clough's departure, 'it's so exactly what we *ought* to be,
you know. That's really my *idea* of a book, not that I know much
about 'em, but if they're simply what you see about you every day,
well, where are you? I mean to say it makes you think. Makes you
sort of overhaul yourself. The way you live kind-of-thing. Bee's a
jolly good sort, of course, and there's the club, that's all right in a
way; but there's something else, and that's where you set us thinking,
old boy. We might all of us be better. That the idea? Anyway, come
and have a quick one at the club.'

Upwester had put Aubrey up for this club of which he spoke,
and at first Aubrey had hardly known what to talk about to the
fellows to whom his friend had introduced him. He was indifferent
at golf, knew little about cars, less about horses, and had never
heard of nine out of ten of the different cocktails that were served
at the smoking-room bar. Neither was Aubrey skilled enough at
poker to play that game for pound points, in absolute silence, for
afternoon after afternoon. Sometimes he dropped out of the conversation altogether, and wandered about the rooms, looking at
the rather surprising prints and pictures that paved the walls, with

trophies of jockeys' caps and sketches done by hilarious artists after midnight filling in the chinks between. But Upwester looked after the new member. 'Kneller – writes books, you know – just read one of 'em – top hole' – Aubrey and his job were inseparable on the peer's lips. And when Aubrey, first swearing him to secrecy, confided to him the title of his forthcoming work, Upwester would stand at the bar, with a cocktail that looked like furniture-cream in his hand, and, with a jerk of his elbow, would say, 'D.V., old chap – you know – hope she sells a million!' and would drink. Heart of gold little Upwester had, Aubrey sometimes thought. He still sometimes came home with somebody else's hat on and the visiting cards of people he didn't remember in his pocket, but it is a poor heart that never rejoices. Aubrey had lately had to buy a new hat too.

Upwester first met Delia at that party of Aubrey's with which Clough had refused to have anything to do. The party itself may be described in Upwester's words, which if he repeated once he did so twenty times.

'Now I *like* a party like that. Quiet, sensible talk, nobody one over the eight, no dressing up in pyjamas, no ragging, not to speak of, and everybody off home by half-past two! That's the stuff; makes a break! Must have another. Fresh as paint this morning – thoroughly enjoyed! But look here, my old Ticklers' jam; got a bone to pick with you! You didn't tell me there was a *real* D.V.! I don't want to butt in, but who in smoke is she? Costs a pretty penny to dress *her*, I guess! No business of mine, of course, but she's as smart a thing as I've seen in a month of Sundays. Keeps a shop, you say? So does my sister. Lingerie? Nothing like it! Wish I'd a business head on me! Begin to think I'm no good at cards even – lost fourteen quid to Bertie Murray this afternoon. Time I went slow for a bit; it's Cork Street if I don't. But I did enjoy that party – '

Delia, too, had enjoyed the party, if one could judge from her manner the next afternoon. She snuggled up to Aubrey with a contented little sigh, playing with his buttons and tracing little patterns with her forefinger on the back of his hand.

'It was lovely!' she sighed. 'I felt just a bit shy at first, but everybody was so nice! I love Bee! But I don't think I care for Lord Upwester much. Isn't he rather stupid? Anyway, he's a lord, and I only keep a hat-shop. Is he very rich as well as being a lord?'

She played with his buttons and stroked his hand, but she still deferred her engagement to him. She had so much to think about, she said, and it wouldn't look right, so soon after his breach with Helen. He might call it an understanding if he wished, and she didn't mind wearing his ring, but it would have to be on another finger. It was a lovely ring, she said; and so it should have been, seeing it had cost him a hundred-and-eighty guineas. Yes, he might kiss her, too; she didn't *always* want not to be kissed . . . So he kissed her, and she closed her eyes blissfully. Later he mused on the strangeness of it, that this atomy he had found in a hat-shop, unformed and ready to tremble at a look, should so have found her way to the very core of his heart.

But more and more he worried about the possible effect of all this on his fortunes. In the days of what his critics were presently to call his 'earlier manner' he had considered the public at large to be a very good judge of books, since it bought his own in large numbers – never yet had a man a stroke of good luck but his first endeavour was to persuade himself that he deserved it all and more. But the dropping of those scales from his eyes that had begun that afternoon in Pountney Place had shown him that hardly anybody knew the first single thing about books after all. He saw that famous public of his as a flock of sheep, ready to take any gate if somebody else took it first, refusing it unanimously if the leader jibbed. To buy or bribe or win over that leader was the whole business of authorship as it was practised. To that end literary journals were directed, tea-parties were held, and publishers bought newspaper-space ahead. All was a machine, in which one must either ride or be run over. And in *Delia Vane* Aubrey had challenged the machine. Some piece of grit had found its way into the wheels. That piece of grit was called Truth.

And now what was going to become of him? Any number of things were possible. His credit might be good enough to stand the strain for a time, but publishers work in figures, and the gradual letting-down of his saleability could not be long delayed. He might make a *succès de scandale*, which in the long run would not be good for his credit either, since the public does not like its slaves in two pigeon-holes at once. Or nothing at all might happen. That book of his, his first living book, might be condoned as an escapade, on the understanding that the offence did not happen again. But he could never go back to his former manner. His editions would be a story of diminishing prices – seven-and-six, three-and-six, a shilling, Tauchnitz, and the usual odds-and-ends. Already he was within sight of the bottom of his current account.

It was not a good time to sell his securities. If an idea for another book did not occur to him he must set about writing stories or newspaper articles. Or a little reviewing. He felt just about capable of a little reviewing.

13

'Dearest,' she said to him one night, 'I should so love to go on the stage!'

They were, as it happened, in the stalls of the 'Thalia' at that moment, but Aubrey knew little of what passed across the footlights. He had had a fruitless day of brain-cudgelling, and felt all-in. His tie was carelessly tied, and he would have liked nothing so much as to be at home in bed. But she was full of life and joy

'You see,' she went on – this was during an *entr'acte* and her hand beneath her shawl was light and warm upon his knee – 'you see, Bee's been on the stage and knows all about it. They'll make you a star straight away if you can put up five thousand pounds. Being a star's as easy as falling out of bed if you've got money. I *should* so love to go on the stage, Aubrey!'

At any other time he would have fenced, delayed, laughed the occasion off. But it was now beyond his strength. Miserably he confessed that he neither had five thousand pounds nor knew where to lay his hands on any such sum. Her eyes were sidelong on a curtained doorway with the word 'EXIT' written over it in red electric lights.

'Poor darling!' she said; and then, with a sudden little pressure of her hand upon his knee, 'Oh, look! Isn't that Lord Upwester? I'm sure he's not seen you! Do go and have a drink with him – I don't mind being left alone – '

He left her, but he did not seek Upwester in the bar. Instead he stood alone in a dim crimson corridor, absently flicking the ash of his cigarette into a receptacle on the wall.

Five thousand pounds! By the sale of everything he had he could hardly now have spared her five hundred. He didn't doubt that all she said of the stage was true. Furs ready to step into, a waiting brougham, an expensive flat in town and a country cottage, a horse to give lumps of sugar to with a camera standing by – somebody had to occupy this glittering sphere, and it might as well be she as anybody else. Not a doubt that five thousand pounds would do the trick. But as far as Aubrey Kneller was concerned five thousand pounds might just as well have been the moon.

And if he hadn't the cash, had he anything else to take its place? A year or so before he might have raised money on his mere name; but not now – or at least not after the moment when his book should appear. Already he was conscious that he was going to let his publisher down; should he, while there was still time, add to his iniquity by grabbing a further sum on account, based on his former successes? He would almost have done it – for her. But wearily he turned his face to the crimson wall, burying it in his arms, careless of whether anybody saw him or not. He knew now what that book of his was. It was not a novel, but a bomb. If he had sought to challenge, not only the book-world, but the whole gravely comic convention of the world at large, *Delia Vane* could not have been more exquisitely devised for the purpose. He had betrayed, not only his publishers, but Society. The naked truth in a world that only exists by means of conventions – that was what his brain had been able to conceive and his hand rash enough to write. *Delia Vane* after *Loved I Not Honour More* – it was his death-warrant. They would be quite right in putting him to death. He had set himself on a high place, merely to cast himself down again. There would soon remain to him nothing but the memory of what he had been, and that witching little sweetheart of his sitting down there in the stalls.

That night he gave her a cigarette in his flat before driving her home, and wondered moodily how he was to break these things to her. He could hardly expect her to understand them, since a few months before he would not have understood them himself. He could only trust to her faithfulness and gratitude. Tears came into his eyes at the sight of her, curled up in his huge chair, with one small ankle pushed out towards him, and the gay lining of her cloak making a spread on the chairback behind her. Dear God, if he should lose her now! It was in his heart never to let her out of his flat again. And to think that she smiled, knowing nothing of the agony that surged in his breast! She was smiling at the orange-hued cylinders of his electric fire. She seemed to him to be already on the stage, bowing behind a forest of bouquets, courted, photographed, adored, her name on everybody's lips. And had it been in his power she should have had it all for one of those kisses she knew how to give.

Then she moved. 'I suppose it can't be done,' she sighed.

He did not even ask her what it was that could not be done.

He discharged his taxi at her door in Pountney Place, and set out to walk to King Street, St James's. He passed shelterless, outcast people, and felt himself more outcast than they. He began to count his steps. *Left foot, right foot*: with every step he took there ran a dual set of pictures in his brain. They ran, as it were, in harness, the actual facts of the world's life, the no less actual facts of that other life that no man knows but himself. *Left foot, right foot*: the Annie Thompson who had crept into his book, the Delia Vane who had crept into his heart. *Left foot, right foot*: exit Rosamond, goodbye Helen. *Left foot, right foot*: Upwester and Pat –

Suddenly a cold sweat broke out on Aubrey Kneller's brow. Upwester and Pat! He was passing the doors of the New Universities Club; he sat suddenly down on the Club's steps. Upwester! No, impossible! Though Delia had married Pat in the book, *that* parallel at least could not be carried over into real life! Upwester would never come between Aubrey and this other Delia of his desire! He was a decent little fellow, played the game. Why, he had had drinks with Aubrey, introduced him to his club, invited him to his flat. Nobody did these things and then let a pal down. Upwester was, must be, all right!

Yes, but what about *her*? Could he trust her a yard? Utterly as he loved her he knew he could not. Between his first gift of a hat and this last demand for five thousand pounds there had been wile after wile, stratagem after stratagem. She had pouted and wept and flared up; she had promised and broken her promise; she would marry him and she would not marry him; a dog was not to be hanged on her word. Therefore, however loyal his intentions, what chance would Upwester have if *she* decided to set her cap at *him*? Why had she said when she had first met him that she didn't think she liked him very much? Why had she said that she would go to him for money for her business? Why had her eyes spied him so quickly at the theatre? Because she was a liar, and he loved her. She was a selfish, heartless little schemer, and he loved her. And Upwester would not even have to furnish the five thousand pounds. His title was enough. Lady Upwester was already a star without lifting a finger. And Aubrey could do nothing, nothing, nothing. He could only sit on the steps of the New Universities Club and rock slowly from side to side with his head between his hands.

The next day but one the proofs of his book arrived. Except to correct a few trifling literal errors he barely glanced at them; why read a book that is as inalienably one's own life as the blood that comes and goes from one's heart? Let the proofs go. Half a morning sufficed to despatch them. He registered the packet at the Post Office near St James's Church and put his receipt into his pocket.

But that perforated piece of paper was not a receipt for the parcel. It was a receipt for the body and brain and immortal soul of a man.

14

Not very long after that Aubrey found it necessary to run down to Rickmansworth on business connected with the house he no longer required. He asked Delia to go with him, but she said that she could not leave Pountney Place. He wondered a little at this, as she now had an assistant, but if she couldn't she couldn't, and there was an end of it. He went alone, telling her that he would be back in time to take her out to dinner.

His business was done more quickly than he expected. He was back in King Street again before five o'clock. As he waited on the ground floor for the descending lift, down it came, and Upwester and Delia stepped out of it.

She greeted him with an undisturbed smile, and, with her first words back came his own chickens to roost. For, just as he had formerly pretended to Helen that he had thought an appointment was for half-past four instead of four, so she now said that she had understood him to say he would be back at five. And, anyway, wasn't he back at five? So she had called for him at his flat, and had found all locked up, and just as she had turned away again Lord Upwester had come out of his own door. He knew that it was a tissue of lies from beginning to end; he knew that she knew that he saw through it; but there was nothing to be said. Upwester looked guilty. The three of them walked together as far as the Carlton, and there Upwester left them. Aubrey and Delia descended to the tea-room.

He was silent, but she made up for his taciturnity. Never had her eyes been so active nor her spirits so high. She rallied him on his gloominess, and gave a delighted little laugh at his sudden start when she slyly placed a hot teaspoon on the back of his hand. She adored the Carlton, she said, and wasn't that Gladys Cooper sitting with the good-looking man over there? He roused himself a little, but relapsed again. A great dread possessed him. He drank tea, but could not have swallowed a crumb. She *had* met Upwester by appointment, *was* turning him round her finger, and he *was* going to lose her.

'It is Gladys Cooper!' she rippled. 'Aubrey, darling, if I do go on the stage will you write me a play?'

He said that he couldn't write a play. He didn't think he should ever write anything again.

'Oh, that's only because you're a little tired, darling! Do write me a play, Aubrey, with a large fat part all to myself!'

'Oh, marry me, marry me!' broke in a low groan from him.

'Silly boy, what's the matter with you?' she asked, innocently. 'I can't marry you this minute, can I?'

'Do you love me, *do* you love me?'

'Of course I do. I think you're a perfect duck. You aren't cross with me about anything, are you?'

'Oh, I feel like water!'

'I know,' she sympathised. 'I always used to feel like that. I felt like that when you came into the shop that time. It's a horrid feeling.'

'Marry me tomorrow – the next day – say you will – '

'But there won't be time, darling! I shall have all my things to get! I should hate to get married in a poky sort of way!'

'I'd marry you if you hadn't a penny.'

'Aubrey,' she said slowly, 'don't you trust me?'

He dared go no further on that dangerous ground.

That night he met Upwester at the club. The peer's hang-dog look completely gave him away. Returning home, he tossed all that night in a rage of jealousy. In his thoughts he alternately took Upwester by the throat, threatened him, implored him, laid machiavellian traps for him. He would have them both watched, would watch them himself, until he could account for every moment of their day. He tortured himself with images of their clandestine meeting that afternoon. And from loving Delia he turned to hate of her. He called her vile names. She was a treacherous, cold-blooded, unscrupulous little harpy. She had no intention of marrying him. She was holding out for the highest bid. He had clothed her, fed her, taken her about, loaded her with gifts, financed her business. All was not enough, but she must have five thousand pounds more and a play all about her heartless little self. Let her not try him too far! There was a limit! Flesh and blood could only stand a certain amount –

So he tossed, turning his dreadful new gift of vision into a fiendish instrument with which to torture himself. Sinister gift, that will not let us look on love but we must gaze on hate too! He had better have married Helen. Infinitely happier had he never adventured beyond the easy falsities of life. That was the grief to which he came. He had come, just for once, into contact with knowledge, and saw his ruinous end rushing to meet him. The publication

of *Delia Vane* overshadowed him like an imminent doom. For a
year or two he would scrape along somehow. Oddments of money
would still trickle in. He could compound on his life-insurance
policy. His past services to literature might bring him within the
terms of the Royal Literary Funds. He supposed he would always
have the clothes he stood up in. But for the rest, all the profit of his
life would be the peace and bitterness of truth.

15

His book appeared in September. Bold pronouncements in the book-
columns of the newspapers heralded its appearance, the framed posters
in the tube lifts proclaimed it. He had his cheque in advance and on
account, and it rather more than sufficed to set him straight again at
the bank. His first reviews came to hand. They were brief and colourless. A large edition had been subscribed; all was in readiness for an
immediate reprinting. And then, suddenly, nothing whatever happened. Quietly, undramatically, nothing at all happened. It was as if
Delia Vane was being secretly and silently burked. Openly assassin-
ated it could not be. People could not be prevented from asking for
the latest work of the author of *Loved I Not Honour More*. And no
doubt they did ask. But Aubrey never heard of it.

A week passed, and a fortnight. Papers that might have been
expected to review him still delayed to do so. One paper indeed,
highbrow and obscure, did attack him violently. It rated the book as
a grotesque travesty of life, and said that Mr Kneller's acquaintance
among the baronetage could be but small if he thought that such a
figure as Sir Patrick Archdale existed outside his own delirious imagination. It strongly recommended him to return to the manner of
those spotless ones, Sir Vernon and Sir Hugh.

And that was all. *Delia Vane* simply did not catch on. Nobody
understood it or cared a hang about it. Its announcements disappeared
from the booksellers' windows, other posters replaced it in the tubes.
The trade gave it a perfunctory display, and then relegated it to
the back parts of the shops. His publishers wrote to him complaining
that they could not conceive what had happened. Then apparently it
occurred to somebody in the office to read the book itself. Aubrey
received a peremptory telephone-message telling him he must call at
once. He did so, and there was the devil of a row.

Hitherto (they told him) they had accepted his books in good faith.
He had supplied a saleable article, had built up a magnificent public,

and their relations had been of the happiest. But – they must tell Mr Kneller this plainly – had they known beforehand the character of the work he had now foisted on them, like some stinging creature in a posy of flowers, they would never have dreamed of affixing their imprint to it. They could not imagine what had possessed him. And at the word 'possessed' Aubrey started a little. It was so very near the truth.

'But hang it all,' he broke out, 'what else do you want? Of course a fellow must be possessed by his book! How the devil can *he* possess *it*?'

'Those are technicalities with which we have nothing to do, Mr Kneller. We don't write the book. And it's hardly too much to say that you've let us down grossly and that we have a very heavy load left on our hands.'

'But damn it all, man,' Aubrey had exploded, 'the book's worth all the others put together! No, it isn't even that – it's in a class by itself!'

'So are its sales, Mr Kneller. That's exactly what we're complaining of.'

'Start the advertising again. Surely the public aren't all fools! I tell you there's the stuff of life in that book!'

'We've read it,' was the dry reply.

'Where's a copy? Let me show you!'

'It's no good, Mr Kneller. Your other books were a faithful and charming picture, the mirror held up to nature, but this – '

Aubrey broke into a wild laugh.

'The mirror held up to nature! Are you serious? *Haw, haw, haw*! Sorry to laugh – *haw, haw, haw*! – but it's too comic! *Haw, haw, haw, haw*! Don't mind me, but you see I happen to know Archdale – he's really a fellow called Upwester! And I happen to know Delia too – her real name's Marie! And as for those tailor's-dummies you want me to put in, why, I had 'em in, and I turfed them out again! Where do you suppose books come from? Out of a machine, like a gross of cut nails? I tell you they get born, like a woman with a baby, and all you confounded publishers have to do is to tie the knot and let 'em run about on their own!'

'Well, Mr Kneller, you're entitled to your views, but as this is the last book of your contract you can hardly expect us to renew.'

'Renew!' cried Aubrey excitely. 'Do you think I'd *let* you renew? Do you think I've been through what I have been through for you to hawk my stuff on your coster's barrow? No, sir! You go on publishing as you call it; life and I'll attend to our end of the show! I know what I know, and I laugh at you! My soul's my own – "*HAW, HAW, HAW, HAW, HAW*!" '

And with a wave of his hand he strode out of the office and down the stairs.

He strode straight on to Pountney Place, laughing loudly as he went. Free, free! Or at least he would be free within half an hour from now. For did he not see with translucent clearness what was going to happen? Did he not know, as if it had been shouted in his ears, what Delia was going to tell him! And did he now care the snap of a finger? Not he! Let her marry her peer! He wasn't a bad sort after all. And she, steeped to her lips in smiling deceit, was a born actress. As Lady Upwester she would probably set the London stage on fire. And Aubrey would go to her debut. He would see her from the gallery, join in the acclamations, shout himself hoarse at her triumph. Marry her now? He didn't want to marry her! Some union more mystic even than that of marriage was between her and him. She was Delia Vane, who had given him, not a few kisses, but this boundless liberty with which he could now move through the world. She was his door, not into a house in Rickmansworth, not into a flat in St James's, not into a parlour in Pountney Place, but into the heart of life itself! Know yourself, one other person, and the relation between the two, and you have a base-line from which to find the range of anything there is; and did not Aubrey know himself, her, and that relation? Was she not his very Muse? Had she not given him the note of harmonies that would be music in his soul for ever? Oh, she had, she had, and he must run and thank her!

He turned into Pountney Place. Behind him, past Harrods' and the Oratory, swept the double main stream of life, east and west, west and east, without ceasing. He walked as if on air, laughing for joy as he went. What a quaint, quakerish, demure little street it was, with its windows so oddly half-commercial and half-domestic! The very furniture in the windows of its antique shops seemed to have turned its back on the interiors only for a moment, and would turn round again when it saw that there was nobody outside to look at but Aubrey Kneller! Striped sunblinds, flowers in window-boxes, fanlights, quiet old Hogarth frontages – a novelist might find suggestions in a street like that! That little shop across the way, for example: it had a little whitewashed area, a green-and-white sunblind with the name

Mathilde

in flowing script across it, and a serried row of chimney cowls making ragged the skyline over its coping. On a pedestal in the window stood a single green-and-white hat. He had a fancy he would look at that

hat. He had no particular reason for doing so; he just thought he would. He crossed the street. The front door of the shop stood open, but a door just within it on the right was closed. Under a little brass plate that bore the words 'Please Ring' was an electric button. But Aubrey had no intention of ringing. He hadn't the price of a hat such as that in his pocket. Yet he lingered, not passing the shop immediately.

As he lingered, he faintly heard, from somewhere at the back of the premises, and apparently upstairs, a woman's voice that called some apprentice or junior assistant.

'*Marie-e-e-e*!' the voice died away on the air . . .

The Cigarette Case

'A cigarette, Loder?' I said, offering my case. For the moment Loder was not smoking; for long enough he had not been talking.

'Thanks,' he replied, taking not only the cigarette, but the case also. The others went on talking; Loder became silent again; but I noticed that he kept my cigarette case in his hand, and looked at it from time to time with an interest that neither its design nor its costliness seemed to explain. Presently I caught his eye.

'A pretty case,' he remarked, putting it down on the table. 'I once had one exactly like it.'

I answered that they were in every shop window.

'Oh yes,' he said, putting aside any question of rarity . . . 'I lost mine.'

'Oh? . . . '

He laughed. 'Oh, that's all right – I got it back again – don't be afraid I'm going to claim yours. But the way I lost it – found it – the whole thing – was rather curious. I've never been able to explain it. I wonder if you could?'

I answered that I certainly couldn't till I'd heard it, whereupon Loder, taking up the silver case again and holding it in his hand as he talked, began.

'This happened in Provence, when I was about as old as Marsham there – and every bit as romantic. I was there with Carroll – you remember poor old Carroll and what a blade of a boy he was – as romantic as four Marshams rolled into one. (Excuse me, Marsham, won't you? It's a romantic tale, you see, or at least the setting is.) . . . We were in Provence, Carroll and I; twenty-four or thereabouts; romantic, as I say; and – and this happened.

'And it happened on the top of a whole lot of other things, you must understand, the things that do happen when you're twenty-four. If it hadn't been Provence, it would have been somewhere else, I suppose, nearly, if not quite as good; but this was Provence, that smells (as you might say) of twenty-four as it smells of argelasse and wild lavender and broom . . .

'We'd had the dickens of a walk of it, just with knapsacks – had started somewhere in the Ardèche and tramped south through the vines and almonds and olives – Montélimar, Orange, Avignon, and a fortnight at that blanched skeleton of a town, Les Baux. We'd nothing to do, and had gone just where we liked, or rather just where Carroll had liked; and Carroll had had the *De Bello Gallico* in his pocket, and had had a notion, I fancy, of taking in the whole ground of the Roman conquest – I remember he lugged me off to some place or other, Pourrières I believe its name was, because – I forget how many thousands – were killed in a river-bed there, and they stove in the water-casks so that if the men wanted water they'd have to go forward and fight for it. And then we'd gone on to Arles, where Carroll had fallen in love with everything that had a bow of black velvet in her hair, and after that Tarascon, Nîmes, and so on, the usual round – I won't bother you with that. In a word, we'd had two months of it, eating almonds and apricots from the trees, watching the women at the communal washing-fountains under the dark plane-trees, singing *Magali* and the *Qué Cantes*, and Carroll yarning away all the time about Caesar and Vercingetorix and Dante, and trying to learn Provençal so that he could read the stuff in the *Journal des Félibriges* that he'd never have looked at if it had been in English . . .

'Well, we got to Darbisson. We'd run across some young chap or other – Rangon his name was – who was a vine-planter in those parts, and Rangon had asked us to spend a couple of days with him, with him and his mother, if we happened to be in the neighbourhood. So as we might as well happen to be there as anywhere else, we sent him a postcard and went. This would be in June or early in July. All day we walked across a plain of vines, past hurdles of wattled *cannes* and great wind-screens of velvety cypresses, sixty feet high, all white with dust on the north side of 'em, for the mistral was having its three-days' revel, and it whistled and roared through the *cannes* till scores of yards of 'em at a time were bowed nearly to the earth. A roaring day it was, I remember . . . But the wind fell a little late in the afternoon, and we were poring over what it had left of our Ordnance Survey – like fools, we'd got the unmounted paper maps instead of the linen ones – when Rangon himself found us, coming out to meet us in a very badly turned-out trap. He drove us back himself, through Darbisson, to the house, a mile and a half beyond it, where he lived with his mother.

'He spoke no English, Rangon didn't, though of course, both French and Provençal; and as he drove us, there was Carroll, using him as a Franco-Provençal dictionary, peppering him with questions about the names of things in the patois – I beg its pardon, the language – though there's a good deal of my eye and Betty Martin about that, and I fancy this Félibrige business will be in a good many pieces when Frédéric Mistral is under that Court-of-Love pavilion arrangement he's had put up for himself in the graveyard at Maillanne. If the language has got to go, well, it's got to go, I suppose; and while I personally don't want to give it a kick, I rather sympathise with the Government. Those jaunts of a Sunday out to Les Baux, for instance, with paper lanterns and Bengal fire and a fellow spouting *O blanche Vénus d'Arles* – they're well enough, and compare favourably with our Bank Holidays and Sunday League picnics, but . . . but that's nothing to do with my tale after all . . . So he drove on, and by the time we got to Rangon's house Carroll had learned the greater part of *Magali* . . .

'As you, no doubt, know, it's a restricted sort of life in some respects that a young *vigneron* lives in those parts, and it was as we reached the house that Rangon remembered something – or he might have been trying to tell us as we came along for all I know, and not been able to get a word in edgeways for Carroll and his Provençal. It seemed that his mother was away from home for some days – apologies of the most profound, of course; our host was the soul of courtesy, though he did try to get at us a bit later . . . We expressed our polite regrets, naturally; but I didn't quite see at first what difference it made. I only began to see when Rangon, with more apologies, told us that we should have to go back to Darbisson for dinner. It appeared that when Madame Rangon went away for a few days she dispersed the whole of the female side of her establish- ment also, and she'd left her son with nobody to look after him except an old man we'd seen in the yard mending one of these double-cylindered sulphur-sprinklers they clap across the horse's back and drive between the rows of vines . . . Rangon explained all this as we stood in the hall drinking an *apéritif* – a hall crowded with oak furniture and photographs and a cradle-like bread-crib and doors opening to right and left to the other rooms of the ground floor. He had also, it seemed, to ask us to be so infinitely obliging as to excuse him for one hour after dinner – our postcard had come unexpectedly, he said, and already he had made an appointment with his agent about the *vendange* for the coming autumn . . . We begged him, of course, not to allow us to interfere with his business in the slightest degree. He thanked us a thousand times.

' "But though we dine in the village, we will take our own wine with us," he said, "a wine *surfin* – one of my wines – you shall see – "

'Then he showed us round his place – I forget how many hundreds of acres of vines, and into the great building with the presses and pumps and casks and the huge barrel they call the thunderbolt – and about seven o'clock we walked back to Darbisson to dinner, carrying our wine with us. I think the restaurant we dined in was the only one in the place, and our gaillard of a host – he was a straight-backed, well-set-up chap, with rather fine eyes – did us on the whole pretty well. His wine certainly was good stuff, and set our tongues going . . .

'A moment ago I said a fellow like Rangon leads a restricted sort of life in those parts. I saw this more clearly as dinner went on. We dined by an open window, from which we could see the stream with the planks across it where the women washed clothes during the day and assembled in the evening for gossip. There were a dozen or so of them there as we dined, laughing and chatting in low tones – they all seemed pretty – it was quickly falling dusk – all the girls are pretty then, and are quite conscious of it – you know, Marsham. Behind them, at the end of the street, one of these great cypress wind-screens showed black against the sky, a ragged edge something like the line the needle draws on a rainfall chart; and you could only tell whether they were men or women under the plantains by their voices rippling and chattering and suddenly a deeper note . . . Once I heard a muffled scuffle and a sound like a kiss . . . It was then that Rangon's little trouble came out . . .

'It seemed that he didn't know any girls – wasn't allowed to know any girls. The girls of the village were pretty enough, but you see how it was – he'd a position to keep up – appearances to maintain – couldn't be familiar during the year with the girls who gathered his grapes for him in the autumn . . . And as soon as Carroll gave him a chance, he began to ask *us* questions, about England, English girls, the liberty they had, and so on.

'Of course, we couldn't tell him much he hadn't heard already, but that made no difference; he could stand any amount of that, our strapping young *vigneron*; and he asked us questions by the dozen, that we both tried to answer at once. And his delight and envy! . . . What! in England did the young men see the young women of their own class without restraint – the sisters of their friends *même* – even at the house? Was it permitted that they drank tea with them in the afternoon, or went without invitation to pass the *soirée*? . . . He had all the later Prévosts in his room, he told us (I don't doubt he had the earlier ones also); Prévost and the Disestablishment between them must be playing the mischief with the convent system of education for young girls; and our young man was – what d'you call it? – "Co-ed" – co-educationalist – by Jove, yes! . . . He seemed to marvel that we should have left a country so blessed as England to visit his dusty, wild-lavender-smelling, girl-less Provence . . . You don't know half your luck, Marsham . . .

'Well, we talked after this fashion – we'd left the dining-room of the restaurant and had planted ourselves on a bench outside with Rangon between us – when Rangon suddenly looked at his watch and said it was time he was off to see this agent of his. Would we take a walk, he asked us, and meet him again there? he said . . . But as his agent lived in the direction of his own home, we said we'd meet him at the house in an hour or so. Off he went, envying every Englishman who stepped, I don't doubt . . . I told you how old – how young – we were . . . Heigho! . . .

'Well, off goes Rangon, and Carroll and I got up, stretched ourselves, and took a walk. We walked a mile or so, until it began to get pretty dark, and then turned; and it was as we came into the blackness of one of these cypress hedges that the thing I'm telling you of happened. The hedge took a sharp turn at that point; as we came round the angle we saw a couple of women's figures hardly more than twenty yards ahead – don't know how they got there so suddenly, I'm sure; and that same moment I found my foot on something small and white and glimmering on the grass.

'I picked it up. It was a handkerchief – a woman's – embroidered –

'The two figures ahead of us were walking in our direction; there was every probability that the handkerchief belonged to one of them; so we stepped out . . .

'At my "*Pardon, madame*" and lifted hat one of the figures turned her head; then, to my surprise, she spoke in English – cultivated English. I held out the handkerchief. It belonged to the elder lady of the two, the one who had spoken, a very gentle-voiced old lady, older by very many years than her companion. She took the handkerchief and thanked me . . .

'Somebody – Sterne, isn't it? – says that Englishmen don't travel to see Englishmen. I don't know whether he'd stand to that in the case of Englishwomen; Carroll and I didn't . . . We were walking rather slowly along, four abreast across the road; we asked permission to introduce ourselves, did so, and received some name in return which, strangely enough, I've entirely forgotten – I only remember that the ladies were aunt and niece, and lived at Darbisson. They shook their heads when I mentioned M. Rangon's name and said we were visiting him. They didn't know him . . .

'I'd never been in Darbisson before, and I haven't been since, so I don't know the map of the village very well. But the place isn't very big, and the house at which we stopped in twenty minutes or so is probably there yet. It had a large double door – a double door in two senses, for it was a big *porte-cochère* with a smaller door inside it, and an iron grille shutting in the whole. The gentle-voiced old lady had already taken a key from her reticule and was thanking us again for the little service of the handkerchief; then, with the little gesture one makes when one has found oneself on the point of omitting a courtesy, she gave a little musical laugh.

' "But," she said with a little movement of invitation, "one sees so few compatriots here – if you have the time to come in and smoke a cigarette . . . also the cigarette," she added, with another rippling laugh, "for we have few callers, and live alone – "

'Hastily as I was about to accept, Carroll was before me, professing a nostalgia for the sound of the English tongue that made his recent protestations about Provençal a shameless hypocrisy. Persuasive young rascal, Carroll was – poor chap . . . So the elder lady opened the grille and the wooden door beyond it, and we entered.

'By the light of the candle which the younger lady took from a bracket just within the door we saw that we were in a handsome hall or vestibule; and my wonder that Rangon had made no mention of what was apparently a considerable establishment was increased by the fact that its tenants must be known to be English and could be seen to be entirely charming. I couldn't understand it, and I'm afraid hypotheses rushed into my head that cast doubts on the Rangons – you know – whether *they* were all right. We knew nothing about our young planter, you see . . .

'I looked about me. There were tubs here and there against the walls, gaily painted, with glossy-leaved aloes and palms in them – one of the aloes, I remember, was flowering; a little fountain in the middle made a tinkling noise; we put our caps on a carved and gilt console table; and before us rose a broad staircase with shallow steps of spotless stone and a beautiful wrought-iron handrail. At the top of the staircase were more palms and aloes, and double doors painted in a clear grey.

'We followed our hostesses up the staircase. I can hear yet the sharp clean click our boots made on that hard shiny stone – see the

lights of the candle gleaming on the handrail . . . The young girl –
she was not much more than a girl – pushed at the doors, and we
went in.

'The room we entered was all of a piece with the rest for rather
old-fashioned fineness. It was large, lofty, beautifully kept. Carroll
went round for Miss . . . whatever her name was . . . lighting candles
in sconces; and as the flames crept up they glimmered on a beautifully polished floor, which was bare except for an Eastern rug here
and there. The elder lady had sat down in a gilt chair, Louis Fourteenth I should say, with a striped rep of the colour of a petunia; and
I really don't know – don't smile, Smith – what induced me to lead
her to it by the finger-tips, bending over her hand for a moment as
she sat down. There was an old tambour-frame behind her chair, I
remember, and a vast oval mirror with clustered candle-brackets
filled the greater part of the farther wall, the brightest and clearest
glass I've ever seen . . . '

He paused, looking at my cigarette case, which he had taken into
his hand again. He smiled at some recollection or other, and it was a
minute or so before he continued.

'I must admit that I found it a little annoying, after what we'd
been talking about at dinner an hour before, that Rangon wasn't
with us. I still couldn't understand how he could have neighbours
so charming without knowing about them, but I didn't care to insist
on this to the old lady, who for all I knew might have her own
reasons for keeping to herself. And, after all, it was our place to
return Rangon's hospitality in London if he ever came there, not,
so to speak, on his own doorstep . . . So presently I forgot all about
Rangon, and I'm pretty sure that Carroll, who was talking to his
companion of some Félibrige junketing or other and having the air
of Gounod's *Mireille* hummed softly over to him, didn't waste a
thought on him either. Soon Carroll – you remember what a pretty
crooning, humming voice he had – soon Carroll was murmuring
what they call "seconds", but so low that the sound hardly came
across the room; and I came in with a soft bass note from time to
time. No instrument, you know; just an unaccompanied murmur
no louder than an Aeolian harp; and it sounded infinitely sweet and
plaintive and – what shall I say? – weak – attenuated – faint – "pale"
you might almost say – in that formal, rather old-fashioned *salon*,
with that great clear oval mirror throwing back the still flames of
the candles in the sconces on the walls. Outside the wind had now
fallen completely; all was very quiet; and suddenly in a voice not

much louder than a sigh, Carroll's companion was singing *Oft in the Stilly Night* – you know it . . . '

He broke off again to murmur the beginning of the air. Then, with a little laugh for which we saw no reason, he went on again.

'Well, I'm not going to try to convince you of such a special and delicate thing as the charm of that hour – it wasn't more than an hour – it would be all about an hour we stayed. Things like that just have to be said and left; you destroy them the moment you begin to insist on them; we've every one of us had experiences like that, and don't say much about them. I was as much in love with my old lady as Carroll evidently was with his young one – I can't tell you why – being in love has just to be taken for granted too, I suppose . . . Marsham understands . . . We smoked our cigarettes, and sang again, once more filling that clear-painted, quiet apartment with a murmuring no louder than if a light breeze found that the bells of a bed of flowers were really bells and played on 'em. The old lady moved her fingers gently on the round table by the side of her chair . . . oh, infinitely pretty it was . . . Then Carroll wandered off into the *Qué Cantes* – awfully pretty – "It is not for myself I sing, but for my friend who is near me" – and I can't tell you how like four old friends we were, those two so oddly met ladies and Carroll and myself . . . And so to *Oft in the Stilly Night* again . . .

'But for all the sweetness and the glamour of it, we couldn't stay on indefinitely, and I wondered what time it was, but didn't ask – anything to do with clocks and watches would have seemed a cold and mechanical sort of thing just then . . . And when presently we both got up neither Carroll nor I asked to be allowed to call again in the morning to thank them for a charming hour . . . And they seemed to feel the same as we did about it. There was no "hoping that we should meet again in London" – neither an *au revoir* nor a goodbye – just a tacit understanding that that hour should remain isolated, accepted like a good gift without looking the gift-horse in the mouth, single, unattached to any hours before or after – I don't know whether you see what I mean . . . Give me a match somebody . . .

'And so we left, with no more than looks exchanged and finger-tips resting between the back of our hands and our lips for a moment. We found our way out by ourselves, down that shallow-stepped staircase with the handsome handrail, and let ourselves out of the double door and grille, closing it softly. We made for the village without speaking a word . . . Heigho! . . . '

Loder had picked up the cigarette case again, but for all the way his eyes rested on it I doubt whether he really saw it. I'm pretty sure he didn't; I knew when he did by the glance he shot at me, as much as to say 'I see you're wondering where the cigarette case comes in.' . . . He resumed with another little laugh.

'Well,' he continued, 'we got back to Rangon's house. I really don't blame Rangon for the way he took it when we told him, you know – he thought we were pulling his leg, of course, and he wasn't having any; not he! There were no English ladies in Darbisson, he said . . . We told him as nearly as we could just where the house was – we weren't very precise, I'm afraid, for the village had been in darkness as we had come through it, and I had to admit that the cypress hedge I tried to describe where we'd met our friends was a good deal like other cypress hedges – and, as I say, Rangon wasn't taking any. I myself was rather annoyed that he should think we were returning his hospitality by trying to get at him, and it wasn't very easy either to explain in my French and Carroll's Provençal that we were going to let the thing stand as it was and weren't going to call on our charming friends again . . . The end of it was that Rangon just laughed and yawned . . .

' "I knew it was good, my wine," he said, "but – " a shrug said the rest. "Not so good as all that," he meant . . .

'Then he gave us our candles, showed us to our rooms, shook hands, and marched off to his own room and the Prévosts.

'I dreamed of my old lady half the night.

'After coffee the next morning I put my hand into my pocket for my cigarette case and didn't find it. I went through all my pockets, and then I asked Carroll if he'd got it.

' "No," he replied . . . "Think you left it behind at that place last night?"

' "Yes; did you?" Rangon popped in with a twinkle.

'I went through all my pockets again. No cigarette case . . .

'Of course, it was possible that I'd left it behind, and I was annoyed again. I didn't want to go back, you see . . . But, on the other hand, I didn't want to lose the case – it was a present – and Rangon's smile nettled me a good deal, too. It was both a challenge to our truthfulness and a testimonial to that very good wine of his . . .

' "Might have done," I grunted . . . "Well, in that case we'll go and get it."

' "If one tried the restaurant first – ?" Rangon suggested, smiling again.

' "By all means," said I stuffily, though I remembered having the case after we'd left the restaurant.

'We were round at the restaurant by half-past nine. The case wasn't there. I'd known jolly well beforehand it wasn't, and I saw Rangon's mouth twitching with amusement.

' "So we now seek the abode of these English ladies, *hein*?" he said.

' "Yes," said I; and we left the restaurant and strode through the village by the way we'd taken the evening before . . .

'That *vigneron*'s smile became more and more irritating to me . . . "It is then the *next* village?" he said presently, as we left the last house and came out into the open plain.

'We went back . . .

'I was irritated because we were two to one, you see, and Carroll backed me up. "A double door, with a grille in front of it," he repeated for the fiftieth time . . . Rangon merely replied that it wasn't our good faith he doubted. He didn't actually use the word "drunk" . . .

' "*Mais tiens*," he said suddenly, trying to conceal his mirth. "S*i c'est possible . . . si c'est possible* . . . a double door with a grille? But perhaps that I know it, the domicile of these so elusive ladies . . . Come this way."

'He took us back along a plantain-groved street, and suddenly turned up an alley that was little more than two gutters and a crack of sky overhead between two broken-tiled roofs. It was a dilapidated, deserted *ruelle*, and I was positively angry when Rangon pointed to a blistered old *porte-cochère* with a half-unhinged railing in front of it.

' "Is it that, your house?" he asked.

' "No," says I, and "No," says Carroll . . . and off we started again . . .

'But another half-hour brought us back to the same place, and Carroll scratched his head.

' "Who lives there, anyway?" he said, glowering at the *porte-cochère*, chin forward, hands in pockets.

' "Nobody," says Rangon, as much as to say "look at it!" "M'sieu then meditates taking it?" . . .

'Then I struck in, quite out of temper by this time.

' "How much would the rent be?" I asked, as if I really thought of taking the place just to get back at him.

'He mentioned something ridiculously small in the way of francs.

' "One might at least see the place," says I. "Can the key be got?"

'He bowed. The key was at the baker's, not a hundred yards away, he said . . .

'We got the key. It was the key of the inner wooden door – that grid of rusty iron didn't need one – it came clean off its single hinge when Carroll touched it. Carroll opened, and we stood for a moment motioning to one another to step in. Then Rangon went in first, and I heard him murmur *"Pardon, Mesdames . . . "*

'Now this is the odd part. We passed into a sort of vestibule or hall, with a burst lead pipe in the middle of a dry tank in the centre of it. There was a broad staircase rising in front of us to the first floor, and double doors just seen in the half-light at the head of the stairs. Old tubs stood against the walls, but the palms and aloes in them were dead – only a cabbage-stalk or two – and the rusty hoops lay on the ground about them. One tub had come to pieces entirely and was no more than a heap of staves on a pile of spilt earth. And everywhere, everywhere was dust – the floor was an inch deep in dust and old plaster that muffled our footsteps, cobwebs hung like old dusters on the walls, a regular goblin's tatter of cobwebs draped the little bracket inside the door, and the wrought-iron of the hand-rail was closed up with webs in which not even a spider moved. The whole thing was preposterous . . .

' "It is possible that for even a less rental – " Rangon murmured, dragging his forefinger across the hand-rail and leaving an inch-deep furrow . . .

' "Come upstairs," said I suddenly . . .

'Up we went. All was in the same state there. A clutter of stuff came down as I pushed at the double doors of the *salon*, and I had to strike a stinking French sulphur match to see into the room at all. Underfoot was like walking on thicknesses of flannel, and except where we put our feet the place was as printless as a snowfield – dust, dust, unbroken grey dust. My match burned down . . .

' "Wait a minute – I've a *bougie*," said Carroll, and struck the wax match . . .

'There were the old sconces, with never a candle-end in them. There was the large oval mirror, but hardly reflecting Carroll's match for the dust on it. And the broken chairs were there, all gutless, and the rickety old round table . . .

'But suddenly I darted forward. Something new and bright on the table twinkled with the light of Carroll's match. The match went out, and by the time Carroll had lighted another I had stopped. I wanted Rangon to see what was on the table . . .

' "You'll see by my footprints how far from that table *I've* been," I said. "Will you pick it up?"

'And Rangon, stepping forward, picked up from the middle of the table – my cigarette case.'

* * *

Loder had finished. Nobody spoke. For quite a minute nobody spoke, and then Loder himself broke the silence, turning to me.

'Make anything of it?' he said.

I lifted my eyebrows. 'Only your *vigneron's* explanation – ' I began, but stopped again, seeing that wouldn't do.

'*Any*body make anything of it?' said Loder, turning from one to another.

I gathered from Smith's face that he thought one thing might be made of it – namely, that Loder had invented the whole tale. But even Smith didn't speak.

'Were any English ladies ever found to have lived in the place – murdered, you know – bodies found and all that?' young Marsham asked diffidently, yearning for an obvious completeness.

'Not that we could ever learn,' Loder replied. 'We made enquiries too . . . So you all give it up? Well, so do I . . . '

And he rose. As he walked to the door, myself following him to get his hat and stick, I heard him humming softly the lines – they are from *Oft in the Stilly Night* –

> I seem like one who treads alone
>   Some banquet-hall deserted,
> Whose guests are fled, whose garlands dead,
>   And all but he – departed!

The Rope in the Rafters

I

For the last seven miles of his journey James Hopley's hopes had sunk lower and ever lower till now, at the gates of the château itself, he heartily wished he had never left the clinic in Paris. The driver of the single-horse *voiture* had descended from the seat and with the rain beating on his back was struggling with the rusty fastenings. One of the gates had come away from its masonry, and the pair of them were only held together by the lock in the middle and a turn or two of old dog-chain, and even when he had got them apart he had to hold them so while he led the horse through by the bridle. With one of his eyes, for the other was of glass, James Hopley looked through the streaming panes at the desolate and unkempt avenue. Then he groaned. The château itself had come into view. The whole of one end of it was a skeleton of scaffolding. New windows were being broken through, a new chimneystack was being built. The rain beat down on dumps of broken brick and débris and laths torn out of walls, the yew trees dripped on barrows and wheeling-planks and weeds. A Henri Quatre château in the depths of the country! This was the place Blanche and the doctors had said would do him all the good in the world!

For many years past Blanche's kindnesses to him had been innumerable. She had written to him when nobody else had, had remembered him when the rest of the world had forgotten him. This loan of her château was only the most recent of her benefactions. But there was one thing she would not do. She would keep her memory of him as he had been. Never, never would she see him again. And he sometimes felt that this was her greatest kindness of all.

By a terrace door in an angle of the façade the driver tugged at an iron bellrod. After a longish interval the door was opened by an elderly, bald, greybearded man in a red baize apron, behind whom stood a meagre woman in black. These were evidently the Marsacs, who were to look after him during his convalescence. Without a word the man reached behind him for a huge umbrella and came forward to hold it over James. From under its edge James saw a long terrace frontage with tall windows and more tall windows above them. In an inner lobby a second door stood half open. The man in the apron had returned to fetch his belongings.

Then happened something that seemed little short of a miracle. Stepping forward James suddenly found himself in a lofty room with panelled and tapestried walls, vast armoires, and a wide stone hearth on which, behind massive firedogs, a great wood fire burned. Near it a small period table was laid for one, with cutlery, a napkin and a large jar of montbretia. By a glass stood a tall bottle of wine with the cork invitingly half drawn. Outside the mud and the rain and inside – this! He stood looking round the surprising room and then turned to the woman, who with eyes averted was waiting for her orders.

'You seem to have been busy, Madame Marsac,' he said.

The woman had a voice as harshly shrill as that of a parrot. But busy! Only the day before yesterday nothing, not a chair, and then, *mon Dieu*, everything arriving by road from Paris at once! Busy!

And if Madame Marsac had been busy here his friend Blanche had been no less busy at the auction-rooms of the Hôtel Drouot in Paris. *Chez* Drouot one can buy for a song ancient and elephantine pieces of furniture that no modern room will take, and here they were, the tapestries and leather-backed chairs, tall oil-lamps of bronze and onyx, a battle-piece big enough for a wall at Versailles, porcelain vases as large as those of the Forty Thieves. But James Hopley had put out his hand to the bottle with the half-drawn cork. Even a *gueule cassée*, blown up by high explosive in the war and not dug out of the earth again for a week, may still like the inner warmth of a glass of wine. So here was to Blanche. Her white-elephant of a château was not turning out so badly after all.

2

That afternoon, the rain still continuing, he took a walk round this place that had been so generously put at his disposal. Strictly speaking it was not so much a château as a hunting-box, of two tall storeys and a hipped and dormered roof above that, with one row of windows facing the terrace and the other looking across the neglected park to the river that joined the sea some dozen miles away. But it was the topmost floor of all that instantly seized James Hopley's imagination. What a place for a couple of boys to have played hide-and-seek in! Except for the roof itself this upper portion had never in fact been completed. Floorboards ended suddenly, leaving bare the joists and the drop to the storey below. The dormers were infrequent and the light already falling, and when presently he began to strike matches as likely as not a sigh of wandering air blew them out again. He would in fact be wise to get to the safety of the lower levels before it became quite dark.

And suddenly he was checked. Something had struck him lightly in the face.

A bat? There might well be bats up there. And his matches were getting few, but he shielded one carefully in his hands. The object that had struck him was a rope, that swung from a beam overhead and disappeared in the shadows below. Still, with workmen about a place a rope was no unusual thing to find, and he turned away.

But by this time he had got confused about the building's plan. He descended to the mansard level again and found a door that opened on stairs similar to those he had come up by. He groped his way down these and in the darkness pushed at another door at the bottom. And the next moment he was in a high, lamplighted, kitchen sort of room, stacked half way to the ceiling with packing-cases and crates from which the paper and straw protruded. The lamp shone full on the bald head of the man in the red baize apron, who with the meagre woman his wife was sitting at a bare table having a frugal meal. He had stumbled into the caretaker's quarters.

He was about to apologise when suddenly he stopped. The woman, catching sight of him, had let out a harsh, ringing cry, and had clapped her hands before her eyes. The man's hand, too, had closed swiftly on the lighted lamp as if he would have hurled it. But he picked it up shakily instead, rising to his feet as he did so. His voice was strongly under control.

'Monsieur has no doubt missed his way; it is here,' he said, and lamp in hand advanced to a door in a corner. He led the way across a draughty apartment empty except for sacks of cement, and opened another door. James was back in the large room that had first welcomed him, but this time from the fireplace end.

Mortified, dispirited, the slow recovery of weeks undone again at a single stroke, he sank into one of the leather-backed chairs. Always, always his face, and so he supposed it must be to the end. For in Paris, when the yearly performances were given, and the cap was passed round for the benefit of those afflicted as he was, be sure you would not find James Hopley standing next to the kiosk where his own picture-postcard was for sale, showing off his grafts and his paraffin-wax and his seared cheek, with the glass eye glittering as hard as a doll's in the middle of it all. Much more then, meeting people for the first time and in a place like this, he ought not to have shown himself without warning, appearing from nowhere at the foot of a flight of private stairs. But he made no mention of the incident when presently the woman came in to lay the period table for his supper. By that time he was busily writing. He was still writing when she came in to clear away. And as it is on this writing of James Hopley's that this tale of him is largely based, a word had better be said about it.

The shiny, black-backed exercise-book before him was the fifth of the series. They contained his own account of his case apart from anything the doctors might have to say about it, and as they were written for his own eye only, they leave out much more than they put in. Naturally he did not tell himself things he already knew. But once in a while some unexpected result cropped up, and at present he was noting down this unfortunate beginning with the Marsacs. He passed his hand over his brow as he finished it, then closed his book, took his candle, and at a little after nine o'clock slowly mounted the echoing stairs to bed.

His bedroom, too, was Hôtel Drouot, with much ormolu and alabaster and cracked and faded gilding. It had two beds, a yard or so apart, as if Blanche had made ready either for married guests or for a single person like himself, and on a small commode between them stood the second candlestick. James Hopley had had a long journey and was tired. He threw his dressing-gown across the second bed and got into the first one. There, having blown out his candle, he lay awake listening to the hundred noises of the gaunt place.

Outside the rain beat down without ceasing. Somewhere a door must have been left open, for he found himself waiting for a recurrent banging. Outside in the corridor vague gusts entered by the window-piercings, and somewhere on the scaffolding something flapped. Slowly that mortifying picture faded, of a woman who hid her face and screamed while a man's hand went to a lighted lamp. He yawned, drew up his knees, and slipped over the edge of sleep.

He was awakened by a sound different from any he had been listening to. It seemed to come from immediately overhead and so heavy was the thud of it that it brought him upright on his pillow, startled and listening.

But when a sound wakes you from sleep, and is not repeated, it is not difficult to persuade yourself that you have dreamed it after all. James sank slowly back to his pillow again. But he was next conscious of a sudden alteration in the air; a strong odour seemed to have found its way into the room, and at the same time he was aware of a new sound, that came from somewhere in the room itself. It came from the direction of the other bed, and it was the sound of deep and painful breathing.

But it was on the sharp, pervading smell that his attention was first of all concentrated. Two of its components he could have accounted for readily enough. They were wet earth and freshly-bruised grass, and there was plenty of both outside. But to these was added something else. It was the smell of the chest and arms of a man. Then he gave his attention to the breathing again.

Matches stood on the commode beside him, but he did not immediately put out his hand to them. Even the striking of a match would have been an interruption. Sometimes the sounds of the breathing died down, and then suddenly they fought, as if for life, filling the room with their noise. And James Hopley had never been in this château in his life before, but either that was the breathing of somebody he had known or else in some other way it broke suddenly through out of the dark tomb of the past. For it is the first time only that we forget. Set the chord vibrating again and thenceforward it continues to vibrate as long as we have a memory at all. In the darkness James lay listening to the breathing for a while longer; then he put out his hand for the matches.

But he instantly drew it back again, so many degrees colder was the air. It was in fact a minute or more before he managed to light one of the candles. The other bed was unchanged in appearance, with his dressing-gown still across it just as he had thrown it down. But brr, it was cold! The cold, that pungent smell of sweat, the breathing.

He had put one foot out of bed and advanced his ear. He advanced it so close that he almost expected to feel the breath on his cheek. Then he placed his hand on the coverlet.

But that apparently he ought not to have done. There was the sigh of one who wakes from temporary forgetfulness to the intolerable burden of life again. The chilliness drew away. The breathing became fainter and died. The air cleared. The candle burned on as if nothing had happened.

3

Most of us like our bedrooms to ourselves. If we must share them we would rather do so with somebody who does not smell quite so strongly nor bring quite such a coldness into the air. But comparatively few of us have been through the ordeal James Hopley had been through. The main structure of our frame has not been so shattered that as a frame it can suffer no more, but only in its remaining separate fragments. Account for it as you will, James Hopley did not shrink from something that would have sent most of us back to Paris by the very next train. It was in fact a slight disappointment to him that for the remainder of the night he was undisturbed. And he was busily writing it all down in his *cahier* before he had well swallowed his coffee the next morning.

Towards the middle of the morning, however, he was interrupted by the announcement of a visitor. The *curé* of the place had lost no time in coming to enquire after the health of Madame Blanche in Paris and to hope that M. Hopley himself had recovered from the fatigue of his journey. At least these were the reasons he gave for his call. James had no doubt he had others. One was probably curiosity, and James, who noticed such things, marked him creditably highly for his composure in the presence of skin-grafting and paraffin-wax. But for all that the *curé* had not talked for ten minutes before he was hinting that the château was perhaps not the best place for a convalescent to be staying in at that particular moment.

'When this rain stops the men will be at work again,' he said, fingering his little silver cross. 'And I see that one of your occupations is writing, which requires quiet. I cannot think you will be comfortable here. Come to me at my little house if you feel inclined. I should even be happy if you would spend some considerable time with me. My garden is pleasant and my apples are ripe. Also it would be society for me. Here – so near the river – the air is not salubrious.'

This was generous, and James thanked the *curé*; but at the same time it looked a little like letting the cat out of the bag, and presently he was asking about the château itself, its history, legends, associations. It seemed a natural thing to do.

But he did not find the *curé* communicative. No place like that was without its hundred legends, some with a basis of truth, others the merest gossip, he said. Three houses had stood on those foundations before the present one. One story was that the wounded were brought to this château after the battle of Arcques. There were rumours concerning it during the Terror. Later, if vulgar report was to be believed, it had a history of smuggling. Its skeletons were best left in its cupboards. And that was about as much as the *curé* would commit himself to. Again he recommended his own vicarage. He accepted a glass of wine, but declined to stop and share James's midday meal, and James accompanied him as far as the rusty gates.

He found it interesting that the battle of Arcques had been fought in the neighbourhood. He did not know what weather that battle had taken place in, but a battle can be an earthy affair, with much trampled grass, and they who take part in it are exceedingly likely to sweat. But James could not believe that a battle fought nearly three hundred years ago had very much to do with himself. Had nothing happened in this country of France since then? The Terror was not exactly yesterday either. As for smuggling . . . well, these people ought to know best, but he gave a shrug. The incident had made far too deep an impression on him to be dismissed like that. If it were merely that some desperado had been pistolled or knocked on the head while running a bale or two of wool from England, Blanche would have been proud of her ghost and would have told him in her letters. Walking slowly with head down and hands behind his back he fell into a deep musing.

Nevertheless he discovered the château's possibilities with regard to contraband that very afternoon. He found them in the cellars. These were a series of vaults on ancient foundations of flint, with great bays branching off them, a bakehouse, a laundry, wine-cellars with the old wooden bins still mouldering in them, and in the very middle of the house he nearly walked into an unrailed and unguarded well. A rope in the rafters to hang him and a well down here to drown him? But no. On examination he found the well to be a dry one. Then, making a swift calculation, he shone his electric torch up into the vaulting. There were signs that at some time or other, it had been cut through, and a tour of the other floors a little later in the day showed the remains of other trap-doors, boarded up and long disused, but all in a vertical line between the rope and the well. With a river across the park and the sea only a few miles away here was a depot for contraband ready made. But still he shook his head. Somewhere not far away there was a truer explanation than that. The rain was beginning to stop. Perhaps a turn outside would clear his thoughts and give some inner James Hopley a chance to say what he had to say. He descended the worn and grey and lichened steps at the end of the terrace. He walked along the edge of the shrub-grown moat, past the gnarled old orchard, and through knee-deep thistles down the slope of the park to the river. There, by the muddy, sliding water, that ought to provide good fishing when it cleared, he cast about as it were for a rise in his own mind.

His habit of avoiding all company but his own had made of this mind a sparsely-furnished but a severely-ordered one. Accordingly he began at the right end, namely, with the people he knew something about. First there was the *curé*. He was kind, hospitable and well-mannered. James was as touched by the offer of his house and orchard as if he had thought of availing himself of it. But the *curé* after all had to steer a middle course between two worlds, and vague talk about Arcques, the Terror and smuggling was all James was likely to get out of him. Next there was Marsac. Marsac was getting on in years. He lived rent-free, the produce of the gardens was enough for him and his wife, and if he lost this job he would not find it easy to get another at his time of life. He would therefore put up with midnight bumps and alterations of temperature in a part of the house he was not called upon to occupy. Then there was Blanche herself. She was spending a lot of money on her purchase and would be coming to live there in the spring. As for the workmen, he hadn't seen them yet, but, like Marsac, they would not be likely to quarrel with their bread-and-butter.

But must every place affect everybody in precisely the same way and degree? Was there nothing in what a man brought to it? It was no light experience that James Hopley was bringing to this chateau of his friend's. A smell at which anybody else would simply have opened a window was for him charged with dreadful memories. Coldness to him was not a mere momentary discomfort but the coldness of all mortality, disturbed breathing the suffering of a human frame that could bear no more. Was it then to be wondered at that after that first night he was ready to appropriate to himself anything unusual there might be about that château, its past, its present, or anything else it might have in store? He continued his walk under the alders of the swollen river, sometimes wondering whether the air was really as insalubrious as the *curé* has said, but always returning to his thought . . . that if a man brought more to a place than he found there he already knew a good deal more about it than anybody else could tell him.

4

There is only one sure way of being present at the birth of a legend. That is to be oneself its origin. James Hopley left the river that afternoon with a highly remarkable idea in his head.

It had to do with this queer business of revived memory. Show a man for example a drawing of a person he has seen perhaps once; the chances are that he will have forgotten the person; but he will remember the drawing. So with the happenings of last night. Should they happen a *second* time then that would be a momentous and ineradicable event. It was not impossible that out of the sheer force of the stirring-up a third would follow, and a fourth. This was the idea James Hopley left the river with that afternoon.

But it was only the beginning of it. Something far more pregnant followed. It had been in 1916 that he had been blown up and had disappeared from the world for exactly seven days and seven nights. Then had come his recent and unaccountable relapse in Paris. Therefore he was now a man who experiments upon the string of an instrument. Touch it never so lightly in the right place and you were answered by its harmonic. It might be a harmonic of a jangled and horrible discord, scraped rawly out on that open string of 1916, but it would be identical in its notes and duration, faithful in its other correspondences. Seven nights of actually-lived-through hell then, seven nights of its etherealised repetition now. What was to happen after that does not seem to have troubled him very much. What would come would come, and it could hardly be worse than what had been. And oh, what a lot about this twilit edge of things he would know by that seventh night! As he took his candle to go to bed it seemed already strange to him that he had only been in that château of his own reawakened memories a little more than twenty-four hours.

But as he was turning down the bronze lamps the door beyond the fireplace opened and Marsac stood in the entry. And James was already finding Marsac not at all a bad fellow. He had intelligence above the average, and also a stolid sort of courage. Therefore he paused in his going to bed to exchange a word with him.

'It seems a pity to leave that fire,' he said pleasantly, for its flames played richly on the tapestries and the high tinted ceiling. 'I was just going upstairs.'

'Until the workmen have finished it is not possible to put a fire upstairs for monsieur. Madame wrote suddenly, and there was little time to make ready,' Marsac replied.

'Did Madame then think I had married without telling her? There are two beds,' James said, his single eye on the caretaker's face to see how he took it.

But Marsac made no sign. 'It was as easy to put two as one, and she did not say how long monsieur might be staying.'

'Because the place is not salubrious? It is what Monsieur le Curé said. For that reason he invited me to stay with him.'

At that Marsac did go near to betraying himself. 'Then no doubt monsieur will do so?' he asked quickly.

'I? Visit?' said James, and Marsac became the restrained domestic again.

'Monsieur is comfortable here? There is nothing else he requires tonight?'

'Nothing. Good night,' and as the caretaker finished the putting out of the lamps the ceiling and tapestries looked the friendlier because of all that James Hopley knew for certain awaited him in the bedchamber upstairs.

That night he again threw his dressing-gown across the second bed and blew out his candle. But as he lay there awake he knew now what he was waiting for.

On the following morning a young workman in a blouse and peaked cap mounted a ladder and chanced to put his head into a window-aperture that opened to the long corridor inside. Suddenly a door immediately across the corridor opened, and James Hopley stood there. The workman descended hastily to where a couple of carpenters were sawing at a trestle under a portion of the scaffolding. He took off the peaked cap and passed his sleeve across his brow.

'Have you seen?' he whispered, glancing involuntarily over his shoulder.

'Has who seen what?' an older man demanded, pausing in his sawing.

'What has arrived. *Mon Dieu*! Jean the Smuggler will not have it all his own way in the château now!'

'It is the English *gueule cassée*. Mathilde Marsac told me. You have seen him?'

'If I have seen him! . . . ' exclaimed the young man.

'What is he like?'

'Like! What is a nightmare like when it promenades itself by day? I will tell you what he is like . . . '

He did so. One of his listeners made a grimace, the other nodded.

'It is what Mathilde Marsac said. She saw him arrive, looking over her husband's shoulder. She saw him as he stood there in the salon, looking round. And that very same night, just as she was having her supper, the door of the back stairs opened and he stood there, his face like a cinder with a piece of glass in it . . . '

But the second carpenter was a more matter-of-fact sort of fellow. 'Mathilde Marsac!' he scoffed. 'Mathilde's knees knock together if she has to pass the churchyard in the daylight!'

'And is it not in the daylight that I have seen him, not five minutes ago?' the young workman demanded. 'The night is the night. Such things belong to it. But at the beginning of the day . . . '

'Bah, poor devil! Marsac told me – Madame Blanche wrote it in the letter to say he was coming – that he will not go back to his own country because of those who might remember him there. Perhaps some woman – perhaps Madame herself – who knows? *Va*! Mathilde Marsac and our Francis here, now they have *both* seen Jean the Smuggler,' and the speaker reached for his saw again.

But Francis the mason had seen what he had seen, and moved off to find another audience.

He had in fact seen, though without knowing anything about it, an exceedingly startling development. It was one that James Hopley himself, writing at that moment his 'roofer' to Blanche (and for what a roof!), had as yet no inkling of. For James was flushed with success. He had predicted an astonishing thing, and lo, it had straightway come true to the letter. But something else had come no less true with it. He had had no particular reason for looking at himself in the glass more attentively than usual that morning. All that he remembered of his getting up was that as he had stepped out of his room some young workman or other had hastily withdrawn his face from a window-opening. But James had in fact made his first serious mis-assumption. He had taken it for granted that the work of the doctors was now done once for all, past possibility of slipping back. An actual *physical retrogression* had been the last thing he had foreseen. Yet swift as a returned blow this had taken place within a few hours, and if it continued the inner ravage would but make the plastic superimpositions the more ghastly as time went on. It mattered little now what he wrote in or left out of his diary. The thing had already begun to write itself terribly on his face.

He was in fact already planning the next steps of his adventure at that very moment. He must try to take this room-fellow of his by surprise. What for example would happen if he were to change the position of the beds? If, approaching carefully, he tried whether that harsh breathing would stir the flame of a candle? Dim a looking-glass? If he spoke suddenly and loudly, setting subtle traps in his questions? But now that all was well afoot there was plenty of time. He did not notice that his midday meal was brought in that day not by Madame Marsac, but by her husband. But he did remember the workman who had looked across the corridor at him and, looking up, asked the caretaker his name.

'A brown-eyed, timid-looking young man in a blouse and a peaked cap,' he said. 'He was standing halfway up a ladder.'

'That would be Francis, the mason,' Marsac replied.

'Francis the mason. I see. They are good fellows, the workmen here?'

Marsac would not express an opinion. They were *comme ci comme ça* . . . all sorts.

'It is doubtless a fine thing for the village that Madame Blanche has acquired this property.'

'No doubt it brings money.'

'And will bring more when she herself comes and begins to entertain.'

'The château has had its lean years. It is but just it should have its prosperous ones,' Marsac replied.

'I sincerely hope it may have,' said James, resuming his work, and the caretaker withdrew.

His work for the moment was to address Francis the mason in a sort of written monologue. James in fact talked to him with his fountain-pen as if he had been actually there. You are young, Francis (he wrote), and for the young one makes allowances. When you are as old as our friend Marsac here you will not look at a man for a moment like that and then draw back as if you had seen a ghost. You have perhaps finished your service, but wait till you have seen a war. They will make you a hundred ghosts there quicker than you can put your head through an opening and take it away again. Ghosts may not be all you think, friend Francis. Much depends on how much you bring with you. Are you married? Have you children? Children grow up and women grow old, and if that's all, death's the end. But is it the end? That's what I'm trying to find out. In a very few nights I'm hoping to know. Would you like to know too? You look the sort it might be easy to tell. You may not be the first to be told. Madame Marsac looks like being that. But would you like to be the second?

And when a man sets out during his lifetime to find out what happens to him when he dies, a few days and nights are little enough for the task before him.

5

His first serious check awaited him on his fifth afternoon. It began with something that he afterwards called himself fool and dunderhead not to have thought of before. Did *he* only breathe at night? Had *he* never lain down for a rest in the middle of the afternoon? Also up to then he had been content to write of this visitor of his that after a certain time he 'went'. But where did he go? Even he couldn't go simply nowhere. This is what happened.

At about five o'clock that afternoon he needed something – it was nothing more than a clean handkerchief – that chanced to be in his bedroom, and went upstairs to get it. And this time he does not stint his description of what happened the moment he opened the bedroom door. He is, in fact, unpleasantly explicit, so we will simply say that the signs were at their maximum strength. And it was as he stood looking wonderingly down on that flat empty bed of suffering that he had his inspiration. *Where* did the fellow take himself off to when he was disturbed? Hitherto his manner towards his guest had varied. There had been all those stealthy experiments to try. But even at his most intent he had shown a measure of consideration. Now he twitched off the coverlet abruptly. This fellow went back to the battlefield of Arcques when he left the bed, did he? To the Quartier St Antoine or the Bastille? To a cave of the confederates of this smuggling gang? Well, wherever he went this time he would have to pass James Hopley at the door before he did so. James stood in the entry, waiting for the chill waft to pass before his face.

For it was by the coldness and the overpowering smell that he followed. After a moment or two these became less strong, but in the corridor the scent was still breast-high. Along the passage he followed in the direction of the stairs that led to the mansard, up the stairs into the space beneath the roof. He followed in cold blood, not into bat-haunted shadows now, but in pallid dusty daylight that showed up every detail of every post and beam. He came to where the floorboards ended and the drop to the stage below could be seen. Then the odour left him as cleanly as if it had fallen in one dense body over the edge, and he stood looking stupidly at the rope that dangled from the beam overhead.

Stupidly yet with eyes suddenly cleared, for he remembered now how that rope had been the first thing to greet him on his arrival at the house. With workmen about its presence had not struck him as sinister then, but now it beckoned to him like some dreadful lure. '*Your* life?' the gently-swaying, sinuous thing seemed to whisper. 'It cannot be that you value life? When you remember yourself as you were twenty years ago? Have you forgotten? *The Past was the Best, the Present is Worse, the Worst is to Come*! Twenty years ago you lived every minute, because you knew how few the minutes might be. If anything should happen at least a whole man would get it in head or stomach or groin. The feel of your body was like wine to you, you made friends of a sudden. Where are your friends now? Can you find one, where before every man had a wave of the hand for you, though you never saw him again? The best of them are dead. They would be glad to be dead if they could see today what they died for. It would at least be decent that all should be dead before men began to think of carnage again. But they are subtly at work, even those who saw it – security, rights, the glorious past, our immortal story, the heritage our fathers died for, our glory still to be. And what of the multitude who will believe anything if only the lie is big and noisy enough? Who cling to their leaders who prepared the evil, and saw the evil through, and made a worse evil to follow it, and are even now tired and helpless before an evil by the side of which the other would be good? Have you seen it once and want to see it again? Do you *want* to live, James? In this world as it is? *The Past was the Best, the Present is Worse, the Worst is to Come*. Look at me, James, and ask yourself if you want to live.' All this, and a thousand times more, the rope seemed to be saying to James Hopley as it hung there, gently swaying from the beam overhead.

And suddenly James Hopley covered his face with his hands. Blasted and blackened as he was, he *did* want to live. And he was afraid of that waving, beckoning thing. He turned and ran. He ran from some inner vision of what would happen to him unless he packed his bags and left that château at once. He ran to the door of his own room and put his hand on the knob, but even then he drew it back again with a cry. The door had been opened at the same moment from inside.

'Monsieur!' he heard Marsac's voice, hard and shaken.

'What . . . what . . . are you doing here?'

'*Mon Dieu* . . . if there is more of this I shall have to leave the service of monsieur . . . '

'I asked you . . . what are you . . . '

'I came to open the window of the room. It is not sanitary. The room needs air.'

'Why do *you* do these things? Why do *you* now serve my meals? How is it that I do not see Madame?'

'It is that Madame is not well. She has gone away for a few days.'

'And why do you look at me like that?'

'Like what, monsieur?' But he dropped his eyes. As James Hopley's face was then he had reason.

'As you are looking. As that young workman looked. As M. le curé looked. As the doctors looked when I was ill.'

'I, monsieur? If I am lacking in respect for monsieur – '

'Do you mean that I am changed?'

They were still face to face in the doorway, one inside the room, the other out. Suddenly Marsac stood aside for James to enter. He spoke soothingly.

'As I was unpacking this morning I found a folding bed. I will put it into the room downstairs. The summer is getting late. At night there is a nip in the air.'

'That is not answering my questions.'

'As monsieur says, he has been ill. First I will get a clothes-brush to remove that dust. Then I will set out a glass of wine downstairs.'

'Get the wine,' said James Hopley, abruptly turning his back.

But half an hour later, downstairs with the bottle of wine in front of him, and a glass of it already swallowed, he was able to take charge of his thoughts again. Marsac was fussing over him, making excuses to come in and out, and after the second glass James became as politic as he had recently been unnerved. Marsac was closing a placard. James spoke to him in conciliatory tones.

'I did not know that Madame Marsac was not well.'

Marsac replied that it was nothing, a slight *crise de nerfs*. He was used to it in Madame.

'Is it that the château does not suit her?'

'We cannot all pick and choose where we live. It may be so. She is from a town, from Rouen.'

'Then after Rouen she finds this . . . ?'

'What, monsieur?'

'Come,' said James Hopley with sudden friendliness. 'This château is a very old place. Many people have lived and died here. When many people have lived and died in a place it is – it is as a place is when many people have lived and died there.'

Marsac's knotted hands were twisting his red baize apron. He looked up. 'Monsieur is speaking of the health of Madame?'

'Naturally. And of the château.'

'Monsieur has then heard some rumour?'

'It may be rumour. It is that that I am asking you. Come, Marsac, be frank. If this place was not agreeable to me I would tell you. Does a room need air? Then give it air. It is cold and not as other rooms? Then choose a different one. I am content with the room I am in. Sit down.'

But the caretaker preferred to stand. He nodded assentingly, however, at James's words. He, too, had no time for *des riens*, he said. How many rooms were there, except those built yesterday, in which somebody had not died? Did it matter how they died? One can but die. It was not dying, but living that Marsac found difficult.

'So this room I am sleeping in . . . ?'

With that Marsac's tongue was loosed and he told the story without further ado.

'Since monsieur takes so rational a view of it, and as my grandfather told the story . . . yes,' he said. 'At one time this place was notorious for smuggling. Monsieur will not have noticed, but I can show him places where the floors have been cut through, to allow the pulley at the top of the house to be used for the well in the cellars below. There were trap-doors, and they stored the bales in the well. Rather than be taken one man – he is known still as Jean the Smuggler – tried to hang himself. The rope broke, the trap-door gave way under his weight, and he fell through into monsieur's room. Nothing can be seen, however, as the ceiling has since been plastered many times.'

James Hopley did not often smile, but his face gave one of its twitches now. Always 'the ceiling had been plastered over' – always there was the gap between the event and the first record of it. And what were the next record, and the next, and the next, but so many successive plasterings? Stones were never very long in place before the legends began to follow. So why begin with Arcques? According to the *curé*, portions of the foundations went back centuries before then. It amused James to make little trimmings of his own to the château's history.

'At least this poor fellow had a struggle for his life!'

'One's life is one's life. Doubtless one struggles.'

'No doubt after a flight across the fields, hiding under the haystacks and taking shelter in the ditches?'

'It is probable that to get to the château he would cross fields. He is said to have swum the river. I myself remember one place that few would pass alone after dark.'

'Because of this *suicidé*?'

'One supposes so. But there are some who will believe anything.'

'All the same these things make history.'

Marsac gave a shrug. 'As I say, one can but die once. Perhaps it is well. And with Madame away I have the work of two to do. Monsieur will not let me make up the bed for him downstairs?'

'I am very well where I am.'

'I will ask the men about the chimney. It will then be possible to have a fire upstairs,' and Marsac shuffled off to his own quarters. James Hopley filled his glass again.

One can but die! Now who had told the excellent Marsac that? And the legend of the smuggler who had come through the ceiling of his room! What tomfoolery would they be talking next? And as it was not a joke he could share with the first-comer he shared it with his *cahier* that night.

There is in fact one passage he wrote that had better be transcribed exactly as he wrote it, lest another pen should seem to have mis-interpreted him. It is the first clear indication we have of the lengths to which this ingrowing mind of his was prepared to go. He writes, in cold ink:

Since that visit of mine to the top of the house this afternoon I am at least face to face with something real. But as for 'A man can but die', who except Marsac says so? If all who ever lived are completely dead what is all the talk about? Since the world began has no man ever been *partially* dead? Never? It seems to me a good deal to say. I am not thinking of Lazarus. Unless he was wholly dead there was no miracle. And I am leaving out Trans-lation, for these 'were not' and death does not enter into it. But say that a few exist in this residual and partial state. On what level do these manifest, and to whom? Assuredly to somebody they meet on the same level. So take such a man as I am, neither one thing nor the other. I am, as you might say, either death warmed up or life cooled down. In that case there is only a margin of difference between him, scarcely dead, and me, scarcely alive. He is as much a man as I, I as much a ghost as he. For all I know I am in the direct line of succession. It is merely that in that case I should like to know. And by the way, a rather curious thing has occurred to me. A set of words has been running in my head for this last hour that I have not the faintest recollection of having heard before. Textually they are the same every time they come, and they do not strike one as an accidental jingle. They are: *The Past was the Best, the Present is Worse, the Worst is to Come.* Needless to say I haven't invented them, and they seem to come from a very, very long way off. Where?

So here was a man, calmly arguing, and with a certain show of logic, the possibility of becoming a ghost himself. If (he seems to have asked) this Jean the Smuggler had been preceded by a spectre from the Terror, and that by an invisible shape from Arcques, and the Arcques phantom by a dim line of others, why should the Ghost-age stop there? As for his quotation, that indeed is slightly puzzling. Very few fragments of this ancient Maya philosophy remain, and such as there are are not likely to have come James Hopley's way. But somehow the words, coming like the phantoms out of abysses of time, add a credit to his other speculations.

But with all his logic he had forgotten one thing. This was that ghosts do not appoint themselves. It is still the consensus of human tongues that makes the ghost, and in the end all came back, not to James, but to the men and women of the neighbourhood.

As usually happens, it was pure accident that brought this to a head, on the Sunday after his arrival at the château. So far he had taken his walks within the limits of the château's own lands, and he ought to have known that he was taking risks in venturing farther abroad on the day when the masons and carpenters rested from their work of the week. But it was a tempting day for a stroll, and he happened to find himself at a dilapidated postern with fields of wheat and half-cut lucerne beyond that rose up a small hill. There was nobody about, nor unless an unseen cock crowed, any sign of life to be seen, and passing out of the postern he began the ascent of the hill.

And a man may commune with a rope about the vileness of man and the things he does on earth but he cannot see the wheat waving over its poppies and cornflowers, nor the humble thyme and bed-straw and rest-harrow that make a world of dowdy beauty of the stubble, and remain altogether unmoved in heart. Acute noises of busy insects sounded in James Hopley's ears, the quick eyes of a bird looked into his for a moment, and close to his foot a clod stirred that was a hedgehog. And for all he knew he might be looking at it for the last time. Something came into his throat. This was all of life he would really miss. There had indeed been a time . . . but what was time to all this untramelled homeliness? The speck of an insect settling on his hand: its momentary agony were he to destroy it would be as long as any agony James Hopley had endured, but its joy in the glowing minutes of the sun was as long. It was endless as those kisses women gave to all men but to him, seeming to keep them alive for ever during the unmeasured minute their eyelids dropped and quivered. O, if a man could but have had the floweriness and the love and put all the fiendishness away. And in that very moment he found himself at the top of the hill, looking down the other slope of it. The slender spire of the church rose against the next hillside, and past it the road straggled among the compact farms. But there was also something else going on. In a small field just this side of the church the people of the village seemed to have been spilt together in a little hollow as if out of a scoop. Marsac had said nothing to James Hopley about a *fête*, but there it was, in full progress. Half a dozen canvas booths had been set up, with tiny flags and gay banners of bunting. Rustic games were in full swing, and the short crack of airguns where the boys shot for tinsel prizes, and he could distinguish the *curé*, short and black in his soutane, moving among the mothers and marshalling the children for their short races. A hedge surrounded the field. It was pure hunger of heart that made James long to draw a little nearer. If he liked to use the slight shoulder of the hill as cover he might be able to do so unseen. Cautiously he descended, and presently, standing in a dry ditch with foxgloves and cow-parsley up to his knees, was peering through a gap.

Almost the first thing he saw seemed to have been put there specially for him. On a fluttering strip of homely unsized calico, the home-made letters all blurred, he read: '*Anciens Combattants de la Guerre*'. There with their half-legs and sticks and empty sleeves and war-medals they moved about, and God knows they could have had James's English one-pound note had anybody told him of the occasion. But these were decent mutilations, mutilations that made a man hold his head up and brought him honour among his friends and the awed regard of their children. James, putting the tangle of convolvulus aside with his hand, could only stand there out of sight, looking on.

He never knew whose eyes had been the first to see him. By ill-luck it was a child who suddenly screamed. And though an instant later James Hopley was no longer there a mother was already at the child's side. Other mothers, too, had come up and were gently shaking the child, demanding what it had seen to terrify it. But the child could only sob and gulp and cling to its mother. By that time James, no longer thinking of concealment, was walking with downhung head and hands before his face up the hill again. Once he turned. Down in the field he saw them as they watched him, hands that pointed him out. One urchin had lifted a toy gun to his shoulder and James heard the minute crack. Where the stooks began he dropped behind them out of sight. Below him he saw the broken postern he had come out by. Better if he had remained on the other side of it.

For men might understand and grant that after all war was like that, and women always had their men behind them, but let James Hopley come unawares upon a child and its father and mother alike turned on him eyes that blazed. Had this accursed *mutilé* then not the decency to stay within doors? Must he stare even at children so that his dreadful visage haunted them at night? Who was he, this corpse that Madame had sent here to die? He who prowled about the château after dark, so that even good Mathilde Marsac would not stay a day longer in the place? Where was Mathilde? Run and get her! She was the one to question the child; poor little Leonie, she could not tell her own mother, but she would tell Mathilde, who had come over just the same way herself. 'Francis! Charles! You saw the foreigner, the English *gueule cassée*; tell us what kind he is, this animal who frightens children!'

And Francis the mason was able to say that he had looked through a window-piercing into the corridor, and it was well the ladder had been secured at the top or he and the ladder must have come down together, such a glaring face had this stranger turned on him. And Charles could tell them more than that, for he had seen him in his room, dressing himself, putting his face on, for that, *bien sur*, was not the face he slept in, but another, that he took off and put on the bedside commode before he hid himself under the sheets. But a third had presently left that far behind. This Englishman, this horror, he said, had a glass eye, which God knows does sometimes happen to a *copain* in a war without anybody thinking the worse of him, but he does not get a malevolent soul in the war too. Not only had he a glass eye, *ce cadavre*, but he played devil's tricks with it. Let them ask Jacques Martin when he returned! Jacques would tell them how he had met this *misérable* three days ago down by the river, at a certain spot they knew of . . . yes, the selfsame spot. He had been under the alders, just as he had hidden under the hedge to frighten the child. And Jacques himself had seen him take out the glass eye and polish it with a handkerchief and put it back into its socket again, and then he had screwed up the other eye, pretending to take that out and polish it too, and had glared at Jacques with them both. What did Jacques do? You may well ask! He looked round for the nearest billet of wood. But before he could find one he had gone, this English miscreant . . . gone and not to be found, though Jacques had shaken every bush round about for half an hour. As for him, who spoke, he wished that somebody would write a letter to Madame in Paris, telling her she must remove her *revenant* or get somebody else to wheel her barrows. When Madame bought people's labour she did not buy their nerves too. *Mon Dieu*, he wanted a cognac now, the turn Jacques Martin's story had given him . . .

So the workmen retired to the inn, there to discuss their relations with Madame Blanche; but James Hopley sat among his tapestries and porcelain vases, his spirit broken. What was the world but a place where little girls had fits at the sight of him and youngsters of ten pointed their toy guns at him? *Anciens Combattants de la Guerre*! It was time to make room. He saw by Marsac's face when he came in that what had happened had already got round to him. And Marsac now had not even the excuse that he had his wife to look after, but he merely brought in James's supper, saw to it that he had a good fire, and left him again. Drawing near to the fire-dogs and stretching out his hands as if they had been cold and stiff already, James Hopley did not even write in his book.

6

Whenever James Hopley looked back on those days of 1916 he looked back on a world of men each with a face and name and rank and regimental number and a separate history of his own. And that had been a good time to know a man in, for you had learned more about him in half an hour than in all the years since the Armistice. But in this harmonic repetition of it all every one of these trifling, all-important things was missing. He had now spent four nights in that Hôtel Drouot room upstairs, knowing with a certainty that had increased every night *what* this roomfellow of his was, but without getting an inch nearer to knowing *who*. He sat long that night over the fire. The flames seemed to make the stiff figures of the tapestries start softly forward and retire again, they gave a dim life and motion to the battlepiece that was big enough for a wall at Versailles, but no friendly face started forth out of the fire to look at James himself. Curse the fellow! James had done his utmost to make himself known to him; why couldn't he have done the same? If James had been through that storm of khaki and flame and gas and mud and chloride-of-lime once he could go through it again, but he would not do so alone. He would have a pal with him the next time. Well there was another chance tonight. Perhaps his pal would have changed his mind. Sluggishly he rose.

His pal had changed his mind. Throughout that night the second bed remained unvisited. In the room itself nothing whatever happened. James lay awake till the first streaks of daylight. Then, exhausted, he fell into a doze.

But he was roused by a rude enough shock an hour or so later. There was a shattering of glass. Something rolled across the floor and came to rest. Turning his head on his pillow James saw that it was a stone. They were going to stone him out of the château now.

And what was he going to do about that? There had been a time when he wouldn't have had to ask himself. The whole village could have gone to the devil before he would have budged. There were plenty of ways in which he could have retaliated. But what was the good? It wasn't the hostility of the village that mattered. It was this utter, heartbreaking failure of the night. Yet where in this shadowy business had he miscalculated? He went over it all again, but could not find that anywhere he had made a mistake. Was then some presumption being punished in him? Some sin? He asks himself, searching his heart.

I cannot see what great wrong I have ever done in my life. Looking back on it I have a thousand meannesses and petty acts to beg forgiveness for, but it hasn't been an important enough life for a big sin. Not even important enough for big suffering either, for this is not true suffering. There is a gallantry in defying anguish, but this is only wincing under the blow when it comes and waiting for the next. I had hoped for something a little braver. I would have stood up to it, gone out to meet it. Next Wednesday was to have been the crux. And I have one more night. If nothing happens I shall feel like . . .

But what he would feel like in that case is heavily scored out. Again he quotes his bit of Maya about the Best and the Worst, and within a couple of hours is writing:

And now Marsac is leaving me. He has just told me so. I told him he couldn't just step out like that but would at least have to find me somebody else, but he shook his head. Nobody else would come. But he has consented to stay another week. Then in my place he would go too, he says. In my place! . . . Am suddenly interrupted. Here comes the curé along the terrace.

But this time he was not the amiable *curé* who had come to ask after Madame Blanche in Paris and to invite James to come and stay with him at the vicarage. He had his most unyielding clerical face on, so much so that not ten minutes had passed before he was asking James whether he would not like to pray.

'To pray? Why?' James asked.

The *curé* looked him resolutely in the face. 'Have you no enemies?'

With that James answered the *curé* in his own tone. – 'None who have not made themselves so.'

'Is it likely the whole village is wrong?'

'Must I pray for the man who threw a stone through my window this morning?'

The *curé* frowned as he turned his little silver cross in his fingers. The throwing of the stone was evidently news to him, for he dropped a little of his austerity.

'It is as I said. This air is not suitable for you. It is best to speak plainly as to the terrible thing that has happened to you. For your physical hurt, so much worse (believe me) in this short time, there is, alas, no doctor. If they have done all they can for you in Paris it is the will of God. But if your soul is sick there is always prayer. Will you kneel with me?'

'So the village says my soul is sick too?'

'I must close my ears if you boast of your own righteousness.'

'If then my soul is sick should we be praying the same prayer, to the same God?'

'My prayer and my God will prevail.'

'Enough. I will not kneel with you.'

The *curé* became austere again. – 'Monsieur, you come here and in less than a week you are troubling my flock. Already it is said of you that if the earth swallowed you it was as it closed upon Dathan and Abiram, who went down quick into the pit. But the incense of God, whose priest I am, rose between the dead and the living. Again I ask you to pray.'

'I live my life alone. I will pray for what is left of it alone.'

'Surely our own *Anciens Combattants* should sympathise and understand?'

'What do they say?'

'That where already a fear was you make it visible. I, I have the protection of my Cross,' he turned it in his fingers again, 'but if others think you are the Devil I cannot be the shepherd of my flock without entering into their thoughts.'

Suddenly, too exhausted for further disputation, James dropped heavily into a chair. It was precisely as he had thought. This *curé* had his middle course between two worlds to steer. Well, let them have it their own way. He closed his eyes.

'I am sure you meant kindly in coming, monsieur.'

'It was my duty. Your case shall be pleaded with them too. At least no more stones shall be thrown. Since you will not pray with me I will pray for you alone.'

But he spoke to the air. James was asleep. When he opened his eyes again the *curé* had gone.

But during that short interval of forgetfulness James had had a curious dream. He had dreamed that he was upstairs in his room, packing his bags to return to Paris. With the manifestations cut abruptly off, what was there left to stay for? Marsac had advised him to go. The *curé* told him plainly that he was looked on as the Devil and a fear made visible. So he was packing up to leave it all.

But as in his dream he moved about his bedroom he suddenly found himself looking for his water-bottle. Somehow his familiar civilian attire had changed itself into articles of wartime equipment. There they lay spread out on the second bed, his greatcoat, his haversack, his intrenching-tool, his tin hat, his gas-mask. Looking down at himself he saw the puttees on his legs, his stained knees, the skirts of his frayed tunic. His revolver was in the holster at his waist, the breach of his rifle was oiled, the piece of rag was tied over its muzzle. His ten-days' leave was up. Waterloo, the night train and the escorted crossing. Where the devil was that water-bottle? There was something stronger than water in it. Ah, there it was, on the alabaster-topped washstand; fool that he was, it wasn't his water-bottle but his gas-mask that he had lost. It had been on the second bed there only a moment ago. Curse things for getting lost like this, and him in a hurry with the boat-train to catch.

And suddenly in his dream he was standing before the gilded glass above his mantelpiece, staring at himself. He might well look for his mask; he had it on all the time. Christ, what a picture of all-hell it was with its goggles and its swines snout, its offal-like windpipe re-entering his own entrails, its integument tucked like putrid wrinkled flesh into his collar . . .

And all at once he gulped as if a hand had closed hard on his heart. That that he was looking at was not the mask. It was his face. He woke with a cry.

It was small wonder he frightened the village if even in a dream he could frighten himself. Fear made visible? But he was angry now. What fear? Why, the fear they had always had, the rats! The fear that they were bold to laugh at in the daytime, but that at nightfall drew them close together in the inn, to tell one another over their cognac that it took more than a shadow to frighten them. But because they *did* fear the shadow they cast about to give it a substance, and in James they found one ready-made and to hand. Within a week he was no less a personage than the Devil himself And at the thought of this there smote through the dun clouds that enveloped James's mind a piercing, dazzling ray. The Devil? *He?* Why, if they thought that, then it was in his power to *be* the Devil! Suddenly he laughed outright. Wretched little souls without imagination, who wanted all but the picturesquely wounded to take themselves out of sight so that they might be able to talk with a better conscience about the glorious past and the heritage their fathers had died for! At least the rope had told leaner, starker truth than that! He had turned and run from it before. Would he turn and run from it now?

And that non-appearance of the night before: what had ailed James that he had looked on *that* as a calamity? Was it not in truth the very opposite? What had become of James's theory of first and second times if it applied to appearances *and not to non-appearances also?* Suddenly he exulted. That first night of unsupported loneliness had been sent to test him. It had been sent to try whether he was yet goblin enough to stand alone. And he had stood alone. His very face was now hardly recognisable as a face, and it had been as much as the *curé* had been able to do to look at it without blenching. A fear made visible? He broke into a peal of laughter that startled himself and ended abruptly. Give James a *second* night of tranquillity and the ghost in him would be marvellously strong. No threadbare story of Jean the Smuggler, but he, James Hopley and the Devil they attributed to him, would be the unsettling of the *curé's* flock. Oh, let *no* chill or smell or breathing come tonight to mar the rich perfection of it! He was eager to begin that deep, dreamless sleep at once.

That night he went to bed supperless and slept like the dead.

7

As a small child, just before they drew his nursery curtains late in the afternoon, James Hopley had sometimes stood at the window, looking at the mimic fire that had seemed to burn in mid-air outside, magically and all by itself. People in the street seemed to walk through it unscathed, and young James himself had only had to take a step this way or that and out the fire had gone altogether. It had of course been only the reflection of the fire in the room, and yet to James its reality had been such that the illusion had stuck with him through life. He had of course had different names for it at different times. At one time he had called it ambition, but he had never been equipped for that, and ambition hadn't lasted very long. Then he had known it by the name of love, and had wondered that others didn't stop to warm their hands at this wonderful thing of his too, till one day one of them had, and out that had gone too. And he had called it knowledge, and pleasure, and a number of other things, and now he was wondering what form it was going to take next. He had also been counting up how many pages remained in his *cahier*, for it was his intention to go on writing to the very last moment. There were fifteen of them, and his normal handwriting was on the small side. Fifteen should be enough, and as he looked on the blank pages he wondered what would be found on them at that time tomorrow.

He had arrived at the château on a Wednesday, and at six o'clock on the following Tuesday afternoon he was watching the work-men depart. One or two of them glanced backwards over their shoulders, but James kept out of their sight, by a tall onyx lamp near the fireplace. Then, when the last of them had disappeared, he took a walk round Blanche's domain. His senses were more than ordinarily sharpened, his single eye was as alert as if he had been making a final inspection of the property before taking possession of it. He noted what a great deal of work still remained to be done. The old orchard there would have to be grubbed up and replanted, the cleaning out of the choked moat would take weeks yet, sum-mers must pass before the gardens took on orderliness, scores of summers before the restored portions of the building began to assimilate with the older work. But assimilate in time they would, and it would be an odd thing now if James Hopley had no part at all in the place that was to be. There was at least one little girl in the village who, become a grandmother, would be able to tell how, in

broad daylight, the château's spectre had mopped and mowed at
her through a hedge, giving such a turn to her thoughts that they
had never really got over it, and an aged man by a fireside would
nod gravely and say that that was quite true, for he himself had seen
it too, half way up the hill behind the church there, and had pointed
a gun at it, and it had fled.

The sun was going redly down behind the scaffold-poles. It dyed
the new chimney-stack rose-pink, and presently, when the empty
window-holes were glazed, they would fling back the gold too. It was
a short life at the best, and when the hour came it shrank to such a
small handful of days as to make one wonder what it had all been
about. And suddenly, like an announcement of that hour, a bell with
a curiously harsh iron clang broke in on his thoughts. Now where
had that bell come from? That was new. Was it something else that
Blanche had picked up at the Hôtel Drouot? Probably, and Marsac,
unable to find him in the house, was telling him supper was ready.
He had a feeling that Marsac ought to provide a rather special supper
that night. Slowly he ascended the steps to the terrace.

As all Blanche's friends know, she did not move into that château
on the following spring. To the dismay of the men of the village, but
also as a final confirmation had one been needed, the work was
discontinued abruptly, and in the Paris newspapers an advertisement
appeared, that a Henri Quatre château, partly furnished and needing
only a little restoration, was for sale, no reasonable offer refused and
possession at purchaser's own convenience. No tenant has yet concluded the bargain. Several have been down to visit the property,
which now has not even a caretaker, and the last applicant, a wealthy
man in the motor business, was buttonholed on his way back to his
car by a bald, bearded, elderly man, who said that his name was
Marsac, that he lived in the little shack behind the inn, could tell
monsieur such and such things about the château, and for the rest
did such odd jobs as were to be had while his wife looked after the
young children of the women who worked in the fields. What passed
between Marsac and the motor-magnate is not known, but the car
drove away and has not been seen since.

So things draw to a close of themselves. One persists in giving his
account of the affair, another his, and so on, but when it is all
weighed up those cahiers of James Hopley's are the only direct
testimony that remains, a stop-watch record of what passed, set
down in the moment of its passing. They are written in pencil,

apparently as he sat up in bed. His first entry is timed 11.30, with all still outside and all quiet in the gilt and alabaster room. His pulse was normal, his breathing easy, and he had not drunk any wine. In these circumstances his personal narrative ends and the new legend begins.

11.45 ... Nothing yet, but it is still early. Am writing to kill time as I wait. Of course that was all nonsense about taking my revenge by haunting these poor people. I have other things to think about now. But I don't think I should care to be the *curé* of a place like this, though I expect that about Dathan and Abiram came from Madame Marsac. She has that sort of look now I come to think of it. Poor Marsac! He's taken this rather badly. I could see he was in two minds about giving notice. He didn't want to stay but he didn't want to go either. Quite a bond between us in exactly one week. I shall remember Marsac. That is if one does remember these things afterwards.

12.15 ... Still nothing, but wonder what's just brought Tommy Allinson into my head. He got his at Loos. But he got it clean and quick, not like me and this other chap. You don't have relapses years afterwards and go into a clinic when you've been drilled through the head. Funny I can remember Tommy's name and any number of other names but not this fellow's. Always on the tip of my tongue. Some name like Hobbs. Briggs. Crabbe. A tough devil he was anyway, pinned in the darkness under that beam like that. Still breathing when they got him out; gave a shriek, I remember, and that hour before they came for me seemed longer than all the rest put together. Australian, sergeant, Fifth Division. Afterwards at Horseferry Road they thought I was loopy, asking for a man and knowing no more who than that, no name, no number, no unit, nothing. But they were tough, all those Aussies. That night-raid when they blackened their faces and put cogwheels and bits of iron on pick-handles. In the trench that other time, when they found a whole section of them dead with women's underclothes on. Didn't he come from Brisbane now? Hell, why didn't I think of that before? Big husky chap, scar over right eye, swore like blazes and came from Brisbane. Why didn't I tell them that at Horseferry Road? Higgs. Biggs. Some short name.

12.30 ... Keep looking up at the trapdoor Marsac says they've plastered up. But I know he's not always punctual to the tick. Wait. What's that? Thought I heard something. Whee-e-e-o-o-o-ooo – *bump*! It's nothing. Only Jerry waking up. Half an hour and he'll stop. You can set your watch by Jerry. Worth a quid to see what we're doing to him when it's our turn. Something pretty dirty a fellow who managed to get away told me. Wait a bit though . . . that *was* something upstairs . . .

12.55 . . . [*note: this entry consists of the hour only*]

1.30 . . . Can't say I'm sorry that's over. Hell, but it was good and solid on top of us that time! The other must have been the last lot of earth settling. Why can't it stop where it's put instead of shifting and rumbling to itself like a man's belly? That get you any, digger? Don't like his being so quiet. There's something pushing against my right foot that wasn't there before. First you can't move, then it loosens up, and you're afraid to lift a finger. Christ, that bastard's woke up. He's at it again. Hell, give it a rest, man. Am I on a bloody feather-bed either? Something crawling over your face? They don't charge you anything extra for that. I haven't got any legs that I can feel. Day or night? How in the goddamn blazes do I know? What do you think I am, a sundial? Stop it or you'll start another bloody vibration or something. Phoo, you stink, or somebody does! Any more of us here? Same old smell, boys, good for you, doesn't make you think too much of yourself. For the love of God stop it, man! Listen, that was picks. Shovels. Voices. I heard 'em . . . damn you, I tell you I heard 'em! Oh my God, he's stopped! Passed out this time I guess. Are you there? You . . . what's your name . . . you from Botany Bay . . .

2.05 . . . That thing by my right leg's a box of some kind. Just managed to get my hand down to it. Anyway it's wood; iron's colder. Ammunition-box, perhaps, with the rope handle come loose. Stop. This is getting exciting. There's too much of it for an ammunition-box. Perhaps an end of broken waggon with a trace on it. Never know what you find when a dump blows up. Yards of it! Wonder if I could work an end over to him and tell him to make it fast to the timber. Hi, cobber, are you awake? Got a hand loose? There's a rope here. A rope, man, do you hear? Lots of it. Then get your hands free and scratch a way out. A rope end coming over . . . no hurry . . . haul in and try again . . . we've all the time there is . . .

2.15 . . . This is queer. The place has got all turned round and there's a light and I can see. Where did that candle come from? What am I doing in bed? Don't you begin seeing things that aren't there, my son, or you're done. You've been blown up. Two

beds mean you're seeing double, and bedrooms don't stink like
this. No, making it fast to the beam's no good. Wants a dead
prise-up with a lever, shall be crushing the poor devil to pulp if I
begin to haul. He's dead off again now. Off for good if he's lucky.
You have ten minutes' nap, digger. Do you all the good in the
world, as Blanche says. I was a rotten swine to wake you up that
afternoon; regular dog in the manger, didn't want the bed myself
and wouldn't let you have it. Let a man sleep when he can. Sleep
himself right off the map. Go out like a candle. Funny place this,
a candle one minute and not the next. And that candle's nearly
out. Better put another one in . . .

He didn't need those fifteen pages after all. Indeed his closing
words are in a scrawl so agitated that something dire must have
happened. One conjecture is that in putting in the new candle he
upset the candlestick on the other bed, scaring this companion of his
away; there is in fact a small trace of wax, on the counterpane, though
no scorching. The *cahier* was found the next morning face downwards on the floor between the beds, the one tossed, the other as
smooth as if it had been newly made. It ends almost illegibly, with
the words scattered all over the page.

*Damnation quiet he stirred no he's only turned over wait no he's
getting up the door listen I've found a rope the Past the Present to Come
wait wait . . .* '

*   *   *

There was one point of the roof-gutter that the plank cradle did not
quite reach, but Francis the mason thought that by lashing it to the
nearest point of the scaffolding he could cant it sufficiently and so
save himself the trouble of setting it up anew. He called to Marsac,
who was passing below.

'Marsac! Have you a rope handy?'

'Descend by the ladder and get in at the window-piercing. You will
find one in the rafters there,' and he passed on to prepare M. Hopley's coffee. Francis descended and scrambled through the aperture.

He found the rope, or what was left of it, for it was newly broken.
Francis looked up at the centre rafter, where it had jumped from the
sheave of the pulley and jammed, and then down at the unboarded
floor. There below he saw the rest of it, but it was attached to
something. The something wore a pair of pyjamas, and its feet were
bare. Francis fled.

In his own quarters Marsac was pouring boiling water into a metal jug. He looked round as Francis the mason entered.

'You found the rope?' But the young mason could only stammer . . . 'Yes . . . and you . . . in the night . . . you heard nothing?'

At something in his tone Marsac's bearded face too had turned the colour of butcher's fat on a slab . . . 'What? Heard what?'

'The *gueule cassée* . . . *suicidé* . . . *il s'est pendu* . . . it is the work of Jean the Smuggler . . . he does not do it himself . . . always he makes them do it . . . go and see . . . '

But at that moment the door at the foot of the back stairs swung slowly, silently, emptily open. And Jean the Smuggler was apparition enough for Francis the mason, but not for Henri Marsac. Suddenly the caretaker gave a harsh cry, as his wife had done before him. The jug of M. Hopley's morning coffee was still in his hand. All at once he hurled it across the apartment full into the vacant doorway, as before he had almost thrown a lighted lamp. Then he fell in a heap across a chair, and lay there shuddering. The metal pot crashed against the edge of the open door and fell to the floor. Slowly, what was left of the coffee spread out in an irregular pool about it. 'I shall remember Marsac,' James Hopley had written. He had remembered him.

Resurrection in Bronze

THE CLAY

I

'The clay is the birth, the wax is the death, but the bronze is the resurrection.' John Brydon had forgotten where the saying came from, but as his strong fingers bent and twisted his bits of lead and wire the words repeated themselves from time to time in his head, not insistently enough to take his thoughts off what he was doing, but like something heard from afar, too remote to disturb, a rather pleasing echo in possession. He stepped back to look at his work. 'The clay is the birth,' but this was still the darkness before the birth. The turntable under the powerful electric light carried no more than the reinforcement that would take the clay's weight. That wiry scrabble had not even the outlines of a skeleton. In John Brydon's mind it was merely so much balance, proportion, so many rigid calculations from a centre of gravity that must be determined now and held to till the end.

But how fiercely the vision of the thing to be burned in his brain you had only to look at his face to see. A step back, a breath that was almost a hiss – hold it – a step forward – and there! By and by *that* would be something for the child to kick in the womb with! *There* was his brother taken by the heel, had there been a brother! The power before the glory. Of the monument that should tower like a king over lesser memorials, setting a capital a-flutter with flags and its air a-throb with military music, so far only that handful of lead and wire existed.

John Brydon had made himself an eyeshade of brown paper against the strong overhead light, and its peak jutted fiercely forward, throwing his face into shadow. But it was only a little less prominent than his hook of a nose, that stuck out from his face as if it, like his fingers, would have been at the work. And giant of a man as he was he shook with the tenseness of his stringing up. Again came the hiss as he stepped back. For a minute he stood frowning, uncertain. And then

suddenly he relaxed. It would do. Half an hour's rest now before he
started with his clay.

Clay or plasticine? He had chosen the clay. 'The clay is the birth',
and he had prepared it earlier in the day. He hitched up his plaster-
splashed working blouse and groped in the pocket underneath for
cigarettes. He lighted one, and glanced towards a low couch half
hidden behind a curtain as if he would have lain him down. But no. It
would be a better rest to keep his mind, not off, but just a little aslant
of his work. Instead he began to walk about the studio, pausing here
and there, but always before work of his own. The work of no artist
alive or dead approached in its importance to John Brydon the work
that lay ahead of him, and he himself was the man he would have to
drive, to scourge, and if necessary to break rather than that work
should not be done.

It was the chance of his lifetime, and he had waited half his
lifetime for it. And he had not waited patiently nor with submission,
content to wait his turn, but arrogantly and in bitterness, waking up
to it each morning as a man wakes to the morning of his revenge.
He had removed the eyeshade, showing the jutting nose and the
mouth that pitied neither others nor himself. But ultimate victory
was there too. He had all he had ever asked for – his chance. If he
failed he only would be to blame. Others – for of necessity he would
need the help of others – would fail him at their peril. Many said of
him that he had no belief, only the stubborn, intractable strength of
a working-hate. But now he knew that somewhere within him an
angel had been watching all the time, an angel not to be thanked for
opportunities, but to be praised in the seizing of them. And he
would praise after his own fashion though it took blasphemy to
bring it about.

To whom had he owed it that he was the only man in England
who had had the honour of being invited? He did not know. The
official letter, in French, had come like a bolt from the blue, with
the arms of an Embassy at the top and the signature of some
assistant-secretary at the foot, and with it had come the conditions,
the specifications, the photographs of the site, the architects' elevations, the tracings, the blue-prints, the rest of the data. So either
some hitherto indifferent person had come tardily to his senses
or there was a better man in the world somewhere than John
Brydon had been aware of. But ultimately he owed it to nobody
but himself, and it was his succession of past selves that he was
considering now as he moved round the studio from piece to

piece, the eyeshade still dangling in his hand, the brow beneath his grizzled hair deeply corrugated. Not that self, for example – he was standing before the startling head of a Faun that some fool of a critic had said was only startling because he had stolen it from the archaic Greek. He had not, and the fellow would have been told so had any critic been worth John Brydon's breath. Critics! If a man was feeble enough they could pick him up when he fell, but not all the critics in the world could stop a man who knew his way and went it. And as with the Faun, so with the Ixion and others, in plaster, bronze, plaster waxed over, some still in clay under their wet swaddlings. All inclined to violence, something torn from the side rather than born in natural labour, *pour épater*, useless now. They had served their purpose in training him for this the opportunity of his life. He did not thirst for fame. As for decorations, they might have them who cared for such things. Money? Perhaps that was coming rather nearer. That was power as even the veriest fool understood it, and even when he had paid for the granite and bronze, the fees of his assistants and subordinates, the casting, the transport, the foundations, the setting up, the margin would be an ample one. But no less important than the money was the time. At the best two months was little enough for all he had to do. Over by the couch behind the curtain was a packed bag. He crossed to it and began to unpack it. A small stock of shirts and collars; a couple of suits of pyjamas; a large supply of handkerchiefs and a spare suit – he would need little more, since except for meals it would be at least a week before he set foot out of the studio again. And even for simple meals he could telephone.

And now for a little letter-writing, for there was plenty of that. He must think in advance of the three-ply set-up of his forty-foot statue's surroundings, the parterres and approaches and the great domed Senate behind, of his perspective-drawings hardly less important than the maquette itself; of climate, of weathering, of the dozen other things that must be seen to when nations are in jealous competition, and each wants the feather in its own cap and sets its agents to work beneath the surface, so that the soul of the artist sickens but the State boasts itself in its son. John Brydon knew nothing about the State and cared less. What he cared about was his gamble with his life, for he knew that that thing that existed in his mind would either ride away in triumph the moment it was uncovered or fail completely. And he was not going to fail.

'The clay is the birth, the wax is the death, but the bronze is the resurrection.' He began to put the clay on his armature that very night.

2

When a man has a dream of that sort in his head the earlier stages of his work are likely to be incomprehensible to the casual visitor. He may even seem to be wasting his time, and certainly he is best left alone. John Brydon wanted nothing but to be left alone. Least of all did he wish to be approached by his wife, for he knew only too well what would happen. She would come with sympathy, encouragement, and that hit-or-miss understanding of hers. It was this last that made him never sure of her. Even when she praised the right thing he had to lock up that mouth of his far more tightly than if she could always have been depended on to praise the wrong one. In that sense there was seldom rest for his mind in her company, and the gap between them was bridged only by his great tenderness for his ten-years-old daughter, Mara.

Winifred Brydon appeared at the studio when the clay on the armature was some four days old. She had brought him flowers and a bundle of American magazines, for as a writer for such publications she pulled her weight in the family boat too. By this time the group on the turntable had taken some semblance of shape, but was still little more than an abstract mass, capable of a score of final constructions. It was before this that she stood, fair-haired, cool, wifely, solicitous, smelling of her Surrey garden, for Brydon would not have his child brought up in a town.

'What a splendid beginning, darling!' she said. 'I had to come up to bring Mara to the Bannisters' party, and thought I'd call. I shall fetch her again at six o'clock – at six o'clock mind, Mara,' she added to the child.

John Brydon did not reply. He was looking at his plaster base again from which he had just dismounted the group it was to sustain. Out of that base was to spring the vitality of his whole design, and he was not satisfied with it. If that was wrong everything was wrong. His wife went on.

'Those nice Crawshaw children are to be there. You remember you said what nice children they were. What is that?' and she pointed to the irregular quadrilateral block he was knitting his brows over.

'The base,' he replied. 'I've just dismounted it.'

'Because the lines aren't straight up? I can see from here they aren't straight up. But that won't be very difficult, will it?'

'They aren't meant to be straight,' John replied. 'It's what's called a batter. Every plane is battered except one. That's the one, isn't it,' and he pointed it out to her, frowning at the thing again.

'I see,' she said, her fair head on one side. 'Now I'll take myself off and let you get on with your work for a bit. It's only just round in South Kensington. I'll pop in again in about half an hour.'

His answer was to pick up his daughter and to hold her against his breast. 'Have a good time at the party, sweetheart,' he whispered. 'I'll try to get down home for a weekend presently. That – when a thing's out of the vertical – is called a batter. I know it's not right yet, but it will be,' and setting her down he once more fixed his eyes on his work. Waving her hand from the door his wife sought the family car.

With the group mounted on it again that base looked like giving trouble. It was the trunk up which the living sap of his idea coursed, and if it was right as it was then everything else was wrong. And suddenly he drew in his breath with a hiss again. It required courage, but he reached for a straightedge and a black crayon. He glared for a moment at the base, and then ruled a slashing line that would mean whole inches off the plaster and a new casting. The new line threw the whole group still further out, and what he had to do must be done now or not at all. Stiffening himself, and with hands as strong and steady as those of a surgeon, he grasped the whole superstructure, forced it bodily over as a bonesetter forces a bone into its proper place, and hissed again as he stepped back. Had he ruined it? No, the armature was unstrained and the gravity-centre still came over the base of support. But phew! He was glad *that* was over! A man doesn't want to do a thing like that oftener than he needs! He dropped into a chair to rest.

He was not aware that in order to save him the trouble of going down again his wife had left both upper and lower doors open. Suddenly she was standing before him.

'Darling, you're tired,' she said.

'No,' he answered. 'I've just taken a bit of a risk, that's all. Did you get Mara safely there?'

'Yes. But I can see you're tired. Would you like me to make you a cup of tea?'

'I should like one.'

'It won't take five minutes. I hope you're eating properly. I know you haven't too much time to do it in, but a breakdown won't help you,' and she went into the studio's small kitchen.

He heard the little plop as she lighted the gas ring and the clink of cups and saucers. Except that a woman came in in the mornings he did these things for himself, and often they went undone. His absence from home put a good deal on Winifred, and it was good of her to come up and fuss about him like this. But he rather wished she hadn't come to stay for the whole three hours of Mara's party. Surely she had friends she could have called on? He knew that at present he was not fit company for anybody.

She entered with the tray. She had taken off a small *bergère* hat and was looking for somewhere to put the tray down. She did so on a small table she drew up to the couch half hidden behind the curtain. Then she poured out the tea.

'Come and have it while it's hot,' she said. 'Leave that thing just for a few minutes; surely you've time for a cup of tea! What do you say you call it when it isn't straight up?'

'Battered.'

'And what have you made those thick black lines on it for?'

'It will be to cut down and a new base made.'

'Oh dear,' she said, patting the fair hair, 'it seems almost as bad as having a baby!'

And that, coming as it did near the truth, was precisely the kind of remark she was least successful at. She had made him sit down on the couch by her side. Having a baby? The clay the birth? Perhaps it was like that, and she knew what having the other sort of baby meant. But she knew nothing about this gestation of his. Any normal woman could have done what she had done, but for this birth of his John Brydon had been singled out from all the artists of the land. Again she was right in her hit-or-miss way, and John Brydon was silent. And suddenly he drank his tea at a gulp. It was time he got back to his turntable.

But she filled his cup again. She had leaned a little towards him, and there was a softer note in her voice as she sighed, 'Oh dear, I do wish life wasn't all work! I've had a trying time, too. Didn't you say something about coming home for the weekend?'

'Let me get a firm hold on this thing first.'

'But surely you have. It's a wonderful start. And Mara does so miss you.'

'Remember it's got to be finished in less than two months.'

'Will you get it done any quicker by *never* leaving it for an hour?' Her voice was softer still, and her hand was on the sleeve of his working-blouse. 'It is so dull with only me and Mara, John – '

'Don't, Winifred,' he muttered, and she pouted. 'I can see you don't mean to come, and it will be at least a week before I can get up to town again – '

'Dear,' he said gently, 'let me tell you what I'm doing. As it is I'm breaking every rule of the competition. I'm doing far more than they ask for. To begin with I'm making it bigger, and strictly speaking they could turn me down on that alone. Then plaster would have done, and I'm giving them bronze. If it doesn't cost too much I shall give them a granite base too. You see, I'm stealing every little advantage I can for the sake of the first impression. I may even have to ask them for a little more time. But even then it will mean working all day and half the night.'

'I almost wish you'd never – no, of course I don't mean that, but – John – ' and her lids dropped and her hand crept closer to his breast.

And he had known what was coming ever since he had opened the door to her. More than that, it was her right and due. She even had means of enforcing it, for he knew what happened when husbands disregarded these natural occasions. The woman brought other weapons to bear. Negligence and preoccupation are not safe when the answer is to make jealous. Her arms were close about him and she lay on his breast quite still. She was still desirable enough for any husband, she smelt of her garden. He was glancing at his work on the turntable, but her touch on his cheek caused him to turn his eyes away, and she drew his face down. It was five o'clock, and she was going back to the Bannisters' for Mara at six. After that it would be a week before he saw her again. Very well. Be it so. He bent his head and kissed her.

3

When little things began to go wrong with that scale-model of John Brydon's the mishaps at first were to the accessories rather than to the clay itself, and they did not originate with John, but in the errors of his assistants. They were minor errors, but none the less a check. For example, the workman to whom he entrusted the re-making of the base somehow got wrong in a measurement, and as the work had to be done yet a third time it might as well be the finished article while they were about it. He had decided against granite. Special lacquers were cheaper and would have to serve. He put it in hand, hoping that no further hitch of the kind would occur.

But he was also beginning to worry about that extension of time it became plain enough he would have to ask for. Knowing how long these things take he wrote to the Embassy without losing any time. But as the days went on nothing happened, and since it would have been rash at this juncture to have approached the Government concerned direct he must give the Embassy officials yet a little longer. And say that these things were trifles and all in the day's work. There followed something that was not a trifle. Those all-important perspectives, that were to 'force' an angle on a committee probably incapable of choosing one for itself as a conjurer 'forces' a card, gave him no confidence whatever as they progressed. An inferior design, perspectived as it should be, would certainly be chosen before his own.

Another difficulty too became the more serious the nearer it approached. His group included a horse, and a man may be as well grounded in human anatomy as John Brydon was and still have everything to learn about the comparative branches of the science. He made ready to go to school again. Books on the subject began to litter his couch, photographs and charts of equine types. He sent for semi-skeletonised plaster casts. Reins and bits and a headstall were slung across an angle of his walls. Further details of equipment and uniform (for which he had written) still did not arrive, but he remembered a man who possessed the skirted coat he wanted, a girl who had been a riding-mistress and had boots that for the moment would serve. These he made to sit for him, on an improvised steed of two padded chair-backs with a length of cord for the leathers, and by the time John Brydon had finished with his male sitter he had to be lifted like a cripple to the ground again. The girl was less fortunate. Not being a professional model she was on her mettle, he was too absorbed in his work to notice what was happening, and she had not even to be lifted off. She fell off of herself, and did not come to the studio again. But John Brydon had got what he wanted.

Then something far more than all these things put together began to weigh on him. Iron-framed as he was, he was setting everything on one cast, and he began to be aware of a creeping staleness in himself, due to lack of proper exercise and work for too many hours at a stretch. That, unless it was seen to, would mean the end of everything, and his method of dealing with it was this –

He bought an alarm-clock and began to arrange his work in watches, the day and the night through, much as sailors do. In order that he should not be inopportunely awakened he telephoned to his wife in Surrey. She was not to ring him up unless the occasion was an urgent one, and on no account was she to come up to the studio without due announcement. He went into his reasons at some length, but she made no comment on them. Her short reply was 'Very well.' He felt himself a brute, but she assured him again that she 'quite understood', and he returned to his turntable.

But with all these increasing worries he had his bits of luck too. He was not exactly a sociable man, but for all that he had a few influential friends, who usually had a way of being no less grim than himself, and among these was a distinguished horse-surgeon, head of a great establishment. This friend was called into collaboration, for it was not likely that fault would be found with John Brydon's horse after the approval of such an authority as he. In the establishment's riding school grooms began to parade horses of the required type, while the sculptor took photographs and made notes, and one day John Brydon chanced to mention to his friend his apprehension about the Embassy's ignoring of his letters, and the always possible other machinations that might be going on without his knowledge. It was well that he did so. Sir George told him that there happened to be in London at that moment a personage who might be of the greatest service to him, and as a result he spent an evening away from his studio for the first time since he had set up his armature. In order to do this he had to telephone for his evening clothes to be sent to him. They arrived, and he ordered a taxi to the door, for from prolonged standing his feet were beginning to give him trouble. But he returned late that evening satisfied that his interests were thenceforward in good hands, and, lying down for a minute, fell asleep in his evening clothes.

Two days later his wife, breaking his injunction, appeared again at the studio. Her reason for coming happened to be sufficient – just sufficient – but a glance at her told him that again it was not her real reason. She would have to take her real reason back to the country with her. But now she had a weapon as well, and as she looked round the studio her eyes by fell chance on a second one. It was a half-full whisky bottle, for when your alarm-clock buzzes in your ear at four in the morning and you wish it wouldn't, a stiff half-tumbler of whisky will kick you up to work again. She made no comment on the bottle, but allowed herself a half-serious one on his personal appearance.

'John, you haven't shaved today!' she said.

'No,' he answered, and after a moment added, 'nor yesterday.'

'I shouldn't have thought that took very long. How did you enjoy your party?'

'What party?'

'The one you wanted your evening clothes for. I hope you shaved for that!' She laughed a little as she said it, but it was not the kind of laugh that mends matters. 'Do you know, for a few minutes that evening I was almost jealous!'

'It was very far from being what you'd call a party if you only knew,' he informed her, his mind running over it again.

'Anyway you went, but when Mara and I want you to come home for a weekend – ' she did not finish.

And of course it was all plain enough the way she saw it. It was now nearly a month since he had been near his home. No public announcement had yet been made that an international competition of magnitude among a few chosen artists was under way. Except to a very few his absence was therefore unexplained. When his neighbours in Surrey asked what had become of him it was she who had to answer as best she could. Mara too would doubtless be stopped and asked pleasantly, 'how her father was getting on'. And more than all that. A desirable and still young woman with many friends, capable at a pinch of earning her own living, with no more encumbrance than a daughter well on the way to young womanhood herself and a house to whom she can ask anybody she pleases, need not find time hang heavy on her hands. It is not unknown that her husband will even pay her an occasional visit by way of a pleasant surprise. John Brydon knew that she had the cards in her hand if she chose to play them.

Yet he knew too that a more menacing shape than any hanging-about young man stood between himself and his wife. They happened to be standing side by side in front of the turntable. At the farther end of the studio was a tall, moveable glass in which he was able to see the effect of his work at double the distance the actual size of the studio allowed. And lifting his eyes he saw them in the glass, her, himself, with the statue between them. And the distance was not so great but that he saw too the expression on her face. It was not he who was jealous, but she, and this work of his was the hated rival. She was hardening her heart against the thing that was served before her, that had broken up his days and nights, was shaking the foundations of his health, for the trouble in his feet was no better, and even when she did bring the gift of her arms to him thrust her out of the place. Again she could claim to be right – and all at once her eyes met his in the distant glass. That they should meet all those yards away when they stood shoulder to shoulder was in itself a further widening of the gulf that had opened between them. In that moment his heart

was bursting to close that gulf again, to tell her that trusting to his
strength and constitution he *had* perhaps begun a little immoder-
ately, that staleness had come on him before he had been prepared
for it, that he *had* shouldered a burden bigger than had been asked of
him – but oh, if she only realised the importance of it to them all,
how much it mattered to him, how little the future would hold for
him if he failed in this! . . . But she had turned abruptly away and
tucked the fair hair under the little *bergère* hat. Almost gaily she acted
her little part.

'Well, I'll get along,' she said. 'I don't want to be too late because
of Mara. Besides, I have the Phillipsons coming in tonight. They're
bringing that young nephew who's just back from Kenya; you
remember him, don't you? Bertie. Before he went away he used to
think he was a little in love with me. He must be twenty-six now.
Don't come down. Let me know if you want anything else sent, and
good hunting. Of course if you *don't* win the thing after all this
it will be simply tragic, but don't let's think of that. Shall I give
your love to the Phillipsons? All sorts of people are asking what's
become of you. Goodbye – '

The door closed behind her, and a few moments later he was
thumbing and paring his clay again, but his heart was heavy. Poor,
shut-out, hurt, gallant little Winifred, ready to fight back, with
nothing better than her flimsy little invention of Bertie Phillipson to
fight with! But no finger-tipping, after-tea-calling, young man had
made the breach between them. She might pretend it was Bertie.
Pique her enough and presently she might even make it Bertie. But
John Brydon, looking at his statue, knew what it really was.

THE WAX

I

One morning John Brydon woke on his couch, put his foot to the
ground, and then, drawing it back again, found it swollen out of
recognisable shape. Its fellow was the same. He made his way to the
telephone and rang up a doctor.

The doctor diagnosed its condition as one of oedema, and oedema
is also sometimes known as waterlogging. In the form in which it
had fastened on John Brydon his blood, helped by gravity, had
determined to his feet and his heart was not strong enough to pump
it back again. For a heavy man he had been standing too much, the

doctor said, and he must lie up and give his feet a complete rest. He then asked whether his patient had been drinking to excess lately.

John Brydon cursed this latest piece of ill-luck and made such answers as he could. He had been drinking, he replied, not to excess but according to necessity, and as for lying up, that at present was not possible to be done. Whereupon the doctor pointed out that in that case that oedema also was likely to follow as a necessary consequence, and it was much that John Brydon did not lose his temper. He dismissed the doctor, and in his socks, moving carefully on the outer edges of his feet, hobbled back to his turntable.

But oedema or no oedema, one weight was now off his mind. Over the Embassy's head he had received a telegram granting him a month's extension of time. But against that there was to set that more-than-enough on which he had embarked, that began to open up fresh vistas of labour with every step his work advanced. Well, there was nothing for it but to go on going forward, and, standing there before his group, he saw that his toil had not been for nothing. Sketch or more than sketch, it was a comely birth. It was not now something upon a base; had the base been taken away its proportion and intention would still have been invisibly there, had the superstructure been removed the base would have beckoned that other half of itself back again. And seeing all this he allowed himself ten minutes of luxurious nothingness. Closing his eyes he saw the processes still to come. He saw his work, not in the sober-hued clay, but as if the clay had put on its winding-sheet; it was blank white plaster, cold as a cold heart, raw, upstart, at the unloveliest stage of all. Then the plaster too disappeared; it was embedded in a shapeless boulder-like mass within which was the mould, as if the child and the womb had changed places. Again, and the matrix was a matrix of gelatine for the image in foundry-wax. Translation and re-translation, the stuff of the child now the womb, the womb's shape now the child again, but ever a step nearer to the end that had been the first conception of all . . . and suddenly he gave an exclamation of pain. He had closed his eyes once too often and given a little stumble. With his feet in that condition it would not do for him to go to sleep standing up. Awake again he felt behind him for a chair and sank into it. A cigarette and a few minutes with his feet up on the banker there and he would be all right. Half an hour perhaps. His alarm clock was over there on the mantelpiece, but he could trust himself to wake.

An hour later his telephone bell rang, but he did not hear it. He was dreaming that he was in his Surrey garden, lying out on a long chair with his head on a pillow, and Winifred and Mara were bringing out tea. He remembered the dream when, two-and-a-half hours later, he woke.

Since his wife had left him with that sprightly little reminder that a young man called Bertie Phillipson was back home from Kenya she had not been near the studio. Only once had she even telephoned, and that was about something he had now forgotten. Unless some model rang his bell, to have the door shut in her face the moment he learned her business, his daily woman was the only woman he saw, and even she was in trouble of her own and often had to leave her work to accumulate. But one afternoon his bell rang, and going to the door he saw on the landing not Winifred, but his daughter Mara. Or was something the matter with his eyes that she stood there alone? But no, it was Mara, looking at him with startled but unafraid eyes. He made a sign for her to come in, for for the moment he did not trust himself to speak. Then when he had closed the door again, and with his hand on the edge of a banker to steady himself, he eased himself down to his knees and stretched out his arms.

'My little girl!' he laughed to himself. 'I mean my big girl. You see you're getting so big – and heavy – I can't take you up in my arms. Let me look at you,' and, kneeling, he held her away at arms length.

'Father, aren't you well?' she asked, looking at him steadily. His nose stood out above a three-days' growth, the eyes on either side of it were bloodshot, so bloated were his feet that his socks would pull on no higher than his ankle bones, and his working blouse, which he had not changed, was patterned with nameless stains.

'I shall be all right in a few days, dear. I've been working rather hard. What good wind brings you here?'

'Mother was coming up to do some shopping and I said might I come. I said I wanted to see it,' and she glanced up at the turntable. 'She said she didn't think she'd have time to see you because she'd such a lot of things to do, but I said couldn't I have half a crown, because I know the way, so she dropped me outside, and it's only a shilling in a taxi to the Bannisters', and I've got the half-crown.'

'Do you mean she's not coming back here for you?' Because as long as he and the Bannisters had each a telephone she was, whether she knew it or not.

'She didn't say so. Perhaps she thought you'd come with me in the taxi.'

He did not reply, but helped himself to his feet again. 'It's lovely of you to come, Mara. There's the thing. Can you see from there?'

And she was his, his, not only in the shape of her firm body, but in her intelligence and understanding too. He must not expect too much of her yet, but what she did say he could lean on with his full weight; she wouldn't be sometimes right and sometimes wrong without knowing the difference herself. He dreaded the day when she should be grown up. He would have had her grow up just so far and then stop, his. She stood in her still-short skirt and straw hat, looking at his group.

'Is that bottom part granite?' she asked.

'No, darling. Granite would have taken too long and cost rather a lot, especially if the men had happened to make a mistake, as they did before. That's only imitation.'

'Did they make a mistake because of the batters?'

'Exactly. They look simple, but they're very, very complicated.'

'But I thought the rest was going to be in bronze.'

'It is. We haven't come to the bronze yet. The bronze comes last of all. It has to die first.'

'To die? What has it got to die for?'

'First it has to be turned into wax, the same thing you're looking at now, but wax, hollow, only about so thick, with a thing called a core inside it so it doesn't break. And then you bury it and you never see it again.'

'Why must you bury it?'

'You bury it in fireclay, that sets hard like plaster. It's just a shell of wax, held fast between two walls of fireclay, but exactly the shape you're looking at now.'

'I don't think I quite understand about the burying.'

'Listen. When they've done what I say they put the whole thing into a furnace. There are holes and places for the gases to escape out of and every scrap of wax is melted away. Then there's nothing between the two walls of fireclay.'

She looked puzzled, but he went on.

'They have the bronze ready melted, terribly hot and as thin as milk, and they run it into the space where the wax used to be. Then days later, when it's got cool again, they break the mould away and there it is, bronze. Have you understood?'

'I think I have now.'

'Could you tell me what they do?'

With no more than a falter or two she repeated the lost-wax process as he had just described it to her.

'Good. Would you like to see it done when everything's ready?'

'Oh yes! Can I bring Sammie?' Sammie was her spaniel dog.

'If you keep him on a lead.'

'Will mother be there?'

'Of course, if she'd care to come. I should like her to come.'

He watched her as she turned away and began to walk about the studio and saw that she was looking at the floor. It was unsightly with ash and the trodden ends of cigarettes, papers he had been using, unwashed glasses pushed aside. Then she went into the kitchen, and it was from the kitchen that she called to him.

'Oh, father! There is such a lot of washing-up!'

'I know. Mrs Day hasn't been able to do it. Her baby's very ill.' Then a few minutes later, as he heard the clatter of crockery and the running of water, 'What are you doing?'

'I'm going to wash them up,' she replied.

He let her. His heart was full that he should be served by her. And he thought he knew why she had been allowed to come that afternoon. Winifred's setting of her down at the door had been an olive-branch. Not for a moment had he believed in her figment of young men back from Kenya. She felt it more than he did, for he always had his work, and it was an indignity to both of them that she should come as far as the door and let the child come up alone. She must come and fetch her. He crossed to the telephone and got the Bannisters' number.

But the understanding must still hold till the statue was out of the studio for good. If she would agree to that her presence once more would be a comfort and a promise. It was not much of a life as things were, but surely between them they could make the best of it for a little longer.

In the little kitchen Mara continued to wash up.

She came that same afternoon. She came with a little air of being almost a stranger that was very taking. And she would have accepted almost any condition if only because of her shock at his stumbling walk and altered appearance. Had she known he was like that (she told him) she would have been long before. Now if he would let her she would bring him soup in a thermos and things to eat that only needed warming up and she would be as quiet as a mouse while he worked. Should she bring their own doctor with her? But at the mention of the doctor he shook his head quickly. No, no doctors. He knew what doctors would say about him. Doctors were of no use to John Brydon at this juncture. What matter if he collapsed completely as long as the work was finished? Winifred and Mara did not leave till nearly seven o'clock, and then only because of the car's lights. And his first four hours' sleep that night were among the purely peaceful things he afterwards remembered.

2

She was as good as her word. During the first week she came twice, bringing Mara again on the second occasion, and it made the place home to see her moving here and there, sitting in a chair reading one of her magazines, scribbling for an hour perhaps, cool, fresh, with the air of her Surrey garden about her, trying not to let him know she was there. But he was now past the stage when he had wanted to throw something if anybody spoke to him, and it was good for him too that he had to shave and to pull himself a little together. But alas, there was still no sitting down for him. He must be on those swollen, aching, bandaged feet every hour he was at work. Sometimes he suffered so that he had to ring her up early and to ask her, if she had thought of coming up that day, not to do so. But sometimes, when his moulder came in with his assistant and the bronze-founder to see whether he could be given a date yet – for the wax and the subsequent stages were rapidly approaching – the studio had almost a festive air, so many people seemed to be assembled. Cavani the master-moulder, despite his advancing years, was a fount of merriment in himself. He would solemnly admonish Mara that if she wished to be happy she must on no account marry anybody but a good Italian, who would play the mandolin under her window and show her Venice by moonlight and make love to her that would be like quicksilver in her veins; and when Mara with an unsmiling face asked what this last meant Winifred would laugh and play with the child's hair and say that she wasn't to take any notice of Mr Cavani, for she would know all about it one day. She would then glance softly across at John.

The first time since the truce that he saw one of these glances he turned his head away. One of his reasons for doing this was that she must not think his work was at an end even when it was delivered over to the moulders. What about his set-up, those worrying per-spectives, the margin he must allow for the possible mistakes of others, the final stages on the bronze itself? But there came a day when she appeared, not with Mara, but alone. A parcel addressed to her had preceded her; she had asked whether it might be sent there, for it was from a dressmaker, and to have it sent straight to the studio would save time in case alterations had to be made. On her arrival she proceeded to open the parcel there and then. And a young man from Kenya or elsewhere, though he may hope for no profit of it himself, can set something aglow, for this time the frown above his great nose was a deep one. *That* was outside the bargain, that that he had no choice but to see now. Never did a model show herself quite like that. And many a man would have turned away with indifference, telling himself that it was only his wife. Not so John Brydon. It was because she was his wife that she had this power. Immodest modesty of those we marry, so to play on us and afterwards if needs be to turn round and ask us what then we married them for! Had she advanced to him like that, with those cool bare arms and that less cool breast, anything might have happened. But having kindled the torch she hid its light away again without allaying its heat. She slipped the new frock over her head and stood before him.

'Isn't there something to fasten somewhere at the back?'

'My hands are all clay and plaster. You'd better do it yourself. And draw that curtain,' he replied.

But she opened her eyes wide. – 'Why, what's the matter?'

'Nothing.' But it is love's hypocrisy to ask like that what the matter is.

'Aren't you going to tell me how you like it? I was thinking of you when I chose it.'

His right foot gave him a twinge at which he winced. – 'I think you'd do better to forget me for the present,' he said between his teeth.

'Why – John!' She had stepped back, but she was still shining softly at him through her clothing. 'Didn't you want me to come today?'

'Come whenever you like – ' but again the twinge took him.

A blush as unannounced as that of a young girl came into her cheeks, and she turned abruptly away.

'I shall send it back to the shop and tell them I don't want it,' she said, drawing the curtain. Her voice came from behind it. 'I'm sure I don't know what I've done. I've tried to do everything you say. I didn't bring Mara because I know it worries you to have a lot of people about. I can't think all this is necessary. Other people have work to do too.'

To have answered her would only have been to provoke further words, but now they came of themselves.

'It's all that thing you're doing!' He heard the rustle of tissue-paper and knew she was putting the frock back into its carton. 'I'm going back to the shop straight away. It's no good buying frocks for people who don't look at them. And I thought we were friends again. I shall go where I'm wanted. I can't believe *all* these competitors of yours are treating their wives like this.'

And in that the chances were that she was right, but the words that stuck with him long after she had gone were that it 'was all that thing he was doing'.

Moulding as elaborate as that that his group would require was not his trade, but he had resolved that nothing was going to be done except under his own eye, and on the day when his clay went out of the studio he was at least able to rest his feet for a few hours. He did not trouble to change out of his blouse; he took a taxi to the moulder's, which was no great distance away, and there, lying out on an improvised chair with his feet propped up on another, he watched the preparations for the wax. He half raised himself on one elbow when they brought in his model, his heart in his mouth for fear it should slip from the hands of the man who carried it. If anything should happen to it now! But nothing went amiss. The men knew their job better than he could teach it to them. While it was going forward there was little to look at, and there, in the moulder's work-shop, surrounded by claybins and buckets and trestles and a crowded graveyard of grimy saints and imps and gargoyles of all ages and sizes, again he fell off into a doze.

'Looks just about all in if you ask me,' commented an assistant whose hands and forearms dripped with plaster. 'What he wants is somebody to look after him.'

'He's getting near the finish of it now.'

'But he says he's got to start on another job straight away.'

'Says! *He* isn't starting on any new job, not yet a bit he isn't! I know all about them feet. I've had it.'

'Yours was beer, my lad.'

'And *he's* been knocking 'em back a bit this last month and more. It beats me how he's done his work with it all.'

'He wouldn't have done it without.'

'But when they have to get stiffer and stiffer before you can get any kick out of them, that ain't so good.'

'Well . . . isn't that mould about ready to come off?' and the man with the plastered forearms dipped them in a bucket, wiped them on a piece of sacking, and proceeded to untie the rope that knotted the piece-mould firmly together.

The perfect wax that was delivered at Brydon's studio a couple of days later was in colour a dull restful red, a boon to Brydon's eyes after the hateful white of the plaster that, thank God, he had now looked on for the last time. But it was there only at a cost that brought his heart into his mouth every time he looked at the thing. He had not even been in the moulder's shop when the all but fatal accident had happened. For without warning, as yet inexplicably, and through nobody's fault or negligence, some portion of the inner roof of the workshop had waited till that very last moment, and then, with a rush of plaster and a splintering of thick glass, had come down in a thick cloud of dust. Mercifully the newly-made wax had been well out of harm's way, but not so the gelatine mould within which it had lain and the plaster cast from which that mould had been made. These had lain deep under a barrowful of fallen débris. That – that there was now no means of replacement – was the thought that made him feel faint a dozen times a day. The premises were covered by insurance, but what would be the use of insurance to John Brydon if anything happened to that dull red waxen image now? He could only bow his head in gratitude that at least his wax had been spared. He must now guard it as he would have guarded his last hope of heaven, and it would have surprised those who thought they knew John Brydon as a man without beliefs if they could have come upon him a few minutes after he had been told what had happened – on his knees on his studio floor, not because of his throbbing feet this time, but committing his statue thenceforward into the charge of its own special angel, lest human or inanimate spite should pursue him still further.

After that came the hour when, looking at it from all angles, in all lights, with the help of slanting mirrors, from the sight-level of the turntable on which it stood, he saw that it was good. Few but he would ever know how good it was.

Others would see, a couple of years hence, under a high foreign sun, an uplifted shape against skyline and dome and palm, on a pedestal of specially quarried granite that revealed itself with every hour of the sun as if a flower opened and closed itself, but they would know nothing of that faithful service of a vision that in less than ten weeks had changed John Brydon from an erect and iron-framed man into a bent huddle, his feet swathed in dusters, longing now for nothing except that the rest should be quickly over. And now that by a miracle his wax was spared it would not be long. He had no fear that Cavani, born and inured to bronze, the last of a long line that had served fire and metal before him, would fail him. So now to the last leisurely details. He got out his penknife and reached for the oil-bottle.

And now that his wax was to die he had promised Mara that she should see it before it went. What about Winifred? Yes, Winifred too; had it not been she who had likened his toil to the labour of bearing a child in the flesh? It was this experience shared between them, and nothing that any young man from Kenya could claim a share in, that sent him to the telephone. She herself answered, and her voice was as musical as a harp. Had he really, really finished? Only a day or two more? Oh, she was glad and oh, how she was longing to see it! Then would he be coming home? Might she come up tomorrow. Should she bring Mara? The child had a slight cold, but . . . oh, very well. She would wrap her up well and put the hood of the car up. She was in bed – yes, she would say good night for him. And she hoped that he, too, would have a good sleep, for she was sure he had earned it. He heard the click as she hung up the receiver. He tried to remember what flowers would be out in his Surrey garden now.

3

His first question was about his daughter's cold. Winifred answered lightly.

'It's nothing really, except that if you begin to get them at this time of the year they're sometimes difficult to shake off. But *that* isn't going to be the funeral, is it, darling?'

'The funeral?' said John Brydon, not understanding, and she laughed.

'All the way coming up she's been asking about the funeral. Tell him, Mara.'

His daughter was looking at his wax. – 'You said it had to die,' she said, and smiled.

'It isn't going to die here. It will go to the foundry for that. Cavani will see to the burying. How long has she had this cold?'

'A couple of days. We went to a party at the Phillipsons' and I think she caught a slight chill there. We can't stay in the house *all* the time, just us two women,' she laughed.

Mara was asking what the inscriptions on the base meant, for the stately thing now bore its stately name in three languages. One of these he could not read himself but he translated the others.

'There are a lot of things to learn,' said the child, and her father put his hand on her head.

'There are. It's all learning, and by the time you've learned it you're almost too tired to want to do it. If only you could begin, Mara, young and fresh, knowing what I know – ' and he sighed.

'Can't I if I'm taught?'

'No. Only life can teach you, and by the time you've learned it you're old. Was it a nice party at the Phillipsons?'

'No,' said the child, shortly, and then asked when Mr Cavani was going to bury the wax.

His wife had moved away and was looking at the other works that stood against the studio walls. She had seen them fifty times before, and it was difficult to see what her interest in them could be now. She paused before the Ixion, the Faun, other works, and then stood before a half-finished bust still in the clay. Apparently he had abandoned it, for it was hard and dry and fissured for lack of cloths and water. It was in fact the 'next job' the moulder's assistant had spoken of.

'Why,' she exclaimed, stepping back, 'that's the Sir Henry, isn't it?'

'Yes,' he mumbled.

'But what's happened to it? Didn't you cover it up? I thought it – '

'I know,' he muttered. 'It was stupid of me. I'd simply so much on my mind I forgot all about it. I remembered it the other day. I shall start on it the moment I've finished this.'

'Oh – ' she said, and bit her lip and stopped.

But her tone was enough. He was to have been well paid for the Sir Henry, and at once, but he had set it aside, and for the past weeks she had been the main support of the Surrey end of their home.

'What's the date?' she asked abruptly. 'Will there be *time* to do another one?'

'Just, if I start at once. What I want to know is all there, and Cavani will make a special effort with the bronze. There will be just time.'

But she had turned her back on the Sir Henry and had given herself an angry shake. She spoke with sudden asperity.

'Well, there's only one thing to be said about it.'

'What's that, Winifred?' he asked, his heart sinking.

'That I wish you'd told me sooner. I'm not a sculptor, but I could at least have poured an occasional jug of water over the thing. It seems to me that *everything* has had to stand aside for that one-in-a-thousand chance you've spent all these weeks over.'

'Not one-in-a-thousand,' he answered, suddenly more tired than he had been yet. 'At the worst it's one in a dozen. You may call it evens if you like. And I'm hoping for something better than that.'

'Oh, I've no doubt the whole dozen of you are all *hoping*!' she flashed at him with sudden scorn.

And it was as if she swept away his chance already. No dream-shape against domes and pediments for her, but only a profitable, ready-money job neglected and no time left now to do it in. Even propped up on crutches he would not be able to do it in the time. Once more she was right. She had stepped forward.

'I really do think this is about the last straw, John,' she said in a tremulous voice. 'There are lots of things I've kept to myself because I didn't want to upset you, but there was that bust, nearly finished and as good as paid for. How much was it? Two hundred and fifty guineas? Burying yourself week after week here I think you forget what the house and everything costs. I don't get paid in hundreds of guineas. I pick it up a guinea or two at a time and then have to wait for it. If I'd thought for a moment you'd let the thing get into that state I'd have come up and *made* you finish it.'

'I know,' he said, passing his hand over his eyes. 'It's what I ought to have done. It was only fair to you. But there's still time, and this won't be in guineas or hundreds – it will be in thousands – '

At that she let her scorn have its way. It came out in a torrent.

'*Will* be, he says! All he has to do is to shut himself up here, and never see anybody, never listen to a word of advice, but make himself a cripple and drink himself stupid and say it *will* be – !'

'I know I had to drink,' he answered in a low voice. 'But I didn't drink myself stupid. I drank myself something very different if you only knew. There aren't many living sculptors whose work I don't know, and I don't think you'll find one whose chances are much brighter than mine. That's all I mean when I said "I will". I hope and think it will.'

'And if it doesn't?'

His answer was so humble that it hardly seemed his. – 'I shall still have done it and be glad.'

Suddenly the scorn left her voice. It is difficult to find a name for the thing that took its place. In it were mingled truth and falsity, the present deadlock of duty and affection, her despite of the wreck he had made of himself, her own exemplary patience, all his absence and denial. These could be seen in her face as warring ingredients can be seen fuming and annihilating one another in a test-tube. And that fragrance of her Surrey garden might cling about her, but it was no incense to that waxen thing on the stand that had come between them. What rubbish had he been telling Mara about the wax being the death, so that she talked in the car about funerals? At least it was not going to be Winifred Brydon's death! It had made too much mischief already. The test-tube hissed and cracked as she spoke.

'And you think it's enough to say that even if it comes to nothing you'll "have done it and be glad!" Who else is glad? Is Mara glad? Am I glad? Will the servants be glad if their wages aren't paid? Mara and I, we're just two people who're told to stay away till you want us, and when you do it's to run your errands and do your washing-up! And it's different with Mara, because she's still a child, but am *I* supposed to sit still like Penelope till you come back? And when you do come the place won't be any better than a nursing-home! If those thousands were in your pocket now it wouldn't be worth it! Just look at yourself in that glass! You tell me that if I'm good I shall have *that* to look at every time I come to the table! I'm *not* good! I'm not going to be good! Please yourself what you do! Take yourself and that thing you seem to think the world of – '

Crippled and in pain as he was he could almost certainly have stopped what came next. That he made no attempt to stop it showed how inconceivable it was to him that such a thing could be done. Nor perhaps was she herself entirely accountable. She may have told herself that if only out of instinct he would still seize her hand. But petulance, rage or whatever it was, out her hand shot. The wax stood loose and unfastened on its base, and a touch was enough. Even when he saw it totter he must have thought that some last-moment miracle would happen to save it. Then, too late, he came to violent life. He started forward. It was to die, but not that way! An age passed before he heard the dull, mile-away thud, followed by an appalling stillness. Scraping the edge of the turntable in its fall it hung for a moment over the edge of a chair-seat, and then finished its journey to the floor.

'*Mother! Look out!*'

It was as well that she should do so now that the incredible thing had forced itself on his understanding. Yet he was delaying for a moment, as if to choose for himself the most delectable out of a thousand revenges. He was crouching forward almost double. The great hands at the ends of his half-extended arms were hooked to seize. His face was thrust forward, his teeth were bared to the gums, and his nose was like the scythe on the axle of a battle-chariot. Then he sprang.

But how could a man attempt such a leap with feet as John Brydon's were? He missed it at the very take-off. She and the child were at the door before he fell his length on the floor and lay there. After that a blackness descended on him.

He had no means of knowing whether it was day or night when at last he stirred again. His lights frequently burned the twenty-four hours through, and from where he lay no hint of daylight appeared beyond the studio blinds. But something in his head remained awake, for he was spared the anguish of remembering a little at a time. It came back to him instantaneously and whole, that half-checked push of her hand, the totter on the turntable, its disappearing over the edge, the impact on the floor. Without moving his head he knew exactly where the wreckage lay. But first things first. He must make sure of his own condition. Cautiously he tried one foot against the other to see how much they had suffered from that impossible leap he had attempted. He decided that they were not much worse than before. And all at once he found his brain working with extraordinary clearness. It directed him to the easiest way to his feet and to the telephone. Before he did anything else he must know the time and the day of the week, for how was he to know that he had not missed a day? But he had not. It was 10.32 p.m., Wednesday the fourteenth. Next he dialled a number, and almost immediately a voice replied from the other end. Yes, that was Dr Hood speaking. Come now, at once? A few more words and then a 'Very good'; the doctor would be round in half an hour. John Brydon shuffled over to his couch, took off his blouse and the waistcoat underneath, and rolled up both his sleeves from his forearms. His brain was still working beautifully ahead, and he rolled up his sleeves for a very crafty reason. The doors had been so left that when the doctor came he could let himself in, and John Brydon had still twenty minutes or so to work out the details of his plan.

First of all he must clear his mind of everything that had passed by means of a good sleep, and that was a simple matter. Doctors had a dozen things that would do that. But what was the other stuff, not the stuff that sends a man to sleep, but that keeps him awake, for a week or ten days if necessary, and keyed up to the last ounce of his strength all the time? He had no medical knowledge, but few men reach his age without picking up a smattering here and there, possibly dangerously wrongly. But he put that aside. Now or never was the time to take a risk. There was heroin then, and there was cocaine. Everybody had heard of these, and some had even seen a collapsed young man or woman, spent with excess, and lo, an absence of less than ten minutes, that stab of whatever it was, and back they were, bright-eyed, laughing, the life and soul of the party once more. Something of that kind was the stuff, and doctors carried these precious, perilous drugs, usually in a case that looked like an attaché-case. If they lost them they commonly lost the lot and not one selected phial or tube. And naturally the final bit of craftiness would have to be left to the chances of the moment. That was why John Brydon had rolled up both his sleeves, one arm for the needle while the other hand was left free for the theft. If Hood put the case down on the couch, one position; if he set it down on the floor, another; if he left it yards away across the studio John Brydon would have to think of some other way. And he must put all his emphasis on his need of sleep. Not a word about keeping awake, awake for another week if necessary.

The doctor arrived, let himself in, and put the case down on a banker. John Brydon was sitting up on the edge of the couch, ready to turn in any position. The doctor advanced to him with a professionally cheerful, 'Well, and what have *you* been doing to yourself?'

'Still the oedema. Give me something to make me sleep. I don't care if I sleep for a month.'

'Still the oedema? Let's have a look at it. Hm!' he cogitated when he had done so. 'Well, you'll be resting while you're asleep. A month you say? We'll start with a night anyway. How do you react to these things taken internally?'

'No use to me at all. I'm afraid I've been taking too many things internally. Give it me in my arm.'

And with that the doctor, turning away, did the very thing John Brydon was praying he would do. He returned and set the case down on the floor, admirably within reach. John Brydon rolled over on his left side and held out his right arm for the shot.

And the attention of a doctor who pinches up a bit of loose tissue is for the moment occupied, but Hood was no busier than John Brydon was. With his head half over the edge of the couch and his left hand free he could study the contents of the case almost at his leisure. There they were in their small variously-shaped bottles, digitalin, heroin, strychnine, morphia, others he didn't know – and what were those, the pill-like things that stared straight at him as if put there purposely for his taking? The bottle was turned half way round, so that he could only read the first four letters of the label: 'Barb-something.' Now what was that? Barbituric? Barbituric acid? A little knowledge is a dangerous thing, but it is all a man has to depend on when his wax, his irreplaceable wax . . . but he put that thought hurriedly out of his head. Barbituric acid. He had heard of that stuff somewhere. He seemed to remember someone out of the distant

past saying that something with a name remarkably like that was
powerful yet manageable stuff, well up to the job unless too much of it
defeated itself. Anyway he wasn't going to take it without getting it
checked over; the first thing to do was to get hold of it. The doctor
had the sleepy-stuff ready. He jabbed the needle into John's right arm
and wiped the place with a bit of cotton wool, watching it meanwhile.
'There you are,' he said, 'and unless you've something to get up for
you'd better stay where you are. I'll see to your light. You'll sleep all
right tonight. If you don't give me a ring in the morning.'

He drew the coverlet over John, and John turned over to sleep; but
he kept the little bottle concealed in the palm of his hand till the
sound of the doctor's footsteps had died away down the stairs.

THE BRONZE

I

Since that attempted leap that had brought him his length along
the floor John Brydon's thoughts and actions had been those of a
machine that continues to function of its own momentum. The old,
controlling John Brydon had been as it were on a journey. For
example, he had not once been near that broken wax to ascertain the
extent of the catastrophe that had befallen him. But he woke, twenty
hours later, completely in charge of himself again, and lay there on
his back without moving, recalling everything that had happened.

And his very first thought cut so deep into the profundities of our
life itself as almost to frighten him. For almost up to the moment of
the accident his wax had had no armature of wire or lead that by a
heroic effort of will and hands he could have wrenched back into its
former position had anything gone wrong. Had he followed the
customary procedure the thing would have been no more than a shell
with a thin lining of fireclay to stiffen it, insufficient to withstand the
slightest shock. Then all at once the accident had happened, and
now, but for something else, his model would have lain behind him
on the floor, unmendable by him or anybody else.

It was the something else that filled him now with an almost
terrified hope. He did not even remember giving the curt order.
Cavani had been strongly against it. It was not the practise of his
craft, he had said. The thing might crack, warp, burst, anything;
experience had taught that a just-sufficient lining of fireclay was best,
not the whole core run in before the outside support was ready to

hold everything together. But in that moment John Brydon had been conscious of his angel close about him. 'Do not answer him, but do as I say,' that angel had whispered in his ear, and he had turned an authoritative front to Cavani. Its life was his life, and he had withstood the founder. 'I've no doubt you're entirely right, but – fill it in,' he had commanded, and now, lying on his back on his couch with his nose as imperious as that of an eagle, he could only remember that they had shaken their heads but had done his bidding.

But what else had that angelic whisper meant? It had meant that, foreseeing the disaster, his Guide had also seen the hope and promise beyond. So certain now was he of the solidity of that core and that all would be well in the end that suddenly he got up from his couch, washed himself in cold water, and walked without a falter to where the empty turntable stood.

As the scene of a crime is left undisturbed till the arrival of the police, so at first he stood looking down at the mangled thing only. But after a time he knelt and took the group carefully in his hands. As he did so a spasm twitched his face. At a first glance it was not much better than the worst he had feared. And the core, on which everything depended, was the one thing he could not see. Unless that was intact all would fall to pieces in the firing. But the chance of its resurrection it was going to have. Handling it as tenderly as one handles a sick child John Brydon made a soft place for it on his lap. His fingers might have been manipulating a still-beating heart. He turned his ear into a stethoscope, listening for the minutest crack or crepitation, for he dreaded to believe the almost-too-good-to-be-true thing – that the group's fall had been so broken, first by the scrape along the edge of the turntable, and next by the padding of the chair seat, that the inside still held together.

But it was a dismaying sight at best. Take a plastic substance like wax and drop it on the floor and each point of contact becomes the tip of a nose that is flattened against a windowpane. What further jarring and straining the thing had sustained might take a week to discover. Half his surface-planes, detail, harness, trappings, had gone. He spent the greater part of that day in tapping, listening, palpitating with sensitive fingers, making notes on a piece of paper, and at the end of it was still making heart-rending discoveries. His faith in his angel was becoming a memory already. His heart sank lower and lower.

But he now had a remedy against that. It was in the small bottle he had stolen from the doctor's bag. No more drink; he had drunk himself through the stupid stage into steadiness, and alcohol would no longer serve. So first to make sure of the action of this other stuff. His family doctor in Surrey was also his friend, and he could put his questions in such a way that they would not betray him. He rang up the number, and at the third attempt got him. Tanner answered in an oddly serious voice, and something told John Brydon that the seriousness was not because of the questions he was being asked. But there was no time to waste. He found out more or less what he wanted to know about the properties of the drug, and as for its administering and dosage there were always certain precepts of common sense, even about these things. The maximum effect out of the minimum dose – that was what he was after. Alcohol had so taken away his appetite that he did not feel the need of food. When he did he could order it. Now for another look at those multiple injuries he had noted down on his piece of paper, and to work again.

That night, turning on his powerful overhead light and putting his brown paper shade over his deep-sunk eyes again, with throbbing feet of which he did not feel the pain, a jaded brain that must recapture a first fresh vision, and nothing but a drug and the half-forgotten echo of an angel's promise to keep him to it, he once more set up his crippled wax on its base.

2

If during the days and nights that followed anybody had asked John Brydon anything about his wife it is doubtful whether he would have taken the question in. This was not because of anything out of the doctor's bag. As the eye has its blind spot till the focus is adjusted again, so in this one portion of it had his memory. The blank extended, though less completely, to his daughter. There had been a time for Mara and there would be again, but not yet. That his wife had committed a cowardly assassination and that he had turned on her with bared teeth to rend her, these things sometimes occurred to him, but they were gone again almost in the moment of their coming. When the work was finished anything you like. Till then he had peace.

But a family doctor is a family doctor, and is likely to be the doctor of more families than one. Tanner, going his rounds in his car, must have heard whatever gossip there might be about John Brydon's prolonged absence from his home, and when John Brydon had telephoned to him to ask him the properties of a certain drug he had no doubt noticed the care with which his sometime patient had confined himself to that one subject. One afternoon John Brydon's telephone rang.

'Is that you, John? Tanner speaking,' came the voice.

The sculptor waited for the message.

'Are you there? How are you? Everything all right?'

'I'm all right, thanks,' said John Brydon.

'Any chance of seeing you down here soon?'

'If you mean within the next week or so I'm afraid not.'

'Would you like me to come up and see you?'

'Why?' What had Tanner got hold of now? 'Is anything the matter? with Mara?'

'Mara's all right, but – '

'But what?'

'I'm not quite so sure about your wife.'

'Is she ill?'

'Nothing organically wrong. She's . . . but look here, there are things we can't discuss over the telephone – '

'If she's ill surely you can look after her?'

'Listen. We're pretty good friends. Shall I run up and see you tomorrow?'

But if Tanner came up tomorrow he might notice a number of things John Brydon didn't want noticed. He would certainly break in on precious time, and if John Brydon, keyed up as he was, once allowed himself to relax he might never reach the tension again. And that settled it. Mara was all right. There was nothing organically the matter with Winifred. He answered that he was engaged tomorrow.

'Very soon after then?' came the voice.

'If she isn't well look after her. I'm very busy. I'll come down as soon as I can. I'll give you a ring,' and John Brydon hung up the receiver again.

But the effects of that telephone conversation continued long after their cause was removed. What (he had to ask himself) was to happen when his work was finished? If his time was to be wasted like this would it ever be finished? Suppose he did finish it, his core failed him after all, and it cracked up in the furnace? Was he to take up his life again exactly as he had left it? As if nothing had happened? Was *that* his duty? To forgive? Oh, he was not going to harbour any bitterness. She had his forgiveness now if it was any good to her, that was to say if she could ever forgive herself. 'Till death us do part?' That was something he had vowed at the altar, and there was always that way out; gas, the razor, an overdose, the shot – there were as many ways out as there were flowers in her Surrey garden. But if there had really been anything he could have done for her Tanner would have told him. She simply didn't understand, never had understood; didn't know that she was pressing on him with her thoughts now, as before she had fluttered about him with her body. If she would only let him finish his work there were plenty of things he had to be forgiven too, and he must be getting on with it. Tanner's call, for no reason that he could see except to ask him how was he and when he was coming home and to tell him that his wife wasn't very well but there was nothing really the matter with her, had been distraction enough. Did she expect to be very well after . . . but he must be careful about that. That sounded a little as if he had *not* forgiven her. He crossed to the wall-cupboard where he kept the little bottle.

Apart from the core, the stuff had enabled him to do a miracle of repairing. That night, in order to bring out the detail under the strong light, he had given the thing a light sheen of oil, and this had woken up the lovely dead rose almost as if it had been the bronze itself. But at what a cost to John Brydon he had only to look in the glass to see. And as he stood there, sunken-chested with the cramped standing that was easiest for his feet, half-bearded, dead-eyed, hollow-cheeked but indomitable, he forgot that it was not afternoon, and glanced across at the glass against the wall, remembering how he and she had stood in that same spot with the statue between them. And his grim mouth relented. Forgiveness? How can one forgive something that hasn't happened? It had been still in the clay then, and was it not in the wax again now? What did the horrible gulf in between matter? That was all a nightmare. She had *not* done it. What was not a nightmare was that that was about him now, the two of them side by side, with Mara standing serious-eyed between them, remembering what he had told her about the batters. She was Winifred and he was John, and the child had come forth from her even as his group was born of himself. 'Almost like having a baby.' Was it not true, as true at heart as herself? Oh, let her wait a little, just a little longer! It had not been easy for him either. And she and Mara were coming to see the last stage of all. He frowned for a moment; had he told Mara the date? Then he remembered. Of course he hadn't. The date had had to be altered, anyway. But he would be able to tell her in a very few days. He would ring up Tanner. It would be better to telephone to Tanner rather than to his own home, because – because – because of something that for the moment escaped him. Of course there would have to be some sort of an explanation between him and Winifred. A man can't have his work knocked about in a fit of temper like that, and as Tanner said there were some things you couldn't talk about over the telephone. So he would telephone to Tanner. Then Mara would come, bringing Winifred with her. He would have his hair cut and be shaved. And they had better all meet at the foundry. That way it would be less like asking her to come. Only a few days now – only a few more days. And now for that bridle and reins. They would have to be re-made afterwards, but he wanted to see the line, the glint, the last little touches of realism that give life to all the rest.

But first he went to the cupboard in the wall again.

3

Not one in a hundred of the people who passed the end of the narrow alley ever suspected that such a place as a bronze-foundry existed there. All that they saw was a little cluster of London cottages so poor as almost to be called a slum, with doors mostly open and children at play outside them. But near the end on the right was an inconspicuous entry with a heavy iron ring-knocker. You knocked at this, and the door was opened by a humorous-looking Italian in old boots and a smock and with a tall paper cap on his head like that of a chef. This was Cavani, master-founder and last of a line of founders, for in spite of his talk of Venice by moonlight and love that turned the blood to quicksilver in the veins he had no son. The chambers of his foundry were three. The first of these, like the moulding-shop, was a crowded jumble of grimy figures and grotesques and reliefs and moulds and portions of castings of all descriptions. The second was a top-lighted anteroom, a mortuary of a place where the wax victim was made ready for the final sacrifice. But it was in neither of these that John Brydon stood, waiting for the knock at the door that would tell him that Mara had been brought in the car. He had descended by four unrailed wooden steps into a dungeon below, stifling with the fumes of coke, the walls of sooty stone. He had supported himself between two heavy sticks, and his mouth drew tighter every time he looked at the watch on his wrist. If she – they – didn't come in a very few minutes they could not be waited for.

Besides being a dungeon the place resembled a medieval torture-chamber too. Large-scale work requires room, but it had not been

possible to add to the height of Cavani's foundry. The depth was in
the pit beneath that made the floor seem insecure to the feet and
sounded hollow when John Brydon stumped across it on his two
sticks. Not that there was much floor-space at the best, for coke had
slipped from its loose mounds, wood rolled down from its stack-
ing, iron moulds for ingots lay among cinders and slack, everywhere
were solidified splashes of molten metal. You were careful what you
touched on that floor, for you might put your foot or hand on
something black that only a few minutes before had glowed dull
red. Strange instruments of iron looked down from the walls, irons
with rings and double handles, irons like the shackles of a bilboes,
pokers, hooks, tongs, scrapers. Two great semicircular hearths of
pale firebrick seemed *cachots* for some choice and peculiar pain. And
at one end of the suffocating place, left half uncovered by an iron
ventilation-plate, was the firepit itself tinting the air and the walls
about it with a jewel-like upward glow.

John Brydon looked at his watch again and then spoke to Cavani.
'How long can you give them yet?'

'Only five, ten minutes, Mr Brydon,' the Italian answered. 'The
flame is beginning to change. You cannot delay a fire that has been
four days making itself.'

'What the devil's become of them?' muttered John Brydon, and
walked over to where his labour of months lay buried.

For there was now nothing to be seen of it. A strong octagon of
heavy timbers a yard high enclosed it, closely packed with sand, from
which a pudding-shaped mound rose, with a ridiculous little twist of
newspaper in its orifice. Hidden as the secret channels of the human
body was the system of ducts and vents for the fiery vapours, the pins
that kept core and case at their distance. The death was over, the
obsequies were complete. By what a precarious thread the hope of
the resurrection hung Cavani and John Brydon knew. Cavani had
ceased to speak of it; who would add to the weight that that broken
man on his two sticks carried already? Three days for the thing to
cool, another day to chip off the mould, and he would know the best
or the worst that could happen. And he could wait no longer. He
made a sign with his finger and two assistants whose paper caps were
a dust of bronze-filings advanced to the fire pit. One of them had a
pair of tongs, the other a long iron scraper. There was a clanging of
metal as the covering plate was dragged on one side.

John Brydon too had advanced. He stood looking down into the
beautiful horror in the heart of which, like a semi-transparent egg in

an infernal nest, the crucible of bronze lay. For beauty it had in that last perfection of still heat. Over its surface blonde gases licked and played, as if diamond and amethyst and amber had rarefied themselves together; sulphur yielded up its last and thinnest blue; but underneath the sevenfold fire slept like a top. Throw a cup of water into it and a gun would go off; pour in a bucketful and up would go the roof. The assistant had thrust in the tongs and seized the lip of the crucible. He tipped it forward for the other man to cream it of its surface of scum, and the beautiful beast opened an eye of baleful, flower-like periwinkle. But the attendant removed his implement again. Still a few minutes. He left the covering plate where it was as a cook leaves open the door of an oven, and at that moment John Brydon heard a sound outside. It was the stopping of a car. There was a knock at the door. Mara – both of them – had come.

Cavani had to receive them, for John Brydon on his two sticks was little more than a living tripod. Neither was the floor about the firepit cool, and he had to stand first on this foot and then on that, nursing the supporting one with the other. He heard Cavani's voice in the anteroom above. He was jesting with Mara, asking her whether she had met her handsome Italian yet. He waited for them to appear.

Mara came first, and never had he seen his child's face like that before. In her arms she carried her spaniel dog, and it was at once plain that she had taken the whole responsibility of the family on her young shoulders. It was only after a moment that her mother's face appeared behind her; she might have been a nurse or a servant, ready to wait outside till she should be sent for. And now he knew why Tanner had spoken like that. They were pitiful, those eyes that neither looked at him nor away from him. And as she still hesitated Mara set the dog down. She felt behind her for her mother's hand and came down the steps.

'Sammie is on his lead, father,' she said, while her mother stumbled a little, as if she was just up after a month in bed.

'Look where you walk, and don't touch anything,' said John Brydon. 'We couldn't have waited any longer. Better pick Sammie up and stand over here. Now, Cavani, as soon as you like.'

There was no time for further greetings, for a third assistant had come in and Cavani had taken charge. Brydon found a place for them on one side. One of the long torture-bars had been laid in position on the floor, its two-handled end towards Cavani, for when you are handling metal so changed by heat that it seems almost an impiety that man should have dared to meddle with it so, you cannot have two minds in control. They were getting down more irons from the wall.

'Not too near,' said John Brydon. 'Down there, that's the bronze,' and Mara peered cautiously down into the pit where the crucible lay like a rosy petal. 'They'll pour it into that little hole over there, where the bit of newspaper's sticking up.'

'Has the wax all gone now?'

'Nobody'll see that wax any more. Nobody wants to see any of us any more when we've done our work. Keep close to mother, and you'd better come over here now. I must see this,' and he slipped something into his mouth.

With the tongs they were preparing to lift the crucible from the pit. Suddenly, as if the stillness of the fire protested against being disturbed, the pit became a bursting sunspot. Half way up its walls the vapours leapt, and the throat shut itself tightly against the blast of coke. Up the crucible came, a plucked out heart, to pulse for only a few moments before it was quenched in the tomb of the mould. 'There's still a little more crust to come off – keep back in case of a splash,' muttered John Brydon over his shoulder.

They were already flaking it off, a splash at a time, casting it behind them, showing the unsullied metal beneath. John Brydon was holding his breath. The colour, the timing, the implements, the cunning of men – down the centuries nothing had altered, all was as in the days of Benvenuto, as in the days of Michael Angelo himself. One more splash that went a little further this time – Winifred stepped back. Mara with the spaniel still clasped to her breast, had moved closer to her father.

'Now watch,' he whispered in her ear.

Cavani had lifted the double handle, and the other man the single end of the iron. The half-transparent crucible sat in the ring midway between them. A hand twitched the bit of paper from the orifice of the mould, and steadily the vessel and its ardent contents were raised. One last pollution of scum – that too must be skimmed off – the man put out the rod to do it.

Not an eye saw the thing in the moment of its happening, not an ear heard a cry. But eyes saw and ears heard the terrible sequel that followed hardly a moment later, and in that den of heat every heart turned to ice. A blaze and a roaring rushed up from the pit. A heedless step sideways to see better, a fragment of something too hot for a woman's thin sole, a whiff of coke, an instant's giddiness, something else of which Tanner knew the reason – but almost better to have been there than to read about it at ease in an armchair. It was not as if mortal man could have done anything. A minute or little more sufficed, and then the foundry seemed to grow suddenly inky dark. Winifred was not there.

John Brydon on his sticks was the first to move. He could not move far nor easily, for his daughter had cast her arms about him and buried her face against his body. Only the spaniel whimpered and looked piteously up at him. And when certain drugs have their way with a man who shall say how many lives he is living simultaneously, how many emotions crowd themselves on him in one moment of time? Dragging the child and the dog with him he had taken a step forward. The man who still held the iron was looking at him with a face that few who knew him would have known for his. Over the pit John Brydon's lips were shaping words, a name.

'Winifred – my loved Win – Win – '

But the words, seemed to run straight into other words, that came he knew not whence. They came from his childhood perhaps, some story heard at his mother's knee, of a certain faithful three whose names were Shadrach and Meshach and Abednego. Even in their coats and hosen and their hats they had been cast in, but the smell of it had not passed upon them, neither had the fire had any power over them. And had not an angel, peering down into the pit, seen a Fourth walking among them, and did not an angel stand by John Brydon's side now? Suddenly, thrusting the child aside, he stood up at his full height. Swiftly in the thick air his finger made the Sign of the Cross. The next words came in a rapid gabble.

' "*I am the Resurrection and the Life* – " '

Then his voice cracked as thunder cracks when it is flung back from a low cloud.

'You there! What's your name! Cavani! What are you doing?' His stick beat the air in an agony of impatience. '*It's cooling in the crucible*! There's a crust on it already! Quick – what are you waiting for? Run it in I tell you – run it in – '

And Cavani, his face a mask behind which there was no looking, nodded to the man at the other end of the iron. By a miracle that bronze might come out, but nothing less than an angel would have looked after John Brydon if it did. From the lip of the crucible the metal began to pour in a steady, ponderous flow.

The Woman in the Way

Note – There lived in England, in the middle of the Seventeenth Century, a man called Ruddle, a parson by calling, who wrote down on paper that he saw, with his own eyes, the things here described, and did not add that he considered it high time he prepared to take his leave of the world. All I know of this Reverend Mr Ruddle is to be found in the *History of the Princes, Lords Marcher, etc. of Powys Fadog*, by Mr Hughes of Clochfaen (London, Richards, 1881), vol.1, pp.246 et seq. The passages here printed in italics are precisely as Mr Ruddle wrote them. The rest is my own. Mr Ruddle begins.

I

In the beginning of the year 1665 a disease happened in this town of Launceston and some of my scholars died of it. Among others who fell under its malignity was John Elliott, the eldest son of Edward Elliott, of Treberse, Esq., a stripling of about sixteen years of age, but of uncommon parts and ingenuity. At his own particular request I preached at the funeral, which happened on the 20th day of June. In my discourse I spoke some words in commendation of the young gentleman, such as might endear his memory to those who knew him, and withal tend to preserve his example to those who went to school with him and were to continue after him. An ancient gentleman who was then in the church was much affected with the discourse, and often heard to repeat one expression I then used out of Virgil: 'Et puer ipse fuit cantari dignus.'

Mr Ruddle then goes on to tell us that no sooner was the service over than he was accosted at the church-door by the ancient gentleman just mentioned (on whom he had never before set eyes in his life), who, with unusual importunity, begged the minister to come with him to his house and stay the night. The request could hardly be granted, as the parson considered himself to be bound to the bereaved parents for the remainder of the day. Accordingly he 'rescued himself' from the old gentleman's kindness – for the invitation had been courteously expressed.

But the would-be host persisted; and this is the first of a series of pictures Mr Ruddle gives us that need but a touch to make them glow – the group of the Elliotts and their friends at the church-door, the dead boy's fellow-students, the ring of less-directly interested spectators, and, in the middle of it, the parson, button-holed by an importunate stranger almost before the bell had ceased to toll. We can imagine the parson as saying, as he extricated himself, that this was no moment for intrusion. Nor would he even promise to go on the following day.

'Then at least, sir, give me your promise that you will come on the day after,' the old gentleman urged, in some such words.

Whereupon the parson asked the nature of this business that could brook so little delay.

But even this was evaded. The other only begged him over and over again to come, while none was more puzzled than the parson himself 'to know whence this sudden flush of friendship should arise'.

But in the end he gave way. He promised to pay his visit on the next day but one, and the old gentleman, with profuse thanks, bowed and departed.

But this was only a beginning. Apparently Mr Ruddle stayed in the Elliotts' house that night, for it was there, on the very next day, that a messenger from the same old gentleman sought him out and begged him to come forthwith. The distance that the messenger had travelled could have been no very great one, for, on Mr Ruddle's bluntly refusing, he was back again, if you will believe it, in the afternoon. It was surely pardonable in the parson that by this time he showed a flash of temper.

'Tell your master,' he charged the servant, 'that it does not suit my convenience, and if that does not content him, and he will still give no reason why I should visit him, then I will not come at all.'

However, he finally went, as originally arranged and in view of all this urgency he must have been more than a little astonished to find himself received, not by his host, nor by any member of his family, but by a second clergyman, who had very little the air of being there by accident. Parson Ruddle does not hide his impression that the stage had been carefully set, and it was, in fact, from this brother of the coat that he had the first inkling of why he had been summoned.

First [says Mr Ruddle] *he began to inform me of the infelicity of the family in general, and then gave instance of the youngest son. He related*

*what a hopeful sprightly lad he lately was, and how melancholick and
sottish he was now grown. Saith he, 'The poor boy believes himself to
be haunted with ghosts, and is confident that he meets with an evil spirit
in a certain field about half a mile from this place, as often as he goes that
way to school.'*

At which point, and 'as observing their cue most exactly', up at last
came the old gentleman and his lady, and made haste to confirm all
that had been said.

But apparently they did not do this to Mr Ruddle's entire satisfaction, if we are right in reading a certain reserve into his next
words.

*It was the main drift of all these three to persuade me that either the boy
was lazy, and glad of an excuse to keep from the school, or that he had a fetch
upon his father to get money and new clothes, that he might range to
London after a brother he had there.*

And this strikes one as a sensible view. The parents will have none
of this ghost-seeing, and neither will we. In fact we should have
expected Mr Ruddle, who so far has seemed a level-headed man and
skilled in the ways of boys withal, to be of the same opinion.

But not so. He found the thing 'strange but not incredible', and for
a moment we wonder whether we have not been mistaken in him
after all.

However, the obvious thing to do in the circumstances was to see
the boy himself. As part of the invitation these people had forced on
him Mr Ruddle was staying the night in the house. Perhaps he was a
little tired, perhaps he had found a little more than met the eye in the
peculiar manner of his reception. However it was, he proposed to put
off seeing the boy until the following morning.

But here he 'perceived another spring that their courtesy had laid
for him.' The 'spring' must have been more in the manner than the
words, for it was surely not unnatural that the mother should want
no more delay. The three men, two of them parsons and the third
the old gentleman, had been talking a little apart. Suddenly the
mother stepped forward to them, with the request that the boy
should be seen there and then.

So, *drawing off the company to an orchard hard by, she went herself and
brought him to me, and left him with me.*

We are given the actual date of this interview. It was the twenty-
second day of June, in the late afternoon or early evening. And it
gives us a curious sense of the nearness of all these events that we
have even authority for the weather – the extraordinary heat and

dryness of the day that was closing, the sultry stillness of the air, so that chimney-smoke rose straight up, the low flashes of summer lightning, the mutterings of thunder. The fruit would be forming in that Cornish orchard, and the last of the browning petals would sprinkle the grass underfoot. As these were evidently people of some substance, it is no far flight of fancy to add a fruit-wall or so, gardens with walks between the parched flowers, and the sun either behind the gables of the house or flashing on their windows like gold. In spite of the two-and-a-half centuries that lie like a dark glass in between, these things still show faint but true through Parson Ruddle's tale.

And so, walking up and down that orchard, he and the boy had what nowadays would be called their psychoanalytic talk together.

He instantly discovered that it 'needed no policy to screw himself into the youth's heart.' Quite the other way.

He most openly, and with all obliging candour, did aver that he loved his books and desired nothing more than to be bred a scholar: that he had not the least respect for any of womankind, as his mother gave out: and that the only request he would make to his parents was that they would but believe his constant assertions concerning the woman he was disturbed with in the field called the Higher Broom Quartils. He told me, with all naked freedom and a flood of tears, that if any man (making a bow to me) would but go with him to the place, he might be convinced that the thing was real.

And then this, with the totally unexpected shock of its concluding words.

This woman which appears to me (said he) lived a neighbour here to my father, and died about eight years since. Her name was Dorothy Dingley. She never speaks to me: but passeth by hastily, and always leaves the footpath to me, and she commonly meets me – this is the shocking thing –

– she commonly meets me twice or three times in the length of the field.

2

At what may be called the sheer mechanical novelty of the encounter – not to go any further – one puts down the Reverend Mr Ruddle's record at this point and tries to collect one's thoughts. The ingenious cruelty of the idea makes us catch our breath. Of course we do not believe a word of it. It is merely something that the boy told Mr Ruddle, who passes it on at his own risk. He takes no responsibility except that of a tale-bearer, and to find him a mere carrier of gossip is a little disappointing after our first impression of him. In the meantime, we are merely asked to believe that, in a certain part of the county of Cornwall, at intervals between the June of 1664 and the June of the following year, the factor of space was annihilated, and something existed in a place that was already naturally and normally occupied.

And the factor of time went too; for if, as this boy said, the hallucination happened to him two or three times in the length of a field, why not oftener? Why not at every step he took? Why not a running stream of apparitions, so continuous, that this woman-shape did not 'appear' at all, but was merely permanently there, constant in its ubiquity?

It appeared that the boy himself had a hazy sort of recollection of the person of this Dorothy Dingley. 'Though the shape of the face was in my memory, yet I could not recall the name of the person, but did suppose it was some woman who lived thereabout, and had frequent occasion that way.' This, at any rate, we unreservedly believe, for it is of the very texture of our young memories. The boy was about eight years old when Mistress Dingley died. Ask a boy of eight what is his earliest memory and you will get an answer of sorts. But ask him the same question at sixteen and already he is at a loss. He will not so much remember as re-echo his former statement. It is not at all surprising that this boy should remember only tardily that the woman whose shape he saw was dead. The word 'dead' conveyed nothing to him. So at first he had no fear. He saw so little to be afraid of that he often spoke to this woman whose business brought her so frequently that way. It was only slightly disconcerting that he never had any reply.

But the first day of fear was rapidly approaching. This day must have been the very first day when she met him, not once, but twice. That must have been fear to demonstration, and with the shock of it there must have vanished all possibility of this wayfarer being an ordinary woman. And in his fear he changed his way to school, 'taking the under horse-road, and then she always met me in the narrow lane, between the quarry park and the nursery, which – ' we read it in its unstressed simplicity, – 'which was worse.' Evidently, then, her business was with the boy himself, and was not confined to the field that lay between his home and his school.

All this, he told the parson, had been going on for a year. No need to dwell on the increasingly familiar daily dread of those twelve

months. Enough that from a merry sprightly lad he had become
sottish and melancholick.

I prayed continually that God would either free me from it, or let me
know the meaning of it. Night and day, sleeping and waking, the shape was
ever running in my mind, and I often did repeat these places in Scripture
(with which he took a small Bible out of his pocket): 'Thou scarest me with
dreams and terrifiest me through visions': and 'In the morning thou shalt
say, Would God it were evening, and at evening thou shalt say, Would God
it were morning, for the fear of thine heart wherewith thou shalt fear and
for the sight of thine eyes with which thou shalt see.'

And when at last the whole thing came out, it was not the boy
himself who told his parents. Besides the brother who had ranged to
London, there was a middle brother, who, we note in passing, is the
only member of the family Mr Ruddle sees fit to name. We fasten on
it, as it were, that this lad's name was William. Boy-like, the unhappy
youth told his trouble first to brother William. And brother William
told his father and mother.

Already we can guess which of these it was who wore the breeches
in that troubled house. It was the mother who had fetched the boy
from the orchard, insisting that Parson Ruddle should see him at
once. It was the mother, we may be sure, who, hearing that a man so
understanding with boys was in the neighbourhood, had despatched
her ancient husband to young Elliott's funeral, with orders to
bring this Mr Ruddle back. Her command had lain behind the old
gentleman's almost unmannerly importunity, she had scolded him
when he had returned with no parson by his side. She, and surely
nobody else, had sent off the messenger who had twice pestered the
parson while he was still in the Elliotts' house. And since she had a
son of school age, she was presumably a good deal younger than
her Latin-mumbling spouse. Disingenuousness and reluctance and
reserve had characterised Parson Ruddle's reception. Putting two
and two together, does it not seem likely that what the mother was
manoeuvring for was this – to get all the help the parson could give
her, but to give him as little information as possible in return? A
secretive lady, one would say, who liked to keep things in her own
hands. A managing lady, who ordered her husband about and wanted
things done there and then. An anxious lady, the mother of one
son who had ranged to London with new clothes on his back and
money in the pockets of them, and of another who showed signs of
following in his footsteps. But a lady, above all, at her wits' end what
to do, since she sent for parsons with one breath and with the next

sharply charged her son with malingering and bade him be off to school. And to school he went.

'*But always*,' says the unhappy lad, '*I met the Woman in the Way*.'

The talk between the parson and the boy lasted for close on two hours. At the end of it Mr Ruddle had definitely taken sides. He confesses that on his return to the house he was short with the parents. He tells us that the mother, 'whose inquisitiveness had missed us', wanted to speak to him. He 'gave her a convenience' – he could hardly do less – but it is noteworthy that he said not one word about the agreement to which he and the boy had come; which was, that they should go together to these uneasy Quartils at six o'clock of the following morning, to see, if they could, this presence that certainly had no business to be there.

3

Mr Ruddle is presently about to make a number of tremendous assertions. Let us, before he does so, clear the ground a little for him. After that he is more than welcome to have it to himself.

He was going with the boy to enquire into the alleged comings and goings of somebody he had never known. The boy's own recollections in the matter were vague and confused. But the parents had been well acquainted with the original of this troublesome thing. She was spoken of as a neighbour, they had attended her funeral. So she can hardly have been a simple dairymaid or the daughter of a Cornish hind. She must have been a person of at least respectable degree, and not impossibly of some minor consideration and standing. She had died eight years before, when the boy who was now sixteen had been eight years old.

And, now that he was sixteen, she seemed to have singled him out for her undesired companionship. Had she troubled other boys of the neighbourhood it would quickly have become notorious. The middle brother, William, was left in peace. And already we wonder whether we ought even to wonder what her motive was. Already we scent a warning in the air – and have half a mind to drop the curtain on this obscure family history of so long ago. But even as we hesitate a new actor seems to step on the scene. He is the elder brother who has ranged away to London.

A disease had happened in Launceston – they are Mr Ruddle's opening words – of which some of his scholars had died. So quietly, so naturally has the story begun that for the moment it did not occur to us that this was the year of the Plague. Nor, for that matter, is it to be found in the records that Launceston, so far away, was one of the places from which the fugitives from London were driven back at the pitchfork's point. But everywhere terror and foreboding stalked up and down the land, and war was awake upon the seas. Ways were foul, communications bad, home best. Add to this that London, youth, money and new clothes were very much the same then that they are today. Few and far between must have been the letters that that Cornish mother received from her prodigal in the afflicted city. He might have been dead for months and she none the wiser.

Nor do sons become prodigals all in a moment. Sad mothers see it coming. There were innocent rustic junketings in Cornwall as else-where, but there were also pleasures less innocent. And what can a mother do when she sees her son, on the verge of manhood, weary-ing of his surroundings and fretting to range away? She will pray, supplicate, try to stay him with her arms. All that is past shall be forgotten so he will but remain with her. She will exhaust herself that his father's house shall be a pleasant place for him, and will look about among the neighbouring families of standing in search of a girl of her own choosing, whose arms may keep him where her own have failed. Mothers were so, are so, and will always be so.

Therefore let us picture a similar situation today. Let us suppose that, today, a mother sought a desirable wife for her restless son – but found that the young man had already contracted a less desir-able infatuation of his own. And say that all had begun innocently enough, and that half the danger lay in the mother's own apprehen-sion. And say that this undesired young woman happened to be of such a condition that she could not well be denied the house merely because she was disliked. Do we not instantly see what would happen? Can we not picture how smilingly the bidden but unwelcome guest would sit at the board, yet how secretly armed, as if with a steel shirt under her smock? Can we not see how, under her demure looks, she would hungrily wait for the slightest occasion of offence? Would not every word be given its particular con-struction and every glance be wrested to a private meaning? We not only see; we almost hear the indignant words shaping themselves in her breast. Not good enough for their spark of a son, she! ('Yes, madam; I thank you, madam!') Permitted the house, but as some-thing between the servants and themselves! ('No, madam; indeed you are too kind, madam!') How long would such a situation con-tinue? Not long. Something would presently happen. The visits to the house would cease. Clandestine meetings would take their place. This, too, would come to the ears of the mother. The fat would be in the fire, would flare. The young woman would march down the path with angry words in her ears and her heart already seething with schemes of revenge. This is what would happen today, and even in two-hundred-and-fifty years the ways of the heart in love and hate do not greatly change.

Assume, then – for it commits us to no conclusion from which we cannot withdraw at any moment – that Dorothy Dingley had been such an one. Suppose her to have been of intermediate condition, with goods enough to keep her in idleness and no more, come into her small property too young, grown up to do as she pleased with none to check her. No need to say that she was ill-intentioned or ill-conditioned. The sense of grievance under which she laboured might have been a perfectly legitimate one. She need not even have been greatly drawn to their son. For all that – hoity-toity! It was not as if she herself was going a-begging! Far from it! There were young farmers in plenty to whom her middling fortune would be riches undreamed-of! She could have her pick of a dozen of them!

So, misjudged and injured, would not such a young woman be willing, as the saying is, to give these people something to talk about? Can we not hear her scoffing laugh? *They*, to set themselves up! *That* woman, with her pottering old dotard of a husband! Much joy of love she had had, to marry for an orchard or so and a few gables! Let her take care – others were as good as she, and with blood in their veins too! Her son? That young cock with his hackle up? She wouldn't have wasted a look on him except to anger that old-man's-nurse, his mother! A turn of the head would fetch him – a glance and she could have him at her feet –

So it may have been – or it may not. She may have been one who should have been stripped and flogged at the cart's-tail amid the execrations of every mother of growing sons thereabouts – or she may not. She may have run from him, been caught and kissed, struggled and broken free again – or not. She may have given him the ribbon from her breast or the garter from her knee, and laughed at him and called him boy the more he tried to show himself a man – or none of these things may be true. But if she did not some other woman did, in 1665 as today. We do not know whether the youth went off to London flushed with success or in dudgeon and despite. We do not know whether the Plague took or spared him. We do not know of what illness Dorothy Dingley herself died. We only know that the bell had tolled for her as her mortal remains had been lowered into the grave, and that now, eight years later, or seven, if we reckon off the year it had lasted, something of her that was *not* dead met a younger brother in the Way.

Let Parson Ruddle now speak again.

4

Before five o'clock in the morning the lad was in my chamber, and very brisk. I arose and went with him. The field he led me to I guessed to be about twenty acres, in an open country and about three furlongs from the house. We went into the field, and had not gone above a third part before the spectrum, in the shape of a woman, with all the circumstances he had described to me in the orchard the day before (as much as the suddenness of its appearance and evanition would permit me to discover) met us and passed us by. I was a little surprised at it and though I had taken up a firm resolution to speak to it yet I had not the power, nor indeed durst I look back, yet I took care not to show my fear to my pupil and guide: and therefore telling him that I was satisfied in the truth of his complaint, we walked to the end of the field and returned, nor did the ghost meet us at that time more than once.

With these words Parson Ruddle burns his boats. He can no longer shelter behind the boy's account. He has seen for himself, takes the whole thing on his own shoulders, and we know exactly where we are. If we now meet with lies, they are his lies and not the lad's.

And, after the first instinctive gesture of fear, he was merely 'a little surprised'. You or I might marvel that grass and common yellow broom should grow in that dreadful place at all. We might stand in amazement that honeysuckle and roses should dare to flower in the hedges of that awful sunken lane. But apparently the whole landscape could rock horrifically before this parson's eyes, and, barring a natural shiver, he was merely 'a little surprised'. Perhaps the terrific implication of it all sank in later . . .

And now comes a break in the narrative. Word was brought to Mr Ruddle that urgent private affairs demanded his presence elsewhere. He left, promising to be back in a week's time. This promise he was unable to keep, for his wife was taken ill. It is the first we hear that he had a wife. We have already made up our minds that Mrs Ruddle had a very remarkable husband.

However [he says] *my mind was upon the adventure; I studied the case; and about three weeks after that went again, resolving, by the help of God, to see the utmost.*

By this time the boy would be almost blithe again. He had found a sympathetic friend, able to help and returning presently. But heavy care weighed on that anxious, close-lipped woman, his mother. For the parson said not a word to her or her spouse of what he had seen. All that she knew was that her boy, who a year before had gone gaily singing about the house was a mere shadow of his former self. And he was now sixteen, which is the turn and change in a boy's life. In love with some wench? Not unlikely; but with which wench? The neighbourhood was not so populous that he could keep such a secret for long. True, he denied it, but what boy would not? So once more the same thing would happen that we might expect today. She would watch his comings and goings. She would ask him questions of which the drift did not appear. She would lay little traps for him, would send him on errands in order that she might discover in which quarters he lingered unusually long. Names would be slyly introduced in his presence, bits of gossip repeated to see whether he changed countenance. In a word, the history of the prodigal eldest brother would be enacted all over again.

Then one day the boy, who had never swerved from his story of what happened to him in the field, would let fall some little detail at which the mother would prick up her ears. One sees her turn suddenly pale. Of *what* appearance did he say this woman was who met him? *What* shape of face? *What* colour of brows? *How* tall! Of *what* carriage?

And then would come the sickening hour when it appeared that the boy's description corresponded exactly with that of the woman who had already stepped between her and one of her sons.

It is of course all supposing: nothing on earth but supposing. But it is supposing in terms of known reality. Women have been known to transfer their favours from one brother to another. But when in the history of the world before did one do so from the grave? And when did one so diabolically bide her time, waiting as it were for the ripe moment when her victim did not know what ailed him, but only that women were disturbingly different from anything he had supposed? Up to that point evil influences had been powerless against his innocence. It may be that this influence had had no choice but to wait for those seven years. But the seven years were at an end, and — lo! the hour at last! Gently, then, at first, not to frighten the quarry!

Give place to him – remember that *he* comes from a house with gables and orchards, while *you* are of inferior condition! Do not answer him if he speaks, Dorothy Dingley – remember that your voice is not quite what an ordinary woman's voice should be, for it is no perfected piece of work, but only a flimsy figure, the making of which you have busied yourself about for so long! And above all, be wary about that first time you meet him, not once, but twice again after that! He might shy at that! For he is of a different make from that ruffling blade of a brother of his! That one was only too ready to be drinking and cockfighting and wenching; but this is a pious, studious lad, with a quick and timid fancy for you to play on! Play on it, then, and be evens with that hated woman with the nodding old husband! She thought she could treat you thus and thus, did she? She had come to your funeral with weeds upon her body but triumph and joy in her heart? She had thought she had heard the last of you when the bell clanged out its note? Indeed no! You knew a trick worth two of that, Dorothy Dingley! Never mind the middle boy, young William! First the firstborn, then the youngest, will serve your turn! *She* to set herself up? Ha, ha! Let her wait a bit – let her wait a bit –

For how can one more surely pierce a mother's heart than by means of the last son she will bear?

If these things were true – but *only* if they were true – then neither Plague nor Fire was the remarkablest thing that happened in England in those years.

5

Mr Ruddle came back on the 27th day of July, five weeks within a day after the funeral of young Elliott of Treberse. And whatever those 'studies' of his in the meantime had been, his mind was now made up. He had had enough of these people who first called him in and then kept things back from him. He had had enough of the second parson too, supposing (as is likely) that he also had known this Mistress Dingley and so was in the plot. This time he was going to the Quartils alone. In fact the very next morning found him there.

But the enterprise was in part a failure. It proved one thing, however, namely, that the thing could show itself in the boy's absence. Says the parson:

The spectre appeared much about the same place as before, about ten feet distant on my right hand. But this time it moved more quickly,

inasmuch as I had no time to speak to it, as I had determined with myself
beforehand.

And then at last the parson decided to take the parents into consultation. He did so that very night, proposing that they should all
visit the unclean field together on the morrow. He did so as they sat
by candlelight round the board – or it may have been as they took the
evening air in the porch – or perhaps it was as they paced the flagged
paths, with the hush of the violet evening about them and the large
moon (for it was late in the month) beginning to look over the hill. If
the other parson (who somehow strikes one as a bit of a shuffler) was
there he was not included in the invitation, or else was unable to
accept it, for he did not make one of the party. They talked far
into the night – or maybe for a short time only. They went to bed to
sleep – or perhaps to toss restlessly until the first signs of dawn. All
was thus, or thus, or after some other fashion. And it is noticeable
that from this point on Mr Ruddle becomes increasingly reticent
about the whole affair.

And yet so charged with import are the few things he does allow
to pass him, and so actinically do they project themselves down to
our own day, that they kindle as it were glimmers for a little way
about them in the surrounding darkness, so that we feel sure of just
a little more than we have actual warrant for. And as presently we
shall have to refrain altogether from guessing, we will make the
most of our time.

First, then, Mr Ruddle, who had twice seen this Mistress Dingley's
shape, does not mention whether she had or had not beauty. This
is understandable. Seeing the action he was about to take, earthly
considerations such as these would be far from his mind. Indeed
beauty would be a positive discommendation in his eyes, as one snare
the more to tangle the wayward foot and the erring eye. So he would
be silent about it.

Next, neither does the boy say that she was hideous, which he
would certainly have done had she had the appearance of a bogey. In
the beginning at any rate he was not afraid of her good-morning. So
may not a measure of good looks, whether of a malignant cast or
otherwise, be taken as not impossible?

Again, supposing that prodigal in London had been the mere
slave of a petticoat: were there not dairymaids and village wenches
enough for the lifting up of such a young squire's finger? And if
the beauty be not denied, would it not be a somewhat different
beauty from that of these rustic rivals who milked and churned and

scoured the pans? A paler, more harmonious beauty, menacing or benign, with the slender hand going bail for the whole lovely arm, and the foot for the hidden rest? Or deny the beauty altogether: does not one daily see *un*beautiful women who do not lack other gifts – the parleying eye, the displayed breast, the gait that bids follow? Dare we give these attributes to this being who, though dead, was not at rest? Singular in that, what other dreadful uniqueness might she not possess? Dead and yet not dead – dead as it were with one eye open, vigilant and baleful – lurking where two worlds met, rejected in some part of her body by the one and unaccepted in her spirit by the other –

So what awful ambiguity have we here? When have we heard of these pestilent creatures before? What ancient unhallowed legends break in upon us that we had supposed to belong to the limbo of things blessedly lost? Who was this Lilith, pale predecessor of Eve – of sweetest Eve, man's proper mate, who interposed between Adam and this wickedness, thrusting it out into the voids of the upper air? Who and what were those others, those Lamiae, so inimical to the race of man that to destroy it in its innocent beginnings was their delight? Who and what were those other lean and hungry shapes, of devil-women and succubi, of vampires and sirens and draggers-down of the bodies and souls of men? Was the year 1665 *not* then a Year of Grace? Had redemption suddenly failed? Did these horrible concepts come into their own again as part of the dark inheritance of man?

Now it is that we realise how much better it would be to let the whole matter rest.

But will it let us rest? Why, if not for the glory of his Maker, did Parson Ruddle write down his narrative at all? He must have intended something, or why should we now look on the world with changed eyes?

For the shreds and remnants of just such things are still hauntingly about us. We do occasionally see, flesh in our midst, these women from whose eyes something underived looks out, something out of line, carried over as it were from Chaos, omitted from the inventory of Creation, never since wholly absorbed into the Divine Order. It flickers like half-quenched wildfire at intervals through the world, throwing its murky beam into the forgotten recesses of our nature. It mocks our love and compassion; and men have been known to swear that they have seen that woman-shape, dark and pallid, and with beautiful baleful brows huddled close like the black 'berry' of a swan, that has been able to make its way to their bedside in the dead of night, though the door of the chamber was bolted and barred. 'It was a dream,' they still their fears afterwards; but it was no dream while it stood there, offering the key of the Nadir between its cruel lips, the discarnate kiss of sin.

And if in Babylon or Sidon, why not in Launceston when Plague walked the earth and death was let loose? Was Mr Ruddle a liar that he should write these things down? Or was he beguiled or bemused? If you think so, read his words. Come with him to the Quartils once more. For this was the manner of his going there:

The morning being come, lest we should alarm the family of servants, they [the parents] *went under the pretence of seeing a field of wheat, and I took my horse, and fetched a compass another way, and so met at the stile we had appointed. Thence we all four walked leisurely into the Quartils, and had passed above half the field before the ghost made its appearance. It then came over the stile just before us, and moved with that swiftness that by the time we had gone six or seven steps it passed. I immediately turned my head and ran after it, with the young man by my side; we saw it pass over the stile at which we entered, but no farther. I stept upon the hedge at one place and he at another, but could discern nothing; whereas I dare aver that the swiftest horse in England could not have conveyed himself out of sight in that short space of time. Two things I did note in this day's appearance* (1) *That a spaniel dog that followed the company unregarded did bark and run away as the spectrum passed by.* (2) *That the motion of the spectre was not gradatim, or by steps and moving of the feet, but a kind of gliding, as children upon ice or a boat down a swift river.*

That stricken field at six o'clock of a July morning, the spaniel barking, and a clergyman and a youth making a dash for different parts of a hedge to see what had become of something that apparently had the power of omnipresence –

The spectre's own haste to be gone, as if itself now saw reason for fear –

No. It is enough. Criticism has nothing further to say. Visibility, gliding, the dog – we accept them all. It comes in the end to this, that Parson Ruddle saw what he says he saw. And we ourselves are as near to that field as ever we wish to be.

And we have finished with our prying too. We are content that thereafter Parson Ruddle should hold the stage, alone and to the end. *The parents* [we read] *were strangely affrighted, who had known this Dorothy Dingley in her lifetime and now plainly saw her features. After that they went no more.* We can well believe it. We do not want to know what kind of a look that was that passed between the mother and this persecutor of her sons. It must have been livid with recognition, hate and farewell.

6

If only we possessed a picture of the parson, in his broad hat and starched bands and high-heeled shoes! If only we had the description of somebody who knew him in the flesh as he lived! But there remains nothing of him but his plain honest English style and the directness and truth-speaking and simplicity of heart that shine through it. With these and 'such lawful means as God hath discovered, and learned men have successfully practised in these uncommon cases', he was prepared to undertake his inconceivable task. And he lost no time about it.

The next morning, being Thursday, I went out very early by myself and walked about an hour's space in meditation and prayer in the field next adjoining the Quartils. Soon after five I stepped over the stile into the disturbed field.

And there is no need for him to point that commanding finger, bidding us leave him. If we dared we would not stay. Already we have 'listened in' on this ancient story too presumptuously, and must down on our knees for the violation we have done. Terror, like Apollyon, straddled across the breadth of that Way, and it was for Parson Ruddle to beware lest his own soul should be spilt. And we know as we turn away that he was facing the powers of darkness, not for the succour of a tormented boy, not for the quiet of a Cornish field, but in some sort for the safety and peace of heart of all mankind alive or to be.

'O Lord make speed to save us.'

'O Lord make haste to help us.'

'Let us pray.'

The rest is set down without comment.

I had not gone above thirty or forty paces before the ghost appeared at the farther stile. I spake to it with a loud voice, in some such sentences as the way of these dealings directed me; whereupon it approached but slowly, and when I came near it moved not. I spake again, and it answered in a voice neither very audible nor intelligible. I was not in the least terrified, and therefore persisted, until it spake again and gave me satisfaction. The discourse lasted about a quarter of an hour. But the work could not be finished at this time; wherefore the same evening, an hour after sunset, it met me again in the same place. After a few words on each side, it quietly vanished, and neither doth appear since, nor ever will more, to any man's disturbance.

> The sparrow hath found her an house,
> And the turtle a nest where she may lay her young.

It may be that, in the Year of Grace 1935, we take down an old book from a shelf, and read, in the Form '*Quae ordo dicitur Domum a Daemone perturbatum liberandi*', how, not by Christ only, nor by His apostles, but by all holy men and women, the upright become to the evil spirits a new hell and a burning furnace of eternal horror, so that they flee from every corner, and God is ever glorified. But this adds nothing to the relation of Parson Ruddle, who ends:

These things are true; and I know them to be so with as much certainty as eyes and ears can give me; and until I can be persuaded that my senses do deceive me about their proper object, and by that persuasion deprive myself of the strongest inducement to believe the Christian religion, I must and will assert that these things in this paper are true.

EXPLICIT

The Smile of Karen

(to June)

I

Although the sleigh had come to a standstill, I do not think that half the people in it had any idea of what was happening. All that they seemed to hear, besides their own cheerful voices, was the dull rush of the torrent below and a little clamour of bells whenever a horse moved his head. But another sound, a leisurely 'Cric-crac, cric-cric', had seemed to me to grow more formidable every moment, and I had climbed out of the sleigh and was watching the man who was the cause of it.

We could hardly have come upon the timber-cart at a more perilous spot. The road at that point, besides being deep in snow, was not more than ten feet wide, and the timber-cart had the right to the inside berth, the one with the sheer face of precipitous rock that seemed to rise to the skies. Only a low parapet separated the sleigh from the abyss of tree-tops below. The problem was how to pass.

The largest tree was sixty feet if it were an inch, and if that could be cleared all would be well. It was against the tree that the young man in the velvet jacket and voluminous corduroys had set the jack. Without haste, a pound or so at a time, he was slowly pumping power into it, with the wall of rock to take the resistance. I learned soon enough that he could neither read nor write. This that he was doing was his revelation of himself, his signature upon the world. A slip of the jack, a fragment of ice, a faltering of the man's nerve, and there was no second chance. He knew it, and he, his task, and the way he set himself to it, made on me an impression of fatalistic beauty that has never left me.

Imperceptibly, relentlessly, the tree became bowed like a cata-pult. At every grind it gave on the rock's face my heart leaped into my mouth. But he only stepped back once or twice to see how much more there was to do, and then bent to the ratchet again. The handsome black brows under the black wideawake were hardly knitted.

'Cric-cric, cric-cric, cric-cric . . . ' Still he went on, though the tree could have whisked us into the abyss as easily as a finger flicks a pea.

'Cric-cric, cric-cric, cric-cric . . . '

And even did he bend the tree sufficiently to allow the sleigh to pass, he still had the task of rendering the dreadful engine harmless again.

We did pass, or I should not be writing about Walther Blum. The passengers did not resume their chatter, because they had barely interrupted it. An hour later we had arrived at our destination, but I confess that my dreams that night were of elemental things – of masses and weights and forces and how man tames the devils that abide in them. I was haunted by thoughts of the precarious margins of safety by which we live, and by the still more precarious assumption that a man will never fail of having himself in control. And, above all, there seemed to hang between me and the night a slightish figure in a black velvet jacket and baggy corduroys, with handsome dark brows over dark fatalistic eyes, who himself seemed to possess something of that very inimicality of the Nature against which he wrought. As long as things went well he held, as a dam holds; but if they went ill he was himself a tree to break, with a dreadful sound, a rock to come thundering down.

2

It has more than once happened to me that a powerfully received impression has been followed almost immediately by another one, as if in some way I myself were specially attuned and open to it. I am of a restless disposition, and did not propose to make any long stay in Haarheim; and if Walther Blum (as I presently learned his name to be) had made such an impression on me, and was indeed a timber-carrier, well, these fellows spend three-quarters of their lives on the road, and the chances were that I should never see him again. But I did see him again, and, as it happened, within a couple of nights of that perilous exploit of his with the jack.

I am permitted a moderate amount of walking, though not 'winter sports'; and as hotel life has long since lost its attraction for me, I like to turn my back on the ringing *eisbahn* and to seek the higher slopes, where the clearings and the sawmills are, and the hydraulic mains lean on the mountains like rods against a wall, and, higher still, where the kites circle, and a thousand trees can be cut and the face of the landscape is hardly changed. With the close of the season the hotels shut down, direction and staff and clientèle move elsewhere; but the timbermen and the men of the power-stations and the cattlemen and sawyers remain. In the meantime their wives sweep the floors and carry the pails and make the beds at the hotels.

It was in these high regions that I saw Walther Blum again. And I say that I saw him at night, though in that electricity-flooded country of snowy tops and wooded scarps, 'artificial day' would serve as well, since they hold midnight carnivals on the *eisbahn* under the great sputtering arcs, while frequently lights burn unheeded at noon. There was, in fact, a carnival that night, and I relied on its illumination to guide me home again, for to tell the truth I had no very clear idea where I was. It was in order to ascertain this that I was making towards another light, along a rough, snowy track that skirted a clearing.

The light was a sort of blurred square, as if the window were draped with some curtain-stuff, and as I drew nearer I saw that it came from the window of a house or hut of logs, apparently of two rooms that communicated. The communicating door must have been open, for a remnant of light was visible in the second window also. And then I saw what it was that veiled the first window. They were icicles. They made another bloated pane outside the inner one, some of them three fingers thick, others mere films, as if it had thawed and blown a gale and frozen again simultaneously, and one liquefying finger had passed its drops on to the next. This shutter of ice gave the place an uncared-for look, for it could have been cleared away in a couple of minutes, and even the light within was no certain indication that there was anybody there. I therefore approached the window before knocking at the door.

I dimly saw that a hatted man sat inside at a table, alone. The naked incandescent was immediately above his head, and he appeared to be moving something smoothly and regularly a few inches along the table, to and fro. The rest was a mere distorted blur, through which it was impossible that he should have seen me, and I turned away quietly enough; but suddenly I heard the moving of his chair and his voice that called:

'Is that you, Karen?'

The next moment the door was flung open and I stood full in the light.

In the German I make shift with, I told him that I had missed my way and would be grateful if he would direct me to the Haarheim Palast. He stood aside to allow me to enter.

'Come in,' he said, and he closed the door behind me.

It was a rough and neglected interior, and it gave the impression of having been shut up for some time. The walls were of yellow pine, and there was probably an air-space between them and the outer logs. The furniture consisted of the table I had seen, a couple of chairs, a sort of home-made settee with blankets and a great-coat on it, a rack of crockery, a stopped fretwork clock, and the stove. There was not so much as a print on the walls, but ranged along a narrow shelf were the usual trifles in carved wood – paper-knives, boxes, blotters, toy cattle, a bear, and the rest of the things people buy in the picture-postcard shops and bring home as mementoes. To make these things was evidently his way of passing the evenings, as indeed the litter on the table showed, for the light shone down on a handful of chisels and a small saw; and, mingled with chips and sawdust, on a newspaper he couldn't read, stood a loaf of black bread and half a sausage. The oilstone was there too, for the smooth, regular move-ment I had seen through the icicled window had been the sharpening of his penknife.

He showed no sign of recognising me as the passenger who had got out of the sleigh to watch him at work with the jack. He had taken off his wide hat, and its removal showed a broad brow beneath thick rumpled hair, the low growth of which made more emphatic still the handsomeness of his brows. His youthful face – he could not have been more than five- or six-and-twenty – was weathered to a clear even brown, and possibly he shaved twice a week or so, for his small moustache was continued downwards in a soft smudge, which seemed to give a richness to the fine line of his jaw. His eyes were very bright, and even his wide corduroys did not conceal his powerful grace of movement as he crossed to get the other chair for me.

'You are from the Haarheim Palast, Herr Doktor?' he said.

I told him yes, but that there was a carnival that had not greatly amused me, and I had taken a walk instead. I also told him that I was neither Doktor nor Professor, but he continued to call me 'Herr Doktor' till the end.

'There are many people there?' he asked.

'In the hotel? It is full. They are even sleeping in the bathrooms.'

'So. So. I was told so. It all makes work.'

'And brings money to Haarheim?' I suggested.

'People lived here before the Palast was built,' he answered moodily.

Then, as I looked again round the poor and brilliantly lighted interior, my eyes were attracted by something that apparently he had made a hasty effort to conceal. Although the table was strewn with fresh chippings, no trinket-box or paper-knife was to be seen; but half hidden behind the newspaper on which the bread and sausage stood was the object on which he had been at work. I saw the head and shoulders of a small wooden statuette.

There was that about the glimpse that made me wish to see more, and in matters of that kind I permit myself a little curiosity. He did not appear to have seen my glance.

'I interrupted you at work?' I said.

'No, Herr Doktor, my time is my own.'

'You carve these animals and things?'

'Everybody here carves them. They are made in every house.'

'I am a kind of artist too. May I see that?' And I nodded towards the figure.

His bright eyes were mistrustfully on mine. Thinking it might help matters if I gave him my name, which is known here and there, I did so; but he only shook his head. He had never heard it. Nevertheless, the fact that apparently I had a name worth giving seemed to impress him, and his eyes dropped. He muttered something I didn't catch. He took up the penknife, as if he would have resumed his sharpening. And then suddenly he yielded. He rose, pushed the newspaper aside, and placed the statuette in my hands.

I suppose I am about the last man in the world to lose my head over a work of art. It has always seemed to me that the more claims a thing makes the higher must be the standard by which it is judged, and this is to reduce the number of the world's masterpieces considerably. Masterpieces? Why do I mention the word? A masterpiece has detachment, and this statuette had none. Its merit was vehemently the other way. It banished the very word 'classic'. It was as much his own as his own reluctant speech. If his fatalistic handling of the jack had impressed me, all that I could now do was to stare at the piece of wood in my hands. And as I like to be tight about my facts, let me first give its dimensions.

It was a woman's figure, about ten inches high, in the attitude of dancing. Allowing a minimum for wastage, the block in which it had slept before it came to life was about 11 by 4 by 5 inches. Call it 12 by 6 by 6 inches, or a quarter of a cubic foot. Those, I say, were the dimensions of the original block. But the figure itself contained nothing like that. Perhaps 6 cubic inches for the trunk and head, 4 for the thighs and legs, and 2 for the arms – total, 12: out of 432 cubic inches all but 12 had had to be laboriously cut away before the figure emerged, and that at the risk of an oversawing or a fracture at any moment. 'What on earth made you choose wood?' one wanted to cry to him. 'Why, you could have set up a wire armature in an hour. Is there no clay in Haarheim? Couldn't you have bought a pound or two of wax on one of your timber-journeys to the towns? Why this immense toil? Are you truly of a nature so tormented by itself that if no difficulties exist you must create them?'

For that was precisely what it looked like. He had gone wilfully out of his way to postpone the consummation of his work as long as possible. But now that the thing was finished, or almost so, I had to admit that it was neither wood nor wax, but flesh. The tendon of that supporting ankle would be hard between the fingers, a thumb run up that spine would feel the vertebrae. Feet, ankles, neck were exquisitely finished. But the face, the face only, was left. The cheeks remained rough and pitted by the tool. And in some obscure way this was a relief. For the figure was not merely a statuette of a woman. It was of one *given* woman, in all the idiom of her beauty, and to have given her a face would have been to shout her name as well.

'Where,' I asked slowly, 'did you learn all this?'

He did not seem to understand. 'To carve wood? Everybody here carves wood. Our fathers carved wood, and their fathers.'

'Yes, paper-knives and Noah's Ark cows. But *this*? You have then studied?'

He shook his head. At the schools? No.

'But, man! I know what I am saying. One can get a resemblance, even of anatomy. Nine people out of ten are deceived. But not the tenth. It is *not* Nature, where you can trace the effect back to the cause. It is Art, where, if you do not understand the cause, the effect cannot possibly be right.'

For the anatomy of that piece of wood left not a single anatomical question unanswered. The heads of the gastrocuemius *would* swell so, the soleus behave so, the thin, taut flank stretch precisely so.

'I can set bones,' he said, as if in apology. 'Often there are accidents in the woods. Then they send for me.'

'But are you not often away?'

'Not now. That is finished. Josef Speck broke his leg. I set it and took his team till he was well. Now I am back. I help the second forester.'

'I saw you on the road, when the sleigh could not pass.'

'I did not see you, Herr Doktor.'

'I saw you bend the pole with the jack.'

'So?' he said indifferently. 'Something had to be done.'

'Tell me,' I said after a pause, 'why you carved the figure in wood when there were easier ways, why make it so difficult for yourself?'

He hesitated, at a loss for words. He muttered: 'I don't know. How should I know? I am not as the Herr Doktor. It was as it was. It is still as it is. It has always been so. And it is more difficult than you know. More difficult – more difficult . . . ' His voice sank, and then his manner changed. He had questions to put to me too, quick little questions, so far as I could see without import.

'Is it pleasant at the Palast?'

I shrugged my shoulders. 'Hotels are very much alike.'

'You are staying there long?'

'Most likely not. No. Not long.'

'They are' – the bright eyes were earnestly on mine as he used the German equivalent – 'they are run off their feet there? I mean the service?'

'I really don't know. The hotel is full. I don't suppose they employ more people than they have work for.'

'No. I believe they work late,' he said, frowning, his fingers drumming on the table again.

Light began to dawn on me. His first words on hearing my foot on the snow outside had been, 'Is that you, Karen?' His questions about the hotel, the service, the degree of its busyness, could only mean that he had a wife at the hotel and was expecting her home. I was looking intently at the tool-marked space where the statuette's face should have been.

'Why don't you finish it?' I asked him.

He fixed me with his stare, as if I had committed an impertinence, which quite possibly I had.

'What?' he demanded.

'The hands, the feet, are wonderfully done. You have even put life into the braiding of the hair. Why leave the face like that?'

I have seldom seen a man's expression change so swiftly. A fire seemed to blaze up in him. Something looked for a moment out of his eyes that made me afraid, not, understand, for myself, but for the latent things so imperfectly safeguarded in himself. I have stood on a spot where they say the crust of the earth is only twelve feet thick, and the ground rings hollow to your tread. Sulphurous vapours trickle up from the crevices, and to run a torch along them is to wake the whole region into activity. I felt that I was experimenting with some such torch now. His voice, which had been a pleasant soft guttural, became strained and harsh.

'Why?' he said, with sudden loudness. 'The Herr Doktor asks me why? Why, indeed! I will tell you. It is because she smiles! Always she smiles! Once she did not smile, not, at least, like that, and I was happy. Now she smiles, and it drives me mad . . . '

And with an abrupt movement he was on his feet and struggling into the greatcoat that lay on the settee.

I protested that it was not necessary that he should accompany me. It would suffice if he indicated the way. But his voice fell to a mutter again.

'No. I will come. There is a branch of the paths – I will come. I will come to the hotel. It is nothing. Often I have been later than this. We will leave the light. There is a branch of two paths – she knows it too; if the Herr Doktor will please . . . '

Together we passed out of the hut, leaving the light burning behind us.

Yes, it seemed clear enough – all but one thing. He had been sitting up for this wife, who worked at the hotel, and was now going to fetch her, as a husband should. But the other thing remained. Most husbands are happy in the smiles of their wives, but he was not. Once she had not smiled, or not after that fashion, and he said he had been happy. Now she smiled, smiled always, and he left that portion of his carving blank and expressionless. What sort of a smile was that? I wondered deeply as we trudged together along the cart-track at the wood's edge and began to descend by rounded, monotonous hummocks of snow.

But he said not another word. At the junction of the tracks of which he had spoken he paused for a moment, looking along both portions. Then he took the right-hand one, which was obviously the more direct. A quarter of an hour later I fancied I had picked up my bearings again, and told him so, but still he tramped on at my side without replying. A little later still we came upon ski-tracks, and in one quarter the night seemed to have paled perceptibly. We rounded a shoulder of the mountain and gained its crest. Over the pines below was a mist of light, from which faint sounds reached us. They were still keeping up the carnival. We dropped down the track to the Palast Hotel.

A plantation straggles upwards from the rear of the hotel premises, and as we approached this Walther Blum began to tread more carefully. His care increased as the lights of the servants' quarters at the back began to appear through the trees. Most of the lower windows were in darkness, for the kitchens were hardly likely to be troubled again at that hour of the night, but the floors above shone out brightly enough, and through corridor windows a shadow could even be seen to pass from time to time. My own room was in the front of the hotel, where the long balconies are, and one can look down on the *eisbahn*. From this now came a confused babble of sound – music, a faint rattle of applause, the thin hum of skates. A swept path ran round the hotel in that direction. I was about to thank Walther Blum and to take this path when from the darkness there came the sound of a door being softly closed. Two low voices were heard, the one a woman's, the other a man's.

'No, go in now,' the woman's voice was saying. 'If he says he came to meet me I shall say I went the other way round.'

'*Dis bonsoir.*'

'No, not now – be careful – return to the bar – '

'The colleague Otto is there; just ten minutes, in the wood – '

'No, I say – '

We had drawn into the shadow of the trees. For all her protests, there was the sound of a kiss. A door closed, and in the semi-darkness a shadow was seen to steal away. The shadow went, not in the direction by which Blum and I had come, but by the other path. I looked round for Blum.

He was not there. He was a dozen yards away. And he was hurrying, not after the woman, but by the shorter way we had taken, as if he wished to reach home first.

3

Unless one has need of something and rings for it, one usually sees little of one's chambermaid, and I had no idea who performed this office for me at the Haarheim Palast. Indeed, it was at my own risk if I concluded that Walther Blum's wife was a chambermaid at all, and not employed in some other branch of the service. My data for her identification were, on the one hand, uniquely ample, and on the other, scanty to a degree. For all practical purposes they resolved themselves into one distinguishing feature – hair braided in a thick coronal round the head, as if two heavy plaits had been brought forward and woven together.

I have already remarked how, before what later seems a hidden plan is unfolded and revealed, trifling events add themselves to one another with increasing swiftness, until the last trifling accident or two have almost the force of a foregone conclusion. I was not thinking of Walther Blum when I rang my bell some two mornings later. Nor could I possibly know that, just as he had been doing an injured timber-driver's job in an emergency, so she now was temporarily taking over somebody else's duties. She knocked and entered in answer to my ring; and she was so indubitably the woman of the statuette that I could have called her by her name: Karen.

To my astonishment she seemed to be hardly more than seventeen. Young to be married, I thought, and to a husband in whom was something – I do not know if 'timeless' is the right word; I mean something that the years can neither add to nor take away from. She was blue-eyed, fair as Ceres, and had a mouth like a sealed rose. If, hastily summoning and dismissing a recollection, I found her on the small side, these things, after all, are more a matter of proportion than of actual size. Her ample blue-print skirt filled the doorway like a bell, and her expression was one of petulant gravity, as if, young as she was, she must struggle with things beyond her years, while resenting and hating them. It was right too that she should be a chambermaid. She fitted in better with linen-closets and brush-cupboards than if she had worn a smart apron or sat behind a cash-desk. And I confess that it came over me with a shock that not only could she apparently hold her vows loosely, but was also capable of telling her husband that she had gone one way home when, in fact, she had taken another.

I had no excuse for detaining her, and I told her what I wanted; but I missed not a single one of her movements as she stooped to the pile of linen on the floor and began to sort it. Then she looked up.

'The *gnädiger* Herr has made a list?' she asked in good German.

'No.'

'Then I will count it.'

So at least she could read and write. I continued to watch her as she made her list. Once she turned her head, and it was the identical turn of the statuette; and the wreath of the honey-fair hair was the same; but her face was hidden. She gathered the linen together, placed it on a towel, and knotted the corners crosswise. She rose with the bundle.

'The *gnädiger* Herr would wish them quickly?' she said, the grave, resentful eyes on mine.

'As quickly as possible.'

'It is done in the hotel. It will be ready at half past eight o'clock on Thursday evening. I shall do it myself.'

The door closed on her and her bundle.

So this was Karen of the smile! Certainly I had seen little smile enough, but possibly she was not yet restored to a smiling humour, for had I been a woman I should not have cared to return to that hut with the icicled window and tell such a husband as Walther Blum a pack of lies in his teeth. I would as soon not have gone home at all. I wondered what her life with him was up there. He had been away on the road. She too, so far as I could gather, was temporarily under-taking other duties. But these were interruptions to the routine. Soon the hotel would close. She would return home, and all day long he would not be far away – merely in some neighbouring portion of the forest, helping the second forester. A couple of strokes with a brush-handle and that raffle of icicles would come splintering down. The interior would be set to rights. Normal cohabitation would go on as before.

But I checked my thoughts, suddenly still. Everything as before! How then had that been? Since she was certainly not yet eighteen, there could not have been a great deal of 'before'. And why should his statuette, so betrayingly evidential in everything else, keep that blank, mocking, unfeatured face? What was this reason he gave of a smile? A smile is a peaceful, happy thing. So much can it do that, let a man but have it, and a load falls from him, as the mass of late snow, slipping away, suddenly shows the green all new and tender beneath. Yet he had said it himself. She smiled, and the chisel was arrested in his hand. She smiled, and every other perfection that those few cubic inches of wood contained become anonymous. She smiled, and at the mere recollection of it he broke out in fury before a stranger. 'Why? I will tell you why! *Because* she smiles! Once she did not smile, and I was happy. Now she smiles always, always smiles and it is driving me mad!'

Sufficiently occupied with these thoughts, I turned my attention to the other man.

For I already knew who *he* was. Even the few words I had over-heard at the back of the hotel had had that caressing yet acrid Neapolitan timbre. He was Nicolo, the white-jacketed waiter in the American bar, and his type is repugnant to me. He could not hide the fulsome meanings in his strongly staring black eyes, nor keep the vain and conquering smile from his shaven lips. Shaven? He was shaven *au bleu*. He must have shaved twice a day to keep the indigo so smoothly down. I learned that he did, in fact, shave for the second time before coming on to serve the evening cocktails, for, seeking a way up to the roof early one evening to see what the view was like up there, I came by chance upon the little room where daily the barber attended, and there was Nicolo, with the napkin tucked about the cauliflower of soap, his head back, and that ineffable smile on his face at something imaginary between him and the ceiling. His teeth, too, were as white as his barman's jacket, and as he polished his glasses behind the counter he might have been under glass himself, so sleek and unspotted a picture did he make.

In the circumstances I saw no reason why, over my modest *apéritif*, I should not find out as much about Nicolo as I could.

I soon had him marked down as a diligent fellow, with ambitions. A German-Swiss hotel is no bad stepping-stone from Naples to London, and Nicolo was making the most of his time. He was continually checking his stock, marking bottles, and copying the remaining quantities into a little book; and he had another book, too, with coloured edges, in French, German, Italian and English. It was a book of cookery recipes, and his short straight nose was never out of it. One of these days he was going to have his own hotel. Every *pfennig* of change that was pushed back to him as *trinkgeld* was set aside, and presently he would be leaving Haarheim, not to return. He would take his cookery-book with him in his trunk, and his hard-boiled shirts, and his black bows and starched white jackets. But he would not take his mistress, if she were that. Why pay excess on superfluous luggage? There were mistresses enough in London for a handsome, far-seeing, ambitious fellow such as our Nicolo.

So there was dapper Nicolo, with his English lessons in his spare hours, and his serenely insolent way of looking at women, and his smooth, plump hands that would let them go like so many water-drops when he reached for a towel. And there was Walther Blum, muttering, morose, half-savage as regarded one part of his nature, the other half mingled flame and passion and nameless desire. And apparently Nicolo got the kisses and Walther got the smiles. It doesn't matter by what processes I pieced all this together. I hardly think I did piece it together. It fell together of itself. It was simply the final assembly of elements that had long been preparing, and I doubt if anything could have changed the complete pattern into which they finally fell. On my walks, at my solitary table in the corner, leaning over the balcony at night and watching the waltzings and acrobatics on the *eisbahn*, I pondered much about it all, and one of the resolutions to which I came was that when Karen brought my linen back at half past eight o'clock on the Thursday evening I would be there to have, if possible, a word with her.

4

For I am no stranger to hotels, and I know what their promises about laundry usually amount to. It comes when it comes. But here was a promise much more precisely made. It was made even to the half-hour. She was doing it herself, and it was to be in my room at half past eight. Of course it might not come, but I was inclined to dismiss that. There were too many things against it. Say, for one thing, she was in love with this fellow. At half past eight the hotel, including myself, would be dining. The bedrooms would long since have been made ready for the night, except for the final touches that would only take a few minutes. And at half past eight Otto, as I knew, relieved Nicolo at the American bar. It was the one interval of the day that they might reasonably expect to have to themselves. That, briefly, was my guess at the position.

Yet I was dissatisfied with my guess. It seemed to condemn her too summarily. There must be some reason for the hate and resentfulness that dwelt so contradictorily side by side with the gravity in her clear eyes, and I began to play with hypotheses. Suppose, I argued to myself, that she had been married a year. If she had had even a little happiness during that year it was as much as could have been expected from a man so palpably at odds with the world and human life as he found it as Walther Blum. The chances were that he avoided his kind, or classed them, too, as phenomena with the trees and the rocks and the snows. He must have been a very difficult man to live with.

Yet it was a woman he had married, not a rock or a tree; and there had been something very steadfast in the eyes she had turned up to me as she had packed my linen on the floor. Apparently this man, who took life hardly himself, had passed a hard portion on to her too, and she had flown to one who took it more easily, cajoled her, flattered her, and would turn her off the moment he got what he wanted. In that case I was sorry for her, but except to tell her to make the best of her Walther and leave the other alone, I should not have known how to advise her.

I had intended to be in my room when Karen came at half past eight on Thursday; as it turned out I had no choice in the matter. A slight indisposition necessitated my seeing the doctor that afternoon; I was told that a couple of days in bed would set me right; and to bed I was sent. I had been in bed some hours when I heard Karen's tap at the door.

One minor difficulty at least was out of the way. I could not very well have detained her had she wished to finish the errand and be gone, but she, if she chose, might in the circumstances linger as long as she wished. She came in with my parcel. She wore the same little jacket and wide blue print skirt as before. In anybody else I should have called her salutation a curtsey, but in her it was somehow both given and withheld. Then, in the act of setting down the parcel, she paused.

'The *gnädiger* Herr is not well?' she asked, as if she had only just noticed that I was in bed.

I told her that it was nothing, and that I should be all right in a couple of days.

'Is it the *gnädiger* Herr's pleasure that I should count the linen and put it away?'

'If you would be so kind, Karen.'

She unfastened the parcel, checked its contents, and began to open drawers. She did not ask where anything was to be put, but went about her light task smoothly and efficiently. Only towards the end of her shirt-and-collar sorting did she delay a little. Then she turned, with the last of the washing still in her hand.

'The *gnädiger* Herr then knows my name?'

'Yes. You are Karen, the wife of Walther Blum. I have spoken with your husband.'

'You know him?' The limpid blue eyes were on mine, and she seemed to have forgotten the third-personal address.

'Very slightly,' I answered, though I felt this to be, in some odd way, untrue. 'Among others, I am not at all sure that he didn't save my life.'

Most people would have asked how that had come about, but she only knitted the brows above the blue eyes. She put away the last of the linen and closed the drawer. I thought she was about to leave. But she stood there with her hands on her hips (she seemed incapable of an attitude that was not alive with grace, and her hands and wrists in particular were full of the most moving beauty), the small foot under the bell-shape of blue-print tapping, her teeth catching at that half-rose of a lower lip. No wonder Blum had given forth her shape so passionately in his wood. I could hardly take my eyes from her. And then her own eyes, which had been on the polished floor, met mine again.

'I am also grateful to your husband for directing me when I had missed my way,' I went on.

And that she did take up. 'When?' she demanded, almost imperiously.

'Let me see. Four nights ago.'

She betrayed herself completely in her next question, for I might have met him anywhere; but she didn't seem to care. 'And you went in?' she challenged me.

'Yes,' I answered. There was no need to say where. She herself went straight to the point.

'And he walked back to the hotel with you?'

'Yes . . . Though I didn't say so.'

Still she didn't seem to care, though she bit her lip again. I would have given a fortune to have known all that was passing behind those rounds of palest blue under the wreath of fairest hair, but a very little I thought I did know. I had been in her husband's house four nights before. He had walked back to the hotel with me, and she herself had slipped away like a shadow by another path. There must have been – let us call it a situation – when she had climbed the mountain and pushed at the door of that solitary hut again. And above all, if I had been inside I had seen the statuette.

'The *gnädiger* Herr speaks the truth,' she said; 'since I knew all that,' she added, with a lift of her head.

Then suddenly it came out, as if somebody else spoke for me. Up to that moment it had not entered my head to ask such a question.

'Why do you smile, Karen? I want to know why you smile.'

Ah! the eyes seemed to say. So I knew that too! Well, if I already knew it it saved the time and trouble of explanation. All could be understood without further ado. Nevertheless, she repeated my question.

'Why do I smile?'

'Why do you smile?'

'You have been in the house?'

'I said so.'

'And you saw – it?'

I spoke slowly: 'By "it" you mean the thing that doesn't smile?'

'I knew you had seen it. It never will smile. It will never be finished. But I – I shall smile the more . . . So he told you that too?'

'He told me that you smiled, and that it drove him mad.'

'It is no worse to be mad than to be killed, as I have been killed,' she answered, with compressed lips. 'One can be killed, and yet go on living.'

Killed! She in the bloom and freshness of her seventeen short years! . . . But girls have these fancies. In another year or two she would be laughing at them herself. I leaned up on my pillow and looked at her attentively.

'What do you mean, Karen?'

She returned my look disdainfully, as if I and all like me were things of so little importance that the truth could be flung to us as one tosses a bone to a dog. But her hands had left her hips, and were clenched at her sides.

'Why should I not tell you? Why should I not tell everybody? It is only *he* who doesn't understand!' broke from her. 'Listen! Do you know how old I am? I am seventeen and a half years old. And I have been married to Walther Blum one year – one whole year! I didn't want to marry him. He made me marry him. We didn't even belong to the same valley. He lived in one valley and I in another, with the Huldhorn between. Among us we marry in the same valley – because of the mountain, because of the Huldhorn. Hardly a man can pass the cornice in the winter. Even in the summer it is a toil. So our young men marry the girls at home. But he came over, down into our village from the skies. He came over whatever the weather was, with runners on his feet that he had made himself. He could have settled among us, for he lived alone, but he would not. He told me that he would not come every night, but I soon learned what *that* meant. It meant that he might not arrive every night. But he set out every night. I asked him once, when he was very late, whether he had got lost, but he said he had a compass in his breast. I used to open the shutters and look up at the crest of the hill for his lantern.'

So he had made even his love difficult to the verge of impossibility! Her words pictured it all the more vividly because of their very abruptness – him in his hut making ready his lantern; his setting-out; the diamonded night sky overhead or else the blinding scurries of snow; the soft sliding thunder of a distant avalanche, the creep round the cornice of the Huldhorn; the pause to look down on the handful of houses that made the hamlet – and all guided by that in his breast that he called a compass. I saw the child of sixteen peering past the

shutter for the winking light of his lantern. And I was quite prepared
to hear that she had been afraid of him even then.

'My parents were against it, *gnädiger* Herr,' she went on more
quietly. 'They said it was not natural that he should not be able to get
a girl without coming over the mountain. But he said: Get a girl! He
had seen them – girls. They were nothing. If *those* were girls, then *I*
was something else, and he wanted me, whatever I was, if those
others were girls He said that my smile made him warm even on the
cornice of the Huldhorn. My father said that was high-falutin talk,
and not good. Let him come and make his home among us and then
it would be time to talk, my father said. And the Herr Pastor, who
was also my schoolmaster, said the same. But I began not to listen to
them. At first, all the same, I didn't want to marry Walther. I told
him not to come. But he made me marry him, *gnädiger* Herr. He
gave me no peace. There is no peace where he is. If there is a
moment's peace an avalanche follows. And when I learned that he set
out every night, then the nights when he didn't arrive were terrible. I
felt that I had killed him by not marrying him sooner. I was very
young, *gnädiger* Herr. I am older now. And so I married him.'

That, too, I could believe – that he had made her marry him. He
had compelled her a little at a time, as he had loaded up that sixty-
foot tree, forcing it to bend. And suddenly she stamped her small
foot so that the blue-print bell shook with the passionate gesture.

'And what was it? *Lieber Gott*! Do the other men do so to the other
girls? Why, then, do they not die? But I have seen them laughing,
these young married girls; how can they do it? I tell you, you who lie
there, that it was endless! Always it was so, always, always . . . And
there, with the Huldhorn between, where was there to run to? And
what was the good of crying? No, I do not wish! He broke me, he
broke me. It arrived that he might do as he wished; what did I care?
Then he reproached me; but it no longer mattered to me. Nothing
mattered. And so I was contented, thinking I knew the worst.

'But I did *not* know the worst, you who lie there!' she cried, in a
voice that mounted. 'Having broken my body he began to break
my mind too! I had had lessons from the Herr Pastor. I could read
and write; I could speak a little French; and he could neither read
nor write nor speak French. And because I could not answer his
questions he called me a fool! His questions, *lieber Gott*! He did not
understand them himself. They were not questions! I have heard him
say that he did not know what it was he wanted to know! How, then,
should I know? He called us all fools. Even the Herr Pastor he called

a fool. He said that we knew no more than he, and that if he learned
to read and write he would be the greatest fool of all. And when one
is called a fool sufficiently one ceases to open one's mouth. Days
passed when I never spoke to him. Even at night I never spoke to
him. All was without words or speech, since he wished it so. Why
should one speak when one is a fool?'

Poor, hapless pair! What was there to say? I said what I could.

'Much is laid on him, Karen.'

'What is laid on him? How, laid on him?' she flashed.

'It hasn't got a name. He is right in saying that the Herr Pastor
knows no more of the reason of everything than he. Nevertheless, it
is fastened on him as they fasten the trees to the carts – with a chain
and a winch.'

'It is on *me* that it is fastened!' she cried. 'Listen to me! Listen
heedfully! What had I left? My beauty remained. I do not mean my
beauty as at first, though he might please himself about that. My
beauty to his eyes remained. That was all – all! And his eyes never left
me. They followed me about like the piercings in a dark shutter. And
then the other – all else – stopped. I existed in his eyes only. I was his
Gliederpuppe, his thing that he copied from. Even in mid-winter I
must go about – yes, even when I was sweeping up his chippings or
cooking the supper . . . but the *gnädiger* Herr has seen. Soon I ceased
to blush. That was not his first statuette. Many he cast into the stove,
saying it was all they were fit for – more true to say it was all *I* was fit
for! I was a fool. That other was finished. But this remained. I had
married a man who growled over pieces of wood. I was something
to turn into a piece of wood. If I could tell you, you who lie there
listening – if I could tell you – '

I put up my hand to calm her. It was not necessary to tell me; the
statuette had done that. I thought of that lonely hut far up the
Huldhorn. Terrible houses of men, of which we see the outside only!
A mansion in a London square, a crowded Paris tenement, a cabin on
a vineyard's slope, a log-hut high and lonely in a world of snows –
just once in a while a chink opens, a curtain is left a little aside. One
learns the reasons why a will was made, why a divorce-action was
entered, why a crime was committed. Then the chink closes again
and the curtain slips back into its place. But one has seen. I saw in
Walther Blum a man scourged by life and his station in it, dwelling
in solitude of soul up there, saturating his eyes with anguishing and
untranslatable beauty, and with curses casting his wretched images
into the stove. I saw a young girl, shy with the shyness of young

girls, modest with a peasant's flinching modesty, shrivelling Semele-like under the fierce heat of a passion elemental and beyond her comprehension, forced to yield up her very superficies as her sole remaining value. Comprehend it? Because she did not comprehend it, it was the last violation. The little he had left her of her own, to do as she pleased with, he used up in order that the eyes of strangers might know as much of her as he. I had seen. Anybody might see. And she no longer cared.

'But all this, Karen – it might explain why you weep. It does not explain why you smile,' I said, after a long silence.

'Does it not?' she taunted me. 'To you, no, perhaps; but *he* knows! Listen! It is not all. I now give way to him in everything. From here to here' – she put out one foot and, with a gesture terrible in its very slightness, lightly touched her chin – '*that* is his. He may look at it, embrace it, burn it, cut it with knives. I now run to let him do as he wishes with it. "Yes, Walther; assuredly, Walther," I say – for we speak now. But he pays. There is still something in me he cannot touch.' And the smile, with all its hideous meanings for him, stole over the young rose of a mouth. 'Is it not so, *gnädiger* Herr? And when he groans and weeps and prays for that something – for the *gnädiger* Herr is right when he says it has no name, but it is that he wants – is not that alone enough to make the smile come? For I cannot give that something now if I would. It is me, but it is not mine. He has all the rest instead. And so it is even wifely to smile.'

'If it drives him mad, Karen?' I asked gravely. For I had remembered Nicolo's absence from the American bar. 'If it drives him – or you – to something desperate?'

She now spoke quite lightly with a little stretch of herself. 'At least it would be an end . . . Please would the *gnädiger* Herr like me to send the valet as I go down?'

'No, Karen.'

'Or any service – ?'

'There is nothing, thank you. But I should like to see you again.'

With the smile still about her mouth, the steady, scornful look in her clear eyes, and her hands upon her hips again, she said a mocking and a bitter thing: 'The *gnädiger* Herr has only to ring.'

'Karen! . . . Why do you not go to your home over the Huldhorn for a short time?'

'I come here instead,' she answered; and the next moment she was gone, leaving me gazing at the 'Flight into Egypt' carved in high relief in brown wood on the wall opposite my bed.

5

How much better for Walther Blum, I thought, could he have contented himself with work of that kind, carving what every peasant in
the district carved, the edelweiss paper-knives, the clock faces, and
the other objects of the stationers' shops! But what was the good of
thoughts like that? He was what he was, and who shall justify the
ways of man to woman, of woman to man? It was much more to the
point that apparently his wife was carrying on this intrigue with the
Neapolitan. Or was it not an intrigue at all? Was it, so to speak, part
of the smile? Was it designed to show him that all that he had
destroyed in her might still revive at the beck of somebody else?

Our conversation, which I have abbreviated, had taken some time.
If she had had an assignation with Nicolo at half past eight she had
certainly not kept it. She might or might not be with him now. It was
truly no affair of mine. And yet I felt restless and anxious.

My indisposition was a short one. After two days I was up and
about again. I received the congratulations of such of the guests as
had any interest in me, and was told that I had missed little during
my lying-up. The weather had broken. A strong thaw had set in. The
eisbahn was a deserted waste, and there were trunks at the door of the
hotel – for those who were not departing immediately were preparing to do so, and within a few days the clientèle would probably be
diminished by half. The signs of the winter's end were not confined
to the guests. There was a stir in the natural life of the district too.
Down the lower slopes one saw more cattle, and multitudinous
sounds of deliquescence and break-up were everywhere. Upstairs
in the hotel they were already closing unneeded rooms, and downstairs Nicolo, checking his stock and poring over his book in four
languages, had the American bar to himself.

The incident to which I am coming happened at five o'clock
one afternoon upstairs in the already half-empty hotel. They were
stripping beds and rolling up the bolsters and mattresses, and as a
portion of the staff had already been discharged the rest of the
remaining personnel was bearing a hand. Among them was Nicolo,
in his shirt-sleeves, a plump cock among the print-skirted hens,
smiling, showing his white teeth, and within an hour of his second
daily shave. His jests, as he dragged out the mattresses and carried
the stacks of sheets, caused an incessant tittering among the maids,
and I suppose it is because I have no such success with women as he
that I liked him less than ever.

Something had taken me to my room, which was, of course, untouched, and I had seen all this in passing. I did whatever it was that had brought me up, and came out again. A few yards along the corridor stood an addition to the group. Walther Blum had joined it.

He was standing by the half-open door of a linen-room, watching his wife and Nicolo as they folded a blanket between them. For two reasons I did not pass on: I was interested in the situation, and I had a fancy to pass the time of day with Blum. Thus, as I lingered, I heard what passed between Nicolo and Karen Blum, in French.

'When one folds blankets you know what happens?' the Neapolitan was saying.

Karen shook the plaited head.

'It cannot happen this time, for a reason. The reason stands there watching us. But one folds, so – and so' – the blanket was halved and quartered as the two holders of it approached – 'and the one who takes the blanket takes something else also.'

'What?'

'Ah, so little when one thinks of the rest! (*Comme il fait les yeux féroces!*)'

'*Il fait toujours les yeux féroces.*'

'*Mais les tiens . . .* ' His own black bull's-eyes rolled to her clear rounds, and the look itself was the kiss of which he spoke. She made way for me to pass, and I sought Blum.

The man from Naples was certainly taking risks. I myself should hesitate before I provoked on a man's face the sort of look that was on Blum's. When I greeted him he did not at first speak. When he did speak it was not in answer to my greeting.

'The Herr Doktor speaks languages. What was that he was saying?' he said under his breath.

'I heard nothing. What brings you here, Blum?'

'Those things that the Herr Doktor does not hear bring me here,' he replied grimly. 'There is no longer any reason why she should remain. Half of them have left already. It is time she left.'

'It is only a matter of a few days.'

'I have come to fetch her today,' he answered curtly.

At that moment there was a further interesting passage between the pair who folded the blankets. She had loaded him with a pile of them for carrying away, and the pile bulged and tottered. He looked back over his shoulder.

'Give a hand or they will be down and all to fold again,' he panted, for he was of a sedentary habit, and the blankets had lodged stiffly against some small projection of the wall. She tripped after him.

But she did not reach him. Blum's voice was raised.

'Karen!'

She turned. One would have thought she had not known of his presence.

'Yes, Walther?'

'You are to come home. You are to come now. Go and make yourself ready.'

It was peremptory, perhaps a little unreasonable; but she ignored that. The look she turned on him was not mere yielding; it was the deliberate strangling of a will of any kind set against his. Already she was close on him, hastening to whatever room she occupied. At me she did not glance. The look was all for him – as also was the smile that accompanied it.

'Yes, Walther.'

'Go and pack your box. I will carry it up the mountain.'

'Yes, Walther.'

'At once. Get your wages and wait for me.'

'Yes, Walther.' The next moment she was gone.

I thought for a moment that Walther Blum was going to seek out Nicolo there and then, for he stood irresolute, watching him with wrathful, smouldering eyes. But all at once he turned away. I thought he was going to take some domestics' staircase or other, but he didn't. In his black jacket and spacious corduroys, though carrying his broad hat in his hand, he marched down the main staircase, as if he had been staying in the hotel. I followed him, and on the broad outer verandah called his name. He turned.

'Herr Doktor?'

'Could I have a word with you?'

He bowed, for he had the peasant's courtesy.

'Properly speaking, what I want to say is none of my business, unless I can be of use. But you yourself spoke of it one night, and since then an accident has brought about a talk with your wife also.'

'She shall come away today,' he muttered.

'But you speak as if she had left your roof. She has returned late perhaps, but she has worked late. There has been much to do. You will remember that you asked me the question.'

He made no reply, and again I wondered what had passed be-tween them on the night when he had overheard her words to

Nicolo and been a witness to their kiss. The next moment he had told me.

'I have warned her!' he cried. 'That man, anybody can see what he is! Would I had the shaving of him; I would make the blade keen for *that*! . . . What was he saying in that language?' he demanded once more.

'I scarcely heard. It was harmless.'

'It was *not* harmless! Those eyes do not go with harmless things!'

I was much of the same opinion, but, 'He is going away in a week,' I said. 'Do not think of him.'

But the empty verandah boomed with Walther Blum's outbreak.

'In a week! And what does *that* mean? He has not possessed her. I made her tell me that night, and it would have given her pleasure to say yes, but she does not lie. He has not possessed her. But there is still time! All these months he has planned it, and he has one week left! I do not wish to kill. It is better to take her away. But if, within a week, I find him one yard above that plantation's edge . . . ' He stopped.

This was a dangerous turn for things to take. Not only was he capable of doing it; he was capable of finding, out of that chaotic, tormented mind of his, overwhelming reason why it should be done. If the lore of the Herr Pastor over the mountain was ignorance and confusion to him, he would make as little of a Commandment. Neither was it safe that he should boom out menaces of this kind under the verandah of the Haarheim Palast Hotel.

'Your wife will not come out this way,' I said. 'Will you take a little walk?' And to make sure of his doing so I took his arm. We turned by the path that led round the hotel, under the plantation beyond which, if Nicolo went a single yard, it would be at his own risk. A little way up the plantation was an old wooden cattle-trough, with the bent and rusty remains of the pipe that had fed it. It was half full of snow, but we should see from there when Karen came out, and its thick, worn edge made a seat. We sat down side by side.

We might have been waiting for Karen and nothing else, for we were as silent as if our minds had been unoccupied. It would have been like him not to speak at all. It was therefore I who took the word.

'Walther,' I said, using the name for the first time, 'to what kind of a life do you take Karen when she goes up there?'

'To mine,' he said. 'To the only one I have. But she gets the whole of it. *I* want no light-o'-love!' he added contemptuously.

'But is it necessary to give her the whole of it? May not the whole be too much? She is very young.'

His eyes were past the hotel, over the valley furrowed with white, thinned and mottled into dark, unsightly patches. Soon the gentian and anemone would smile there and the sweet, cold freshets thread themselves downward under the grass, and the tonk of the bells be borne on the wind. And he seemed to be thinking of gentler things than murder, too, for he began to speak in a voice from which the anger had died away.

'It may be so, Herr Doktor,' he said. 'It should not be so, for what is to love if it is not to give? But sometimes I ask myself whether only I am right, and I cannot answer. It is *here*' – he placed a clenched hand on his breast – 'and if I feel it there, how can I lie to myself and say I do not feel it? We cannot all be right, I and they. Then come times when I tell myself that it is easy for them to say "I give all", when their all perhaps is so little. And yet again there are times when I rage, and say they are wrong, were they as countless as the pines, and only I understand. Is that too much, Herr Doktor?'

'Much too much.'

'When I love her?'

'Love her a little less, Walther.'

The brown hand gripped the remains of the rusty trough-pipe, and I could see its fierce tension. Then his head sank suddenly to his breast. He spoke in a shaky voice.

'Herr Doktor, I have no words of my own. The words I have are carved and filed smooth by others. They are a great number, the others, and I am only one, and ignorant at that. Therefore I do not say I loved her, Herr Doktor. She happened to me. I say she happened to me. She happened to me as rain happens, or sun, or the fall of the tree, or the avalanche. She happened as sickness happens, or healing, or thirst, or hunger. Sometimes, when she looked beautiful, I could even love myself a little, that I should be the cause of her looking beautiful. She lived in the valley over the Huldhorn. What was the Huldhorn? I have crossed it in all weathers. They do not love, these young men who will not take the trouble if the one they love lives a couple of pastures away! Herr Doktor, if I have no words to speak of these things, was it not word enough to cross the Huldhorn for her? I could have carried her, too, as I shall carry her box today. So she happened to me in that valley.

'And I said to myself, "Have a care, Walther Blum! You are rude and unlettered. *They* have been to school with the Herr Pastor!

Therefore contradict nobody. If they seem to you to talk foolish and vain things, things that will not bear examination, say nothing. Look at Karen instead. Look at her as she takes down the platters, as she serves the cheese, as she kisses her father before going to bed. Look at her as if she were the mountain air you breathed, the mountain pool in which you swam." All the way back over the Huldhorn it remained with me. Beauty is agony to me, Herr Doktor. She cannot move a hand but I feel that no woman's hand has ever moved so before. And even these are words, that other people use. Let them pass. They are nothing . . . ah!'

What else he would have said I cannot tell, for at that moment there was a little bustle at the back of the hotel. Nicolo appeared, bearing in front of him a small trunk of metal, corded. Karen followed, in a queer, stiff, little round hat. Nicolo set the trunk on the ground, with a gesture that seemed to say, Ach, but that was heavy! Blum had risen. I continued to sit where I was. He dropped down through the plantation and joined the pair at the door. As far as I could see he did not look at Nicolo. He threw the box up to his shoulder and made a gesture of his head to his wife. A few minutes later they had passed me, she a few paces in front, he with the corded box on his shoulder, on their way to their home among the melting snows.

6

It chanced that I had an acquaintance at the hotel who was among the last to leave, and I might well have left with him; but for reasons I need not go into it was not to be so, and I went to see him off instead. The station is twelve miles away, and whereas we had come in sleighs, we went back in Swiss carts. I said goodbye to my friend, and the heads of the horses were turned homeward again. Halfway back I saw Walther Blum. He was sitting on a timber-cart. The vehicles passed without incident. I think he saw me, but was not sure. He gave no sign of recognition.

'Has Josef Speck fallen ill again?' I asked of the driver. Josef Speck was the man whose leg Blum had set, driving his cart for him until his recovery.

'No, *gnädiger* Herr. Josef Speck is well and on his journey.'

'Then what does Walther Blum going to the town?'

The man laughed. 'Oh, Walther Blum is unaccountable, *gnädiger* Herr. Nobody asks himself why Walther Blum does anything.'

We drove on.

As I look back oh this incident I find it difficult to justify the apprehension I felt. Walther Blum was on a timber-cart, going to the town; why should he not be on a timber-cart, going to the town? He was not even driving, but sitting by the driver's side; why, if he had business that way, should he not take the chance of a lift? For all I knew he was going to dispose of his paper-knives and blotters and fretwork clock-faces. If he were away for a couple of days it would be lonely for his wife, but they do not mind loneliness up there, and possibly he had sent her to her people. It was as natural that Walther Blum should be taking a journey on a cart as that I myself should be saying goodbye to my friend.

None the less, I could not get rid of it like that. 'Nobody asks why Walther Blum does anything,' my driver had just said; but I asked. Say he was not going away at all. Say he merely wished it to be supposed he had gone away. Say, in short, that he was setting a trap for Nicolo. Had it been possible, I would have bidden my driver turn and follow Walther Blum wherever he went. That was not possible. But something else was. I couldn't follow Walther Blum, but I could keep an eye on Nicolo. He would not know he was being watched, and watched, moreover, for his own health and safety.

It was the first thing I did on my return to the hotel to walk into the American bar. He happened to be there. Disliking him as I did, I nevertheless made myself talk to him.

'So another has left, Nicolo,' I said, with an assumption of cheerfulness. 'It is drawing near the end.'

'Monsieur will be the last,' he said, busily polishing.

'When do you go to London?'

'In four days, monsieur.'

'Well, this country is beautiful in the winter, and beautiful in the summer, but it is not much in between.'

He showed his close white teeth in a smile. 'It is monsieur who sees the country,' he said. 'We of the staff work too long hours to see much of it.'

'But you go up the mountain sometimes for a walk and to breathe the air?'

'Not I, monsieur. I do not like the cold. I like Capri and Sorrento and the sun on Naples bay.'

And, having ascertained that he was in the hotel, I left him, but did not go too far away.

I well believed that he was not fond of mountain climbing. He might even have to run the gauntlet of jests if he, the smooth, lazy one, were seen toiling up past the plantation during the day. For many reasons he would prefer the night. And I had no evidence that he intended to go at all. But I was persuaded by something more subtly strong than evidence. There were vast gaps in my information. I only knew in outline what had passed between Blum and his wife on that first night of all. That she and Nicolo exchanged kisses I did know, but not every kiss is an adultery, and it would be an unfeeling heart that found no forgiveness for her. But while I did not know the details, I did know the sum and result of them. Blum himself was satisfied that no guilty act had been committed. At the same time, he was equally satisfied that the attempt would be made, and had cunningly and deliberately provided the opportunity. If Nicolo did not climb the mountain it was even possible that he might prevail on her to make a pretext to come to the hotel. Or nothing at all might happen.

But as the day wore on and I wandered aimlessly about the precincts of the hotel, I thought so less and less.

I come now to the moment when Nicolo did leave the hotel, setting his face up the mountain. With the passing of time I can survey the events of that evening almost calmly; but time has had to pass. I have ceased to call myself a young man. I apprehend, too constantly, the meaning of such words as causation and fatality and absence of design. I have learned how events themselves take charge and fall into inhuman and unpremeditated patterns. I think it was so with Walther and Karen Blum. As she had 'happened' to him, so the world had happened to him and he to the world, and there was no escape from the dreadful logic of the upshot. It had to be so, and it was so, and I had to be a witness of it.

Nicolo did not steal out of the hotel like a man on a guilty errand. He strolled out, apparently with no other purpose than to take the air. He wore his waiter's black trousers, but had changed his white jacket for one of purplish cloth, and on his head was a green velours hat with feathers in it. To English eyes his appearance was incongruous yet somehow dandified, and he himself was evidently well content with it. All this I saw from where I stood at the verandah's end. He sauntered round to the back of the hotel, and I ascended quickly to my room. Not that there was any hurry. I had to let him get ahead. I do not carry firearms, but if I had had a pistol I should certainly have slipped it into my pocket. For moral effect, naturally.

He was not quite out of sight when I descended; he was well up the plantation, giving a backward glance, as if he wondered how much longer it was necessary to keep up appearances. I stepped out of his line of vision. There was one chance and one only that I should lose him, and even that did not matter – for if he took the longer and less steep of the two paths that met again farther on, I could take the other one and be there before him. That might be the best. At least I should escape the hateful appearance of watching another man unobserved. As he was of a corpulent build he probably would take the easier path. In fact, he did so, and I the other.

I made haste. If Blum should appear he would hardly resent it that one such as I should be found alone with his wife, and if he did not appear Nicolo would be likely to find an empty house at the end of his journey. It may seem odd, but it seemed somehow part of what I have called the pattern that I made no attempt to divert Nicolo himself. He was a contemptible fellow, and must take his chance. He was away to the right, somewhere over the shoulder of the hill, and as I passed the point that he too would presently have to pass, I quickened my pace to something like a run, that he might not see me ahead.

More snow than in the valleys still lay on the ground, and as I reached the beginning of the dark clearing the ghostly mass of the Huldhorn rose miles ahead, just discernible. Not a quarter of a mile away Blum's light showed, almost as watery as on my first visit – for I discovered that the icicles had not been broken away, but still formed a screen, though a perforated and attenuated one only. This time I did not look in. I walked up to the door and knocked. Only when I had done so did it occur to me that my knock might be taken for the knock of somebody else.

There was no reply, and I knocked more loudly. Still I had no answer, though I heard a muffled sound within. There was nothing for it but the window. I advanced and looked through a ribbed and ragged hole.

Karen sat there alone. She sat where her husband had sat, under the powerful incandescent, and her round eyes appeared to be staring straight into mine. But I don't think they saw. She was rigid, as if the sound of my knock had frozen both the sight and speech of her. The table at which she sat was empty. On the little shelf stood the row of wooden cattle and carved knives, but I did not see the statuette. I called; I gave my name; and as if my name had been a magic word, she broke into life. She sprang up and disappeared for an instant from my view. I heard the shooting of a bolt. By this time I was at the door. She flung it open, dragged me in, and shot the bolt again almost in one movement. Then she clasped both her hands on one of my shoulders, and I had to save her from falling.

'Oh, the dear God has sent you!' she moaned on my breast. 'Do not go. Keep me so. Keep me so till morning, for God knows what is going to happen this night!'

'I know what is going to happen this night if you will, Karen. You cannot stay here alone. Put your things on and come with me back to the hotel.'

She shook convulsively. 'I cannot! I dare not! I was told I must stay here! Stay here with me!'

'Certainly I will stay with you; but who told you you must stay here?'

'He told me – Walther – '

'But he has gone to the town?'

'He has not gone to the town. I do not know where he is. But he is not far away. He was here an hour ago. He has kept me here all day, that I might neither go nor send word to the hotel.'

'Why should you wish to send word to the hotel, Karen? Word to whom, and about what?'

But she only said, 'Oh! Oh! Oh!' and crushed herself harder against me.

'When I knocked, Karen, did you think it might be somebody else, that you did not answer?' I asked.

I felt her nod.

'Walther?' (The door had been bolted, and the visitor might have been he.)

'No.'

'The somebody else – has he ever been here?'

'Never – never – never!' she said, with a passion that utterly convinced me.

'You know what I mean?' I whispered.

'Yes.'

'Then shall I go and turn him back?'

She bounded from my arms in fright. 'What! Then he is coming?'

'There may be time to warn him.'

She sank to the floor. 'If he is on the mountain Walther can run like a hare and leap like the chamois – '

And I remembered Blum's words: 'If he steps a yard beyond the plantation . . . '

It had been plain enough before; it was bright as a sunburst now. My first unworthy idea, that Blum had turned his house into a mousetrap and baited it with a piece of cheese, was utterly wrong.

Nobody was luring Nicolo. He was free to stay away. But he was free *only* as long as he stayed away. Once he set foot on those mountain wastes he entered a cage of which the door closed behind him. What chance had he, the keeper of an American bar, against a man who could run like a hare and leap like a chamois? . . . And yet a panic took me too. I must have caught it from her, sunk to a huddle on the floor. I could not see a human being walk into an open trap like that. I must warn him. I sprang to the bolt of the door.

But I was too late. I heard the faint sound of a distant scream. I flung open the door with such force that the wall shook.

'*Eee-eee-eee!*' It was the tight-drawn, inarticulate scream of pure terror, and it came from somewhere in the wood. He had sought safety in the wood – and from a pursuing woodsman!

'*Eee-eee-eee!*' Again came the squeal. My shadow streamed from the doorway, and the beginning of the wood beyond was illuminated as if by the headlights of a car.

Karen had stopped her ears.

'*Eee-eee-eee!*'

And then, a little way within the wood, I saw him, if that shadow was he. The sounds of the last scream had died away, as if he had merely continued to scream as a child screams, having once began. He seemed to be listening. Blum I did not see. This made matters no better. Better to see Blum than to know all the time that he was near, stealing noiselessly from tree to tree, ushering, shepherding, getting his man where he wanted him.

'*Eee-eeee-eeee!* . . . *Eeee-eeee-eeee!*'

Such an added extreme of terror would have seemed inexpressible, but he did it. The next moment he was flying straight for the hut, as a moth makes for a lamp. His arms were above his head, and Blum was after him.

Do not tell me how feeble was my effort to bang the door between the two. I cannot leap like a chamois nor cover the mountains like a hare. Loudly the door swung to and back again. As it did so something fell to the floor with a little snap. I do not know on what ledge or shelf it had been standing, but it was Blum's statuette, and the violent jar of the door had brought it down. Breathing easily, Blum slowly bolted the door.

'Walther,' I cried sharply, 'open that door! No harm is done! Let the fellow go!'

He did not appear to hear me. His bright eyes were on the other's white and sweating face.

'Then I will open it.' And I took a step forward.

But I seemed merely to precipitate the thing I wished to forestall. Even in a light-built man I should not have thought so swift a movement possible. I fell back with a ringing head and one useless elbow, and Blum was not calm now. He was trembling and his face was advanced towards the Neapolitan's.

'So you thought you would come? The coast was clear? Just one little peep past the plantation before you left?'

Nicolo was licking his lips. His purple jacket was fouled and burred, and his green velours hat had gone.

'You said to yourself, "Walther Blum is away, and his wife must be lonely, and it would be neighbourly to sit with her an hour"?'

I saw Nicolo's fleeting look at the window. I read his thoughts; a sudden leap to the table and a header, through icicles and all – Blum could have done it – it was all there was to do. It was, as a matter of fact, Nicolo who struck first, a desperate and futile blow. He did not even succeed in getting on to the table. He was caught and tripped, and in a moment both men were on the floor.

Karen had fallen back behind the stove, with eyes that peeped dreadfully between her fingers. And there was no more screaming now. Blum had his left forearm under the Neapolitan's nape, and his right palm was pressed on his forehead. He was looking at him earnestly, attentively. And he had ceased to speak. Why should he speak? Words were things used up and outworn by others. To creep in midwinter round the cornice of the Huldhorn had been one of his words. And this was his companion word, that he was doing now.

Then my heart stood still as I saw the slow grope of his powerful hand along the floor. In a flash I knew beforehand what he intended to do. I tried to kick at the hand, but once more I was too late. I looked wildly round. Karen had sunk to the floor by the stove, but I saw her raise her head.

And that at least – her seeing what I foresaw – I *could* stop. Those blue, already overburdened eyes were not made for *that*. I do not know whether or not I was in time. I sprang to the middle of the room and with my unhurt hand dashed out the incandescent.

I dash out the light from this page too. As the player rises from the board without making the final move, as the pattern is all there without the addition of the last piece of all, so let it be with the tale. Say – I do not know – that the whole thing took ten minutes, half an hour, an hour, before the silence came. It was in the dead silence that

I heard Blum get up from the floor. I heard his feet pass me, heard his groping in some cupboard behind me. There were sounds as he did something in the middle of the room.

Then suddenly the hut was flooded with the light of the new bulb he had fitted.

My eyes rested on Karen first. She lay on her back, wide-eyed and still. I had heard no sound from her – believe me, if you had been there you would have had ears for one set of sounds only – but deep in her breast was Walther's slenderest carving-chisel. He was standing there, but he had not yet seen her; he was looking down at his other piece of work. I think, when I remember the cleared table at which Karen had sat, that he had intended to make a man-to-man business of it. He had cleared away all other weapons, intending to finish him with his hands, and Karen had probably hidden the thin chisel somewhere about her. But what I saw I seemed already to have known. Only the arm of the statuette was to be seen – the one that had broken off when it had fallen from behind the door. All else of that thing of loveliness was indistinguishable from the rest of the red on the floor. Blum had broken it to splinters in cramming it where he conceived it to belong – where he had conceived the smile itself to belong – in between Nicolo's white teeth and down his throat.

Two Trifles

From The Ghost Book (*Hutchinson, 1927*) *compiled by*
Lady Cynthia Asquith

I

THE ETHER-HOGS

With one foot thrust into an angle to brace himself against the motion of the ship, the twin telephone-receivers about his head, and one hand on the transmitting key, while the other hovered over screws and armatures, the young wireless operator was trying to get into tune. He had had the pitch, but had either lost it again, or else something had gone wrong on the ship from which that single urgent call had come. The pear-shaped incandescent light made cavernous shadows under his anxiously drawn brows; it shone harshly on dials and switchboards, on bells and coils, and milled screws and tubes; and the whole white-painted room now heeled slowly over this way, and then steeved as violently back the other, as the liner rolled to the storm.

The operator seemed to be able to get any ship except the one he wanted. As a keyed-up violin-string answers to tension after tension, or as if a shell held to the ear should sing, not one Song of the Sea, but a multitude, so he fluctuated through level after level of the diapason of messages that the installation successively picked up. They were comically various, had the young operator's face not been so ghastly anxious and set. 'Merry Christmas . . . the *Doric* . . . buy Erie Railroads . . . Merry Christmas . . . overland from Marseilles . . . closing price copper . . . good night . . . Merry Christmas' – the night hummed with messages as a telephone exchange hums; and many decks overhead, and many scores of feet above that again, his own antennae described vast loops and arcs in the wintry sky, and from time to time spoke with a roar that gashed the night.

But of all the confusion of intercourse about him, what follows is a Conference that the young wireless operator did *not* hear.

The spirits of the Special Committee on Ethereal Traffic and Right of Way were holding an Extraordinary General Meeting. They were holding it because the nuisance had finally become intolerable. Mortal messages tore great rents through space with such a reckless disregard of the Ethereal Regulations that not a ghost among them was safe. A spectre would be going peacefully about his haunting; there would come one of these radio-telegraphic blasts; and lo! his essence would be shattered into fragments, which could only be reassembled after the hideous racket had passed away.

And by haunting they meant, not merely the old-fashioned terrorising by means of white sheets and clanking fetters, nor yet only the more modern forms of intimidation that are independent of the stroke of midnight and the crowing of the first cock, but also benigner suggestions – their gentle promptings to the poets of the world, their whispered inspirations to its painters, their care for the integrity of letters, their impulses to kindliness, their spurs to bravery, and, in short, any other noble urging that earth-dwellers know, who give their strength and labour for the unprofitable things they believe without ever having seen them.

A venerable spirit with a faint aura of silver beard still clinging about him spoke.

'I think we are agreed something must be done,' he said. 'Even now, one of the most amiable junior ghosts of my acquaintance, on his way with a *motif* to a poor tired musician, was radio'd into flinders, and though his own essence is not permanently harmed, his inspiration was shocked quite out of him, and may never be recovered again.'

'That is so,' another bore witness. 'I happened to be projecting myself not far from the spot, and saw the whole occurrence – poor fellow! he had no chance whatever to escape. It was one of these "directive" messages, as they call them, and no ghost of his grade could have stood up for a moment against it.'

'But it is the universal messages, sent out equally in all directions, that are the most serious menace to our state,' another urged.

'Quite so. We have a chance of getting out of the way of the directive ones, but the others leave us no escape.'

'Look – there goes one now,' said another, suddenly pointing; 'luckily it's far enough away.'

There was an indignant clamour.

'Vandals!' 'Huns!' 'Hooligans!' 'Shame!'

Then a female spirit spoke. It was known that she owed her condition to a motor accident on earth.

'I remember a name the grosser ones used to have for those who exceeded the speed limit in their motorcars. They were called road-hogs. In the same way the creators of these disturbances ought to be called ether-hogs.'

There was applause at this, which the young wireless operator, still seeking his pitch, mistook for the general radio-commotion about him.

'Yes,' the female spirit went on (she had always been a little garrul-ous under encouragement), 'I was afflicted with deafness, and in that horrible instrument they call an Insurance Policy I had to pay an extra premium on that account; dear, dear, the number of times my heart jumped into my mouth as their cars whizzed by!'

But at this point two attendant spirits, whose office it was, gently but firmly 'damped' her, that is, merged into her and rarefied her astral coherence; they had heard her story many, many times before. The deliberations continued.

Punitive measures were resolved on. With that the question arose, of whom were they to make an example?

'Take a survey,' said the spirit with the aura of silver beard; and a messenger was gone, and immediately back again, with the tidings that at that very moment a young operator, in an admirably suscept-ible condition of nerves, was seeking to compass a further outrage.

'Good,' said the venerable one, dismissing his minion again. 'We have now to decide who shall haunt him. The Chair invites suggestions.'

Now the selection of a haunter is always a matter for careful thought. Not every ghost can haunt everybody. Indeed, the superior attenuations have often difficulty in manifesting themselves at all, so that in practice a duller spirit becomes their deputy. Thus it is only the less ghostly ghosts we of earth know, those barely yet weaned from the breast of the world, and that is the weakness of haunting from the ghostly point of view. The perfect message must go through the imperfect channel. The great ghosts may plan, but the coarser ones execute.

But as this is not unknown on earth also, we need hardly dwell on it.

Now the Committee had no more redoubtable haunter in certain respects than it had in the spirit of an old Scottish engineer, who had suffered translation in the middle days of steam. True, they had to watch him rather carefully, for he had more than once been suspected of having earthly hankerings and regrets; but that, a demerit in one sense, meant added haunting-efficacy in another, and no less a spirit than Vanderdecken himself had recommended him for a certain class of seafaring commission. He was bidden to appear, and his errand was explained to him.

'You understand,' they said a little severely when all had been made clear. 'Your instructions are definite, remember, and you are not to exceed them.'

'Ay, ay, sir,' said that blunt ghost. 'I kenned sail, and I kenned steam, and I ha' sairved on a cable-ship. Ye canna dae better than leave a' tae me.'

There was the ring, at any rate, of sincere intention in his tone, and they were satisfied.

'Very well,' said the presiding spirit. 'You know where to find him. Be off.'

'Ay, ay, sir – dinna fash yersel' – I'll gi'e the laddie a twisting!'

But at that moment a terrific blast from the Cape Cod Station scattered the meeting as if it had been blown from the muzzle of a gun.

And you are to understand that the foregoing took no time at all, as earthly time is reckoned.

2

'Oh, get out of my way, you fool! I want the ship that called me five minutes ago – the *Bainbridge*. Has she called you? . . . O Lord, here's another lunatic – wants to know who's won the prize fight! Are you the *Bainbridge*? Then buzz off! . . . You there – have you had a call from the *Bainbridge*? Yes, five minutes ago; I think she said she was on fire, but I'm not sure, and I can't get her note again! You try – shove that Merry Christmas fool out – B-a-i-n . . . No, but I think – I say I think – she said so – perhaps she can't transmit any more . . .'

Dot, dash – dot, dash – dot, dash –

Again he was running up and down the gamut, seeking the ship that had given him that flickering uncertain message, and then – silence.

A ship on fire – somewhere –

He was almost certain she had said she was on fire –

And perhaps she could no longer transmit –

Anyway, half a dozen ships were trying for her now.

It was at this moment, when the whole stormy night throbbed with calls for the *Bainbridge*, that the ghost came to make an example of the young wireless operator for the warning of Ethereal Trespassers at large.

Indeed, the ships were making an abominable racket. The Morse tore from the antennae through the void, and if a homeless spectre missed one annihilating wavelength he encountered another. They raged. What was the good of their being the Great Majority if they were to be bullied by a mortal minority with these devastating devices at its command?

Even as that ghostly avenger, in a state of imminent precipitation, hung about the rocking operating-room, he felt himself racked by disintegrating thrills. The young operator's fingers were on the transmitting key again.

'Can't you get the *Bainbridge*? Oh, try, for God's sake . . . Are you there? Nothing come through yet? . . . *Doric*. Can't you couple? . . . '

Lurch, heave; crest, trough; a cant to port, an angle of forty-five degrees to starboard; on the vessel drove, with the antennae high overhead describing those dizzy loops and circles and rendering the night with the sputtering Morse.

Dot, dash – dot, dash – dot, dash –

But already that old ghost, who in his day had known sail and steam and had served on a cable-ship, had hesitated even on the brink of manifestation. He knew that he was only a low-grade ghost, charged rather than trusted with an errand, and their own evident mistrust of him was not a thing greatly to strengthen his allegiance to them. He began to remember his bones and blood, and his past earthly passion for his job. He had been a fine engineer, abreast of all the knowledge of his day, and what he now saw puzzled him exceedingly. By virtue of his instantaneousness and ubiquity, he had already taken a complete conspectus of the ship. Much that he had seen was new, more not. The engines were more powerful, yet essentially the same. In the stokeholds, down the interminable escalades, all was much as it had formerly been. Of electric lighting he had seen more than the beginnings, so that the staring incandescents were no wonder to him, and on the liner's fripperies of painted and gilded saloons and gymnasium and staterooms and swimming baths he had wasted little attention. And yet even in gathering himself for visibility he had hesitated. He tried to tell himself why he did so. He told himself that, formidable haunter as he was, it is no easy matter to haunt a deeply preoccupied man. He told himself that he would be able to haunt him all the more soundly did he hold off for awhile and find the hauntee's weak spot. He told himself that his superiors (a little condescending and sniffy always) had after all left a good deal to his discretion. He told himself that, did he return with his errand unaccomplished, they would at all events be no worse off than they had been before.

In a word, he told himself all the things that we mere mortals tell ourselves when we want to persuade ourselves that our inclinations and our consciences are one and the same thing.

And in the meantime he was peering and prying about a little moving band of wires that passed round two wooden pulleys geared to a sort of clock, with certain coils of wire and a couple of horseshoe magnets, the whole attached to the telephone clasped about the young ether-hog's head. He was tingling to know what the thing was for.

It was, of course, the Detector, the instrument's vital ear.

Then the young man's finger began to tap on the transmitter key again.

'*Doric* . . . Anything yet? . . . You're the *Imperator*? . . . Are you calling the *Bainbridge*?'

Now the ghost, who could not make head or tail of the Detector, nevertheless knew Morse; and though it had not yet occurred to him to squeeze himself in between the operator's ears and the telephone receiver, he read the transmitted message. Also he saw the young man's strained and sweating face. He wanted some ship – the *Bainbridge*; from the corrugations of his brows, a grid in the glare of the incandescent, and the glassy set of his eyes, he wanted her badly; and so apparently did those other ships whose mysterious apparatus harrowed the fields of ether with long and short –

Moreover, on board a ship again that wistful old ghost felt himself at home – or would do so could he but grasp the operation of that tapping key, of that air-wire that barked and oscillated overhead, and of that slowly-moving endless band that passed over the magnets and was attached to the receivers about the young ether-hog's ears.

Whatever they thought of him who had sent him, he *had* been a person of no small account on earth, and a highly skilled mechanic into the bargain.

Suddenly he found himself in temptation's grip. He didn't want to haunt this young man. If he did, something might go wrong with that unknown instrument, and then they might not get this ship they were hunting through the night.

And if he could only ascertain *why* they wanted her so badly, it would be the simplest thing in space for a ghost to find her.

Then, as he nosed about the Detector, it occurred to him to insinuate a portion of his imponderable fabric between the receiver and the young man's ear.

The next moment he had started resiliently back again, as like pole repels like pole of the swinging needle. He was trembling as no radio-message had ever set him trembling yet.

Fire! A ship on fire! –

That was why these friendly young engineers and operators were blowing a lot of silly ghosts to smithereens! –

The *Bainbridge*, on fire! –

What did all the ghosts of the Universe matter if a ship was on fire?

That faithless emissary did not hesitate for an instant. The ghostly Council might cast him out, if they liked; he didn't care; they should be hogged till Domesday if, on all the seas of the world, a single ship was on fire! A ship on fire? He had once seen a ship on fire, and didn't want, even as a ghost, to see another.

Even while you have been reading this he was off to find the *Bainbridge*.

Of course he hadn't really to go anywhere to find her at all. Low-class and ill-conditioned ghost as he was, he still had that property of ubiquity. An instantaneous double change in his own tension and he was there and back again, with the *Bainbridge's* bearings, her course, and the knowledge that it was still not too late. The operator was listening in an agony into the twin receivers; a thrill of thankfulness passed through the ghost that he had not forgotten the Morse he had learned on the cable-ship. Swiftly he precipitated himself into a point of action on the transmitter key.

Long, short – long, short – long, short –

The operator heard. He started up as if he had been hogged himself. His eyes were staring, his mouth horridly open. What was the matter with his instrument?

Long, short – long, short – long, short –

It was not in the telephone. The young man's eyes fell on his own transmitter key. It was clicking up and down. He read out 'Bainbridge', and a bearing, and of course his instrument was spelling it out to the others.

Feverishly he grabbed the telephone.

Already the *Doric* was acknowledging. So was the *Imperator*.

He had sent no message –

Yet, though it made him a little sick to think of it, he would let it stand. If one ship was fooled, all would be fooled. At any rate he did not think he had dreamed that *first* call, that first horrifying call of 'Bainbridge – fire!'

He sprang to the tube and called up the bridge.

They picked them up from the *Bainbridge's* boats towards the middle of Christmas morning; but that unrepentant, old seafaring spectre, returning whence he had come, gave little satisfaction to his superiors. Against all their bullying he was proof; he merely repeated doggedly over and over again, 'The laddie's nairves o' steel! Ower and ower again I manifested mysel' tae him, but it made na mair impression on him than if I'd tried to ha'nt Saturn oot o' his Rings! It's my opeenion that being a ghaistie isna what it was. They hae ower mony new-fangled improvements in these days.'

But his spectral heart was secretly sad because he had not been able to make head or tail of the Detector.

I

'Oh, Egbert,' the White Lady implored, 'let me beg of you to abandon this mad, wicked idea!' Sir Egbert the Dauntless was in the act of passing himself through the wainscot of the North Gallery; he turned, half on this side of the panel, half already in the Priest's Hole in the thickness of the wall.

'No, Rowena,' he replied firmly. 'You saw fit to cast doubts upon my courage before all the Family Ancestors, and now I intend to do it. If anything happens to me my essence will be upon your head.'

The Lady Rowena wailed. In her agitation she clasped her hands awry, so that they interpenetrated.

'Nay, Egbert, I did but jest! On earth you were known as the Dauntless; our descendants are proud of you; cannot you forget my foolish words?'

'No,' replied Sir Egbert, sternly. 'Though it cost me my Non-existence I will spend the night in a Human Chamber!'

'Egbert – Egbert – stay – not *that* one – *not* the Parson's! Think – should he exorcise you! – '

'Too late; I have spoken!' said Sir Egbert, with an abrupt wave of his hand. He vanished into the Fifth Dimension. No sooner had he done so than the general lamentation broke out.

'Oh, he'll Be, he'll Be, I *know* he'll Be!' the White Lady sobbed.

To be re-confined in Matter, so that there is no speech save with a tongue and no motion save with limbs – to be once more subject to the Three Dimensions of the grosser life – is the final menace to the spectral Condition.

'Poor chap – I fancied I detected a trace of Visibility about him already,' grim Sir Hugo muttered.

'Oh, it's playing with Flesh!' another cried, with a shiver.

'Almost Human folly!'

'Already his glide isn't what it was,' said the melancholy Lady Annice, who on Earth had been a famous attender at funerals.

'I shall never behold his dear Aura again,' moaned the White Lady, already half opaque herself. 'It will be the Existence of me!'

'If only it had not been a Parson's Chamber,' said the Lady Annice, with mournful relish.

'Here – catch her quick – she's solidifying!' half a dozen of them cried at once.

It was with difficulty that they brought the White Lady even to a state of semi-evaporation again.

2

It was midnight, and the Parson snored. He turned uneasily in his sleep. Perhaps already he was conscious of Sir Egbert's presence.

Sir Egbert himself dared approach no nearer to the Mortal Bed than the lattice. Fear had given him the pink gossamer look that is the perilous symptom of veins and blood, and he knew that he received faintly the criss-crossed shadow of the lattice. To save his Nonentity he could not have glided up the shaft of moonlight that streamed in at the window.

Suddenly a violent Hertzian Wave passed through Sir Egbert's ether. He jumped almost clear out of his Dimension. The Parson had opened his eyes. To Be or not to Be? Had he seen him?

He had. His horrible embodied eyes were on the poor harmless Spectre. The two looked at one another, the one quailing in the moonlight, the other sitting in all the horror of Solidity bolt upright in bed.

Then the Mortal began to practise his fearsome devices.

First he gave the hoarse cry that all ghosts dread, and Sir Egbert felt himself suddenly heavier by a pound. But he remembered his name – the Dauntless. He would not yield.

Then the Parson's teeth began to chatter. He gibbered, and Sir Egbert wondered whether this was the beginning of the Exorcism. If it was, he would never see the happy old Ancestral Gallery again, never hold his dear Rowena in perfect interpermeation again – never pass himself through a Solid again – never know again the jolly old lark of being nowhere and everywhere at once.

'Mercy, Mercy!' he tried to cry; and indeed his voice all but stirred the palpable air.

But there was no mercy in that grisly Parson. His only reply was to shoot the hair up on his head, straight on end.

Then he protruded his eyes.

Then he grinned.

And then he began to talk as it were the deaf and dumb alphabet on his fingers.

Sir Egbert's semi-Substance was like reddish ground glass; it was the beginning of the agony. How near to the Mortal Precipitation he was he knew when suddenly he found himself thinking, almost with fright, of his own dear White Lady. *She was a Ghost.*

Then the Mortal began to gabble words. It was the Exorcism.

Oh, why – why – why had Sir Egbert not chosen a Layman?

The gabbling continued. Colour – warmth – weight – these settled down on Sir Egbert the Dauntless. He half Was. And as he continued steadily to Become, the words increased in speed. Sir Egbert's feet felt the floor; he cried; a faint windy moan came. The Parson bounded a foot up on the bed and tossed his pillow into the air.

Could nothing save Sir Egbert?

Ah, yes. They that lead a meek and blameless Non-existence shall not be cast down; they shall not be given over at last to the terrors of the Solid and Known. From somewhere outside in the moonlight there came a shrill sound.

It was the crowing of a Cock.

The Parson had had the pillow over his face. It fell, and he looked again.

Nothing was there.

Sir Egbert, back in his comfortable Fourth Dimension, was of the loved indivisible texture of his dear White Lady again.

The Master of the House

I

The draft agreement, as old Mr Wetherby explained it, contained one clause that nine people out of ten would have hesitated to accept. The owner of the property was to remain on undisturbed, he, his manservant and his Alsatian dog. Andy Peckover did in fact demur. He was the eldest of the three brothers, the Sikh, and whatever place they took would be in his name.

'Why the dog?' he asked. 'Why not the cat and the canary? Do you often put dogs in your agreements?'

'My dear Andy,' Mr Wetherby replied, who had been their father's solicitor before them, 'in the Law we learn to be surprised at nothing. Up there' – and he indicated the japanned boxes that resembled black marble slabs with white epitaphs – 'there are much odder things than that.'

'But we don't want a lodger hanging about. Place wouldn't be our own.'

'He has his own quarters in a wing part. He undertakes that as far as possible you shall – let me see – yes, here it is – you shall be unaware of his presence.' And he put the draft into Andy's hand that he might see for himself.

Andy's thick brows were bent over the paper. – 'Why is it in those words – I mean "unaware of his presence"?'

'His way of putting it, I suppose.'

'Who is he?'

'Except that he is a Mr Laban, and that he lives a very retired life, I know nothing about him. He writes through his solicitors. If he has an establishment he can no longer afford to maintain – ' Mr Wetherby spread his hands.

Andy pushed the paper away and stretched himself. After weeks of hanging about London he wanted exercise. – 'Better call it off, I think,' he said.

At that a girl's voice gave a deep resigned sigh. She was Eve, the youngest of them all.

'So now we start all over again! Oh, how sick I am of the words, "Please Admit Bearer to View" and "This Portion to be Left at the Residence"!'

'We only want it for a year,' said Davy. He came next in age to herself, and, like Andrew, was a soldier.

'Ten months – two have gone. We shall never all have leave together again like this. And this lovely English spring – oh, that apple-orchard and the forget-me-nots!' Eve sighed.

'For goodness' sake let's settle something – '

'Think of some of the places we've seen – '

'If we're going to wait for Andrew to make up his mind – '

And after all they had come home to an England nettle-rashed with contractors' bungalows on the one hand and melancholy with huge shuttered mansions on the other, to be had rent-free by any-body who would pay the wages of a minimum number of servants. Every place they had 'viewed' had been either too vast to be thought of or too small to be of use. But here was a modest property of eight or ten acres, standing high on heathy land, at a rental within their means, and the references all ready to take up. Andy got up with a mighty stretch of his spare frame.

'Well, there seems rather a lot of Alsatian dog and invisibility about it,' he capitulated, 'but Eve'll have the place to run, so if she's satisfied – want me to sign anything?'

'Not now. I'll have the agreement prepared and sent round to you in a few days,' Mr Wetherby replied.

And sent round it was, and Andy signed it, condition and all.

During their weeks of house-hunting trains had served their turn, with an omnibus or a station taxi at the other end; but if they were going into the heart of the country, that is to say four miles from a village, they must have means of their own of getting about. The tall Sikh Major walked into a motor showroom one day and asked the price of a car in the window. They told him, and he produced his cheque-book and fountain-pen. He was then asked the very latest date at which he could accept delivery.

'I want to take it away with me,' said Andy.

Wondering where this tall man in the loose grey clothes had been spending his time, the salesman smiled. – 'I'm afraid we have to take our orders in rotation, sir. Of course we always do our utmost to expedite.'

'I can give you till Friday.'

The salesman said something about two months. – 'And when you let us have the pleasure of giving you a trial run, sir – '

But he found himself talking to the air. Andy had put his fountain-pen back into his pocket and had walked out of the shop.

He thought he had seen in Great Portland Street the sort of place he wanted. It was a place where cars not strictly new were sold. He walked there, and, entering the shop, stood looking at a small blue-bodied 8 h.p. Fiat. A youth with a cigarette between his lips strolled up to him.

'Is that car for sale?' Andy asked.

'I should say so.'

'Do you want to sell it?'

The youth looked up as if he was about to say No, he'd rather take it home to keep rabbits in, but apparently thought better of it. – 'Of course I want to sell it,' he said.

'Then take that cigarette out of your mouth and show it to me.'

Both these things were done. After a number of questions Andy asked the price.

'That depends on how many payments, sir.'

'One payment. Now.'

At this unprecedented way of buying a car the youth had to consult a superior. The price was £160. Out came Andy's fountain-pen again.

'Fill it up with petrol, and have it running at the door at four o'clock. Facing south,' he added.

This was the car in which, on a sunny day in May, accompanied by Eve and a first instalment of personal belongings, Major Peck-over drove to the house that had been rented for the remainder of the year.

It stood within a screen of Surrey pines, through which glimpses could be had of the wide-spreading vale below. A quarter of a mile of sandy lane led to it, losing itself in a heathy common, and the drive wound in such a way that the house did not actually appear till one was upon it. Then one saw that it was really approached from the back. The place was being thoroughly aired. The door under the white-pillared Victorian porch stood wide open; so did the series of doors within; and the eye travelled as it were through a shining interior tunnel, along the staircased hall, through a far drawing-room, and out to the gardens beyond, which were the house's real front. On the left a spacious flagged yard with stables was crossed by a high wall with a closed door in it. Where the path passed round to the right three ground-floor bow-windows resembled stucco crinolines, the wearers of which were apparently leaning in at the windows above.

The Peckovers were not taking up residence for some days yet, but it looked as if somebody was already moving out. By the porch stood a wheel-barrow, with a corded tin trunk on it. Andy glanced at this, and then called to a figure that appeared from behind the stairs.

'Are you Mr Laban's man?'

But the man called to somebody unseen, 'They're here, Jane,' and came forward. He took the shafts of the barrow and trundled the load away. A moment later a woman appeared, with a black veil pushed up under her black bonnet and black kid gloves on her hands. She carried a bunch of iron keys.

'I'll show you which is which, miss, on account of some of the labels being a bit rubbed,' she said. 'Then it will be time for me to be getting along.'

'But,' Eve exclaimed, taken aback, 'you were to stay till we came, and then to get me daily help till I could get proper maids from the Registry Office!'

'And so I have, miss, the best I could, though Mrs Hodgson and her girl aren't quite what I could have wished. And begging your pardon, miss, it was understood by *me* for today, and here you are – '

'Yes, but not to stay – '

The housekeeper considered. She was a person who would rather do a little more than her duty than fall short of it, and there was a later train.

'Well, seeing Mrs Hodgson hasn't come yet, and it's a misunderstanding, perhaps I'd better tell him,' she said, and hastened after the man with the barrow. Andy lifted packages from the Fiat. The housekeeper returned, and the two women entered the house together.

Immediately Eve forgot the little domestic hitch. After parched India, this vernal freshness! There was hardly a window in the place that did not look out on some near or distant prospect of English beauty. The apple-blossom was more fully out, less ruddy than when she had last seen it, but the lovers' colour of the forget-me-nots was the same, and beauty had marched on beauty as the bright regiments of the spring had succeeded one another. In front of the crinolined windows white broom broke into cloudlets, as if a child had exploded a paper bag of petals, and over it the laburnum showered its gold. The hawthorn was opening its clenched buds, the lilac was already tipped with purple-black. The sky was of baby-ribbon blue; and if the grass of the tennis-court was ankle-deep, had she not three able-bodied brothers to set to work with scythe and cutter? After the baked compounds with their marigolds and hibiscus, this!

'And I understand that's where the maids will sleep,' the house-keeper said, pointing to outbuildings that were prolonged into the garden. 'Mr Laban and his man has what I'm told used to be their quarters.'

'You're told?' Eve asked. 'Then you haven't been here very long?'

'Only since February, miss. I did all myself, a room at a time. A little a day makes a lot in the end when you aren't interfered with.'

'Then this is the first time Mr Laban's let his house?'

'There's many that's glad to have a smaller roof over their heads these days, though changes come hard when you're on in years like him.'

'What kind of a man is Mr Laban?'

The housekeeper's black-gloved fingers were at her lips.

'Well,' she deliberated, 'it isn't a deal I've seen of him. Nor his man. If it wasn't for the dog you'd hardly know there was a soul in the place. The man does the buying, not that that's a deal either. He never gave me a hand even with the carpets. But I'm not one that can't bear their own company. I'm a bookish woman. Give me a good Mrs Henry Wood and the time flies . . . Now *this* is the room I should pick for myself if I was you, miss – '

If she meant the view from the window she was to be congrat-ulated on her taste. It was the most inspiring outlook of all. There was a gap in the pines. The stages by which the land fell away were hidden, and neither Crome nor Cox ever painted a horizon so bluely stretching away as that that was revealed. The few yards between the trees framed fifty miles of arable and pasture and villages that ended in '-shott'. A gatepost hid three-quarters of a distant wood, its fellow a couple of farms. And as far away as could be seen a train crept from the south, trailing its tiny cater-pillar of smoke.

'You'd call that a picture, wouldn't you, miss?' the housekeeper was saying. 'So why windows should be blocked up, with a bit of scenery like that to look at . . . hark, that'll be Mrs Hodgson. Would you like to see her now, miss?'

A glance at Mrs Hodgson and Eve's mind was made up. She was quite unemployable, her fifteen-years-old daughter to all appear-ances a halfwit. Whenever the child was spoken to she went through a sort of callisthenic exercise, which was to dip her black-stockinged knees, at the same time raising her finger-tips to her shoulders. Eve sought her brother.

'How long shall you be?' she asked, 'I've got to call in Willowmere –

unless you wish to clean all those boots yourself, that is.' And she explained the domestic situation.

'Just ready.'

'And do drive slowly through these lovely lanes – '

Twenty minutes later Andy was slackening speed under the meeting boughs and pausing at the gates of buttercup fields. Willowmere, with its high pavement and white-penned market-place, delighted Eve hardly less, and it was quite unlike India that at the little Registry Office with its two rounded windows they also sold bacon and peppermint and cards of darning-wool.

'How many servants will be required, miss?' Mrs Hickman asked.

'Three, and I want them immediately, please.'

Mrs Hickman looked at this urgent young woman, who must have her maids three at a time and immediately. She saw a blunt-featured, capable young face, with eyes that were clear because they had nothing to conceal, and cropped boyish hair under the sort of flat hat that goes with a hunting-stock.

'How many in family did you say, miss?'

'My three brothers and myself. Mr Laban has his own man.'

'Is *that* the house! – It's a longish way out.'

'There's the motor-bus.'

'They like to be handy for the pictures of an evening. Who might I ask have you been having?'

'As we don't come in till next Friday I've not had anybody. There was some misunderstanding about dates, and the regular house-keeper has left.'

'Ah, that'd be that Portsmouth woman. She wasn't engaged through me. And different people has different ideas, but I shouldn't fancy moving house on a Friday myself – '

With which words and a shrug, Mrs Hickman promised to do her best.

2

Not Andy, but Mickie, the brother in the Political, drove Eve down on the following Friday. Mickie, though three years younger than his elder brother, looked older, partly by reason of a scar that ran down the length of one cheek, but more because of responsibilities shared with few, and experiences it was best to be silent about. Mickie too had the quick light Peckover eyes, and as the car drew up at the front door that was at the back they shot a glance in the direction of an exceedingly tall man in black, who hurried across the yard with a large clay-coloured dog dragging by a thong behind him. The door in the high wall closed after them.

'What *are* you doing, Mickie?' Eve exclaimed; for Mickie had thrown a leg over the side of the car and had taken a light run across the yard. He was trying the door that had just closed.

'Why did you do that?' Eve asked again, when he returned.

'What? Run after that fellow? Thought he might give me a hand with these things. Never mind.'

And after all there was nothing that he and his sister couldn't carry between them.

The house was ready for occupation. In the little smoking-room the glasses of the Landseers were brightly polished, in the dining-room to the left of the porch the large duplex oil-lamp was filled, and stood on the mahogany table. Across the hall, in the men's hat-and-coat lobby, clean towels hung, and in the morning-room bluebells stood on a piano as yellow as a tortoise-shell cat. Mickie carried Eve's dress-baskets up to the room the former housekeeper had so strongly recommended. It was a large two-windowed room, with a paper of faded vertical stripes that gave to the hand like a drum by reason of its many superimpositions. Two steel-engravings of Rome hung from nails with china heads. The mantelpiece was of white marble, and there were watch-pockets over the pillows of the large mahogany bed. Eve advanced to the window. Beautiful, beautiful view! She would have that to look at, throughout a whole changing summer! She opened the window wide, breathing in the air, while the sash-weights knocked in their cases and the lace curtains floated inwards. A jolly, great-grandfatherly sort of house, with its old bell-fittings and curly-backed sofas! Who minded oil-lamps for an hour of a summer's evening, when the birds sang half the night and moths and beetles flew in at the open windows?

It was as she turned away from the view that she noticed something she had not noticed before. It was as faint as the plate-marks on the steel-engravings of Rome, and for that matter was a little like them. It was to the right of the fireplace, and the shadow from the window and the vertical stripes of the paper combined to conceal it. The papering of the walls had been continued over the surface of a communicating door.

Eve paused, and then put out her hand. At any rate the papering was not recent, for it was as parchment with old layers as the rest. It was in fact not the door at all that caused her suddenly to wonder. It was something she had heard – something the housekeeper had said –

All at once she had it. 'You'd call that a picture, wouldn't you now? So why windows should be blocked up, with a bit of scenery like that to look at – ' the housekeeper had said.

What window had been blocked up? She had been repeatedly round the house, and had found no blocked window.

She went downstairs and walked out into the garden. It was true, though anybody might have looked a score of times and never have noticed it. If the housekeeper had not had it to clean she might not have noticed it either. There were four windows overlooking the garden in which she stood, the two of her own room, another to the left, and a fourth, to the extreme right. It was on this that her eyes were fixed. At a glance it was precisely like the others. It had lace curtains, a little dingy perhaps, and a short roller-blind. But there *was* a difference. Eve found herself looking up into a lidded eye. It was bricked or boarded up behind.

Well, there was nothing in that. Eve seemed to remember something from her school days about Mr Gladstone and a window-tax. They had left the curtains up to preserve the look of the place. The shut-off portion of the house was a mere prolongation, and it would have other windows. It was merely odd that the one chosen for obliteration should have been the one with the glorious view.

In the hall Mrs Hodgson was busy with a broom, sweeping up packing-litter. Eve, returning to the house, stopped to speak to her. Give Mrs Hodgson's tongue a chance and it was sometimes difficult to stop. It ran on now, about the motor-bus she and her daughter had to take mornings and evenings, making a long hard day of it, and how poorly Alice had been on her feet since her last bad go, though the doctor said she would grow out of it; and much more.

'So it will have to be backwards and forwards till you're suited, miss, which I'm sure the panel must be sick of the child's face by this time, well one day and bad again the next – mercy, if she isn't at it again!'

Indeed the girl who could give that scream, instantly muffled, was a fit candidate for a doctor. In any setting it would have been discordant; in that pleasant hall, full of homely litter and flowery light, it was doubly harsh.

'What's the matter?' Eve exclaimed.

Mrs Hodgson seemed to make little of something in which none the less she took a secret pride.

'It's being in a strange place, miss. That's nothing to some I've heard her out with. You've got to see she doesn't bite her tongue;

many's the bit of firewood I've stuck in or anything else I could lay hand on. Then I go on with my work and take no notice.'

'You take no notice! Come at once!'

The child had not bitten her tongue. They merely found her in the kitchen, with her back to the window, and a straw marketing-bag pressed to her eyes. These, when the bag was taken away, proved to be lustreless but dry, and she could not or would not give any reason for the scream.

'It's no good asking her. You get used to it,' said the mother, as one who knew.

But Eve hoped that the Registry would soon send proper maids rather than that she should have to get used to sounds so startling.

Andy and Davy came down that afternoon, and the four walked round the gardens, considering the work to be done.

There was occupation enough. Presumably Mr Laban had not let his house to strangers until the force of circumstances had compelled him, and while his housekeeper had made something of the interior, the outside had evidently been too much for his man. The flower-beds were neglected, the grass of the tennis-court ankle-deep. Weeding was to be done, hedges were to trim, mountains of rubbish to burn. Eve wanted the masses of jasmine cut away that darkened the dining-room window, blown-down pine-cones here, everywhere to be gathered up. Half the glass of the cold frames was broken, and what was growing inside them she did not know.

'Bags I the tennis-court,' said Davy. 'I wonder if that fellow's anywhere about?'

'What fellow?'

'Uncle Laban's man. I want to know where I can borrow a scythe.'

'He isn't our man,' Andy reminded him.

'I know that, but surely he can tell us where to borrow a scythe. And I haven't seen any gardening tools yet.'

'That's all right. They're in one of the sheds.'

'What I mean is, surely *somebody'll* show us round. They can't simply chuck a place at us and leave us to it.'

'Come, we've hardly been in ten minutes.'

And Davy, who always looked out for the next job before he had started the one in hand, departed to the kitchen-garden to make a bonfire there and then.

Indeed, if Mr Laban's man might reasonably have been expected to spare the newcomers half an hour, Mr Laban himself might equally have been expected at least to give them a greeting. But they saw nothing of him that day, nor on the day that followed, nor on the day after that. A week passed, and except for themselves there was no sign of a living soul in the place. And only once during that week did any approach the dwelling from the outside world. This was when a tradesman's van crunched along the drive and drew up before the closed door in the wall. Mickie happened to be doing something to the car in the yard. It was he who saw the door open and the goods delivered. Then the door closed again, and silence and invisibility descended once more.

The Peckovers were a singularly united family. Separately, Eve had spent months on end with each of her brothers, keeping house for them at their various stations; and now that by something like a miracle all three of them had got leave together she had looked forward to a summer of unalloyed delight. Later, she was inclined to date the first cloud from that evening when she and Davy went seriously into the matter of the tennis-court.

With its surrounding netting it would cost at least twenty pounds to set up, and the question was whether after all it was worth it. Davy, looking like a Fred Walker picture as he leaned in his shirt and breeches on the scythe he had borrowed from the farm along the lane, weighed the pros and cons.

'Cost a fortune in balls if we don't have netting,' he mused, 'and on the other hand, Evelet, here we are, three well-set-up young men, not to mention yourself, ornaments to any neighbourhood, and there must be a dozen houses with courts round about. Suppose some of the local denizens will be calling on us.'

'We shall have to have the Trevelyans here for one thing, and they'll have to be amused.'

'Wonder if old fish-netting would come cheaper,' Davy meditated. 'I found a lot of larch-poles that would do for posts. I say, if you're going in you might get the catalogue – it's in the smoke-room – ' he called after her as she turned to the house.

The smoke-room was the bow-windowed room with the Landseers, next to the lobby. Its door stood partly open, and as she approached it she heard her brother Michael's voice, apparently concluding some recital.

' – depend on this, that at the very first sign of anything I'll have a few of my people down in two shakes of a lamb's tail.'

'That's always supposing he's your man,' came Andrew's voice.

'I'm not mistaken. He's my friend of the temple. And I'm not the man to take such a thing seriously unless – ' he broke off abruptly as Eve entered.

There was a moment of dead embarrassed silence. Andy broke in.

'Want something, Eve?'

'Yes. Gamage's catalogue.'

'David had it last.'

'He says he left it in here. What's this about a temple?'

'A temple? What about a temple?'

'Mickie was saying something about a temple, and having somebody here in two shakes of a lamb's tail.'

'Quite mistaken, my dear. We were talking about polo.'

'And you said you took something seriously – '

'Of course. Polo has to be taken seriously. What's Davy doing?'

'He's over by the tennis-court. And at least he isn't saying things and then saying he didn't say them,' Eve returned as she passed out of the door.

3

She didn't like being treated as if she was a child. Leaving the house, she did not rejoin Davy on the tennis-court. She sought the orchard instead. It was an evening of purest beauty, with a sky full of amethyst light and the apple-petals fallen among the forget-me-nots like faint kissing lips, but she had no eyes for the evening. She was cross. Why had they put her off like that? Hadn't she ears? They *had* been talking about a temple, having somebody down, and taking something seriously. And it wasn't the first time Mickie had behaved like that. Why had he slid out of the car and stolen across the yard after that man that day? Why was that window blocked up? Why had that child screamed like that? And why, except that apparently a cart came once a week with provisions, did never a sound come from the other portion of the house? Oh, she knew that every one of these questions could be answered. Who took any notice of what a halfwit child did? If people got on very well with a window closed why spend money on opening it again? What more convenient than to place a standing order with tradespeople when the village was four miles away? And wasn't it natural, seeing a man crossing a yard, to ask him to bear a hand with a trunk?

But these were *not* answers. Mickie and Andy had *not* been talking about polo. And Mickie *had* run to that door as if he wished to see somebody while remaining unobserved himself. And as for the window, it almost looked as if it had been sealed, not to shut a beautiful view out, but to shut something in.

Supper that even – cold supper, for Mrs Hodgson and her daughter had departed, and they had to wait upon themselves and one another – was a scrambling sort of meal. It was not worth changing clothes for, and except that Davy put a collar on they did not change. The trifling family jests were mostly Davy's, and became even more so as the meal went on. If Mickie and Andy were hiding something from her it looked as if they were hiding it from Davy too. She glanced at Mickie past the duplex lamp. More than ever did he seem Andy's senior, more haunted with responsibility, with deeper histories in his eyes. She had only the very vaguest notion of where he had got that scar: it had almost healed when she had first seen it. And she wished he wouldn't wear what she called that going-away look – the kind of look people have who hope their friends will remember them, but must put up with it if they do not.

'I say, Eve,' said Davy, cheerfully rising to change plates, 'when you do get maids get some we can look at. When I see old Mother What's-her-Name I nearly choke with virtue.'

'I'm doing my best,' said Eve, who was beginning to dislike the very look of food that Mrs Hodgson had touched. 'She has to bring the child, because she can't leave her alone in the house.'

She wished, however, that she had not mentioned the child. The child reminded her of only one thing – that sudden scream. And now for the first time the scream made her conscious of something else, namely that in an hour or two, candle in hand, she would have to make her way to a room in one corner of which was a papered-over door, and beyond that a window that showed lace curtains and roller-blinds to the world but allowed the world to see nothing in return.

Suddenly Andy spoke. – 'When do the Trevelyans want you to go and stay with them, Eve?'

Eve was still a little hurt. – 'They haven't asked me,' she replied.

'You don't wait for the Trevelyans to ask you, do you?'

'Of course I could get myself asked, but till we get servants – '

'Of course. Nobody says go tomorrow. But we can look after ourselves, and they'll expect you before long.'

'Anybody'd think you were trying to get me out of the house,' said Eve with a nervous laugh; and it was so obviously the truth that a silence fell.

After supper they walked in the garden; that is to say Eve walked in the garden, while Andy and Davy cleared away. In the circular space of a flagged Dutch walk was a sundial, but now the day was in ashes overhead, and its gnomon slept. It was by the sundial that she came upon Mickie. He seemed lost in thought. He looked up.

'Hallo, Eve. Didn't hear you coming.'

She spoke without preface. – 'Mickie, what's the matter?'

'Matter? What matter?'

'I want to talk to you, and not to be shut up.'

'Dear, I'm not shutting you up.'

'You are. And first of all I want to know why you followed that man across the yard that day.'

Mickie's finger was rubbing the edge of the gnomon, tracing patterns on the dial. – 'Do you mean the day you and I came down together?' he asked.

'Yes. You were out of the car without even opening the door, and followed him across the yard.'

'My legs are long enough.'

'Then the way you were talking in the smoke-room when I came in.'

'Fellow was half choking that dog,' said Mickie reflectively.

'What have you and Andy got between you?'

Mickie passed his arm about her. But he didn't tell her what she wanted to know.

'Got between us? Well, we've got a sister for one thing. And I say, you're cold. Baths in this house aren't any too hot, and this is only spring. What about a tune on that marmalade piano?'

'Mickie, *must* you shut me out like this?' she pleaded.

'Shut you out? Look here, this house-hunting's been too much for you. Why don't you do as Andy says and go to the Trevelyans for a week or two?'

'You *do* want to get me out!' broke from Eve. 'But I'm not going, and if it's anything to do with this house I shouldn't dream of going!'

'This house? Why this house?' Mickie asked quickly.

'I *won't* be treated like a child!' she said passionately as she broke away. 'If you keep things to yourself so shall I!'

Yet what after all had she to tell?

Little as it was, she wished later that she had told him there and then, for, to anticipate matters by a few hours, her sleep that night was not without incident. The candles were kept in a row on the table at the foot of the stairs. Eve took hers and ascended to her room. With a taper she lighted her lamp, glancing once at the plate-mark to the right of the mantelpiece and then resolutely resisting the temptation to look again. She undressed, put out her light, and got into bed. She had hardly expected to go to sleep at once, but she did so, easily and immediately. Outside the moon rode high. Because of its height it shone only a little way into the room, and even then the rays that entered the two windows were further dimmed by the lace curtains. So Eve's eyes, when sometime or other during the night she suddenly opened them, were unsure of themselves. A bright light makes the immediate shadow obscurer, but an intercepted one veils all in a dim clarity. It was into this dim clarity, a little below her bed-foot, that her eyes were bent.

Even as she looked she could hardly have sworn to it. Her door was closed, but there seemed to have announced himself from somewhere, entered from somewhere, somebody she had certainly never seen before. As if a process had been dispensed with, she felt that she could equally have been with her lids closed. He was a shrunken old man, who seemed almost too weak to bear the weight of his shabby old brown dressing-gown. His short white beard was thin and ragged, and his white hair fell about his face. And there was that of unutterable appeal about him, a cry, not to judgment, but to the unquestioning mercy that is in us all, that made Eve wellnigh throw out her arms in pity. 'I don't know what it is you need, you poor old thing!' she wanted to cry. 'Tell me what it is! Tell me what we can do! It isn't right they should use you so! Tell me what they have been doing to you! Tell me how you can be helped!' But she lay there, still and gazing, not uttering a word. And as she gazed something happened. Deeply muffled, but from somewhere quite close at hand, there came the low warning 'Woof!' of a dog. He at whom Eve looked seemed to hear it too. The piteous eyes were turned in a last imploring look. Then, just as she had turned down her lamp on going to bed, all grew dim. Just as she had puffed across the lamp chimney, all went out. And there was the dim lacy moonlight on the floor again.

But what Michael George Peckover, of the Indian Political Service, still standing by the sundial, was deeply wondering, was how in the Name of Darkness that fellow Binian came to be here.

4

'Andy, I'm writing a note,' said Eve in the morning-room the next day, after breakfast.

'Post it in town for you if you like,' Andy replied. 'Did I tell you Mickie and I were going up for the day? Davy'll drive us to the station.'

'I don't want it posted. I shall send it by hand. I'm asking Mr Laban to have dinner with us.'

'Hm! That's an idea,' Andy remarked. 'One rather gathered he wished to be left alone though.'

'No. I think that that's simply his sensitiveness. He thought it was what *we* should prefer. Here's a poor old man, driven to let his house to strangers – '

'You seem to know a good deal about him! Who's going to wait on him? Us? Mrs Hodgson?'

Eve had got up that morning with something glowing and exalted in her heart, that took no account of anything but itself. She had actually been on the point of writing her letter, forgetful that that would be to ask a guest to a servantless house.

'Of course. I'd forgotten.'

'No particular hurry. Leave it for a few days,' said Andy. 'Mrs Hodgson – hang it all – '

'Then perhaps I'd better come into Willowmere with you and have another try,' Eve sighed, her dream of the night before as if it had never been.

But who knows by what slender accidents fortune may bring her good to pass? Eve had not known her brothers were going to London that day. She might well not have accompanied them as far as Willowmere. But the fortune was this, nothing less – that entering Mrs Hickman's Registry Office, she saw two fresh and buxom young women already there, whose frank and friendly eyes were turned on hers for a moment and then away again.

'Yes, I've had an enquiry from Lady Onslow – ' Mrs Hickman was saying, when Eve stepped forward.

'Can either of you cook?' she asked.

One girl whispered to the other, who spoke.

'Yes, 'm.'

'Are you looking for a place?'

'Yes, 'm. Both of us.'

'When are you free?'

'We consider ourselves free now, miss, but we should like a few days.'

'I have a car outside. Would you care to come and look at the place now, to see whether you would like it?'

There was a further exchange of whispering. It ended in a 'Yes, 'm.'

'But – ' Mrs Hickman's outraged voice broke in, and Eve turned.

'You put my name down in your books and promised I should come first,' she said. 'Here I find you sending maids somewhere else. Come along, you two.'

'And mind you, you might want maids after this!' Mrs Hickman called after her as she left the shop. 'Then perhaps you'll come to me again!'

So Eve bore off her prizes in triumph, and found that they were ready to take up service in a week.

They came, in fact, within the week. They were twins, and where one went the other went. They were especially delighted at the thought of their own separate quarters. It would be a pleasure to the eye to see them about the place. Davy at least was of this opinion. In fact, by one prompt stroke, Eve's troubles were diminished by half. Dinner to Mr Laban or to anybody else would now be no trouble at all. Blithely she paid Mrs Hodgson and the callisthenic daughter off. She didn't a bit mind bearing a hand herself. She counted Rose and Laura among her friends.

She did not tell her brothers her real reason for wishing to have Mr Laban to dinner. Strong as her inner conviction was, she had still no certainty. Curiously enough, however, both Mickie and Andy fell in with her idea quite remarkably readily. They gave various reasons. The old gentleman was no doubt longing to be asked, they said. Since he could not make the first advance it was their duty to make it for him. The position would soon become laughable. Let the new maids find their feet and have him by all means . . . It was glorious May weather; never had English skies better behaved themselves. The air was nutty with the smell of hawthorn, the cuckoo called, the birds sang. Davy too sang as he scythed, not the tennis-court, which he had characteristically left half-finished, but a rough patch behind the orchard:

> Two men went to mow,
>> Went to mow a meadow,
> Two men, one man and his dog
>> Went to mow a meadow.

Andy was busy with the Fiat. Mickie appeared to have a good many letters to write and papers to consult. Eve was occupied with seedsmen's catalogues and her maids.

Then one evening she sat down and wrote her note.

Thereupon a curious little question rose. How was it going to be delivered?

THE MASTER OF THE HOUSE

'It seems a bit stiff just to put it in the post,' said Eve. 'But all that part is locked up, and what are we to do?'

'He must get letters. He got Wetherby's.'

'Wetherby wrote through his solicitors.'

'Then he must get his solicitor's.'

'Give it to me. I'll see it's delivered,' Mickie said suddenly.

None the less it was three days before a reply came. Shortly before midday one of the old pothook bells in the kitchen clanged. Laura glanced up at the wagging pendulum, threw off her apron, and hurried along the hall. Instantly a large clay-coloured dog sought the shelter of the house. 'That object beats that dog,' Laura said to her sister afterwards.

The 'object' who had jerked the dog back was as tall as a flagstaff and thin as a hayrake – six feet six inches in height and hardly broad enough to cast a shadow. He had a muddy complexion, and eyes so deeply buried that they resembled half-healed wounds in dough. His black clothes hung scarecrow-wise from his shoulder-arch, and in the middle of a padded tie that crept up his choker collar a dull red stone lurked. Without a word he handed in a note.

'Is there an answer?' Laura asked.

'It is an answer,' he said huskily.

The next moment he was hauling the reluctant dog across the yard again.

The terms of Mr Laban's note gave rise to a certain amount of discussion. The letter was passed from hand to hand.

'At any rate he accepts,' said Eve.

'But does he?' Andy rejoined. 'He seems to leave it open. "My health permitting – if I am well enough on the day," he says.'

'He's very old,' Eve pleaded. 'The housekeeper told me he was very old,' she added as an afterthought.

'Let's look at it again.' And Andy read:

DEAR MISS PECKOVER

I shall be glad to come, my health permitting. I hope to come if I am well enough on the day. I want to come, but I have to be very careful. In hope. – AMBROSE LABAN

' "In hope, Ambrose Laban". Are we supposed to prepare for him whether he comes or not?' Andy asked.

'Not a word about anything else – hoping we're comfortable here and so on.'

'He'll say all that when he comes,' Eve protested; and except to remark that their guest seemed to have a gift for putting things oddly Andy said no more.

Even for a guest who might at the last moment fail to appear preparations had to be made, and Eve set about them with minute attention. She mused over that letter as she did so. The master of a house who lets it to strangers may well be a guest in that house: but the note's abruptness? Its indecision? Had it been written surreptitiously, while some other back was turned, it could not have been more hurriedly or timidly expressed. But somehow it seemed to fall in with her dream. All her life her instincts had been to comfort and help. For years she had looked after brothers very well able to look after themselves. Should she now turn a deaf ear to the entreaty of a weak old man? No; her preparations must be special. He must be given food light enough for his delicate stomach. She made Davy drive her into Willowmere for fruit and such wine as was to be had, she had the mahogany table polished till it shone like glass. She herself gathered the flowers for its centre – a large china bowl of primroses that looked as if somebody had left a Russian ballet wig there. And she took away the duplex lamp. There were old plated candlesticks in the house. She set candles in them, with little inexpensive creamy shades. For the rest, the windows, now cleared of jasmine, would give enough of clear evening light. All the time she thought of the pity of it, that a man in his closing years should have to sit at his own table and be fed by strangers.

And as Mr Laban would be shown first into the drawing-room, she had a bright wood fire lighted there. It remained now only to wait and see whether he would appear. And it was because she wished to receive him alone that she made jobs with bottles for her brothers and waited in the drawing-room.

At half-past seven she heard the ringing of the bell. Rosie stood aside as she made her announcement.

'Mr Laban.'

But Eve had not expected that the large Alsatian dog would follow at her guest's heels.

And now that he had come, was he or was he not the person of her dream? He was – and yet he was not quite. The difference puzzled her. His clothes – those of course were accounted for. She had not expected him to come to dinner in a sagging old dressing-gown. But his man did not seem to have turned him out with any special care. The shoulders of his crumpled dinner-jacket bore traces of dust and a white hair or two, and Eve wondered when he had last worn the garment. New laces had been put into his cracked old varnished shoes, and of his two studs one was different from the other. He gave in short an impression of moth-ball and brown paper. On the other hand he had taken certain pains with his hair and beard. The first had been cut after a fashion, the second trimmed to something approaching a point. His manner was nervous and unsure. Eve had advanced to greet him. His very first words took her utterly aback. He had glanced timidly at the dog.

'I trust I explained sufficiently in my letter,' he faltered in a voice that seemed to echo a gentle and educated past. 'We are inseparables, Jacomb and I. My man is out this evening, and Jacomb is never left alone.'

What had surprised Eve was that the letter had not contained one single word about the dog.

But she recovered herself. Poor old dear, his memory was evidently faulty.

'I'm so glad you were well enough to come,' she smiled. 'It's strange to live under the same roof and never meet. Do sit down. My brothers will be here in a moment.'

'Thank you, thank you.' Mr Laban sat down and stretched out frail white hands to the blaze. 'I hope – I hope you are comfortably settled here. As I think I said in my note, I have to live somewhere, and I have had misfortunes – misfortunes. I wished you to feel that it was entirely your own – entirely your own – ' and he glanced round at his belongings – the chintz sofas, the chairs, the cabinets, and finally at the dog.

Eve, wondering what next he would imagine he had put into that remarkable note, was about to hope that they for their part did not disturb him, when Andy entered, followed by Mickie and Davy. There were handshakes, conventional sounds of pleasure. Eve announced that as Mr Laban was going to eat from his own plates and drink from his own glasses she was going to put him at the head of the table. Dinner was announced. She placed her hand lightly on their guest's creased sleeve. Her brothers followed. The dog, unbidden, brought up the rear.

Mr Laban, at the head of the table, presided like a shy child at its own birthday-party. He gazed at the clock in the corner and seemed to be listening to its half-forgotten voice. Poor forlorn old fellow! was it after all kind to thrust him back into these memories? To one thing only he seemed to cling pathetically. That was the dog. The animal had stationed itself at its master's side as if from long habit. To have nothing but a dog to turn to at the end of his days! No wonder his hand strayed from time to time to the creature's head.

The talk was of the neighbourhood, the news of the day, their own relations as landlord and tenants. But even this languished. It was long since Mr Laban had paid calls or received any. Of the happenings of the outside world he appeared to be almost totally ignorant. He was vague, timorous, uncertain of memory. Indeed Eve presently found herself reduced to the topic of servants and her various difficulties concerning them. Gaily she related how she had borne off her present treasures from under Mrs Hickman's very nose. And in the matter of servants Mr Laban showed a certain interest.

'I am fortunate too,' he said in a halting voice. 'Without my man Binian I do not know what I should do. I would not part with Binian. The nursing he has given me, the attendance, the care – '

Eve wondered whether Mr Laban knew of the roughness with which this treasured servant treated the dog, but Mr Laban continued.

'My needs are few. I never married. My man and my dog suffice me. This evening is the first time I have left my room for many months. And when Binian has to go out Jacomb looks after me – don't you, Jacomb?' And again his hand went to the animal's head.

It was an unprepossessing enough brute. Sometimes the Peckovers had discussed Alsatians. They agreed in thinking them an unsettled breed, liable to go back to origin. But there was no doubt of Jacomb's interest in his master. With his mouth half open in a canine laugh and his large prick ears on a level with the table, he seemed to be listening intelligently to every word that was said. He moved his head from side to side, looking from face to face. But what the devil was the creature doing there at all?

Meanwhile the whole company was trying not to notice with what voracity this frail old man ate.

'Thank you, I will – this bread sauce is excellent – if one of your maids made it – your cook – I of course live exceedingly simply – Binian does admirably all I require – '

And he was off on the virtues of his servant again, as if he found it impossible to say too much in his praise.

It was at this point that Mickie spoke, for the first time during the meal.

'By the way, sir. Speaking of your man. Was he ever in India? His is not a face one forgets, and I seem to have seen it before.'

Mr Laban seemed suddenly agitated. His knife made a tremulous little rattling on his plate. He spoke almost warmly.

'Binian has travelled. He may have been in India. He is a man of remarkable parts. I do not mind confessing that I bow to his opinion in a great many things. I believe he has been to India. As you say, he is a man not readily forgotten. Is there any reason why he should not have been in India?'

'Has he any idea of going back?'

A silence had fallen. Mickie had taken too sudden charge of the conversation. It amounted to the judicial examination of a guest. Eve was surprised at Mickie. Mr Laban seemed on the point of breaking down.

'I – I – know little about it,' he faltered. 'I don't think Binian would leave me. It is hard to answer questions about a faithful and trusted servant. He and I – '

Suddenly every eye at the table was watching a remarkable demonstration of affection on the part of the Alsatian dog.

They had never seen anything quite like it. Since Mickie's question the animal's eyes had not been removed from his master's face. Now it suddenly reared itself up. It placed one paw on Mr Laban's breast, and with the other beat up and down in the air, as if it sought the other shoulder to embrace. Its ears were set sharply forward, its tail swung from side to side. The lean jaw was laughing to the very condyles, the long thin tongue was curled as it reached for its master's face. Its pantings of pleasure filled the room.

And then with a soft gruff bark it sank to the floor again.

'Aren't you well, sir?'

It was Davy who had sprung up and was leaning over the chair where Mr Laban had swayed a little. The others too had half-risen, and were looking at the old man. He was cloudy-white, his hand fumbled at his breast, and in his eyes were the supplication and anguish of Eve's dream.

'I – I – am better,' the words came faintly at last. 'I – my health. I ought not to have come. I was not well enough. I have to be – careful. I must go. I hope – '

It was not to be thought of that he should be allowed to go like that. Why indeed should they not keep him for the night? For a few days? Start up the car and fetch a doctor? What was there to return to that lonely wing for? But already he had got totteringly on his feet, while the dog waited for him at the door. He must go, he must go, he said. Binian would probably be back by now. Binian knew what was best to be done – nobody understood him like Binian. And seeing him indissuadable they ceased to press him. They offered to go round and see if Binian had returned. But at this he took fright again.

'No, no – I much prefer it – it would be kinder – I can manage – I am used – my apologies – I hoped – '

They were already in the hall. They were helping him on with his old silk hat and muffler. At the porch he tried feebly to push them back.

'It is only the length of the house – gentlemen, I beg you – '

Notwithstanding which Mickie and Andy accompanied him as far as the door in the wall. He refused even to take out his key till they had left him. From the porch they watched the closing of the door behind him and his dog.

In the drawing-room the four Peckovers stood looking at one another in silence. Then Andy approached Eve.

'Eve, we want you to do something. Not just to go to the Trevelyans. To go to the Trevelyans tomorrow.'

Eve spoke quite calmly. – 'No. I'm going to stay here and be told everything.'

'We'd rather you went.'

'I'm not going.'

'Then tell her, Michael. Tell Davy too.'

Mickie sat down. His hand was at his scarred cheek. He seemed tired.

'Very well. Perhaps it would be best. We're all in the risk. I have an idea that somebody's trying to get past us with a little elementary lycanthropy, that's all,' he said.

5

Davy was the first to find his voice. – 'Like what?'

'Lycanthropy.'

'What's that?'

'Sort of hocus-pocus . . . catch hold of Eve, there – '

For a sound had suddenly come from the other part of the house that caused their hearts to bound and then stand still. Something was happening to the animal. The maids had heard it too, for the drawing-room door was thrown open, and they stood there white-faced. From behind the walls came another long-drawn howl, and then silence. They waited, but the sounds were not repeated. Mickie turned to the maids.

'It's all right. Mr Laban wasn't very well. His man is looking after him. One of them has probably trodden on the dog. Good night.'

The maids withdrew, and all eyes were turned to Mickie again.

'I shall have to leave a certain amount out,' he began. 'Departmental for one thing, and some of it isn't put on record at all. The fact is I had a good deal to do with the fellow being turned out of India.'

'What, that manservant?' Davy asked.

'Yes. The Binian all the talk was about.'

'Turned out what for?'

'For knowing more than he ought. Going native for one thing. Dabbling in Tantric for another.'

And again Davy wanted to know what that was.

It was a vile word, for a vile thing. A little harmless table-rapping, a fortune told over the cards or palmistry with a soft hand held – these would have gone better with the quietly-burning lamp on the table, the chintz chairs, the cut-steel fender. For this was England in Maytime, and not the land they had left, where mysteries stand behind seen things as shadows stand behind the light.

'If you don't know, so much the better for you,' Mickie replied. 'It's not altogether unheard-of in England either. I seem to remember something about a police-visit and a bowl of human blood not very far from Clapham Junction a few years ago.'

'The devil they did!' was all Davy could find to say, and Mickie went on.

'So as that kind of man can do simply incalculable political mischief, I was told off to find out what I could about him. Had to catch my hare first. This took time. It took some months as a matter of fact. But in the end – ' Mickie didn't say after what occurrences, though the memento on his cheek seemed to say it for him, ' – anyway it was in Benares. Among the Pilgrims. Bathing at the bottom of the steps. Yes, he's been about a lot. Quite extraordinary at dialects; disguises too. He wasn't called Binian then. He'd quite a number of names.' Mickie mused, seemed to be telling them over.

'Go on about seeing him in Benares.'

'I saw him in quite a number of places after that. No need to go into it. I found out quite a lot about him before he knew we were interested in him. Do you know Dakhta Lal?'

'No.'

'There's a temple there, among the tulsi-trees. A particularly unpleasant Kali among other things, and paintings on the walls – call 'em ritualistic. And that time he beat me. Somehow he'd got away even with that height of his. I hadn't a notion it was him till he spoke. Did I say that I happened to be disguised that day too?'

'Thank God I've nothing worse than a bit of safe soldiering to do,' Andy muttered.

'I didn't like his speaking first,' Mickie continued. 'And in English, especially after . . . anyway. It showed he'd scented us, and me in particular. "I don't often come across a native who speaks English like you," was one of his sneers. Then he got on to the wall paintings. Those that we'll call ritualistic. It was all there, he said – whatever it was. Seemed to be taking in the Hindu Gods on his way to the Hindu Devils. I've no doubt it's an immensely complicated study. Quite as difficult as getting yourself into the Calendar of Saints. Prayer and fasting, only the wrong way round . . .'

'Don't leave quite so much out!' said Davy, but Mickie's narrative became even more fragmentary.

'And he couldn't resist showing off a bit either. Wanted to put the fear into me straight away. Listen. There's a bathing-ghat just below the temple. We went there. He slipped out of his clothes. He went in. He went under. I timed him. He was under two hours and a half by my watch. Then he came out again. He put his face close to mine. He stank of mud. He spoke for all the world as if we'd been continuing a conversation. "And even if you *do* get me away to England you won't be able to keep me there," he said. "I may be only a novice, but I know enough for *that*!" That's the fellow we've got under this roof. And now' – Mickie seemed to be putting a world of recollections aside – 'I want you to tell me something. Is it usual for a man to bring his dog into the dining-room the first time he's asked to dinner?'

Eve was lying on the sofa with closed eyes. She spoke without opening them.

'He seemed to think he'd mentioned that in his letter.'

'But there was nothing about it in his letter.'

'No.'

'Then tell me something else. We all four saw Mr Laban and his dog tonight. And we've all four seen Binian and the dog.'

'No. I haven't set eyes on the gentleman yet,' Davy interposed.

'Well, Eve and I have. So have the maids. Has anybody seen them all three together?'

'Here, I say!' said Davy, startled.

'*Has* anybody?'

Not one of them had seen the master of the house, his manservant and the Alsatian dog all at the same time.

Suddenly Davy broke into a laugh, if a sound so violent could be called a laugh. Then he sat up, serious-faced and apologetic.

'Sorry everybody. I don't know what made me do that.'

'I doubt if we shall see them all three,' said Mickie quietly. 'It's my private belief that there are only two of them, and they were both here tonight.'

Whereupon he invited them to run over the events of the evening.

'Let's assume for the moment there are only two. Which of them was master of the other tonight?'

'Oh Lord!'

'The dog's being here at all? All that rigmarole about the virtues of Binian? The way the brute jumped up and licked him? The way it glared at me when I asked if Binian was going back to India? What happened then?'

This time it was Davy whose mind rushed to embrace the incredible thing.

'Good God! It barked! I can hear it now! And he turned faint and said he must go!'

'And could we keep him? Would he let us send for a doctor? Would he let us see him home?'

'No!'

'And before he'd been gone a quarter of an hour, that howl that brought the maids in?'

'What was that?' Davy asked breathlessly.

'I don't know. I only know what I think.'

'What do you think?'

'The wrench when they change places again,' Mickie replied.

Davy made one last clutch to save his foundering mind. – 'Come,' he expostulated weakly, 'you'll be saying next they can raise the dead!'

'They say,' Mickie answered slowly, 'they can raise the unborn. If metamorphosis at all, what's the odds?'

And – if metamorphosis at all – why not? Since the birth of Time has not man's mind veered and fluctuated among these very beliefs? Are we of today so much wiser? Life is a fluid. It may coagulate in a rock, creep sluggishly in a tree, but muscle and vein, hidden root and the beating heart, are no more than its apparatus. Is every species immutably established? How came it to be so? By the power of a Holy Word? Is there no Unholy Negation? What is a dog? How big is a dog? What is its weight, what its colour? How come the lap-dog and

the mastiff to be equally dogs? And granted that which was not able
to stabilise itself went into Creation's limbo long ago, is there no
abhorrent art that can call it back, the simulacrum of an hour? And
granted such an art, where would it find the weak link but in a creature
that has lately ceased to be feral while attaining only a precarious
domesticity? Browne speaks of 'the public soul of all things'. The
mind turns away from the thought of a public body, lent and borrowed
and kept in circulation. Yet there can be no choosing among miracles.
Accept one accept all. It might indeed be as Mickie said.

'And what do you say it's called?' Davy asked with an exhausted sigh.

'Lycanthropy.'

'And the other trick?'

'Tantric.'

'But what – what do they want to do a silly thing like that for?'

'From Binian's point of view? I told you what he said to me. Said if
we got him to England we shouldn't be able to keep him. Well, we
couldn't bring home the charge we wanted, but we deported him on
something else. And in England he's got to live. Somebody's got to
pay his wages. So what would suit him better than to get hold of
some harmless old semi-invalid who lived alone, get himself fixed
up as his servant, and – continue his interrupted studies? He can
produce Mr Laban when necessary. After all there's got to *be* a Mr
Laban. He must have a certain amount of business to transact. There
had to be a Mr Laban to let us this house.'

'That was rather taking a chance, wasn't it?'

'Probably wanted the money. Another thing. That letter. All hurried
and frazzled. Said he *wanted* to come. Said he *hoped* to come. Used
exactly the same words again just as he was leaving. The rest was all
testimonials to Binian. But that sounded like a message for us.'

'Slipped another note in! Then by the time he really passes his
Higher Proficiency – ?'

'An old man will be on his way back to India, travelling with an
Alsatian dog,' Mickie replied.

6

A thoughtful Eve walked the next morning on the common. She had
dozed and waked again all night in the drawing-room, with Davy
to keep her company, yet she was not in the least tired. Instead,
something seemed to have happened to time. Long experiences,
protracted processes of thought, passed over her while the second-
hand of her watch crept round once. Similarly with her perceptions.

She seemed to take in a hundred things at once, the sulphur butter-flies that played about her, the smell of bruised thyme that rose to her nostrils. The wide vale below lay thankful in the sun, as if its very farms and copses praised the sweet orderliness of created things. In those cottages women were at work, in the schools children were being taught in the fear of God. Men swung their horses at the turn of the field, the tradesmen's vans delivered the groceries. Everybody was aware of the friendly presence of his neighbour, and dogs were dogs and nothing else.

She was standing still, with the breeze rippling her cropped head; she turned to look back at the house. But the pines hid it, seemed to whisper 'Hush!' about it. How foolish it had been to suppose even for a moment that one could be under the same roof with a person and not be aware of that person's presence! The very announce-ment should have been its own warning. It was like having a dead person in the house; the dead make no noise, but it is useless to pretend they aren't there. Was she afraid? Of course she was afraid. But it was of something vaster than the house she was afraid. She would have been no less afraid, perhaps more afraid, anywhere else. Therefore having said she was afraid she must forget it. If she were even to change her room her fear might become a panic. And that would be dangerous.

Mickie and Andy had again gone to London. Davy, who had driven them, ought to be back by now. Moreover, it would be as well for her to occupy herself, like those women in the farms down there. Perhaps the hands of her watch would move a little more quickly then. Suddenly she turned her back on the sheep-dotted slope where the clumsy baby-lambs called, and sought the shady lane. Conscious that she was walking slowly towards the house, she walked more quickly. She reached the pine-sheltered drive. Half way down it she stopped dead. Violent and uncouth noises were coming from the direction of the yard.

She reached the turn. In the middle of the yard Rose and Laura stood. Davy had returned, and was in the act of taking a run at the closed door in the wall. It was from behind the door that the noises came. Half a dozen dogs seemed to be tearing one another to pieces.

Davy played polo twice a week, squash the same, tennis all the time, with an occasional bout of fives. When he set his twelve-and-a-half-stone of toughness to the charge something had to give way. There was a crash, and an iron staple was heard to go clinking along the ground. Instantly the noises ceased, and a door banged.

Eve had run forward. Davy was trying the door that had banged. He turned, saw her, and rejoined her.

'What happened?' she asked breathlessly.

'Dog had a convulsion or something. I was only just back.'

Eve sought her maids. She had it in breathless half sentences.

'I said to Laura first time I saw him – "He thrashes that dog, he does," I said – '

'If you'd heard it, miss – '

'Like shouting it was – '

'I'll swear there was two voices – '

'Thump-thump, raging and tearing – '

'It was Laura's morning upstairs, and I ran up to her all of a shake – '

'And I bumped into her as I was running down – '

'And even in the garden we could hear it over the roof – '

'And then Mr David drove up in the car – '

'That howl last night too – '

'And we were going to ask if we could have that spare room next to yours, miss – '

'Because we won't be able to stay if there's going to be these goings-on – '

'Yes, yes,' said the distracted Eve.

But it was two o'clock before lunch was served that day.

In the afternoon Rose and Laura took down their beds, and Davy helped them to carry mattresses and what-not past the orchard end to the main portion of the house. He made use of the opportunity to examine the room they were leaving. It was a pleasant sort of loft, such as is found over garages, and its window looked past the close hedge that, with the wall at the other side, shut off Mr Laban's wing. Over this hedge Davy saw the upper portion of his private door, with a pointed window above it that seemed to be obscured with some sort of *décalco-manie*. Possibly one large room, possibly two smaller ones, lay behind it. If there was a chamber below it apparently had no light at all.

Davy stood in thought. His was a mind that liked to get things over and done with, and here you had a fellow who in some way or other had provided himself with a sort of dog, that he sometimes took a night's lodging in himself, but more often used in order to lock up his master. If that was so the thing was fairly simple. All that need be done was to come upon Mr Laban *plus* dog, put a bullet through the brute, and – well Davy didn't quite know what would happen after that, but something would be bound to happen. At least if that wasn't the idea he didn't know what was.

But he hesitated. He hesitated because he was a little nervous of the glimpse he had had that morning. For supposing the thing didn't always work cleanly and completely? Suppose one wasn't always completely master, nor the other utterly helpless? He no longer sang his song about the two men and the dog. He didn't want to kill the wrong one, nor yet to blow a hole through a sort of amalgam of the two. And how the old fellow had tucked his supper away last night! Just as if he had been getting his strength up for something! Getting his strength up to shut up Binian in the dog! How had the struggle ended? Either might be master at that very moment.

Davy left the loft. He walked round the house and entered the yard by the broken door. He strode to the private door and knocked loudly with his knuckles. He waited for a couple of minutes, and then knocked more loudly still. He thought he heard a faint voice within.

'It's Captain Peckover. Will you please come down?'

After all, what more natural than that they should call to enquire after the health of an old man who had been ill?

Several more minutes passed. Then feet were heard on wooden stairs within. The door opened. Binian stood there.

So this piece of emaciation was the famous Binian! It was much that such a mummy should bear a name at all. Two hours in a river? He might have been there two months, and just hauled out; and the fishes had had his eyes, for Davy couldn't see any. He clung to the lintel with his fingers, like something that hung on to the bar of a pit-cage, going up or down. And he had almost completely lost his voice.

'Yes, sir?' he whispered.

'Can I see Mr Laban?'

'I'm afraid Mr Laban isn't very well, sir.'

'I know. That's why I want to see him.'

'I'm afraid he's not to be seen, sir.'

'I've come to apologise for a broken door. I heard such an infernal hubbub in here this morning that I thought something was wrong, and burst open the door.'

'I didn't hear anything, sir.'

'Something was the matter with your dog.'

For a moment Davy saw the eyes at the bottom of the puckers. – 'Mr Laban will be sorry you were disturbed, sir.'

'I not only heard it. I saw it.'

The extremity of his exhaustion notwithstanding, something in the abominable cadaver seemed to stiffen. – 'Mr Laban's very partic-ular about who enters these parts of the premises, sir.'

And the door began to close, as if a corpse drew to the lid of his coffin. But Satan himself could not have bettered the look Davy had through the last inch of it.

The yard door remained unrepaired during the whole of the next day. The inmates of that portion of the house must have slept the clock several times round. But on the morning after it was found to be set up again, and Rose and Laura, descending to light the fires, saw through the kitchen window the tall black-coated figure, with the dog once more at his heels. A small shed had been reserved for the storage of the master's outside belongings, and it was from this shed that Binian was returning, carrying several pieces of iron. During that morning muffled knockings were heard, and Davy, interested in these knockings, sought his observation-post in the loft. The door under the decalcomanied window stood open, and Binian could be seen behind it, with a large screwdriver in his hand. The door closed for a moment, but opened again, as if he was ascertaining some fit or dimension, and at one of his movements something fell, with a clang of iron. It was an hour before the door finally closed and did not open again. Apparently he had to secure the door that he himself could get out. But it might be a matter of difficulty for anybody outside to get in.

7

People who live through vast experiences what time it takes the hand of a watch to travel one minute cannot long remain at that point of tension. There are silences that make us long to shriek in order to break them, and the Thing that Grows had got hold of Eve. It sprouted a fresh tentacle at every denial of its existence. Andy suggested, for example, that if she would not go to the Trevelyans she might ask Rachel Trevelyan to come and stay with them. To have told him, as she wanted to tell him, that she would not dream of asking Rachel or anybody else to such a house, would have been the truth. But she couldn't admit that. She sat down and wrote to Rachel – a pointless letter, all about nothing, with never a word of invitation in it. Again, it got on her nerves that Davy went about cheerfully whistling. She knew that it was all for her benefit, and that his eyes and ears were sharpened all the time. None the less it drove her to the piano herself, to play a few bars and stop, her fingers on the keys, as if waiting for something. And she herself had either to pretend to her maids or else lose them. Yet day followed day, night

night, without anything happening. Worst of all, Davy's song ran fantastically in her head. A man and a dog; two men and a dog, always two, never three; and always the other one. She began to feel that her thoughts were not her own. They were being manipulated, palpated, read. It is after this fashion that the Thing that Grows works. You yourself do its work for it. Neither Laban nor Binian was Master of that House. The Devil was Master of that House in which Eve had thought to spend her English summer.

So Andy and Mickie put their heads together about it.

Eve, heavy-eyed and listless, did not know what kept Davy so busy in the stable next the garage. But money spent on a tennis-court would be money said goodbye to, whereas money spent on a horse would be recoverable later on. The horse arrived – a sleek sixteen-hands chestnut, with saddle and bridle and blanket complete, and Eve got out her russet jodhpurs and mounted.

'But am I to ride all by myself?' she asked as she patted the glossy neck.

'Can't afford a horse apiece. Off you go, and look out for the rabbit-holes,' they replied.

And off she went, and her first day's stiffness was the beginning of her return to health.

She did not ride alone for very many days. Within a week she returned shortly before lunch accompanied by a cavalier whom she introduced to her brothers as Mr Struddy Rimington. He was received with civility, and asked if he lived in the neighbourhood. He did not. He was putting up at the Royal Foresters, he said. He had the air of a man capable of looking after himself in most emerg-encies; he was admirably breeched and gaitered, and sat his black like a centaur; but the question was where Eve had picked him up? Eve answered that it was really the horses that had made themselves known to one another.

'And I think he's the kind of man it was possible to have asked to stay to lunch,' she reproached them when he had gone.

'Who is he? One never knows,' said Andy.

'How very English you've got. Nobody'd suppose you'd lived in India! Anyway it's stupid to see a person morning after morning and treat them as if they had the plague!'

'What's he doing at the Foresters? What's his job? Sorry to have to do the heavy father, but if we are going to have the fellow in to smoke a pipe – '

'He smokes cigarettes. Balkans.'

This at least had Davy's approval. – 'Balkans at sixteen bob a hundred, hacks every day and stops at the Foresters – fellow to know,' he said.

'And I'm *not* in the habit of picking up any stranger, even if he is on a horse,' said Eve with dignity as she marched away.

The whole incident, in short, went off smoothly and according to plan.

A few days later Mr Struddy Rimington was asked to stay to lunch. On a close inspection he was perhaps not quite so young as he looked; he might have been twenty-eight or nine. The black was not his own; it belonged to the Foresters' stables. Save during the week-ends the Foresters was practically empty, he said, and he admitted that there was an expensive sort of bleakness about it.

'Pleasant little place you have here,' he remarked. 'I should like to ask you to show me round one time.'

'Come and have a walk round now,' said Mickie of the worn scarred face.

And when it appeared that Mr Struddy Rimington too had stayed with the Trevelyans he was free to come in whenever he liked.

Eve's eyes grew bright again and her step springy once more. How should they not, with a horse under her, the sunny English heath to gallop over, and Mr Struddy Rimington for company? Her jodhpurs and little round hat became her daily attire. Rose and Laura began to lay the extra place without being told. They exchanged looks behind their mistress's back. It was to be gathered that something or other had their entire approval.

Then came a day when Mr Struddy Rimington said that fair was fair, and he'd really no false shame about such things, but the hospitality was getting a bit one-sided, and what about their dining at the Foresters with him? For that matter, why not that very evening? Pack the maids off to the cinema or somewhere – what about it?

Nothing could be pleasanter. Laura and Rose were given their late passes. Eve and her brothers wedged themselves into the little Fiat. The Royal Foresters was a bare mile away. They set off, and for the first time during their occupation the house, as far as the tenants were concerned, was empty.

How restful was the Foresters after that Victorian dwelling with the faded furniture and the shut-off wing! Its utter lack of atmosphere or association of any kind was a release. Only the gardens were older than the day before yesterday. Its entrance-hall was Waring and

Gillow baronial, with an arched fireplace and massive iron dogs; its aperitif-lounge shone with leather and glass and parquet. The mantelpieces of the dining-room were architectural elevations of red mahogany, and the ceiling from which depended the electric chandeliers was coffered and pargetted. When bells rang waiters had apparently to come from immense distances, and the wine-waiter from farthest away of all. Dogs haunted it not – Visitors were Respectfully Requested to arrange for the feeding of their dogs outside. Nothing whatever haunted it. It was magnificently modern and immune.

But a White Lady might have haunted the old garden on which their table looked out. Its hedges were solid walls of clipped box, on which sentinel-shapes like chessmen were posted at intervals. Their black-green seemed to clarify the sky to a crystal translucency, in which a thin moon was already sinking. Not as much as a daisy spotted the shaven lawn. And to complete the English peace, some-where a quiet bell was calling folk to week-night Service.

'This do, Miss Peckover?' said Struddy, showing the table by the wide-open window. 'And by the way, what *do* I call you all?'

'Heaven knows why we were all named after Saints,' Andy re-marked. 'Parents hoped for the best, I suppose.'

'Mine's the worst,' said Eve; 'Eve Mary Agatha Monica is my calamity. So you've plenty to choose from.' And dinner began.

Not only did the Victorian house seem a world away; Eve's whole precious life might have been the life of another Eve. Always she had done things for her brothers; the thought that she might one day do something for herself had only newly come to her. Something of her history was folded up and laid away, something else unpacked, shining out of its wrappings like a new treasure. Dear boys! How fond she would always remain of them, how close their business would always be to her! Those were the things that could never be taken away. Andy and Davy would go back to their soldiering, Mickie to his peculiar trade; but she would remain here. It was all settled in her heart. She could have laughed for the sureness of it. There was something of 'their sort' about him, the family valuation of what were the essentials, what the asides. She saw Andy looking at him. When Andy disapproved of a thing people were aware of it. She did not think Andy disapproved.

A waiter approached the host. He was wanted at the telephone. He excused himself, and until his return the party ceased to be a party, and became a family sitting once more.

After dinner they walked in the box-walled garden. The church bell had long since ceased, the young moon had disappeared. Overhead the rooks were assembling, and the inky chessmen stood rigid against an infinity of fading gold. Eve had taken Davy's arm. The other three men were across the lawn. She had nothing to say to Davy; she just wanted to take his arm. It was a strong and jolly arm to take.

They continued to walk and to talk, now grouped together, now split up again. Eve neither found herself alone with Struddy nor sought to be. It grew late, and she said something about home.

'Heaps of time yet,' Struddy answered. 'Come inside and have a whisky-and-soda.'

It was eleven o'clock, and a second whisky-and-soda had gone the way of the first, before Davy fetched the car. The headlights swung round the orderly gravel of the hotel sweep. Eve was packed in, and Davy took the wheel.

'Tomorrow – ' said Eve with a wave of her hand, and the Royal Foresters Hotel was lost behind them in the night.

A few moments brought them home. Eve, first ascertaining that Rose and Laura had returned, went straight to her room. She lighted her lamp and began to prepare for bed. She had no fear of the room now. Only because her heart had been empty had the devils of fear crept in. Now, whatever lurked behind that closed door –

Instinctively her eyes went to the door.

Something had been done to it. High up in one corner a tiny shadow showed where she could have sworn no shadow had been before. Lamp in hand, she advanced. A small triangular flap projected slightly forward. She held the lamp closer to the vertical stripes. A sharp knife had been run all round the plate-mark, cutting cleanly through the super-impositions of papering. Pull that flap forward a little more, loosen the top edge, and use a little strength, and the surface could be stripped away and the door exposed. Somebody, with or without an Order to View, had been in her room, and this was the Portion that had been left on the Premises.

8

When man makes to himself a machine so powerful that to set it in motion may well be not to know how to stop it again, he must have at hand a second machine, more controllable for ordinary purposes. Armies are not mobilised when a punitive expedition is all that is required. Which is probably the reason why all at once letters began to arrive addressed to Ambrose Laban, Esquire.

The first of these was delivered with the Peckover letters. On the postman's next visit Andy handed the letter back to him.

'Nothing to do with anybody here,' he said.

'I've knocked, sir, but I can't get any answer,' the man replied.

'How have you delivered Mr Laban's letters before?'

'Here, sir. Those he had. The housekeeper took them in. There hasn't been many since then.'

'What's done with letters that aren't delivered?'

'They're opened and sent back to the sender, sir.'

'Then that's what you'd better do with this one,' said Andy.

Let the Post Office work for its living. If Mr Laban remained obdurate in his non-existence it would then be time to bring heavier pressure to bear.

For nobody wanted uniformed policeman fussing about the place. Reporters and photographers were even less desired. All that was sought was the fixation of Ambrose Laban, Esquire, in his proper personal shape, and the seizure of a dog in the presence of responsible witnesses.

'Have you many like Struddy at the I.O.?' Andy asked of Mickie.

'No, Struddy's our bright particular star in that line,' Mickie replied.

'Eve, any notion of why we were all pushed out to the Foresters that night?'

'Don't think so,' and there was a pause.

'But how do we know *he* didn't hear them?' Andy asked presently. 'They went through the whole house. Moving about her room, for instance?'

'We don't know. We aren't dealing with the knowable. He may anticipate everything we do.'

'Well, Davy's room's ready for Struddy, and I've changed with Eve. Struddy got his chit?'

'Got it this morning.'

'Then all we can do's to wait.'

The 'chit' that Struddy Rimington, of His Majesty's India Office, London, had got, was signed by a Secretary of State, and countersigned by the Head of another Department. Precisely how it stood with regard to Habeas Corpus was not yet ascertainable – for who knew what form the corpus would take? The words 'alive or dead' did not occur in it – for is a man alive or dead during the two-and-a-half hours he sleeps in the bed of an Indian river? Nevertheless, on information received from Michael George Peckover, of the same Service, wide discretionary powers were vested in the holder of the document.

And copies of Enclosure (B) had been sent to Ambrose Laban, Esquire, and a certain Stephen Binian, at their last-known addresses, and from the circumstances of their sending would be deemed to have been duly delivered.

'So he'd better tread on the gas,' said Struddy; and Davy, who had moved his bed over to the loft, reported that a light had shown behind the decalcomanied window from sunset till daybreak. Andy, from Eve's room, corroborated, that all night the sounds of moving about had not ceased. 'Packing up for his master like a good servant, and exit Mr Laban and his dog together,' he added.

He appeared to be right. The next morning, without any attempt at concealment, Binian and the dog crossed the yard and went out. He was away several hours. That afternoon a horse and cart approached along the drive. It drew up at the door that Davy had broken. Binian and the driver put a number of boxes on it, and the cart started back for Willowmere.

Within half an hour Struddy Rimington was informed that the labels of the boxes bore the name of Ambrose Laban, and that their destination was Waterloo.

'Pass the Time Table, Mickie,' he said.

The afternoon trains were slow ones, the evening trains good: but before he could take a train a feeble old man, leading a powerful dog, would have to get to Willowmere. Struddy chuckled. If a taxi came to the house all they would have to do would be to stop Mr Laban, to regret deeply and politely that they had a warrant for the arrest of his manservant, and to request that he be produced. But that was not very likely to happen. Binian was too wide awake for that. The last train left Willowmere at 10.26. Mr Laban could not walk the four miles to the station. But he would be able to reach the end of the lane on foot. A hundred to one a vehicle would be found waiting there towards ten o'clock.

'And with Davy over the way and Andy in the kitchen,' said Struddy, who had now taken command. ' – well, I mean, better call it another dinner with me – '

So Rose and Laura were once more given leave of absence and in the kitchen Andy cut beef sandwiches. Mickie was given a roving commission, and went frequently into the room with the paper door. As for Eve, the director of operations was giving her an entirely unrequired lesson in night-driving. Driving a car by night, he said, was a very different thing from driving a car by day, and driving between lights was most difficult of all. Except to say 'Really?' Eve kept her mouth shut, and took the wheel of the Fiat. With the twilight deepening about her and the startled moths vivid in the beam of the headlights, she drove up and down the Willowmere road, with other lights, white and red, meeting or passing them from time to time.

Suddenly she gave a soft laugh. – 'You *are* so ridiculously simple, Struddy!' she said. 'As if I hadn't guessed long ago what all this was about!'

'All what?'

'Oh, everything! At the moment this getting me out of the way, while you cruise up and down looking for a taxi you expect.'

'Don't talk. You're driving.'

'And your staying at the Foresters, and "What am I to call you fellows?" as if you'd never set eyes on them before!'

'Mind the ditch – better turn at that gate – '

'Suppose I hadn't looked at you that morning?'

He dropped his voice suddenly. – 'Let that fellow get past – I think I'll take the wheel – '

Quickly they changed places, keeping behind the taillight that had just passed. The ruby glowed on the number-plate of one of the station taxis. At the lane's end it slowed down. Struddy sounded no horn. Eve felt the Fiat's swift picking up. A quarter of a mile of double hedge rushed past like the wind. They swung in at the gate, did an outside-edge along the drive. Struddy stopped short of the porch, and the car came to a standstill in the middle of the fairway, headlights whitely blazing.

'Don't move her – stay here and keep the lights on,' Struddy ordered, and was off.

In Eve's old room he spoke to Mickie in a whisper.

'All right. Taxi's waiting for him. Anything happened?'

Something happened even as he spoke. From behind the papered door, shattering the silence of so many days, the voice of the dog was again raised in a howl of uttermost anguish. Another howl followed it, and another, and another. Again there were the sounds of a violent struggle, the crash of objects falling. The Devil had broken loose.

Bertie had dashed for a chair and mounted it. His hands were at the upper edge of the cut. *Rrrrrp!* There was a hollow rending, drowned by the clamour of the dog. *Rrrrrp!* The upper panels of a brown and yellow grained door were revealed. In Mickie's hand was a revolver.

'Both together – '

And as the two men hurled themselves on the door the faint sound of Davy's whistle reached them from the direction of the loft.

In the room in which they stood Eve's bedroom lamp burned, but it showed little through the gap where the door had been. Other lights burned there, dim smoking yellow wicks, and already there was a smell that should have warned them. But the two men had fallen back, their eyes fixed on the swollen clay-yellow mass that rolled and writhed and tore itself. God in Heaven, the size of it! Its head seemed small and toylike – and yet it was the head of a large Alsatian dog, with jaws that foamed and clashed. On its back it bucked, its tail straight as a rod.* And mingled with the rest of the uproar were mouthings that resembled words.

And the room in which the horror leapt and bounded and fought? Mickie knew it, with its painted obscenities on the walls, its side-shrines on which the lamps fumed with an evil smell, and the hideous four-armed image at the farther end that threatened to strike them down. It was the temple at Dakhta Lal. He had set up the abominable apparatus of his worship here – if it was his worship, and not another blasphemy added to the rest.

And at the lane's end a taxi was waiting to take him back. As a dog he would travel, when he had evicted his master from that monstrous counter-changing shape. But as Davy's whistle sounded again the two watching men became conscious of that smell and an unwonted heat. There came a sudden crackle as of musketry, and a dull light shone up the stairs past the four-armed image. The distended animal seemed conscious of it too, for it redoubled its efforts. And of a sudden, as if tinder had been already prepared down below, up rushed the bright flame, flooding the painted walls with light.

---

* 'But to come to these three symptoms then whereof I spake; I account the one of them to be the incredible strength of the possessed creature which will farre exceed the strength of sixe of the wightest and wodest of any other men that are not so troubled. The next is the boldning up so far of the patient's brest and bellie with such an unnatural sturring and vehement agitation within them; and such an ironie hardness of his sinewes so stiffly bended out, that it were not possible to pricke out, as it were, the skinne of any other person so farre . . . The last is the speaking of sundrie languages, which the patient is known by them that were acquaint with him neuer to have learned, and that with an uncouth and hollow voice; and all the time of his speaking, a greater motion being in his breast than in his mouth.' – (*Demonologie*, James I)

Mickie had seized the bedroom jug, but it might as well have been a teacup. There was a hissing and a cloud of steam. It puffed up like incense, hiding for a moment the four-armed Kali, and in that same moment the creature's ravings ceased. The stairs were a bonfire, for which an Alsatian dog was making a leap. Mickie's revolver cracked twice, but Mickie himself didn't for a moment suppose he had hit. And at Kali's feet a white-bearded old man lay motionless.

It was next morning, at the Royal Foresters, where Mr Laban had been taken. He had died during the night without regaining consciousness. A mile away the house was still smoking, with half Willowmere standing by, but whether any discovered the image of Kali or not would depend entirely on what that image was made of. Davy had told his portion of the story.

'I heard Eve and Struddy come back in the car. I knew by the lick they came at there was something doing, and of course I heard all that racket going on. It was when I saw the light I thought it was time to do something.'

'The fire?'

'Yes. Down below. The door had seemed closed, but it wasn't. It was left open a couple of inches. I saw the light through the crack, and dashed down and round by the yard. That was open too, and I saw the car in the drive. I remembered the waterbutt, but of course there wasn't a bucket, and anyway the stairs were well alight.'

'You saw it come out?'

'It dashed right past me, across the yard. I hared after the brute. Saw it in the headlights – saw it take a slash at Eve – Lord, if it had got her! Then it was gone.'

The smoke of the house rose over the sentinelled hedge. All else of the heavens was of morning purity. One blind of the Royal Foresters was drawn, but only an old man lay behind it, perhaps happier than he had ever been. In the aperitif lounge of the hotel policemen were closing their notebooks on written statements. These were unimpeachably correct, and amounted to a surmise that a lamp had overturned in Mr Laban's quarters. Of Mr Laban's man the Peckover brothers knew nothing at all.

Along the length of the box-hedge Eve and Struddy were pacing back and forth. The brothers, their statements ended, saw them approach across the lawn. At the open window by which they had dined all met. Struddy was beginning to speak, but Eve said it without words. Beginning with Andy, she lifted her face to each of her brothers in turn. She kissed them. She had always been very, very fond of them. She would be fonder than ever of them now.

But a large, clay-coloured Alsatian dog, probably badly burned, is urgently wanted by the India Office. The Surrey Police have the matter in hand.

Tragic Casements

I

Eustace Corydon had put up his greenhouse during the winter months, and at a cost of next to nothing. A lucky find of second-hand glass, a few flagstones, and the old sections that had been lying in the woodshed for years, and now where the old lobby had been they had a conservatory-lounge to sit in and a look-out over the bird-haunted morfa that stretched away to the estuary and the sea.

It seemed an age since their daughter Patricia's last homecoming. As she had spent Christmas with Anne, so now she had brought Anne home with her, and they were to sleep in the garden hut up at the orchard's edge. But they had had a long and exhausting day of it, the morfa-view would keep till the morning, and the best welcome to the pair of them was to give them their supper and pack them off early to their garden beds.

Anne, four years older than Patricia, was a town-mouse. Her garden in London had iron railings round it, and if she heard stirrings after she had gone to bed they were those of the policeman on his nightly round, his light resting on locks and fastenings as he passed. But here the nearest police station was five miles away. It had honeysuckle up its wall, through which hardly once in five years did some disturbing black word like REWARD peep, and to sleep out of doors came as naturally to Patricia as to a fledgling in its nest.

But tonight fitful summer lightning made a tremolo of the sky, and the silver half-shilling of the moon gave the newly-painted sashwork of this greenhouse that she saw for the first time a white and wakeful look. Broken up by the slight irregularities of its panes, it was a moon seen in water, all bits and pieces, that twinkled and played tictac as the half-shilling changed its position overhead. She missed the old lobby and the black water-butt that had always stood there. The hut had roller-shutters, adjustable against wind and rain; she wanted to close them against the moon

too, and though at last she slept, at some hour of that dark overlap
between moonlessness and the dawn, Anne heard a quavering voice
from the other bed.

'Anne, are you awake?'

'Yes, I was watching that star.'

'Stay awake and talk, Anne. I don't want to go to sleep again and I
want someone to talk to.'

'Paddy! You've been asleep for hours!'

'I'd the most horrid dream. People were moving about the front
of the house, and two awful men looked round the shutter at us,
and one of them said we were asking for it, and the other said
nobody'd hear from the house, and tomorrow I'm going back to my
old room – '

Anne's answer was to slip into the other bed and take the tall
schoolgirl into her arms. They might sleep in gardens who wished.
She had been awake those two hours, and from Paddy's bed she
could still see her star and think her nightly thoughts of Denzil. He
was Patricia's six-foot soldier brother, and since last Christmas they
had been engaged to be married.

Back debts of the night are quickly paid when day comes with
its cheerful solvency. After breakfast the next morning the new
greenhouse was inspected, its wicker chairs sat in, its view of the
morfa through the field-glasses admired. By the old passageway
it communicated with the house, a step across the new crazy path,
and they were in the garden itself, and what a little pet of a house
and garden they were, this pocket-sized estate of Eustace Corydon's, that twenty years before had been no more than a couple
of labourer's cottages in a field! Passing motorists slowed down
involuntarily at the bend of the road that brought it into view. They
did so at the sudden picture it made, with its wisteria-plumed white
gable, the maroon of its prunus, its boughs heavy with damson and
cherry and plum, and its apples ripening against the wooded hillside behind. Ladies from London said they wanted to cut it out to
frame it and take it back with them. But Eustace Corydon sold
them strawberries instead, and booked profitable mail-orders for
its asparagus next year.

And now, with the fruit season upon them, these Corydons had no
time for lounging in greenhouses. They were places to pass through,
dressed in their oldest clothes, laden with trugs and baskets, to fill
them with their ladders set against the trees, their heads not to be
seen for leafage as they conversed from tree to tree. Their picnic

meals were carried out to them, they spent their days out of doors, and the most constant occupant of their new conservatory chairs was Tiger the cat, sleeping off on some cushion his hunting debauch of the night before. Even the creeping-jinny in its overhead wire basket was removed, because it trailed in their faces every time they passed.

So for a picture of family peace at the end of the day, let the ladies from London cut that out, too, and frame it, supper over and everybody fit to be seen again, the candles in their silver sticks and the firelight upon their faces, more to eke out their scanty electricity than for any need they had of its glow. If no bee droned or wasp buzzed in their new greenhouse they had all the bees and wasps they wanted during the day; if not as much as a blade of grass pushed through the cracks of their crazy-pavement, what were a few hyacinths or shirley poppies that they should miss them? That evening Eustace Corydon had just picked up the newspaper he had had no time to look at all day. At the wireless Patricia had been dashing like a non-stop train through Europe's stations till she had been ordered to leave the knob alone, but not by her mother. She, gentle soul, must have ear-aid, and her battery was in her lap as she and Anne turned back the corners of a thick book of patterns they had had to send to London for. That gaping oblong at the farther end of the room, just beyond the range of the firelight, would need curtains before the winter came. Then suddenly Eustace Corydon was seen to lower the edge of his paper.

'Is that wireless properly turned off?' he asked.

Anne got up to see, but no leakage came from the wireless; she returned to her patterns and Eustace Corydon resumed his reading. But a few minutes later his *Times* was lowered again.

'Has Freda gone to bed, or has she got somebody in the kitchen with her?' he asked.

'Freda's gone to bed. I heard her go up twenty minutes ago,' Patricia sulked. *She* could read a book and listen to the wireless, too.

But even Mrs Corydon's head turned at the next. From some-where inside the house there had come the squeaking scrape of wood on stone and a creaking as of wicker under a weight. The muffled jingling vibration that followed it resembled nothing so much as the dropping of a tray laden with crockery, and snatching a candle from the table, Eustace Corydon had disappeared by the uncurtained doorway.

He was gone some minutes, during which time nobody spoke. Then he reappeared.

'Who turned Tiger out?' he demanded.

'I did,' and again it was Patricia.

'Has anybody been in the greenhouse since?'

Nobody had been in the greenhouse since.

'Then who left the outer door open?' But Patricia was on her feet, her eyes on the uncurtained passageway, her hands at her heart.

'Father, I *know* I didn't! – I *remember* locking it. I was *careful* to lock it – '

So, seeing her agitation, her father said nothing about the rest; the basket-chair he had found overturned, and the hook from which the creeping-jinny had been removed lying upon the floor, with a ball of garden raffia by its side.

2

A War Department jeep with a nosey-parker antenna gave three short staccato pips. A kitbag was set down by the roadside and a tail-light disappeared as the jeep continued on its northward way.

But Anne's SOS was answered, and with last night's hearth not yet swept and the seed-pearls of the night still grey on web and twig, she was down in the garden and in his arms.

So entered young Denzil in his battledress with the captain's stars, Captain Corydon of Field Security (MI5), who asked no more of Command HQ than to be turned loose with his earphoned jeep, and his mobile section of sixteen hand-picked men. And, their first embrace over, she had expected a thousand questions and was ready with her thousand answers, but not a question did he ask. He had come to see for himself; he only laughed, held her back at arm's-length, drew her close again, and the day was broadening and bird answering bird before he even said: 'Well, what about a little snoop round before anybody's awake?'

But a new lock had been fitted to the greenhouse door and a chain to arrest its opening with a warning jar. Its none too clean windows showed only a disorder of baskets inside, heaped on the wicker chairs, with his father's gumboots on the floor. In the workshop along the alley was a quantity of leftover glass, noticeable among it the lower half of a landing-light of mid-Victorian decalcomania, diapered with cut stars and surrounded by squares of gloomy crimson and deep eye-bath blue. But suddenly Anne stood still, listening, with her fingers at her lips. She didn't want to be caught by Freda, creeping in the back-way with nothing on but her dressing-gown and pyjamas, and she lifted her face.

'Quickly . . . then shall I tell them you're here?'

But the barkings and boundings of Ianto, released from the chain, had already told them that.

* * *

'Which farm was this, father?'

He might have left the old room only yesterday, and his mother's ears needed no aid when *he* spoke from his accustomed place at the breakfast-table. Paddy, at his side, hardly took her eyes off him and his battle-dress. But his father? He showed his years, yet his eyes had a restless, rejuvenated brightness as he described that hilltop auction where he had found his greenhouse glass. He elaborated, dwelt on details, made a regular set-piece of it with its furniture and effects carried out into the yard, and the folk of the region assembled in their nondescript vehicles to buy, and Denzil's eyes sought Anne's across the table. 'Eye-wash?' they questioned, but there was no stopping his father now.

'You see, Den, I'd heard there might be a wind-pump going cheap. We can't depend on this stream of ours, the pump might have given us an extra volt or two, but you should have seen the thing! As old iron I wouldn't have given half-a-crown for it! So I was coming away again, in a pretty savage temper, when in the cowhouse I spotted this glass – '

And now it was the glass and the state he had found it in, all mired and dropped on by the birds and by some oversight not even in the catalogue –

'But I doubt if you'd know the farm. It's up at the back of beyond – you can see Hungerton and half the county from up there – but I was telling you about this glass. The tenant, I forget his name, had died within the month. There were a lot of old flagstones, too; it seemed Roberts had left the cataloguing to his clerk, but he was there to do the best he could for the estate; I got the lot at my own price, and I don't know what it was about that auction that made such an impression on me. I still can't get it out of my head; a stranger's goods and chattels, not like these parts, where they know the pedigree of every chest and corner-cupboard. Even the looking-glasses on the chests-of-drawers seemed to be peering about them, wondering who their next owner was to be, so what about this for an idea? Anne's been working in the garden like a black. Nobody seemed to know anything about this fellow, and it's quite a panorama from up there. So take the field-glasses and off you go, the pair of you, and make a day of it.'

So if young Denzil could steal upon his family like a thief in the night others could do the same, and the summer weather always hatched them out like flies, the roadsters with their sacks, the vagrants who came to the door for hot water for their tea and left their chalk-marks behind, the sleepers under haystacks, and the known characters whom the public houses would serve with one drain drink and no more. If poachers were the trouble, set tripwires with cans that jangled. In the house black cotton could be made to tell a tale. It would do those greenhouse windows no harm to clean them, and lest it should be supposed he was watching from his sleeping-hut, make a dummy of his kitbag and watch from somewhere else.

But first the bicycles and a day of it up in the hills with Anne.

3

A day of it! They had made a day-and-a-half of it; tomorrow they would both be stiff as boards, and he had changed his mind about the dummy in the bed, for he lay there himself, scene after scene of that long day still racing through his head.

The miles between farm and farm, but at last the farm they sought, the farm where his father had found his glass, dwelling and barn in one, and little need of a decalcomania landing-window with its door-step its only stair.

Jaffers, the name of the late tenant had been; a retired police-sergeant from Hungerton, with some idea of bulb-growing in his head; but that was as much as they could tell him, and he would have to go to Hungerton for the rest –

Hungerton through the field-glasses, pale and aerial so far away, but when you got there a county town with its traffic lights and studded crossings, its constabulary headquarters and its assize court, its public park and its county asylum, and its garden-city penitentiary where its old gaol had been.

His quick question to Anne – were her legs good for it and chance the train back? Her nodded 'Yes'.

And what a still night to be recalling it all, with everybody asleep and the gable below glimmering of its own whiteness and the wist-eria without shadow –

It was at that moment that the light appeared in the greenhouse and in his plimsolls he was off the bed.

. But it was such a light as a night-traveller sees as he scans the breathed-on windows of the train for a seat within. Dimly haloed, it was being raised, lowered, directed now into this corner, now that, and suddenly it grew dim, flickered, disappeared. He stepped back till his feet were on grass, looked up, waited. The light reappeared on the ceiling of his parents' room, was blown out, and the front of the house was in darkness again.

But now he too heard the sounds that had brought his father from his bed. Suddenly topping the hedge, the moon, a hump-backed orange with its waning, was looking at him like a punch-drunk bruiser's eye. It made a blackness of the hedge-bottom beneath it, but in the blackness something stirred. As in the whispering-gallery one steps suddenly into the unseen focus of audition, so a voice spoke and a second voice answered it.

'Tottenham Fields – ' the first voice said.

'Ten miles out o' Bath – ' said the second.

Then he sprang as suddenly back as if he had been catapulted.

For London had ended at Holborn when last a battered knave-of-spades hat, a mask and a horse-pistol a foot-and-a-half long had been seen in Tottenham Fields. There had been no jeeps with antennae when that second, with his dingy wisp of necklace and the skirted coat too big for him, had taken the night air as far away as Bath. And had he truly seen them? He had felt no contact. For an instant's flicker only they had passed between him and the moon. Then only the moon was there.

But what was this that was happening in his father's garden? The scent had gone from the stocks, there was a smell of compost in the air. A fret from the morfa had drifted over it, above the level of which only the tall sunflowers reared their tarnished heads like the half-obliterated coronas of an eclipse. And how came it that half the length of the garden away he should see so much more plainly than he had seen that shadowy pair of the hedge close at hand? As through the honeysuckle of the police-station the disturbing word peeped, so the dimness of the garden was faintly populous with shapes that flitted and moved. The herbaceous border was an ambush of comings and goings, not a bush or shrub but something lurked behind it, and stare at them and they were gone. But get them into the eye-corner and they took on phantasmal substance, gait, separateness and glimpses of clothing.

Yet they were no contemporaries of one another, for the first of them to draw earthly breath must have been dead a century before the greater number were born, nor had they any air of knowing one another, but rather of making acquaintance as they met. Against the Victoria plum a garden ladder had been left, and they were making for it as if some common memory drew them, to some place they must revisit, some scene re-enact, and as they approached it now a hairtie was to be distinguished among them, now a pocket-flap, a triple cape, a buckled hat of the Regency, a peg-leg, an eye-patch, a spotted belcher. And, shelled as peas as they were, etiolated and spent, the rattling of resuscitation that rose from them was in the thieves' patter and caggermagger of centuries ago.

And now, as they grew ever more visible the nearer they drew to the ladder, there were mob-caps and mutches among them, quilted petticoats and tawdry finery, and a glimmer of light was breaking upon Denzil Corydon. They were their hussies and fancy-women, their decoys of the inns and fairs, and they had turned them off in style in those days. They had made a public holiday of it, with gingerbread and oranges and last dying speeches, and if he had been a popular desperado he had had twenty light o' loves to make his sufferings short under that ladder where in her corduroy slacks Anne had picked her fruit. But as he had fallen back from the highwaymen of the hedge, so his heart gave a bound now. From the greenhouse behind him there had come a sharp, tingling crack, and there was no mistaking the sound that followed it. It was the muffled yet forceful pressure upon a window that is being tampered with, and in his plimsolls he sprang to the crazy pavement.

One by one he knew those panes by this time, and now he was ready to take a long look at their pedigree too. The first of them was the flawed pane that gave their faces the mumpish look as they passed, the next the one where for economy of glass two pieces had been cut to overlap. Steamed and trickling, they had haloed his father's candle, but now for the moon, they were a reflecting outer surface only, and again it was a moon in bits and pieces, that light-soiled moon of the small hours that by the time sleeping mankind wakes is no more than a vanishing wafer in the sky. There was nothing remarkable about the third pane, but putting his hand to the fourth he drew it quickly back again. Something adhered to his fingers. It was the panel that adjoined the door, and when he advanced his hand again it passed clean through it. A quarter-circle had been cut out, the stickiness was that of the fly-paper or plaster that had muffled the blow, and through the hole the knob and chain could be reached. Stooping, he looked in.

4

For all its suffocation of breathing and sweat the interior was as chill as that morgue where, behind their thin film of running water, the unidentified dead lay, each with his dreadful photograph and particulars at his head. They are the bodies dragged from the river, and the suicide no relative claims, and now he would not have swapped his glimmer of a hunch for a thousand pounds!

No geraniums in their pots, *no* basket chairs, but a prison antechamber, muddily moonshot, its thick air scarcely breathable for the huddled squalor that lay there on its floor!

In the garden he had felt no mortal chill. For all he knew they were still at it about their ladder under the victoria plum, re-enacting their bygone charade with the marsh-fret for their artificial backcloth. The fellow of Tottenham Fields bade only the sunflowers stand and deliver, that swaggering beau of the Bath Road danced his minuet in feather-dustered wax, downstairs at Madame Tussaud's show.

But here was the foetid gaol-delivery itself, and how many were they as they cursed and laughed and quarrelled and gesticulated and shivered in their fevers there? But he drew back for air. He would as soon have made an inventory of the Black Museum itself, the tiny bottles with the poison still in them, the hacked razors and flattened bullets that had done the deed, as separate these from their sessions and calendars, their circuits and sentences, their remands in custody and puttings-off till the next assize.

Yet he was not old enough to remember that old gaol at Hungerton, where now the garden-city penitentiary stood. He had only heard of its grim exercise-yard, with the rusty *chevaux-de-frises*, and now out of the sordid anonymity individual faces were beginning to emerge, black-list faces, with family likenesses and rememberable names. A bare century had passed since the oldest in crime of these had picked 'em up on Hungerton's rumbling treadmill in his dingy yellow with the broad-arrows, and now he too heard what Anne had heard before Patricia, his father before himself –

Tramp-tramp-tramp of feet on stone, shuffle-shuffle-shuffle along Hungerton's grey corridors, with faces turned to the wall as the Governor passed –

Rubbings and fumblings on sash and glass, glass that still kept the associations and echoes of it, glass that no scouring would cleanse –

Glass from a whole county's areas and sculleries and half-floors and privies, decalcomania windows opened by sluts of skivvies and the undersized lad popped in –

But now he himself had been seen at the quarter-circle with the moonlight on his face, and there was a surge and a pressing forward, and the palms of house-breakers and enterers smeared away the steaming as at every pane there appeared a face –

And somewhere among them, at large in the house, was a rogue of today, to be taken with the sticky stuff still on his fingers –

Putting his hand through the hole, he slid back the knob of the door.

But into what chaos and hurly-burly of atmospherics had he stepped? He was in his jeep again, his antenna useless, jammed in a cacophony of interference. He was driving in fog by night again, behind lights that showed the motes and particles of the opacity only. A focus of audition, this?

But an extraordinary thing was happening. Slowly the whole perimeter seemed to be revolving upon itself, the focus seeking *him* out, tuning itself into *his* ear, *his* intelligence, and suddenly like a belch the harsh colloquy broke through.

'It was Flattie Jaffers pinched me, but wait till *my* feet hit the flagstones again!'

'They ain't got no right to put a man on solitary in *that* cell,' and an old lag's jeering laugh.

'It's only Sammy Smithers, and who takes any notice of Sammy? *I* seen 'im 'ang hisself twice in '16!'

'He ain't going to hang hisself when *I'm* doing solo there. *Hi, grab him, don't let him get on that chair –* '

But there was the scraping of a garden-chair on stone, a jarring of frame-work, a concussion like the dropping of a heavily-laden tray. Something hurtled past Denzil Corydon as the pane with the hole in it was shivered into a thousand fragments. At the leaping flash of his three-cell torch the prison had gone, and only for a moment had there lingered in the air a pendant shape with neck awry, in a prisoner's parti-coloured boiler suit, hideously convulsed. Now he had eyes only for his father, standing in the inner doorway with a second flower-pot poised ready to hurl, the overturned chair, and the Woolworth hook and skein of garden raffia on the floor.

At noon of the following day they telephoned from the honey-suckled police-station that they had their roadster safely under lock and key. Judging it best to beat it while the going was good, the elusive one whose comings and goings had been cloaked by the flurry of ghostly gaolbirds had hurriedly let himself out by the front door again, only to walk into the constable's waiting arms. But at five o'clock the telephone had rung again. In taking a cup of tea into the station's single cell the constable's tender-hearted wife had closed its door with her foot only. So the miscreant had soaked his sticky fingers in it, drunk what remained, and by the time she had returned for the empty cup had been once more at large. At any rate, that was the tale that they were giving out, and unless he had thumbed a lift they were bound to get him again within a milestone or two.

But about the rest they are freely communicative. It is the police practice, they say, to remove the exhibit intact, pane, finger-prints and all. They remembered Jaffers, and saw no reason at all why a retiring member of the force with a fancy for bulb-farming should not pick up a job lot of done-with old glass as well at a prison demolition as anywhere else. But Eustace Corydon's white gable has no greenhouse today. It lies in five fathoms of water, a mile to seaward of the bar. Motorists still slow down to exclaim at the beauty of his garden. But let any lady from London speak of cutting anything out and framing it, and she is listened to in polite silence.